Strange Tales from a Chinese Studio

Eerie and Fantastic
Chinese Stories
of the Supernatural

PU SONGLING

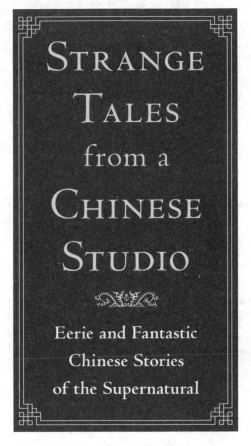

STRANGE
TALES
from a
CHINESE
STUDIO

Eerie and Fantastic
Chinese Stories
of the Supernatural

TRANSLATED BY HERBERT
A. GILES

WITH A NEW FOREWORD BY
VICTORIA CASS

TUTTLE Publishing
Tokyo | Rutland, Vermont | Singapore

ABOUT TUTTLE
"Books to Span the East and West"

Our core mission at Tuttle Publishing is to create books which bring people together one page at a time. Tuttle was founded in 1832 in the small New England town of Rutland, Vermont (USA). Our fundamental values remain as strong today as they were then—to publish best-in-class books informing the English-speaking world about the countries and peoples of Asia. The world has become a smaller place today and Asia's economic, cultural and political influence has expanded, yet the need for meaningful dialogue and information about this diverse region has never been greater. Since 1948, Tuttle has been a leader in publishing books on the cultures, arts, cuisines, languages and literatures of Asia. Our authors and photographers have won numerous awards and Tuttle has published thousands of books on subjects ranging from martial arts to paper crafts. We welcome you to explore the wealth of information available on Asia at www.tuttlepublishing.com.

Published by Tuttle Publishing, an imprint of Periplus Editions (HK) Ltd.

www.tuttlepublishing.com

Copyright © 2010 Periplus Editions (HK) Ltd.

Library of Congress Cataloging-in-Publication Data
Pu, Songling, 1640-1715.
  [Liao zhai zhi yi. English.]
  Strange tales from a Chinese studio / The Herbert A. Giles
translation of Songling Pu's Masterpiece with a new foreword by Victoria Cass.
      447 p. ; 20 cm.
  ISBN 978-0-8048-4138-2 (pbk.)
1. Short stories, Chinese--Translations into English.
2. China--Social life and customs--Fiction.
I. Giles, Herbert Allen, 1845-1935. II. Cass, Victoria Baldwin. III. Title.
  PL2722.U2L513 2010
  895.1'30108--dc22

                2010012480

This Edition ISBN 978-0-8048-4908-1

Distributed by

North America, Latin America & Europe
Tuttle Publishing
364 Innovation Drive
North Clarendon, VT 05759-9436 U.S.A.
Tel: 1 (802) 773-8930
Fax: 1 (802) 773-6993
info@tuttlepublishing.com
www.tuttlepublishing.com

Japan
Tuttle Publishing
Yaekari Building, 3rd Floor, 5-4-12 Osaki
Shinagawa-ku, Tokyo 141 0032
Tel: (81) 3 5437-0171
Fax: (81) 3 5437-0755
sales@tuttle.co.jp
www.tuttle.co.jp

Asia Pacific
Berkeley Books Pte. Ltd.
3 Kallang Sector #04-01
Singapore 349278
Tel: (65) 6741-2178
Fax: (65) 6741-2179
inquiries@periplus.com.sg
www.periplus.com

First edition
23 22 21 20 19   6 5 4 3 2
1910CM

Printed in China

Contents

To My Grandchildren

Penelope Esbell Laurence
Margaret Valerie St. Giles
Sylvia Sarah Giles
Rosamond St. Giles
Austin Loudon Valentine St. Giles
John Allen Laurence
Audrey Laurence

Foreword

THERE—exactly as I had expected—in all its reality, was the book, *The Guideways of Mountains and Seas*; and before my eyes, I could actually see the beasts: the man-faced monster, Snake with Nine Faces. There too was Lord Zhang—One-footed Ox-monster—who looked like a sack. And then I saw Xing Tian—Creature of No Head—who used his nipples as his eyes and his navel as his mouth, and danced with his spear and his shield.[1]

Lu Xun (1881–1936)

When Pu Songling died on February 25, 1715, in the seventy-first year of the Qing Dynasty (1644–1911), the collection of tales he called *Strange Tales of the Make-Do Studio* was given over to his sons in a stack of one hundred and ten loose-leaf sheets, hand-written and unpublished.[2] Now, almost three centuries later, there are hundreds more versions of *Strange Tales* than there were of original pages: from the many editions in the nineteenth century, to the modern printings throughout Asia, and then the favorite tales recreated in varying media: plays and storyteller performance, films and their sequels, television shows and serials: as well as, finally, the approximately forty versions in translation. The one hundred and ten pages have replicated like a magic trick: the ghosts and shape-shifters, lovers and demons emerging confidently from those simple hand-written origins into the modern world. How could Pu Songling's life have prefigured this; constrained by poverty and modest in manner, he was a private, deeply ethical man of conservative accomplishments who was both dedicated to his family and decidedly provincial. But he did call himself "Historian of the Strange;" and perhaps in "the lantern-light that dims and wants to gutter"—as he described the setting of his work—he might have imagined the wild re-duplication of the creatures he concocted.

Certainly, he knew them well. They came from that small terrain that was his home, and Pu Songling was a man deeply tied to home. Indeed, his Pu-family compound in Zichuan, where he had grown up with his brothers and sisters, was painfully dear to him. It was a great grief to him when the three siblings were forced—by family strife—to divide the property and live apart. But "the gossip and blame, chatter and arguments" of the

---

1   Lu Xun, "Ah Chang yu *Shan hai jing*" (Ah Chang and the *Guideways of Mountains and Seas*), *Lu Xun Sanshinian ji*, Hong Kong: Xinyi chubanshe, 1968. p. 368–370.
2   Allan Barr, "The Textual Transmission of Liaozhai zhiyi," HJAS vol. 44, No. 2 (Dec., 1984). p. 520

sisters-in law against Pu's wife could not be quieted. His father divided the compound and split up the fields, buildings and furnishings, "setting aside the broken bits" as they argued possession. "My wife stood by in silence," Pu Songling recalled, "disconsolate and resigned, as it was all divided up."[3] And his new home, small, broken down, barely adequate for his wife Liu, and his son Pu Ro—and later his three children—remained his home until his death in 1715, over fifty years later.

But the town he barely left, as well as the countryside around, provided a Daoist Gourd of magical encounters. The farm fields and roadways, market towns and villages, all supplied the characters for his miniature dramas.[4] Wives and mothers, fathers and siblings in scenes of domestic life are the heroes close at hand for many of his stories. His portraits are intimate: "When I was a little boy I went one day to the prefectural city," he recalls. "It was the time of the Spring Festival," and there at the Spring Performance, "I saw a magician traveling with his own small boy."[5] Pu Songling gathers anecdotes from friends as well: and from friends of friends. Stories are personally relayed to him by word of mouth. "Han Gongfu of Yucheng, told me that he was one day traveling..."[6] His Strange Tales are local in source, coming to him from a web of voices around him.

Greatest of all the local mysteries were the fox shape-shifters, an extended tribe of mischief-makers, enigmatic neighbors of human kind. They were a known phenomenon of Pu Songling's home province; "Shandong proliferates in foxes," said one intellectual.[7] They could be persistent and troublesome: alternately human or fox, they borrowed and stole, seduced and confused, and were not always easy to detect within your own compound, although a bushy tail beneath a cloak was a give-away. Householders were often bothered by the fox. "His family was under fox influence," Pu Songling noted blandly, "Many strange things having happened before."[8] But a fox is a moral shape-shifter as well. Foxes could be helpful; one fox wife of a

3   Pu Songling, "Shu Liu Shi xingshi" (On the Events in the Life of Madame Liu), http://blog.sina.com.cn/zyc666

4   For a discussions of the Shandong landscape and historical events of Pu Songling's time, see Jonathan D. Spence, *The Death of Woman Wang*, New York: Viking, 1978; and Chang Chun-shu and Chang Hsueh-lun, *Redefining History: Ghosts, Spirits, and Human Society in P'u Sung-ling's World, 1640–1715*. Ann Arbor, MI: University of Michigan Press, 1998, pp, 52–62

5   Pu Songling, "Tou tao," *Liaozhai zhiyi*, Shanghai: Shanghai guji chubanshe, 1978, pp. 32–34. Also: "Theft of the Peach," in Pu Songling, *Strange Tales from a Chinese Studio*, translated by Herbert A. Giles, North Clarendon, VT: Tuttle Publishing, 2010, 104.

6   "A Strange Companion," Giles, *Strange Tales*. 87.

7   Victoria Cass, *Dangerous Women, Warriors, Grannies and Geishas of the Ming*, Lanham Maryland: Rowman and Littlefield, 1999, p. 93: citing Lang Ying, *Qixiu leigao*, Beijing 1961, p. 705.

8   "A Strange Companion," Giles, *Strange Tales*, 87.

human "knew when harvests would be good or bad." And one fox tutor was a dedicated teacher, though he went out every night and came back without using the door. Danger is always possible: but so are help and fortune. Too amiably human, the fox evades easy censure.

According to some critics these protean creatures usefully symbolize human ambivalence. They epitomize alien emotions and conflicting values—obsession and compulsion, fear and dread—echoing mythic constructs of the conflicted self.[9] Pu Songling does make sly references to the ambivalent nature of human response: "We don't like his kind!" says one father of an impertinent fox who asks to marry his daughter.[10] But exactly what "kind" they were—human or demonic, beneficent or harmful—left room for much ambiguity. Like the foxes themselves, Pu Songling evades easy interpretation. His attitude suggests the witty reply Charles Dickens gave when characterizing his own ghost stories: "My own mind is perfectly unprejudiced and impressible on the subject of ghosts—I do not in the least pretend that such things cannot be."

Pu Songling, however, was not always the charmed observer. Many of his accounts are informed by a dark imagination and a knowledge that was darker still. A fox-demon was one type of strangeness, but stranger still was the savagery of the powerful. Pu Songling witnessed astonishing cruelties. He was born in 1640, four years before the conquest of China by the Manchu, and lived in the period of Manchu stabilization, a time referred to as "The Troubles,"[11] when Shandong was ravaged by battles between the Manchu overlords and local loyalists. Pu Songling wrote boldly of this madness. He named names; and many of these stories were excised from editions. "In 1674, during the time of the Rebellion against the Manchu, the Qing forces were on a punitive expedition to the South when they swept into the town, destroying everything.... At that time it was the rainy season and the fields werc flooded and had become lakes. The people had no place

---

9   For multiple and fascinating discussions of fox shape shifters, especially female foxes, see especially: Allan Barr, "Disarming Intruders: Alien Women in *Liaozhai zhiyi*," HJAS, 49.2 (Dec. 1989): 501–517. Judith T. Zeitlin, *Historian of the Strange: Pu Songling and the Chinese Classical Tale*. Stanford: Stanford University Press, 1983. Li Wai-yee,. *Enchantment and Disenchantment: Love and Illusion in Chinese Literature*. Princeton: Princeton University Press, 1993. Luo Hui, "The Ghost of Liaozhai: Pu Songling's Ghostlore and Its History of Reception," Ph D thesis, University of Toronto, 2009. (Luo Hui provides a treatment as well of the film versions that are based on the stories). And Rania Hunington *Alien Kind: Foxes and Late Imperial Chinese Narrative*, Cambridge, MA the Harvard University Asian Center 2003. For a brief, but pithy overview see John Minford's introduction to his translation: Pu Songling, *Strange Tales from a Chinese Studio* tr. John Minford. London: Penguin, 2006.
10   "The Fight with the Foxes," Giles, *Strange Tales*. 35.
11   Pu Songling, *Strange Tales from a Chinese Studio* tr. John Minford. London: Penguin, 2006, p. xvi.

to hide so they made off on rafts into the growths of sorghum. The soldiers realized this and stripped off their clothes and rode out on horseback into the water. They chased the women down and raped them."

More familiar cruelties appalled him too: corrupt officials revolted him. He called these grandees "wolves" and allowed himself a corrosive disdain. "When I see officials behave thus, my sense of deep disgust seeps like damp into the very marrow of my bones."[12] His contempt could have as well a personal bite to it. Pu Songling's own life was scarred by failure. His fourteen attempts—lasting over forty-six years—to pass the second level of the civil service exams was deeply humiliating to him, a humiliation he described as "the seven transformations of a candidate." "When he first arrives in the examination hall, he drags himself along exhausted under his load of bags; at that stage he is a beggar." In successive stages he is a "prisoner, an insect larva, a sick bird, or a monkey on a leash."[13]

This writer, so easily charmed by cleverness, so tolerant and catholic in his views of folk life, finds a voice that is, by contrast, redolent with an intense and inward fury. Nor is this voice a casual experiment; it is his own self-declared métier. In his eloquent preface to Strange Tales he pretends to an inheritance: the grim perspective of earlier morose solitaries. "Madly I continue my own Accounts of the Netherworld," he professes, claiming the same bleak landscape that they faced: "The wind sighs coldly outside and the chill on the table is like ice." He summons up the executed minister Han Fei who wrote his own grim assessments in a state of fury: "Drinking my wine and taking up my brush, I push on to complete these writings of 'Solitary Rage.'"[14] This "solitary rage" is not, for Pu Songling, a writer's pose; it is, in many of his stories, his vision.

***

One of the great men of letters Wang Shizhen, (1634–1711), in between his duties as President of the Censorate and Director of the Board of Punishments, read the loose sheets of the manuscript, *Strange Tales of the Make-do Studio*, and was delighted with it. He wrote a poem for Pu Songling, expressing his respect.

---

12   "Mad Priest," Giles, *Strange Tales*, CXXXVI, comments by "Historian of the Strange" are in "Dian daoren," Pu Songling, *Liaozhai zhiyi*, Shanghai: Shanghai guji chubanshe, 1978, p. 961.
13   Pu Songling, "Author's Preface," *Liaozhai zhiyi*, Shanghai: Shanghai guji chubanshe, 1978, p. 3.
14   Pu Songling, "Wang Zi'an," *Liaozhai zhiyi*, Shanghai: Shanghai guji chubanshe, 1978, p. 1238–1248.

Bean arbor, gourd trellis, silken rain.
Idle words, idly spoken, idly heard—
Like Su the Poet and Teller of Tales,
Of whom we are both so fond!
The world's debates disdained;
We loved to hear the songs of ghosts,
Issuing from the graves of autumn.[15]

Wang Shizhen admires the manuscript for what he knows it is: a masterpiece by a refined classicist. Pu Songling is a worthy descendent, says Wang, of the great essayist, poet and official-scholar, Su Dongpo; Wang is not alone in this assessment. The list of learned readers who championed this work is impressive. From its earliest appearance in manuscript through its publication in the late Qing, the literati praised this book as another fine example of classical tales, finding in it a blending of the two well know genres: tales of the anomalous (zhiguai) and accounts of the strange (chuanqi). Clearly, their expectations were not to hear the voice of the folk artist, nor the impassioned narrator of the horrific, but were to acquire an additional dose of the unexplained, in the manner of long established genres. Pu Songling was not unclear in this regard; his voice was tuned pitch perfect to the tastes of the literati. Thus he called himself by a sobriquet instantly evocative of classical predecessors. In his comments that follow his stories he calls himself: "Historian of the Strange."

If his stories reflected the tastes of polite society, this is not surprising. Pu Songling was a literatus steeped in elite traditions. Pu was erudite, educated in the Confucian classics, as were his sons and grandsons. Failing to achieve civil service rank, he became alternately a private secretary and private tutor. These were modest forms of employment, of ambiguous social status; yet his life as minor litcratus was rich in intelligent companionship. He worked as tutor for thirty-six years for Bi Jiyou. As patriarch in one of the most important families in Shandong, Bi had a grand estate with a famous library; and both he and his wife were early and loyal enthusiasts of *Strange Tales*. Pu Songling's personal friends were literati; they were writers as well as officials. Gao Heng (1612–1697) served in Beijing in the Imperial Academy and in the Bureau of Punishments and was a companion and enthusiast of *Strange Tales*. Pu Songling, like all literati of standard

---

15   Pu Songling, *Strange Tales from a Chinese Studio*, John Minford trans., London: Penguin, 2006, p. 462.

experience, belonged to a literary society, the Poetry Society of Ancient Chu. Pu Songling was also prolific. He did write about vernacular concerns, but he wrote or compiled extensively on recondite matters in educated language. He wrote six volumes of classical poetry, and tens of volumes on miscellaneous matters for the governing class, such as *The Handbook for Scholars on Essentials of Daily Life and Intellectual Activities*. Finally, as a teacher, he produced texts. The grandsons of Bi Jiyou used his *Essentials of Elementary Learning and Selections from the Zhuang Zi and Lie Zi*, written specifically for them.[16] He was an intellectual.

Not surprisingly, his stories, for all their off hand charm, are exemplars: crisp, elegant, rich in vocabulary, allusive, classical. His style is brilliant. A genius with voice and pace, he draws the reader into a fantasy-construct with the mild, disarming perspective of the innocent provincial, a persona without coyness or ironic distance. Then come the shifts: the small changes in voice—from farmer to fox, back to farmer—creating miniscule, but essential, displacements. These are not so much disorientations, as serial re-orientations, that slip the reader into an exotic world of the other, to see through their eyes. Pace figures in as well. The extreme economy of the narration, reinforced by the classical density, keeps the tale clipped. Sweeping along with rapid shifts in perspective, the tale is finished in one sitting, ending before you can reason your way back to a proper disbelief, leaving you with a kind of useful knowledge, albeit of short duration, that you have been, and can be, taken off guard again. The brilliance of his style was no secret. He was known as the master of the light touch. Feng Zhenluan, writing in 1818, praised his polished subtlety: "the whole story is like that" he said, "fragmentary, inconclusive, loose, delicate, exquisite."[17]

Of course, he is writing in a medium with well-known classical models, yet his tales of the strange are not slavish copies. Indeed, Pu Songling knew the rules and he broke them. He was a fearless writer, manipulating the boundaries of the genre in ways that might be called experimental. He employed highly self-aware techniques of the meta-novel, bending the genre. One scholar notes that in his stories there is a "continual blurring of literal and figurative truth."[18] His characters step in and out of fictional constructs. The "author," his friends, his fictional characters, the subjects of paintings, people from dream sequences, and the strange beings of magic,

16   Chang Chun-shu and Chang Hsueh-lun, *Redefining History: Ghosts, Spirits, and Human Society in P'u Sung-ling's World, 1640–1715*. Ann Arbor, MI: University of Michigan Press, 1998, pp, 52–62
17   Minford, 542.
18   Zeitlin p. 166.

all exchange positions. In "The Fox Dream" Pu Songling creates a story with Bi Yi'an as protagonist, claiming Bi is a real person, the nephew of his employer. This already ambiguous character in his own strange tale falls in love with one of the fox women of an earlier story in the collection. The tale becomes "a tangle of connections," with "layers of dream ...(that) seem to be continually erasing themselves,"[19] all related in elegant, classical rhetoric. This is a writer of immense sophistication.

Literati tastes were highly accommodating to this "tangle of connections." Reality-shifts, unexpected shocks, ironic knowledge and enlightenment: all these were the common coin of the day. In the Late Ming (1368–1644) and Early Qing educated men and women commonly voiced a revulsion for rational perceptions and praised the eccentric, the wild and the mad; poets and essayists loved the spirit of "Crazy Zen," as it was termed. The wonder tale was similarly the right medium for this koan perspective; the inverted worlds of magic were the madness cure, the absurdity cure, designed to eliminate bad habits such as thinking. Pu Songling's tales, with their changing identities and shifting realities, their sudden revelations of worlds within worlds, their dream sequences that reveal higher realities, and the layering of truths within truths, were well attuned to this inside-out logic. They were deemed useful to rout the horror of a life poisoned in small degrees. Pu Songling clearly knew this. Of his own stories, he said, "Foolishness is my core nature," and, "My madness is solid—impossible to refuse!"[20] One of his poems reads like a small manifesto for the strange tale that is laced with Zen. In his "Spring in the Rain Soaked Garden" he says that his "wild talk of ancient ghosts" recreates the Zen enigma.

> I study the way of Su Dongpo to stir away melancholy
> With my wild talk of ancient ghosts.
> The Master of Clarity takes his seat,
> Shunning fine phrases he renews the way of Zen.[21]

For all the talk of Zen, however, Pu Songling's tales are, at heart, ghost stories; but they are ghost stories with a twist. As Henri Maspero pointed out, the word ghost (*gui*) suggests the word return (also *gui*), for the ghost is the creature who, despite the rupture of death, unnaturally returns to

---

19   Zeitlin p. 176.
20   *Pu Songling*, "Author's Preface," *Liaozhai zhiyi*, Shanghai: Shanghai guji chubanshe, 1978, p. 3.
21   Luo Hui, p. 71, but with my own translation.

the living, refusing release from the vestiges of earlier lives. A gui-ghost is literally a "revenant." Pu Songling's tales are indeed tales of the malign revenant, not of ghosts, but of deceptive truths and soured mentalities, of shallow visions that seal the self in narrow borders. The tales banish what Pu Songling's friend Gao Heng referred to as, "men whose eyes are as tiny as peas," and "who get lost in the forest when they see a single leaf."[22]

Zen tales of shifting visions clearly exercise the lazy self. A Daoist monk provides a hiding place for two lovers. They suddenly shrink and hide up inside his copious sleeve. They, of course, write poems to each other, and when the Daoist examines his robe, he finds their poems written on the silk in "lines of words as tiny as lice."[23] Inside-out, microcosm macrocosm: his *Strange Tales* press us to change our vision of reality. They also fuse grand spiritual visions with small emotional accommodations, as the intimate seems to matter as much as the philosophical. One man becomes deeply obsessed with a painting, and then becomes the painting: obsessions create deep empathy, a movement of the spirit beyond the self, for as the poet Howard Nemerov noted, "What you look at hard looks back at you." Even Pu Songling's state of "solitary rage" is shifted. In "The Three States of Existence"[24] the Jade God, Lord of the Underworld, master of all punishments allotted in Hell, is scandalized by the loathing an examination candidate feels for the examiner who failed him. "When will ye have done with your wrongs and animosities?" asks the appalled god. With clearly a nod to his own fury at failing the exams, Pu Songling mocks the rage that survives three cycles of rebirth; and then, as storyteller, he calmly resolves it. Indeed, the small resolutions—among women and men, among siblings, and among generations—are as weighty, and as pleasurable to exorcise, as any Zen leap into another consciousness. Whether human scaled or grandiose, an amplitude of spirit informs the tales. The one punishable offense is rigidity.

Pu Songling began working on the *Strange Tales of the Make-do Studio* in about 1671 shortly after his third failure at stage two of the examination. He then spent the next thirty-five years gathering, writing, editing, polishing, rewriting and re-polishing the remaining tales: five hundred in all.[25] Though it was not published in his lifetime, it was a success in 1766

---

22   Zeitlin, p. 23.
23   Pu Songling, "Gong xian," *Liaozhai zhiyi,* Shanghai: Shanghai guji chubanshe, 1978, p. 895–901 Zeitlin discusses pp 197.
24   "The Three States of Existence," Giles, *Strange Tales,* 75.
25   The number in the collection is unstable: Chang and Chang state that the most comprehensive

when his grandson—with financial help—had the blocks cut in order to print the sheets that had been preserved for over fifty years.

It seems a harsh existence that Pu Songling led with his fourteen attempts at the Examinations, stopping only after his mother died when, at his wife's urging, he set aside that hard ambition. Yet his decades as schoolmaster cannot have been wasted; and it is impossible not to feel grateful for his forty-six years as classicist and instructor. Perhaps his life in classrooms, though a fall back position for failed candidates, was in his mind when he wrote the tales. Like the textbooks he prepared, the *Strange Tales from a Chinese Studio* is another primer of sorts, one donated to generations unknown to him: a meticulously shaped, classically elegant, exercise book in spiritual agility, composed in the spirit of his earlier primer, *The Essentials of Elementary Learning*, that he had written for the grandsons of Bi Jiyou.

Victoria Cass
Baltimore, Maryland

version has five hundred, although more commonly used editions have 431. See Chang Chun-shu and Chang Hsueh-lun, *Redefining History: Ghosts, Spirits, and Human Society in P'u Sung-ling's World, 1640–1715*. Ann Arbor, MI: University of Michigan Press, 1998, p 2, p. 44, p. 61. See Chang and Chang as well for an excellent history of his career during this period. For discussion of the history of the publication see also, Allan Barr, "The Textual Transmission of Liaozhai zhiyi," HJAS vol 44, No. 2 (Dec., 1984). p. 530–34.

Introduction

THE barest skeleton of a biography is all that can be formed from the very scanty materials which remain to mark the career of a writer whose work has been for the best part of two centuries as familiar throughout the length and breadth of China as are the tales of the "Arabian Nights" in all English-speaking communities. The author of "Strange Stories" was a native of Zichuan, in the province of Shandong. His family name was Pu; his particular name was Songling; and the designation or literary epithet by which, in accordance with Chinese usage, he was commonly known among his friends, was Liuxian, or "Last of the Immortals." A further fancy name, given to him probably by some enthusiastic admirer, was Liuquan, or "Willow Spring;" but he is now familiarly spoken of simply as Pu Songling. We are unacquainted with the years of his birth or death; however, by the aid of a meager entry in the *History of Zi-Quan* it is possible to make a pretty good guess at the date of the former event. For we are there told that Pu Songling successfully competed for the lowest or bachelor's degree before he had reached the age of twenty; and that in 1651 he was in the position of a graduate of ten years' standing, having failed in the interim to take the second, or master's, degree. To this failure, due, as we are informed in the history above quoted, to his neglect of the beaten track of academic study, we owe the existence of his great work; not, indeed, his only production, though the one by which, as Confucius said of his own "Spring and Autumn,"[26] men will know him. All else that we have on record of Pu Songling, besides the fact that he lived in close companionship with several eminent scholars of the day, is gathered from his own words, written when, in 1679, he laid down his pen upon the completion of a task which was to raise him within a short period to a foremost rank in the Chinese world of letters. Of that record I here append a close translation, accompanied by such notes as are absolutely necessary to make it intelligible to non-students of Chinese.

---

26 Annals of the Lu State.

Author's Own Record

"CLAD in wistaria, girdled with ivy;"[27] thus sang Qu Ping[28] in his *Falling into Trouble.*[29] Of ox-headed devils and serpent Gods,[30] he of the long-nails[31] never wearied to tell. Each interprets in his own way the music of heaven;[32] and whether it be discord or not, depends upon antecedent causes.[33] As for me, I cannot, with my poor autumn firefly's light, match myself against the hobgoblins of the age.[34] I am but the dust in the sunbeam, a fit laughing-stock for devils.[35] For my talents are not those of Gan Bao,[36] elegant explorer of the records of the Gods; I am rather animated by the spirit of Su Dongpo,[37] who loved to hear men speak of the supernatural. I get people to commit what they tell me to writing and subsequently I dress it up in the form of a story; and thus in the lapse of time my friends from all quarters have supplied me with quantities of material, which, from my habit of collecting, has grown into a vast pile.[38]

Human beings, I would point out, are not beyond the pale of fixed laws, and yet there are more remarkable phenomena in their midst than in the country of those who crop their hair;[39] antiquity is unrolled before us, and many tales are to be found therein stranger than that of the nation

---

27 Said of the bogies of the hills, in allusion to their clothes. Here quoted with reference to the official classes, in ridicule of the title under which they hold posts which, from a literary point of view, they are totally unfit to occupy.
28 A celebrated statesman (332–295 BCE) who, having lost his master's favor by the intrigues of a rival, finally drowned himself in despair. The annual Dragon Festival is said by some to be a "search" for his body. The term *San Lü* used here was the name of an office held by Qu Ping.
29 A poem addressed by Qu Ping to his Prince, after his disgrace. Its non-success was the immediate cause of his death.
30 That is, of the supernatural generally.
31 A poet of the Tang dynasty whose eyebrows met, whose nails were very long, and who could write very fast.
32 "You know the music of earth," said Zhuang Zi; "but you have not heard the music of heaven."
33 That is, to the operation of some influence surviving from a previous existence.
34 This is another hit at the ruling classes. Xi Kang, a celebrated musician and alchemist (223–262 CE), was sitting one night alone, playing upon his lute, when suddenly a man with a tiny face walked in, and began to stare hard at him, the stranger's face enlarging all the time. "I'm not going to match myself against a devil!" cried the musician, after a few moments, and instantly blew out the light.
35 When Liu Quan, Governor of Wuling, determined to relieve his poverty by trade, he saw a devil standing by his side, laughing and rubbing its hands for glee. "Poverty and wealth are matters of destiny," said Liu Quan; "but to be laughed at by a devil—," and accordingly he desisted from his intention.
36 A writer who flourished in the early part of the fourth century, and composed a work in thirty books entitled *Supernatural Researches.*
37 The famous poet, statesman, and essayist, who flourished 1036–1101 CE.
38 "And his friends had the habit of jotting down for his unfailing delight anything quaint or comic that they came across."—The World on Charles Dickens, July 24, 1878.
39 It is related in the *Historical Record* that when Tai Po and Yu Zhong fled to the southern savages they saw men with tattooed bodies and short hair.

of Flying Heads.[40] "Irrepressible bursts, and luxurious ease,"[41]—such was always his enthusiastic strain. "Forever indulging in liberal thought,"[42]— thus he spoke openly without restraint. Were men like these to open my book, I should be a laughing-stock to them indeed. At the crossroad[43] men will not listen to me, and yet I have some knowledge of the three states of existence[44] spoken of beneath the cliff;[45] neither should the words I utter be set aside because of him that utters them.[46] When the bow [47] was hung at my father's door, he dreamed that a sickly-looking Buddhist priest, but half covered by his stole, entered the chamber. On one of his breasts was a round piece of plaster like a *cash*;[48] and my father, waking from sleep, found that I, just born, had a similar black patch on my body. As a child, I was thin and constantly ailing, and unable to hold my own in the battle of life. Our own home was chill and desolate as a monastery; and working there for my livelihood with my pen,[49] I was as poor as a priest with his alms-bowl.[50] Often and often I put my hand to my head[51] and exclaimed, "Surely he who sat with his face to the wall[52] was myself in a previous state of existence;" and thus I referred my non-success in this life to the influence of a destiny surviving from the last. I have been tossed hither and thither in the direction of the ruling wind, like a flower falling in filthy places; but the

---

40   A fabulous community, so called because the heads of the men are in the habit of leaving their bodies, and flying down to marshy places to feed on worms and crabs. A red ring is seen the night before the flight encircling the neck of the man whose head is about to fly; at daylight the head returns. Some say that the ears are used as wings; others that the hands also leave the body and fly away.

41   A quotation from the admired works of Wang Bo, a brilliant scholar and poet, who was drowned at the early age of twenty-eight, 676 CE.

42   I have hitherto failed in all attempts to identify the particular writer here intended. The phrase is used by the poet Li Taibo and others.

43   The cross-road of the "Five Fathers" is here mentioned, which the commentator tells us is merely the name of the place.

44   The past, present, and future life of the Buddhist system of metempsychosis.

45   A certain man, who was staying at a temple, dreamt that an old priest appeared to him beneath a jade-stone cliff, and, pointing to a stick of burning incense, said to him, "That incense represents a vow to be fulfilled; but I say unto you, that ere its smoke shall have curled away, your three states of existence will have been already accomplished." The meaning is that time on earth is as nothing to the Gods.

46   This remark occurs in the fifteenth chapter of the Analects or Confucian Gospels.

47   The birth of a boy was formerly signalled by hanging a bow at the door; that of a girl, by displaying a small towel—indicative of the parts that each would hereafter play in the drama of life.

48   See note 7 in tale number 2.

49   Literally, "plowing with my pen."

50   "The *patra* or bowl, used by Buddhist mendicants, in imitation of the celebrated alms-dish of Shâkyamuni Buddha.

51   Literally, "scratched my head," as is often done by the Chinese in perplexity or doubt.

52   Alluding to Bôdhidharma, who came from India to China, and tried to convert the Emperor Wu Di of the Liang dynasty; but, failing in his attempt, because he insisted that real merit lay not in works but in purity and wisdom combined, he retired full of mortification to a temple at Sung-shan, where he sat for nine years before a rock, until his own image was imprinted thereon.

six paths[53] of transmigration are inscrutable indeed, and I have no right to complain. As it is, midnight finds me with an expiring lamp, while the wind whistles mournfully without; and over my cheerless table I piece together my tales,[54] vainly hoping to produce a sequel to the *Infernal Regions*.[55] With a bumper I stimulate my pen, yet I only succeed thereby in "venting my excited feelings,"[56] and as I thus commit my thoughts to writing, truly I am an object worthy of commiseration. Alas! I am but the bird, that dreading the winter frost, finds no shelter in the tree; the autumn insect that chirps to the moon, and hugs the door for warmth. For where are they who know me?[57] They are "in the bosky grove, and at the frontier pass"[58] —wrapped in an impenetrable gloom!

From the above curious document the reader will gain some insight into the abstruse, but at the same time marvelously beautiful, style of this gifted writer. The whole essay—for such it is, and among the most perfect of its kind—is intended chiefly as a satire upon the scholarship of the age; scholarship which had turned the author back to the disappointment of a private life, himself conscious all the time of the inward fire that had been lent him by heaven. It is the keynote of his own subsequent career, spent in the retirement of home, in the society of books and friends; as also to the numerous uncomplimentary allusions which occur in all his stories relating to official life. Whether or not the world at large has been a gainer by this instance of the fallibility of competitive examinations has been already decided in the affirmative by the millions of Pu Songling's own countrymen, who for the past two hundred years have more than made up to him by a posthumous and enduring reverence for the loss of those earthly and ephemeral honors which he seems to have coveted so much.

---

53   The six *gâti* or conditions of existence, namely: angels, men, demons, hungry devils, brute beasts, and tortured sinners.

54   Literally, "putting together the pieces under the forelegs (of foxes) to make robes." This part of the fox-skin is the most valuable for making fur clothes.

55   The work of a well-known writer, named Lin Yiqing, who flourished during the Song Dynasty.

56   Alluding to an essay by Han Fei, a philosopher of the third century BCE, in which he laments the iniquity of the age in general, and the corruption of officials in particular. He finally committed suicide in prison, where he had been cast by the intrigues of a rival minister.

57   "Confucius (*Anal,* xiv.) said, " Alas! there is no one who knows me (to be what I am)."

58   The great poet Du Fu (712–770 CE) dreamt that his greater predecessor, Li Taibo (705–762 CE) appeared to him, "coming when the maple-grove was in darkness, and returning while the frontier-pass was still obscured!"—that is, at night, when no one could see him; the meaning being that he never came at all, and that those "who know me (Pu Songling)" are equally non-existent.

Strange Stories from a Chinese Studio, known to the Chinese as the *Liao-zhai Zhiyi,* or more familiarly, the *Liaozhai,* has hardly been mentioned by a single foreigner without some inaccuracy on the part of the writer concerned. For instance, the late Mr. Mayers states in his *Chinese Reader's Manual,* p. 176, that this work was composed "circa A.D. 1710," the fact being that the collection was actually completed in 1679, as we know by the date attached to the "Author's Own Record" given above. I should mention, however, that the *Liao Zhai* was originally, and for many years, circulated in manuscript only. Pu Songling, as we are told in a colophon by his grandson to the first edition, was too poor to meet the heavy expense of block-cutting; and it was not until so late as 1740, when the author must have been already for some time a denizen of the dark land he so much loved to describe, that his aforesaid grandson printed and published the collection now universally famous. Since then many editions have been laid before the Chinese public, the best of which is that by Dan Minglun, a Salt Commissioner, who flourished during the reign of Dao Guang, and who in 1842 produced, at his own expense, an excellent edition in sixteen small octavo volumes of about 160 pages each. And as various editions will occasionally be found to contain various readings, I would here warn students of Chinese who wish to compare my rendering with the text, that it is from the edition of Dan Minglun, collated with that of Yu Ji, published in 1766, that this translation has been made. Many have been the commentaries and disquisitions upon the meaning of obscure passages and the general scope of this work; to say nothing of the prefaces with which the several editions have been ushered into the world. Of the latter, I have selected one specimen, from which the reader will be able to form a tolerably accurate opinion as to the true nature of these always singular and usually difficult compositions. Here it is:

Tang Meng-Lai's Preface

THE common saying, "He regards a camel as a horse with a swelled back," trivial of itself, may be used in illustration of greater matters. Men are wont to attribute an existence only to such things as they daily see with their own eyes, and they marvel at whatsoever, appearing before them at one instant, vanishes at the next. And yet it is not at the sprouting and falling of foliage, nor at the metamorphosis of insects that they marvel, but only at the manifestations of the supernatural world; though of a truth, the

whistling of the wind and the movement of streams, with nothing to set the one in motion or give sound to the other, might well be ranked among extraordinary phenomena. We are accustomed to these, and therefore do not note them. We marvel at devils and foxes: we do not marvel at man. But who is it that causes a man to move and to speak?—to which question comes the ready answer of each individual so questioned, "*I* do." This "I do," however, is merely a personal consciousness of the facts under discussion. For a man can see with his eyes, but he cannot see what it is that makes him see; he can hear with his ears, but he cannot hear what it is that makes him hear; how, then, is it possible for him to understand the rationale of things he can neither see nor hear? Whatever has come within the bounds of their own ocular or auricular experience men regard as proved to be actually existing; and only such things.[59] But this term "experience" may be understood in various senses. For instance, people speak of something which has certain attributes as *form,* and of something else which has certain other attributes as *substance*; ignorant as they are that form and substance are to be found existing without those particular attributes. Things which are thus constituted are inappreciable, indeed, by our ears and eyes; but we cannot argue that therefore they do not exist. Some persons can see a mosquito's eye, while to others even a mountain is invisible; some can hear the sound of ants battling together, while others, again, fail to catch the roar of a thunder-peal. Powers of seeing and hearing vary; there should be no reckless imputations of blindness. According to the schoolmen, man at his death is dispersed like wind or fire, the origin and end of his vitality being alike unknown; and as those who have seen strange phenomena are few, the number of those who marvel at them is proportionately great, and the "horse with a swelled back" parallel is very widely applicable. And ever quoting the fact that Confucius would have nothing to say on these topics, these schoolmen half discredit such works as the *Qijie zhiguai* and the *Yu chuji* ignorant that the Sage's unwillingness to speak had reference only to persons of an inferior mental caliber; for his own *Spring and Autumn* can hardly be said to be devoid of all allusions of the kind. Now Pu Liuxian devoted himself in his youth to the marvelous, and as he grew older was

---

59 "Thus, since countless things exist that the senses *can* take account of, it is evident that nothing exists that the senses can *not* take account of."—The "Professor" in W. H. Mallock's *New Paul and Virginia.*

This passage recalls another curious classification by the great Chinese philosopher Han Wengong. "There are some things which possess form but are devoid of sound, as, for instance, jade and stones; others have sound, but are without form, such as wind and thunder; others, again, have both form and sound, such as men and animals; and lastly, there is a class devoid of both, namely, *devils and spirits.*"

specially remarkable for his comprehension there of; and being moreover a most elegant writer, he occupied his leisure in recording whatever came to his knowledge of a particularly marvelous nature. A volume of these compositions of his formerly fell into my hands, and was constantly borrowed by friends; now, I have another volume, and of what I read only about three-tenths was known to me before. What there is, should be sufficient to open the eyes of those schoolmen, though I much fear it will be like talking of ice to a butterfly. Personally, I disbelieve in the irregularity of natural phenomena, and regard as evil spirits only those who injure their neighbors. For eclipses, falling stars, the flight of herons, the nest of a mainah, talking stones, and the combats of dragons, can hardly be classed as irregular; while the phenomena of nature occurring out of season, wars, rebellions, and so forth, may certainly be relegated to the category of evil. In my opinion the morality of Pu Liuxian's work is of a very high standard, its object being distinctly to glorify virtue and to censure vice; and as a book calculated to elevate mankind, it may be safely placed side by side with the philosophical treatises of Yang Xiong[60] which Huan Dan[61] declared to be so worthy of a wide circulation.

With regard to the meaning of the Chinese words *Liaozhai Zhiyi*, this title has received indifferent treatment at the hands of different writers. Dr. Williams chose to render it by "Pastimes of the Study," and Mr. Mayers by "The Record of Marvels, or Tales of the Genii;" neither of which is sufficiently near to be regarded in the light of a translation. Taken literally and in order, these words stand for "Liao—library—record—strange," "Liao" being simply a fanciful name given by our author to his private library or studio. An apocryphal anecdote traces the origin of this selection to a remark once made by himself with reference to his failure for the second degree. "Alas!" he is reported to have said, "I shall now have no resource (*Liao*) for my old age;" and accordingly he so named his study, meaning that in his pen he would seek that resource which fate had denied to him as an official. For this untranslatable "Liao" I have ventured to substitute "Chinese," as indicating more clearly the nature of what is to follow. No such title as "Tales of the Genii" fully expresses the scope of this work, which embraces alike weird stories of Taoist devilry and magic, marvelous accounts of impossible countries beyond the sea, simple scenes of Chinese everyday life, and notices of extraordinary natural phenomena. Indeed, the

---

60 53 BCE–18 AD
61 13 BCE–56 AD

author once had it in contemplation to publish only the more imaginative of the tales in the present collection under the title of "Devil and Fox Stories;" but from this scheme he was ultimately dissuaded by his friends, the result being the heterogeneous mass which is more aptly described by the title I have given to this volume. In a similar manner, I too had originally determined to publish a full and complete translation of the whole of these sixteen volumes; but on a closer acquaintance many of the stories turned out to be quite unsuitable for the age in which we live, forcibly recalling the coarseness of our own writers of fiction in the eighteenth century. Others, again, were utterly pointless, or mere repetitions in a slightly altered form. From the whole, I therefore selected one hundred and sixty-four of the best and most characteristic stories, of which eight had previously been published by Mr. Allen in the *China Review,* one by Mr. Mayers in *Notes and Queries on China and Japan,* two by myself in the columns of the *Celestial Empire,* and four by Dr. Williams in a now forgotten handbook of Chinese. The remaining one hundred and forty-nine have never before, to my knowledge, been translated into English. To those, however, who can enjoy the *Liaozhai* in the original text, the distinctions between the various stories in felicity of plot, originality, and so on, are far less sharply denned, so impressed as each competent reader must be by the incomparable *style* in which even the meanest is arrayed. For in this respect, as important now in Chinese eyes as it was with ourselves in days not long gone by, the author of the *Liaozhai* and the rejected candidate succeeded in founding a school of his own, in which he has since been followed by hosts of servile imitators with more or less success. Terseness is pushed to extreme limits; each particle that can be safely dispensed with is scrupulously eliminated; and every here and there some new and original combination invests perhaps a single word with a force it could never have possessed except under the hands of a perfect master of his art. Add to the above, copious allusions and adaptations from a course of reading which would seem to have been co-extensive with the whole range of Chinese literature, a wealth of metaphor and an artistic use of figures generally to which only the writings of Carlyle form an adequate parallel; and the result is a work which for purity and beauty of style is now universally accepted in China as the best and most perfect model. Sometimes the story runs along plainly and smoothly enough; but the next moment we may be plunged into pages of abstruse text, the meaning of which is so involved in quotations from and allusions to the poetry or history of the past three thousand years as to be recoverable only after diligent perusal of the commentary and much searching in other works of reference. In illustration of the popularity of this book, Mr. Mayers once stated that "the porter at his gate, the boatman at his midday rest, the chair-coolie at his stand, no less than the man of letters among his books, may be seen poring with delight over the elegantly-narrated marvels of the *Liaozhai*;" but he would doubtless have withdrawn this statement in later years, with the work lying open before him. During many years in China, I made a point, when feasible, when passing by someone reading, to glance at the volume in his hand; and at my various stations in China I always kept up a borrowing acquaintance with the libraries of my private or official servants; but I can safely affirm that I never once detected the *Liaozhai* in the hands of an ill-educated man. In the same connection, Mr. Mayers observed that "fairy-tales told in the style of the *Anatomy of Melancholy* would scarcely be a popular book in Great Britain;" but except in some particular points of contact, the styles of these two works could scarcely claim even the most distant of relationships.

Such, then, is the setting of this collection of *Strange Tales from a Chinese Studio,* many of which contain, in addition to the advantages of style and plot, a very excellent moral. The intention of most of them is, in the actual words of Tang Meng-lai, "to glorify virtue and to censure vice,"—always, it must be borne in mind, according to the Chinese and not to a European interpretation of these terms. As an addition to our knowledge of the folk-lore of China, and as a guide to the manners, customs, and social life of that vast Empire, my translation of the *Liaozhai* may not be wholly devoid of interest. It has now been carefully revised, all inaccuracies of the first edition having been, so far as possible, corrected.

—HERBERT A. GILES
CAMBRIDGE, *July* 1908

1. Examination for the Post of Guardian Angel[1]

MY eldest sister's husband's grandfather, named Song Dao, was a graduate.[2] One day, while lying down from indisposition, an official messenger arrived, bringing the usual notification in his hand and leading a horse with a white forehead to summon him to the examination for his master's degree. Mr. Song here remarked that the Grand Examiner had not yet come, and asked why there should be this hurry. The messenger did not reply to this, but pressed so earnestly that at length Mr. Song roused himself, and getting upon the horse rode with him. The way seemed strange, and by-and-by they reached a city which resembled the capital of a prince. They then entered the Prefect's *yamen*,[3] the apartments of which were beautifully decorated; and there they found some ten officials sitting at the upper end, all strangers to Mr. Song, with the exception of one whom he recognized to be the God of War.[4] In the verandah were two tables and two stools, and at the end of one of the former a candidate was already seated, so Mr. Song sat down alongside of him. On the table were writing materials for each, and suddenly down flew a piece of paper with a theme on it, consisting of the following eight words: "One man, two men; by intention, without intention." When Mr. Song had finished his essay, he took it into the hall. It contained the following passage: "Those who are virtuous by intention, though virtuous, shall not be rewarded. Those who are wicked without intention, though wicked, shall receive no punishment." The presiding deities praised this sentiment very much, and calling Mr. Song to come forward, said to him, "A Guardian Angel is wanted in Honan. Go you and take up the appointment." Mr. Song no sooner heard this than he bowed his head and wept, saying, "Unworthy though I am of the honor you have conferred upon me, I should not venture to decline it but that my aged mother has reached her seventh decade, and there is no one now to take care of her. I pray you let me wait until she has fulfilled her destiny, when I will hold myself at your disposal." Thereupon one of the deities, who seemed to be the chief, gave instructions to search out his mother's term of life,

---

1   The tutelar deity of every Chinese city.
2   That is, he had taken the first or bachelor's degree. I shall not hesitate to use strictly English equivalents for all kinds of Chinese terms. The three degrees are literally, (1) Cultivated Talent, (2) Raised Man, and (3) Promoted Scholar.
3   The official residence of a mandarin above a certain rank.
4   The Chinese Mars. A celebrated warrior, named Guan Yu, who lived about the beginning of the third century of our era. He was raised after death to the rank of a God, and now plays a leading part in the Chinese Pantheon.

and a long-bearded attendant forthwith brought in the Book of Fate. On turning it over, he declared that she still had nine years to live; and then a consultation was held among the deities, in the middle of which the God of War said, "Very well. Let Mr. graduate Zhang take the post, and be relieved in nine years' time." Then, turning to Mr. Song, he continued, "You ought to proceed without delay to your post; but as a reward for your filial piety, you are granted a furlough of nine years. At the expiration of that time you will receive another summons." He next addressed a few kind words to Mr. Zhang; and the two candidates, having made their *kotow*, went away together. Grasping Mr. Song's hand, his companion, who gave "Zhang Qi of Changshan" as his name and address, accompanied him beyond the city walls and gave him a stanza of poetry at parting. I cannot recollect it all, but in it occurred this couplet:

> With wine and flowers we chase the hours,
> In one eternal spring:
> No moon, no light, to cheer the night,
> Thyself that ray must bring.

Mr Song here left him and rode on, and before very long reached his own home; here he awaked as if from a dream, and found that he had been dead three days,[5] when his mother hearing a groan in the coffin, ran to it and helped him out. It was some time before he could speak, and then he at once inquired about Changshan, where, as it turned out, a graduate named Zhang had died that very day.

Nine years afterwards, Mr. Song's mother, in accordance with fate, passed from this life; and when the funeral obsequies were over, her son, having first purified himself, entered into his chamber and died also. Now his wife's family lived within the city, near the western gate; and all of a sudden they beheld Mr. Song, accompanied by numerous chariots and horses with carved trappings and red-tasselled bits, enter into the hall, make an obeisance, and depart. They were very much disconcerted at this, not knowing that he had become a spirit, and rushed out into the village to make inquiries, when they heard he was already dead. Mr. Song had an account of his adventure written by himself; but unfortunately after the insurrection it was not to be found. This is only an outline of the story.

---

5   Catalepsy, which is the explanation of many a story in this collection, would appear to be of very common occurrence among the Chinese. Such, however, is not the case.

2. The Talking Pupils

AT Changan there lived a scholar, named Fang Dong, who though by no means destitute of ability, was a very unprincipled rake, and in the habit of following and speaking to any woman he might chance to meet. The day before the spring festival of Clear Weather,[6] he was strolling about outside the city when he saw a small carriage with red curtains and an embroidered awning, followed by a crowd of waiting-maids on horseback, one of whom was exceedingly pretty, and riding on a small palfrey. Going closer to get a better view, Mr. Fang noticed that the carriage curtain was partly open, and inside he beheld a beautifully dressed girl of about sixteen, lovely beyond anything he had ever seen. Dazzled by the sight, he could not take his eyes off her; and, now before, now behind, he followed the carriage for many a mile. By-and-by he heard the young lady call out to her maid, and, when the latter came alongside, say to her, "Let down the screen for me. Who is this rude fellow that keeps on staring so?" The maid accordingly let down the screen, and looking angrily at Mr. Fang said to him, "This is the bride of the Seventh Prince in the City of Immortals going home to see her parents, and no village girl that you should stare at her thus." Then taking a handful of dust, she threw it at him and blinded him. He rubbed his eyes and looked around, but the carriage and horses were gone. This frightened him, and he went off home, feeling very uncomfortable about the eyes. He sent for a doctor to examine his eyes, and on the pupils was found a small film, which had increased by next morning, the eyes watering incessantly all the time. The film went on growing, and in a few days was as thick as a cash.[7] On the right pupil there came a kind of spiral, and as no medicine was of any avail, the sufferer gave himself up to grief and wished for death. He then bethought himself of repenting of his misdeeds, and hearing that the *Guangming* Sutra could relieve misery, he got a copy and hired a man to teach it to him. At first it was very tedious work, but by degrees he became more composed, and spent the whole day in a posture of devotion, telling his beads. At the end of a year he had arrived at a state of perfect calm, when one day he heard a small voice, about as loud as a fly's, calling out from his left eye: "It's horridly dark in here." To this he heard a reply

---

6   One of the twenty-four solar terms. It falls on or about the 5th of April, and is the special time for worshipping at the family tombs.

7   The common European name for the only Chinese coin, about twenty of which go to a penny. Each has a square hole in the middle, for the convenience of stringing them together; hence the expression "strings of cash."

from the right eye, saying, "Let us go out for a stroll, and cheer ourselves up a bit." Then he felt a wriggling in his nose which made it itch, just as if something was going out of each of the nostrils; and after a while he felt it again as if going the other way. Afterwards he heard a voice from one eye say, "I hadn't seen the garden for a long time: the epidendrums are all withered and dead." Now Mr. Fang was very fond of these epidendrums, of which he had planted a great number, and had been accustomed to water them himself; but since the loss of his sight he had never even alluded to them. Hearing, however, these words, he at once asked his wife why she had let the epidendrums die. She inquired how he knew they were dead, and when he told her she went out to see, and found them actually withered away. They were both very much astonished at this, and his wife proceeded to conceal herself in the room. She then observed two tiny people, no bigger than a bean, come down from her husband's nose and run out of the door, where she lost sight of them. In a little while they came back and flew up to his face, like bees or beetles seeking their nests. This went on for some days, until Mr. Fang heard from the left eye, "This roundabout road is not at all convenient. It would be as well for us to make a door." To this the right eye answered, "My wall is too thick: it wouldn't be at all an easy job." "I'll try and open mine," said the left eye," and then it will do for both of us." Whereupon Mr. Fang felt a pain in his left eye as if something was being split, and in a moment he found he could see the tables and chairs in the room. He was delighted at this and told his wife, who examined his eye and discovered an opening in the film, through which she could see the black pupil shining out beneath, the eyeball itself looking like a cracked pepper-corn. By next morning the film had disappeared, and when his eye was closely examined it was observed to contain two pupils. The spiral on the right eye remained as before; and then they knew that the two pupils had taken up their abode in one eye. Further, although Mr. Fang was still blind of one eye, the sight of the other was better than that of the two together. From this time he was more careful of his behavior, and acquired in his part of the country the reputation of a virtuous man.[8]

---

8   The belief that the human eye contains a tiny being of the human shape is universal in China. It originated, of course, from the reflection of oneself that is seen on looking into the pupil of anybody's eye or even, with the aid of a mirror, into one's own.

3. The Painted Wall

A JIANGXI gentleman, named Meng Longtan, was lodging at the capital with a Mr. Zhu, M.A., when one day chance led them to a certain monastery, within which they found no spacious halls or meditation chambers, but only an old priest in *déshabillé*. On observing the visitors, he arranged his dress and went forward to meet them, leading them around and showing whatever there was to be seen. In the chapel they saw an image of Zhi Gong, and the walls on either side were beautifully painted with life-like representations of men and animals. On the east side were pictured a number of fairies, among whom was a young girl whose maiden tresses were not yet confined by the matron's knot. She was picking flowers and gently smiling, while her cherry lips seemed about to move, and the moisture of her eyes to overflow. Mr. Zhu gazed at her for a long time without taking his eyes off, until, at last he became unconscious of anything but the thoughts that were engrossing him. Then, suddenly he felt himself floating in the air, as if riding on a cloud, and found himself passing through the wall,[9] where halls and pavilions stretched away one after another, unlike the abodes of mortals. Here an old priest was preaching the Law of Buddha, surrounded by a large crowd of listeners. Mr. Zhu mingled with the throng, and after a few moments perceived a gentle tug at his sleeve. Turning around, he saw the young girl above-mentioned, who walked laughing away. Mr. Zhu at once followed her, and passing a winding balustrade arrived at a small apartment beyond which he dared not venture farther. But the young lady, looking back, waved the flowers she had in her hand as though beckoning him to come on. He accordingly entered and found nobody else within. Then they fell on their knees and worshipped heaven and earth together,[10] and rose up as man and wife, after which the bride went away, bidding Mr. Zhu keep quiet until she came back. This went on for a couple of days, when the young lady's companions began to smell a rat and discovered Mr. Zhu's hiding-place. Thereupon they all laughed and said, "My dear, you are now a married woman, and should leave off that maidenly *coiffure*." So they gave her the proper hair-pins and head ornaments, and bade her go bind her hair, at which she blushed very much but said nothing. Then one of them cried out, "My sisters, let us be off. Two's company, more's none." At this

---

9   Which will doubtless remind the reader of "Alice through the Looking-glass, and what she saw there."
10   The all-important item of a Chinese marriage ceremony; amounting, in fact, to calling God to witness the contract.

they all giggled again and went away.

Mr. Zhu found his wife very much improved by the alteration in the style of her hair. The high top-knot and the coronet of pendants were very becoming to her. But suddenly they heard a sound like the tramping of heavy-soled boots, accompanied by the clanking of chains and the noise of angry discussion. The bride jumped up in a fright, and she and Mr. Zhu peeped out. They saw a man clad in golden armor, with a face as black as jet, carrying in his hands chains and whips, and surrounded by all the girls, He asked, "Are you all here?" "All," they replied. "If," said he, "any mortal is here concealed amongst you, denounce him at once, and lay not up sorrow for yourselves." Here they all answered as before that there was no one. The man then made a movement as if he would search the place, upon which the bride was dreadfully alarmed, and her face turned the color of ashes. In her terror she said to Mr. Zhu, "Hide yourself under the bed," and opening a small lattice in the wall, disappeared herself. Mr. Zhu in his concealment hardly dared to draw his breath; and in a little while he heard the boots tramp into the room and out again, the sound of the voices getting gradually fainter and fainter in the distance. This reassured him, but he still heard the voices of people going backwards and forwards outside; and having been a long time in a cramped position, his ears began to sing as if there was a locust in them, and his eyes to burn like fire. It was almost unbearable; however, he remained quietly awaiting the return of the young lady without giving a thought to the why and wherefore of his present position.

Meanwhile, Meng Longtan had noticed the sudden disappearance of his friend, and thinking something was wrong, asked the priest where he was. "He has gone to hear the preaching of the Law," replied the priest. "Where?" said Mr. Meng. "Oh, not very far," was the answer. Then with his finger the old priest tapped the wall and called out, "Friend Zhu! what makes you stay away so long? "At this, the likeness of Mr. Zhu was figured upon the wall, with his ear inclined in the attitude of one listening. The priest added, "Your friend here has been waiting for you some time;" and immediately Mr. Zhu descended from the wall, standing transfixed like a block of wood, with starting eye-balls and trembling legs. Mr. Meng was much terrified, and asked him quietly what was the matter. Now the matter was that while concealed under the bed he had heard a noise resembling thunder and had rushed out to see what it was.

Here they all noticed that the young lady on the wall with the maiden's tresses had changed the style of her *coiffure* to that of a married woman. Mr.

Zhu was greatly astonished at this and asked the old priest the reason.

He replied, "Visions have their origin in those who see them: what explanation can I give?" This answer was very unsatisfactory to Mr. Zhu; neither did his friend, who was rather frightened, know what to make of it all; so they descended the temple steps and went away.

4. Planting a Pear Tree

A COUNTRYMAN was one day selling his pears in the market. They were unusually sweet and fine flavored, and the price he asked was high. A Taoist[11] priest in rags and tatters stopped at the barrow and begged one of them. The countryman told him to go away, but as he did not do so he began to curse and swear at him. The priest said, "You have several hundred pears on your barrow; I ask for a single one, the loss of which, Sir, you would not feel. Why then get angry?" The lookers-on told the countryman to give him an inferior one and let him go, but this he obstinately refused to do. Thereupon the beadle of the place, finding the commotion too great, purchased a pear and handed it to the priest. The latter received it with a bow and turning to the crowd said, "We who have left our homes and given up all that is dear to us[12] are at a loss to understand selfish niggardly conduct in others. Now I have some exquisite pears which I shall do myself the honor to put before you." Here somebody asked, "Since you have pears yourself, why don't you eat those?" "Because," replied the priest, "I wanted one of these pips to grow them from." So saying he munched up the pear; and when he had finished took a pip in his hand, unstrapped a pick from his back, and proceeded to make a hole in the ground, several inches deep, wherein he deposited the pip, filling in the earth as before.

---

11 That is, of the religion of *Tao*, a system of philosophy founded some six centuries before the Christian era by a man named Laozi, "Old boy," who was said to have been born with white hair and a beard. It is now but a shadow of its former self, and is corrupted by the grossest forms of superstition borrowed from Buddhism, which has in its turn adopted many of the forms and beliefs of Taoism, so that the two religions are hardly distinguishable one from the other. "What seemed to me the most singular circumstance connected with the matter, was the presence of half a dozen Taoist priests, who joined in all the ceremonies, doing everything that the Buddhist priests did, and presenting a very odd appearance, with their topknots and cues, among their closely shaven Buddhist brethren. It seemed strange that the worship of Sakyamuni by celibate Buddhist priests, with shaved heads, into which holes were duly burned at their initiation, should be participated in by married Taoist priests, whose heads are not wholly shaven, and have never been burned."— *Initiation of Buddhist Priests at Kooshan*, by S. L. B.

Taoist priests are credited with a knowledge of alchemy and the black art in general.

12   A celibate priesthood belongs properly to Buddhism, and is not a doctrine of the Taoist church.

He then asked the bystanders for a little hot water to water it with, and one among them who loved a joke fetched him some boiling water from a neighboring shop. The priest poured this over the place where he had made the hole, and every eye was fixed upon him when sprouts were seen shooting up, and gradually growing larger and larger. By-and-by, there was a tree with branches sparsely covered with leaves; then flowers, and last of all fine, large, sweet-smelling pears hanging in great profusion. These the priest picked and handed around to the assembled crowd until all were gone, when he took his pick and hacked away for a long time at the tree, finally cutting it down. This he shouldered, leaves and all, and sauntered quietly away. Now, from the very beginning, our friend the countryman had been amongst the crowd, straining his neck to see what was going on, and forgetting all about his business. At the departure of the priest he turned around and discovered that every one of his pears was gone. He then knew that those the old fellow had been giving away so freely were really his own pears. Looking more closely at the barrow, he also found that one of the handles was missing, evidently having been newly cut off. Boiling with rage, he set out in pursuit of the priest, and just as he turned the corner he saw the lost barrow-handle lying under the wall, being in fact the very pear-tree the priest had cut down. But there were no traces of the priest—much to the amusement of the crowd in the market-place.

5. The Taoist Priest of Laoshan

There lived in our village a Mr. Wang, the seventh son in an old family. This gentleman had a *penchant* for the Taoist religion; and hearing that at Laoshan there were plenty of Immortals,[13] shouldered his knapsack and went off for a tour thither. Ascending a peak of the mountain he reached a secluded monastery, where he found a priest sitting on a rush mat, with long hair flowing over his neck, and a pleasant expression on his face. Making a low bow, Wang addressed him thus: "Mysterious indeed is the doctrine: I pray you, Sir, instruct me therein." "Delicately nurtured and wanting in energy as you are," replied the priest, "I fear you could not

---

13   The "angels" of Taoism—immortality in a happy land being the reward held out for a life on earth in accordance with the doctrines of Tao.

Taoist priests are believed by some to possess an elixir of immortality in the form of a precious liquor; others again hold that the elixir consists solely in a virtuous conduct of life.

support the fatigue." "Try me," said Wang. So when the disciples, who were very many in number, collected together at dusk, Wang joined them in making obeisance to the priest, and remained with them in the monastery. Very early next morning the priest summoned Wang, and giving him a hatchet sent him out with the others to cut firewood. Wang respectfully obeyed, continuing to work for over a month until his hands and feet were so swollen and blistered that he secretly meditated returning home. One evening when he came back he found two strangers sitting drinking with his master. It being already dark, and no lamp or candles having been brought in, the old priest took some scissors and cut out a circular piece of paper like a mirror, which he proceeded to stick against the wall. Immediately it became a dazzling moon, by the light of which you could have seen a hair or a beard of corn. The disciples all came crowding around to wait upon them, but one of the strangers said, "On a festive occasion like this we ought all to enjoy ourselves together." Accordingly he took a kettle of wine from the table and presented it to the disciples, bidding them drink each his fill; whereupon our friend Wang began to wonder how seven or eight of them could all be served out of a single kettle. The disciples, too, rushed about in search of cups, each struggling to get the first drink for fear the wine should be exhausted. Nevertheless, all the candidates failed to empty the kettle, at which they were very much astonished, when suddenly one of the strangers said, "You have given us a fine bright moon; but it's dull work drinking by ourselves. Why not call Changao[14] to join us?" He then seized a chop-stick and threw it into the moon, whereupon a lovely girl stepped forth, from its beams. At first she was only a foot high, but on reaching the ground lengthened to the ordinary size of woman. She had a slender waist and a beautiful neck, and went most gracefully through the Red Garment figure.[15] When this was finished she sang the following words:

Ye fairies! ye fairies! I'm coming back soon,
Too lonely and cold is my home in the moon.

Her voice was clear and well sustained, ringing like the notes of a flageolet, and when she had concluded her song she pirouetted around and jumped up on the table, where, with every eye fixed in astonishment upon

---

14   The beautiful wife of a legendary chieftain named Hou Yi, who flourished about 2500 BCE She is said to have stolen from her husband the elixir of immortality, and to have fled with it to the moon.
15   The name of a celebrated *pas seul* of antiquity.

her, she once more became a chop-stick. The three friends laughed loudly, and one of them said, "We are very jolly tonight, but I have hardly room for any more wine. Will you drink a parting glass with me in the palace of the moon?" They then took up the table and walked into the moon, where they could be seen drinking so plainly that their eyebrows and beards appeared like reflections in a looking-glass. By-and-by the moon became obscured; and when the disciples brought a lighted candle they found the priest sitting in the dark alone. The viands, however, were still upon the table and the mirror-like piece of paper on the wall. "Have you all had enough to drink?" asked the priest; to which they answered that they had. "In that case," said he, "you had better get to bed, so as not to be behind-hand with your wood-cutting in the morning." So they all went off, and among them Wang, who was delighted at what he had seen, and thought no more of returning home. But after a time he could not stand it any longer; and as the priest taught him no magical arts he determined not to wait, but went to him and said, "Sir, I have traveled many long miles for the benefit of your instruction. If you will not teach me the secret of Immortality, let me at any rate learn some trifling trick, and thus soothe my cravings for a knowledge of your art. I have now been here two or three months, doing nothing but chop firewood, out in the morning and back at night, work to which I was never accustomed in my own home." "Did I not tell you," replied the priest, "that you would never support the fatigue? Tomorrow I will start you on your way home." "Sir," said Wang, "I have worked for you a long time. Teach me some small art, that my coming here may not have been wholly in vain." "What art?" asked the priest. "Well," answered Wang, "I have noticed that whenever you walk about anywhere, walls and so on are no obstacle to you. Teach me this, and I'll be satisfied." The priest laughingly assented, and taught Wang a formula which he bade him recite. When he had done so he told him to walk through the wall; but Wang, seeing the wall in front of him, didn't like to walk at it. As, however, the priest bade him try, he walked quietly up to it and was there stopped. The priest here called out, "Don't go so slowly. Put your head down and rush at it." So Wang stepped back a few paces and went at it full speed; and the wall yielding to him as he passed, in a moment he found himself outside. Delighted at this, he went in to thank the priest, who told him to be careful in the use of his power, or otherwise there would be no response, handing him at the same time some money for his expenses on the way. When Wang got home, he went about bragging of his Taoist friends and his contempt for walls in general; but as his wife disbelieved his story, he set about going through the performance as before. Stepping back from the wall, he rushed at it full speed with his head down; but coming in contact with the hard bricks, finished up in a heap on the floor. His wife picked him up and found he had a bump on his forehead as big as a large egg, at which she roared with laughter; but Wang was overwhelmed with rage and shame, and cursed the old priest for his base ingratitude.

6. The Buddhist Priest of Changqing

AT Changqing there lived a Buddhist priest of exceptional virtue and purity of conduct, who, though over eighty years of age, was still hale and hearty. One day he fell down and could not move; and when the other priests rushed to help him up, they found he was already gone. The old priest was himself unconscious of death, and his soul flew away to the borders of the province of Henan. Now it chanced that the scion of an old family residing in Henan had gone out that very day with some ten or a dozen followers to hunt the hare with falcons;[16] but his horse having run away with him he fell off and was killed. Just at that moment the soul of the priest came by and entered into the body, which thereupon gradually recovered consciousness. The servants crowded around to ask him how he felt, when opening his eyes wide, he cried out, "How did I get here? "They assisted him to rise, and led him into the house, where all his ladies came to see him and inquire how he did. In great amazement he said, "I am a Buddhist priest. How came I hither? "His servants thought he was wandering, and tried to recall him by pulling his ears. As for himself, he could make nothing of it, and closing

16   This form of sport may still be seen in the north of China. A hare being started, two Chinese gray-hounds (which are very slow) are slipped from their leash in pursuit. But, as the hare would easily run straight away from them, a falcon is released almost simultaneously. The latter soars to a considerable height, and then swoops down on the hare, striking it a violent blow with the "pounce," or claw. This partially stuns the hare, and allows the dogs to regain lost ground, by which time the hare is ready once more, and off they go again. The chase is ended by the hare getting to earth in a fox's burrow, or being ultimately overtaken by the dogs. In the latter case the heart and liver are cut out on the spot, and given to the falcon; otherwise he would hunt no more that day. Two falcons are often released, one shortly after the other. They wear hoods, which are removed at the moment of flying, and are attached by a slip-string from one leg to the falconer's wrist. During the night previous to a day's hunting they are not allowed to sleep. Each falconer lies down with one falcon on his left wrist, and keeps up an incessant tapping with the other hand on the bird's head. This is done to make them fierce. Should the quarry escape, a hare's skin is thrown down, by which means the falcons are secured, and made ready for a further flight. Occasionally, but rarely, the falcon misses its blow at the hare, with the result of a broken or injured "arm."

his eyes refrained from saying anything further. For food he would only eat rice, refusing all wine and meat; and avoided the society of his wives.[17] After some days he felt inclined for a stroll, at which all his family were delighted; but no sooner had he got outside and stopped for a little rest than he was besieged by servants begging him to take their accounts as usual. However, he pleaded illness and want of strength, and no more was said. He then took occasion to ask if they knew the district of Changqing, and on being answered in the affirmative expressed his intention of going thither for a trip, as he felt anxious about those he had left to their own resources, at the same time bidding the servants look after his affairs at home. They tried to dissuade him from this on the ground of his having but recently risen from a sick bed; but he paid no heed to their remonstrances, and on the very next day set out. Arriving in the Changqing district, he found everything unchanged; and without being put to the necessity of asking the road, made his way straight to the monastery. His former disciples received him with every token of respect as an honored visitor; and in reply to his question as to where the old priest was, they informed him that their worthy teacher had been dead for some time. On asking to be shown his grave, they led him to a spot where there was a solitary mound some three feet high, over which the grass was not yet green. Not one of them knew his motives for visiting this place; and by-and-by he ordered his horse, saying to the disciples, "Your master was a virtuous priest. Carefully preserve whatever relics of him you may have, and keep them from injury." They all promised to do this, and he then set off on his way home. When he arrived there, he fell into a listless state and took no interest in his family affairs. So much so, that after a few months he ran away and went straight to his former home at the monastery, telling the disciples that he was their old master. This they refused to believe, and laughed among themselves at his pretensions; but he told them the whole story, and recalled many incidents of his previous life among them, until at last they were convinced. He then occupied his old bed and went through the same daily routine as before, paying no attention to the repeated entreaties of his family, who came with carriages and horses to beg him to return. About a year subsequently, his wife sent one of the servants with splendid presents of gold and silk, all of which he refused with the exception of a single linen robe. And whenever any of his old friends

---

17   Abstinence from wine and meat, and celibacy, are among the most important rules of the Buddhist church, as specially applied to its priesthood. At the door of every Buddhist monastery may be seen a notice that "No wine or meat may enter here!" Even the laity are not supposed to drink wine.

passed this monastery, they always went to pay him their respects, finding him quiet, dignified, and pure. He was then barely thirty, though he had been a priest for more than eighty years.[18]

7. The Marriage of the Fox's Daughter

A PRESIDENT of the Board of Civil Office,[19] named Yin, and a native of Licheng, when a young man, was very badly off, but was endowed with considerable physical courage. Now in this part of the country there was a large establishment, covering several acres, with an unbroken succession of pavilions and verandahs, and belonging to one of the old county families; but because ghosts and apparitions were frequently seen there, the place had for a long time remained untenanted, and was overgrown with grass and weeds, no one venturing to enter in even in broad daylight. One evening when Yin was carousing with some fellow-students, one of them jokingly said, "If anybody will pass a night in the haunted house, the rest of us will stand him a dinner." Mr. Yin jumped up at this, and cried out, "What is there difficult in that?" So, taking with him a sleeping-mat, he proceeded thither, escorted by all his companions as far as the door, where they laughed and said, We will wait here a little while. In case you see anything, shout out to us at once." "If there are any goblins or foxes," replied Yin, "I'll catch them for you." He then went in, and found the paths obliterated by long grass, which had sprung up, mingled with weeds of various kinds. It was just the time of the new moon, and by its feeble light he was able to make out the door of the house. Feeling his way, he walked on until he reached the back pavilion, and then went up on to the Moon Terrace, which was such a pleasant spot that he determined to stop there. Gazing westwards, he sat for a long time looking at the moon—a single thread of light embracing in its horns the peak of a hill[20]—without hearing anything at all unusual; so, laughing to himself at the nonsense people talked, he spread his mat upon the floor, put a stone under his head for a pillow, and lay down to sleep. He

---

18   Having renewed his youth by assuming the body of the young man into which his soul had entered.

19   One of the "Six Boards" (now Seven) at the capital, equivalent to our own War Office, Board of Works, etc.

20   Which, of course, is impossible.

had watched the Cow-herd and the Lady[21] until they were just disappearing, and was on the point of dropping off, when suddenly he heard footsteps down below coming up the stairs. Pretending to be asleep, he saw a servant enter, carrying in his hand a lotus-shaped lantern,[22] who, on observing Mr. Yin, rushed back in a fright, and said to someone behind, "There is a stranger here!" The person spoken to asked who it was, but the servant did not know; and then up came an old gentleman, who, after examining Mr. Yin closely, said, "It's the future President: he's as drunk as can be. We needn't mind him; besides, he's a good fellow, and won't give us any trouble." So they walked in and opened all the doors; and by-and-by there were a great many other people moving about, and quantities of lamps were lighted, until the place was as light as day. About this time Mr, Yin slightly changed his position, and sneezed; upon which the old man, perceiving that he was awake, came forward and fell down on his knees, saying, "Sir, I have a daughter who is to be married this very night. It was not anticipated that Your Honor would be here. I pray, therefore, that we may be excused." Mr. Yin got up and raised the old man, regretting that, in his ignorance of the festive occasion, he had brought with him no present.[23] "Ah, Sir," replied the old man, "your very presence here will ward off all noxious influences; and that is quite enough for us." He then begged Mr. Yin to assist in doing the honors, and thus double the obligation already conferred. Mr. Yin readily assented, and went inside to look at the gorgeous arrangements they had made. He was here met by a lady, apparently about forty years of age, whom the old gentleman introduced as his wife; and he had hardly made his bow when he heard the sound of flageolets,[24] and some one came hurrying in, saying, "He has come!" The old gentleman flew out to meet this personage, and Mr. Yin also stood up, awaiting his arrival. In no long time, a bevy of people with gauze lanterns ushered in the bridegroom himself, who seemed to be about seventeen or eighteen years old, and of a most refined and prepossessing appearance. The old gentleman bade him pay his respects first to their worthy guest; and upon his looking towards Mr. Yin, that gentleman came forward to welcome him on behalf of the host. Then followed ceremonies between the old man and his son-in-law; and when these were over, they all sat down to supper. Hosts of waiting-maids brought in profuse quantities of wine and meats, with bowls

---

21   The Chinese names for certain stars: $\beta\gamma$ Aquilae and α Lyrae.
22   Lanterns very prettily made to resemble all kinds of flowers are to be seen at the Chinese New Year.
23   This is, as with us, obligatory on all friends invited to a marriage.
24   The accompaniment of all weddings and funerals in China.

and cups of jade or gold, until the table glittered again. And when the wine had gone around several times, the old gentleman told one of the maids to summon the bride. This she did, but some time passed and no bride came. So the old man rose and drew aside the curtain, pressing the young lady to come forth; whereupon a number of women escorted out the bride, whose ornaments went *tinkle tinkle* as she walked along, sweet perfumes being all the time diffused around. Her father told her to make the proper salutation, after which she went and sat by her mother. Mr. Yin took a glance at her, and saw that she wore on her head beautiful ornaments made of kingfisher's feathers, her beauty quite surpassing anything he had ever seen. All this time they had been drinking their wine out of golden goblets big enough to hold several pints, when it flashed across him that one of these goblets would be a capital thing to carry back to his companions in evidence of what he had seen. So he secreted it in his sleeve, and pretending to be tipsy,[25] leaned forward with his head upon the table as if going off to sleep. "The gentleman is drunk," said the guests; and by-and-by Mr. Yin heard the bridegroom take his leave, and there was a general trooping downstairs to the "tune of a wedding march." When they were all gone the old gentleman collected the goblets, one of which was missing, though they hunted high and low to find it. Someone mentioned the sleeping guest; but the old gentleman stopped him at once for fear Mr. Yin should hear, and before long silence reigned throughout. Mr. Yin then arose. It was dark, and he had no light; but he could detect the lingering smell of the food, and the place was filled with the fumes of wine. Faint streaks of light now appearing in the east, he began quietly to make a move, having first satisfied himself that the goblet was still in his sleeve. Arriving at the door, he found his friends already there; for they had been afraid he might come out after they left, and go in again early in the morning. When he produced the goblet they were all lost in astonishment; and on hearing his story, they were fain to believe it, well knowing that a poor student like Yin was not likely to have such a valuable piece of plate in his possession.

Later on Mr. Yin took his doctor's degree, and was appointed magistrate over the district of Fei-qiu, where there was an old-established family of the name of Zhu. The head of the family asked him to a banquet in honor of his arrival, and ordered the servants to bring in the large goblets. After

---

25 The soberest people in the world, amongst whom anything like sottishness is comparatively unknown, think it no disgrace, but rather complimentary, to get pleasantly tipsy on all festive occasions; and people who are physically unable to do so frequently go so far as to hire substitutes to drink for them. Mandarins specially suffer very much from the custom of being obliged to take "wine" with a large number of guests. For further on this subject, see note 258 in tale number 54.

some delay a slave-girl came and whispered something to her master which seemed to make him very angry. Then the goblets were brought in, and Mr. Yin was invited to drink. He now found that these goblets were of precisely the same shape and pattern as the one he had at home, and at once begged his host to tell him where he had had these made. "Well," said Mr. Zhu, "there should be eight of them. An ancestor of mine had them made, when he was a minister at the capital, by an experienced artificer. They have been handed down in our family from generation to generation, and have now been carefully laid by for some time; but I thought we would have them out today as a compliment to your Honor. However, there are only seven to be found. None of the servants can have touched them, for the old seals of ten years ago are still upon the box, unbroken. I don't know what to make of it." Mr. Yin laughed, and said, "It must have flown away! Still, it is a pity to lose an heirloom of that kind; and as I have a very similar one at home, I shall take upon myself to send it to you." When the banquet was over, Mr. Yin went home, and taking out his own goblet, sent it off to Mr. Zhu. The latter was somewhat surprised to find that it was identical with his own, and hurried away to thank the magistrate for his gift, asking him at the same time how it had come into his possession. Mr. Yin told him the whole story, which proves conclusively that although a fox may obtain possession of a thing, even at a distance of many hundred miles, he will not venture to keep it altogether.[26]

8. Miss Jiaonuo

KONG XUELI was a descendant of Confucius.[27] He was a man of considerable ability, and an excellent poet.[28] A fellow-student, to whom he was much attached, became magistrate at Tiantai, and sent for Kong to join him. Unfortunately, just before Kong arrived his friend died, and he found

---

26   The wedding-party was, of course, composed entirely of foxes, this animal being believed by the Chinese to be capable of appearing at will under the human form, and of doing either good or evil to its friends or foes. These facts will be prominently brought out in several of the stories to follow.
27   Lineal descendants of Confucius are to be found at this day living together as a clan, near their founder's mausoleum in Shandong. The head of the family is a hereditary *gong* or "duke," and each member enjoys a share of the revenues with which the family has been endowed, in well-merited recognition of the undying influence of China's greatest sage.
28   More or less proficiency in the art of poetry is an absolutely essential qualification for all who present themselves at the great competitive tests by which successful candidates are admitted to Chinese official life.

himself without the means of returning home; so he took up his abode in a Buddhist monastery, where he was employed in transcribing for the priests. Several hundred paces to the west of this monastery there was a house belonging to a Mr. Shan, a gentleman who had known better days, but who had spent all his money in a heavy lawsuit; and then, as his family was a small one, had gone away to live in the country and left his house vacant. One day there was a heavy fall of snow which kept visitors away from the monastery; and Kong, finding it dull, went out. As he was passing by the door of the house above-mentioned, a young man of very elegant appearance came forth, who, the moment he saw Kong, ran up to him, and with a bow, entered into conversation, asking him to be pleased to walk in. Kong was much taken with the young man, and followed him inside. The rooms were not particularly large, but adorned throughout with embroidered curtains, and from the walls hung scrolls and drawings by celebrated masters. On the table lay a book, the title of which was "Jottings from Paradise;" and turning over its leaves, Kong found therein many strange things. He did not ask the young man his name, presuming that as he lived in the Shan family mansion, he was necessarily the owner of the place. The young man, however, inquired what he was doing in that part of the country, and expressed great sympathy with his misfortunes, recommending him to set about taking pupils. "Alas!" said Kong, "who will play the Mæcenas to a distressed wayfarer like myself?" "If," replied the young man, "you would condescend so far, I for my part would gladly seek instruction at your hands." Kong was much gratified at this, but said he dared not arrogate to himself the position of teacher, and begged merely to be considered as the young man's friend. He then asked him why the house had been shut up for so long; to which the young man replied, "This is the Shan family mansion. It has been closed all this time because of the owner's removal into the country. My surname is Huangfu, and my home is in Shaanxi; but as our house has been burnt down in a great fire, we have put up here for a while." Thus Mr. Kong found out that his name was not Shan. That evening they spent in laughing and talking together, and Kong remained there for the night. In the morning a lad came in to light the fire; and the young man, rising first, went into the private part of the house. Mr. Kong was sitting up with the bed-clothes still huddled around him, when the lad looked in and said, "Master's coming!" So he jumped up with a start, and in came an old man with a silvery beard, who began to thank him, saying, "I am very much obliged to you for your condescension in becoming my son's tutor. At present he writes a villainous hand; and

I can only hope you will not allow the ties of friendship to interfere with discipline." Thereupon, he presented Mr. Kong with an embroidered suit of clothes, a sable hat, and a set of shoes and stockings; and when the latter had washed and dressed himself he called for wine and food. Kong could not make out what the valances of the chairs and tables were made of; they were so very bright-colored and dazzling. By-and-by, when the wine had circulated several times, the old gentleman picked up his walking-stick and took his leave. After breakfast the young man handed in his theme, which turned out to be written in an archaic style, and not at all after the modern fashion of essay-writing. Kong asked him why he had done this, to which the young man replied that he did not contemplate competing at the public examinations. In the evening they had another drinking-bout, but it was agreed that there should be no more of it after that night. The young man then called the boy and told him to see if his father was asleep or not; adding that if he was, he might quietly summon Miss Perfume. The boy went off, first taking a guitar out of a very pretty case; and in a few minutes in came a very nice-looking young girl. The young man bade her play the *Death of Shun*;[29] and seizing an ivory plectrum she swept the chords, pouring forth a vocal melody of exquisite sweetness and pathos. He then gave her a goblet of wine to drink, and it was midnight before they parted. Next morning they got up early and settled down to work. The young man proved an apt scholar: he could remember what he had once read, and at the end of two or three months had made astonishing progress. Then they agreed that every five days they would indulge in a symposium, and that Miss Perfume should always be of the party. One night when the wine had gone into Kong's head, he seemed to be lost in a reverie; whereupon his young friend, who knew what was the matter with him, said. "This girl was brought up by my father. I know you find it lonely, and I have long been looking out for a nice wife for you." "Let her only resemble Miss Perfume," said Kong, "and she will do." "Your experience," said the young man, laughing, "is but limited, and, consequently, anything is a surprise to you. If Miss Perfume is your *beau ideal*, why, it will not be difficult to satisfy you."

Some six months had passed away, when one day Mr. Kong took it into his head that he would like to go out for a stroll in the country. The

---

29   One of the two celebrated but legendary rulers of China in the golden ages of antiquity. Yao— who abdicated 2357 BCE—nominated as his successor a young and virtuous husbandman named Shun, giving him both his daughters in marriage. At the death of Shun, these ladies are said to have wept so much that their tears literally drenched the bamboos which grew beside their husband's grave; and the speckled bamboo is now commonly known as the bamboo of Shun's wives.

entrance, however, was carefully closed; and on asking the reason, the young man told him that his father wished to receive no guests for fear of causing interruption to his studies. So Kong thought no more about it; and by-and-by, when the heat of summer came on, they moved their study to a pavilion in the garden. At this time Mr. Kong had a swelling on the chest about as big as a peach, which, in a single night, increased to the size of a bowl. There he lay groaning with the pain, while his pupil waited upon him day and night. He slept badly and took hardly any food; and in a few days the place got so much worse that he could neither eat nor drink. The old gentleman also came in, and he and his son lamented over him together. Then the young man said, "I was thinking last night that my sister, Jiaonuo, would be able to cure Mr. Kong, and accordingly I sent over to my grandmother's asking her to come. She ought to be here by now." At that moment a servant entered and announced Miss Jiaonuo, who had come with her cousin, having been at her aunt's house. Her father and brother ran out to meet her, and then brought her in to see Mr. Kong. She was between thirteen and fourteen years old, and had beautiful eyes with a very intelligent expression in them, and a most graceful figure besides. No sooner had Mr. Kong beheld this lovely creature than he quite forgot to groan, and began to brighten up. Meanwhile the young man was saying, "This respected friend of mine is the same to me as a brother. Try, sister, to cure him." Miss Jiaonuo immediately dismissed her blushes, and rolling up her long sleeves approached the bed to feel his pulse.[30] As she was grasping his wrist, Kong became conscious of a perfume more delicate than that of the epidendrum; and then she laughed, saying, "This illness was to be expected; for the heart is touched. Though it is severe, a cure can be effected; but, as there is already a swelling, not without using the knife." Then she drew from her arm a gold bracelet which she pressed down upon the suffering spot, until by degrees the swelling rose within the bracelet and overtopped it by an inch and more, the outlying parts that were inflamed also passing under, and thus very considerably reducing the extent of the tumor: With one hand she opened her robe and took out a knife with an edge as keen as paper, and pressing the bracelet down all the time with the other, proceeded to cut lightly around near the root of the swelling. The dark blood gushed forth, and stained the bed and the mat; but Mr. Kong

---

30   Volumes have been written by Chinese doctors on the subject of the pulse. They profess to distinguish as many as twenty-four different kinds, among which is one well known to our own practitioners—namely, the "thready" pulse; they, moreover, make a point of feeling the pulses of *both* wrists.

was delighted to be near such a beauty— not only felt no pain, but would willingly have continued the operation that she might sit by him a little longer. In a few moments the whole thing was removed, and looked like a growth which had been cut off a tree. Here Miss Jiaonuo called for water to wash the wound, and from between her lips she took a red pill as big as a bullet, which she laid upon the flesh, and; after drawing the skin together, passed around and around the place. The first turn felt like the searing of a hot iron; the second like a gentle itching; and at the third he experienced a sensation of lightness and coolness which penetrated into his very bones and marrow. The young lady then returned the pill to her mouth, and said, "He is cured," hurrying away as fast as she could. Mr. Kong jumped up to thank her, and found that his complaint had quite disappeared. Her beauty, however, had made such an impression on him that his troubles were hardly at an end. From this moment he gave up his books, and took no interest in anything. This state of things was soon noticed by the young man, who said to him, "My brother, I have found a fine match for you." "Who is it to be?" asked Kong. "Oh, one of the family," replied his friend. Thereupon Mr. Kong remained some time lost in thought, and at length said, "Please don't!" Then turning his face to the wall, he repeated these lines:

Speak not of lakes and streams to him who once has seen the sea; The clouds that circle Wu's peak are the only clouds for me.[31]

The young man guessed to whom he was alluding, and replied, "My father has a very high opinion of your talents and would gladly receive you into the family, but that he has only one daughter, and she is much too young. My cousin, Asong, however, is seventeen years old, and not at all a bad-looking girl. If you doubt my word, you can wait in the verandah until she takes her daily walk in the garden, and thus judge for yourself." This Mr. Kong acceded to, and accordingly saw Miss Jiaonuo come out with a lovely girl—her black eyebrows beautifully arched, and her tiny feet encased in phoenix-shaped shoes—as like one another as they well could be. He was of course delighted, and begged the young man to arrange all preliminaries; and the very next day his friend came to tell him that the affair was finally settled. A portion of the house was given up to the bride and bridegroom, and the marriage was celebrated with plenty of music and hosts of guests, more like a fairy wedding than anything else. Mr. Kong was very happy, and

---

31   By a famous poet, named Yuan Zhen, 779–831 CE.

began to think that the position of Paradise had been wrongly laid down, until one day the young man came to him and said, "For the trouble you have been at in teaching me, I shall ever remain your debtor. At the present moment, the Shan family lawsuit has been brought to a termination, and they wish to resume possession of their house immediately. We therefore propose returning to Shaanxi, and as it is unlikely that you and I will ever meet again, I feel very sorrowful at the prospect of parting." Mr. Kong replied that he would go too, but the young man advised him to return to his old home. This, he observed, was no easy matter; upon which the young man said, "Don't let that trouble you: I will see you safe there." By-and-by his father came in with Mr. Kong's wife, and presented Mr. Kong with one hundred ounces of gold; and then the young man gave the husband and wife each one of his hands to grasp, bidding them shut their eyes. The next instant they were floating away in the air, with the wind whizzing in their ears. In a little while he said, "You have arrived," and opening his eyes, Kong beheld his former home. Then he knew that the young man was not a human being. Joyfully he knocked at the old door, and his mother was astonished to see him arrive with such a nice wife. They were all rejoicing together, when he turned around and found that his friend had disappeared. His wife attended on her mother-in-law with great devotion, and acquired a reputation both for virtue and beauty, which was spread around far and near. Some time passed away, and then Mr. Kong took his doctor's degree, and was appointed Governor of the Jail in Yan'an. He proceeded to his post with his wife only, the journey being too long for his mother, and by-and-by a son was born. Then he got into trouble by being too honest an official, and threw up his appointment; but had not the wherewithal to get home again. One day when out hunting he met a handsome young man riding on a nice horse, and seeing that he was staring very hard looked closely at him. It was young Huangfa. So they drew bridle, and fell to laughing and crying by turns—the young man then inviting Kong to go along with him. They rode on together until they had reached a village thickly shaded with trees, so that the sun and sky were invisible overhead, and entered into a most elaborately-decorated mansion, such as might belong to an old-established family. Kong asked after Miss Jiaonuo, and heard that she was married; also that his own mother-in-law was dead, at which tidings he was greatly moved. Next day he went back and returned again with his wife. Jiaonuo also joined them, and taking up Kong's child, played with it, saying, "Your mother played us truant." Mr. Kong did not forget to thank her for her former kindness to him, to which she replied, "You're a great man now.

Though the wound has healed, haven't you forgotten the pain yet?" Her husband, too, came to pay his respects, returning with her on the following morning. One day the young Huangfu seemed troubled in spirit, and said to Mr. Kong, "A great calamity is impending. Can you help us?" Mr. Kong did not know what he was alluding to, but readily promised his assistance. The young man then ran out and summoned the whole family to worship in the ancestral hall, at which Mr. Kong was alarmed, and asked what it all meant. "You know," answered the young man, "I am not a man but a fox. Today we shall be attacked by thunder;[32] and if only you will aid us in our trouble, we may still hope to escape. If you are unwilling, take your child and go, that you may not be involved with us." Mr. Kong protested he would live or die with them, and so the young man placed him with a sword at the door, bidding him remain quiet there in spite of all the thunder. He did as he was told, and soon saw black clouds obscuring the light until it was all as dark as pitch. Looking around, he could see that the house had disappeared, and that its place was occupied by a huge mound and a bottomless pit. In the midst of his terror, a fearful peal was heard which shook the very hills, accompanied by a violent wind and driving rain. Old trees were torn up, and Mr. Kong became both dazed and deaf. Yet he stood firm until he saw in a dense black column of smoke a horrid thing with a sharp beak and long claws, with which it snatched someone from the hole, and was disappearing up with the smoke. In an instant Kong knew by her clothes and shoes that the victim was no other than Jiaonuo, and instantly jumping up he struck the devil violently with his sword, and cut it down. Immediately the mountains were riven, and a sharp peal of thunder laid Kong dead upon the ground. Then the clouds cleared away, and Jiaonuo gradually came around, to find Kong dead at her feet. She burst out crying at the sight, and declared that she would not live since Kong had died for her. Kong's wife also came out, and they bore the body inside. Jiaonuo then made Asong hold her husband's head, while her brother pried open his teeth with a hair-pin, and she herself arranged his jaw. She next put a red pill into his mouth, and bending down breathed into him. The pill went along with the current of air, and presently there was a gurgle in his throat, and he came around. Seeing all the family about him, he was disturbed as if waking from a dream. However, they were all united together, and fear

---

32 The Chinese believe that wicked people are struck by the God of Thunder, and killed in punishment for some hidden crime. They regard lightning merely as an arrangement with a mirror by which the God is enabled to see his victim.

gave place to joy; but Mr. Kong objected to five in that out-of-the-way place, and proposed that they should return with him to his native village. To this they were only too pleased to assent—all except Jiaonuo; and when Mr. Kong invited her husband, Mr. Wu, as well, she said she feared her father and mother-in-law would not like to lose the children. They had tried all day to persuade her, but without success, when suddenly in rushed one of the Wu family's servants, dripping with perspiration and quite out of breath. They asked what was the matter, and the servant replied that the Wu family had been visited by a calamity on the very same day, and had every one perished. Jiaonuo cried very bitterly, at this, and could not be comforted; but now there was nothing to prevent them from all returning together. Mr. Kong went into the city for a few days on business, and then they set to work packing-up night and day. On arriving at their destination, separate apartments were allotted to young Mr. Huangfu, and these he kept carefully shut up, only opening the door to Mr. Kong and his wife.

Mr. Kong amused himself with the young man and his sister Jiaonuo, filling up the time with chess,[33] wine, conversation, and good cheer, as if they had been one family. His little boy, Huan, grew up to be a handsome young man, but with a touch of the fox in his composition; so that when he showed himself abroad, he was immediately recognised as the son of a fox.

9. Magical Arts

A CERTAIN Mr. Yu was a spirited young fellow, fond of boxing and trials of strength. He was able to take two kettles and swing them around about with the speed of the wind. Now, during the reign of Chong Zheng,[34] when up for the final examination at the capital, his servant became seriously ill. Much troubled at this, he applied to a necromancer in the market-place[35]

---

33   Chinese "chess" is similar to, but not identical with, our game. The board is divided by a river, and the king is confined to a small square of moves on his own territory. The game *par excellence* in China is *weiqi* (go), an account of which I contributed to the *Temple Bar* magazine for January 1877.

34   The last emperor of the Ming dynasty. Began to reign 1628 CE.

35   The trade of fortune-teller is one of the most flourishing in China. A large majority of the candidates who are unsuccessful at the public examinations devote their energies in this direction; and in every Chinese city there are regular establishments whither the superstitious people repair to consult the oracle on every imaginable subject—not to mention hosts of itinerant soothsayers, both in town and country, whose stock-in-trade consists of a trestle-table, pen, ink, and paper, and a few other mysterious implements of their art. The nature of the response, favorable or otherwise, is determined by an inspection of the year, month, day, and hour at which the applicant was born, taken in combination with other

who was skillful at determining the various leases of life allotted to men. Before he had uttered a word, the necromancer asked him, saying, "Is it not about your servant, Sir, that you would consult me?" Mr. Yu was startled at this, and replied that it was. "The sick man," continued the necromancer, "will come to no harm; you, Sir, are the one in danger." Mr. Yu then begged him to cast his nativity, which he proceeded to do, finally saying to Mr. Yu, "You have but three days to live! Dreadfully frightened, he remained some time in a state of stupefaction, when the necromancer quietly observed that he possessed the power of averting this calamity by magic, and would exert it for the sum of ten ounces of silver. But Mr. Yu reflected that Life and Death are already fixed,[36] and he didn't see how magic could save him. So he refused, and was just going away, whereupon the necromancer said, "You grudge this trifling outlay. I hope you will not repent it." Mr. Yu's friends also urged him to pay the money, advising him rather to empty his purse than not secure the necromancer's compassion. Mr. Yu, however, would not hear of it, and the three days slipped quickly away. Then he sat down calmly in his inn to see what was going to happen. Nothing did happen all day, and at night he shut his door and trimmed the lamp; then, with a sword at his side, he awaited the approach of death.

By-and-by, the clepsydra[37] showed that two hours had already gone without bringing him any nearer to dissolution; and he was thinking about lying down, when he heard a scratching at the window, and then saw a tiny little man creep through, carrying a spear on his shoulder, who, on reaching the ground, shot up to the ordinary height. Mr. Yu seized his sword and at once struck at it; but only succeeded in cutting the air. His visitor instantly shrank down small again, and made an attempt to escape through the crevice of the window; but Yu redoubled his blows and at last brought him to the ground. Lighting the lamp, he found only a paper man,[38] cut right

---

particulars referring to the question at issue.

36   A firm belief in predestination is an important characteristic of the Chinese mind. "All is destiny" is a phrase daily in the mouth of every man, woman, and child, in the empire. Confucius himself, we are told, objected to discourse to his disciples upon this topic; but it is evident from many passages in the *Lun Yu*, or *Confucian Gospels* [Book VI. ch. 8, Book xiv. ch. 38, etc.], that he believed in a certain pre-arrangement of human affairs, against which all efforts would be unavailing.

37   An appliance of very ancient date in China, now superseded by cheap clocks and watches. A large clepsydra, consisting of four copper jars standing on steps one above the other, is still, however, to be seen in the city of Canton, and is in excellent working order, the night-watches being determined by reference to its indicator in the lower jar. By its aid, coils of "joss-stick," or pastille, are regulated to burn so many hours, and are sold to the poor, who use them both for the purpose of guiding their extremely vague-notions of time, and for lighting the oft-recurring tobacco-pipe.

38   "Paper men" are a source of great dread to the people at large. During the year 1876 whole provinces were convulsed by the belief that some such superstitious agency was at work to deprive innocent

through the middle. This made him afraid to sleep, and he sat up watching, until in a little time he saw a horrid hobgoblin creep through the same place. No sooner did it touch the ground than he assailed it lustily with his sword, at length cutting it in half. Seeing, however, that both halves kept on wriggling about, and fearing that it might get up again, he went on hacking at it. Every blow told, giving forth a hard sound, and when he came to examine his work, he found a clay image all knocked to pieces. Upon this he moved his seat near to the window, and kept his eye fixed upon the crack. After some time, he heard a noise like a bull bellowing outside the window, and something pushed against the window-frame with such force as to make the whole house tremble and seem about to fall. Mr. Yu, fearing he should be buried under the ruins, thought he could not do better than fight outside; so he accordingly burst open the door with a crash and rushed out. There he found a huge devil, as tall as the house, and he saw by the dim light of the moon that its face was as black as coal. Its eyes shot forth yellow fire: it had nothing either upon its shoulders or feet; but held a bow in its hand and had some arrows at its waist. Mr. Yu was terrified; and the devil discharged an arrow at him which he struck to the ground with his sword. On Mr. Yu preparing to strike, the devil let off another arrow which the former avoided by jumping aside, the arrow quivering in the wall beyond with a smart crack. The devil here got very angry, and drawing his sword flourished it like a whirlwind, aiming a tremendous blow at Mr. Yu. Mr. Yu ducked, and the whole force of the blow fell upon the stone wall of the house, cutting it right in two. Mr. Yu then ran out from between the devil's legs, and began hacking at its back—whack! whack! The devil now became furious, and roared like thunder, turning around to get another blow at his assailant. But Mr. Yu again ran between his legs, the devil's sword merely cutting off a piece of his coat. Once more he hacked away— whack!—whack! and at length the devil came tumbling down flat. Mr. Yu cut at him right and left, each blow resounding like the watchman's wooden gong,[39] and then, bringing a light, he found it was a wooden image about

persons of their tails; and the so-called "Pope" of the Taoist religion even went so far as to publish a charm against the machinations of the unseen. It ran as follows: "Ye who urge filthy devils to spy out the people: the Master's spirits are at hand and will soon discover you. With this charm anyone may travel by sunlight, moonlight, or starlight all over the earth." At one time popular excitement ran so high that serious consequences were anticipated; and the mandarins in the affected districts found it quite as much as they could do to prevent lynch-law being carried out on harmless strangers who were unlucky enough to give rise to the slightest suspicion.

Taoist priests are generally credited with the power of cutting out human, animal, or other figures, of infusing vitality into them on the spot, and of employing them for purposes of good or evil.

39 Watchmen in China, when on their nightly rounds, keep up an incessant beating on what, for want

as tall as a man. The bow and arrows were still there, the latter attached to its waist. Its carved and painted features were most hideous to behold; and wherever Mr. Yu had struck it with his sword, there was blood. Mr. Yu sat with the light in his hand until morning, when he awoke to the fact that all these devils had been sent by the necromancer in order to kill him, and so evidence his own magical power. The next day, after having told the story far and wide, he went with some others to the place where the necromancer had his stall; but the latter, seeing them coming, vanished in the twinkling of an eye. Someone observed that the blood of a dog would reveal a person who had made himself invisible, and Mr. Yu immediately procured some and went back with it. The necromancer disappeared as before, but on the spot where he had been standing they quickly threw down the dog's blood. Thereupon they saw his head and face all smeared over with blood, his eyes glaring like a devil's; and at once seizing him, they handed him over to the authorities, by whom he was put to death.

10. Joining the Immortals

A Mr. Zhou, of Wen-Teng had in his youth been fellow-student with a Mr. Cheng, and a firm friendship was the result. The latter was poor, and depended very much upon Zhou, who was the elder of the two. He called Zhou's wife his "sister," and had the run of the house just as if he was one of the family. Now this wife happening to die in child-bed, Zhou married another named Wang; but as she was quite a young girl, Cheng did not seek to be introduced.[40] One day her younger brother came to visit her, and was being entertained in the "inner" apartments[41] when Cheng chanced to call. The servant announced his arrival, and Zhou bade him ask Mr. Cheng in. But Cheng would not enter, and took his leave. Thereupon Zhou caused the entertainment to be moved into the public part of the house, and, sending after Cheng, succeeded in bringing him back. They had hardly sat down before someone came in to say that a former servant of the establishment had been severely beaten at the magistrate's yamên; the facts of the case being

---

of a better term, we have called a wooden gong. The object is to let thieves know they are awake and on the look-out.
40   This is a characteristic touch. Only the most intimate of friends ever see each other's wives.
41   Where the women of the family live, and into which no stranger ever penetrates. Among other names by which a Chinese husband speaks of his wife, a very common one is "the inner [wo]man."

that a cow-boy of the Huang family connected with the Board of Rites had driven his cattle across the Zhou family's land, and that words had arisen between the two servants in consequence; upon which the Huang family's servant had complained to his master, who had seized the other and had sent him in to the magistrate's, where he had been bambooed. When Mr. Zhou found out what the matter was, he was exceedingly angry, and said, "How dares this pig-boy fellow behave thus? Why, only a generation ago his master was my father's servant! He emerges a little from his obscurity, and immediately thinks himself I don't know what!" Swelling with rage, he rose to go in quest of Huang, but Cheng held him back, saying, "The age is corrupt: there is no distinction between right and wrong. Besides, the officials of the day are half of them thieves, and you will only get yourself into hot water." Zhou, however, would not listen to him; and it was only when tears were added to remonstrances that he consented to let the matter drop. But his anger did not cease, and he lay tossing and turning all night. In the morning he said to his family, "I can stand the insults of Mr. Huang; but the magistrate is an officer of the Government, and not the servant of influential people. If there is a case of any kind, he should hear both plaintiff and defendant, and not act like a dog, biting anybody he is set upon. I will bring an action against the cow-boy, and see what the magistrate will do to him." As his family rather egged him on, he accordingly proceeded to the magistrate's and entered a formal plaint; but that functionary tore up his petition, and would have nothing to do with it. This roused Zhou's anger, and he told the magistrate plainly what he thought of him, in return for which contempt of court he was at once seized and bound. During the forenoon Mr. Cheng called at his house, where he learnt that Zhou had gone into the city to prosecute the cow-boy, and immediately hurried after him with a view to stop proceedings. But his friend was already in the jail, and all he could do was to stamp his foot in anger. Now it happened that three pirates had just been caught; and the magistrate and Huang, putting their heads together, bribed these fellows to say that Zhou was one of their gang, whereupon the higher authorities were petitioned to deprive him of his status as a graduate,[42] and the magistrate then had him most unmercifully bambooed.[43] Mr. Cheng gained admittance to the jail, and,

---

42   Until which he would be safe, by virtue of his degree, from the degrading penalty of the bamboo.

43   This is the instrument commonly used for flogging criminals in China, and consists of a strip of split bamboo planed down smooth. Strictly speaking there are two kinds, the *heavy* and the *light*; the former is now hardly if ever used. Until the reign of Kang Xi all strokes were given across the back; but that humane Emperor removed the *locus operandi* lower down, "for fear of injuring the liver or the

after a painful interview, proposed that a petition should be presented direct
to the Throne. "Alas!" said Zhou, "here am I bound and guarded, like a
bird in a cage. I have indeed a young brother, but it is as much as he can
do to provide me with food." Then Cheng stepped forward, saying, "I will
perform this service. Of what use are friends who will not assist in the
hour of trouble?" So away he went, and Zhou's brother provided him with
money to defray his expenses. After a long journey he arrived at the capital,
where he found himself quite at a loss as to how he should get the petition
presented. However, hearing that the Emperor was about to set out on
a hunting tour, he concealed himself in the market-place, and when His
Majesty passed by, prostrated himself on the ground with loud cries and
gesticulations. The Emperor received his petition, and sent it to the Board
of Punishments,[44] desiring to be furnished with a report on the case. It was
then more than ten months since the beginning of the affair, and Zhou, who
had been made to confess[45] to this false charge, was already under sentence
of death; so that the officers of the Board were very much alarmed when
they received the Imperial instructions, and set to work to re-hear the case
in person. Huang was also much alarmed, and devised a plan for killing
Mr. Zhou by bribing the jailers to stop his food and drink; so that when
his brother brought provisions he was rudely thrust back and prevented
from taking them in. Mr. Cheng complained of this to the Viceroy of the
province, who investigated the matter himself, and found that Zhou was in
the last stage of starvation, for which the jailers were bambooed to death.
Terrified out of his wits, Huang, by dint of bribing heavily, succeeded in
absconding and escaping a just punishment for his crimes. The magistrate,
however, was banished for perversion of the law, and Zhou was permitted to
return home, his affection for Cheng being now very much increased. But
ever after the prosecution and his friend's captivity, Mr. Cheng took a dismal
view of human affairs, and one day invited Zhou to retire with him from the
world. The latter, who was deeply attached to his young wife, threw cold
water on the proposition, and Mr. Cheng pursued the subject no farther,
though his own mind was fully made up. Not seeing him for some days
afterwards, Mr. Zhou sent to inquire about him at his house; but there they
all thought he was at Zhou's, neither family, in fact, having seen anything
of him. This looked suspicious, and Zhou, aware of his peculiarity, sent off

lungs."
44   See note 18 in tale number 7.
45   It is a principle of Chinese jurisprudence that no sentence can be passed until the prisoner has
confessed his guilt—a principle, however, frequently set aside in practice.

people to look for him, bidding them search all the temples and monasteries in the neighborhood. He also from time to time supplied Cheng's son with money and other necessaries.

Eight or nine years had passed away, when suddenly Cheng re-appeared, clad in a yellow cap and stole, and wearing the expression of a Taoist priest. Zhou was delighted, and seized his arm, saying, "Where have you been? —letting me search for you all over the place." "The solitary cloud and the wild crane," replied Cheng, laughing, "have no fixed place of abode. Since we last met my equanimity has happily been restored." Zhou then ordered wine, and they chatted together on what had taken place in the interval. He also tried to persuade Cheng to detach himself from the Taoist persuasion, but the latter only smiled and answered nothing. "It is absurd!" argued Zhou. "Why cast aside your wife and child as you would an old pair of shoes?" "Not so," answered Cheng; "if men wish to cast me aside, who is there who can do so now?" Zhou asked where he lived, to which he replied, "In the Great Pure Mansion on Mount Lao." They then retired to sleep on the same bed; and by-and-by Zhou dreamt that Cheng was lying on his chest so that he could not breathe. In a fright he asked him what he was doing, but got no answer; and then he woke up with a start. Calling to Cheng and receiving no reply, he sat up and stretched out his hand to touch him. The latter, however, had vanished, he knew not whither. When he got calm, he found he was lying at Cheng's end of the bed, which rather startled him. "I was not tipsy last night," reflected he; "how could I have got over here?" He next called his servants, and when they came and struck a light, lo! he was Cheng. Now Zhou had had a beard, so he put up his hand to feel for it, but found only a few straggling hairs. He then seized a mirror to look at himself, and cried out in alarm: "If this is Mr. Cheng, where on earth am I?" By this time he was wide awake, and knew that Cheng had employed magic to induce him to retire from the world. He was on the point of entering the ladies' apartments; but his brother, not recognising who he was, stopped him, and would not let him go in; and as he himself was unable to prove his own identity, he ordered his horse that he might go in search of Cheng. After some days' journey he arrived at Mount Lao; and, as his horse went along at a good rate, the servant could not keep up with him. By-and-by he rested awhile under a tree, and saw a great number of Taoist priests going backwards and forwards, and among them was one who stared fixedly at him. So he inquired of him where he should find Cheng; whereat the priest laughed and said, "I know the name. He is probably in the Great Pure Mansion." When he had given this answer he went on his way, Zhou following him with his eyes about a stone's-throw, until he saw him speak with some one else, and, after saying a few words, proceed onwards as before. The person whom he had spoken with came on to where Zhou was, and turned out to be a fellow-townsman of his. He was much surprised at meeting Zhou, and said, "I haven't seen you for some years. They told me you had gone to Mount Lao to be a Taoist priest. How is it you are still amusing yourself among mortals? 'Zhou told him who he really was; upon which the other replied, "Why, I thought the gentleman I just met was you! He has only just left me, and can't have got very far." "Is it possible," cried Zhou, "that I didn't know my own face?" Just then the servant came up, and away they went full speed, but could not discover the object of their search. All around them was a vast desert, and they were at a loss whether to go on or to return. But Zhou reflected that he had no longer any home to receive him, and determined to carry out his design to the bitter end; but as the road was dangerous for riding, he gave his horse to the servant, and bade him go back. On he went cautiously by himself, until he spied a boy sitting by the wayside alone. He hurried up to him and asked the boy to direct him where he could find Mr. Cheng. "I am one of his disciples," replied the lad; and, shouldering Zhou's bundle, started off to show the way. They journeyed on together, taking their food by the light of the stars, and sleeping in the open air, until, after many miles of road, they arrived in three days at their destination. But this Great Pure locality was not like that generally spoken of in the world. Though as late as the middle of the tenth moon, there was a great profusion of flowers along the road, quite unlike the beginning of winter. The lad went in and announced the arrival of a stranger, whereupon Mr. Cheng came out, and Zhou recognised his own features. Cheng grasped his hand and led him inside, where he prepared wine and food, and they began to converse together. Zhou noticed many birds of strange plumage, so tame that they were not afraid of him; and these from time to time would alight on the table and sing with voices like Pan-pipes. He was very much astonished at all this, but a love of mundane pleasures had eaten into his soul, and he had no intention of stopping. On the ground were two rush-mats, upon which Cheng invited his friend to sit down with him. Then about midnight a serene calm stole over him; and while he was dozing off for a moment, he seemed to change places with Cheng. Suspecting what had happened, he put his hand up to his chin, and found it covered with a beard as before. At dawn he was anxious to return home, but Cheng pressed him to stay; and when three days had gone by Cheng said to him, "I pray you take a little rest now: tomorrow I will set you on your way." Zhou had barely closed his eyelids before he heard Cheng call out, "Everything is ready for starting!" So he got up and followed him along a road other than that by which he had come, and in a very short time he saw his home in the distance. In spite of Zhou's entreaties, Cheng would not accompany him so far, but made Zhou go, waiting himself by the roadside. So the latter went alone, and when he reached his house, knocked at the door. Receiving no answer, he determined to get over the wall, when he found that his body was as light as a leaf, and with one spring he was over. In the same manner he passed several inner walls, until he reached the ladies' apartments, where he saw by the still burning lamp that the inmates had not yet retired for the night. Hearing people talking within, he licked a hole in the paper window[46] and peeped through, and saw his wife sitting drinking with a most disreputable-looking fellow. Bursting with rage, his first impulse was to surprise them in the act; but seeing there were two against one, he stole away and let himself out by the entrance-gate, hurrying off to Cheng, to whom he related what he had seen, and finally begged his assistance. Cheng willingly went along with him; and when they reached the room, "Zhou seized a big stone and hammered loudly at the door. All was then confusion inside, so Zhou hammered again, upon which the door was barricaded more strongly than before. Here Cheng came forward with his sword,[47] and burst the door open with a crash. Zhou rushed in, and the man inside rushed out; but Cheng was there, and with his sword cut his arm right off. Zhou rudely seized his wife, and asked what it all meant; to which she replied that the man was a friend who sometimes came to take a cup of wine with them. Thereupon Zhou borrowed Cheng's sword and cut off her head,[48] hanging up the trunk on a tree in the courtyard. He then went back with Cheng. By-and-by he awaked and found himself on the bed, at which he was somewhat disturbed, and said, "I have had a strangely confused dream, which has given me a fright." "My brother," replied Cheng, smiling, "you look upon dreams as realities: you mistake realities for dreams." Zhou asked what he meant by these words; and then Cheng showed him his

---

46 Wooden frames covered with a semi-transparent paper are used all over the northern provinces of China; in the south, oyster-shells, cut square and planed down thin, are inserted tile-fashion in the long narrow spaces of a wooden frame made to receive them, and used for the same purpose. But glass is gradually finding its way into the houses of the well-to-do, large quantities being made at Canton and exported to various parts of the empire.
47 Every Taoist priest has a magic sword, corresponding to our "magician's wand."
48 In China, a man has the right to slay his adulterous wife, but he must slay her paramour also; both or neither. Otherwise, he lays himself open to a prosecution for murder. The act completed, he is further bound to proceed at once to the magistrate of the district and report what he has done.

sword besmeared with blood. Zhou was terrified, and sought to destroy himself; but all at once it occurred to him that Cheng might be deceiving him again. Cheng divined his suspicions, and made haste at once to see him home. In a little while they arrived at the village gate, and then Cheng said, "Was it not here that, sword in hand, I awaited you that night? I cannot look upon the unclean spot. I pray you go on, and let me stay here. If you do not return by the afternoon, I will depart alone." Zhou then approached his house, which he found all shut up as if no one was living there; so he went into his brother's.

The latter, when he beheld Zhou, began to weep bitterly, saying, "After your departure, thieves broke into the house and killed my sister-in-law, hanging her body upon a tree. Alas! Alas! The murderers have not yet been caught." Zhou then told him the whole story of his dream, and begged him to stop further proceedings; at all of which his brother was perfectly lost in astonishment. Zhou then asked after his son, and his brother told the nurse to bring him in; whereupon the former said, "Upon this infant are centred the hopes of our race.[49] Tend him well; for I am going to bid adieu to the world." He then took his leave, his brother following him all the time with tears in his eyes to induce him to remain. But he heeded him not; and when they reached the village gate his brother saw him go away with Cheng. From afar he looked back and said, "Forbear, and be happy!" His brother would have replied; but here Cheng whisked his sleeve, and they disappeared. The brother remained there for some time, and then went back overwhelmed with grief. He was an unpractical man, and before many years were over all the property was gone and the family reduced to poverty.

---

49   The importance of male offspring in Chinese social life is hardly to be expressed in words. To the son is confided the task of worshipping at the ancestral tombs, the care of the ancestral tablets, and the due performance of all rites and ceremonies connected with the departed dead. No Chinese man will die, if he can help it, without leaving a son behind him. If his wife is childless he will buy a concubine; and we are told on page 41, vol. xiii., of the *Liaozhai*, that a good wife, "who at thirty years of age has not borne a child should forthwith pawn her jewelry and purchase a concubine for her husband; for to be without a son is hard indeed!" Another and a common resource is to adopt a nephew; and sometimes a boy is bought from starving parents, or from a professional kidnapper. Should a little boy die, no matter how young, his parents do not permit even him to be without the good offices of a son. They adopt some other child on his behalf; and when the latter grows up it becomes his duty to perform the proper ceremonies at his baby father's tomb. Girls do not enjoy the luxury of this sham posterity. They are quietly buried in a hole near the family vault, and their disembodied spirits are left to wander about in the realms below uncared for and unappeased. It must not be inferred, however, from this that the position of woman in China is low, as such is far from being the case. Every mother shares in the ancestral worship, and her name is recorded on the tombstone, side by side with that of her husband. Hence it is that Chinese tombstones are always to the memory either of a father or of a mother, or of both, with occasionally the addition of the grandfather and grandmother, and sometimes even that of the generation preceding.

Zhou's son, who was growing up, was thus unable to secure the services of a tutor, and had no one but his uncle to teach him. One morning, on going into the school-room, the uncle found a letter lying on his desk addressed to himself in his brother's handwriting. There was, however, nothing in it but a finger-nail about four inches in length. Surprised at this, he laid the nail down on the ink-slab while he went out to ask whence the letter had come. This no one knew; but when he went back he found that the ink-stone had been changed into a piece of shining yellow gold. More than ever astonished, he tried the nail on copper and iron things, all of which were likewise turned to gold. He thus became very rich, sharing his wealth with Cheng's son; and it was rumored that the two families possessed the secret of transmutation.[50]

11. The Fighting Quails

WANG CHENG belonged to an old family in Pingyuan, but was such an idle fellow that his property gradually disappeared, until at length all he had left was an old tumble-down house. His wife and he slept under a coarse hempen coverlet, and the former was far from sparing her reproaches. At the time of which we are speaking the weather was unbearably hot; and Wang went to pass the night with many other of his fellow-villagers in a pavilion which stood among some dilapidated buildings belonging to a family named Zhou. With the first streaks of dawn his comrades departed; but Wang slept well on until about nine o'clock, when he got up and proceeded leisurely home. All at once he saw in the grass a gold hair-pin; and taking it up to look at it, found engraved thereon in small characters: "The property of the Imperial family." Now Wang's own grandfather had married into the Imperial family,[51] and consequently he had formerly possessed many similar articles; but while he was thinking it over up came an old woman in search of the hair-pin, which Wang, who though poor was honest, at once produced

---

50   The belief that a knowledge of alchemy is obtainable by leading the life of a pure and perfect Taoist is one of the numerous additions in later ages to this ancient form of religion. See note 11 in tale 4.
51   The direct issue of the Emperors of the present dynasty and their descendants in the male line for ever are entitled to wear a yellow girdle in token of their relationship to the Imperial family, each generation becoming a degree lower in rank, but always retaining this distinctive badge. Members of the collateral branches wear a red girdle, and are commonly known as *gioros*. With the lapse of two hundred and fifty years, the wearers of these badges have become numerous, and in many cases disreputable; and they are now to be found even among the lowest dregs of Chinese social life.

and handed to her. The old woman was delighted, and thanked Wang for his goodness, observing that the pin was not worth much in itself, but was a relic of her departed husband. Wang asked what her husband had been; to which she replied, "His name was Wang Jianzhi, and he was connected by marriage with the Imperial family." "My own grandfather!" cried Wang, in great surprise; "how could you have known him?" "You, then," said the old woman, "are his grandson. I am a fox, and many years ago I was married to your grandfather; but when he died I retired from the world. Passing by here I lost my hairpin, which destiny conveyed into your hands." Wang had heard of his grandfather's fox-wife, and believing therefore the old woman's story, invited her to return with him, which she did. Wang called his wife out to receive her; but when she came in rags and tatters, with unkempt hair and dirty face, the old woman sighed, and said, "Alas! alas! has Wang Jianzhi's grandson come to this? "Then looking at the broken, smokeless stove, she added, "How, under these circumstances, have you managed even to support life?" Here Wang's wife told the tale of their poverty, with much sobbing and tears; whereupon the old woman gave her the hair-pin, bidding her go pawn it, and with the proceeds buy some food, saying that in three days she would visit them again. Wang pressed her to stay, but she said, "You can't even keep your wife alive; what would it benefit you to have me also dependent on you?" So she went away, and then Wang told his wife who she was, at which his wife felt very much alarmed; but Wang was so loud in her praises, that finally his wife consented to treat her with all proper respect. In three days she returned as agreed, and, producing some money, sent out for a hundredweight of rice and a hundredweight of corn. She passed the night with them, sleeping with Mrs. Wang, who was at first rather frightened, but who soon laid aside her suspicions when she found that the old lady meant so well towards them. Next day the latter addressed Wang, saying, "My grandson, you must not be so lazy. You should try to make a little money in some way or another." Wang replied that he had no capital; upon which the old lady said, "When your grandfather was alive, he allowed me to take what money I liked; but not being a mortal, I had no use for it, and consequently did not draw largely upon him. I have, however, saved from my pin-money the sum of forty ounces of silver, which has long been lying idle for want of an investment. Take it, and buy summer cloth, which you may carry to the capital and re-sell at a profit." So Wang bought some fifty pieces of summer cloth; and the old lady made him get ready, calculating that in six or seven days he would reach the capital. She also warned him, saying,

Be neither lazy nor slow—
For if a day too long you wait,
Repentance comes a day too late.

Wang promised all obedience, and packed up his goods and went off. On the road he was overtaken by a rain-storm which soaked him through to the skin; and as he was not accustomed to be out in bad weather, it was altogether too much for him. He accordingly sought shelter in an inn, but the rain went on steadily until night, running over the eaves of the house like so many ropes. Next morning the roads were in a horrible state; and Wang, watching the passers-by slipping about in the slush, unable to see any path, dared not face it all, and remained until noon, when it began to dry up a little. Just then, however, the clouds closed over again, and down came the rain in torrents, causing him to stay another night before he could go on. When he was nearing the capital, he heard to his great joy that summer cloth was at a premium; and on arrival proceeded at once to take up his quarters at an inn. There the landlord said it was a pity he had come so late, as communications with the south having been only recently opened, the supply of summer cloth had been small; and there being a great demand for it among the wealthy families of the metropolis, its price had gone up to three times the usual figure. "But," he added, "two days ago several large consignments arrived, and the price went down again, so that the late comers have lost their market." Poor Wang was thus left in the lurch, and as every day more summer cloth came in, the value of it fell in a corresponding ratio. Wang would not part with his at a loss, and held on for some ten days, when his expenses for board and lodging were added to his present distress. The landlord urged him to sell even at a loss, and turn his attention to something else, which he ultimately did, losing over ten ounces of silver on his venture. Next day he rose in the morning to depart, but on looking in his purse found all his money gone. He rushed away to tell the landlord, who, however, could do nothing for him. Someone then advised him to take out a summons and make the landlord reimburse him; but he only sighed, and said, "It is my destiny, and no fault of the landlord's." Thereupon the landlord was very grateful to him, and gave him five ounces of silver to enable him to go home. He did not care, however, to face his grandmother empty-handed, and remained in a very undecided state, until suddenly he saw a quail-catcher winning heaps of money by fighting his birds, and selling them at over 100 *cash* a-piece. He then determined to lay out his five ounces of silver in quails, and pay back the landlord out of the profits. The latter approved very highly of this plan, and not only agreed to lend him a room, but also to charge him little or nothing for his board. So Wang went off rejoicing, and bought two large baskets of quails, with which he returned to the city, to the great satisfaction of the landlord, who advised him to lose no time in disposing of them. All that night it poured in torrents, and the next morning the streets were like rivers, the rain still continuing to fall. Wang waited for it to clear up, but several days passed and still there were no signs of fine weather. He then went to look at his quails, some of which he found dead and others dying. He was much alarmed at this, but was quite at a loss what to do; and by the next day a lot more had died, so that only a few were left, which he fed all together in one basket. The day after this he went again to look at them, and lo! there remained but a single quail. With tears in his eyes he told the landlord what had happened, and he, too, was much affected. Wang then reflected that he had no money left to carry him home, and that he could not do better than cease to live. But the landlord spoke to him and soothed him, and they went together to look at the quail. "This is a fine bird," said the landlord, "and it strikes me that it has simply killed the others. Now, as you have got nothing to do, just set to work and train it; and if it is good for anything, why, you'll be able to make a living out of it." Wang did as he was told; and when the bird was trained, the landlord bade him take it into the street and gamble for something to eat. This, too, he did, and his quail won every main; whereupon the landlord gave him some money to bet with the young fellows of the neighborhood. Everything turned out favorably, and by the end of six months he had saved twenty ounces of silver, so that he became quite easy in his mind and looked upon the quail as a dispensation of his destiny.

Now one of the princes was passionately fond of quail-fighting, and always at the Feast of Lanterns anybody who owned quails might go and fight them in the palace against the Prince's birds. The landlord therefore said to Wang, "Here is a chance of enriching yourself by a single stroke; only I can't say what your luck will do for you." He then explained to him what it was, and away they went together, the landlord saying, "If you lose, burst out into lamentations; but if you are lucky enough to win, and the Prince wishes, as he will, to buy your bird, don't consent. If he presses you very much, watch for a nod from me before you agree." This settled, they proceeded to the palace, where they found crowds of quail-fighters already on the ground; and then the Prince came forth, heralds proclaiming to the multitude that any who wished to fight their birds might come up. Some man at once stepped forward, and the Prince gave orders for the quails to be released; but at the first strike the stranger's quail was knocked out of time. The Prince smiled, and by-and-by won several more mains, until at last the landlord said, "Now's our time," and went up together with Wang. The Prince looked at their bird and said, "It has a fierce-looking eye and strong feathers. We must be careful what we are doing." So he commanded his servants to bring out Iron Beak to oppose Wang's bird; but, after a couple of strikes, the Prince's quail was signally defeated. He sent for a better bird, but that shared the same fate; and then he cried out, "Bring the Jade Bird from the palace!" In a little time it arrived, with pure white feathers like an egret, and an unusually martial appearance. Wang was much alarmed, and falling on his knees prayed to be excused this main, saying, "Your Highness's bird is too good. I fear lest mine should be wounded, and my livelihood be taken from me." But the Prince laughed and said, "Go on. If your quail is killed I will make it up to you handsomely." Wang then released his bird, and the Prince's quail rushed at it at once; but when the Jade Bird was close by, Wang's quail awaited its coming head down and full of rage. The former made a violent peck at its adversary, and then sprang up to swoop down on it. Thus they went on up and down, backwards and forwards, until at length they got hold of each other, and the Prince's bird was beginning to show signs of exhaustion. This enraged it all the more, and it fought more violently than ever; but soon a perfect snowstorm of feathers began to fall, and, with drooping wings, the Jade Bird made its escape. The spectators were much moved by the result; and the Prince himself, taking up Wang's bird, examined it closely from beak to claws, finally asking if it was for sale. "My sole dependence," replied Wang, "is upon this bird. I would rather not part with it." "But," said the Prince, "if I give you as much as the capital, say, of an ordinary tradesman, will not that tempt you?" Wang thought some time, and then answered, "I would rather not sell my bird; but as your Highness has taken a fancy to it I will only ask enough to find me in food and clothes." "How much do you want?" inquired the Prince; to which Wang replied that he would take a thousand ounces of silver. "You fool!" cried the Prince; "do you think your bird is such a jewel as all that?" "If your Highness," said Wang, "does not think the bird a jewel, I value it more than that stone which was priced at fifteen cities." "How so?" asked the Prince. "Why," said Wang, "I take my bird every day into the market-place. It there wins for me several ounces of silver, which I exchange for rice; my family, over ten in number, has nothing to fear from either cold or hunger. What jewel could do that?" "You shall not lose anything," replied the Prince; "I will give you two hundred ounces." But Wang would not consent, and then the Prince added another hundred; whereupon Wang looked at the landlord, who, however, made no sign. Wang then offered to take nine hundred; but the Prince ridiculed the idea of paying such a price for a quail, and Wang was preparing to take his leave with the bird, when the Prince called him back, saying, "Here! here! I will give you six hundred. Take it or leave it as you please." Wang here looked at the landlord, and the landlord remained motionless as before. However, Wang was satisfied himself with this offer, and being afraid of missing his chance, said to his friend, "If I get this price for it I shall be quite content. If we go on haggling and finally come to no terms, that will be a very poor end to it all." So he took the Prince's offer, and the latter, overjoyed, caused the money to be handed to him. Wang then returned with his earnings, but the landlord said to him, "What did I say to you? You were in too much of a hurry to sell. Another minute, and you would have got eight hundred." When Wang got back he threw the money on the table and told the landlord to take what he liked; but the latter would not, and it was only after some pressing that he would accept payment for Wang's board. Wang then packed up and went home, where he told his story and produced his silver, to the great delight of all of them. The old lady counselled the purchase of a quantity of land, the building of a house, and the purchase of implements; and in a very short time they became a wealthy family. The old lady always got up early in the morning and made Wang attend to the farm, his wife to her spinning; and rated them soundly at any signs of laziness. The husband and wife henceforth lived in peace, and no longer abused each other, until at the expiration of three years the old lady declared her intention of bidding them adieu. They both tried to stop her, and with the aid of tears succeeded in persuading her; but the next day she had disappeared.[52]

12. The Painted Skin

AT Taiyuan there lived a man named Wang. One morning he was out walking when he met a young lady carrying a bundle and hurrying along

---

52   Quail fighting is not so common now in China as it appears to have been formerly. Cricket-fighting is, however, a very favorite form of gambling, large quantities of these insects being caught every year for this purpose, and considerable sums frequently staked on the result of a contest between two champions.

by herself. As she moved along with some difficulty,[53] Wang quickened his pace and caught her up, and found she was a pretty girl of about sixteen. Much smitten, he inquired whither she was going so early, and no one with her. "A traveler like you," replied the girl, "cannot alleviate my distress; why trouble yourself to ask?" "What distress is it?" said Wang; "I'm sure I'll do anything I can for you." "My parents," answered she, "loved money, and they sold me as concubine into a rich family, where the wife was very jealous, and beat and abused me morning and night. It was more than I could stand, so I have run away." Wang asked her where she was going; to which she replied that a runaway had no fixed place of abode. "My house," said Wang, "is at no great distance; what do you say to coming there?" She joyfully acquiesced; and Wang, taking up her bundle, led the way to his house. Finding no one there, she asked Wang where his family were; to which he replied that that was only the library. "And a very nice place, too," said she; "but if you are kind enough to wish to save my life, you mustn't let it be known that I am here." Wang promised he would not divulge her secret, and so she remained there for some days without anyone knowing anything about it. He then told his wife, and she, fearing the girl might belong to some influential family, advised him to send her away. This, however, he would not consent to do; when one day, going into the town, he met a Taoist priest, who looked at him in astonishment, and asked him what he had met. "I have met nothing," replied Wang. "Why," said the priest, "you are bewitched; what do you mean by not having met anything?" But Wang insisted that it was so, and the priest walked away, saying, "The fool! Some people don't seem to know when death is at hand." This startled Wang, who at first thought of the girl; but then he reflected that a pretty young thing as she was couldn't well be a witch, and began to suspect that the priest merely wanted to do a stroke of business. When he returned, the library door was shut, and he couldn't get in, which made him suspect that something was wrong; and so he climbed over the wall, where he found the door of the inner room shut too. Softly creeping up, he looked through the window and saw a hideous devil, with a green face and

---

53   Impeded, of course, by her bound feet. This practice is said to have originated about 970 CE, with Yao Niang, the concubine of the pretender Li Yu, who wished to make her feet like the "new moon." The Manchu or Tartar ladies never adopted this custom, and therefore the Empresses of modern times have had feet of the natural size; neither is it in force among the Hakkas or among the hill-tribes of China and Formosa and others. The practice was forbidden in 1664 by the Manchu Emperor, Kang Xi; but popular feeling was so strong on the subject that four years afterwards the prohibition was withdrawn, A vigorous attempt is now being made to secure natural feet for the Chinese girl, with more chance of success.

jagged teeth like a saw, spreading a human skin upon the bed and painting it with a paint brush. The devil' then threw aside the brush, and giving the skin a shake out, just as you would a coat, threw it over its shoulders, when lo! it was the girl. Terrified at this, Wang hurried away with his head down in search of the priest, who had gone he knew not whither; subsequently finding him in the fields, where he threw himself on his knees and begged the priest to save him. "As to driving her away," said the priest, "the creature must be in great distress to be seeking a substitute for herself;[54] besides, I could hardly endure to injure a living thing."[55] However, he gave Wang a fly-brush, and bade him hang it at the door of the bedroom, agreeing to meet again at the Qingdi temple. Wang went home, but did not dare enter the library; so he hung up the brush at the bedroom door, and before long heard a sound of footsteps outside. Not daring to move, he made his wife peep out; and she saw the girl standing looking at the brush, afraid to pass it. She then ground her teeth and went away; but in a little while came back, and began cursing, saying, "You priest, you won't frighten me. Do you think I am going to give up what is already in my grasp?" Thereupon she tore the brush to pieces, and bursting open the door, walked straight up to the bed, where she ripped open Wang and tore out his heart, with which she went away. Wang's wife screamed out, and the servant came in with a light; but Wang was already dead and presented a most miserable spectacle. His wife, who was in an agony of fright, hardly dared cry for fear of making a noise; and next day she sent Wang's brother to see the priest. The latter got into a great rage, and cried out, "Was it for this that I had compassion on you, devil that you are?" proceeding at once with Wang's brother to the house, from which the girl had disappeared without anyone knowing whither she had gone. But the priest, raising his head, looked all around, and said, "Luckily she's not far off." He then asked who lived in the apartments on the south side, to which Wang's brother replied that he did; whereupon the priest declared that there she would be found. Wang's

---

54   The disembodied spirits of the Chinese *Inferno* are permitted, under certain conditions of time and good conduct, to appropriate to themselves the vitality of some human being, who, as it were, exchanges places with the so-called "devil." The devil does not, however, reappear as the mortal whose life it has become possessed of, but is merely born again into the world; the idea being that the amount of life on earth is a constant quantity, and cannot be increased or diminished, reminding one in a way of the great modern doctrine of the conservation of energy. This curious belief has an important bearing that will be brought out in a subsequent story.

55   Here again is a Taoist priest quoting the Buddhist commandment, "Thou shalt not take life." The Buddhist laity in China, who do not hesitate to take life for the purposes of food, salve their consciences from time to time by buying birds, fishes, etc., and letting them go, in the hope that such acts will be set down on the credit side of their record of good and evil.

brother was horribly frightened and said he did not think so; and then the priest asked him if any stranger had been to the house. To this he answered that he had been out to the Qingdi temple and couldn't possibly say: but he went off to inquire, and in a little while came back and reported that an old woman had sought service with them as a maid-of-all-work, and had been engaged by his wife. "That is she," said the priest, as Wang's brother added she was still there; and they all set out to go to the house together. Then the priest took his wooden sword, and standing in the middle of the courtyard, shouted out, "Base-born fiend, give me back my fly-brush!" Meanwhile the new maid-of-all-work was in a great state of alarm, and tried to get away by the door; but the priest struck her and down she fell flat, the human skin dropped off, and she became a hideous devil. There she lay grunting like a pig, until the priest grasped his wooden sword and struck off her head. She then became a dense column of smoke curling up from the ground, when the priest took an uncorked gourd and threw it right into the midst of the smoke. A sucking noise was heard, and the whole column was drawn into the gourd; after which the priest corked it up closely and put it in his pouch.[56] The skin, too, which was complete even to the eyebrows, eyes, hands, and feet, he also rolled up as if it had been a scroll, and was on the point of leaving with it, when Wang's wife stopped him, and with tears entreated him to bring her husband to life. The priest said he was unable to do that; but Wang's wife flung herself at his feet, and with loud lamentations implored his assistance. For some time he remained immersed in thought, and then replied, "My power is not equal to what you ask. I myself cannot raise the dead; but I will direct you to some one who can, and if you apply to him properly you will succeed." Wang's wife asked the priest who it was; to which he replied, "There is a maniac in the town who passes his time grovelling in the dirt. Go, prostrate yourself before him, and beg him to help you. If he insults you, show no sign of anger." Wang's brother knew the man to whom he alluded, and accordingly bade the priest adieu, and proceeded thither with his sister-in-law.

They found the destitute creature raving away by the roadside, so filthy that it was all they could do to go near him. Wang's wife approached him on her knees; at which the maniac leered at her, and cried out, "Do you love me, my beauty?" Wang's wife told him what she had come for, but he only laughed and said, "You can get plenty of other husbands. Why raise the dead one to life?" But Wang's wife entreated him to help her; whereupon

---

56 This recalls the celebrated story of the fisherman in the *Arabian Nights*.

he observed, "It's very strange: people apply to me to raise their dead as if I was king of the infernal regions." He then gave Wang's wife a thrashing with his staff, which she bore without a murmur, and before a gradually increasing crowd of spectators. After this he produced a loathsome pill which he told her she must swallow, but here she broke down and was quite unable to do so. However, she did manage it at last, and then the maniac, crying out, "How you do love me!" got up and went away without taking any more notice of her. They followed him into a temple with loud supplications, but he had disappeared, and every effort to find him was unsuccessful. Overcome with rage and shame, Wang's wife went home, where she mourned bitterly over her dead husband, grievously repenting the steps she had taken, and wishing only to die. She then bethought herself of preparing the corpse, near which none of the servants would venture, and set to work to close up the frightful wound of which he died.

While thus employed, interrupted from time to time by her sobs, she felt a rising lump in her throat, which by-and-by came out with a pop and fell straight into the dead man's wound. Looking closely at it, she saw it was a human heart; and then it began as it were to throb, emitting a warm vapor like smoke. Much excited, she at once closed the flesh over it, and held the sides of the wound together with all her might. Very soon, however, she got tired, and finding the vapor escaping from the crevices, she tore up a piece of silk and bound it around, at the same time bringing back circulation by rubbing the body and covering it up with clothes. In the night she removed the coverings, and found that breath was coming from the nose; and by next morning her husband was alive again, though disturbed in mind as if awaking from a dream, and feeling a pain in his heart. Where he had been wounded there was a cicatrix about as big as a cash, which soon after disappeared.

13. The Trader's Son

In the province of Hunan there dwelt a man who was engaged in trading abroad; and his wife, who lived alone, dreamt one night that someone was in her room. Waking up, she looked about, and discovered a small creature which on examination she knew to be a fox; but in a moment the thing had disappeared, although the door had not been opened. The next evening she asked the cook-maid to come and keep her company; as also her own son, a boy of ten, who was accustomed to sleep elsewhere. Towards the middle of the night, when the cook and the boy were fast asleep, back came the fox; and the cook was woken up by hearing her mistress muttering something as if she had nightmare. The former then called out, and the fox ran away; but from that moment the trader's wife was not quite herself. When night came she dared not blow out the candle, and bade her son be sure and not sleep too soundly. Later on, her son and the old woman having taken a nap as they leant against the wall, suddenly woke up and found her gone. They waited some time, but she did not return, and the cook was too frightened to go and look after her; so her son took a light, and at length found her fast asleep in another room. She didn't seem aware that anything particular had happened, but she became queerer and queerer every day, and wouldn't have either her son or the cook to keep her company anymore. Her son, however, made a point of running at once into his mother's room if he heard any unusual sounds; and though his mother always abused him for his pains, he paid no attention to what she said. Consequently, everyone thought him very brave, though at the same time he was always indulging in childish tricks. One day he played at being a mason, and piled up stones upon the window-sill, in spite of all that was said to him; and if anyone took away a stone, he threw himself on the ground, and cried like a child, so that nobody dared go near him. In a few days he had got both windows blocked up and the light excluded; and then he set to filling up the chinks with mud. He worked hard all day without minding the trouble, and when it was finished he took and sharpened the kitchen chopper. Everyone who saw him was disgusted with such antics, and would take no notice of him. At night he darkened his lamp, and, with the knife concealed on his person, sat waiting for his mother to mutter. As soon as she began he uncovered his light, and, blocking up the doorway, shouted out at the top of his voice. Nothing, however, happened, and he moved from the door a little way, when suddenly out rushed something like a fox, which was disappearing through the door when he made a quick movement and cut off about two inches of its tail, from which the warm blood was still dripping as he brought the light to bear upon it. His mother hereupon cursed and reviled him, but he pretended not to hear her, regretting only as he went to bed that he hadn't hit the brute fair. But he consoled himself by thinking that although he hadn't killed it outright, he had done enough to prevent it coming again. On the morrow he followed the tracks of blood over the wall and into the garden of a family named He; and that night, to his great joy, the fox did not reappear. His mother was meanwhile prostrate, with hardly any life in her, and in the midst of it all his father came home. The boy told him what had happened, at which he was much alarmed, and sent for a doctor to attend his wife; but she only threw the medicine away, and cursed and swore horribly. So they secretly mixed the medicine with her tea and soup, and in a few days she began to get better, to the inexpressible delight of both her husband and son. One night, however, her husband woke up and found her gone; and after searching for her with the aid of his son, they discovered her sleeping in another room. From that time she became more eccentric than ever, and was always being found in strange places, cursing those who tried to remove her. Her husband was at his wits' end. It was of no use keeping the door locked, for it opened of itself at her approach; and he had called in any number of magicians to exorcise the fox, but without obtaining the slightest result. One evening her son concealed himself in the He family garden, and lay down in the long grass with a view to detecting the fox's retreat. As the moon rose he heard the sound of voices, and, pushing aside the grass, saw two people drinking, with a long-bearded servant pouring out their wine, dressed in an old dark-brown coat. They were whispering together, and he could not make out what they said; but by-and-by he heard one of them remark, "Get some white wine for tomorrow," and then they went away, leaving the long-bearded servant alone. The latter then threw off his coat, and lay down to sleep on the stones; whereupon the trader's son eyed him carefully, and saw that he was like a man in every respect except that he had a tail. The boy would then have gone home; but he was afraid the fox might hear him, and accordingly remained where he was until near dawn, when he saw the other two come back, one at a time, and then they all disappeared among the bushes. On reaching home his father asked him where he had been, and he replied that he had stopped the night with the He family. He then accompanied his father to the town, where he saw hanging up at a hat-shop a fox's tail, and finally, after much coaxing, succeeded in making his father buy it for him. While the latter was engaged in a shop, his son, who was playing about beside him, availed himself of a moment when his father was not looking and stole some money from him, and went off and bought a quantity of white wine, which he left in charge of the wine-merchant. Now an uncle of his, who was a sportsman by trade, lived in the city, and thither he next betook himself. His uncle was out, but his aunt was there, and inquired after the health of his mother. "She has been better the last few days," replied he; "but she is now very much upset by a rat having gnawed a dress of hers, and has sent me to ask for some poison." His aunt opened the cupboard and gave him about the tenth of an ounce in a piece of paper, which he thought was very little; so, when his aunt had gone to get him something to eat, he took the opportunity of being alone, opened the packet, and abstracted a large handful. Hiding this in his coat, he ran to tell his aunt that she needn't prepare anything for him, as his father was waiting in the market, and he couldn't stop to eat it. He then went off; and having quietly dropped the poison into the wine he had bought, went sauntering about the town. At nightfall he returned home, and told his father that he had been at his uncle's. This he continued to do for some time, until one day he saw among the crowd his long-bearded friend. Marking him closely, he followed him, and at length entered into conversation, asking him where he lived. "I live at Beicun," said he; "where do you live?" "I," replied the trader's son, falsely, "live in a hole on the hillside." The long-bearded man was considerably startled at his answer, but much more so when he added, "We've lived there for generations: haven't *you*?" The other man asked his name, to which the boy replied, "My name is Hu.[57] I saw you with two gentlemen in the He family garden, and haven't forgotten you." Questioning him more fully, the long-bearded man was still in a half-and-half state of belief and doubt, when the trader's son opened his coat a little bit, and showed him the end of the tail he had bought, saying, "The like of us can mix with ordinary people, but unfortunately we can never get rid of this." The long-bearded man then asked him what he was doing there, to which he answered that his father had sent him to buy wine; thereupon the former remarked that that was exactly what he had come for, and the boy then inquired if he had bought it yet or not. "We are poor," replied the stranger, "and as a rule I prefer to steal it." "A difficult and dangerous job," observed the boy. "I have my masters' instructions to get some," said the other, "and what am I to do?" The boy then asked him who his masters were, to which he replied that they were the two brothers the boy had seen that night. "One of them has bewitched a lady named Wang; and the other, the wife of a trader who lives near. The son of the last-mentioned lady is a violent fellow, and cut off my master's tail, so that he was laid up for ten days. But he is putting her under spells again now." He was then going away, saying he should never get his wine; but the boy said to him, "It's much easier to buy than steal. I have some at the wineshop there which I will give to you. My purse isn't empty, and I can buy some more." The long-bearded man hardly knew how to

---

57   *Hu* is the sound of the character for "fox;" it is also the sound of quite a different character, which is used as a surname.

thank him; but the boy said, "We're all one family. Don't mention such a trifle. When I have time I'll come and take a drink with you." So they went off together to the wine-shop, where the boy gave him the wine, and they then separated. That night his mother slept quietly and had no fits, and the boy knew that something must have happened. He then told his father, and they went to see if there were any results; when lo! they found both foxes stretched out dead in the arbour. One of the foxes was lying on the grass, and out of its mouth blood was still trickling. The wine-bottle was there; and on shaking it they heard that some was left. Then his father asked him why he had kept it all so secret; to which the boy replied that foxes were very wise, and would have been sure to scent the plot. Thereupon his father was mightily pleased, and said he was a perfect Ulysses[58] for cunning. They then carried the foxes home, and saw on the tail of one of them the scar of a knife-wound. From that time they were left in peace; but the trader's wife became very thin, and though her reason returned, she soon died of consumption. The other lady, Mrs. Wang, began to get better as soon as the foxes had been killed; and as to the boy, he was taught riding and archery[59] by his proud parent, and subsequently rose to high rank in the army.

14. Judge Lu

AT Lingyang there lived a man named Zhu Erdan, whose literary designation[60] was Xiaoming. He was a fine manly fellow, but an egregious dunce, though he tried hard to learn. One day he was taking wine with a number of fellow-students, when one of them said to him, by way of a joke,

---

58   The name of the Chinese type was Chen Ping.
59   Skill in archery was until quite lately *de rigueur* for all Manchus, and for those who would rise in the Chinese army.
60   Every Chinese man and woman inherits a family name or surname. A woman takes her husband's surname, followed in official documents by her maiden name. Children usually have a pet name given to them soon after birth, which is dropped after a few years. Then there is the *ming* or name, which once given is unchangeable, and by which the various members of a family are distinguished. But only the Emperor, a man's father and mother, and certain other relatives are allowed to use this. Friends call each other by their literary designations or "book-names," which are given generally by the teacher to whom the boy's education is first entrusted. Brothers and sisters and others have all kinds of nick-names, as with us. Dogs and cats are called by such names as "Blacky," "Whitey," "Yellowy," "Jewel," "Pearly," etc., etc., Junks are christened "Large Profits," "Abounding Wealth," "Favorite of Fortune," etc., etc. Places are often named after some striking geographical feature; *e.g.*, Hankou— "mouth of the Han river," *i.e.*, its point of junction with the Yangtze; or they have fancy names, such as *Fujian*— "happily established;" *Tianjin*— "Heaven's ford;" or names implying a special distinction, such as *Nanjing*— "southern capital;" *Shandong*— "east of the mountains," etc.

"People credit you with plenty of pluck. Now, if you will go in the middle of the night to the Chamber of Horrors,[61] and bring back the Infernal Judge from the left-hand porch, we'll stand you a dinner." For at Lingyang there was a representation of the Ten Courts of Purgatory, with the gods and devils carved in wood, and almost lifelike in appearance; and in the eastern vestibule there was a full-length image of the Judge with a green face, and a red beard, and a hideous expression in his features. Sometimes sounds of examination under the whip were heard to issue during the night from both porches, and persons who went in found their hair standing on end from fear; so the other young men thought it would be a capital test for Mr. Zhu. Thereupon Zhu smiled, and rising from his seat went straight off to the temple; and before many minutes had elapsed they heard him shouting outside, "His Excellency has arrived!" At this they all got up, and in came Zhu with the image on his back, which he proceeded to deposit on the table, and then poured out a triple libation in its honor. His comrades, who were watching what he did, felt ill at ease, and did not like to resume their seats; so they begged him to carry the Judge back again. But he first poured some wine upon the ground, invoking the image as follows: "I am only a foolhardy, illiterate fellow: I pray your Excellency excuse me. My house is close by, and whenever your Excellency feels so disposed I shall be glad to take a cup of wine with you in a friendly way." He then carried the Judge back, and the next day his friends gave him the promised dinner, from which he went home half-tipsy in the evening. But not feeling that he had had enough, he brightened up his lamp, and helped himself to another cup of wine, when suddenly the bamboo curtain was drawn aside, and in walked the Judge. Mr. Zhu got up and said, "Oh, dear! Your Excellency has come to cut off my head for my rudeness the other night." The Judge parted his thick beard, and smiling, replied, "Nothing of the kind. You kindly invited me last night to visit you; and as I have leisure this evening, here I am." Zhu was delighted at this, and made his guest sit down, while he himself wiped the cups and lighted a fire.[62] "It's warm weather," said the Judge; "let's drink the wine cold." Zhu obeyed, and putting the bottle on the table, went

---

61   The name given by foreigners in China to the imitation of the ten torture-chambers of purgatory, as seen in every *Chenghuang* or municipal temple. The various figures of the devil-lictors and the tortured sinners are made either of clay or wood, and painted in very bright colors; and in each chamber is depicted some specimen of the horrible tortures that wicked people will undergo in the world to come. I have given in the first *Appendix* a translation of the *Yuli chao zhuan*, a celebrated Taoist work on this subject, which should at any rate be glanced at by persons who would understand the drift some of these stories.

62   To heat the wine, which is almost invariably taken hot.

out to tell his servants to get some supper. His wife was much alarmed when she heard who was there, and begged him not to go back; but he only waited until the things were ready, and then returned with them. They drank out of each other's cups,[63] and by-and-by Zhu asked the name of his guest. "My name is Lu," replied the Judge; "I have no other names." They then conversed on literary subjects, one capping the other's quotation as echo responds to sound. The Judge then asked Zhu if he understood composition; to which he answered that he could just tell good from bad; whereupon the former repeated a little infernal poetry which was not very different from that of mortals. He was a deep drinker, and took off ten goblets at a draught; but Zhu, who had been at it all day, soon got dead drunk and fell fast asleep with his head on the table. When he woke up the candle had burnt out and day was beginning to break, his guest having already departed; and from this time the Judge was in the habit of dropping in pretty often, until a close friendship sprang up between them. Sometimes the latter would pass the night at the house, and Zhu would show him his essays, all of which the Judge scored and underlined as being good for nothing. One night Zhu got tipsy and went to bed first, leaving the Judge drinking by himself. In his drunken sleep he seemed to feel a pain in his stomach, and waking up he saw that the Judge, who was standing by the side of the bed, had opened him and was carefully arranging his inside. "What harm have I done you," cried Zhu, "that you should thus seek to destroy me?" "Don't be afraid," replied the Judge, laughing; "I am only providing you with a more intelligent heart."[64] He then quietly put back Zhu's viscera, and closed up the opening, securing it with a bandage tied tightly around his waist. There was no blood on the bed, and all Zhu felt was a slight numbness in his inside. Here he observed the Judge place a piece of flesh upon the table, and asked him what it was. "Your heart," said the latter, "which wasn't at all good at composition, the proper orifice being stuffed up.[65] I have now provided you with a better one, which I procured from Hades, and I am keeping yours to put in its place."[66] He then opened the door and took his leave. In the morning Zhu undid the bandage, and looked at his waist, the wound on which had quite healed up, leaving only

---

63   In token of their mutual good feeling.

64   The Chinese as a nation believe to this day that the heart is the seat of the intellect and the emotions.

65   The heart itself is supposed to be pierced by a number of " eyes," which pass right through; and in physical and mental health these passages are believed to be clear.

66   See note 54 in tale number 12.

a red seam. From that moment he became an apt scholar, and found his memory much improved; so much so, that a few days afterwards he showed an essay to the Judge for which he was very much commended. "However," said the latter, "your success will be limited to the master's degree. You won't get beyond that." "When shall I take it?" asked Zhu. "This year," replied the Judge. And so it turned out. Zhu passed first on the list for the bachelor's degree, and then among the first five for the master's degree. His old comrades, who had been accustomed to make a laughing-stock of him, were now astonished to find him a full-blown M.A., and when they learned how it had come about, they begged Zhu to speak to the Judge on their behalf. The Judge promised to assist them, and they made all ready to receive him; but when in the evening he did come, they were so frightened at his red beard and flashing eyes that their teeth chattered in their heads, and one by one they stole away. Zhu then took the Judge home with him to have a cup together, and when the wine had mounted well into his head, he said, "I am deeply grateful to your Excellency's former kindness in arranging my inside; but there is still another favor I venture to ask which possibly may be granted." The Judge asked him what it was; and Zhu replied, "If you can change a person's inside, you surely could also change his face. Now my wife is not at all a bad figure, but she is very ugly. I pray your Excellency try the knife upon her." The Judge laughed, and said he would do so, only it would be necessary to give him a little time. Some days subsequently, the Judge knocked at Zhu's door towards the middle of the night; whereupon the latter jumped up and invited him in. Lighting a candle, it was evident that the Judge had something under his coat, and in answer to Zhu's inquiries, he said, "It's what you asked me for. I have had great trouble in procuring it." He then produced the head of a nice-looking young girl, and presented it to Zhu, who found the blood on the neck was still warm. "We must make haste," said the Judge, "and take care not to wake the fowls or dogs."[67] Zhu was afraid his wife's door might be bolted; but the Judge laid his hand on it and it opened at once. Zhu then led him to the bed where his wife was lying asleep on her side; and the Judge, giving Zhu the head to hold, drew from his boot a steel blade shaped like the handle of a spoon. He laid this across the lady's neck, which he cut through as if it had been a melon, and the head fell over the back of the pillow. Seizing the head he had

---

67 The *Xi yuan lu,* a well-known work on Chinese medical jurisprudence and *an officially authorized book,* while giving an absurd antidote against a poison that never existed, gravely insists that it is to be prepared at certain dates only, "in some place quite away from women, fowls, and dogs."

brought with him, he now fitted it on carefully and accurately, and pressing it down to make it stick, bolstered the lady up with pillows placed on either side. When all was finished, he bade Zhu put his wife's old head away, and then took his leave. Soon after Mrs. Zhu waked up, and perceived a curious sensation about her neck, and a scaly feeling about the jaws. Putting her hand to her face, she found flakes of dry blood; and much frightened called a maid-servant to bring water to wash it off. The maid-servant was also greatly alarmed at the appearance of her face, and proceeded to wash off the blood, which colored a whole basin of water; but when she saw her mistress's new face she was almost frightened to death. Mrs. Zhu took a mirror to look at herself, and was staring at herself in utter astonishment, when her husband came in and explained what had taken place. On examining her more closely, Zhu saw she had a well-featured pleasant face, of a high order of beauty; and when he came to look at her neck, he found a red seam all around, with the parts above and below of a different colored flesh. Now the daughter of an official named Wu was a very nice-looking girl, who, though nineteen years of age, had not yet been married, two gentlemen who were engaged to her having died before the day.[68] At the Feast of Lanterns,[69] this young lady happened to visit the Chamber of Horrors, whence she was followed home by a burglar, who that night broke into the house and killed her. Hearing a noise, her mother told the servant to go and see what was the matter; and the murder being thus discovered, every member of the family got up. They placed the body in the hall, with the head alongside, and gave themselves up to weeping and waning the live-long night. Next morning, when they removed the coverings, the corpse was there, but the head had disappeared. The waiting-maids were accordingly flogged for neglect of duty, and consequent loss of the head, and Mr. Wu brought the matter to the notice of the Prefect. This officer took very energetic measures, but for three months no clue could be obtained; and then the story of the changed head in the Zhu family gradually reached Mr. Wu's ears. Suspecting something, he sent an old woman to

---

68   It was almost a wonder that she got a second *fiancé*, few people caring to affiance their sons in a family where such a catastrophe has once occurred. The death of an engaged girl is a matter of much less importance, but is productive of a very curious ceremony. Her betrothed goes to the house where she is lying dead and steps over the coffin containing her body, returning home with a pair of the girl's shoes. He thus severs all connection with her, and her spirit cannot haunt him as it otherwise most certainly would do.

69   Held annually on the 15th of the first Chinese month—*i.e.,* at the first full moon of the year, when colored lanterns are hung at every door. It was originally a ceremonial worship in the temple of the First Cause, and dates from about the time of the Han dynasty, or nearly two thousand years ago.

make inquiries; and she at once recognized her late young mistress's features, and went back and reported to her master. Thereupon Mr. Wu, unable to make out why the body should have been left, imagined that Zhu had slain his daughter by magical arts, and at once proceeded to the house to find out the truth of the matter; but Zhu told him that his wife's head had been changed in her sleep, and that he knew nothing about it, adding that it was unjust to accuse him of the murder. Mr. Wu refused to believe this, and took proceedings against him; but as all the servants told the same story, the Prefect was unable to convict him. Zhu returned home and took counsel with the Judge, who told him there would be no difficulty, it being merely necessary to make the murdered girl herself speak. That night Mr. Wu dreamt that his daughter came and said to him, "I was killed by Yang Danian, of Suqi. Mr. Zhu had nothing to do with it; but desiring a better-looking face for his wife, Judge Lu gave him mine, and thus my body is dead while my head still lives. Bear Zhu no malice." When he awaked, he told his wife, who had dreamt the same dream; and thereupon he communicated these facts to the officials. Subsequently, a man of that name was captured, who confessed under the bamboo that he had committed the crime; so Mr. Wu went off to Zhu's house, and asked to be allowed to see his wife, regarding Zhu from that time as his son-in-law. Mrs. Zhu's old head was fitted on to the young lady's body, and the two parts were buried together. Subsequent to these events Mr. Zhu tried three times for his doctor's degree, but each time without success, and at last he gave up the idea of entering into official life. Then when thirty years had passed away, Judge Lu appeared to him one night, and said, "My friend, you cannot live forever. Your hour will come in five days' time." Zhu asked the Judge if he could not save him; to which he replied, "The decrees of Heaven cannot be altered to suit the purposes of mortals. Besides, to an intelligent man life and death are much the same.[70] Why necessarily regard life as a boon and death as a misfortune?" Zhu could make no reply to this, and forthwith proceeded to order his coffin and shroud; and then, dressing himself in his grave-clothes,[71] yielded up the ghost. Next day, as his wife was weeping

---

70　It was John Stuart Mill who pointed out that the fear of death is due to "the illusion of imagina-tion, which makes one conceive oneself as if one were alive and feeling oneself dead" (*The Utility of Religion*).

71　"Boards of old age" and "Clothes of old age sold here" are common shop-signs in every Chinese city; death and burial being always, if possible, spoken of euphemistically in some such terms as these. A dutiful son provides, when he can afford it, decent coffins for his father and mother. They are gener-ally stored in the house, sometimes in a neighboring temple; and the old people take pleasure in seeing that their funeral obsequies are properly provided for, though the subject is never raised in conversaover his bier, in he walked at the front door, to her very great alarm. "I am now a disembodied spirit," said Zhu to her, "though not different from what I was in life; and I have been thinking much of the widow and orphan I left behind." His wife, hearing this, wept until the tears ran down her face, Zhu all the time doing his best to comfort her. "I have heard tell," said she, "of dead bodies returning to life; and since your vital spark is not extinct, why does it not resume the flesh?" "The ordinances of Heaven," replied her husband, "may not be disobeyed." His wife here asked him what he was doing in the infernal regions; and he said that Judge Lu had got him an appointment as Registrar, with a certain rank attached, and that he was not at all uncomfortable. Mrs. Zhu was proceeding to inquire further, when he interrupted her, saying, "The Judge has come with me; get some wine ready and something to eat." He then hurried out, and his wife did as he had told her, hearing them laughing and drinking in the guest chamber just like old times come back again. About midnight she peeped in, and found that they had both disappeared; but they came back once in every two or three days, often spending the night, and managing the family affairs as usual. Zhu's son was named Wei, and was about five years old; and whenever his father came he would take the little boy upon his knee. When he was about eight years of age, Zhu began to teach him to read; and the boy was so clever that by the time he was nine he could actually compose. At fifteen he took his bachelor's degree, without knowing all this time that he had no father. From that date Zhu's visits became less frequent, occurring not more than once or so in a month; until one night he told his wife that they were never to meet again. In reply to her inquiry as to whither he was going, he said he had been appointed to a far-off post, where press of business and distance would combine to prevent him from visiting them any more. The mother and son clung to him, sobbing bitterly, but he said, "Do not act thus. The boy is now a man, and can look after your affairs. The dearest friends must part some day." Then, turning to his son, he added, "Be an honorable man, and take care of the property. Ten years hence we shall meet again." With this he bade them farewell, and went away.

Later on, when Wei was twenty-five years of age, he took his doctor's degree, and was appointed to conduct the sacrifices at the Imperial tombs. On his way thither he fell in with a retinue of an official, proceeding along

---

tion. Chinese coffins are beautifully made; and when the body has been in for a day or two, a candle is closely applied to the seams all around to make sure it is air-tight—any crack, however fine, being easily detected by the flickering of the flame in the escaping gas. Thus bodies may be kept unburied for a long time, until the geomancer has selected an auspicious site for the grave.

with all the proper insignia,[72] and, looking carefully at the individual sitting in the carriage, he was astonished to find that it was his own father. Alighting from his horse, he prostrated himself with tears at the side of the road; whereupon his father stopped and said, "You are well spoken of. I now take leave of this world." Wei remained on the ground, not daring to rise; and his father, urging on his carriage, hurried away without saying any more. But when he had gone a short distance, he looked back and unloosing a sword from his waist, sent it as a present to his son, shouting out to him, "Wear this and you will succeed." Wei tried to follow him; but, in an instant, carriage, retinue, and horses had vanished with the speed of wind. For a long time his son gave himself up to grief, and then seizing the sword began to examine it closely. It was of exquisite workmanship, and on the blade was engraved this legend: "*Be bold, but cautious; round in disposition, square in action.*"[73] Wei subsequently rose to high honors, and had five sons named Chen, Qian, Wu, Hun, and Shen. One night he dreamt that his father told him to give the sword to Hun, which he accordingly did; and Hun rose to be a Viceroy of great administrative ability.

15. Miss Yingning; or, The Laughing Girl

At Luodian, in the province of Shandong, there lived a youth named Wang Zifu, who had been left an orphan when quite young. He was a clever boy, and took his bachelor's degree at the age of fourteen, being quite his mother's pet, and not allowed by her to stray far away from home. One young lady to whom he had been betrothed having unhappily died, he was still in search of a wife when, on the occasion of the Feast of Lanterns, his cousin Wu asked him to come along for a stroll. But they had hardly got beyond the village before one of his uncle's servants caught them up and told Wu he was wanted. The latter accordingly went back; but Wang, seeing plenty of nice girls about and being in high spirits himself, proceeded on alone. Amongst others, he noticed a young lady with her maid. She had

72   Gongs, red umbrellas, men carrying boards on which the officer's titles are inscribed in large characters, a huge wooden fan, etc., etc.
73   "Be like a cash" (see note 7 in tale number 2) is a not uncommon saying among the Chinese, the explanation of which rests upon the fact that a cash is "round in shape and convenient for use," which words are pronounced identically with a corresponding number of words meaning "round in disposition, square in action." It is, in fact, a play on words.

just picked a sprig of plum-blossom, and was the prettiest girl he had ever heard of, her smiling face being very captivating. He stared and stared at her quite regardless of appearances; and when she had passed by, she said to her maid, "That young fellow has a wicked look in his eyes." As she was walking away, laughing and talking, the flower dropped out of her hand; and Wang, picking it up, stood there disconsolate as if he had lost his wits. He then went home in a very melancholy mood; and, putting the flower under his pillow, lay down to sleep. He would neither talk nor eat; and his mother became very anxious about him, and called in the aid of the priests.[74] By degrees, he fell off in flesh and got very thin; and the doctor felt his pulse and gave him medicines to bring out the disease. Occasionally, he seemed bewildered in his mind, but in spite of all his mother's inquiries would give no clue as to the cause of his malady. One day when his cousin Wu came to the house, Wang's mother told him to try and find out what was the matter; and the former, approaching the bed, gradually and quietly led up to the point in question. Wang, who had wept bitterly at the sight of his cousin, now repeated to him the whole story, begging him to lend some assistance in the matter. "How foolish you are, cousin," cried Wu; "there will be no difficulty at all, I'll make inquiries for you. The girl herself can't belong to a very aristocratic family to be walking alone in the country. If she's not already engaged, I have no doubt we can arrange the affair; and even if she is unwilling, an extra outlay will easily bring her around.[75] You make haste and get well: I'll see to it all." Wang's features relaxed when he heard these words; and Wu left him to tell his mother how the case stood, immediately setting on foot inquiries as to the whereabouts of the girl. All his efforts, however, proved fruitless, to the great disappointment of Wang's mother; for since his cousin's visit Wang's color and appetite had returned. In a few days Wu called again, and in answer to Wang's questions falsely told him the affair was settled. "Who do you think the young lady is?" said he. "Why, a cousin of ours, who is only waiting to be betrothed; and though you two are a little near,[76] I dare say this difficulty may be overcome." Wang was

---

74   Sickness being supposed to result from evil influences, witchcraft, etc., just as often as from more natural causes.

75   The rule which guides betrothals in China is that "the doors should be opposite" —*i.e.*, that the families of the bride and bridegroom should be of equal position in the social scale. Any unpleasantness about the value of the marriage presents, and so on, is thereby avoided.

76   Marriage between persons of the same surname, except in special cases, is forbidden by law, for such are held to be blood relations, descended lineally from the original couple of that name. Inasmuch, however, as the line of descent is traced through the male branches only, a man may marry his cousins on the maternal side without let or hindrance except that of sentiment, which is sufficiently strong to keep these alliances down to a minimum.

overjoyed, and asked where she lived; so Wu had to tell another lie, and say, "On the south-west hills, about ten miles from here." Wang begged him again and again to do his best for him, and Wu undertook to get the betrothal satisfactorily arranged. He then took leave of his cousin, who from this moment was rapidly restored to health. Wang drew the flower from underneath his pillow, and found that, though dried up, the leaves had not fallen away. He often sat playing with this flower and thinking of the young lady; but by-and-by, as Wu did not reappear, he wrote a letter and asked him to come. Wu pleaded other engagements, being unwilling to go; at which Wang got into a rage and quite lost his good spirits; so that his mother, fearing a relapse, proposed to him a speedy betrothal in another quarter. Wang shook his head at this, and sat day after day waiting for Wu, until his patience was thoroughly exhausted. He then reflected that ten miles was no great distance, and that there was no particular reason for asking anybody's aid; so, concealing the flower in his sleeve, he went off in a huff by himself without letting it be known. Having no opportunity of asking the way, he made straight for the hills; and after about ten miles' walking, found himself right in the midst of them, enjoying their exquisite verdure, but meeting no one, and with nothing better than mountain paths to guide him. Away down in the valley below, almost buried under a densely luxuriant growth of trees and flowers, he espied a small hamlet, and began to descend the hill and make his way thither. He found very few houses, and all built of rushes, but otherwise pleasant enough to look at. Before the door of one, which stood at the northern end of the village, were a number of graceful willow trees, and inside the wall plenty of peach and apricot trees, with tufts of bamboo between them, and birds chirping on the branches. As it was a private house, he did not venture to go in, but sat down to rest himself on a huge smooth stone opposite the front door. By-and-by he heard a girl's voice from within calling out Xiaorong; and noticing that it was a sweet-toned voice, set himself to listen, when a young lady passed with a bunch of apricot-flowers in her hand, which she was sticking into her bent-down head. As soon as she raised her face she saw Wang, and stopped putting in the flowers; then, smothering a laugh, she gathered them together and ran in. Wang perceived to his intense delight that she was none other than his heroine of the Feast of Lanterns; but recollecting that he had no right to follow her in, was on the point of calling after her as his cousin. There was no one, however, in the street, and he was afraid lest he might have made a mistake; neither was there anybody at the door of whom he could make inquiries. So he remained there in a very restless state until the sun was well down in the west, and his hopes were almost at an end, forgetting all about food and drink. He then saw the young lady peep through the door, apparently very much astonished to find him still there; and in a few minutes out came an old woman leaning on a stick, who said to him, "Whence do you come. Sir? I hear you have been here ever since morning. What is it you want? Aren't you hungry?" Wang got up, and making a bow, replied that he was in search of some relatives of his; but the old woman was deaf and didn't catch what he said, so he had to shout it out again at the top of his voice. She asked him what their names were, but he was unable to tell her; at which she laughed and said, "It is a funny thing to look for people when you don't know their names. I am afraid you are an unpractical gentleman. You had better come in and have something to eat; we'll give you a bed, and you can go back tomorrow and find out the names of the people you are in quest of." Now Wang was just beginning to get hungry, and, besides, this would bring him nearer to the young lady; so he readily accepted and followed the old woman in. They walked along a paved path banked on both sides with hibiscus, the leaves of which were scattered about on the ground; and passing through another door, entered a courtyard full of trained creepers and other flowers. The old woman showed Wang into a small room with beautifully white walls and a branch of a crab-apple tree coming through the window, the furniture being also nice and clean. They had hardly sat down when it was clear that someone was taking a peep through the window; whereupon the old woman cried out, "Xiaorong! make haste and get dinner," and a maid from outside immediately answered "Yes, ma'am." Meanwhile, Wang had been explaining who he was; and then the old lady said, "Was your maternal grandfather named Wu?" "He was," replied Wang. "Well, I never!" cried the old woman; "he was my uncle, and your mother and I are cousins. But in consequence of our poverty, and having no sons, we have kept quite to ourselves, and you have grown to be a man without my knowing you." "I came here," said Wang, "about my cousin, but in the hurry I forgot your name." "My name is Qin," replied the old lady; "I have no son: only a girl, the child of a concubine, who, after my husband's death, married again[77] and left her daughter with me. She's a clever girl, but has had very little education; full of fun and ignorant of the sorrows of life. I'll send for her by-and-by to make your acquaintance." The maid then brought in the dinner—a well-grown fowl—and the old woman pressed him to eat. When they had finished, and the things were taken

---

77   A very unjustifiable proceeding in Chinese eyes, unless driven to it by actual poverty.

away, the old woman said, "Call Miss Ning," and the maid went off to do so. After some time there was a giggling at the door, and the old woman cried out, "Yingning! your cousin is here." There was then a great tittering as the maid pushed her in, stopping her mouth all the time to try and keep from laughing. "Don't you know better than to behave like that?" asked the old woman, "and before a stranger, too." So Yingning controlled her feelings, and Wang made her a bow, the old woman saying, "Mr. Wang is your cousin; you have never seen him before. Isn't that funny?" Wang asked how old his cousin was, but the old woman didn't hear him, and he had to say it again, which sent Yingning off into another fit of laughter. "I told you," observed the old woman, "she hadn't much education; now you see it. She is sixteen years old, and as foolish as a baby." "One year younger than I am," remarked Wang. "Oh, you're seventeen, are you? Then you were born in the year ——, under the sign of the horse"[78] Wang nodded assent, and then the old woman asked who his wife was, to which Wang replied that he had none. "What! a clever, handsome young fellow of seventeen not yet engaged?[79] Yingning is not engaged either: you two would make a nice pair if it wasn't for the relationship." Wang said nothing, but looked hard at his cousin; and just then the maid whispered to her, "It is the fellow with the wicked eyes! He's at his old game." Yingning laughed, and proposed to the maid that they should go and see if the peaches were in blossom or not; and off they went together, the former with her sleeve stuffed into her mouth until she got outside, where she burst into a hearty fit of laughing. The old woman gave orders for a bed to be got ready for Wang, saying to him, "It's not often we meet: you must spend a few days with us now you are here, and then we'll send you home. If you are at all dull, there's a garden behind where you can amuse yourself, and books for you to read." So next day Wang strolled into the garden, which was of moderate size, with a well-kept lawn and plenty of trees and flowers. There was also an arbor consisting of three posts with a thatched roof, quite shut in on all sides by the luxuriant vegetation. Pushing his way among the flowers, Wang heard a noise from one of the trees, and looking up saw Yingning, who at once burst out

---

78 The Chinese years are distinguished by the names of twelve animals—namely, rat, ox, tiger, hare, dragon, serpent, horse, sheep, monkey, cock, dog, and boar. To the common question, "What is your honorable age?" the reply is frequently, "I was born under the—;" and the hearer by a short mental calculation can tell at once how old the speaker is, granting, of course, the impossibility of making an error of so much as twelve years.

79 Parents in China like to get their sons married as early as possible, in the hope of seeing themselves surrounded by grandsons, and the family name in no danger of extinction. Girls are generally married at from fifteen to seventeen.

laughing and nearly fell down. "Don't! don't!" cried Wang, " you'll fall!" Then Yingning came down, giggling all the time, until, when she was near the ground, she missed her hold, and tumbled down with a run. This stopped her merriment, and Wang picked her up, gently squeezing her hand as he did so. Yingning began laughing again, and was obliged to lean against a tree for support, it being some time before she was able to stop. Wang waited until she had finished, and then drew the flower out of his sleeve and handed it to her. "It's dead," said she; "why do you keep it?" "You dropped it, cousin, at the Feast of Lanterns," replied Wang, "and so I kept it." She then asked him what was his object in keeping it, to which he answered, "To show my love, and that I have not forgotten you. Since that day when we met, I have been very ill from thinking so much of you, and am quite changed from what I was. But now that it is my unexpected good fortune to meet you, I pray you have pity on me." "You needn't make such a fuss about a trifle," replied she, "and with your own relatives, too. I'll give orders to supply you with a whole basketful of flowers when you go away." Wang told her she did not understand, and when she asked what it was she didn't understand, he said, "I didn't care for the flower itself; it was the person who picked the flower." "Of course," answered she, "everybody cares for their relations; you needn't have told me that." "I wasn't talking about ordinary relations," said Wang, "but about husbands and wives." "What's the difference? "asked Yingning. "Why," replied Wang, "husband and wife are always together." "Just what I shouldn't like," cried she, "to be always with anybody."[80] At this juncture up·came the maid, and Wang slipped quietly away. By-and-by they all met again in the house, and the old woman asked Yingning where they had been; whereupon she said they had been talking in the garden. "Dinner has been ready a long time. I can't think what you have had to say all this while," grumbled the old woman. "My cousin," answered Yingning, "has been talking to me about husbands and wives." Wang was much disconcerted, and made a sign to her to be quiet, so she smiled and said no more; and the old woman luckily did not catch her words, and asked her to repeat them. Wang immediately put her off

---

80   This scene should for ever disabuse people of the notion that there is no such thing as "making love" among the Chinese. That the passion is just as much a disease in China as it is with us will be abundantly evident from several subsequent stories; though by those who have lived and mixed with the Chinese people, no such confirmation will be needed. I have even heard it gravely asserted by an educated native that not a few of his countrymen had "died for love" of the beautiful Miss Lin, the charming but fictitious heroine of the so-called *Dream of the Red Chamber*.

Playgoers can here hardly fail to notice a very striking similarity to the close of the first act of Sir W. S. Gilbert's "Sweethearts."

with something else, and whispered to Yingning that she had done very wrong. The latter did not see that; and when Wang told her that what he had said was private, answered him that she had no secrets from her old mother. "Besides," added she, "what harm can there be in talking on such a common topic as husbands and wives?" Wang was angry with her for being so dull, but there-was no help for it; and by the time dinner was over he found some of his mother's servants had come in search of him, bringing a couple of donkeys with them. It appeared that his mother, alarmed at his non-appearance, had made strict search for him in the village; and when unable to discover any traces of him, had gone off to the Wu family to consult. There her nephew, who recollected what he had previously said to young Wang, advised that a search should be instituted in the direction of the hills; and accordingly the servants had been to all the villages on the way until they had at length recognized him as he was coming out of the door. Wang went in and told the old woman, begging that he might be allowed to take Yingning with him. "I have had the idea in my head for several days," replied the old woman, overjoyed; "but I am a feeble old thing myself, and couldn't travel so far. If, however, you will take charge of my girl and introduce her to her aunt, I shall be very pleased." So she called Yingning, who came up laughing as usual; whereupon the old woman rebuked her, saying, "What makes you always laugh so? You would be a very good girl but for that silly habit. Now, here's your cousin, who wants to take you away with him. Make haste and pack up." The servants who had come for Wang were then provided with refreshment, and the old woman bade them both farewell, telling Yingning that her aunt was quite well enough off to maintain her, and that she had better not come back. She also advised her not to neglect her studies, and to be very attentive to her elders, adding that she might ask her aunt to provide her with a good husband. Wang and Yingning then took their leave; and when they reached the brow of the hill, they looked back and could just discern the old woman leaning against the door and "gazing towards the north."[81] On arriving at Wang's home, his mother, seeing a nice-looking young girl with him, asked in astonishment who she might be; and Wang at once told her the whole story. "But that was all an invention of your cousin Wu's!" cried his mother; "I haven't got a sister, and consequently I can't have such a niece." Yingning here observed, "I am not the daughter of the old woman; my father was named Qin and died when I was a little baby, so that I can't remember

---

81   *q.d.* Looking sorrowfully after them.

anything." "I *had* a sister," said Wang's mother, "who actually did marry a Mr. Qin, but she died many years ago, and can't be still living, of course." However, on inquiring as to facial appearance and characteristic marks, Wang's mother was obliged to acknowledge the identity, wondering at the same time how her sister could be alive when she had died many years before. Just then in came Wu, and Yingning retired within; and when he heard the story, remained some time lost in astonishment, and then said, "Is this young lady's name Yingning?" Wang replied that it was, and asked Wu how he came to know it. "Mr. Qin." answered he, "after his wife's death was bewitched by a fox, and subsequently died. The fox had a daughter named Yingning, as was well known to all the family; and when Mr. Qin died, as the fox still frequented the place, the Taoist Pope[82] was called in to exorcise it. The fox then went away, taking Yingning with it, and now here she is." While they were thus discussing, peals of laughter were heard coming from within, and Mrs. Wang took occasion to remark what a foolish girl she was. Wu begged to be introduced, and Mrs. Wang went in to fetch her, finding her in an uncontrollable fit of laughter, which she subdued only with great difficulty, and by turning her face to the wall. By-and-by she went out; but, after making a bow, ran back and burst out laughing again, to the great amusement of all the ladies. Wu then said he would go and find out for them all about Yingning and her queer story, so as to be able to arrange the marriage; but when he reached the spot indicated, village and houses had all vanished, and nothing was to be seen except hill-flowers scattered about here and there. He recollected that Mrs. Qin had been buried at no great distance from that spot; he found, however, that the grave had disappeared, and he was no longer able to determine its position. Not knowing what to make of it all, he returned home, and then Mrs. Wang, who thought the girl must be a disembodied spirit, went in and told her what Wu had said. Yingning showed no signs of alarm at this remark; neither did she cry at all when Mrs. Wang began to condole with her on no longer having a home. She only laughed in her usual silly way, and fairly puzzled them all. Sharing Miss Wang's room, she now began to take her part in the duties of a daughter of the family; and as for needlework, they had rarely seen anything

---

82   The semi-divine head of the Taoist religion, wrongly called the Master of Heaven. In his body he is supposed to reside the soul of a celebrated Taoist, an ancestor of his, who actually discovered the elixir of life and became an immortal some eighteen hundred years ago. At death, the precious soul above-mentioned will take up its abode in the body of some youthful member of the family to be hereinafter revealed. Meanwhile, the present Pope makes a very respectable income from the sale of charms, by working miracles, and so forth; and only about 1877 he visited Shanghai, where he was interviewed by several foreigners.

like hers for fineness. But she could not get over that trick of laughing, which, by the way, never interfered with her good looks, and consequently rather amused people than otherwise, amongst others a young married lady who lived next door. Wang's mother fixed an auspicious day for the wedding, but still feeling suspicious about Yingning, was always secretly watching her. Finding, however, that she had a proper shadow,[83] she had her dressed up when the day came, in all the finery of a bride; and would have made her perform the usual ceremonies, only Yingning laughed so much she was unable to kneel down.[84] They were accordingly obliged to excuse her, but Wang began to fear that such a foolish girl would never be able to keep the family counsel. Luckily, she was very reticent and did not indulge in gossip; and moreover, when Mrs. Wang was in trouble or out of temper, Yingning could always bring her around with a laugh. The maid-servants, too, if they expected a whipping for anything, would always ask her to be present when they appeared before their mistress, and thus they often escaped punishment. Yingning had a perfect passion for flowers. She got all she could out of her relations, and even secretly pawned her jewels to buy rare specimens; and by the end of a few months the whole place was one mass of flowers. Behind the house there was one especial tree[85] which belonged to the neighbors on that side; but Yingning was always climbing up and picking the flowers to stick in her hair, for which Mrs. Wang rebuked her severely, though without any result. One day the owner saw her, and gazed at her some time in rapt astonishment; however, she didn't move, deigning only to laugh. The gentleman was much smitten with her; and when she smilingly descended the wall on her own side, pointing all the time with her finger to a spot hard by, he thought she was making an assignation. So he presented himself at nightfall at the same place, and sure enough Yingning was there. Seizing her hand, to tell his passion, he found that he was grasping only a log of wood which stood against the wall; and the next thing he knew was that a scorpion had stung him violently on the finger. There was an end of his romance, except that he died of the wound during the night, and his family at once commenced an action against Wang for having a witch-wife. The magistrate happened to be a great admirer of Wang's talent, and knew him

---

83 Disembodied spirits are supposed to have no shadow, and but very little appetite. There are also certain occasions on which they cannot stand the smell of sulphur. Fiske, in his *Myths and Myth-makers* (page 230), says, "Almost universally, ghosts, how ever impervious to thrust of sword or shot of pistol, can eat and drink like Squire Westerns."

84 See note 10 in tale number 3.

85 The Muh-siang or Rosa *Banksiæ*, R. Br.

to be an accomplished scholar; he therefore refused to grant the summons, and ordered the prosecutor to be bambooed for false accusation.[86] Wang interposed and got him off this punishment, and returned home himself. His mother then scolded Yingning well, saying, "I knew your too playful disposition would some day bring sorrow upon you. But for our intelligent magistrate we should have been in a nice mess. Any ordinary hawk-like official would have had you publicly interrogated in court; and then how could your husband ever have held up his head again?" Yingning looked grave and swore she would laugh no more; and Mrs. Wang continued, "There's no harm in laughing as long as it is seasonable laughter; "but from that moment Yingning laughed no more, no matter what people did to make her, though at the same time her expression was by no means gloomy. One evening she went in tears to her husband, who wanted to know what was the matter. "I couldn't tell you before," said she, sobbing; "we had known each other such a short time. But now that you and your mother have been so kind to me, I will keep nothing from you, but tell you all. I am the daughter of a fox. When my mother went away she put me in the charge of the disembodied spirit of an old woman, with whom I remained for a period of over ten years. I have no brothers: only you to whom I can look. And now my foster-mother is lying on the hill-side with no one to bury her and appease her discontented shade. If not too much, I would ask you to do this, that her spirit may be at rest, and know that it was not neglected by her whom she brought up." Wang consented, but said he feared they would not be able to find her grave; on which Yingning said there was no danger of that, and accordingly they set forth together. When they arrived, Yingning pointed out the tomb in a lonely spot amidst a thicket of brambles, and there they found the old woman's bones. Yingning wept bitterly, and then they proceeded to carry her remains home with them, subsequently interring them in the Qin family vault. That night Wang dreamt that the old woman came to thank him, and when he waked he told Yingning, who said that she had seen her also, and had been warned by her not to frighten Mr. Wang. Her husband asked why she had not detained the old lady; but Yingning replied, "She is a disembodied spirit, and would be ill at ease for any time surrounded by so much life."[87] Wang then inquired after Xiaorong, and his wife said, "She

---

86 Strictly in accordance with Chinese criminal law.
87 These disembodied spirits are unable to stand for any length of time the light and life of this upper world, darkness and death being as it were necessary to their existence and comfort.

was a fox too, and a very clever one. My foster-mother kept her to wait on me, and she was always getting fruit and cakes for me, so that I have a friendship for her and shall never forget her. My foster-mother told me yesterday she was married."

After this, whenever the great fast-day[88] came around, husband and wife went off without fail to worship at the Qin family tomb; and by the time a year had passed she gave birth to a son, who wasn't a bit afraid of strangers, but laughed at everybody, and in fact took very much after his mother.

16. The Magic Sword

NING NAICHEN was a Zhejiang man, and a good-natured, honorable fellow, fond of telling people that he had only loved once. Happening to go to Jinhua, he took shelter in a temple to the north of the city; very nice as far as ornamentation went, but overgrown with grass taller than a man's head, and evidently not much frequented. On either side were the priests' apartments, the doors of which were ajar, with the exception of a small room on the south side, where the lock had a new appearance. In the east corner he espied a group of bamboos, growing over a large pool of water-lilies in flower; and, being much pleased with the quiet of the place, determined to remain; more especially as, the Grand Examiner being in the town, all lodgings had gone up in price. So he roamed about waiting until the priests should return; and in the evening a gentleman came and opened the door on the south side. Ning quickly made up to him, and with a bow informed him of his design. "There is no one here whose permission you need ask," replied the stranger; "I am only lodging here, and if you don't object to the loneliness, I shall be very pleased to have the benefit of your society." Ning was delighted, and made himself a straw bed, and put up a board for a table, as if he intended to remain some time; and that night, by the beams of the clear bright moon, they sat together in the verandah and talked. The stranger's name was Yan Chixia, and Ning thought he was a student up for the provincial examination, only his dialect was not that of a Zhejiang man. On being asked, he said he came from Shaanxi; and there was an air of straightforwardness about all his remarks. By-and-by, when their conversation was exhausted, they bade each other good night and

---

88   The day before the annual spring festival.

went to bed; but Ning, being in a strange place, was quite unable to sleep; and soon he heard sounds of voices from the room on the north side. Getting up, he peeped through a window, and saw, in a small courtyard the other side of a low wall, a woman of about forty with an old maid-servant in a long faded gown, humped-backed and feeble-looking. They were chatting by the light of the moon, and the mistress said, "Why doesn't Xiaoqian come?" "She ought to be here by now," replied the other. "She isn't offended with you, is she?" asked the lady. "Not that I know of," answered the old servant; "but she seems to want to give trouble." "Such people don't deserve to be treated well," said the other; and she had hardly uttered these words when up came a young girl of seventeen or eighteen, and very nice looking. The old servant laughed, and said, "Don't talk of people behind their backs. We were just mentioning you as you came without our hearing you; but fortunately we were saying nothing bad about you. And, as far as that goes," added she, "if I were a young fellow, why, I should certainly fall in love with you." "If *you* don't praise me," replied the girl, "I'm sure I don't know who will; "and then the lady and the girl said something together, and Mr. Ning, thinking they were the family next door, turned around to sleep without paying further attention to them. In a little while no sound was to be heard; but, as he was dropping off to sleep, he perceived that somebody was in the room. Jumping up in great haste, he found it was the young lady he had just seen; and detecting at once that she was going to attempt to bewitch him, sternly bade her begone. She then produced a lump of gold which he threw away, and told her to go after it or he would call his friend. So she had no alternative but to go, muttering something about his heart being like iron or stone. Next day, a young candidate for the examination came and lodged in the east room with his servant. He, however, was killed that very night, and his servant the night after; the corpses of both showing a small hole in the sole of the foot as if bored by an awl, and from which a little blood came. No one knew who had committed these murders, and when Mr. Yan came home, Ning asked him what he thought about it. Yan replied that it was the work of devils, but Ning was a brave fellow, and that didn't frighten him much. In the middle of the night Xiaoqian appeared to him again, and said, "I have seen many men, but none with a steel-cold heart like yours. You are an upright man, and I will not attempt to deceive you. I, Xiaoqian, whose family name is Nie, died when only eighteen, and was buried alongside of this temple. A devil then took possession of me, and employed me to bewitch people by my beauty, contrary to my inclination. There is now nothing left in this temple to slay, and I fear that imps will be employed to kill you." Ning was very frightened at this, and asked her what he should do. "Sleep in the same room with Mr. Yan," replied she. "What!" asked he, "cannot the spirits trouble Yan?" "He is a strange man," she answered, "and they don't like going near him." Ning then inquired how the spirits worked. "I bewitch people," said Xiaoqian, "and then they bore a hole in the foot which renders the victim senseless, and proceed to draw off the blood, which the devils drink. Another method is to tempt people by false gold, the bones of some horrid demon; and if they receive it, their hearts and livers will be torn out. Either method is used according to circumstances." Ning thanked her, and asked when he ought to be prepared; to which she replied, "Tomorrow night." At parting she wept, and said, "I am about to sink into the great sea, with no friendly shore at hand. But your sense of duty is boundless, and you can save me. If you will collect my bones and bury them in some quiet spot, I shall not again be subject to these misfortunes." Ning said he would do so, and asked where she lay buried. "At the foot of the aspen-tree on which there is a bird's nest," replied she; and passing out of the door, disappeared. The next day Ning was afraid that Yan might be going away somewhere, and went over early to invite him across. Wine and food were produced towards noon; and Ning, who took care not to lose sight of Yan, then asked him to remain there for the night. Yan declined, on the ground that he liked being by himself; but Ning wouldn't hear any excuses, and carried all Yan's things to his own room, so that he had no alternative but to consent. However, he warned Ning, saying, "I know you are a gentleman and a man of honor. If you see anything you don't quite understand, I pray you not to be too inquisitive; don't pry into my boxes, or it may be the worse for both of us." Ning promised to attend to what he said, and by-and-by they both lay down to sleep; and Yan, having placed his boxes on the window-sill, was soon snoring loudly. Ning himself could not sleep; and after some time he saw a figure moving stealthily outside, at length approaching the window to peep through. Its eyes flashed like lightning, and Ning in a terrible fright was just upon the point of calling Yan, when something flew out of one of the boxes like a strip of white silk, and dashing against the window-sill returned at once to the box, disappearing very much like lightning. Yan heard the noise and got up, Ning all the time pretending to be asleep in order to watch what happened. The former then opened the box, and took out something which he smelt and examined by the light of the moon. It was dazzlingly white like crystal, and about two inches in length by the width of an onion leaf in breadth. He then wrapped it up carefully and put it back in the broken box, saying, "A bold-faced devil that, to dare thus to break my box;" upon which he went back to bed; but Ning, who was lost in astonishment, arose and asked him what it all meant, telling at the same time what he himself had seen. "As you and I are good friends," replied Yan, "I won't make any secret of it. The fact is I am a Taoist priest. But for the window-sill the devil would have been killed; as it is, he is badly wounded." Ning asked him what it was he had there wrapped up, and he told him it was his sword,[89] on which he had smelt the presence of the devil. At Ning's request he produced the weapon, a bright little miniature of a sword; and from that time Ning held his friend in higher esteem than ever.

Next day he found traces of blood outside the window which led around to the north of the temple; and there among a number of graves he discovered the aspen tree with the bird's nest at its summit. He then fulfilled his promise and prepared to go home, Yan giving him a farewell banquet, and presenting him with an old leather case which he said contained a sword, and would keep at a distance from him all devils and bogies. Ning then wished to learn a little of Yan's art; but the latter replied that although he might accomplish this easily enough, being as he was an upright man, yet he was well off in life, and not in a condition where it would be of any advantage to him. Ning then pretending that he had a younger sister buried here, dug up Xiaoqian's bones, and, having wrapped them up in grave-clothes, hired a boat, and set off on his way home. On his arrival, as his library looked towards the open country, he made a grave hard by and buried the bones there, sacrificing, and invoking Xiaoqian as follows: "In pity for your lonely ghost, I have placed your remains near my humble cottage, where we shall be near each other, and no devil will dare annoy you. I pray you reject not my sacrifice, poor though it be." After this, he was proceeding home when he suddenly heard himself addressed from behind, the voice asking him not to hurry; and turning around he beheld Xiaoqian, who thanked him, saying, "Were I to die ten times for you I could not discharge my debt. Let me go home with you and wait upon your father and mother; you will not repent it." Looking closely at her, he observed that she had a beautiful complexion, and feet as small as bamboo shoots,[90] being altogether much prettier now that he came to see her by daylight. So they went together to his home, and bidding her wait awhile, Ning ran in to tell his mother, to the very great surprise of the old lady. Now Ning's wife had

---

89   See note 47 in tale number 10.
90   Which, well cooked, are a very good substitute for asparagus.

been ill for a long time, and his mother advised him not to say a word about it to her for fear of frightening her; in the middle of which in rushed Xiaoqian, and threw herself on the ground before them. "This is the young lady," said Ning; whereupon his mother in some alarm turned her attention to Xiaoqian, who cried out, "A lonely orphan, without brother or sister, the object of your son's kindness and compassion, begs to be allowed to give her poor services as some return for favors shown." Ning's mother, seeing that she was a nice, pleasant-looking girl, began to lose fear of her, and replied, "Madam, the preference you show for my son is highly pleasing to an old body like myself; but this is the only hope of our family, and I hardly dare agree to his taking a devil-wife." "I have but one motive in what I ask," answered Xiaoqian, "and if you have no faith in disembodied people then let me regard him as my brother, and live under your protection, serving you like a daughter." Ning's mother could not resist her straightforward manner, and Xiaoqian asked to be allowed to see Ning's wife, but this was denied on the plea that the lady was ill. Xiaoqian then went into the kitchen and got ready the dinner, running about the place as if she had lived there all her life. Ning's mother was, however, much afraid of her, and would not let her sleep in the house; so Xiaoqian went to the library, and was just entering when suddenly she fell back a few steps, and began walking hurriedly backwards and forwards in front of the door. Ning seeing this, called out and asked her what it meant; to which she replied, "The presence of that sword frightens me, and that is why I could not accompany you on your way home." Ning at once understood her, and hung up the sword-case in another place; whereupon she entered, lighted a candle, and sat down. For some time she did not speak: at length asking Ning if he studied at night or not—"For," said she, "when I was little I used to repeat the Lengyan *sutra*; but now I have forgotten more than half, and, therefore, I should like to borrow a copy, and when you are at leisure in the evening you might hear me." Ning said he would, and they sat silently there for some time, after which Xiaoqian went away and took up her quarters elsewhere. Morning and night she waited on Ning's mother, bringing water for her to wash in, occupying herself with household matters, and endeavoring to please her in every way. In the evening before she went to bed, she would always go in and repeat a little of the *sutra,* and leave as soon as she thought Ning was getting sleepy. Now the illness of Ning's wife had given his mother a great deal of extra trouble—more, in fact, than she was equal to; but ever since Xiaoqian's arrival all this was changed, and Ning's mother felt kindly disposed to the girl in consequence, gradually growing to regard her almost as her own child, and forgetting quite that she was a spirit. Accordingly, she didn't make her leave the house at night; and Xiaoqian, who being a devil had not tasted meat or drink since her arrival,[91] now began at the end of six months to take a little thin gruel. Mother and son alike became very fond of her, and henceforth never mentioned what she really was; neither were strangers able to detect the fact. By-and-by, Ning's wife died, and his mother secretly wished him to espouse Xiaoqian, though she rather dreaded any unfortunate consequences that might arise. This Xiaoqian perceived, and seizing an opportunity said to Ning's mother, "I have been with you now more than a year, and you ought to know something of my disposition. Because I was unwilling to injure travelers I followed your son hither. There was no other motive; and, as your son has shown himself one of the best of men, I would now remain with him for three years in order that he may obtain for me some mark of Imperial approbation[92] which will do me honor in the realms below." Ning's mother knew that she meant no evil, but hesitated to put the family hopes of a posterity into jeopardy. Xiaoqian, however, reassured her by saying that Ning would have three sons, and that the line would not be interrupted by his marrying her. On the strength of this the marriage was arranged, to the great joy of Ning, a feast prepared, and friends and relatives invited; and when in response to a call the bride herself came forth in her gay wedding-dress, the beholders took her rather for a fairy than for a devil After this, numbers of congratulatory presents were given by the various female members of the family, who vied with one another in making her acquaintance; and these Xiaoqian returned by gifts of paintings of flowers, done by herself, in which she was very skillful, the receivers being extremely proud of such marks of her friendship. One day she was leaning at the window in a despondent mood, when suddenly she asked where the sword-case was. "Oh," replied Ning, "as you seemed afraid of it, I moved it elsewhere." "I have now been so long under the influence of surrounding life,"[93] said Xiaoqian, "that I sha'n't be afraid of it any more. Let us hang it on the bed." "Why so?" asked Ning. "For the last three days," explained she, "I have been much agitated in mind; and I fear that the devil at the temple, angry at my escape, may come suddenly and carry me off." So Ning brought the sword-case, and Xiaoqian, after examining it closely,

91   See note 83 in tale number 15.
92   Such as are from time to time bestowed upon virtuous widows and wives, filial sons and daughters, and others. These consist of some laudatory scroll or tablet, and are much prized by the family of the recipient.
93   See note 87 in tale number 15.

remarked, "This is where the magician puts people. I wonder how many were slain before it got old and worn out as it is now. Even now when I look at it my flesh creeps." The case was then hung up, and next day removed to over the door. At night they sat up and watched, Xiaoqian warning Ning not to go to sleep; and suddenly something fell down flop like a bird. Xiaoqian in a fright got behind the curtain; but Ning looked at the thing, and found it was an imp of darkness, with glaring eyes and a bloody mouth, coming straight to the door. Stealthily creeping up, it made a grab at the sword-case, and seemed about to tear it in pieces, when bang!—the sword-case became as big as a wardrobe, and from it a devil protruded part of his body and dragged the imp in. Nothing more was heard, and the sword-case resumed its original size. Ning was greatly alarmed, but Xiaoqian came out rejoicing, and said, "There's an end of my troubles." In the sword-case they found only a few quarts of clear water; nothing else.

After these events Ning took his doctor's degree and Xiaoqian bore him a son. He then took a concubine, and had one more son by each, all of whom became in time distinguished men.

17. The *Shuimang* Plant

THE *shuimang*[94] is a poisonous herb. It is a creeper, like the bean, and has a similar red flower. Those who eat of it die, and become *shuimang* devils, tradition asserting that such devils are unable to be born again unless they can find someone else who has also eaten of this poison to take their place.[95] These *shuimang* devils abound in the province of Hunan, where, by the way, the phrase "same-year man" is applied to those born in the same year, who exchange visits and call each other brother, their children addressing the father's "brother" as uncle. This has now become a regular custom there.[96]

A young man named Zhu was on his way to visit a same-year friend of his, when he was overtaken by a violent thirst. Suddenly he came upon an old woman sitting by the roadside under a shed and distributing tea gratis,[97] and immediately walked up to her to get a drink. She invited him

---

94 Probably the *Illicium religiosum*, S. & Z., is meant.
95 See note 54 in tale number 12.
96 The common application of the term "same-year men" is to persons who have graduated at the same time.
97 This is by no means an uncommon form of charity. During the temporary distress at Canton, in the

into the shed, and presented him with a bowl of tea in a very cordial spirit; but the smell of it did not seem like the smell of ordinary tea, and he would not drink it, rising up to go away. The old woman stopped him, and called out, "Sanniang! bring some good tea." Immediately a young girl came from behind the shed, carrying in her hands a pot of tea. She was about fourteen or fifteen years old, and of very fascinating appearance, with glittering rings and bracelets on her fingers and arms. As Zhu received the cup from her his reason fled; and drinking down the tea she gave him, the flavor of which was unlike any other kind, he proceeded to ask for more. Then, watching for a moment when the old woman's back was turned, he seized her wrist and drew a ring from her finger. The girl blushed and smiled; and Zhu, more and more inflamed, asked her where she lived. "Come again this evening," replied she, "and you'll find me here." Zhu begged for a handful of her tea, which he stowed away with the ring, and took his leave. Arriving at his destination, he felt a pain in his heart, which he at once attributed to the tea, telling his friend what had occurred. "Alas! you are undone," cried the other; "they were *shuimang* devils. My father died in the same way, and we were unable to save him. There is no help for you." Zhu was terribly frightened, and produced the handful of tea, which his friend at once pronounced to be leaves of the *shuimang* plant. He then showed him the ring, and told him what the girl had said; whereupon his friend, after some reflection, said, "She must be Sanniang, of the Kou family." "How could you know her name?" asked Zhu, hearing his friend use the same words as the old woman. "Oh," replied he, "there was a nice-looking girl of that name who died some years ago from eating of the same herb. She is doubtless the girl you saw." Here someone observed that if the person so entrapped by a devil only knew its name, and could procure an old pair of its shoes, he might save himself by boiling them in water and drinking the liquor as medicine. Zhu's friend thereupon rushed off at once to the Kou family, and implored them to give him an old pair of their daughter's shoes; but they, not wishing to prevent their daughter from finding a substitute in Zhu, flatly refused his request. So he went back in anger and told Zhu, who ground his teeth with rage, saying, "If I die, she shall not obtain her transmigration thereby." His friend then sent him home; and just as he reached the door he fell down dead. Zhu's mother wept bitterly over his corpse, which was in due

---

summer of 1877, large tubs of gruel were to be seen standing at convenient points, ready for any poor person who might wish to stay his hunger. It is thus, and by similar acts of benevolence, such as building bridges, repairing, roads, etc., etc., that the wealthy Chinese man strives to maintain an advantageous balance in his record of good and evil.

course interred; and he left behind one little boy barely a year old. His wife did not remain a widow, but in six months married again and went away, putting Zhu's son under the care of his grandmother, who was quite unequal to any toil, and did nothing but weep morning and night. One day she was carrying her grandson about in her arms, crying bitterly all the time, when suddenly in walked Zhu. His mother much alarmed, brushed away her tears, and asked him what it meant. "Mother," replied he, "down in the realms below I heard you weeping. I am therefore come to tend you. Although a departed spirit, I have a wife, who has likewise come to share your toil. Therefore do not grieve." His mother inquired who his wife was, to which he replied, "When the Kou family sat still and left me to my fate I was greatly incensed against them; and after death I sought for Sanniang, not knowing where she was. I have recently seen my old same-year friend, and he told me where she was. She had come to life again in the person of the baby-daughter of a high official named Ren; but I went thither and dragged her spirit back. She is now my wife, and we get on extremely well together." A very pretty and well-dressed young lady here entered, and made obeisance to Zhu's mother, Zhu saying, "This is Sanniang, of the Kou family;" and although not a living being, Mrs. Zhu at once took a great fancy to her. Zhu sent her off to help in the work of the house, and, in spite of not being accustomed to this sort of thing, she was so obedient to her mother-in-law as to excite the compassion of all. The two then took up their quarters in Zhu's old apartments, and there they continued to remain.

Meanwhile Sanniang asked Zhu's mother to let the Kou family know; and this she did, notwithstanding some objections raised by her son. Mr. and Mrs. Kou were much astonished at the news, and, ordering their carriage, proceeded at once to Zhu's house. There they found their daughter, and parents and child fell into each other's arms. Sanniang entreated them to dry their tears; but her mother, noticing the poverty of Zhu's household, was unable to restrain her feelings. "We are already spirits," cried Sanniang; "what matters poverty to us? Besides, I am very well treated here, and am altogether as happy as I can be." They then asked her who the old woman was, to which she replied, "Her name was Ni. She was mortified at being too ugly to entrap people herself, and got me to assist her. She has now been born again at a soy shop in the city." Then, looking at her husband, she added, "Come, since you are the son-in-law, pay the proper respect to my father and mother, or what shall I think of you?" Zhu made his obeisance, and Sanniang went into the kitchen to get food ready for them, at which her mother became very melancholy, and went away home, whence she sent a couple of maid-servants, a hundred ounces of silver, and rolls of cloth and silk, besides making occasional presents of food and wine, so that Zhu's mother lived in comparative comfort. Sanniang also went from time to time to see her parents, but would never stay very long, pleading that she was wanted at home, and such excuses; and if the old people attempted to keep her, she simply went off by herself. Her father built a nice house for Zhu with all kinds of luxuries in it; but Zhu never once entered his father-in-law's door.

Subsequently a man of the village who had eaten *shuimang*, and had died in consequence, came back to life, to the great astonishment of everybody. However, Zhu explained it, saying, "I brought him back to life. He was the victim of a man named Li Jiu; but I drove off Li's spirit when it came to make the other take his place." Zhu's mother then asked her son why he did not get a substitute for himself; to which he replied, "I do not like to do this. I am anxious to put an end to, rather than take advantage of, such a system. Besides, I am very happy waiting on you, and have no wish to be born again." From that time all persons who had poisoned themselves with *shuimang* were in the habit of feasting Zhu and obtaining his assistance in their trouble. But in ten years' time his mother died, and he and his wife gave themselves up to sorrow, and would see no one, bidding their little boy put on mourning, beat his breast, and perform the proper ceremonies. Two years after Zhu had buried his mother, his son married the granddaughter of a high official named Ren. This gentleman had had a daughter by a concubine, who had died when only a few months old; and now, hearing the strange story of Zhu's wife, he came to call on her and arrange the marriage. He then gave his granddaughter to Zhu's son, and a free intercourse was maintained between the two families. However, one day Zhu said to his son, "Because I have been of service to my generation, God has appointed me Keeper of the Dragons; and I am now about to proceed to my post." Thereupon four horses appeared in the court-yard, drawing a carriage with yellow hangings, the flanks of the horses being covered with scale-like trappings. Husband and wife came forth in full dress, and took their seats, and, while son and daughter-in-law were weeping their adieus, disappeared from view. That very day the Kou family saw their daughter arrive, and, bidding them farewell, she told them the same story. The old people would have kept her, but she said, "My husband is already on his way," and, leaving the house, parted from them for ever. Zhu's son was named Ngo, and his literary name was Lichen. He begged Sanniang's bones from the Kou family, and buried them by the side of his father's.

18. Little Zhu

A MAN named Li Hua dwelt at Changzhou. He was very well off, and about fifty years of age, but he had no sons; only one daughter, named Xiaohui, a pretty child on whom her parents doted. When she was fourteen she had a severe illness and died, leaving their home desolate and depriving them of their chief pleasure in life. Mr. Li then bought a concubine, and she by-and-by bore him a son, who was perfectly idolized, and called Zhu, or the Pearl. This boy grew up to be a fine manly fellow, though so extremely stupid that when five or six years old he didn't know pulse from corn, and could hardly talk plainly. His father, however, loved him dearly, and did not observe his faults.

Now it chanced that a one-eyed priest came to collect alms in the town, and he seemed to know so much about everybody's private affairs that the people all looked upon him as superhuman. He himself declared he had control over life, death, happiness, and misfortune; and consequently no one dared refuse him whatever sum he chose to ask of them. From Li he demanded one hundred ounces of silver, but was offered only ten, which he refused to receive. This sum was increased to thirty ounces, whereupon the priest looked sternly at Li and said, "I must have one hundred; not a fraction less." Li now got angry, and went away without giving him any, the priest, too, rising up in a rage and shouting after him, "I hope you won't repent." Shortly after these events little Zhu fell sick, and crawled about the bed scratching the mat, his face being of an ashen paleness. This frightened his father, who hurried off with eighty ounces of silver, and begged the priest to accept them. "A large sum like this is no trifling matter to earn," said the priest, smiling; "but what can a poor recluse like myself do for you?" So Li went home, to find that little Zhu was already dead; and this worked him into such a state that he immediately laid a complaint before the magistrate. The priest was accordingly summoned and interrogated; but the magistrate wouldn't accept his defence, and ordered him to be bambooed. The blows sounded as if falling on leather, upon which the magistrate commanded his lictors to search him; and from about his person they drew forth two wooden men, a small coffin, and five small flags. The magistrate here flew into a passion, and made certain mystic signs with his fingers, which when the priest saw he was frightened, and began to excuse himself; but the magistrate would not listen to him, and had him bambooed to death. Li thanked him for his kindness, and, taking his leave, proceeded home. In the evening, after dusk, he was sitting alone with his wife, when suddenly in popped a little boy, who said, "Ba! why did you hurry on so fast? I couldn't catch you up." Looking at him more closely, they saw that he was about seven or eight years old, and Mr, Li, in some alarm, was on the point of questioning him, when he disappeared, reappearing again like smoke, and, curling around and around, got upon the bed. Li pushed him off, and he fell down without making any sound, crying out, "Ba! why do you do this?" and in a moment he was on the bed again. Li was frightened, and ran away with his wife, the boy calling after them, "Pa! Ma! boo-oo-oo." They went into the next room, bolting the door after them; but there was the little boy at their heels again. Li asked him what he wanted, to which he replied, "I belong to Suzhou; my name is Zhan; at six years of age I was left an orphan; my brother and his wife couldn't bear me, so they sent me to live at my maternal grandfather's. One day, when playing outside, a wicked priest killed me by his black art underneath a mulberry tree, and made of me an evil spirit, dooming me to everlasting devildom without hope of transmigration. Happily you exposed him; and I would now remain with you as your son." "The paths of men and devils," replied Li, "lie in different directions. How can we remain together?" "Give me only a tiny room," cried the boy, "a bed, a mattress, and a cup of cold gruel every day. I ask for nothing more." So Li agreed, to the great delight of the boy, who slept by himself in another part of the house, coming in the morning and walking in and out like any ordinary person. Hearing Li's concubine crying bitterly, he asked how long little Zhu had been dead, and she told him seven days. "It's cold weather now," said he, "and the body can't have decomposed. Have the grave opened, and let me see it; if not too far gone, I can bring him to life again." Li was only too pleased, and went off with the boy; and when they opened the grave they found the body in perfect preservation; but while Li was controlling his emotions, lo! the boy had vanished from his sight. Wondering very much at this, he took little Zhu's body home, and had hardly laid it on the bed when he noticed the eyes move. Little Zhu then called for some broth, which put him into a perspiration, and then he got up. They were all overjoyed to see him come to life again; and, what is more, he was much brighter and cleverer than before. At night, however, he lay perfectly stiff and rigid, without showing any signs of life; and, as he didn't move when they turned him over and over, they were much frightened, and thought he had died again. But towards daybreak he awaked as if from a dream, and in reply to their questions said that when he was with

the wicked priest there was another boy named Gezi;[98] and that the day
before, when he had been unable to catch up his father, it was because he
had stayed behind to bid adieu to Gezi; that Gezi was now the son of an
official in Purgatory named Jiang, and very comfortably settled; and that he
had invited him (Zhan) to go and play with him that evening, and had sent
him back on a white-nosed horse. His mother then asked him if he had seen
little Zhu in Purgatory, to which he replied, "Little Zhu has already been
born again. He and our father here had not really the destiny of father and
son. Little Zhu was merely a man named Yan Zifang, from Jinling, who had
come to reclaim an old debt."[99] Now Mr. Li had formerly traded to Jinling,
and actually owed money for goods to a Mr. Yan; but he had died, and no
one else knew anything about it, so that he was now greatly alarmed when
he heard this story. His mother next asked (the quasi) little Zhu if he had
seen his sister, Xiaohui; and he said he had not, promising to go again and
inquire about her. A few days afterwards he told his mother that Xiaohui
was very happy in Purgatory, being married to a son of one of the Judges;
and that she had any quantity of jewels,[100] and crowds of attendants when
she went abroad. "Why doesn't she come home to see her parents?" asked
his mother. "Well," replied the boy, "dead people, you know, haven't got
any flesh or bones; however, if you can only remind them of something that
happened in their past lives, their feelings are at once touched. So yesterday
I managed, through Mr. Jiang, to get an interview with Xiaohui; and we
sat together on a coral couch, and I spoke to her of her father and mother
at home, all of which she listened to as if she was asleep. I then remarked,
'Sister, when you were alive you were very fond of embroidering double-
stemmed flowers; and once you cut your finger with the scissors, and the
blood ran over the silk, but you brought it into the picture as a crimson
cloud. Your mother has that picture still, hanging at the head of her bed, a
perpetual souvenir of you. Sister, have you forgotten this?' Then she burst
into tears, and promised to ask her husband to let her come and visit you."
His mother asked when she would arrive, but he said he could not tell.
However, one day he ran in and cried out, "Mother, Xiaohui has come, with
a splendid equipage and a train of servants; we had better get plenty of wine
ready." In a few moments he came in again, saying, "Here is my sister," at
the same time asking her to take a seat and rest. He then wept; but none

---

98   It may be necessary here to remind the reader that Zhan's spirit is speaking from Zhu's body.
99   We shall come by-and-by to a story illustrative of this extraordinary belief.
100 The *summum bonum* of many a Chinese woman.

of those present saw anything at all. By-and-by he went out and burnt a quantity of paper money[101] and made offerings of wine outside the door, returning shortly and saying he had sent away her attendants for a while; also that Xiaohui asked if the green coverlet, a small portion of which had been burnt by a candle, was still in existence. "It is," replied her mother, and, going to a box, she at once produced the coverlet. "Xiaohui would like a bed made up for her in her old room," said her (quasi) brother; "she wants to rest awhile, and will talk with you again in the morning."

Now their next-door neighbor, named Zhao, had a daughter who was formerly a great friend of Xiaohui's, and that night she dreamt that Xiaohui appeared with a turban on her head and a red mantle over her shoulders, and that they talked and laughed together precisely as in days gone by. "I am now a spirit," said Xiaohui, "and my father and mother can no more see me than if I was far separated from them. Dear sister, I would borrow your body, from which to speak to them. You need fear nothing." On the morrow, when Miss Zhao met her mother, she fell on the ground before her and remained some time in a state of unconsciousness, at length saying, "Madam, it is many years since we met; your hair has become very white." "The girl's mad," said her mother, in alarm; and, thinking something had gone wrong, proceeded to follow her out of the door. Miss Zhao went straight to Li's house, and there with tears embraced Mrs. Li, who did not know what to make of it all. "Yesterday," said Miss Zhao, "when I came back, I was unhappily unable to speak with you. Unfilial wretch that I was, to die before you and leave you to mourn my loss. How can I redeem such behavior?" Her mother thereupon began to understand the scene, and, weeping, said to her, "I have heard that you hold an honorable position, and this is a great comfort to me; but living as you do in the palace of a Judge, how is it you are able to get away?" "My husband," replied she, "is very kind; and his parents treat me with all possible consideration. I experience no harsh treatment at their hands." Here Miss Zhao rested her cheek upon her hand, exactly as Xiaohui had been wont to do when she was alive; and at that moment in came her brother to say that her attendants were ready to return. "I must go," said she, rising up and weeping bitterly all the time;

---

101 Chinese silver, called sycee (from the Cantonese *sai see*, "fine silk;" because, if pure, it may be drawn out under the application of heat into fine silk threads), is cast in the form of "shoes," weighing from one to one hundred ounces. Paper imitations of these are burnt for the use of the spirits in the world below. The sharp edges of a "shoe" of sycee are caused by the mold containing the molten silver being gently shaken until the metal has set, with a view to secure uniform fineness throughout the lump.

after which she fell down, and remained some time unconscious as before.

Shortly after these events Mr. Li became dangerously ill, and no medicines were of any avail, so that his son feared they would not be able to save his life. Two devils sat at the head of his bed, one holding an iron staff, the other a nettle-hemp rope four or five feet in length. Day and night his son implored them to go, but they would not move; and Mrs. Li in sorrow began to prepare the funeral clothes.[102] Towards evening her son entered and cried out, "Strangers and women leave the room! My sister's husband is coming to see his father-in-law." He then clapped his hands, and burst out laughing. "What is the matter?" asked his mother. "I am laughing," answered he, "because when the two devils heard my sister's husband was coming, they both ran under the bed, like terrapins, drawing in their heads." By-and-by, looking at nothing, he began to talk about the weather, and ask his sister's husband how he did, and then he clapped his hands and said, "I begged the two devils to go, but they would not; it's all right now." After this he went out to the door and returned, saying, "My sister's husband has gone. He took away the two devils tied to his horse. My father ought to get better now. Besides, Xiaohui's husband said he would speak to the Judge, and obtain a hundred years' lease of life both for you and my father." The whole family rejoiced exceedingly at this, and when night came Mr. Li was better, and in a few days quite well again. A tutor was engaged for the (quasi) little Zhu, who showed himself an apt pupil, and at eighteen years of age took his bachelor's degree. He could also see things of the other world; and when anyone in the village was ill, he pointed out where the devils were, and burnt them out with fire, so that everybody got well. However, before long he himself became very ill, and his flesh turned green and purple, whereupon he said, "The devils afflict me thus because I let out their secrets. Henceforth I shall never divulge them again."

19. Miss Quarta Hu

MR. SHANG was a native of Taishan, and lived quietly with his books alone. One autumn night when the Silver River[103] was unusually distinct and the

---

102 Death is regarded as a summons from the authorities of Purgatory; Victors are sent to arrest the doomed man armed with a written warrant similar to those issued on earth from a magistrate's yamên.

103 The Milky Way is known to the Chinese under this name—unquestionably a more poetical one

moon shining brightly in the sky, he was walking up and down under the shade, with his thoughts wandering somewhat at random, when lo! a young girl leaped over the wall, and, smiling, asked him, "What are you thinking about, Sir, all so deeply?" Shang looked at her, and seeing that she had a pretty face, asked her to walk in. She then told him her name was Hu,[104] and that she was called Tertia; but when he wanted to know where she lived, she laughed and would not say. So he did not inquire any further; and by degrees they struck up a friendship, and Miss Tertia used to come and chat with him every evening. He was so smitten that he could hardly take his eyes off her, and at last she said to him, "What *are* you looking at?" "At you," cried he, "my lovely rose, my beautiful peach. I could gaze at you all night long." "If you think so much of poor me," answered she, "I don't know where your wits would be if you saw my sister Quarta." Mr. Shang said he was sorry he didn't know her, and begged that he might be introduced; so next night Miss Tertia brought her sister, who turned out to be a young damsel of about fifteen, with a face delicately powdered and resembling the lily, or like an apricot-flower seen through mist; and altogether as pretty a girl as he had ever seen. Mr. Shang was charmed with her, and inviting them in, began to laugh and talk with the elder, while Miss Quarta sat playing with her girdle, and keeping her eyes on the ground. By-and-by Miss Tertia got up and said she was going, whereupon her sister rose to take leave also; but Mr. Shang asked her not to be in a hurry, and requested the elder to assist in persuading her. "You needn't hurry," said she to Miss Quarta; and accordingly the latter remained chatting with Mr. Shang without reserve, and finally told him she was a fox. However, Mr. Shang was so occupied with her beauty that he didn't pay any heed to that; but she added, "And my sister is very dangerous; she has already killed three people. Anyone bewitched by her has no chance of escape. Happily, you have bestowed your affections on me, and I shall not allow you to be destroyed. You must break off your acquaintance with her at once." Mr. Shang was very frightened, and implored her to help him; to which she replied, "Although a fox, I am skilled in the arts of the Immortals;[105] I will write out a charm for you which you must paste on the door, and thus you will keep her away." So she wrote down the charm, and in the morning when her sister came and saw it, she fell back, crying out, "Ungrateful minx! you've thrown me up for him,

than our own.
104 See note 57 in tale number 13.
105 That is, of the Taoists. See note 11 in tale number 4.

have you? You two being destined for each other, what have I done that you should treat me thus?" She then went away; and a few days afterwards Miss Quarta said she too would have to be absent for a day, so Shang went out for a walk by himself, and suddenly beheld a very nice-looking young lady emerge from the shade of an old oak that was growing on the hillside. "Why so dreadfully pensive?" said she to him; "those Hu girls can never bring you a single cent." She then presented Shang with some money, and bade him go on ahead and buy some good wine, adding, "I'll bring something to eat with me, and we'll have a jolly time of it." Shang took the money and went home, doing as the young lady had told him; and by-and-by in she herself came, and threw on the table a roast chicken and a shoulder of salt pork, which she at once proceeded to cut up. They now set to work to enjoy themselves, and had hardly finished when they heard some one coming in, and the next minute in walked Miss Tertia and her sister. The strange young lady didn't know where to hide, and managed to lose her shoes; but the other two began to revile her, saying, "Out upon you, base fox; what are you doing here?" They then chased her away after some trouble, and Shang began to excuse himself to them, until at last they all became friends again as before.

One day, however, a Shaanxi man arrived, riding on a donkey, and coming to the door said, "I have long been in search of these evil spirits: now I have got them." Shang's father thought the man's remark rather strange, and asked him whence he had come. "Across much land and sea," replied he; "for eight or nine months out of every year I am absent from my native place. These devils killed my brother with their poison, alas! alas! and I have sworn to exterminate them; but I have traveled many miles without being able to find them. They are now in your house, and if you do not cut them off, you will die even as my brother." Now Shang and the young ladies had kept their acquaintanceship very dark; but his father and mother had guessed that something was up, and, much alarmed, bade the Shaanxi man walk in and perform his exorcisms. The latter then produced two bottles which he placed upon the ground, and proceeded to mutter a number of charms and cabalistic formulæ; whereupon four wreaths of smoke passed two by two into each bottle. "I have the whole family," cried he, in an ecstasy of delight; as he proceeded to tie down the mouths of the bottles with pig's bladder, sealing them with the utmost care. Shang's father was likewise very pleased, and kept his guest to dinner; but the young man himself was sadly dejected, and approaching the bottles unperceived, bent his ear to listen. "Ungrateful man," said Miss Quarta from within, "to sit there and make no effort to save me." This was more than Shang could stand, and he immediately broke the seal, but found that he couldn't untie the knot. "Not so," cried Miss Quarta; "merely lay down the flag that now stands on the altar, and with a pin prick the bladder, and I can get out." Shang did as she bade him, and in a moment a thin streak of white smoke issued forth from the hole and disappeared in the clouds. When the Shaanxi man came out, and saw the flag lying on the ground, he started violently, and cried out, "Escaped! This must be your doing, young Sir." He then shook the bottle and listened, finally exclaiming, "Luckily only one has got away. She was fated not to die, and may therefore be pardoned."[106] Thereupon he took the bottles and went his way.

Some years afterwards Shang was one day superintending his reapers cutting the corn, when he descried Miss Quarta at a distance, sitting under a tree. He approached, and she took his hand, saying, "Ten years have rolled away since last we met. Since then I have gained the prize of immortality;[107] but I thought that perhaps you had not quite forgotten me, and so I came to see you once more." Shang wished her to return home with him; to which she replied, "I am no longer what I was that I should mingle in the affairs of mortals. We shall meet again." And as she said this, she disappeared; but twenty years later, when Shang was one day alone, Miss Quarta walked in. Shang was overjoyed, and began to address her; but she answered him, saying, "My name is already enrolled in the register of the Immortals, and I have no right to return to earth. However, out of gratitude to you I determined to announce to you the date of your dissolution, that you might put your affairs in order. Fear nothing; I will see you safely through to the happy land." She then departed, and on the day named Shang actually died. A relative of a friend of mine, Mr. Li Wenyu, frequently met the above-mentioned Mr. Shang.[108]

---

106 Predestination *after the event* is, luckily for China, the form of this superstition which really appeals to her all-practical children. Not a larger percentage than with ourselves allow belief in an irremediable destiny to divert their efforts one moment from the object in view; though thousands upon thousands are ready enough to acknowledge the "will of heaven" in any national or individual calamities that may have befallen. See note 36 in tale number 9.

107 Any disembodied spirit whose conduct for a certain term of years is quite satisfactory is competent to obtain this reward. Thus, instead of being born again on earth, perhaps as an animal, they become angels or good spirits, and live for ever in heaven in a state of supreme beatitude.

108 Our author occasionally ends up with a remark of this kind; and these have undoubtedly had their weight with his too credulous countrymen.

20. Mr. Zhu, the Considerate Husband

AT the village of Zhu in Jiyang, there was a man named Zhu, who died at the age of fifty and odd years. His family at once proceeded to put on their mourning robes, when suddenly they heard the dead man cry out. Rushing up to the coffin, they found that he had come to life again; and began, full of joy, to ask him all about it. But the old gentleman replied only to his wife, saying, "When I died I did not expect to come back. However, by the time I had got a few miles on my way, I thought of the poor old body I was leaving behind me, dependent for everything on others, and with no more enjoyment of life. So I made up my mind to return, and take you away with me." The bystanders thought this was only the disconnected talk of a man who had just regained consciousness, and attached no importance to it; but the old man repeated it, and then his wife said, "It's all very well, but you have only just come to life; how can you go and die again directly?" "It is extremely simple," replied her husband; "you go and pack up everything ready." The old lady laughed and did nothing; upon which Mr. Zhu urged her again to prepare, and then she left the house. In a short time she returned, and pretended that she had done what he wanted. "Then you had better dress," said he; but Mrs. Zhu did not move until he pressed her again and again, after which she did not like to cross him, and by-and-by came out all fully equipped. The other ladies of the family were laughing on the sly, when Mr. Zhu laid his head upon the pillow, and told his wife to do likewise. "It's too ridiculous," she was beginning to say, when Mr. Zhu banged the bed with his hand, and cried out, "What is there to laugh at in dying?" upon which the various members of the family, seeing the old gentleman was in a rage, begged her to gratify his whim. Mrs. Zhu then lay down alongside of her husband, to the infinite amusement of the spectators; but it was soon noticed that the old lady had ceased to smile, and by-and-by her two eyes closed. For a long time not a sound was heard, as if she was fast asleep; and when some of those present approached to touch her, they found she was as cold as ice, and no longer breathing; then, turning to her husband, they perceived that he also had passed away.

This story was fully related to me by a younger sister-in-law of Mr. Zhu's, who, in the twenty-first year of the reign Kang Xi,[109] was employed in the house of a high official named Bi.

---

109 1682 CE.

21. The Magnanimous Girl

AT Jinling there lived a young man named Gu, who had considerable ability but was very poor; and having an old mother, he was very loath to leave home. So he employed himself in writing or painting[110] for people, and gave his mother the proceeds, going on thus until he was twenty-five years of age without taking a wife. Opposite to their house was another building, which had long been untenanted; and one day an old woman and a young girl came to occupy it, but there being no gentleman with them young Gu did not make any inquiries as to who they were or whence they hailed. Shortly afterwards it chanced that just as Gu was entering the house he observed a young lady come out of his mother's door. She was about eighteen or nineteen, very clever and refined-looking, and altogether such a girl as one rarely sets eyes on; and when she noticed Mr. Gu, she did not run away, but seemed quite self-possessed. "It was the young lady over the way; she came to borrow my scissors and measure," said his mother, "and she told me that there was only her mother and herself. They don't seem to belong to the lower classes. I asked her why she didn't get married, to which she replied that her mother was old. I must go and call on her tomorrow, and find out how the land lies. If she doesn't expect too much, you could take care of her mother for her." So next day Gu's mother went, and found that the girl's mother was deaf, and that they were evidently poor, apparently not having a day's food in the house. Gu's mother asked what their employment was, and the old lady said they trusted for food to her daughter's ten fingers. She then threw out some hints about uniting the two families, to which the old lady seemed to agree; but, on consultation with her daughter, the latter would not consent. Mrs. Gu returned home and told her son, saying, "Perhaps she thinks we are too poor. She doesn't speak or laugh, is very nice-looking, and as pure as snow; truly no ordinary girl." There ended that; until one day, as Gu was sitting in his study, up came a very agreeable young fellow, who said he was from a neighboring village, and engaged Gu to draw a picture for him. The two youths soon struck up a firm friendship and met constantly, when it happened that the stranger chanced to see the young lady of over the way. "Who is that?" said he, following her with his eyes. Gu told him, and then he said, "She is certainly pretty, but rather

---

110 The usual occupation of poor scholars who are ashamed to go into trade, and who have not enter-prise enough to start as doctors or fortune-tellers. Besides painting pictures and fans, and illustrating books, these men write fancy scrolls in the various ornamental styles so much prized by the Chinese; they keep accounts for people, and write or read business and private letters for the illiterate masses.

stern in her appearance." By-and-by Gu went in, and his mother told him the girl had come to beg a little rice, as they had had nothing to eat all day. "She's a good daughter," said his mother, "and I'm very sorry for her. We must try and help them a little." Gu thereupon shouldered a peck of rice, and, knocking at their door, presented it with his mother's compliments. The young lady received the rice but said nothing; and then she got into the habit of coming over and helping Gu's mother with her work and household affairs, almost as if she had been her daughter-in-law, for which Gu was very grateful to her, and whenever he had anything nice he always sent some of it in to her mother, though the young lady herself never once took the trouble to thank him. So things went on until Gu's mother got an abscess on her leg, and lay writhing in agony day and night. Then the young lady devoted herself to the invalid, waiting on her and giving her medicine with such care and attention that at last the sick woman cried out, "Oh, that I could secure such a daughter-in-law as you, to see this old body into its grave!" The young lady soothed her, and replied, "Your son is a hundred times more filial than I, a poor widow's only daughter." "But even a filial son makes a bad nurse," answered the patient; "besides I am now drawing towards the evening of my life, when my body will be exposed to the mists and the dews, and I am vexed in spirit about our ancestral worship and the continuance of our line." As she was speaking Gu walked in; and his mother, weeping, said, "I am deeply indebted to this young lady; do not forget to repay her goodness." Gu made a low bow, but the young lady said, "Sir, when you were kind to my mother, I did not thank you; why, then, thank me?" Gu thereupon became more than ever attached to her; but could never get her to depart in the slightest degree from her cold demeanor towards himself. One day, however, he managed to squeeze her hand, upon which she told him never to do so again; and then for some time he neither saw nor heard anything of her. She had conceived a violent dislike to the young stranger above-mentioned; and one evening when he was sitting talking with Gu, the young lady reappeared. After a while she got angry at something he said, and drew from her robe a glittering knife about a foot long. The young man, seeing her do this, ran out in a fright and she after him, only to find that he had vanished. She then threw her dagger up into the air, and whish! a streak of light like a rainbow, and something came tumbling down with a flop. Gu got a light, and ran to see what it was; and lo! there lay a white fox, head in one place and body in another. "There is your *friend*," cried the girl; "I knew he would cause me to destroy him sooner or later." Gu dragged it into the house, and said, "Let us wait until tomorrow to talk it over; we shall then be more calm." Next day the young lady arrived, and Gu inquired about her knowledge of the black art; but she told Gu not to trouble himself about such affairs, and to keep it secret or it might be prejudicial to his happiness. Gu then entreated her to consent to their union, to which she replied that she had already been as it were a daughter-in-law to his mother, and there was no need to push the thing further. "Is it because I am poor?" asked Gu. "Well, I am not rich," answered she, "but the fact is I had rather not." She then took her leave, and the next evening when Gu went across to their house to try once more to persuade her, the young lady had disappeared, and was never seen again.

22. The Boon-Companion

ONCE upon a time there was a young man named Che, who was not particularly well off, but at the same time very fond of his wine; so much so, that without his three stoups of liquor every night, he was quite unable to sleep, and bottles were seldom absent from the head of his bed. One night he had woken up and was turning over and over, when he fancied someone was in the bed with him; but then, thinking it was only the clothes which had slipped off, he put out his hand to feel, and, lo! he touched something silky like a cat, only larger. Striking a light, he found it was a fox, lying in a drunken sleep like a dog; and then looking at his wine bottle he saw that it had been emptied. "A boon-companion," said he, laughing, as he avoided startling the animal, and covering it up, lay down to sleep with his arm across it, and the candle alight so as to see what transformation it might undergo. About midnight, the fox stretched itself, and Che cried, "Well, to be sure, you've had a nice sleep!" He then drew off the clothes, and beheld an elegant young man in a scholar's dress; but the young man jumped up, and making a low obeisance, returned his host many thanks for not cutting off his head. "Oh," replied Che, "I am not averse to liquor myself; in fact they say I'm too much given to it. You shall play Pythias to my Damon;[111] and if you have no objection, we'll be a pair of bottle-and-glass chums." So they lay down and went to sleep again, Che urging the young man to visit him often, and saying that they must have faith in

---

111 Guan Zhung and Bao Shu are the Chinese types of friendship. They were two statesmen of considerable ability, who nourished in the seventh century BCE.

each other. The fox agreed to this, but when Che awoke in the morning his bedfellow had already disappeared. So he prepared a goblet of first-rate wine in expectation of his friend's arrival, and at nightfall sure enough he came. They then sat together drinking, and the fox cracked so many jokes that Che said he regretted he had not known him before. "And truly I don't know how to repay your kindness," replied the former, "in preparing all this nice wine for me." "Oh," said Che, "what's a pint or so of wine?—nothing worth speaking of." "Well," rejoined the fox, "you are only a poor scholar, and money isn't so easily to be got. I must try if I can't secure a little wine capital for you." Next evening, when he arrived, he said to Che, "Two miles down towards the south-east you will find some silver lying by the wayside. Go early in the morning and get it." So on the morrow Che set off, and actually obtained two lumps of silver, with which he bought some choice morsels to help them out with their wine that evening. The fox now told him that there was a vault in his backyard which he ought to open; and when he did so, he found therein more than a hundred strings of cash.[112] "Now then," cried Che, delighted, "I shall have no more anxiety about funds for buying wine with all this in my purse." "Ah," replied the fox, "the water in a puddle is not inexhaustible. I must do something further for you." Some days afterwards the fox said to Che, "Buckwheat is very cheap in the market just now. Something is to be done in this line." Accordingly, Che bought over forty tons, and thereby incurred general ridicule; but by-and-by there was a bad drought and all kinds of grain and beans were spoilt. Only buckwheat would grow, and Che sold off his stock at a profit of one thousand per cent. His wealth thus began to increase; he bought two hundred acres of rich land, and always planted his crops, corn, millet, or what not, upon the advice of the fox secretly given him beforehand. The fox looked on Che's wife as a sister, and on Che's children as his own; but when, subsequently, Che died, it never came to the house again.

23. Miss Lianxiang, the Fox-Girl

THERE was a young man named Sang Ziming, a native of Yizhou, who had been left an orphan when quite young. He lived near the Saffron market, and kept himself very much to himself, only going out twice a day for his

---

112 Say about £10. See note 7 in tale number 2.

meals to a neighbor's close by, and sitting quietly at home all the rest of his time. One day the said neighbor called, and asked him in joke if he wasn't afraid of devil-foxes, so much alone as he was. "Oh," replied Sang, laughing, "what has the superior man[113] to fear from devil-foxes? If they come as men, I have here a sharp sword for them; and if as women, why, I shall open the door and ask them to walk in." The neighbor went away, and having arranged with a friend of his, they got a young lady of their acquaintance to climb over Sang's wall with the help of a ladder, and knock at the door. Sang peeped through, and called out, "Who's there?" to which the girl answered, "A devil!" and frightened Sang so dreadfully that his teeth chattered in his head. The girl then ran away, and next morning when his neighbor came to see him, Sang told him what had happened, and said he meant to go back to his native place. The neighbor then clapped his hands, and said to Sang, "Why didn't you ask her in?" Whereupon Sang perceived that he had been tricked, and went on quietly again as before.

Some six months afterwards, a young lady knocked at his door; and Sang, thinking his friends were at their old tricks, opened it at once, and asked her to walk in. She did so; and he beheld to his astonishment a perfect Helen for beauty.[114] Asking her whence she came, she replied that her name was Lianxiang, and that she lived not very far off, adding that she had long been anxious to make his acquaintance. After that she used to drop in every now and again for a chat; but one evening when Sang was sitting alone expecting her, another young lady suddenly walked in. Thinking it was Lianxiang, Sang got up to meet her, but found that the new-comer was somebody else. She was about fifteen or sixteen years of age, wore very full sleeves, and dressed her hair after the fashion of unmarried girls, being otherwise very stylish-looking and refined, and apparently hesitating whether to go on or go back. Sang, in a great state of alarm, took her for a fox; but the young lady said, "My name is Li, and I am of a respectable family. Hearing of your virtue and talent, I hope to be accorded the honor of your acquaintance." Sang laughed, and took her by the hand, which he found was as cold as ice; and when he asked the reason, she told him that she had always been delicate, and that it was very chilly outside. She then remarked that she intended to visit him pretty frequently, and hoped it would not inconvenience him; so he explained that no one came to see

113 The term constantly employed by Confucius to denote the man of perfect probity, learning, and refinement. The nearest, if not an exact, translation would be "gentleman."
114 Literally, "a young lady whose beauty would overthrow a kingdom," in allusion to an old story which it is not necessary to reproduce here.

him except another young lady, and that not very often. "When she comes, I'll go," replied the young lady, "and only drop in when she's not here." She then gave him an embroidered slipper, saying that she had worn it, and that whenever he shook it she would know that he wanted to see her, cautioning him at the same time never to shake it before strangers. Taking it in his hand he beheld a very tiny little shoe almost as fine-pointed as an awl, with which he was much pleased; and next evening, when nobody was present, he produced the shoe and shook it, whereupon the young lady immediately walked in. Henceforth, whenever he brought it out, the young lady responded to his wishes and appeared before him. This seemed so strange that at last he asked her to give him some explanation; but she only laughed, and said it was mere coincidence. One evening after this Lianxiang came, and said in alarm to Sang, "Whatever has made you look so melancholy?" Sang replied that he did not know, and by-and-by she took her leave, saying they would not meet again for some ten days. During this period Miss Li visited Sang every day, and on one occasion asked him where his other friend was. Sang told her; and then she laughed and said, "What is your opinion of me as compared with Lianxiang?" "You are both of you perfection," replied he, "but you are a little *colder* of the two." Miss Li didn't much like this, and cried out, "*Both of us perfection* is what you say to *me*. Then she must be a downright Cynthia,[115] and I am no match for her." Somewhat out of temper, she reckoned that Lianxiang's ten days had expired, and said she would have a peep at her, making Sang promise to keep it all secret. The next evening Lianxiang came, and while they were talking she suddenly exclaimed, "Oh, dear! how much worse you seem to have become in the last ten days. You must have encountered something bad." Sang asked her why so; to which she answered, "First of all your appearance; and then your pulse is very thready.[116] You've got the devil-disease."

The following evening when Miss Li came. Sang asked her what she thought of Lianxiang, "Oh," said she, "there's no question about her beauty; but she's a fox. When she went away I followed her to her hole on the hillside." Sang, however, attributed this remark to jealousy, and took no notice of it; but the next evening when Lianxiang came, he observed, "I don't believe it myself, but some one has told me you are a fox." Lianxiang asked who had said so, to which Sang replied that he was only joking; and then she begged him to explain what difference there was between a fox and an

115 The Lady of the Moon. See note 14 in tale number 5.
116 See note 30 in tale number 8.

ordinary person. "Well," answered Sang, "foxes frighten people to death, and, therefore, they are very much dreaded." "Don't you believe that!" cried Lianxiang; "and now tell me who has been saying this of me." Sang declared at first that it was only a joke of his, but by-and-by yielded to her instances, and let out the whole story. "Of course I saw how changed you were," said Lianxiang; "she is surely not a human being to be able to cause such a rapid alteration in you. Say nothing; tomorrow I'll watch her as she watched me." The following evening Miss Li came in; and they had hardly interchanged half a dozen sentences when a cough was heard outside the window, and Miss Li ran away. Lianxiang then entered and said to Sang, "You are lost! She is a devil, and if you do not at once forbid her coming here, you will soon be on the road to the other world." "All jealousy," thought Sang, saying nothing, as Lianxiang continued, "I know that you don't like to be rude to her; but I, for my part, cannot see you sacrificed, and tomorrow I will bring you some medicine to expel the poison from your system. Happily, the disease has not yet taken firm hold of you, and in ten days you will be well again." The next evening she produced a knife and chopped up some medicine for Sang, which made him feel much better; but, although he was very grateful to her, he still persisted in disbelieving that he had the devil-disease. After some days he recovered and Lianxiang left him, warning him to have no more to do with Miss Li. Sang pretended that he would follow her advice, and closed the door and trimmed his lamp. He then took out the slipper, and on shaking it Miss Li appeared, somewhat cross at having been kept away for several days. "She merely attended on me these few nights while I was ill," said Sang; "don't be angry." At this Miss Li brightened up a little; but by-and-by Sang told her that people said she was a devil. "It's that nasty fox," cried Miss Li, after a pause, "putting these things into your head. If you don't break with her, I won't come here again." She then began to sob and cry, and Sang had some trouble in pacifying her. Next evening Lianxiang came and found out that Miss Li had been there again; whereupon she was very angry with Sang, and told him he would certainly die. "Why need you be so jealous?" said Sang, laughing; at which she only got more enraged, and replied, "When you were nearly dying the other day and I saved you, if I had not been jealous, where would you have been now?" Sang pretended he was only joking, and said that Miss Li had told him his recent illness was entirely owing to the machinations of a fox; to which she replied, "It's true enough what you say, only you don't see *whose* machinations, However, if anything happens to you, I should never clear myself even had I a hundred mouths; we will, therefore, part. A hundred days hence I shall see you on your bed." Sang could not persuade her to stay, and away she went; and from that time Miss Li became a regular visitor.

Two months passed away, and Sang began to experience a feeling of great lassitude, which he tried at first to shake off, but by-and-by he became very thin, and could only take thick gruel. He then thought about going back to his native place; however, he could not bear to leave Miss Li, and in a few more days he was so weak that he was unable to get up. His friend next door, seeing how ill he was, daily sent in his boy with food and drink; and now Sang began for the first time to suspect Miss Li. So he said to her, "I am sorry I didn't listen to Lianxiang before I got as bad as this." He then closed his eyes and kept them shut for some time; and when he opened them again Miss Li had disappeared. Their acquaintanceship was thus at an end, and Sang lay all emaciated as he was upon his bed in his solitary room longing for the return of Lianxiang. One day, while he was still thinking about her, someone drew aside the screen and walked in. It was Lianxiang; and approaching the bed she said with a smile, "Was I then talking such nonsense? "Sang struggled a long time to speak; and, at length, confessing he had been wrong, implored her to save him. "When the disease has reached such a pitch as this," replied Lianxiang, "there is very little to be done. I merely came to bid you farewell, and to clear up your doubts about my jealousy." In great tribulation, Sang asked her to take something she would find under his pillow and destroy it; and she accordingly drew forth the slipper, which she proceeded to examine by the light of the lamp, turning it over and over. All at once Miss Li walked in, but when she saw Lianxiang she turned back as though she would run away, which Lianxiang instantly prevented by placing herself in the doorway. Sang then began to reproach her, and Miss Li could make no reply; whereupon Lianxiang said, "At last we meet. Formerly you attributed this gentleman's illness to me; what have you to say now? "Miss Li bent her head in acknowledgment of her guilt, and Lianxiang continued, "How is it that a nice girl like you can thus turn love into hate?" Here Miss Li threw herself on the ground in a flood of tears and begged for mercy; and Lianxiang, raising her up, inquired of her as to her past life. "I am a daughter of a petty official named Li, and I died young, leaving the web of my destiny incomplete, like the silkworm that perishes in the spring. To be the partner of this gentleman was my ardent wish; but I had never any intention of causing his death." "I have heard," remarked Lianxiang, "that the advantage devils obtain by killing people is that their victims are ever with them after death. Is this so?" "It is not," replied Miss Li; "the companionship of two devils gives no pleasure to either. Were it otherwise, I should not have wanted for friends in the realms below. But tell me, how do foxes manage not to kill people." "You allude to such foxes as suck the breath out of people?" replied Lianxiang; "l am not of that class. Some foxes are harmless; no devils are,[117] because of the dominance of the *yin*[118] in their compositions." Sang now knew that these two girls were really a fox and a devil; however, from being long accustomed to their society, he was not in the least alarmed. His breathing had dwindled to a mere thread, and at length he uttered a cry of pain. Lianxiang looked around and said, "How shall we cure him?" upon which Miss Li blushed deeply and drew back; and then Lianxiang added, "If he does get well, I'm afraid you will be dreadfully jealous." Miss Li drew herself up, and replied, "Could a physician be found to wipe away the wrong I have done to this gentleman, I would bury my head in the ground. How should I look the world in the face?" Lianxiang here opened a bag and drew forth some drugs, saying, "I have been looking forward to this day. When I left this gentleman I proceeded to gather my simples, as it would take three months for the medicine to be got ready; but then, should the poison have brought anyone even to death's door, this medicine is able to call him back. The only condition is that it be administered by the very hand which wrought the ill." Miss Li did as she was told, and put the pills Lianxiang gave her one after another into Sang's mouth. They burnt his inside like fire; but soon vitality began to return, and Lianxiang cried out, "He is cured!" Just at this moment Miss Li heard the cock crow and vanished,[119] Lianxiang remaining behind in attendance on the invalid, who was unable to feed himself. She bolted the outside door and pretended that Sang had returned to his native place, so as to prevent visitors from calling. Day and night she took care of him, and every evening Miss Li came in to render assistance, regarding Lianxiang as an elder sister, and being treated by her with great consideration

---

117 Miss Lianxiang was there speaking without book, as will be seen in a story later on.

118 The female principle. In a properly-constituted human being the male and female principles are harmoniously combined. Nothing short of a small volume would place this subject, the basis of Chinese metaphysics, in a clear light before the uninitiated reader. Broadly speaking, the *yin* and the *yang* are the two primeval forces from the interaction of which all things have been evolved.

119 *Ber.*—It was about to speak, when the cock crowed.
Hor.—And then it started like a guilty thing
Upon a fearful summons. I have heard,
The cock, that is the trumpet to the morn,
Doth with his lofty and shrill-sounding throat
Awake the God of Day; and, at his warning,
Whether in sea or fire, in earth or air,
The extravagant and erring spirit hies
To his confine. —*Hamlet.*

and kindness. Three months afterwards Sang was as strong and well as ever he had been, and then for several evenings Miss Li ceased to visit them, only staying a few moments when she did come, and seeming very uneasy in her mind. One evening Sang ran after her and carried her back in his arms, finding her no heavier than so much straw; and then, being obliged to stay, she curled herself up and lay down, to all appearance in a state of unconsciousness, and by-and-by she was gone. For many days they heard nothing of her, and Sang was so anxious that she should come back that he often took out her slipper and shook it. "I don't wonder at your missing her," said Lianxiang, "I do myself very much indeed." "Formerly," observed Sang, "when I shook the slipper she invariably came. I thought it was very strange, but I never suspected her of being a devil. And now, alas! all I can do is to sit and think about her with this slipper in my hand." He then burst into a flood of tears. Now a young lady named Yaner, belonging to the wealthy Zhang family, and about fifteen years of age, had died suddenly, without any apparent cause, and had come to life again in the night, when she got up and wished to go out. They barred the door and would not hear of her doing so; upon which she said, "I am the spirit daughter of a petty magistrate. A Mr. Sang has been very kind to me, and I have left my slipper at his house. I am really a spirit; what is the use of keeping me in?" There being some reason for what she said, they asked her why she had come there; but she only looked up and down without being able to give any explanation. Some one here observed, that Mr. Sang had already gone home, but the young lady utterly refused to believe them. The family was much disturbed at all this; and when Sang's neighbor heard the story, he jumped over the wall, and peeping through beheld Sang sitting there chatting with a pretty-looking girl. As he went in, there was some commotion, during which Sang's visitor had disappeared, and when his neighbor asked the meaning of it all, Sang replied laughing, "Why, I told you if any ladies came I should ask them in." His friend then repeated what Miss Yaner had said; and Sang, unbolting his door, was about to go and have a peep at her, but unfortunately had no means of so doing. Meanwhile Mrs. Zhang, hearing that he had not gone away, was more lost in astonishment than ever, and sent an old woman-servant to get back the slipper. Sang immediately gave it to her, and Miss Yaner was delighted to recover it, though when she came to try it on it was too small for her by a good inch. In considerable alarm, she seized a mirror to look at herself; and suddenly became aware that she had come to life again in some one else's body. She therefore told all to her mother, and finally succeeded in convincing her, crying all the time because she was so changed for the worse as regarded personal appearance from what she had been before. And whenever she happened to see Lianxiang, she was very much disconcerted, declaring that she had been much better off as a devil than now as a human being. She would sit and weep over the slipper, no one being able to comfort her; and finally, covering herself up with bed-clothes, she lay all stark and stiff, positively refusing to take any nourishment. Her body swelled up, and for seven days she refused all food, but did not die; and then the swelling began to subside, and an intense hunger to come upon her which made her once more think about eating. Then she was troubled with a severe irritation, and her skin peeled entirely away; and when she got up in the morning, she found that her shoes had fallen off. On trying to put them on again, she discovered that they did not fit her any longer; and then she went back to her former pair, which were now exactly of the right size and shape. In an ecstasy of joy, she grasped her mirror, and saw that her features had also changed back to what they had formerly been; so she washed and dressed herself and went in to visit her mother. Every one who met her was much astonished; and when Lianxiang heard the strange story, she tried to persuade Mr. Sang to make her an offer of marriage. But the young lady was rich and Sang was poor, and he did not see his way clearly. However, on Mrs. Zhang's birthday, when she completed her cycle,[120] Sang went along with the others to wish her many happy returns of the day; and when the old lady knew who was coming, she bade Yaner take a peep at him from behind the curtain. Sang arrived last of all; and immediately out rushed Miss Yaner and seized his sleeve, and said she would go back with him. Her mother scolded her well for this, and she ran in abashed; but Sang, who had looked at her closely, began to weep, and threw himself at the feet of Mrs. Zhang, who raised him up without saying anything unkind. Sang then took his leave, and got his uncle to act as medium between them; the result being that an auspicious day was fixed upon for the wedding. At the appointed time Sang proceeded to the house to fetch her; and when he returned he found that, instead of his former poor-looking furniture, beautiful carpets were laid down from the very door, and thousands of colored lanterns were hung about in elegant designs. Lianxiang assisted the bride to enter, and took off her veil, finding her the same bright girl as ever. She also joined them while drinking the wedding

120 The Chinese cycle is sixty years, and the birthday on which any person completes his cycle is considered a very auspicious occasion. The second emperor of the present dynasty, Kang Xi, completed a cycle in his *reign*, with one year to spare; and his grandson, Qian Long (or Kien Lung) fell short of this only by a single year, dying in the same cyclical period as that in which he had ascended the throne.

cup,[121] and inquired of her friend as to her recent transmigration; and Yaner related as follows: "Overwhelmed with grief, I began to shrink from myself as some unclean thing; and, after separating from you that day, I would not return any more to my grave. So I wandered about at random, and whenever I saw a living being, I envied its happy state. By day I remained among trees and shrubs, but at night I used to roam about anywhere. And once I came to the house of the Zhang family, where, seeing a young girl lying upon the bed, I took possession of her mortal coil, unknowing that she would be restored to life again." When Lianxiang heard this she was for some time lost in thought; and a month or two afterwards became very ill. She refused all medical aid and gradually got worse and worse, to the great grief of Mr. Sang and his wife, who stood weeping at her bedside. Suddenly she opened her eyes, and said, "You wish to live; I am willing to die. If fate so ordains it, we shall meet again ten years hence." As she uttered these words, her spirit passed away, and all that remained was the dead body of a fox. Sang, however, insisted on burying it with all the proper ceremonies.

Now his wife had no children; but one day a servant came in and said, "There is an old woman outside who has got a little girl for sale." Sang's wife gave orders that she should be shown in; and no sooner had she set eyes on the girl than she cried out, "Why, she's the image of Lianxiang!" Sang then looked at her, and found to his astonishment that she was really very like his old friend. The old woman said she was fourteen years old; and when asked what her price was, declared that her only wish was to get the girl comfortably settled, and enough to keep herself alive, and ensure not being thrown out into the kennel at death. So Sang gave a good price for her;[122] and his wife, taking the girl's hand, led her into a room by themselves. Then, chucking her under the chin; she asked her, smiling, "Do you know

---

121 Bride and bridegroom drink wine together out of two cups joined by a red string, typical of that imaginary bond which is believed to unite the destinies of husband and wife long before they have set eyes on each other. Popular tradition assigns to an old man who lives in the moon the arrangement of all matches among mortals; hence the common Chinese expression, "Marriages are made in the moon."

122 The bill of sale always handed to the purchaser of a child in China, as a proof that the child is his *bond fide* property and has not been kidnapped, is by a pleasant fiction called a "deed of gift," the amount paid over to the seller being therein denominated "ginger and vinegar money," or compensation for the expense of rearing and educating up to the date of sale. This phrase originates from the fact that a dose of ginger and vinegar is administered to every Chinese woman immediately after the delivery of her child.

We may here add that the value of male children to those who have no heirs, and of female children to those who want servants, has fostered a regular kidnapping trade, which is carried on with great activity in some parts of China, albeit the penalty on discovery is instant decapitation. Some years ago I was present in the streets of Tianjin when a kidnapper was seized by the infuriated mob, and within two hours I heard that the man had been summarily executed.

me?" The girl said she did not; after which she told Mrs. Sang that her name was Wei, and that her father, who had been a pickle-merchant at Xucheng, had died three years before. Mrs. Sang then calculated that Lianxiang had been dead just fourteen years; and, looking at the girl, who resembled her so exactly in every trait, at length patted her on the head, saying, "Ah, my sister, you promised to visit us again in ten years, and you have not played us false." The girl here seemed to wake up as if from a dream, and, uttering an exclamation of surprise, fixed a steady gaze upon Sang's wife. Sang himself laughed, and said, "Just like the return of an old familiar swallow." "Now I understand," cried the girl, in tears; "I recollect my mother saying that when I was born I was able to speak; and that, thinking it an inauspicious manifestation, they gave me dog's blood to drink, so that I should forget all about my previous state of existence.[123] Is it all a dream, or are you not the Miss Li who was so ashamed of being a devil?" Thus they chatted of their existence in a former life, with alternate tears and smiles; but when it came to the day for worshipping at the tombs, Yaner explained that she and her husband were in the habit of annually visiting and mourning over her grave. The girl replied that she would accompany them; and when they got there they found the whole place in disorder, and the coffin wood all warped. "Lianxiang and I," said Yaner to her husband, "have been attached to each other in two states of existence. Let us not be separated, but bury my bones here with hers." Sang consented, and opening Miss Li's tomb took out the bones and buried them with those of Lianxiang, while friends and relatives, who had heard the strange story, gathered around the grave in gala dress to the number of many hundreds.

I learnt the above when traveling through Yizhou, where I was detained at an inn by rain, and read a biography of Mr Sang written by a comrade of his named Wang Zizhang. It was lent me by a Mr. Liu Zijing, a relative of Sang's, and was quite a long account. This is merely an outline of it.

24. Miss Abao; or, Perseverance Rewarded

IN the province of Guangxi there lived a scholar of some reputation, named Sun Zichu. He was born with six fingers, and such a simple fellow was he

---

123 The power of recalling events which have occurred in a previous life will be enlarged upon in several stories to come.

that he readily believed any nonsense he was told. Very shy with the fair
sex, the sight of a woman was enough to send him flying in the opposite
direction; and once when he was coaxed into a room where there were
some young ladies, he blushed down to his neck and the perspiration
dripped off him like falling pearls. His companions laughed heartily at his
discomfiture, and told fine stories of what a noodle he looked, so that he
got the nickname of Silly Sun.

In the town where our hero resided, there was a rich trader whose
wealth equalled that of any prince or nobleman, and whose connections
were all highly aristocratic.[124] He had a daughter, Abao, of great beauty,
for whom he was seeking a husband; and the young men of position in the
neighborhood were vieing with each other to obtain her hand, but none
of them met with the father's approval. Now Silly Sun had recently lost
his wife; and someone in joke persuaded him to try his luck and send in
an application. Sun, who had no idea of his own shortcomings, proceeded
at once to follow this advice; but the father, though he knew him to be an
accomplished scholar, rejected his suit on the ground of poverty. As the go-
between[125] was leaving the house, she chanced to meet Abao, and related
to her the object of her visit. "Tell him," cried Abao, laughing, "that if he'll
cut off his extra finger, I'll marry him." The old woman reported this to
Sun, who replied, "That is not very difficult;" and, seizing a chopper, cut
the finger clean off. The wound was extremely painful, and he lost so much
blood that he nearly died, it being many days before he was about again.
He then sought out the go-between and bade her inform Miss Abao, which
she did; and Abao was taken rather aback, but she told the old woman to
go once more and bid him cut off the "silly" from his reputation. Sun got
much excited when he heard this, and denied that he was silly; however, as
he was unable to prove it to the young lady herself, he began to think that
probably her beauty was over-stated, and that she was giving herself great
airs. So he ceased to trouble himself about her until the following spring

124 There is nothing in China like an aristocracy of birth. Any man may raise himself from the lowest
level to the highest; and as long as he and his family keep themselves there, they may be considered
aristocratic. Wealth has nothing to do with the question; official rank and literary tastes, separate or
combined, these constitute a man's title to the esteem of his fellows. Trade is looked upon as ignoble
and debasing; and friendly intercourse between merchants and officials, the two great social divisions,
is so rare as to be almost unknown.
125 The medium, without whose good offices no marriage can be arranged. Generally, but not always,
a woman.
   This system of go-betweens is not confined to matrimonial engagements. No servant ever offers
himself for a place; he invariably employs someone to introduce him. So also in mercantile transactions
the broker almost invariably appears upon the scene.

festival,[126] when it was customary for both men and women to be seen abroad, and the young rips of the place would stroll about in groups and pass their remarks on all and sundry. Sun's friends urged him to join them in their expedition, and one of them asked him with a smile if he did not wish to look out for a suitable mate. Sun knew they were chaffing him, but he thought he should like to see the girl that had made such a fool of him, and was only too pleased to accompany them. They soon perceived a young lady resting herself under a tree, with a throng of young fellows crowding around her, and they immediately determined that she must be Abao, as in fact they found she was. Possessed of peerless beauty, the ring of her admirers gradually increased, until at last she rose up to go. The excitement among the young men; was intense; they criticised her face and discussed her feet,[127] Sun only remaining silent; and when they had passed on to something else, there they saw Sun rooted like an imbecile to the same spot; As he made no answer when spoken to, they dragged him along with them, saying, "Has your spirit run away after Abao?" He made no reply to this either; but they thought nothing of that, knowing his usual strangeness of manner, so by dint of pushing and pulling they managed to get him home. There he threw himself on the bed and did not get up again for the rest of the day, lying in a state of unconsciousness just as if he were drunk. He did not wake when called; and his people, thinking that his spirit had fled, went about in the fields calling out to it to return.[128] However, he showed no signs of improvement; and when they shook him, and asked him what was the matter, he only answered in a sleepy kind of voice, "I am at Abao's house;" but to further questions he would not make any reply, and left his family in a state of keen suspense.

Now when Silly Sun had seen the young lady get up to go, he could not bear to part with her, and found himself first following and then walking along by her side without anyone saying anything to him. Thus he went back with her to her home, and there he remained for three days, longing to run home and get something to eat, but unfortunately not knowing the way. By that time Sun had hardly a breath left in him; and his friends,

---

126 See note 6 in tale number 2.
127 The so-called "golden lilies" always come in for a large share of criticism. See note 53 in tale number 12. This term originated with an emperor who reigned in the fifth century, when, in ecstasies at the graceful dancing of a concubine upon a stage ornamented with lilies, he cried out, "Every footstep makes a lily grow."
128 A common custom; *e.g.* in the case of a little child lying dangerously ill, its mother will go outside the door into the garden or field, and call out its name several times, in the hope of bringing back the wandering spirit.

fearing that he was going to die, sent to beg of the rich trader that he would allow a search to be made for Sun's spirit in his house. The trader laughed and said, "He wasn't in the habit of coming here, so he could hardly have left his spirit behind him;" but he yielded to the entreaties of Sun's family, and permitted the search to be made. Thereupon a magician proceeded to the house, taking with him an old suit of Sun's clothes and some grass matting; and when Miss Abao heard the reason for which he had come, she simplified matters very much by leading the magician straight to her own room. The magician summoned the spirit in due form, and went back towards Sun's house. By the time he had reached the door, Sun groaned and recovered consciousness; and he was then able to describe all the articles of toilette and furniture in Abao's room without making a single mistake. Abao was amazed when the story was repeated to her, and could not help feeling kindly towards him on account of the depth of his passion. Sun himself, when he got well enough to leave his bed, would often sit in a state of abstraction as if he had lost his wits; and he was forever scheming to try and have another glimpse at Abao.

One day he heard that she intended to worship at the Shuiyue temple on the 8th of the fourth moon, that day being the Wash-Buddha festival; and he set off early in the morning to wait for her at the roadside. He was nearly blind with straining his eyes, and the sun was already past noontide before the young lady arrived; but when she saw from her carriage a gentleman standing there, she drew aside the screen and had a good stare at him. Sun followed her in a great state of excitement, upon which she bade one of her maids to go and ask his name. Sun told her who he was, his perturbation all the time increasing; and when the carriage drove on he returned home. Again he became very ill, and lay on his bed unconscious, without taking any food, occasionally calling on Abao by name, at the same time abusing his spirit for not having been able to follow her as before. Just at this juncture a parrot that had been long with the family died; and a child, playing with the body, laid it upon the bed. Sun then reflected that if he was only a parrot one flap of his wings would bring him into the presence of Abao; and while occupied with these thoughts, lo! the dead body moved and the parrot flew away. It flew straight to Abao's room, at which she was delighted; and catching it, tied a string to its leg, and fed it upon hemp seed. "Dear sister," cried the bird, "do not tie me by the leg: I am Sun Zichu." In great alarm Abao untied the string, but the parrot did not fly away. "Alas!" said she, "your love has engraved itself upon my heart; but now you are no longer a man, how shall we ever be united together?" "To be near your dear self," replied the parrot, "is all I care about." The parrot then refused to take food from anyone else, and kept close to Miss Abao wherever she went, day and night alike. At the expiration of three days, Abao, who had grown very fond of her parrot, secretly sent someone to ask how Mr. Sun was; but he had already been dead three days, though the part over his heart had not grown cold. "Oh! come to life again as a man," cried the young lady, "and I swear to be yours for ever." "You are surely not in earnest," said the parrot, "are you?" Miss Abao declared she was, and the parrot, cocking its head aside, remained some time as if absorbed in thought. By-and-by Abao took off her shoes to bind her feet a little tighter;[129] and the parrot, making a rapid grab at one, flew off with it in its beak. She called loudly after it to come back, but in a moment it was out of sight; so she next sent a servant to inquire if there was any news of Mr. Sun, and then learnt that he had come around again, the parrot having flown in with an embroidered shoe and dropped down dead on the ground. Also, that directly he regained consciousness he asked for the shoe, of which his people knew nothing; at which moment her servant had arrived, and demanded to know from him where it was. "It was given to me by Miss Abao as a pledge of faith," replied Sun; "I beg you will tell her I have not forgotten her promise." Abao was greatly astonished at this, and instructed her maid to divulge the whole affair to her mother, who, when she had made some inquiries, observed that Sun was well known as a clever fellow, but was desperately poor, "and to get such a son-in-law after all our trouble would give our aristocratic friends the laugh against us."[130] However, Abao pleaded that with the shoe there as a proof against her, she would not marry anybody else; and, ultimately, her father and mother gave their consent. This was immediately announced to Mr. Sun, whose illness rapidly disappeared in consequence. Abao's father would have had Sun come and live with them;[131] but the young lady objected, on the score that a son-in-law should not remain long at a time with the family of his wife,[132] and that as he was poor he would lower himself still more by doing so. "I have accepted him," added she, "and I shall gladly reside in his humble cottage, and share his poor fare without complaint." The marriage

---

129 This process must be regularly gone through night and morning, otherwise the bandages become loose, and the gait of the walker unsteady.

130 I have explained before that any great disparity of means is considered an obstacle to a matrimonial alliance between two families.

131 This is a not unusual arrangement in cases where there are other sons in the bridegroom's family, but none in that of the bride's, especially if the advantage of wealth is on the side of the latter.

132 Such is the Chinese rule, adopted simply with a view to the preservation of harmony.

was then celebrated, and bride and bridegroom met as if for the first time in their lives.[133] The dowry Abao brought with her somewhat raised their pecuniary position, and gave them a certain amount of comfort; but Sun himself stuck only to his books, and knew nothing about managing affairs in general. Luckily his wife was clever in that respect, and did not bother him with such things; so much so that by the end of three years they were comparatively well off, when Sun suddenly fell ill and died. Mrs. Sun was inconsolable, and refused either to sleep or take nourishment, being deaf to all entreaties on the subject; and before long, taking advantage of the night, she hanged herself.[134] Her maid, hearing a noise, ran in and cut her down just in time: but she still steadily refused all food. Three days passed away, and the friends and relatives of Sun came to attend his funeral, when suddenly they heard a sigh proceeding forth from the coffin. The coffin was then opened and they found that Sun had come to life again. He told them that he had been before the Great Judge, who, as a reward for his upright and honorable life, had conferred upon him an official appointment. "At this moment," said Sun, "it was reported that my wife was close at hand,[135] but the Judge, referring to the register, observed that her time had not yet come. They told him she had taken no food for three days; and then the Judge, looking at me, said that as a recompense for her wifely virtues I should be permitted to return to life. Thereupon he gave orders to his attendants to put to the horses and see me safely back." From that hour Sun gradually improved, and the next year went up for his Master's degree. All his old companions chaffed him exceedingly before the examination, and gave him seven themes on out-of-the-way subjects, telling him privately that they had been surreptitiously obtained from the examiners. Sun believed them as usual, and worked at them day and night until he was perfect, his comrades all the time enjoying a good laugh against him. However, when the day came it was found that the examiners, fearing lest the themes they had chosen in an ordinary way should have been dishonestly made public,[136] took a set of fresh ones quite out of the

---

133 They are supposed never to see each other before the wedding-day; but, after careful investigation of the subject, I have come to the conclusion that certainly in seven cases out of ten, the intended bridegroom secretly procures a sight of his future wife. I am now speaking of the higher classes; among the poor, both sexes mix almost as freely as with us.

134 This would still be considered a creditable act on the part of a Chinese widow. It is, however, of exceedingly rare occurrence.

135 Being nearly dead from hanging.

136 This is occasionally done, great influence or a heavy bribe being brought to bear upon the Examiners, of whom there are only two for the Master's degree, and the second of these, or Assistant-Examiner, holds but a subordinate position. See note 392 in tale number 75.

common run—in fact, on the very subjects Sun's companions had given to him. Consequently, he came out at the head of the list; and the next year, after taking his Doctor's degree, he was entered among the Hanlin Academicians.[137] The Emperor, too, happening to hear of his curious adventures, sent for him and made him repeat his story; subsequently summoning Abao and making her some very costly presents.

25. Ren Xiu

REN JIANZHI was a native of Yutai, and a dealer in rugs and furs. One day he set off for Shaanxi, taking with him every penny he could scrape together; and on the road he met a man who told him that his name was Shen Zhuting, and his native place Suqian. These two soon became firm friends, and entered into a masonic bond[138] with each other, journeying on together by the same stages until they reached their destination. By-and-by Mr. Ren fell sick, and his companion had to nurse him, which he did with the utmost attention, but for ten days he gradually got worse and worse, and at length said to Shen, "My family is very poor. Eight mouths depend upon my exertions for food; and now, alas! I am about to die, far from my own home. You and I are brothers. At this distance there is no one else to whom I can look. Now in my purse you will find two hundred ounces of silver. Take half, and when you have defrayed my funeral expenses, use the balance for your return journey; and give the other half to my family, that "they may be able to send for my coffin.[139] If, however, you will take my

---

137 Admission to the Hanlin College is the highest literary honor obtainable by a scholar. Its members are employed in drawing up Government documents, histories, etc.

138 Besides the numerous secret societies so much dreaded by the Government, membership of which is punishable by death, very intimate friends are in the habit of adopting each other as sworn brothers, bound to stand by one another in cases of danger and difficulty, to the last drop of blood. The bond is cemented by an oath, accompanied by such ceremonies as fancy may at the moment dictate. The most curious of all, however, are the so-called "Golden Orchid" societies, the members of which are young girls, who have sworn never to enter into the matrimonial state. To such an extent have these sister-hoods spread in the Guangdong Province, that the authorities have been compelled to prohibit them under severe penalties.

139 The Chinese love to be buried alongside of their ancestors, and poor families are often put to great straits to pay this last tribute of respect and affection to the deceased. At all large cities are to be found temporary burial grounds, where the bodies of strangers are deposited until their relatives can come to carry them away. Large freights of dead bodies are annually brought back to China from California, Queensland, and other parts to which the Chinese are in the habit of emigrating, to the great profit of the steamer companies concerned. Coffins are also used as a means of smuggling, respect for the dead being so great that they are only opened under the very strongest suspicion.

mortal remains with you home to my native place, these expenses need not be incurred." He then, with the aid of a pillow, wrote a letter, which he handed to Shen, and that evening he died. Thereupon Shen purchased a cheap coffin[140] for some five or six ounces of silver; and, as the landlord kept urging him to take away the body, he said he would go out and seek for a temple where it might be temporarily deposited. But he ran away and never went back to the inn; and it was more than a year before Ren's family knew what had taken place. His son was just about seventeen years of age, and had recently been reading with a tutor; but now his books were laid aside, and he proposed to go in search of his father's body. His mother said he was too young; and it was only when he declared he would rather not live than stay at home, that with the aid of the pawn-shop[141] enough money was raised to start him on his way. An old servant accompanied him, and it was six months before they returned and performed the last ceremonies over Ren's remains. The family was thus reduced to absolute destitution; but happily young Xiu was a clever fellow, and when the days of mourning[142] were over, took his Bachelor's degree. On the other hand, he was somewhat wild and very fond of gambling; and although his mother strictly prohibited such diversions, all her prohibitions were in vain. By-and-by the Grand Examiner arrived, and Xiu came out in the fourth class. His mother was extremely angry, and refused to take food, which brought young Xiu to his senses, and he promised her faithfully he would never gamble again. From that day he shut himself up, and the following year took a first-class degree, coming out among the "senior" graduates.[143] His mother now advised him to take pupils, but his reputation as a disorderly fellow stuck to him. and no one would entrust their sons to his care.

Just then an uncle of his, named Zhang, was about to start with

---

140 See note 71 in tale 14. The price of an elaborate Chinese coffin goes as high as £100 or £150.

141 The never-failing resource of an impecunious Chinese man who has any property whatever bearing an exchange value. The pawnshop proper is a licensed institution, where three per cent, *per month* is charged on all loans, all pledges being redeemable within sixteen months. It is generally a very high brick structure, towering far above the surrounding houses, with the deposits neatly packed up in paper and arranged on the shelves of a huge wooden skeleton-like frame, that completely fills the interior of the building, on the top of which are ranged buckets of water in case of fire, and a quantity of huge stones to throw down on any thieves who may be daring enough to attempt to scale the wall. (In Beijing, houses are not allowed to be built above a certain height, as during the long summer months ladies are in the habit of sitting to spin or sew in their courtyards, very lightly clad.) Pawning goods in China is not held to be so disgraceful as with us; in fact, most people, at the beginning of the hot weather, pawn their furs and winter clothes, these being so much more carefully looked after there than they might be at home.

142 Nominally of three years'—really of twenty-eight months'— duration.

143 These are entitled to receive from Government a small allowance of rice, besides being permitted to exercise certain petty functions, for which a certain charge is authorized.

merchandise for the capital, and recommended that Xiu should go along with him, promising himself to pay all expenses, an offer which Xiu was only too pleased to accept. When they reached Linqing, they anchored outside the Custom House, where they found a great number of salt-junks, in fact a perfect forest of masts; and what with the noise of the water and the people it was quite impossible to sleep. Besides, as the row was beginning to subside, the clear rattle of dice from a neighboring boat fell upon Xiu's ear, and before long he was itching to be back again at his old games. Listening to hear if all around him were sound asleep, he drew forth a string of cash that he had brought with him, and thought he would just go across and try his luck. So he got up quietly with his money, and was on the point of going, when he suddenly recollected his mother's injunctions, and at once tying his purse-strings laid himself down to sleep. He was far too excited, however, to close his eyes; and after a while got up again and re-opened his purse. This he did three times, until at last it was too much for him, and off he went with his money. Crossing over into the boat whence the sounds proceeded, he beheld two persons engaged in gambling for high stakes; so throwing his money on the table, he begged to be allowed to join. The others readily consented, and they began to play, Xiu winning so rapidly that soon one of the strangers had no money left, and was obliged to get the proprietor of the boat to change a large piece of silver for him, proceeding to lay down as much as several ounces of silver for a single stake.

As the play was in full swing another man walked in, who after watching for some time at length got the proprietor to change another lump of silver for him of one hundred ounces in weight, and also asked to be allowed to join. Now Xiu's uncle, waking up in the middle of the night, and finding his nephew gone, and hearing the sound of dice-throwing hard by, knew at once where he was, and immediately followed him to the boat with a view of bringing him back. Finding, however, that Xiu was a heavy winner, he said nothing to him, only carrying off a portion of his winnings to their own boat and making the others of his party get up and help him to fetch the rest, even then leaving behind a large sum for Xiu to go on with. By-and-by the three strangers had lost all their ready money, and there wasn't a farthing left in the boat: upon which one of them proposed to play for lumps of silver, but Xiu said he never went so high as that. This made them a little quarrelsome, Xiu's uncle all the time trying to get him away; and the proprietor of the boat, who had only his own commission in view, managed to borrow some hundred strings of cash from another boat, and started them all again. Xiu soon took this out of them; and, as day was beginning to dawn and the Custom House was about to open, he went off with his winnings back to his own boat.

The proprietor of the gambling-boat now found that the lumps of silver which he had changed for his customers were nothing more than so much tinsel, and rushing off in a great state of alarm to Xiu's boat, told him what had happened and asked him to make it good; but when he discovered he was speaking to the son of his former traveling companion, Ren Jianzhi, he hung his head and slunk away covered with shame. For the proprietor of that boat was no other than Shen Zhuting, of whom Xiu had heard when he was in Shaanxi; now, however, that with supernatural aid[144] the wrongs of his father had been avenged, he determined to pursue the man no further. So going into partnership with his uncle, they proceeded north together; and by the end of the year their capital had increased five-fold. Xiu then purchased the status of *jiansheng*,[145] and by further careful investment of his money ultimately became the richest man in that part of the country.

26. The Lost Brother

IN Henan there lived a man named Zhang, who originally belonged to Shandong. His wife had been seized and carried off by the soldiery during the period when Jing Nan's troops were overrunning the latter province;[146] and as he was frequently in Henan on business, he finally settled there and married a Henan wife, by whom he had a son named Na. By-and-by this wife died, and he took another, who bore him a son named Cheng. The last-mentioned lady was from the Niu family, and a very malicious woman. So jealous was she of Na, that she treated him like a slave or a beast of the field, giving him only the coarsest food, and making him cut a large bundle of wood every day, in default of which she would beat and abuse him in a most shameful manner. On the other hand, she secretly reserved all the titbits for Cheng, and also sent him to school. As Cheng grew up, and began to understand the meaning of filial piety and fraternal love,[147] he could not

---

144 One of the strangers was the disembodied spirit of Hsiu's father, helping his son to take vengeance on the wicked Shên.

145 An intermediate step between the first and second degrees, to which certain privileges are attached.

146 1400 CE.

147 The first of the sixteen maxims which form the so-called Sacred Edict, embodies these two all-important family ties. The doctrine of primogeniture is carried so far in China as to put every younger

bear to see this treatment of his elder brother, and spoke privately to his mother about it; but she would pay no heed to what he said.

One day, when Na was on the hills performing his task, a violent storm came on, and he took shelter under a cliff. However, by the time it was over the sun had set, and he began to feel very hungry. So, shouldering his bundle, he wended his way home, where his stepmother, displeased with the small quantity of wood he had brought, refused to give him anything to eat. Quite overcome with hunger, Na went in and lay down; and when Cheng came back from school, and saw the state he was in, he asked him if he was ill. Na replied that he was only hungry, and then told his brother the whole story; whereupon Cheng colored up and went away, returning shortly with some cakes, which he offered to Na. "Where did you get them?" asked the latter. "Oh," replied Cheng, "I stole some flour and got a neighbor's wife to make them for me. Eat away, and don't talk." Na ate them up; but begged his brother not to do this again, as he might get himself into trouble. "I shan't die," added he, "if I only get one meal a day." "You are not strong," rejoined Cheng, "and shouldn't cut so much wood as you do." Next day, after breakfast, Cheng slipped away to the hills, and arrived at the place where Na was occupied with his usual task, to the great astonishment of the latter, who inquired what he was going to do. "To help you cut wood," replied Cheng. "And who sent you?" asked his brother. "No one," said he; "I came of my own accord." "Ah," cried Na, "you can't do this work; and even if you can you must not. Run along home again." Cheng, however, remained, aiding, his brother with his hands and feet alone, but declaring that on the morrow he would bring an axe. Na tried to stop him, and found that he had already hurt his finger and worn his shoes into holes; so he began to cry, and said, "If you don't go home directly, I'll kill myself with my axe." Cheng then went away, his brother seeing him half-way home, and going back to finish his work by himself. He also called in the evening at Cheng's school, and told the master his brother was a delicate boy, and should not be allowed to go on the hills, where, he said, there were fierce tigers and wolves. The master replied that he didn't know where Cheng had been all the morning, but that he had caned him for playing truant. Na further pointed out to Cheng that by not doing as he had told him, he had let himself in for a beating. Cheng laughed, and said he hadn't been beaten;

---

brother in a subordinate position to every elder brother. All property, however, of whatever kind, is equally divided among the sons. [The Sacred Edict was delivered by the great Emperor Kang Xi, and should be publicly read and explained in every city of the Empire on the first and fifteenth of each month.]

and the very next day off he went again, and this time with a hatchet. "I told you not to come," cried Na, much alarmed; "why have you done so?" Cheng made no reply, but set to work chopping wood with such energy that the perspiration poured down his face; and when he had cut about a bundle he went away without saying a word. The master caned him again, and then Cheng told him how the matter stood, at which the former became, full of admiration for his pupil's kind behavior, and no longer prevented him from going. His brother, however, frequently urged him not to come, though without the slightest success; and one day, when they went with a number of others to cut wood, a tiger rushed down from the hills upon them. The wood-cutters hid themselves, in the greatest consternation; and the tiger, seizing Cheng, ran off with him in his mouth. Cheng's weight caused the tiger to move slowly; and Na, rushing after them, hacked away at the tiger's flanks with his axe. The pain only made the tiger hurry off, and in a few minutes they were out of sight. Overwhelmed with grief, Na went back to his comrades, who tried to soothe him; but he said, "My brother was no ordinary brother, and, besides, he died for me; why, then, should I live?" Here, seizing his hatchet, he made a great chop at his own neck, upon which his companions prevented him from doing himself any more mischief. The wound, however, was over an inch deep, and blood was flowing so copiously that Na became faint, and seemed at the point of death. They then tore up their clothes, and, after having bandaged his neck, proceeded to carry him home. His stepmother cried bitterly, and cursed him, saying, "You have killed my son, and now you go and cut your neck in this make-believe kind of way." "Don't be angry, mother," replied Na; "I will not live now that my brother is dead." He then threw himself on the bed; but the pain of his wound was so great he could not sleep, and day and night he sat leaning against the wall in tears. His father, fearing that he too would die, went every now and then and gave him a little nourishment; but his wife cursed him so for doing it, that at length Na refused all food, and in three days he died.

Now in the village where these events took place there was a magician who was employed in certain devil-work among mortals,[148] and Na's ghost, happening to fall in with him, related the story of its previous sorrows, winding up by asking where his brother's ghost was. The magician said he

---

148 Ordinary devils being unable to stand for any length of time the light and life of the upper world, the souls of certain persons are often temporarily employed in this work by the authorities of Purgatory, their bodies remaining meanwhile in a trance or cataleptic fit.

didn't know, but turned around with Na and showed him the way to a city where they saw an official servant coming out of the city gates. The magician stopped him, and inquired if he could tell them anything about Cheng; whereupon the man drew out a list from a pouch at his side, and, after carefully examining it, replied that among the male and female criminals within there was no one of the name of Zhang.[149] The magician here suggested that the name might be on another list; but the man replied that he was in charge of that road, and surely ought to know. Na, however, was not satisfied, and persuaded the magician to enter the city, where they met many new and old devils walking about, among whom were some Na had formerly known in life. So he asked them if they could direct him to his brother; but none of them knew where he was; and suddenly there was a great commotion, the devils on all sides crying out, "Pusa[150] has come! "Then, looking up, Na beheld a most beautiful man descending from above, encircled by rays of glory, which shot forth above and below, lighting up all around him. "You are in luck's way, Sir," said the magician to Na; "only once in many thousand years does Pusa descend into hell and banish all suffering. He has come today." He then made Na kneel, and all the devils began with clasped hands to sing songs of praise to Pusa for his compassion in releasing them from their misery, shaking the very earth with the sound. Pusa himself, seizing a willow-branch, sprinkled them all with holy water; and when this was done the clouds and glory melted away, and he vanished from their sight. Na, who had felt the holy water fall upon his neck, now became conscious that the axe-wound was no longer painful; and the magician then proceeded to lead him back, not quitting him until within sight of the village gate. In fact, Na had been in a trance for two days, and when he recovered he told them all that he had seen, asserting positively that Cheng was not dead. His mother, however, looked upon the story as a make-up, and never ceased reviling him; and, as he had no means of proving his innocence, and his neck was now quite healed, he got up from the bed and said to his father, "I am going away to seek for my brother throughout the universe; if I do not find him, never expect to see me again, but I pray you regard me as dead." His father drew him aside and wept bitterly. However, he would not interfere with his son's design, and Na accordingly set off. Whenever he came to a large town or populous place he used to ask

---

149 Their family name.
150 The Chinese corrupted form of Bodhisatva. Now widely employed to designate any deity of any kind.

for news of Cheng; and by-and-by, when his money was all spent, he begged his way on foot. A year had passed away before he reached Nanjing, and his clothes were all in tatters—as ragged as a quail's tail,[151] when suddenly he met some ten or a dozen horsemen, and drew away to the roadside. Among them was a gentleman of about forty, who appeared to be a mandarin, with numerous lusty attendants and fiery steeds accompanying him before and behind. One young man on a small palfrey, whom Na took to be the mandarin's son, and at whom, of course, he did not venture to stare, eyed him closely for some time, and at length stopped his steed, and, jumping off, cried out, "Are you not my brother?" Na then, raised his head, and found that Cheng stood before him. Grasping each other's hands, the brothers burst into tears, and at length Cheng said, "My brother, how is it you have strayed so far as this?" Na told him the circumstances, at which he was much affected; and Cheng's companions, jumping off their horses to see what was the matter, went off and informed the mandarin. The latter ordered one of them to give up his horse to Na, and thus they rode together back to the mandarin's house. Cheng then told his brother how the tiger had carried him away, and how he had been thrown down in the road, where he had passed a whole night; also how the mandarin, Mr. Zhang,[152] on his return from the capital, had seen him there, and observing that he was no common-looking youth, had set to work and brought him around again. Also how he had said to Mr. Zhang that his home was a great way off, and how Mr. Zhang had taken him to his own home, and finally cured him of his wounds; when, having no son of his own, he had adopted him. And now, happening to be out with his father, he had caught sight of his brother. As he was speaking Mr. Zhang walked in, and Na thanked him very heartily for all his kindness; Cheng, meanwhile, going into the inner apartments to get some clothes for his brother. Wine and food was placed on the table; and while they were chatting together the mandarin asked Na about the number of their family in Henan. "There is only my father," replied Na, "and he is a Shandong man who came to live in Henan." "Why, I am a Shandong man too," rejoined Mr. Zhang; "what is the name of your father's native place?" "I have heard that it was in the Dongchang district," replied Na. "Then we are from the same place." cried the mandarin. "Why did your father go away to Henan?" "His first wife," said Na, "was carried off by soldiers, and my father lost everything he possessed; so, being in the

---

151 The usual similitude for a Chinese tatterdemalion.
152 The surnames Zhang, Wang, and Li correspond in China to our Brown, Jones, and Robinson.

habit of trading to Henan, he determined to settle down there for good." The mandarin then asked what his father's other name was, and when he heard, he sat some time staring at Na, and at length hurried away within. In a few moments out came an old lady, and when they had all bowed to her, she asked Na if he was Zhang Bing-zhi's grandson. On his replying in the affirmative, the old lady wept, and, turning to Mr. Zhang, said, "These two are your younger brothers." And then she explained to Na and Cheng as follows: "Three years after my marriage with your father, I was carried off to the north and made a slave[153] in a mandarin's family. Six months afterwards your elder brother here was born, and in another six months the mandarin died. Your elder brother being his heir, he received this appointment, which he is now resigning. I have often thought of my native place, and have not unfrequently sent people to inquire about my husband, giving them the full particulars as to name and clan; but I could never hear anything of him. How should I know that he had gone to Henan?" Then, addressing Mr. Zhang, she continued, "That was rather a mistake of yours, adopting your own brother." "He never told me anything about Shandong," replied Mr. Zhang; "I suppose he was too young to remember the story." For, in point of age, the elder of the brothers was forty-one; Cheng, the younger, being only sixteen; and Na, twenty years of age. Mr. Zhang was very glad to get two young brothers; and when he heard the tale of their separation, proposed that they should all go back to their father. Mrs. Zhang was afraid her husband would not care to receive her back again; but her eldest son said, "We will cast our lot together; all or none. How can there be a country where fathers are not valued?" They then sold their house and packed up, and were soon on the way to Henan. When they arrived, Cheng

---

153 Slavery, under a modified form, exists in China at the present day. All parents, having absolute power over their children, are at liberty to sell them as servants or slaves to their wealthier neighbors. This is not an infrequent occurrence in times of distress, the children even going so far as to voluntarily sell themselves, and exposing themselves in some public thoroughfare, with a notice affixed to a kind of arrow on their backs, stating that they are for sale, and the amount required from the purchaser. This I have seen with my own eyes. The chief source, however, from which the supply of slaves is kept up is kidnapping. [See note 122 in tale number 23.] As to the condition of the slaves themselves, it is by no means an unhappy one. Their master has nominally the power of life and death over them, but no Chinese man would ever dream of availing himself of this dangerous prerogative. They are generally well fed, and fairly well clothed, being rarely beaten, for fear they should run away, and either be lost altogether or entail much expense to secure their capture. The girls do not have their feet compressed; hence they are infinitely more useful than small-footed women; and, on reaching a marriageable age, their masters are bound to provide them with husbands. They live on terms of easy familiarity with the whole household; and, ignorant of the meaning and value of liberty, seem quite contented with a lot which places them beyond the reach of hunger and cold. Slaves take the surnames of their masters, and the children of slaves are likewise slaves. Emancipation is not uncommon; and Chinese history furnishes more than one example of a former slave attaining to the highest offices of State.

went in first to tell his father, whose third wife had died since Na left, and who now was a desolate old widower, left alone with only his own shadow. He was overjoyed to see Cheng again, and, looking fondly at his son, burst into a flood of tears. Cheng told him his mother and brothers were outside, and the old man was then perfectly transfixed with astonishment, unable either to laugh or to cry. Mr. Zhang next appeared, followed by his mother; and the two old people wept in each other's arms, the late solitary widower hardly knowing what to make of the crowd of men and women-servants that suddenly filled his house. Here Cheng, not seeing his own mother, asked where she was; and when he heard she was dead, he fainted away, and did not come around for a good half-hour. Mr. Zhang found the money for building a fine house, and engaged a tutor for his two brothers. Horses pranced in the stables, and servants chattered in the hall—it was quite a large establishment.

27. The Three Genii

THERE was a certain scholar who, passing through Suqian on his way to Nanjing, where he was going to try for his master's degree, happened to fall in with three other gentlemen, all graduates like himself, and was so charmed with their unusual refinement that he purchased a quantity of wine, and begged them to join him in drinking it. While thus pleasantly employed, his three friends told him their names. One was Jie Qiuheng; the second, Chang Fenglin; and the other, Ma Xichi. They drank away and enjoyed themselves very much, until evening had crept upon them unperceived, when Jie said, "Here we, who ought to have been playing the host, have been feasting at a stranger's expense. This is not right. But, come, my house is close by; I will provide you with a bed." Chang and Ma got up, and, taking our hero by the arm, bade his servant come along with them. When they reached a hill to the north of the village, there before them was a house and grounds, with a stream of clear water in front of the door, all the apartments within being beautifully clean and nice. Jie then gave orders to light the lamps and see after his visitor's servant; whereupon Ma observed, "Of old it was customary to set intellectual refreshments before one's friends; let us not miss the opportunity of this lovely evening, but decide on four themes, one for each of us; and then, when we have finished our essays, we can set to work on the wine."[154] To this the others readily agreed; and each wrote down a theme and threw it on the table. These were next divided amongst them as they sat, and before the second watch[155] was over the essays were all completed and handed around for general inspection; and our scholar was so struck with the elegance and vigor of those by his three friends, that he ran off a copy of them and put it in his pocket. The host then produced some excellent wine, which was drunk by them in such bumpers that soon they were all tolerably tipsy. The other two now took their leave; but Jie led the scholar into another room, where, so overcome was he with wine, that he went to bed in his boots and clothes.

The sun was high in the heavens when our hero awoke, and, looking around, he saw no house or grounds, only a dell on the hill-side, in which he and his servant had been sleeping. In great alarm he called out to the servant, who also got up, and then they found a hole with a rill of water trickling down before it. Much astonished at all this, he felt in his pocket, and there, sure enough, was the paper on which he had copied the three essays of his friends. On descending the hill and making inquiries, he found that he had been to the Grotto of the Three Genii—namely, Crab, Snake, and Frog, three very wonderful beings, who often came out for a stroll, and were occasionally visible to mortal eyes. Subsequently, when our hero entered the examination hall, lo! the three themes set were those of the Three Genii, and he came out at the top of the list.

28. The Singing Frogs

WANG ZISUN told me that when he was at the capital he saw a man in the street who gave the following performance: He had a wooden box, divided by partitions into twelve holes, in each of which was a frog; and whenever he tapped any one of these frogs on the head with a tiny wand, the frog so touched would immediately begin to sing. Someone gave him a piece of silver, and then he tapped the frogs all around, just as if he was striking

---

154 No Chinese wine-party is complete without more or less amusement of a literary character. Capping verses, composing impromptu odes on persons, or places, giving historical and mythological allusions, are among the ordinary diversions of this kind.
155 The Chinese night lasts from 7 P.M. to 5 A.M., and is divided into five watches of two hours each, which are subdivided into five "beats" of the watchman's wooden tom-tom.

a gong; whereupon they all sang together, with their *Do, Ré, Mi, Fa,* in perfect time and harmony.

29. The Performing Mice

MR. WANG also told me that there was a man at Changan who made his living by exhibiting performing mice. He had a pouch on his back in which he kept some ten of these little animals; and whenever he got among a number of people he would fix a little frame on his back, exactly resembling a stage. Then beating a drum he would sing some old theatrical melody, at the first sounds of which the mice would issue forth from the pouch, and then, with masks on their faces, "and arrayed in various costumes, they would climb up his back on to the stage; where, standing on their hind-legs, they would go through a performance portraying the various emotions of joy and anger, exactly like human actors of either sex.[156]

30. The Tiger of Zhaocheng

AT Zhaocheng there lived an old woman more than seventy years of age, who had an only son. One day he went up to the hills and was eaten by a tiger, at which his mother was so overwhelmed with grief that she hardly wished to live. With tears and lamentations she ran and told her story to the magistrate of the place, who laughed and asked her how she thought the law could be brought to bear on a tiger. But the old woman would not be comforted, and at length the magistrate lost his temper and bade her begone. Of this, however, she took no notice; and then the magistrate, in compassion for her great age and unwilling to resort to extremities, promised her that he would have the tiger arrested. Even then she would not go until the warrant had been actually issued; so the magistrate, at a loss what to do, asked his attendants which of them would undertake the job.[157] Upon

---

156 The *rôles* of women are always played in China by men, dressed up so perfectly, small feet and all, as to be quite undistinguishable from real women.
157 All underlings (and we might add overlings) in China being unpaid, it behooves them to make what they can out of the opportunities afforded. In most *yamens*, the various warrants and such documents are distributed to the runners in turn, who squeeze the victims thus handed over to them. For a small bribe they will go back and report "Not at home;" for a larger one "Has absconded," and so on.

this one of them, Li Neng, who happened to be gloriously drunk, stepped forward and said that he would; whereupon the warrant was immediately issued and the old woman went away. When our friend, Li Neng, got sober, he was sorry for what he had done; but reflecting that the whole thing was a mere trick of his master's to get rid of the old woman's importunities, did not trouble himself much about it, handing in the warrant as if the arrest had been made. "Not so," cried the magistrate, "you said you could do this, and now I shall not let you off." Li Neng was at his wits' end, and begged that he might be allowed to impress the hunters of the district.[158] This was conceded; so collecting together these men, he proceeded to spend day and night among the hills in the hope of catching a tiger, and thus making a show of having fulfilled his duty.

A month passed away, during which he received several hundred blows with the bamboo,[159] and at length, in despair, he betook himself to the Chenghuang temple in the eastern suburb, where, falling on his knees, he prayed and wept by turns. By-and-by a tiger walked in, and Li Neng, in a great fright, thought he was going to be eaten alive. But the tiger took no notice of anything, remaining seated in the doorway. Li Neng then addressed the animal as follows: "O tiger, if thou didst slay that old woman's son, suffer me to bind thee with this cord;" and, drawing a rope from his pocket, threw it over the animal's neck. The tiger drooped its ears, and, allowing itself to be bound, followed Li Neng to the magistrate's office. The latter then asked it, saying, "Did you eat the old woman's son?" to which

---

Gatekeepers charge a fee on every petition that passes through their hands; jailers, for a consideration and with proper security, allow their prisoners to be at large until wanted; clerks take bribes to use their influence, honestly or dishonestly, with the magistrate who is to try the case; and all the servants share equally in the gratuities given by anyone to whom their master may send presents. The amount, whatever it may be, is enclosed in a red envelope and addressed to the sender of the present, with the words "Instead of tea," in large characters; the meaning being that the refreshments which should have been set before the servants who brought the gifts have been commuted by a money payment. This money is put into a general fund and equally divided at stated periods.

All Government officers holding a post, from the highest to the lowest, are entitled to a nominal, and what would be a quite inadequate, salary; but no one ever sees this. It is customary to refuse acceptance of it on some such grounds as want of merit, and refund it to the Imperial Treasury.

158 Anybody is liable to be "impressed" at any moment for the service of the Government, Boat owners, sedan-chair and coolie proprietors especially dread the frequent and heavy calls that are made upon them for assistance, the remuneration they receive being in all cases insufficient to defray mere working expenses. But inasmuch as Chinese officials may not seize any men, or boats, or carts, holding passes to show that they are in the employ of a foreign merchant, a lively trade in such documents has sprung up in certain parts of China between the dishonest of the native and foreign commercial circles.

159 Constables, detectives, and others are liable to be bambooed at intervals, generally of three or five days, until the mission on which they are engaged has been successfully accomplished. In cases of theft and non-restoration of the stolen property within a given time, the detectives or constables employed may be required to make it good.

the tiger replied by nodding its head; whereupon the magistrate rejoined "That murderers should suffer death has ever been the law.[160] Besides, this old woman had but one son, and by killing him you took from her the sole support of her declining years. But if now you will be as a son to her, your crime shall be pardoned." The tiger again nodded assent, and accordingly the magistrate gave orders that he should be released, at which the old woman was highly incensed, thinking that the tiger ought to have paid with its life for the destruction of her son.

Next morning, however, when she opened the door of her cottage, there lay a dead deer before it; and the old woman, by selling the flesh and skin, was able to purchase food. From that day this became a common event, and sometimes the tiger would even bring her money and valuables, so that she became quite rich, and was much better cared for than she had been even by her own son. Consequently, she became very well-disposed to the tiger, which often came and slept in the verandah, remaining for a whole day at a time, and giving no cause of fear either to man or beast. In a few years the old woman died, upon which the tiger walked in and roared its lamentations in the hall. However, with all the money she had saved, she was able to have a splendid funeral; and while her relatives were standing around the grave, out rushed a tiger, and sent them all running away in fear. But the tiger merely went up to the mound, and, after roaring like a thunder-peal, disappeared again. Then the people of that place built a shrine in honor of the Faithful Tiger, and it remains there to this day.

31. A Dwarf

IN the reign of Kang Xi, there was a magician who carried about with him a wooden box, in which he had a dwarf not much more than a foot in height. When people gave him money he would open the box and bid the little creature come out. The dwarf would then sing a song and go in again. Arriving one day at Ye, the magistrate there seized the box, and taking it into his *yamen* asked the dwarf whence he came. At first he dared not reply, but on being pressed told the magistrate everything. He said he belonged to a respectable family, and that once when returning home from school he was stupefied by the magician, who gave him some drug which made his

---

160 Extended by the Chinese to certain cases of simple manslaughter."

limbs shrink, and then took him about to exhibit to people. The magistrate was very angry, and had the magician beheaded, himself taking charge of the dwarf. He was subsequently very anxious to get him cured, but unable to obtain the proper prescription.[161]

32. Xiangru's Misfortunes

AT Guangping there lived an old man named Feng, who had an only son called Xiangru. Both of them were graduates; and the father was very particular and strict, though the family had long been poor. Mrs. Feng and Xiangru's wife had died, one shortly after the other, so that the father and son were obliged to do their household work for themselves.

One night Xiangru was sitting out in the moonlight, when suddenly a young lady from next door got on the wall to have a look at him. He saw she was very pretty, and as he approached her she began to laugh. He then beckoned to her with his hand; but she did not move either to come or to go away. At length, however, she accepted his invitation, and descended the ladder that he had placed for her. In reply to Xiangru's inquiries, the young lady said her name was Hongyu, and that she lived next door; so Xiangru, who was much taken with her beauty, begged her to come over frequently and have a chat. To this she readily assented, and continued to do so for several months, until one evening old Mr. Feng, hearing sounds of talking and laughing in his son's room, got up and looked in. Seeing Miss Hongyu, he was exceedingly angry, and called his son out, saying, "You good-for-nothing fellow! poor as we are, why aren't you at your books, instead of wasting your time like this? A pretty thing for the neighbors to hear of!— and even if they don't hear of it, somebody else will, and shorten your life accordingly."[162] Xiangru fell on his knees, and with tears implored forgiveness; whereupon his father turned to the young lady, and said, "A girl who behaves like this disgraces others as well as herself; and if people find

---

161 The Cantonese believe the following to be the usual process: "Young children are bought or stolen at a tender age and placed in a *Qing,* or vase with a narrow neck, and having in this case a movable bottom. In this receptacle the unfortunate little wretches are kept for years in a sitting posture, their heads outside, being all the while carefully tended and fed. . . . When the child has reached the age of twenty or over, he or she is taken away to some distant place and 'discovered' in the woods as a wild man or woman."—*China Mail,* May 15, 1878.

162 Meaning that it would become known to the Arbiter *of* life and death in the world below, who would punish him by shortening his appointed term of years. See tale 131, *The Weiqi Devil.*

this out, we shan't be the only ones to suffer. The old man then went back to bed in a rage, and Miss Hongyu, weeping bitterly, said to Xiangru, "Your father's reproaches have overwhelmed me with shame. Our friendship is now at an end." "I could say nothing," replied he, "as long as my father was here; but if you have any consideration for me, I pray you think nothing of his remarks." Miss Hongyu protested, however, that they could meet no more, and then Xiangru also burst into tears. "Do not weep," cried she, "our friendship was an impossible one, and time must sooner or later have put an end to these visits. Meanwhile, I hear there is a very good match to be made in the neighborhood." Xiangru replied that he was poor; but Miss Hongyu told him to meet her again the following evening, when she would endeavor to do something for him. At the appointed time she arrived, and, producing forty ounces of silver, presented them to Xiangru; telling him that at a village some distance off there was a Miss Wei, eighteen years of age, who was not yet married because of the exorbitant demands of her parents, but that a little extra outlay would secure for him the young lady's hand. Miss Hongyu then bade him farewell, and Xiangru went off to inform his father, expressing a desire to go and make inquiries, but saying nothing about the forty ounces. His father, thinking that they were not sufficiently well off, urged him not to go; however, by dint of argument, he finally persuaded the old man that, at any rate, there was no harm in trying. So he borrowed horses and attendants, and set off to the house of Mr. Wei, who was a man of considerable property; and when he got there he asked Mr. Wei to come outside and accord him a few minutes' conversation. Now the latter knew that Xiangru belonged to a very good family; and when he saw all the retinue that Xiangru had brought with him, he inwardly consented to the match, though he was afraid that perhaps his would-be son-in-law might not be as liberal as he would like. Xiangru soon perceived what Mr. Wei's feelings were, and emptied his purse on the table, at which Mr. Wei was delighted, and begged a neighbor to allow the marriage contract to be drawn up in his house.[163] Xiangru then went in to pay his respects to Mrs. Wei, whom he found in a small, miserable room, with Miss Wei hiding behind her. Still he was pleased to see that, in spite of her homely toilette, the young lady herself was very nice-looking; and, while he was being

---

163 One important preliminary consists in the exchange of the four pairs of characters which denote the year, month, day, and hour of the births of the contracting parties. It remains for a geomancer to determine whether these are in harmony or not; and a very simple expedient for backing out of a proposed alliance is to bribe him to declare that the nativities of the young couple could not be happily brought together.

entertained in the neighbor's house, the old lady said, "It will not be necessary for you, Sir, to come and fetch our daughter. As soon as we have made up a small trousseau for her, we will send her along to you."[164] Xiangru then agreed with them upon a day for the wedding, and went home and informed his father, pretending that the Wei family only asked for respectability, and did not care about money. His father was overjoyed to hear this; and when the day came, the young lady herself arrived. She proved to be a thrifty housekeeper and an obedient wife, so that she and her husband got along capitally together. In two years she had a son, who was called Fuer. And once, on the occasion of the great spring festival, she was on her way to the family tombs, with her boy in her arms, when she chanced to meet a man named Song, who was one of the gentry of the neighborhood. This Mr. Song had been a Censor,[165] but had purchased his retirement, and was now leading a private life, characterized by many overbearing and violent acts. He was returning from his visit to the graves of his ancestors when he saw Xiangru's wife, and, attracted by her beauty, found out who she was; and imagining that, as her husband was a poor scholar, he might easily be induced for a consideration to part with the lady, sent one of his servants to find out how the land lay. When Xiangru heard what was wanted, he was very angry; but, reflecting on the power of his adversary, controlled his passion, and passed the thing off with a laugh. His father, however, to whom he repeated what had occurred, got into a violent rage, and, rushing out, flung his arms about, and called Mr. Song every name he could lay his tongue to. Mr. Song's emissary slunk off and went home; and then a number of men were sent by the enraged Song, and these burst into the house and gave old Feng and his son a most tremendous beating. In the middle of the hubbub Xiangru's wife ran in, and, throwing her child down on the bed, tore her hair and shrieked for help. Song's attendants immediately surrounded her and carried her off, while there lay her husband and his father, wounded on the ground, and the baby squalling on the bed. The neighbors, pitying their wretched condition, helped them up on to the couches, and by the next day Xiangru could walk with a stick; however, his father's anger was not to be appeased, and, after spitting a

---

164 The bridegroom invariably fetches the bride from her father's house, conveying her to his home in a handsomely-gilt red sedan-chair, closed in on all sides, and accompanied by a band of music.

165 The Censorate is a body of fifty-six officials, whose duty it is to bring matters to the notice of the Emperor which might otherwise have escaped attention; to take exception to any acts, including those of his Majesty himself, calculated to interfere with the welfare of the people; and to impeach, as occasion may require, the high provincial authorities, whose position, but for this whole-some check, would be almost unassailable. Censors are popularly termed the "ears and eyes" of the monarch.

quantity of blood, he died. Xiangru wept bitterly at this, and taking his child in his arms, used every means to bring the offenders to justice, but without the slightest success. He then heard that his wife had put an end to her own existence, and with this his cup of misery was full. Unable to get his wrongs redressed, he often meditated assassinating Song in the open street,[166] but was deterred from attempting this by the number of his retainers and the fear of leaving his son with no one to protect him. Day and night he mourned over his lot, and his eyelids were never closed in sleep, when suddenly in walked a personage of striking appearance to condole with him on his losses. The stranger's face was covered with a huge curly beard; and Xiangru, not knowing who he was, begged him to take a seat, and was about to ask whence he came, when all at once he began, "Sir! have you forgotten your father's death, your wife's disgrace?" Thereupon Xiangru, suspecting him to be a spy from the Song family, made some evasive reply, which so irritated the stranger that he roared out, "I thought you were a man; but now I know that you are a worthless, contemptible wretch." Xiangru fell on his knees and implored the stranger to forgive him, saying, "I was afraid it was a trick of Song's: I will speak frankly to you. For days I have lain, as it were, upon thorns, my mouth filled with gall, restrained only by pity for this little one and fear of breaking our ancestral line. Generous friend, will you take care of my child if I fall?" "That," replied the stranger, "is the business of women; I cannot undertake it. But what you wish others to do for you, do yourself; and that which you would do yourself, I will do for you." When Xiangru heard these words he knocked his head upon the ground; but the stranger took no more notice of him, and walked out. Following him to the door, Xiangru asked his name, to which he replied, "If I cannot help you I shall not wish to have your reproaches; if I do help you, I shall not wish to have your gratitude."

---

166 In the *Book of Rites* (I. Pt. i. v. 10), which dates, in its present form, only from the first century BCE, occurs this passage: "With the slayer of his father, a man may not live under the same heaven;" and in the *Family Sayings* (Bk. X. *ab init.*), a work which professes, though on quite insufficient authority, to record a number of the conversations and apophthegms of Confucius not given in the *Lun yu*, or Confucian Gospels, we find the following course laid down for a man whose father has been murdered: "He must sleep upon a grass mat, with his shield, for his pillow; he must decline to take office; he must not live under the same heaven (with the murderer). When he meets him in the court or in the market-place, he must not return for a weapon, but engage him there and then;" being always careful, as the commentator observes, to carry a weapon about with him. Sir John Davis and Dr. Legge agree in stigmatizing this as "one of the objectionable principles of Confucius." It must, however, be admitted that (1) a patched-up work which appeared as we have it now from two to three centuries after Confucius's death, and (2) a confessedly apocryphal work such as the *Family Sayings*, are hardly sufficient grounds for affixing to the fair fame of China's great Sage the positive inculcation of a dangerous principle of blood-vengeance like that I have just quoted.

The stranger then disappeared, and Xiangru, having a presentiment that some misfortune was about to happen, fled away with his child.

When night came, and the members of the Song family were wrapped in sleep, someone found his way into their house and slew the ex-Censor and his two sons, besides a maid-servant and one of the ladies. Information was at once given to the authorities; and as the Song family had no doubt that the murderer was Xiangru, the magistrate, who was greatly alarmed,[167] sent out lictors to arrest him. Xiangru, however, was nowhere to be found, a fact which tended to confirm the suspicions of the Song family; and they, too, despatched a number of servants to aid the mandarin in effecting his capture. Towards evening the lictors and others reached a hill, and, hearing a child cry, made for the sound, and thus secured the object of their search, whom they bound and led away. As the child went on crying louder than ever, they took it from him and threw it down by the wayside, thereby nearly causing Xiangru to die of grief and rage. On being brought before the magistrate he was asked why he had killed these people; to which he replied that he was falsely accused, "For," said he, "they died in the night, whereas I had gone away in the daytime. Besides," added he, "how, with a crying baby in my arms, could I scale walls and kill people?" "If you didn't kill people," cried the magistrate, "why did you run away?" Xiangru had no answer to make to this, and he was accordingly ordered to prison; whereupon he wept and said, "I can die without regret; but what has my child done that he, too, should be punished?" "You," replied the magistrate, "have slain the children of others; how can you complain if your child meets the same fate?" Xiangru was then stripped of his degree[168] and subjected to all kinds of indignities, but they were unable to wring a confession from his lips;[169] and that very night, as the magistrate lay down, he heard a sharp noise of something striking the bed, and, jumping up in a fright, found, by the light of a candle, a small, keen blade sticking in the wood at the head of his couch so tightly that it could not be drawn out. Terribly alarmed at this, the magistrate walked around the room with a spear over his shoulder, but without finding anything; and then, reflecting that nothing more was to be feared from Song, who was dead, as well as his two sons, he laid Xiangru's case before the higher authorities, and obtained

---

167 The Chinese theory being that every official is responsible for the peace and well-being of the district committed to his charge, and even liable to punishment for occurrences over which he could not possibly have had any control.
168 See note 42 in tale number 10.
169 See note 45 in tale number 10.

for him an acquittal. Xiangru was released and went home. His cupboard, however, was empty, and there was nothing except his own shadow within the four walls of his house. Happily, his neighbors took pity on him and supplied him with food; and whenever he thought upon the vengeance that had been wreaked, his countenance assumed an expression of joy; but as often as his misfortunes and the extinction of his family came into his mind, his tears would begin to flow. And when he remembered the poverty of his life and the end of his ancestral line, he would seek out some solitary spot, and there burst into an ungovernable fit of grief. Thus things went on for about six months, when the search after the murderer began to be relaxed; and then Xiangru petitioned for the recovery of his wife's bones, which he took home with him and buried. His sorrows made him wish to die, and he lay tossing about on the bed without any object in life, when suddenly he heard somebody knock at the door. Keeping quiet to listen, he distinguished the sound of a voice outside talking with a child; and, getting up to look, he perceived a young lady, who said to him, "Your great wrongs are all redressed, and now, luckily, you have nothing to ail you." The voice seemed familiar to him, but he could not at the moment recall where he had heard it; so he lighted a candle, and Miss Hongyu stood before him. She was leading a small, happy-looking child by the hand; and after she and Xiangru had expressed their mutual satisfaction at meeting once more, Miss Hongyu pushed the boy forward, saying, "Have you forgotten your father?" The boy clung to her dress, and looked shyly at Xiangru, who, on examining him closely, found that he was Fuer. "Where did he come from?" asked his father, in astonishment, not unmingled with tears. "I will tell you all," replied Miss Hongyu. "I was only deceiving you when I said I belonged to a neighboring family. I am really a fox, and, happening to go out one evening, I heard a child crying in a ditch. I took him home and brought him up; and, now that your troubles are over, I return him to you, that father and son may be together." Xiangru wiped away his tears and thanked her heartily; but Fu'er kept close to Miss Hongyu, whom he had come to regard as a mother, and did not seem to recognise his father again. Before daybreak Miss Hongyu said she must go away; but Xiangru fell upon his knees and entreated her to stop, until at last she said she was only joking, adding that, in a new establishment like theirs, it would be a case of early to rise and late to bed. She then set to work cutting fuel and sweeping up, toiling hard as if she had been a man, which made Xiangru regret that he was too poor to have all this done for her. However, she bade him mind his books, and not trouble himself about the state of their affairs, as they were not likely to die of hunger. She also produced some money, and bought implements for spinning, besides renting a few acres of land and hiring laborers to till them. Day by day she would shoulder her hoe and work in the fields, or employ herself in mending the roof, so that her fame as a good wife spread abroad, and the neighbors were more than ever pleased to help them. In half-a-year's time their home was like that of a well-to-do family, with plenty of servants about; but one day Xiangru said to Miss Hongyu, "With all that you have accomplished on my behalf, there is still one thing left undone." On her asking him what it was, he continued: "The examination for master's degree is at hand, and I have not yet recovered the bachelor's degree of which I was stripped." "Ah," replied she, "some time back I had your name replaced upon the list; had I waited for you to tell me, it would have been too late." Xiangru marveled very much at this, and accordingly took his master's degree. He was then thirty-six years of age, the master of broad lands and fine houses; and Miss Hongyu, who looked delicate enough to be blown away by the wind, and yet worked harder than an ordinary laborer's wife, keeping her hands smooth and nice in spite of winter weather, gave herself out to be thirty-eight, though no one took her to be much more than twenty.

33. Zhang's Transformation

ZHANG YUDAN, of Zhaoyuan, was a wild fellow, who pursued his studies at the Xiao temple. Now it chanced that the magistrate of the district, Mr. Zeng of Sanhan, had a daughter who was very fond of hunting, and that one day young Zhang met her in the fields, and was much struck with her great beauty. She was dressed in an embroidered sable jacket, and rode about on a small palfrey, for all the world like a girl in a picture. Zhang went home with the young lady still in his thoughts, his heart being deeply touched; but he soon after heard, to his infinite sorrow and dismay, that Miss Zeng had died suddenly. Their own home being at a distance,[170] her father deposited the coffin in a temple;[171] the very temple, in fact, where her lover was residing. Accordingly Zhang paid to her remains the same respect he would have offered to a god; he burnt incense every morning, and poured

---

170 No man being allowed to hold office in his own province.
171 This is a very common custom all over China.

out libations at every meal, always accompanied by the following invocation: "I had hardly seen you when your spirit became ever present to me in my dreams. But you passed suddenly away; and now, near as we are together, we are as far apart as if separated by hills and rivers. Alas! Alas! In life you were under the control of your parents; now, however, there is nothing to restrain you, and with your supernatural power, I should be hearing the rustle of your robe as you approach to ease the sorrow of my heart." Day and night he prayed thus, and when some six months had passed away, and he was one night trimming his lamp to read, he raised his head and saw a young lady standing, all smiles, before him. Rising up, he inquired who she was; to which his visitor replied, "Grateful to you for your love of me, I was unable to resist the temptation of coming to thank you myself." Zhang then offered her a seat, and they sat together chatting for some time. From this date the young lady used to come in every evening, and on one occasion said to Zhang, "I was formerly very fond of riding and archery, shooting the musk and slaying the deer; my crime is so great that I can find no repose in death. If you have any friendly feelings towards me, I pray you recite for me the Diamond *sutra*[172] five thousand and forty-eight times, and I will never forget your kindness." Zhang did as he was asked, getting up every night and telling his beads before the coffin, until the occasion of a certain festival, when he wished to go home to his parents, and take the young lady with him. Miss Zeng said she was afraid her feet were too tender to walk far; but Zhang offered to carry her, to which she laughingly assented. It was just like carrying a child, she was so light;[173] and by degrees Zhang got so accustomed to taking her about with him, that when he went up for his examination she went in too.[174] The only thing was she could not travel except at night. Later on, Zhang would have gone up for his master's degree, but the young lady told him it was of no use to try, for it was not destined that he should pass; and accordingly he desisted from his intention. Four or five years afterwards, Miss Zeng's father resigned his appointment, and so poor was he that he could not afford to pay for the removal of his daughter's coffin, but wanted to bury it economically where it was. Unfortunately, he had no ground of his own, and then Zhang came forward and said that a friend of his had a piece of waste land near the temple, and that he might bury it there. Mr. Zeng was very glad to accept, and Zhang kindly assisted him

---

172 Of all the Buddhist *sutras*, this is perhaps the favorite with the Chinese.
173 Contrary to the German notion that the spirit of the dead mother, coming back at night to suckle the child she has left be hind, makes an impress on the bed alongside the baby.
174 Being, of course, invisible to all except himself.

with the funeral—for what reason the former was quite unable to guess. One night after this, as Miss Zeng was sitting by Zhang's side, her father having already returned home, she burst into a flood of tears, and said, "For five years we have been good friends; we must now part. I can never repay your goodness to me." Zhang was alarmed, and asked her what she meant; to which she replied, "Your sympathy has told for me in the realms below. The sum of my *sutras* is complete, and today I am to be born again in the family of a high official, Mr. Lu, of Hebei. If you do not forget the present time, meet me there in fifteen years from now, on the 16th of the 8th moon." "Alas!" cried Zhang, "I am already over thirty, and in fifteen years more I shall be drawing near the wood.[175] What good will our meeting do?" "I can be your servant," replied Miss Zeng, "and so make some return to you. But come, escort me a few miles on my way; the road is beset with brambles, and I shall have some trouble with my dress." So Zhang carried her as before, until they reached a high road, where they found a number of carriages and horses, the latter with one or two riders on the backs of each, and three or four, or even more persons, in every carriage. But there was one richly-decorated carriage, with embroidered curtains and red awnings, in which sat only one old woman, who, when she saw Miss Zeng, called out, "Ah, there you are." "Here I am," replied Miss Zeng; and then she turned to Zhang and said, "We must part here; do not forget what I told you." Zhang promised he would remember; and then the old woman helped her up into the carriage, around went the wheels, off went the attendants, and they were gone. Sorrowfully Zhang wended his way home, and there wrote upon the wall the date mentioned by Miss Zeng; after which, bethinking himself of the efficacy of prayer, he took to reciting *sutras* more energetically than ever. By-and-by he dreamed that an angel appeared to him, and said, "The bent of your mind is excellent indeed, but you must visit the Southern Sea."[176] Asking how far off the Southern Sea was, the angel informed him it was close by; and then waking up, and understanding what was required of him, he fixed his sole thoughts on Buddha, and lived a purer life than before. In three years' time his two sons, Ming and Zheng, came out very high on the list at the examination for the second degree, in spite of which worldly successes Zhang continued to lead his usual holy life. Then one night he dreamed that another angel led him among beautiful halls and palaces,

175 A very ancient expression signifying "the grave," the word "wood" being used by synecdoche for "coffin."
176 The supposed residence of Guanyin, the Chinese Goddess of Mercy, she who "hears prayers," and is the giver of children.

where he saw a personage sitting down who resembled Buddha himself. This personage said to him, "My son, your virtue is a matter of great joy; unhappily your term of life is short, and I have, therefore, made an appeal to God[177] on your behalf." Zhang prostrated himself, and knocked his head upon the ground; upon which he was commanded to rise, and was served with tea, fragrant as the epidendrum. A boy was next instructed to take him to bathe in a pool, the water of which was so exquisitely clear that he could count the fishes swimming about therein. He found it warm as he walked in, and scented like the leaves of the lotus-flower; and gradually the water got deeper and deeper, until he went down altogether and passed through with his head under water. He then waked up in a fright; but from this moment he became more robust and his sight improved. As he stroked his beard the white hairs all came out, and by-and-by the black ones too; the wrinkles on his face were smoothed away, and in a few months he had the beardless face of a boy of fifteen or sixteen. He also grew very fond of playing about like other boys, and would sometimes tumble head over heels, and be picked up by his sons. Soon afterwards his wife died of old age, and his sons begged him to marry again into some good family; but he said he should be obliged to go to Hebei first; and then, calculating his dates, found that the appointed time had arrived. So he ordered his horses and servants, and set off for Hebei, where he discovered that there actually was a high official named Lu. Now Mr. Lu had a daughter, who when born was able to talk,[178] and became very clever and beautiful as she grew up. She was the idol of her parents, and had been asked in marriage by many suitors, but would not accept any of them; and when her father and mother inquired her motives for refusal, she told them the story of her engagement in her former life. "Silly child," said they, reckoning up the time, and laughing at her; "that Mr. Zhang would now be about fifty years of age, a changed and feeble old man. Even if he is still alive, his hair will be white and his teeth gone." But their daughter would not listen to them; and, finding her so obstinate in her determination, they instructed the doorkeeper to admit no strangers until the appointed time should have passed, that thus her expectations might be brought to naught. Before long, Zhang arrived, but the doorkeeper would not let him in, and he went back to his inn in great distress, not knowing what to do. He then took to walking about the fields,

---

177 The great Supreme Ruler, who is supposed to have absolute sway over the various other deities of the Chinese Pantheon.
178 Generally spoken of as an inauspicious phenomenon.

and secretly making inquiries concerning the family. Meanwhile Miss Zeng thought that he had broken his engagement, and refused all food, giving herself up to tears alone. Her mother argued that he was probably dead, or in any case that the breach of engagement was no fault of her daughter's; to none of which, however, would Miss Zeng listen, lying where she was the livelong day. Mr. Lu now became anxious about her, and determined to see what manner of man this Zhang might be; so, on the plea of taking a walk, he went out to meet him in the fields, and to his astonishment found quite a young man. They sat down together on some leaves, and after chatting awhile Mr. Lu was so charmed with his young friend's bearing that he invited him to his house. No sooner had they arrived, than Mr. Lu begged Zhang to excuse him a moment, and ran in first to tell his daughter, who exerted herself to get up and take a peep at the stranger. Finding, however, that he was not the Zhang she had formerly known, she burst into tears and crept back to bed, upbraiding her parents for trying to deceive her thus. Her father declared he was no other than Zhang, but his daughter replied only with tears; and then he went back very much upset to his guest, whom he treated with great want of courtesy. Zhang asked him if he was not the Mr. Lu, of such and such a position, to which he replied in a vacant kind of way that he was, looking the other way all the time and paying no attention to Zhang. The latter did not approve of this behavior, and accordingly took his leave; and in a few days Miss Zeng had cried herself to death. Zhang then dreamed that she appeared to him, and said, "Was it you after all that I saw? You were so changed in age and appearance that when I looked upon your face I did not know you. I have already died from grief; but if you make haste to the little street shrine and summon my spirit back, I may still recover. Be not late!" Zhang then waked, and immediately made inquiries at Mr. Lu's house, when he found that the young lady had been dead two days. Telling her father his dream, they went forth to summon the spirit back; and on opening the shroud, and throwing themselves with lamentations over the corpse, a noise was heard in the young lady's throat, and her cherry lips parted. They moved her on to a bed, and soon she began to moan, to the great joy of Mr. Lu, who took Zhang out of the room and, over a bumper of wine, asked some questions about his family. He was glad to find that Zhang was a suitable match for his daughter, and an auspicious day was fixed for the wedding. In a fortnight the event came off, the bride being escorted to Zhang's house by her father, who remained with them six months before going home again. They were a youthful pair, and people who didn't know the story mistook Zhang's son and daughter-in-law for his father and mother. A year later Mr. Lu died; and his son, a mere child, having been badly wounded by some scoundrels, and the family property being almost gone, Zhang made him come and live with them, and be one of their town family.

34. A Taoist Priest

ONCE upon a time there was a Mr. Han, who belonged to a wealthy family, and was fond of entertaining people. A man named Xu, of the same town, frequently joined him over the bottle; and on one occasion when they were together a Taoist priest came to the door with his alms-bowl[179] in his hand. The servants threw him some money and food, but the priest would not accept them, neither would he go away; and at length they would take no more notice of him. Mr. Han heard the noise of the priest knocking his bowl[180] going on for a long time, and asked his servants what was the matter; and they had hardly told him when the priest himself walked in. Mr. Han begged him to be seated; whereupon the priest bowed to both gentlemen and took his seat. On making the usual inquiries, they found that he lived at an old tumbledown temple to the east of the town, and Mr. Han expressed regret at not having heard sooner of his arrival, so that he might have shown him the proper hospitality of a resident. The priest said that he had only recently arrived, and had no friends in the place; but hearing that Mr. Han was a jovial fellow, he had been very anxious to take a glass with him. Mr. Han then ordered wine, and the priest soon distinguished himself as a hard drinker; Mr. Xu treating him all the time with a certain amount of disrespect in consequence of his shabby appearance, while Mr. Han made allowances for him as being a traveler. When he had drunk over twenty large cups of wine; the priest took his leave, returning subsequently

---

179 This is the Buddhist *patra*, which modern writers have come to regard as an instrumental part of the Taoist religion. See note 11 in tale number 4.
180 To call attention to his presence. Beggars in China accomplish their purpose more effectually by beating a gong in the shop where they ask for alms so loudly as to prevent the shopkeeper from hearing his customers speak; or they vary the performance by swinging about some dead animal tied to the end of a stick. Mendicity not being prohibited in China, there results a system of blackmail payable by every householder to a beggars' guild, and this frees them from the visits of the beggars of their own particular district; many, however, do not subscribe, but take their chance in the struggle as to who will tire out the other first, the shopkeeper, who has all to lose, being careful to stop short of anything like manual violence, which would forthwith bring down upon him the myrmidons of the law, and subject him to innumerable "squeezes."

whenever any jollification was going on, no matter whether it was eating or drinking. Even Han began now to tire a little of him; and on one occasion Xu said to him in raillery, "Good priest, you seem to like being a guest; why don't you play the host sometimes for a change?" "Ah," replied the priest, "I am much the same as yourself—a mouth carried between a couple of shoulders."[181] This put Xu to shame, and he had no answer to make; so the priest continued, "But although that is so, I have been revolving the question with myself for some time, and when we do meet I shall do my best to repay your kindness with a cup of my own poor wine." When they had finished drinking, the priest said he hoped he should have the pleasure of their company the following day at noon; and at the appointed time the two friends went together, not expecting, however, to find anything ready for them. But the priest was waiting for them in the street; and passing through a handsome courtyard, they beheld long suites of elegant apartments stretching away before them. In great astonishment, they remarked to the priest that they had not visited this temple for some time, and asked when it had been thus repaired; to which he replied that the work had been only lately completed. They then went inside, and there was a magnificently-decorated apartment, such as would not be found even in the houses of the wealthy. This made them begin to feel more respect for their host; and no sooner had they sat down than wine and food were served by a number of boys, all about sixteen years of age, and dressed in embroidered coats, with red shoes. The wine and eatables were delicious, and very nicely served; and when the dinner was taken away, a course of rare fruits was put on the table, the names of all of which it would be impossible to mention. They were arranged in dishes of crystal and jade, the brilliancy of which lighted up the surrounding furniture; and the goblets in which the wine was poured were of glass,[182] and more than a foot in circumference. The priest here cried out, "Call the Shi sisters," whereupon one of the boys went out and in a few moments two elegant young ladies walked in. The first was tall and slim like a willow wand; the other was short and very young, both being exceedingly pretty girls. Being told to sing while the company were drinking, the younger beat time and sang a song, while the elder accompanied her on the flageolet. They acquitted themselves admirably; and, when the

181 *Sc.* a "sponge."
182 First manufactured in China 424 CE. The term here used (*boli*) occurs as early as 643 CE, and is of foreign origin.

song was over, the priest, holding his goblet bottom upwards in the air, challenged his guests to follow his example, bidding his servants pour out more wine all around. He then turned to the girls, and remarked that they had not danced for a long time, asking if they were still able to do so; upon which a carpet was spread by one of the boys, and the two young ladies proceeded to dance, their long robes waving about and perfuming the air around. The dance concluded, they leant against a painted screen, while the two guests gradually became more and more confused, and were at last irrecoverably drunk. The priest took no notice of them; but when he had finished drinking, he got up and said, "Pray, go on with your wine; I am going to rest awhile, and will return by-and-by." He then went away, and lay down on a splendid couch at the other end of the room; at which Xu was very angry, and shouted out, "Priest, you are a rude fellow," at the same time making towards him with a view of rousing him up. The priest then ran out, and Han and Xu lay down to sleep, one at each end of the room, on elaborately-carved couches covered with beautiful mattresses. When they woke up, they found themselves lying in the road, Mr. Xu with his head in a dirty drain. Hard by were a couple of rush huts; but everything else was gone.

35. The Fight with the Foxes

IN the province of Zhili, there was a wealthy family in want of a tutor. One day a graduate presented himself at the door, and was asked by the master of the house to walk in; and he conversed so pleasantly that in a short time it was clear to both sides that they were mutually pleased with each other. The tutor said his name was Hu; and when the usual present had been made to him, he was forthwith provided with apartments, and entered very energetically upon his duties, proving himself a scholar of no mean order. He was, however, very fond of roaming, and generally came back in the middle of the night, not troubling himself to knock if the door was locked, but suddenly appearing on the inside. It was therefore suspected that he was a fox, though as his intentions seemed to be harmless, he was treated extremely well, and not with any want of courtesy as if he had been something uncanny. By-and-by he discovered that his master had a daughter,[183] and being desirous of securing the match was always dropping hints to that effect, which his master, on the other hand, invariably pretended not to understand. One day he went off for a holiday, and on the next day a stranger called; who, tying a black mule at the door, accepted the invitation of the master to take a seat within. He was about fifty years of age, very neat and clean in his dress, and gentlemanly in his manners. When they were seated, the stranger began by saying that he was come with proposals of marriage on behalf of Mr. Hu; to which his host, after some consideration, replied that he and Mr. Hu got along excellently well as friends, and there was no object in bringing about a closer connection. "Besides," added he, "my daughter is already betrothed, and I beg you, therefore, to ask Mr. Hu to excuse me." The stranger said he was quite sure the young lady was not engaged, and inquired what might be the objection to the match: but it was all of no avail, until at length he remarked, "Mr. Hu is of a good family; I see no reason why you should have such an aversion to him." "Well, then," replied the other, "I will tell you what it is. We don't like his *species*." The stranger here got very angry, and his host also lost his temper, so that they came to high words, and were already on the way to blows, when the latter bade his servants give the stranger a beating and turn him out. The stranger then retired, leaving his mule behind him; and when they drew near to look at it they found a huge creature with black hair, drooping ears, and a long tail. They tried to lead it away, but it would not move; and on giving it a shove with the hand from behind, it toppled over and was discovered to be only of straw. In consequence of the angry words that had been said, the master of the house felt sure that there would be an attempt at revenge, and accordingly made all preparations; and sure enough the next day a whole host of fox-soldiers arrived, some on horseback, some on foot, some with spears, and others with cross-bows, men and horses trampling along with an indescribable din. The family were afraid to leave the house, and the foxes shouted out to set the place on fire, at which the inmates were dreadfully alarmed; but just then one of the bravest of them rushed forth with a number of the servants to engage the foxes. Stones and arrows flew about in all directions, and many on both sides were wounded; at length, however, the foxes drew off, leaving their swords on the field. These glittered like frost or snow, but when picked up turned out to be only millet-stalks. "Is this all their cunning?" cried their adversary,

---

183 The women's apartments being quite separate from the rest of a Chinese house, male visitors consequently know nothing about their inhabitants.

laughing, at the same time making still more careful preparations in case the foxes should come again. Next day they were deliberating together, when suddenly a giant descended upon them from the sky. He was over ten feet in height by several feet in breadth, and brandished a sword as broad as half a door; but they attacked him so vigorously with arrows and stones that he was soon stretched dead upon the ground, when they saw that he was made of grass. Our friends now began to make light of their fox-foes, and as they saw nothing more of them for three days their precautions were somewhat relaxed. The foxes, however, soon reappeared, armed with bows and arrows, and succeeded in shooting the master of the house in the back, disappearing when he summoned his servants and proceeded to attack them. Then, drawing the arrow from his back, he found it was a long thorn; and thus the foxes went on for a month or so, coming and going, and making it necessary to take precautions, though not really inflicting any serious injury. This annoyed the master of the family very much, until one day Mr. Hu[184] himself appeared with a troop of soldiers at his back, and he immediately went out to meet him. Mr. Hu withdrew among his men, but the master called to him to come forth, and then asked him what he had done that soldiers should be thus brought against his family. The foxes were now on the point of discharging their arrows; Mr. Hu, however, stopped them; whereupon he and his old master shook hands, and the latter invited him to walk into his old room. Wine being served, his host observed, "You, Mr. Hu, are a man of intelligence, and I trust you will make allowances for me. Friends as we were, I should naturally have been glad to form a connection with you; your carriages, however, horses, houses, etc., are not those of ordinary mortals; and even had my daughter consented, you must know the thing would have been impossible, she being still a great deal too young." Mr. Hu was somewhat disconcerted at this, but his host continued, "It's of no consequence; we can still be friends as before, and if you do not despise us earthly creatures, there is my son whom you have taught; he is fifteen years old, and I should be proud to see him connected with you if such an arrangement should be feasible." Mr. Hu was delighted, and said, "I have a daughter one year younger than your son; she is neither ugly nor stupid. How would she do? "His host got up and made a low bow, which Mr. Hu forthwith returned, and they then became the best of friends, forgetting all about the former unpleasantness. Wine was given to Mr. Hu's attendants, and everyone was made happy. The host now inquired

184 See note 57 in tale number 13.

where Mr. Hu lived, that the ceremony of pouring out a libation to the geese[185] might be performed; but Mr. Hu said this would not be necessary, and remained drinking until night, when he went away again. From this time there was no more trouble; and a year passed without any news of Mr. Hu, so that it seemed as if he wished to get out of his bargain. The family, however, went on waiting, and in six months more Mr. Hu reappeared, when, after a few general remarks, he declared that his daughter was ready, and requested that an auspicious day might be fixed for her to come to her husband's home. This being arranged, the young lady arrived with a retinue of sedan-chairs, and horses, and a beautiful trousseau that nearly filled a room.[186] She was unusually respectful to her father and mother-in-law, and the former was much pleased with the match. Her father and a younger brother of his had escorted her to the house, and conversing away in a most refined style they sat drinking until daybreak before they went away. The bride herself had the gift of foreknowing whether the harvest would be good or bad, and her advice was always taken in such matters. Mr. Hu and his brother, and also their mother, often came to visit her in her new home, and were then very frequently seen by people.

36. The King

A CERTAIN Governor of Hunan despatched a magistrate to the capital in charge of treasure to the amount of six hundred thousand ounces of silver. On the road the magistrate encountered a violent storm of rain, which so delayed him that night came on before he was able to reach the next station. He therefore took refuge in an old temple; but, when morning came, he was horrified to find that the treasure had disappeared. Unable to fix the guilt on anyone, he returned forthwith to the Governor and told him the whole story. The latter, however, refused to believe what the magistrate said, and would have had him severely punished, but that each and all of his attendants stoutly corroborated his statements; and accordingly he bade him return and endeavor to find the missing silver. When the magistrate got back to the temple, he met an extraordinary-looking blind

---

185 A very ancient custom in China, originating in a belief that these birds never mate a second time. The libation is made on the occasion of the bridegroom fetching his bride from her father's house.
186 A Chinese trousseau, in addition to clothes and jewels, consists of tables and chairs, and all kinds of house furniture and ornaments.

man, who informed him that he could read people's thoughts, and further
went on to say that the magistrate had come there on a matter of money.
The latter replied that it was so, and recounted the misfortune that had
overtaken him; whereupon the blind man called for sedan-chairs, and told
the magistrate to follow and see for himself, which he accordingly did,
accompanied by all his retinue. If the blind man said east, they went east;
or if north, north; journeying along for five days until far among the hills,
where they beheld a large city with a great number of inhabitants. They
entered the gates and proceeded on for a short distance, when suddenly the
blind man cried "Stop!" and, alighting from his chair, pointed to a lofty
door facing the west, at which he told the magistrate to knock and make
what inquiries were necessary. He then bowed and took his leave, and the
magistrate obeyed his instructions, whereupon a man came out in reply
to his summons. He was dressed in the fashion of the Han dynasty,[187] and
did not say what his name was; but as soon as the magistrate informed
him wherefore he had come, he replied that if the latter would wait a few
days he himself would assist him in the matter. The man then conducted
the magistrate within, and giving him a room to himself, provided him
regularly with food and drink. One day he chanced to stroll away to the
back of the building, and there found a beautiful garden with dense avenues
of pine-trees and smooth lawns of fine grass. After wandering about for
some time among the arbors and ornamental buildings, the magistrate
came to a lofty kiosk, and mounted the steps, when he saw hanging on
the wall before him a number of human skins, each with its eyes, nose,
ears, mouth, and heart.[188] Horrified at this, he beat a hasty retreat to his
quarters, convinced that he was about to leave his own skin in this out-of-
the-way place, and giving himself up for lost. He reflected, however, that
he should probably gain nothing by trying to escape, and made up his
mind to wait; and on the following day the same man came to fetch him,
saying he could now have an audience. The magistrate replied that he was
ready; and his conductor then mounted a fiery steed, leaving the other
to follow on foot. By-and-by they reached a door like that leading into
a Viceroy's *yamen,* where stood on either side crowds of official servants,
preserving the utmost silence and decorum. The man here dismounted
and led the magistrate inside; and after passing through another door they

---

187 Which ended some seventeen hundred years ago.
188 Corresponding with our five " senses," the heart taking the place of the brain, and being regarded
by Chinese doctors as the seat not only of intelligence and the passions, but also of all sensation.

came into the presence of a king, who wore a cap decorated with pearls, and an embroidered sash, and sat facing the south. The magistrate rushed forward and prostrated himself on the ground; upon which the King asked him if he was the Hunan official who had been charged with the conveyance of treasure. On his answering in the affirmative, the King said, "The money is all here; it's a mere trifle, but I have no objection to receive it as a present from the Governor." The magistrate here burst into tears, and declared that his term of grace had already expired: that he would be punished if he went back thus, especially as he would have no evidence to adduce in substantiation of his story. "That is easy enough,"replied the King, and put into his hands a thick letter, which he bade him give to the Governor, assuring him that this would prevent him from getting into any trouble. He also provided him with an escort; and the magistrate, who dared not argue the point further, sorrowfully accepted the letter and took his departure. The road he traveled along was not that by which he had come; and when the hills ended, his escort left him and went back. In a few days more he reached Changsha, and respectfully informed the Governor of what had taken place; but the Governor thought he was telling more lies, and in a great rage bade the attendants bind him hand and foot. The magistrate then drew the letter forth from his coat; and when the Governor broke the seal and saw its contents, his face turned deadly pale. He gave orders for the magistrate to be unbound, remarking that the loss of the treasure was of no importance, and that the magistrate was free to go. Instructions were next issued that the amount was to be made up in some way or other and forwarded to the capital; and meanwhile the Governor fell sick and died.

Now this Governor had had a wife of whom he was dotingly fond; and one morning when they woke up, lo! all her hair was gone. The whole establishment was in dismay, no one knowing what to make of such an occurrence. But the letter above-mentioned contained-that hair, accompanied by the following words: "Ever since you first entered into public life your career has been one of peculation and avarice. The six hundred thousand ounces of silver are safely stored in my treasury. Make good this sum from your own accumulated extortions. The officer you charged with the treasure is innocent; he must not be wrongly punished. On a former occasion I took your wife's hair as a gentle warning. If now you disobey my injunctions, it will not be long before I have your head. Herewith I return the hair as an evidence of what I say." When the Governor was dead, his family divulged the contents of the letter; and some of his subordinates sent men to search for the city, but they only found range upon range of inaccessible mountains, with nothing like a road or path.

37. Engaged to a Nun

AT Yiling, in Hubei, there lived a young man named Zhen Yu, the son of a graduate. He was a good scholar and a handsome fellow, and had made a reputation for himself even before he arrived at manhood. When quite a boy, a physiognomist had predicted that he would marry a Taoist nun; but his parents regarded it only as a joke, and made several attempts to get him a different kind of wife. Their efforts, however, had not hitherto proved successful, the difficulty being to find a suitable match.

Now his maternal grandmother lived at Huanggang; and on one occasion, when young Zhen was paying her a visit, he heard some one say that of the four Yuns at Huangzhou the youngest had no peer. This remark referred to some very nice-looking nuns who lived in a temple[189] a few miles from his grandmother's house; and accordingly Zhen secretly set off to see them, and knocking at the door, was very cordially received by the four ladies, who were persons of considerable refinement. The youngest was a girl of incomparable beauty, and Zhen could not keep his eyes off her, until at last she put her hand up to her face and looked the other way. Her companions now going out of the room to get tea for their visitor, Zhen availed himself of the opportunity to ask the young lady's name; to which she replied that she was called Yunqi, and that her surname was Chen. "How extraordinary!" cried Zhen; "and mine is Pan."[190] This made her blush very much, and she bent her head down, and made no answer; by-and-by rising up and going away. The tea then came in, accompanied by some nice fruit, and the nuns began telling him their names. One was Bai Yunshen, and thirty odd years of age; another was Sheng Yunmian, just twenty; and the third was Liang Yundong, twenty-four or five years old, but the junior in point of religious standing.[191] Yunqi did not reappear, and at length Zhen

---

189 These nunneries, of which there are plenty in China, are well worth visiting, and may be freely entered by both sexes. Sometimes there are as many as a hundred nuns living together in one temple, and to all appearances devoting their lives to religious exercises; report, however, tells many tales of broken vows, and makes sad havoc generally with the reputation of these fair vestals.

190 In corresponding English, this would be: The young lady said her name was Eloisa. "How funny!" cried Zhen, "and mine is Abelard."

191 That is, she was the last to take the vows.

grew anxious to see her again, and asked where she was Miss Bai told him her sister was afraid of strangers, and Zhen then got up and took his leave in spite of their efforts to detain him. "If you want to see Yunqi you had better come again tomorrow," said Miss Bai; and Zhen, who went home thinking of nothing but Yunqi, did return to the temple on the following day. All the nuns were there except Yunqi, but he hardly liked to begin by inquiring after her; and then they pressed him to stay and take dinner with them, accepting no excuses, Miss Bai herself setting food and chop-sticks before him, and urging him to eat. When he asked where Yunqi was, they said she would come directly; but evening gradually drew on, and Zhen rose to go home. Thereupon they all entreated him to stay, promising that if he did so they would make Yunqi come in. Zhen then agreed to remain; the lamps were lighted, and wine was freely served around, until at last he said he was so tipsy he couldn't take any more. "Three bumpers more," cried Miss Bai, "and then we will send for Yunqi." So Zhen drank off his three cups, whereupon Miss Liang said he must also drink three with her, which he did, turning his wine-cup down on the table[192] and declaring that he would have no more. "The gentleman won't condescend to drink with us," said Miss Bai to Miss Liang, "so you had better call in Yunqi, and tell the fair Eloisa that her Abelard is awaiting her." In a few moments Miss Liang came back and told Zhen that Yunqi would not appear; upon which he went off in a huff, without saying a word to either of them, and for several days did not go near the place again. He could not, however, forget Yunqi, and was always hanging about on the watch, until one afternoon he observed Miss Bai go out, at which he was delighted, for he wasn't much afraid of Miss Liang, and at once ran up to the temple and knocked at the door. Yunmian answered his knock, and from her he discovered that Miss Liang had also gone out on business. He then asked for Yunqi, and Yunmian led him into another courtyard, where she called out, "Yunqi! here's a visitor." At this the door of the room was immediately slammed, and Yunmian laughed and told Zhen she had locked herself in. Zhen was on the point of saying something, when Yunmian moved away, and a voice was heard from the other side of the window, "They all want to make me a bait to entice you. Sir; and if you come here again, I cannot answer for my safety. I do not wish to remain a nun, and if I could only meet with a gentleman like you, Mr. Pan, I would be a handmaid to him all the days of my life." Zhen offered his hand and heart to the young lady on the spot; but she reminded him

---

192 The usual signal that a person does not wish to take any more wine.

that her education for the priesthood had not been accomplished without expense. "And if you truly love me," added she, "bring twenty ounces of silver wherewith to purchase my freedom. I will wait for you three years with the utmost fidelity." Zhen assented to this, and was about to tell her who he really was, when Yunmian returned, and they all went out together, Zhen now bidding them farewell and going back to his grandmother's. After this he always had Yunqi in his thoughts, and wanted very much to get another interview with her and be near her once again, but at this juncture he heard that his father was dangerously ill, and promptly set off on his way home, traveling day and night. His father died, and his mother, who then ruled the household, was such a severe person that he dared not tell her what was nearest to his heart. Meanwhile he scraped together all the money he could; and refused all proposals of marriage on the score of being in mourning for his father.[193] His mother, however, insisted on his taking a wife; and he then told her that when he was with his grandmother at Huanggang, an arrangement had been made that he was to marry a Miss Chen, to which he himself was quite ready to accede; and that now, although his father's death had stopped all communications on the subject, he could hardly do better than pay a visit to his grandmother and see how matters stood, promising that if the affair was not actually settled he would obey his mother's commands. His mother consented to this, and off he started with the money he had saved; but when he reached Huanggang and went off to the temple, he found the place desolate and no longer what it had been. Entering in, he saw only one old priestess employed in cooking her food; and on making inquiries of her, she told him that the Abbess had died in the previous year, and that the four nuns had gone away in different directions. According to her, Yunqi was living in the northern quarter of the city, and thither he proceeded forthwith; but after asking for her at all the temples in the neighborhood, he could get no news of her, and returned sorrowfully home, pretending to his mother that his uncle had said Mr. Chen had gone away, and that as soon as he came back they would send a servant to let him know.

Some months after these events, Zhen's mother went on a visit to her own home, and mentioned this story in conversation with her old mother, who, to her astonishment, knew nothing at all about it, but suggested that Zhen and his uncle must have concocted the thing together. Luckily,

---

193 This would carry him well on into the third of the years during which Yunqi had promised to wait for him.

however, for Zhen his uncle was away at that time, and they had no means of getting at the real truth. Meanwhile, Zhen's mother went away to the Lily Hill to fulfil a vow she had made, and remained all night at an inn at the foot of the hill. That evening the landlord knocked at her door and ushered in a young priestess to share the room. The girl said her name was Yunqi; and when she heard that Zhen's mother lived at Iling, she went and sat by her side, and poured out to her a long tale of tribulation, finishing up by saying that she had a cousin named Pan, at Yiling, and begging Zhen's mother to send someone to tell him where she would be found. "Every day I suffer," added she, "and each day seems like a year. Tell him to come quickly, or I may be gone." Zhen's mother inquired what his other name might be, but she said she did not know; to which the old lady replied that it was of no consequence, as, being a graduate, it would be easy to find him out. Early in the morning Zhen's mother bade the girl farewell, the latter again begging her not to forget; and when she reached home she told Zhen what had occurred. Zhen threw himself on his knees, and told his mother that he was the Pan to whom the young lady alluded; and after hearing how the engagement had come about, his mother was exceedingly angry, and said, "Undutiful boy! how will you face your relations with a nun for a wife?" Zhen hung his head and made no reply; but shortly afterwards when he went up for his examination, he presented himself at the address given by Yunqi—only, however, to find that the young lady had gone away a fortnight before. He then returned home and fell into a bad state of health, when his grandmother died and his mother set off to assist at her funeral. On her way back she missed the right road and reached the house of some people named Jing, who turned out to be cousins of hers. They invited her in, and there she saw a young girl of about eighteen sitting in the parlor, and as great a beauty as she had ever set eyes on. Now, as she was always thinking of making a good match for her son, and curing him of his settled melancholy, she i asked who the young lady might be; and they told her that her name was Wang—that she was a connection of their own, and that her father and mother being dead, she was staying temporarily with them. Zhen's mother inquired the name of Miss Wang's betrothed, but they said she was not engaged; and then, taking her hand, she entered into conversation, and was very much charmed with her. Passing the night there, Zhen's mother took her cousin into her confidence, and the latter agreed that it would be a capital match; "but," added she, "this young lady is somewhat ambitious, or she would hardly have remained single so long. We must think about it." Meanwhile, Zhen's mother and Miss Wang got on so extremely well together that they were already on the terms of mother and daughter; and Miss Wang was invited to accompany her home. This invitation she readily accepted, and next day they went back; Zhen's mother, who wished to see her son free from his present trouble, bidding one of the servants tell him that she had brought home a nice wife for him; Zhen did not believe this; but on peeping through the window beheld a young lady much prettier even than Yunqi herself. He now began to reflect that the three years agreed upon had already expired; that Yunqi had gone no one knew whither, and had probably by this time found another husband; so he had no difficulty in entertaining the thought of marrying this young lady, and soon regained his health. His mother then caused the young people to meet, and be introduced to one another; saying to Miss Wang, when her son had left the room, "Did you guess why I invited you to come home with me?" "I did," replied the young lady, "but I don't think you guessed what was *my* object in coming. Some years ago I was betrothed to a Mr. Pan, of Yiling. I have heard nothing of him for a long time. If he has found another wife I will be your daughter-in-law; if not, I will ever regard you as my own mother, and endeavor to repay you for your kindness to me." "As there is an actual engagement," replied Zhen's mother, "I will say no more; but when I was at the Lily Hill there was a Taoist nun inquiring after this Mr. Pan, and now you again, though, as a matter of fact, there is no Mr. Pan in Yiling at all." "What!" cried Miss Wang, "are you that lady I met? I am the person who inquired for Mr. Pan." "If that is so," replied Zhen's mother with a smile, "then your Mr. Pan is not far off." "Where is he?" said she; and then Zhen's mother bade a maid-servant lead her out to her son and ask him. "Is your name Yunqi?" said Zhen, in great astonishment; and when the young lady asked him how he knew it, he told her the whole story of his pretending to be a Mr. Pan. But when Yunqi found out to whom she was talking, she was abashed, and went back and told his mother, who inquired how she came to have two names. "My real name is Wang," replied the young lady; "but the old Abbess, being very fond of me, made me take her own name." Zhen's mother was overjoyed at all this, and an auspicious day was immediatcly fixed for the celebration of their marriage.

38. The Young Lady of Lake Dongting

THE spirits of lake Dongting[194] are very much in the habit of borrowing boats. Sometimes the cable of an empty junk will cast itself off, and away goes the vessel over the waves to the sound of music in the air above. The boatmen crouch down in one corner and hide their faces, not daring to look up until the trip is over and they are once more at their old anchorage.

Now a certain Mr. Lin, returning home after having failed at the examination for Master's degree, was lying down very tipsy on the deck of his boat, when suddenly strains of music and singing began to be heard. The boatmen shook Mr. Lin, but failing to rouse him, ran down and hid themselves in the hold below. Then someone came and lifted him up, letting him drop again on to the deck, where he was allowed to remain in the same drunken sleep as before. By-and-by the noise of the various instruments became almost deafening, and Lin, partially waking up, smelled the delicious scent of perfume filling the air around him. Opening his eyes, he saw that the boat was crowded with a number of beautiful girls; and knowing that something strange was going on, he pretended to be fast asleep. There was then a call for Zhi Cheng, upon which a young waiting-maid came forward and stood quite close to Mr. Lin's head. Her stockings were the color of the kingfisher's wing, and her feet encased in tiny purple shoes, no bigger than one's finger. Much smitten with this young lady, he took hold of her stocking with his teeth, causing her, the next time she moved, to fall forward flat on her face. Someone, evidently in authority, asked what was the matter; and when he heard the explanation, was very angry, and gave orders to take off Mr. Lin's head. Soldiers now came and bound Lin, and on getting up he beheld a man sitting with his face to the South, and dressed in the garments of a king. "Sire," cried Lin, as he was being led away, "the king of lake Dongting was a mortal named Lin; your servant's name is Lin also. His Majesty was a disappointed candidate; your servant is one too. His Majesty met the Dragon Lady, and was made immortal; your servant has played a trick upon this girl, and he is to die. Why this inequality of fortunes?" When the king heard this, he bade them bring him back, and asked him, saying, "Are you, then, a disappointed candidate?" Lin said he was; whereupon the king handed him writing materials, and ordered him to compose an ode upon a lady's head-dress. Some time passed before Lin, who was a scholar of some repute in his own neighborhood, had done more than sit thinking about what he should write; and at length the king upbraided him, saying, "Come, come, a man of your reputation should not take so long." "Sire," replied Lin, laying down his pen, "it took ten years to complete the Songs of the Three Kingdoms; whereby it may be known that the value of compositions depends more upon the labor given to them than the speed with which they are written." The king laughed, and waited patiently from early morning until noon, when a copy of the verses was put into his hand, with which he declared himself very pleased. He now commanded that Lin should be served with wine; and shortly after there followed a collation of all kinds of curious dishes, in the middle of which an officer came in and reported that the register of people to be drowned had been made up. "How many in all?" asked the king. "Two hundred and twenty-eight," was the reply; and then the king inquired who had been deputed to carry it out; whereupon he was informed that the generals Mao and Nan had been appointed to do the work. Lin here rose to take leave, and the king presented him with ten ounces of pure gold and a crystal square,[195] telling him it would preserve him from any danger he might encounter on the lake. At this moment the king's retinue and horses ranged themselves in proper order upon the surface of the lake; and his Majesty, stepping from the boat into his sedan-chair, disappeared from view.

When everything had been quiet for a long time, the boatmen emerged from the hold, and proceeded to shape their course northwards. The wind, however, was against them, and they were unable to make any headway; when all of a sudden an iron cat appeared floating on the top of the water. "General Mao has come," cried the boatmen, in great alarm; and they and all the passengers on board fell down on their faces. Immediately afterwards a great wooden beam stood up from the lake, nodding itself backwards and forwards, which the boatmen, more frightened than ever, said was General Nan. Before long a tremendous sea was raging, the sun was darkened in the heavens, and every vessel in sight was capsized. But Mr. Lin sat in the middle of the boat, with the crystal square in his hand, and the mighty waves broke around without doing them any harm. Thus were they saved, and Lin returned home; and whenever he told his wonderful story, he would assert that, although unable to speak positively as to the facial beauty of the young lady he had seen, he dared say that she had the most exquisite pair of feet in the world.

Subsequently, having occasion to visit the city of Wuchang, he heard

---

195 The instrument used by masons is here meant.

of an old woman who wished to sell her daughter, but was unwilling to accept money, giving out that anyone who had the fellow of a certain crystal square in her possession should be at liberty to take the girl. Lin thought this very strange; and taking his square with him sought out the old woman, who was delighted to see him, and told her daughter to come in. The young lady was about fifteen years of age, and possessed of surpassing beauty; and after saying a few words of greeting, she turned around and went within again. Lin's reason had almost fled at the sight of this peerless girl, and he straightway informed the old woman that he had such an article as she required, but could not say whether it would match hers or not. So they compared their squares together, and there was not a fraction of difference between them, either in length or breadth. The old woman was overjoyed, and inquiring where Lin lived, bade him go home and get a bridal chair, leaving his square behind him as a pledge of his good faith. This he refused to do; but the old woman laughed, and said, "You are too cautious. Sir; do you think I should run away for a square?" Lin was thus constrained to leave it behind him, and hurrying away for a chair, made the best of his way back. When, however, he got there, the old woman was gone. In great alarm he inquired of the people who lived near as to her whereabouts; no one, however, knew; and it being already late he returned disconsolately to his boat. On the way, he met a chair coming towards him, and immediately the screen was drawn aside, and a voice cried out, "Mr. Lin! why so late? "Looking closely, he saw that it was the old woman, who, after asking him if he hadn't suspected her of playing him false, told him that just after he left she had had the offer of a chair; and knowing that he, being only a stranger in the place, would have some trouble in obtaining one, she had sent her daughter on to his boat. Lin then begged she would return with him, to which she would not consent; and accordingly, not fully trusting what she said, he hurried on himself as fast as he could, and, jumping into the boat, found the young lady already there. She rose to meet him with a smile, and then he was astonished to see that her stockings were the color of a kingfisher's wing, her shoes purple, and her appearance generally like that of the girl he had met on lake Dongting. While he was still confused, the young lady remarked. "You stare, Sir, as if you had never seen me before!" but just then Lin noticed the tear in her stocking made by his own teeth, and cried out in amazement," "What! are you Zhi Cheng?" The young lady laughed at this; whereupon Lin rose, and, making her a profound bow, said, "If you are that divine creature, I pray you tell me at once, and set my anxiety at rest." "Sir," replied she, "I will tell you all. That personage you met on the boat was actually the king of lake Dongting. He was so pleased with your talent that he wished to bestow me upon you; but, because I was a great favorite with her Majesty the Queen, he went back to consult with her. I have now come at the Queen's own command." Lin was highly pleased; and washing his hands, burnt incense, with his face towards the lake, as if it were the Imperial Court, and then they went home together.

Subsequently, when Lin had occasion to go to Wuchang, his wife asked to be allowed to avail herself of the opportunity to visit her parents; and when they reached the lake, she drew a hair-pin from her hair, and threw it into the water. Immediately a boat rose from the lake, and Lin's wife, stepping into it, vanished from sight like a bird on the wing. Lin remained waiting for her on the prow of his vessel, at the spot where she had disappeared; and by-and-by, he beheld a houseboat approach, from the window of which there flew a beautiful bird, which was no other than Zhi Cheng. Then someone handed out from the same window gold and silk, and precious things in great abundance, all presents to them from the Queen. After this, Zhi Cheng went home regularly twice every year, and Lin soon became a very rich man, the things he had being such as no one had ever before seen or heard of.

39. The Man Who Was Changed into a Crow

MR. YU RONG was a Hunan man. The person who told me his story did not recollect from what department or district he came. His family was very poor; and once, when returning home after failure at the examination, he ran quite out of funds. Being ashamed to beg, and feeling uncomfortably hungry, he turned to rest awhile in the Wu Wang[196] temple, where he poured out all his sorrows at the feet of the God. His prayers over, he was about to lie down in the outer porch, when suddenly a man took him and led him into the presence of Wu Wang; and then falling on his knees, said, "Your Majesty, there is a vacancy among the black-robes; the appointment might be bestowed on this man." The King assented, and Yu received a suit of black clothes; and when he had put these on he was changed into a crow, and flew away. Outside he saw a number of fellow-crows collected

---

196 The guardian angel of crows.

together, and immediately joined them, settling with them on the masts of the boats, and imitating them in catching and eating the meat or cakes which the passengers and boatmen on board threw up to them in the air.[197] In a little while he was no longer hungry, and, soaring aloft, alighted on the top of a tree, quite satisfied with his change of condition. Two or three days passed, and the King, now pitying his solitary state, provided him with a very elegant mate, whose name was Zhu Qing, and who took every opportunity of warning him when he exposed himself too much in search of food. However, he did not pay much attention to this, and one day a soldier shot him in the breast with a cross-bow; but luckily Zhu Qing got away with him in her beak, and he was not captured. This enraged the other crows very much, and with their wings they flapped the water into such big waves that all the boats were upset. Zhu Qing now procured food and fed her husband; but his wound was a severe one, and by the end of the day he was dead—at which moment he waked, as it were, from a dream, and found himself lying in the temple.

The people of the place had found Mr. Yu to all appearance dead; and not knowing how he had come by his death, and finding that his body was not quite cold, had set someone to watch him. They now learnt what had happened to him, and, making up a purse between them, sent him away home. Three years afterwards he was passing by the same spot, and went in to worship at the temple; also preparing a quantity of food, and inviting the crows to come down and eat it. He then prayed, saying, "If Zhu Qing is among you, let her remain." When the crows had eaten the food they all flew away; and by-and-by Yu returned, having succeeded in obtaining his master's degree. Again he visited Wu Wang's temple, and sacrificed a sheep as a feast for the crows; and again he prayed as on the previous occasion. That night he slept on the lake, and, just as the candles were lighted and he had sat down, suddenly there was a noise as of birds settling, and lo! a beautiful young lady about twenty years of age stood before him. "Have you been quite well since we parted?" asked she; to which Yu replied that he should like to know whom he had the honor of addressing. "Don't you remember Zhu Qing?" said the young lady; and then Yu was overjoyed, and inquired how she had come. "I am now," replied Zhu Qing, "a spirit of the Han river, and seldom go back to my old home; but in consequence of what you did on two occasions, I have come to see you once more." They then

---

197 In order to secure a favorable passage. The custom here mentioned was actually practiced at more than one temple on the Yangtze river, and allusions to it will be found in more than one serious work.

sat talking together like husband and wife reunited after long absence, and Yu proposed that she should return with him on his way south. Zhu Qing, however, said she must go west again, and upon this point they could not come to any agreement. Next morning when Yu woke up, he found himself in a lofty room with two large candles burning brightly, and no longer in his own boat. In utter amazement he arose and asked where he was. "At Hanyang," replied Zhu Qing; "my home is your home; why need you go south?" By-and-by, when it got lighter, in came a number of serving-women with wine, which they placed on a low table on the top of a broad couch; and then husband and wife sat down to drink together. "Where are all my servants?" asked Yu; and when he heard they were still on the boat, he said he was afraid the boat people would not be able to wait. "Never mind," replied Zhu Qing; "I have plenty of money, and I'll help you to make it up to them." Yu therefore remained with her, feasting and enjoying himself, and forgetting all about going home. As for the boatmen, when they walked up and found themselves at Hanyang, they were greatly astonished; and seeing that the servants could find no trace of their missing master, they wished to go about their own business. They were unable, however, to undo the cable, and so they all remained there together for more than a couple of months, by the end of which time Mr. Yu became anxious to return home, and said to Zhu Qing, "If I stay here, my family connections will be completely severed. Besides, as we are husband and wife, it is only right that you should pay a visit to my home." "That," replied Zhu Qing, "I cannot do; and even were I able to go, you have a wife there already, and where would you put me? It is better for me to stop where I am, and thus you will have a second family." Yu said she would be so far off that he could not always be dropping in; whereupon Zhu Qing produced a black suit, and replied, "Here are your old clothes. Whenever you want to see me, put these on and come, and on your arrival I will take them off for you." She then prepared a parting feast for her husband, at which he got very tipsy; and when he woke up he was on board his boat again, and at his old anchorage on the lake. The boatmen and his servants were all here, and they looked at one another in mutual amazement; and when they asked Yu where he had been, he hardly knew what to say. By the side of his pillow he discovered a bundle in which were some new clothes Zhu Qing had given him, shoes, stockings, etc.; and folded up with them was the suit of black. In addition to these he found an embroidered belt for tying around the waist, which was stuffed full of gold. He now started on his way south, and, when he reached the end of his journey, dismissed the boatmen with a handsome present.

After being at home for some months, his thoughts reverted to Hanyang; and, taking out the black clothes, he put them on, when wings immediately grew from his ribs, and with a flap he was gone. In about four hours he arrived at Hanyang, and, wheeling around and around in the air, espied below him a solitary islet, on-which stood a house, and there he proceeded to alight. A maid-servant had already seen him coming, and cried out, "Here's master!" and in a few moments out came Zhu Qing, and bade the attendants take off Mr. Yu's feathers. They were not long in setting him free, and then, hand in hand, he and Zhu Qing went into the house together. "You have come at a happy moment," said his wife, as they sat down to tell each other all the news; and in three days' time she gave birth to a boy, whom they called Hanchan, which means "born on the Han river." Three days after the event all the river-nymphs came to congratulate them, and brought many handsome presents. They were a charming band, not one being over thirty years of age; and, going into the bedroom and approaching the bed, each one pressed her thumb on the baby's nose, saying, "Long life to thee, little one!" Yu asked who they all were, and Zhu Qing told him they belonged to the same family of spirits as herself; "And the two last of all," said she, "dressed in pale lilac, are the nymphs who gave away their girdles at Hankow."[198]

A few months passed away, and then Zhu Qing sent her husband back in a boat to his old home. No sails or oars were used, but the boat sped along of itself; and at the end of the river journey there were men waiting with horses to convey him to his own door. After this he went backwards and forwards very frequently; and in time Hanchan grew up to be a fine boy, the apple of his father's eye. Unhappily his first wife had no children, and she was extremely anxious to see Hanchan; so Yu communicated this to Zhu Qing, who at once packed up a box and sent him back with his father, on the understanding that he was to return in three months. However, the other wife became quite as fond of him as if he had been her own child, and ten months passed without her being able to bear the thought of parting with him. But one day Hanchan was taken violently ill, and died; upon which Yu's wife was overwhelmed with grief, and wished to die too. Yu then set off for Hanyang, to carry the tidings to Zhu Qing; and when he arrived, lo! there was Hanchan, with his shoes and socks off, lying on the

198 Alluding to a legend of a young man meeting two young ladies at Hankow, each of whom wore a girdle adorned with a pearl as big as a hen's egg. The young man begged them to give him these girdles, and they did so; but the next moment they had vanished, and the girdles too.

bed. He was greatly rejoiced at this, and asked Zhu Qing what it all meant. "Why," replied she, "the term agreed upon by us had long expired, and, as I wanted my boy, I sent for him." Yu then told her how much his other wife loved Hanchan, but Zhu Qing said she must wait until there was another child, and then she should have him. Later on Zhu Qing had twins, a boy and a girl, the former named Hansheng and the latter Yupei; whereupon Hanchan went back again with his father, who, finding it inconvenient to be traveling backwards and forwards three or four times in a year, removed with his family to the city of Hanyang. At twelve years of age Hanchan took his bachelor's degree; and his mother, thinking there was no girl among mortals good enough for her son, sent for him to come home, that she herself might find a wife for him, which she did in the person of a Miss Zhiniang, who was the daughter of a spirit like herself. Yu's first wife then died, and the three children all went to mourn her loss, Hanchan remaining in Hunan after the funeral, but the other two returning with their father, and not leaving their mother again.

40. The Flower Nymphs

AT the lower temple on Mount Lao the camellias are twenty feet in height, and many spans in circumference. The peonies are more than ten feet high; and when the flowers are in bloom the effect is that of gorgeous tapestry.

There was a Mr. Huang, of Jiaozhou, who built himself a house at that spot, for the purposes of study; and one day he saw from his window a young lady dressed in white wandering about amongst the flowers. Reflecting that she could not possibly belong to the monastery,[199] he went out to meet her, but she had already disappeared. After this he frequently observed her, and once hid himself in a thick-foliaged bush, waiting for her to come. By-and-by she appeared, bringing with her another young lady dressed in red, who, as he noticed from his distant point of observation, was an exceedingly good-looking girl. When they approached nearer, the young lady in the red dress ran back, saying, "There is a man here!" whereupon Mr. Huang jumped out upon them, and away they went in a scare, with their skirts and long sleeves fluttering in the breeze, and perfuming the air around. Huang pursued them as far as a low wall, where they suddenly vanished from his

---

199 Women, of course, being excluded.

gaze. In great distress at thus losing the fair creatures, he took a pencil and wrote upon a tree the following lines:

> The pangs of love my heart enthrall
> As I stand opposite this wall.
> I dread some hateful tyrant's power,
> With none to save you in that hour.

Returning home he was absorbed in his own thoughts, when all at once the young lady walked in, and he rose up joyfully to meet her. "I thought you were a brigand," said his visitor, smiling; "you nearly frightened me to death. I did not know you were a great scholar whose acquaintance I now hope to have the honor of making." Mr. Huang asked the young lady her name, etc., to which she replied, "My name is Xiangyu, and I belong to Pingkang Xiang; but a magician has condemned me to remain on this hill much against my own inclination." "Tell me his name," cried Huang, "and I'll soon set you free." "There is no need for that," answered the young lady; "I suffer no injury from him, and the place is not an inconvenient one for making the acquaintance of such worthy gentlemen as yourself." Huang then inquired who was the young lady in red, and she told him that her name was Jiangxue, and that they were half-sisters; "and now," added she, "I will sing you a song; but please don't laugh at me." She then began as follows:

> In pleasant company the hours fly fast,
> And through the window daybreak peeps at last.
> Ah, would that, like the swallow and his mate,
> To live together were our happy fate.

Huang here grasped her hand[200] and said, "Beauty without and intellect within—enough to make a man love you and forget all about death, only one day's absence being like the separation of a thousand miles. I pray you

---

200 Although the Chinese do not "shake hands" in our sense of the term, it is a sign of affection to seize the hand of a parting or returning friend. "The Book of Rites," however, lays down the rule that persons of opposite sexes should not, in passing things from one to the other, *let their hands touch;* and the question was gravely put to Mencius (Book IV.) as to whether a man might even pull his drowning sister-in-law out of the water. Mencius replied that it was indeed a general principle that a man should avoid touching a woman's hand, but that he who could not make an exception in such a case would be no better than a wolf. Neither, according to the Chinese rule, should men and women hang their clothes on the same rack, which reminds one of the French prude who would not allow male and female authors to be ranged upon the same bookshelf.

come again whenever an opportunity may present itself." From this time the young lady would frequently walk in to have a chat, but would never bring her sister with her in spite of all Mr. Huang's entreaties. Huang thought they weren't friends, but Xiang said her sister did not care for society in the same way that she herself did, promising at the same time to try and persuade her to come at some future day. One evening Xiangyu arrived in a melancholy frame of mind, and told Huang that he was wanting more when he couldn't even keep what he had got; "for tomorrow," said she, "we part." Huang asked what she meant; and then, wiping away her tears with her sleeve, Xiangyu declared it was destiny, and that she couldn't well tell him. "Your former prophecy," continued she, "has come too true; and now it may well be said of me:

> Fallen into the tyrant's power,
> With none to save me in that hour."

Huang again tried to question her, but she would tell him nothing; and by-and-by she rose and took her leave. This seemed very strange; however, next day a visitor came, who, after wandering around the garden, was much taken with a white peony,[201] which he dug up and carried away with him. Huang now awoke to the fact that Xiangyu was a flower nymph, and became very disconsolate in consequence of what had happened; but when he subsequently heard that the peony only lived a few days after being taken away, he wept bitterly, and composed an elegy in fifty stanzas, besides going daily to the hole from which it had been taken, and watering the ground with his tears. One day, as he was returning thence, he espied the young lady of the red clothes also wiping away her tears alongside the hole and immediately walked back gently towards her. She did not run away, and Huang, grasping her sleeve, joined with her in her lamentations. When these were concluded he invited her to his house, and then she burst out with a sigh, saying, "Alas! that the sister of my early years should be thus suddenly taken from me. Hearing you, Sir, mourn as you did, I have also been moved to tears. Those you shed have sunk down deep to the realms below, and may perhaps succeed in restoring her to us; but the sympathies of the dead are destroyed for ever, and how then can she laugh and talk with us again?" "My luck is bad," said Huang, "that I should injure those I love, neither can I have the good fortune to draw towards me another such a

---

201 The *Pæonia albiflora*, Pall.

beauty. But tell me, when I often sent messages by Xiangyu to you, why did you not come?" "I knew," replied she, "what nine young fellows out of ten are; but I did not know what you were." She then took leave, Huang telling her how dull he felt without Xiangyu, and begging her to come again. For some days she did not appear; and Huang remained in a state of great melancholy, tossing and turning on his bed and wetting the pillow with his tears, until one night he got up, put on his clothes, and trimmed the lamp; and having called for pen and ink, he composed the following lines:

On my cottage roof the evening rain-drops beat;
I draw the blind and near the window take my seat.
To my longing gaze no loved one appears;
Drip, drip, drip, drip: fast flow my tears.

This he read aloud; and when he had finished, a voice outside said, "You want someone to cap your verses there!" Listening attentively, he knew it was Jiangxue and opening the door he let her in. She looked at his stanza and added impromptu:

She is no longer in the room;
A single lamp relieves the gloom;
One solitary man is there;
He and his shadow make a pair.

As Huang read these words his tears fell fast; and then, turning to Jiangxue, he upbraided her for not having been to see him. "I can't come so often as Xiangyu did," replied she, "but only now and then when you are very dull." After this she used to drop in occasionally, and Huang said Xiangyu was his beloved wife, and she his dear friend, always trying to find out every time she came which flower in the garden she was, that he might bring her home with him, and save her from the fate of Xiangyu. "The old earth should not be disturbed," said she, "and it would not do any good to tell you. If you couldn't keep your wife always with you, how will you be sure of keeping a friend?" Huang, however, paid no heed to this, and seizing her arm, led her out into the garden, where he stopped at every peony and asked if this was the one; to which Jiangxue made no reply, but only put her hand to her mouth and laughed.

At New Year's time Huang went home, and a couple of months afterwards he dreamt that Jiangxue came to tell him she was in great trouble, begging him to hurry off as soon as possible to her rescue. When he woke up, he thought his dream a very strange one; and ordering his servant and horses to be ready, started at once for the hills. There he found that the priests were about to build a new room; and finding a camellia in the way, the contractor had given orders that it should be cut down. Huang now understood his dream, and immediately took steps to prevent the destruction of the flower. That night Jiangxue came to thank him, and Huang laughed and said, "It serves you right for not telling me which you were. Now I know you, and if you don't come and see me, I'll get a firebrand and make it hot for you." "That's just why I didn't tell you before," replied she. "The presence of my dear friend," said Huang, after a pause, "makes me think more of my lost wife. It is long since I have mourned for her. Shall we go and bemoan her loss together? "So they went off and shed many a tear on the spot where formerly Xiangyu had stood, until at last Jiangxue wiped her eyes and said it was time to go. A few evenings later Huang was sitting alone, when suddenly Jiangxue entered, her face radiant with smiles. "Good news!" cried she, "the Flower-God,[202] moved by your tears, has granted Xiangyu a return to life. Huang was overjoyed, and asked when she would come; to which Jiangxue replied, that she could not say for certain, but that it would not be long. "I came here on your account," said Huang; "don't let me be duller than you can help." "All right," answered she, and then went away, not returning for the next two evenings. Huang then went into the garden and threw his arms around her plant, entreating her to come and see him, though without eliciting any response. He accordingly went back, and began twisting up a torch, when all at once in she came, and snatching the torch out of his hand, threw it away, saying, "You're a bad fellow, and I don't like you, and I sha'n't have any more to do with you." However, Huang soon succeeded in pacifying her, and by-and-by in walked Xiangyu herself. Huang now wept tears of joy as he seized her hand, and drawing Jiangxue towards them, the three friends mingled their tears together. They then sat down and talked over the miseries of separation, Huang meanwhile noticing that Xiangyu seemed to be unsubstantial, and that when he grasped her hand his fingers seemed to close only on themselves, and not as in the days gone by. This Xiangyu explained, saying, "When I was a flower-nymph I had a body; but now I am only the disembodied spirit of that flower. Do not regard me

---

202 The various subdivisions of the animal and vegetable kingdoms are each believed by the Chinese to be under the sway of a ruler holding his commission from and responsible to the one Supreme Power or God, fully in accordance with the general scheme of supernatural government accepted in other and less civilized communities.

as a reality, but rather as an apparition seen in a dream." "You have come at the nick of time," cried Jiangxue; "your husband there was just getting troublesome." Xiangyu now instructed Huang to take a little powdered white-berry and mixing it with some sulphur, to pour out a libation to her, adding, "This day next year I will return your kindness." The young ladies then went away, and next day Huang observed the shoots of a young peony growing up where Xiangyu had once stood. So he made the libation as she had told him, and had the plant very carefully tended, even building a fence all around to protect it. Xiangyu came to thank him for this, and he proposed that the plant should be removed to his own home; but to this she would not agree, "for," said she, "I am not very strong, and could not stand being transplanted. Besides, all things have their appointed place; and as I was not originally intended for your home, it might shorten my life to be sent there. We can love each other very well here." Huang then asked why Jiangxue did not come; to which Xiangyu replied that they must make her, and proceeded with him into the garden, where, after picking a blade of grass, she measured upwards from the roots of Jiangxue's plant to a distance of four feet six inches, at which point she stopped and Huang began to scratch a mark on the place with his nails. At that moment Jiangxue came from behind the plant, and in mock anger cried out, "You hussy you! what do you aid that wretch for?" "Don't be angry, my dear," said Xiangyu; "help me to amuse him for a year only, and then you sha'n't be bothered any more." So they went on, Huang watching the plant thrive, until by the spring it was over two feet in height. He then went home, giving the priests a handsome present, and bidding them take great care of it. Next year, in the fourth moon, he returned and found upon the plant a bud just ready to break; and as he was walking around, the stem shook violently as if it would snap, and suddenly the bud opened into a flower as large as a plate, disclosing a beautiful maiden within, sitting upon one of the pistils, and only a few inches in height. In the twinkling of an eye she had jumped out, and lo! it was Xiangyu. "Through the wind and the rain I have waited for you," cried she; "why have you come so late?" They then went into the house, where they found Jiangxue already arrived, and sat down to enjoy themselves as they had done in former times. Shortly afterwards Huang's wife died, and he took up his abode at Mount Lao for good and all. The peonies were at that time as large around as one's arm; and whenever Huang went to look at them, he always said, "Some day my spirit will be there by your sides;" to which the two girls used to reply with a laugh, and say, "Mind you don't forget." Ten years after these events,

Huang became dangerously ill, and his son, who had come to see him, was very much distressed about him. "I am about to be born," cried his father; "I am not going to die. Why do you weep?" He also told the priests that if later on they should see a red shoot, with five leaves, thrusting itself forth alongside of the peony, that would be himself. This was all he said, and his son proceeded to convey him home, where he died immediately on arrival. Next year a shoot did come up exactly as he had mentioned; and the priests, struck by the coincidence, watered it and supplied it with earth. In three years it was a tall plant, and a good span in circumference, but without flowers. When the old priest died, the others took no care of it; and as it did not flower they cut it down. The white peony then faded and died; and before long the camellia was dead too.

41. Danan in Search of His Father

Xi CHENGLIE was a Chengdu man. He had a wife and a concubine, the latter named He Zhaorong. His wife dying, he took a second by name Shen, who bullied the concubine dreadfully, and by her constant wrangling made his life perfectly unbearable, so that one day in a fit of anger he ran away and left them. Shortly afterwards Concubine He gave birth to a son, and called him Danan; but as Xi did not return, the wife Shen turned them out of the house, making them a daily allowance of food. By degrees Danan became a big boy; and his mother, not daring to ask for an increase of victuals, was obliged to earn a little money by spinning. Meanwhile, Danan, seeing all his companions go to school and learn to read, told his mother he should like to go too; and accordingly, as he was still very young, she sent him for a few days' probation. He turned out to be so clever that he soon beat the other boys; at which the master of the school was much pleased, and offered to teach him for nothing.[203] His mother, therefore, sent him regularly, making what trifling presents she could to the master; and by the end of two or three years he had a first-rate knowledge of the Sacred Books.[204] One day

---

203 This is by no means uncommon. The debt of gratitude between pupil and teacher is second only to that existing between child and parent; and a successful student soon has it in his power to more than repay any such act of kindness as that here mentioned.

204 Which form the unvarying curriculum of a Chinese education. These are (1) the Four Books, consisting of the teachings of Confucius and Mencius; and (2) the Five Canons (in the ecclesiastical sense of the word) or the Canons of Changes, History, Poetry, the Record of Rites, and Spring and Autumn.

he came home and asked his mother, saying, "All the fellows at our school get money from their fathers to buy cakes. Why don't I?" "Wait until you are grown up," replied his mother, "and I will explain it to you." "Why, mother," cried he, "I'm only seven or eight years old. What a time it will be before I'm grown up." "Whenever you pass the temple of the God of War on your way to school," said his mother, "you should go in and pray awhile; that would make you grow faster." Danan believed she was serious; and every day, going and coming, he went in and worshipped at that temple. When his mother found this out, she asked him how soon he was praying to be grown up; to which he replied that he only prayed that by the following year he might be as big as if he were fifteen or sixteen years old. His mother laughed; but Danan went on, increasing in wisdom and stature alike, until by the time he was ten he looked quite thirteen or fourteen, and his master was no longer able to correct his essays. Then he said to his mother, "You promised me that when I grew up you would tell me where my father is. Tell me now." "By-and-by, by-and-by," replied his mother; so he waited another year, and then pressed her so eagerly to tell him that she could no longer refuse, and related to him the whole story. He heard her recital with tears and lamentations, and expressed a wish to go in search of his father; but his mother objected that he was too young, and also that no one knew where his father was. Danan said nothing; however, in the middle of the day he did not come home as usual, and his mother at once sent off to the school, where she found he had not shown himself since breakfast. In great alarm, and thinking that he had been playing truant, she paid some people to go and hunt for him everywhere, but was unable to obtain the slightest clue to his whereabouts. As to Danan himself, when he left the house he followed the road without knowing whither he was going, until at length he met a man who was on his way to Kuizhou, and said his name was Qian. Danan begged of him something to eat, and went along with him; Mr. Qian even procuring an animal for him to ride because he walked too slowly. The expenses of the journey were all defrayed by Qian; and when they arrived at Kuizhou they dined together, Qian secretly putting some drug in Danan's food which soon reduced him to a state of unconsciousness. Qian then carried him off to a temple, and, pretending that Danan was his son, offered him to the priests[205] on the plea that he had no money to continue his journey. The priests, seeing what a nice-looking boy he was, were only too ready to buy him; and when Qian had got his money he went

205 See note 122 in tale number 23.

away. They then gave Danan a draught which brought him around; but as soon as the abbot heard of the affair and saw Danan himself, he would not allow them to keep him, sending him away with a purse of money in his pocket. Danan next met a gentleman named Jiang, from Luzhou, who was returning home after having failed at the examination; and this Mr. Jiang was so pleased with the story of his filial piety that he took him to his own home at Luzhou. There he remained for a month and more, asking everybody he saw for news of his father, until one day he was told that there was a man named Xi among the Fujian traders. So he bade goodbye to Mr. Jiang, and set off for Fujian, his patron providing him with clothes and shoes, and the people of the place making up a subscription for him. On the road he met two traders in cotton cloth who were going to Fu Qing, and he joined their party; but they had not traveled many stages before these men found out that he had money, and taking him to a lonely spot, bound him hand and foot and made off with all he had. Before long a Mr. Chen, of Yongfu, happened to pass by, and at once unbound him, and giving him a seat in one of his own vehicles, carried him off home. This Mr. Chen was a wealthy man, and in his house Danan had opportunities of meeting with traders from all quarters. He therefore begged them to aid him by making inquiries about his father, himself remaining as a fellow student with Mr. Chen's sons, and roaming the country no more, neither hearing any news of his former and now distant home.

Meanwhile, his mother, the concubine He, had lived alone for three or four years, until the wife, Shen, wishing to reduce the expenses, tried to persuade her to find another husband. As Concubine He was now supporting herself, she steadfastly refused to do this; and then Shen sold her to a Zhong Qing trader, who took her away with him. However, she so frightened this man by hacking herself about with a knife, that when the wounds were healed he was only too happy to get rid of her to a trader from Yanting, who in his turn, after Concubine He had nearly disembowelled herself, readily listened to her repeated cries that she wished to become a nun. However, he persuaded her to hire herself out as housekeeper to a friend of his, as a means of reimbursing himself for his outlay in purchasing her; but no sooner had she set eyes on the gentleman in question than she found it was her own husband. For Xi had given up the career of a scholar, and gone into business; and as he had no wife, he was consequently in want of a housekeeper. They were very glad to see each other again; and on relating their several adventures, Xi knew for the first time that he had a son who had gone forth in search of his father. Xi then asked all the traders and commercial travelers to keep a look-out for Danan, at the same time raising He from the status of concubine to that of wife. In consequence, however, of the many hardships He had gone through, her health was anything but good, and she was unable to do the work of the house; so she advised her husband to buy a concubine. This he was most unwilling to do, remembering too well the former squabbling he had to endure; but ultimately he yielded, asked a friend to buy for him an oldish woman—at any rate more than thirty years of age. A few months afterwards his friend arrived, bringing with him a person of about that age; and, on looking closely at her, Xi saw that she was no other than his own wife Shen!

Now this lady had lived by herself for a year and more when her brother Bao advised her to marry again, which she accordingly agreed to do. She was prevented, however, by the younger branches of the family from selling the landed property; but she disposed of everything else, and the proceeds passed into her brother's hands. About that time a Baoning trader, hearing that she had plenty of money, bribed her brother to marry her to himself; and afterwards, finding that she was a disagreeable woman, took possession of everything she had, and advertised her for sale. No one caring to buy a woman of her age, and her master being on the eve of starting for Kuizhou, took her with him, finally getting rid of her to Xi, who was in the same line of business as himself. When she stood before; her former husband, she was overwhelmed with shame and fear, and had not a word to say; but Xi gathered an outline of what had happened from the trader, and then said to her, "Your second marriage with this Baoning gentleman was doubtless contracted after you had given up all hope of seeing me again. It doesn't matter in the least, as now I am not in search of a wife but only of a concubine. So you had better begin by paying your respects to your mistress here, my wife He Zhaorong." Shen was ashamed to do this: but Xi reminded her of the time when she had been in the wife's place, and in spite of all He's intercession insisted that she should do so, stimulating her to obedience by the smart application of a stick. Shen was therefore compelled to yield, but at the same time she never tried to gain He's favor, and kept away from her as much as possible. He, on the other hand, treated her with great consideration, and never took her to task on the performance of her duties; whilst Xi himself, whenever he had a dinner-party, made her wait at table, though He often entreated him to hire a maid.

Now the magistrate at Yanting was named Chen Zongsi, and once when Xi had some trifling difficulty with one of the neighbors he was further accused to this official of having forced his wife to assume the position of concubine. The magistrate, however, refused to take up the case, to the great satisfaction of Xi and his wife, who lauded him to the skies as a virtuous mandarin. A few nights after, at rather a late hour, the servant knocked at their door, and called out, "The magistrate has come!" Xi jumped up in a hurry, and began looking for his clothes and shoes; but the magistrate was already in their bedroom without either of them understanding what it all meant: when suddenly He, examining him closely, cried out, "It is my son!" She then burst into tears, and the magistrate, throwing himself on the ground, wept with his mother. It seemed he had taken the name of the gentleman with whom he had lived, and had since entered upon an official career. That on his way to the capital[206] he had made a *détour* and visited his old home, where he heard to his infinite sorrow that both his mothers had married again; and that his relatives, finding him already a man of position, had restored to him the family property, of which he had left some one in charge in the hope that his father might return. That then he had been appointed to Yanting, but had wished to throw up the post and travel in search of his father, from which design he had been dissuaded by Mr. Chen. Also that he had met a fortune-teller from whom he obtained the following response to his inquiries: "The lesser is the greater; the younger is the elder. Seeking the cock, you find the hen; seeking one, you get two. Your official life will be successful." Chen then took up his appointment, but not finding his father he confined himself entirely to a vegetable diet, and gave up the use of wine.[207] The above-mentioned case had subsequently come under his notice, and seeing the name Xi, he quietly sent his private servant to find out, and thus discovered that this Xi was his father. At nightfall he set off himself, and when he saw his mother he knew that the fortune-teller had told him true. Bidding them all say nothing to anybody about what had occurred, he provided money for the journey, and sent them back home. On arriving there, they found the place newly painted, and with their increased retinue of servants and horses, they were quite a wealthy family. As to Shen, when she found what a great man Danan had become, she put still more restraint upon herself: but her brother Bao brought an action for the purpose of reinstating her as wife. The presiding official happened to be a man of probity, and delivered the following judgment: "Greedy of gain, you urged your sister to remarry. After she had driven Xi away, she took two fresh husbands. How have you the face to talk about reinstating her as

---

206 To be presented to the Emperor before taking up his post.
207 Hoping thus to interest Buddha in his behalf.

wife?" He thereupon ordered Bao to be severely bambooed, and from this time there was no longer any doubt about Shen's *status*. She was the lesser and He the greater; and yet in the matter of clothes and food He showed herself by no means grasping. Shen was at first afraid that He would pay her out, and was consequently more than ever repentant; and Xi himself, letting bygones be bygones, gave orders that Shen should be called *madam* by all alike, though of course she was excluded from any titles that might be gained for them by Danan.[208]

42. The Wonderful Stone

IN the prefecture of Shuntian[209] there lived a man named Xing Yunfei, who was an amateur mineralogist and would pay any price for a good specimen. One day as he was fishing in the river, something caught his net, and diving down he brought up a stone about a foot in diameter, beautifully carved on all sides to resemble clustering hills and peaks. He was quite as pleased with this as if he had found some precious stone; and having had an elegant sandal-wood stand made for it, he set his prize upon the table. Whenever it was about to rain, clouds, which from a distance looked like new cotton-wool, would come forth from each of the holes or grottoes on the stone, and appear to close them up. By-and-by an influential personage called at the house and begged to see the stone, immediately seizing it and handing it over to a lusty servant, at the same time whipping his horse and riding away. Xing was in despair; but all he could do was to mourn the loss of his stone, and indulge his anger against the thief. Meanwhile, the servant, who had carried off the stone on his back, stopped to rest at a bridge; when all of a sudden his hand slipped and the stone fell into the water. His master was extremely put out at this, and gave him a sound beating; subsequently hiring several divers, who tried every means in their power to recover the stone, but were quite unable to find it. He then went away, having first published a notice of reward, and by these means many were tempted to seek for the stone. Soon after, Xing himself came to the spot, and as he mournfully approached the bank, lo! the water became clear, and he could

---

208 In accordance with Chinese usage, by which titles of nobility are often conferred upon the *dead* parents of a distinguished son.
209 In which Beijing is situated.

see the stone lying at the bottom. Taking off his clothes, he quickly jumped in and brought it out, together with the sandal-wood stand, which was still with it. He carried it off home, but being no longer desirous of showing it to people, he had an inner room cleaned and put it in there. Some time afterwards an old man knocked at the door and asked to be allowed to see the stone; whereupon Xing replied that he had lost it a long time ago. "Isn't that it in the inner room?" said the old man smiling. "Oh, walk in and see for yourself if you don't believe me," answered Xing; and the old man did walk in, and there was the stone on the table. This took Xing very much aback; and the old man then laid his hand upon the stone and said, "This is an old family relic of mine: I lost it many months since. How does it come to be here? I pray you now restore it to me." Xing didn't know what to say, but declared he was the owner of the stone; upon which the old man remarked, "If it is really yours, what evidence can you bring to prove it?" Xing made no reply; and the old man continued, "To show you that I know this stone, I may mention that it has altogether ninety-two grottoes, and that in the largest of these are five words:

A stone from Heaven above."

Xing looked and found that there were actually some small characters, no larger than grains of rice, which by straining his eyes a little he managed to read; also, that the number of grottoes was as the old man had said. However, he would not give him the stone; and the old man laughed, and asked, "Pray, what right have you to keep other people's things?" He then bowed and went away, Xing escorting him as far as the door; but when he returned to the room, the stone had disappeared. In a great fright, he ran after the old man, who had walked slowly and was not far off, and seizing his sleeve entreated him to give back the stone. "Do you think," said the latter, "that I could conceal a stone a foot in diameter in my sleeve?" But Xing knew that he must be superhuman, and led him back to the house, where he threw himself on his knees and begged that he might have the stone. "Is it yours or mine?" asked the old man. "Of course it is yours," replied Xing, "though I hope you will consent to deny yourself the pleasure of keeping it." "In that case," said the old man, "it is back again;" and going into the inner room, they found the stone in its old place. "The jewels of this world," observed Xing's visitor, "should be given to those who know how to take care of them. This stone can choose its own master, and I am very pleased that it should remain with you; at the same time I must inform you that it was in too great a hurry to come into the world of mortals, and has not yet been freed from all contingent calamities. I had better take it away with me, and three years hence you shall have it again. If, however, you insist on keeping it, then your span of life will be shortened by three years, that your terms of existence may harmonize together. Are you willing?" Xing said he was; whereupon the old man with his fingers closed up three of the stone's grottoes, which yielded to his touch like mud. When this was done, he turned to Xing and told him that the grottoes on that stone represented the years of his life; and then he took his leave, firmly refusing to remain any longer, and not disclosing his name.

More than a year after this, Xing had occasion to go away on business, and in the night a thief broke in and carried off the stone, taking nothing else at all. When Xing came home, he was dreadfully grieved, as if his whole object in life was gone; and made all possible inquiries and efforts to get it back, but without the slightest result. Some time passed away, when one day going into a temple Xing noticed a man selling stones, and amongst the rest he saw his old friend. Of course he immediately wanted to regain possession of it; but as the stone-seller would not consent, he shouldered the stone and went off to the nearest mandarin. The stone-seller was then asked what proof he could give that the stone was his; and he replied that the number of grottoes was eighty-nine. Xing inquired if that was all he had to say, and when the other acknowledged that it was, he himself told the magistrate what were the characters inscribed within, also calling attention to the finger marks at the closed-up grottoes. He therefore gained his case, and the mandarin would have bambooed the stone-seller, had he not declared that he bought it in the market for twenty ounces of silver—whereupon he was dismissed.

A high official next offered Xing one hundred ounces of silver for it; but he refused to sell it even for ten thousand, which so enraged the would-be purchaser that he worked up a case against Xing,[210] and got him put in prison. Xing was thereby compelled to pawn a great deal of his property; and then the official sent someone to try if the affair could not be managed through his son, to which Xing, on hearing of the attempt, steadily refused to consent, saying that he and the stone could not be parted even in death. His wife, however, and his son, laid their heads together, and sent the stone to the high official, and Xing only heard of it when he arrived home from

---

210 A common form of revenge in China, and one which is easily carried through when the prosecutor is a man of wealth and influence.

the prison. He cursed his wife and beat his son, and frequently tried to make away with himself, though luckily his servants always managed to prevent him from succeeding.[211] At night he dreamt that a noble-looking personage appeared to him, and said, "My name is Shi Qingxu—(Stone from Heaven). Do not grieve. I purposely quitted you for a year and more; but next year on the 20th of the eighth moon, at dawn, come to the Haidai Gate and buy me back for two strings of cash." Xing was overjoyed at this dream, and carefully took down the day mentioned. Meanwhile the stone was at the official's private house; but as the cloud manifestations ceased, the stone was less and less prized; and the following year when the official was disgraced for maladministration and subsequently died, Xing met some of his servants at the Haidai Gate going off to sell the stone, and purchased it back from them for two strings of cash.

Xing lived until he was eighty-nine; and then having prepared the necessaries for his interment, bade his son bury the stone with him,[212] which was accordingly done. Six months later robbers broke into the vault[213] and made off with the stone, and his son tried in vain to secure their capture; however, a few days afterwards, he was traveling with his servants, when suddenly two men rushed forth dripping with perspiration, and looking up into the air, acknowledged their crime, saying, "Mr. Xing, please don't torment us thus! We took the stone, and sold it for only four ounces of silver." Xing's son and his servants then seized these men, and took them before the magistrate, where they at once acknowledged their guilt. Asking what had become of the stone, they said they had sold it to a member of the magistrate's family; and when it was produced, that official took such a fancy to it that he gave it to one of his servants and bade him place it in the treasury. Thereupon the stone slipped out of the servant's hand and broke into a hundred pieces, to the great astonishment of all present. The magistrate now had the thieves bambooed and sent them away; but Xing's son picked up the broken pieces of the stone, and buried them in his father's grave.

---

211 Another favorite method of revenging oneself upon an enemy, who is in many cases held responsible for the death thus occasioned. The late Sir C. Alabaster told me an amusing story of a Chinese woman who deliberately walked into a pond until the water reached her knees, and remained there alternately putting her lips below the surface and threatening in a loud voice to drown herself on the spot, as life had been made unbearable by the presence of foreign barbarians. This was during the Taiping rebellion.

212 Valuables of some kind or other are often placed in the coffins of wealthy Chinese; and women are almost always provided with a certain quantity of jewels with which to adorn themselves in the realms below.

213 One of the most heinous offences in the Chinese Penal Code.

43. The Quarrelsome Brothers

AT Kunyang there lived a wealthy man named Zeng. When he died, and before he was put in the coffin, tears were seen to gush forth from both eyes of the corpse, to the infinite amazement of his six sons. His second son, Ti, otherwise called Youyu, who had gained for himself the reputation of being a scholar, said it was a bad omen, and warned his brothers to be careful and not give cause for sorrow to the dead—at which the others only laughed at him as an idiot.

Zeng's first wife and eldest son having been carried off by the rebels when the latter was only seven or eight years old, he married a second wife, by whom he had three sons, Xiao, Zhong, and Xin; besides three other sons by a concubine—namely, the above-mentioned Ti, or Youyu, Ren, and Yi. Now the three by the second wife banded themselves together against the three by the concubine, saying that the latter were a base-born lot; and whenever a guest was present and either of them happened to be in the room, Xiao and his two brothers would not take the slightest notice of them. This enraged Ren and Yi very much, and they went to consult with Youyu as to how they should avenge themselves for such slights. Youyu, however, tried every means in his power to pacify them, and would not take part in any plot; and, as they were much younger than he, they took his advice,[214] and did nothing.

Xiao had a daughter, who died shortly after her marriage to a Mr. Zhou; and her father begged Youyu and his other brothers to go with him and give his late daughter's mother-in-law a sound beating.[215] Youyu would not hear of it for a moment; so Xiao in a rage got his brothers Zhong and Xin, with a lot of rowdies from the neighborhood, and went off and did it themselves, scattering the goods and chattels of the family about, and smashing everything they could lay their hands on. An action was immediately brought by the Zhou family, and Xiao and his two brothers were thrown into prison by the angry mandarin, who purposed sending the case before a higher tribunal. Youyu, however, whose high character was well known to that official, interceded for them, and himself went to the Zhou

---

214 Deference to elder brothers is held by the Chinese to be second only in importance to filial piety.

215 In a volume of *Chinese Sketches*, published by me in 1876, occur (p. 129) the following words: "Occasionally a young wife is driven to commit suicide by the harshness of her mother-in-law, but this is of rare occurrence, as the consequences are terrible to the family of the guilty woman. The blood-relatives of the deceased repair to the chamber of death, and in the injured victim's hand they place a broom. They then support the corpse around the room, making its dead arm move the broom from side to side, and thus sweep away wealth, happiness, and longevity from the accursed place for ever."

family and tendered the most humble apologies for what had occurred. The Zhou family, out of respect for Youyu, suffered the case to drop, and Xiao regained his liberty, though he did not evince the slightest gratitude for his brother's exertions. Shortly after, Youyu's mother died; but Xiao and the other two refused to put on mourning for her, going on with their usual feasting and drinking as if nothing had happened. Ren and Yi were furious at this; but Youyu only observed, "What they do is their own indecorous behavior; it does not injure us." Then, again, when the funeral was about to take place, Xiao, Zhong, and Xin stood before the door of the vault, and would not allow the others to bury their mother there. So Youyu buried her alongside the principal grave. Before long Xiao's wife died, and Youyu told Ren and Yi to accompany him to the house and condole with the widower; to which they both objected, saying, "He would not wear mourning for our mother; shall we do so for his wife?"[216] Ultimately Youyu had to go alone; and while he was pouring forth his lamentations beside the bier, he heard Ren and Yi playing drums and trumpets outside the door. Xiao flew into a tremendous passion, and went after them with his own two brothers to give them a good thrashing. Youyu, too, seized a big stick and accompanied them to the house where Ren and Yi were; whereupon Ren made his escape; but as Yi was clambering over the wall, Youyu hit him from behind and knocked him down. Xiao and the others then set upon him with their fists and sticks, and would never have stopped but that Youyu interposed his body between them and made them desist. Xiao was very angry at this, and began to abuse Youyu, who said, "The punishment was for want of decorum, for which death would be too severe. I can neither connive at their bad behavior, nor at your cruelty. If your anger is not appeased, strike me." Xiao now turned his fury against Youyu, and being well seconded by his two brothers, they beat Youyu until the neighbors separated them and put an end to the row. Youyu at once proceeded to Xiao's house to apologise for what had occurred; but Xiao drove him away, and would not let him take part in the funeral ceremonies. Meanwhile, as Yi's wounds were very severe, and he could neither eat nor drink, his brother Ren went on his behalf to the magistrate, stating in the petition that the accused had not worn mourning for their father's concubine. The magistrate issued a warrant; and, besides causing the arrest of Xiao, Zhong, and Xin, he ordered Youyu to prosecute them as well. Youyu, however, was so much cut about the head and face that he could not appear in court, but he wrote out a petition, in

---

which he begged that the case might be quashed; and this the magistrate consented to do. Yi soon got better, the feeling of hatred and resentment increasing in the family day by day; while Ren and Yi, who were younger than the others, complained to Youyu of their recent punishment, saying, "The relationship of elder and younger brothers exists for others, why not for us?" "Ah," replied Youyu, "that is what I might well say; not you." Youyu then tried to persuade them to forget the past; but, not succeeding in his attempt, he shut up his house, and went off with his wife to live somewhere else, about twenty miles away. Now, although when Youyu was among them he did not help the two younger ones, yet his presence acted as some restraint upon Xiao and the other two; but now that he was gone their conduct was beyond all bounds. They sought out Ren and Yi in their own houses, and not only reviled them, but abused the memory of their dead mother, against which Ren and Yi could only retaliate by keeping the door shut against them. However, they determined to do them some injury, and carried knives about with them wherever they went for that purpose.

One day the eldest brother, Cheng, who had been carried off by the rebels, returned with his wife; and, after three days' deliberation, Xiao and the other two determined that, as he had been so long separated from the family, he had no further claims upon them for house-room, etc. Ren and Yi were secretly delighted at this result, and at once inviting Cheng to stay with them, sent news of his arrival to Youyu, who came back directly, and agreed with the others to hand over a share of the property to their elder brother. Xiao and his clique were much enraged at this purchase of Cheng's goodwill, and, hurrying to their brothers' houses, assailed them with every possible kind of abuse. Cheng, who had long been accustomed to scenes of violence among the rebels, now got into a great passion, and cried out, "When I came home none of you would give me a place to live in. Only these younger ones recognized the ties of blood,[217] and you would punish them for so doing. Do you think to drive me away?" Thereupon he threw a stone at Xiao and knocked him down; and Ren and Yi rushed out with clubs and gave the three of them a severe thrashing. Cheng did not wait for them to lay a plaint, but set off to the magistrate on the spot, and preferred a charge against his three brothers. The magistrate, as before, sent for Youyu to ask his opinion, and Youyu had no alternative but to go, entering the *yamen* with downcast head, his tears flowing in silence all the while. The

217 Literally, of hand and foot, to the mutual dependence of which that of brothers is frequently likened by the Chinese.

magistrate inquired of him how the matter stood; to which he replied only by begging His Honor to hear the case; which the magistrate accordingly did, deciding that the whole of the property was to be divided equally among the seven brothers. Thenceforth Ren and Yi became more and more attached to Cheng; and one day, in conversation, they happened to tell him the story of their mother's funeral. Cheng was exceedingly angry, and declared that such behavior was that of brute beasts, proposing at the same time that the vault should be opened and that she should be re-buried in the proper place. Ren and Yi went off and told this to Youyu, who immediately came and begged Cheng to desist from his scheme; to which, however, he paid no attention, and fixed a day for her interment in the family vault. He then built a hut near by, and, with a knife lopping the branches off the trees, informed the brothers that any of them who did not appear at the funeral in the usual mourning would be treated by him in a manner similar to the trees. So they were all obliged to go, and the obsequies were conducted in a fitting manner. The brothers were now at peace together, Cheng keeping them in first-rate order, and always treating Xiao, Zhong, and Xin with much more severity than the others. To Youyu he showed a marked deference, and, whenever he was in a rage, would always be appeased by a word from him. Xiao, too, was always going to Youyu to complain of the treatment he received at Zheng's hands when he did anything that Cheng disapproved of; and then, if Youyu quietly reproved him, he would be dissatisfied, so that at last Youyu could stand it no longer, and again went away and took a `house at a considerable distance, where he remained almost entirely cut off from the others. By the time two years had passed away Cheng had completely succeeded in establishing harmony amongst them, and quarrels were of rare occurrence. Xiao was then forty-six years old, and had five sons; Jiye and Jide, the first and third, by his wife; Jigong and Jiji, the second and fourth, by a concubine; and Jizu, by a slave. They were all grown up, and exactly imitated their father's former behavior, banding themselves together one against the other, and so on, without their father being able to make them behave better. Jizu had no brothers of his own, and, being the youngest, the others bullied him dreadfully; until at length, being on a visit to his wife's family, who lived not far from Youyu's house, he went slightly out of his way to call and see his uncle. There he found his three cousins living peaceably together and pursuing their studies, and was so pleased that he remained with them some time, and said not a word as to returning home. His uncle urged him to go back, but he entreated to be allowed to stay; and then his uncle told him it was not that he grudged his daily food: it was because his father and mother did not know where he was. Jizu accordingly went home, and a few months afterwards, when he and his wife were on the point of starting to congratulate his wife's mother on the anniversary of her birthday, he explained to his father that he should not come home again. When his father asked him why not, he partly divulged his reasons for going; whereupon his father said he was afraid his uncle would bear malice for what happened in the past, and that he would not be able to remain there long. "Father," replied Jizu, "uncle Youyu is a good and virtuous man." He set out with his wife, and when they arrived Youyu gave them separate quarters, and made Jizu rank as one of his own sons, making him join the eldest, Jisan, in his studies. Jizu was a clever fellow, and now enrolled himself as a resident of the place where his uncle lived.[218]

Meanwhile, his brothers went on quarrelling among themselves as usual; and one day Jigong, enraged at an insult offered to his mother, killed Jiye. He was immediately thrown into prison, where he was severely bambooed, and in a few days he died. Jiye's wife, whose maiden name was Feng, now spent the days of mourning in cursing her husband's murderer; and when Jigong's wife heard this, she flew into a towering passion, and said to her, "If your husband is dead, mine isn't alive." She then drew a knife and killed her, completing the tragedy by herself committing suicide in a well.

Mr. Feng, the father of the murdered woman, was very much distressed at his daughter's untimely end; and, taking with him several members of the family with arms concealed under their clothes, they proceeded to Xiao's house, and there gave his wife a most terrific beating. It was now Cheng's turn to be angry. "The members of my family are dying like sheep," cried he; "what do you mean by this, Mr. Feng?" He then rushed out upon them with a roar, accompanied by all his own brothers and their sons; and the Feng family was utterly routed. Seizing old Feng himself, Cheng cut off both his ears; and when his son tried to rescue him, Jiji ran up and broke both his legs with an iron crowbar. Every one of the Feng family was badly wounded, and thus dispersed, leaving old Feng's son lying in the middle of the road. The others not knowing what to do with him, Cheng took him under his arm, and having thrown him down in the Feng village, returned home, giving orders to Jiji to go immediately to the authorities and enter their plaint the first.[219]

---

218 Any permanent change of residence must be notified to the District Magistrate, who keeps a running census of all persons within his jurisdiction.

219 To be thus beforehand with one's adversary is regarded as *prima facie* evidence of being in the right.

The Feng family had, however, anticipated them, and all the Zengs were accordingly thrown into prison, except Zhong, who managed to escape. He ran away to the place where Youyu lived, and was pacing backwards and forwards before the door, afraid lest his brother should not have forgiven past offences, when suddenly Youyu, with his son and nephew, arrived on their return from the examination. "What do you want, my brother?" asked Youyu; whereupon Zhong prostrated himself at the roadside, and then Youyu, seizing his hand, led him within to make further inquiries. "Alas! alas!" cried Youyu, when he had heard the story, "I knew that some dreadful calamity would be the result of all this wicked behavior. But why have you come hither? I have been absent so long that I am no more acquainted with the local authorities; and if I now went to ask a favor of them, I should probably only be insulted for my pains. However, if none of the Feng family die of their wounds, and if we three may chance to be successful in our examination, something may perhaps be done to mitigate this calamity."[220] Youyu then kept Zhong to dinner, and at night he shared their room, which kind treatment made him at once grateful and repentant. By the end of ten days he was so struck with the behavior of the father, sons, uncle, nephew, and cousins, one towards the other, that he burst into tears, and said, "Now I know how badly I behaved in days gone by." His brother was overjoyed at his repentance, and sympathized with his feelings, when suddenly it was announced that Youyu and his son had both passed the examination for master's degree, and that Jizu was *proxime accessit*. This delighted them all very much. They did not, however, attend the *Fu Tai's* congratulatory feast,[221] but went off first to worship at the tombs of their ancestors.

Now, at the time of the Ming dynasty a man who had taken his master's degree was a very considerable personage,[222] and the Fengs accordingly began to draw in their horns. Youyu, too, met them half-way. He got a friend to convey to them presents of food and money to help them in recovering from their injuries, and thus the prosecution was withdrawn. Then all his brothers implored him with tears in their eyes to return home, and, after burning incense with them,[223] and making them enter into a bond with

---

220 By means of the *status* which a graduate of the second degree would necessarily have.

221 A sham entertainment given by the *Fu Tai*, or governor, to all the successful candidates. I say *sham*, because the whole thing is merely nominal; a certain amount of food is contracted for, but there is never anything fit to eat, most of the money being embezzled by the underlings to whose management the banquet is entrusted.

222 Much more so than at present.

223 Thereby invoking the Gods as witnesses. A common method of making up a quarrel in China is to send the aggrieved party an olive and a piece of red paper in token that peace is restored. Why the *olive*

him that bygones should be bygones, he acceded to their request. Jizu, however, would not leave his uncle; and Xiao himself said to Youyu, "I don't deserve such a son as that. Keep him, and teach him as you have done hitherto, and let him be as one of your own children; but if at some future time he succeeds in his examination, then I will beg you to return him to me." Youyu consented to this; and three years afterwards Jizu did take his master's degree, upon which he sent him back to his own family.

Both husband and wife were very loath to leave their uncle's house, and they had hardly been at home three days before one of their children, only three years old, ran away and went back, returning to his great-uncle's as often as he was recaptured. This induced Xiao to remove to the next house to Youyu's, and, by opening a door between the two, they made one establishment of the whole. Cheng was now getting old, and the family affairs devolved entirely upon Youyu, who managed things so well that their reputation for filial piety and fraternal love was soon spread far and wide.

44. The Young Gentleman Who Couldn't Spell[224]

AT Jiaping there lived a certain young gentleman of considerable talent and very prepossessing appearance. When seventeen years of age he went up for his bachelor's degree; and as he was passing the door of a house, he saw within a pretty-looking girl, who not only riveted his gaze, but also smiled and nodded her head at him. Quite pleased at this, he approached the young lady and began to talk, she, meanwhile, inquiring of him where he lived, and if alone or otherwise. He assured her he was quite by himself; and then she said, "Well, I will come and see you, but you mustn't let any one know." The young, gentleman agreed, and when he got home he sent all the servants to another part of the house, and by-and-by the young lady arrived. She said her name was Wenji, and that her admiration for her host's noble bearing had made her visit him, unknown to her mistress. "And gladly," added she, "would I be your handmaid for life." Our hero was delighted, and proposed to purchase her from the mistress she mentioned; and from this time she was in the habit of coming in every other day or so.

---

should be specially employed I have in vain tried to ascertain.
224 Of course there is no such thing as spelling, in our sense of the term, in Chinese. But characters are frequently written with too many or too few strokes, and may thus be said to be incorrectly spelt.

On one occasion it was raining hard, and, after hanging up her wet cloak upon a peg, she took off her shoes, and bade the young gentleman clean them for her. He noticed that they were newly embroidered with all the colors of the rainbow, but utterly spoilt by the soaking rain; and was just saying what a pity it was, when the young lady cried out, "I should never have asked you to do such menial work except to show my love for you." All this time the rain was falling fast outside, and Wenji now repeated the following line:

A nipping wind and chilly rain fill the river and the city.

"There," said she, "cap that." The young gentleman replied that he could not, as he did not even understand what it meant. "Oh, really," retorted the young lady, "if you're not more of a scholar than that, I shall begin to think very little of you." She then told him he had better practice making verses, and he promised he would do so.

By degrees Miss Wenji's frequent visits attracted the notice of the servants, as also of a brother-in-law named Song, who was likewise a gentleman of position; and the latter begged our hero to be allowed to have a peep at her. He was told in reply that the young lady had strictly forbidden that any one should see her; however, he concealed himself in the servants' quarters, and when she arrived he looked at her through the window. Almost beside himself, he now opened the door; whereupon Wenji, jumping up, vaulted over the wall and disappeared. Song was really smitten with her, and went off to her mistress to try and arrange for her purchase; but when he mentioned Wenji's name, he was informed that they had once had such a girl, who had died several years previously. In great amazement Song went back and told his brother-in-law, and he now knew that his beloved Wenji was a disembodied spirit. So when she came again he asked her if it was so; to which she replied, "It is; but as you wanted a nice wife and I a handsome husband, I thought we should be a suitable pair. What matters it that one is a mortal and the other a spirit?" The young gentleman thoroughly coincided in her view of the case; and when his examination was over, and he was homeward bound, Wenji accompanied him, invisible to others and visible to him alone. Arriving at his parents' house, he installed her in the library; and the day she went to pay the customary bride's visit to her father and mother,[225] he told his own mother the whole story. She

---

225 A ceremonial visit made on the third day after marriage.

and his father were greatly alarmed, and ordered him to have no more to do with her; but he would not listen to this, and then his parents tried by all kinds of devices to get rid of the girl, none of which met with any success. One day our hero had left upon the table some written instructions for one of the servants, wherein he had made a number of mistakes in spelling, such as *paper* for *pepper, jinjer* for *ginger,* and so on; and when Wenji saw this, she wrote at the foot:

Paper for pepper do I see?
Jinjer for ginger—can it be?
Of such a husband I'm afraid;
I'd rather be a servant-maid.

She then said to the young gentleman, "Imagining you to be a man of culture, I hid my blushes and sought you out the first.[226] Alas, your qualifications are on the outside; should I not thus be a laughing-stock to all?" She then disappeared, at which the young gentleman was much hurt; but not knowing to what she alluded, he gave the instructions to his servant, and so made himself the butt of all who heard the story.

45. The Tiger Guest

A YOUNG man named Gong, a native of Minzhou, on his way to the examination at Xi'an, rested a while in an inn, and ordered some wine to drink. Just then a very tall and noble-looking stranger walked in, and, seating himself by the side of Gong, entered into conversation with him. Gong offered him a cup of wine, which the stranger did not refuse; saying, at the same time, that his name was Miao. But he was a rough, coarse fellow; and Gong, therefore, when the wine was finished, did not call for any more. Miao then rose, and observing that Gong did not appreciate a man of his capacity, went out into the market to buy some, returning shortly with a huge bowl full. Gong declined the proffered wine; but Miao, seizing his arm to persuade him, gripped it so painfully that Gong was forced to drink a few more cups, Miao himself swilling away as hard as he could go out of a soup-plate, "I am not good at entertaining people," cried

---

226 Contrary to all Chinese notions of modesty and etiquette.

Miao, at length; "pray go on or stop just as you please." Gong accordingly put together his things and went off; but he had not gone more than a few miles when his horse was taken ill, and lay down in the road. While he was waiting there with all his heavy baggage, revolving in his mind what he should do, up came Mr. Miao; who, when he heard what was the matter, took off his coat and handed it to the servant, and lifting up the horse, carried it off on his back to the nearest inn, which was about six or seven miles distant. Arriving there he put the animal in the stable, and before long Gong and his servant arrived too. Gong was much astonished at Mr. Miao's feat; and, believing him to be superhuman, began to treat him with the utmost deference, ordering both wine and food to be procured for their refreshment. "My appetite," remarked Miao, "is one that you could not easily satisfy. Let us stick to wine." So they finished another stoup together, and then Miao got up and took his leave, saying, "It will be some time before your horse is well; I cannot wait for you." He then went away.

After the examination several friends of Gong's invited him to join them in a picnic to the Flowery Hill; and just as they were all feasting and laughing together, lo! Mr. Miao walked up. In one hand he held a large flagon, and in the other a ham, both of which he laid down on the ground before them. "Hearing," said he, "that you gentlemen were coming here, I have tacked myself on to you, like a fly to a horse's tail."[227] Gong and his friends then rose and received him with the usual ceremonies, after which they all sat down promiscuously.[228] By-and-by, when the wine had gone around pretty freely, someone proposed capping verses; whereupon Miao cried out, "Oh, we're very jolly drinking like this; what's the use of making oneself uncomfortable?" The others, however, would not listen to him, and agreed that as a forfeit a huge goblet of wine should be drunk by any defaulter. "Let us rather make death the penalty," said Miao; to which they replied, laughing, that such a punishment was a trifle too severe; and then Miao retorted that if it was not to be death, even a rough fellow like himself might be able to join. A Mr. Jin, who was sitting at the top of the

---

227 Alluding to a well-known expression which occurs in the *Historical Record,* and is often used in the sense of deriving advantage from connection with some influential person.

228 Without any regard to precedence, which plays quite as important a part at a Chinese as at a Western dinner-party. In China, however, the most honored guest sits at (what may be called) the head of the table, the host at the foot: I say "what may be called," as Chinese dining tables are almost invariably square, and position alone determines which is the head and which the foot. They are usually made to accommodate eight persons; hence the fancy name "eight-angel table," in allusion to the eight famous angels, or Immortals, of the Taoist religion. (See note 13 in tale number 5.) Occasionally, round tables are used; especially in cases where the party consists of some such number as ten.

line, then began:

From the hill-top high, wide extends the gaze—

upon which Miao immediately carried on with:

Redly gleams the sword o'er the shattered vase.[229]

The next gentleman thought for a long time, during which Miao was helping himself to wine; and by-and-by they had all capped the verse, but so wretchedly that Miao called out, "Oh, come! if we aren't to be fined for these,[230] we had better abstain from making any more." As none of them would agree to this, Miao could stand it no longer, and roared like a dragon until the hills and valleys echoed again. He then went down on his hands and knees, and jumped about like a lion, which utterly confused the poets, and put an end to their lucubrations. The wine had now been around a good many times, and being half tipsy each began to repeat to the other the verses he had handed in at the recent examination,[231] all at the same time indulging in any amount of mutual flattery. This so disgusted Miao that he drew Gong aside to have a game at "guess-fingers;"[232] but as they went on droning away all the same, he at length cried out, "Do stop your rubbish, fit only for your own wives,[233] and not for general company." The others were much abashed at this, and so angry were they at Miao's rudeness that they went on repeating all the louder. Miao then threw himself on the ground in a passion, and with a roar changed into a tiger, immediately springing upon

---

229 It is almost impossible to give in translation the true spirit of a Chinese antithetical couplet. There are so many points to be brought out, each word of the second line being in opposition both in tone and sense to a corresponding word in the first, that anything beyond a rough rendering of the idea conveyed would be superfluous in a work like this. Suffice it to say that Miao has here successfully capped the verse given; and the more so because he has introduced, through the medium of "sword" and "shattered vase," an allusion to a classical story in which a certain Wang Tun, when drunk with wine, beat time on a vase with his sword, and smashed the lip.

230 This is the *vel ego vel Cluvienus* style of sarcasm, his own verse having been particularly good.

231 Many candidates, successful or otherwise, have their verses and essays printed, and circulate them among an admiring circle of friends.

232 Accurately described in Tylor's *Primitive Culture*, Vol. I., p. 75:— "Each player throws out a hand, and the sum of all the fingers shown has to be called, the successful caller scoring a point; practically each calls the total before he sees his adversary's hand." The insertion of the word "simultaneously" after "called" would improve this description. This game is so noisy that the Hong kong authorities have forbidden it, except within certain authorized limits, between the hours of 11 p.m. and 6 a.m.—Ordinance No. 2 of 1872.

233 This delicate stroke is of itself sufficient to prove the truth of the oft-quoted Chinese saying, that all between the Four Seas are brothers.

the company, and killing them all except Gong and Mr. Jin. He then ran off roaring loudly. Now this Mr. Jin succeeded in taking his master's degree; and three years afterwards, happening to revisit the Flowery Hill, he beheld a Mr. Ji, one of those very gentlemen who had previously been killed by the tiger. In great alarm he was making off, when Ji seized his bridle and would not let him proceed. So he got down from his horse, and inquired what was the matter; to which Ji replied, "I am now the slave of Miao, and have to endure bitter toil for him. He must kill someone else before I can be set free.[234] Three days hence a man, arrayed in the robes and cap of a scholar, should be eaten by the tiger at the foot of the Canglong Hill. Do you on that day take some gentleman thither, and thus help your old friend." Jin was too frightened to say much, but promising that he would do so, rode away home. He then began to consider the matter over with himself, and, regarding it as a plot, he determined to break his engagement, and let his friend remain the tiger's devil. He chanced, however, to repeat the story to a Mr. Jiang who was a relative of his, and one of the local scholars; and as this gentleman had a grudge against another scholar, named You, who had come out equal with him at the examination, he made up his mind to destroy him. So he invited You to accompany him on that day to the place in question, mentioning that he himself should appear in undress only. You could not make out the reason for this; but when he reached the spot there he found all kinds of wine and food ready for his entertainment. Now that very day the Prefect had come to the hill; and being a friend of the Jiang family, and hearing that Jiang was below, sent for him to come up. Jiang did not dare to appear before him in undress, and borrowed You's clothes and hat; but he had no sooner got them on than out rushed the tiger and carried him away in its mouth.

46. The Sisters

HIS EXCELLENCY the Grand Secretary Mao came from an obscure family in the district of Ye, his father being only a poor cow-herd. At the same place there resided a wealthy gentleman, named Zhang, who owned a burial-

---

234 The "substitution" theory, by which disembodied spirits are enabled to find their way back to the world of mortals. A very interesting and important example of this belief occurs in a later story (No. 106.), for which place I reserve further comments.

ground in the neighborhood; and someone informed him that while passing by he had heard sounds of wrangling from within the grave, and voices saying, "Make haste and go away; do not disturb His Excellency's home." Zhang did not much believe this; but subsequently he had several dreams in which he was told that the burial-ground in question really belonged to the Mao family, and that he had no right whatever to it. From this moment the affairs of his house began to go wrong;[235] and at length he listened to the remonstrances of friends and removed his dead elsewhere.

One day Mao's father, the cow-herd, was out near this burial-ground, when, a storm of rain coming on, he took refuge in the now empty grave, while the rain came down harder than ever, and by-and-by flooded the whole place and drowned the old man. The Grand Secretary was then a mere boy, and his mother went off to Zhang to beg a piece of ground wherein to bury her dead husband. When Zhang heard her name he was greatly astonished; and on going to look at the spot where the old man was drowned, found that it was exactly at the proper place for the coffin. More than ever amazed, he gave orders that the body should be buried there in the old grave, and also bade Mao's mother bring her son to see him. When the funeral was over, she went with Mao to Mr. Zhang's house, to thank him for his kindness; and so pleased was he with the boy that he kept him to be educated, ranking him as one of his own sons. He also said he would give him his eldest daughter as a wife, an offer which Mao's mother hardly dared accept; but Mrs. Zhang said that the thing was settled and couldn't be altered, so then she was obliged to consent. The young lady, however, had a great contempt for Mao, and made no effort to disguise her feelings; and if any one spoke to her of him, she would put her fingers in her ears, declaring she would die sooner than marry the cow-boy. On the day appointed for the wedding, the bridegroom arrived, and was feasted within, while outside the door a handsome chair was in waiting to convey away the bride, who all this time was standing crying in a corner, wiping her eyes with her sleeve, and absolutely refusing to dress. Just then the bridegroom sent in to say he was going,[236] and the drums and trumpets struck up the wedding march, at which the bride's tears only fell the faster as her hair hung dishevelled down

235 Such is the dominant belief regarding the due selection of an auspicious site, whether for a house or grave; and with this superstition deeply ingrained in the minds of the people, it is easy to understand the hold on the public mind possessed by the pseudo-scientific professors of *fengshui*, or the geomantic art.

236 The bridegroom leads off the procession, and the bride follows shortly afterwards in an elaborately-gilt sedan-chair, closed in on all sides so that the occupant cannot be seen.

her back. Her father managed to detain Mao awhile, and went in to urge his daughter to make haste, she weeping bitterly as if she did not hear what he was saying. He now got into a rage, which only made her cry the louder; and in the middle of it all a servant came to say the bridegroom wished to take his leave. The father ran out and said his daughter wasn't quite ready, begging Mao to wait a little longer; and then hurried back again to the bride. Thus they went on for some time, backwards and forwards, until at last things began to look serious, for the young lady obstinately refused to yield; and Mr. Zhang was ready to commit suicide for want of anything better. Just then his second daughter was standing by upbraiding her elder sister for her disobedience, when suddenly the latter turned around in a rage, and cried out, "So you are imitating the rest of them, you little minx; why don't you go and marry him yourself?" "My father did not betroth me to Mr. Mao," answered she, "but if he had I should not require you to persuade me to accept him." Her father was delighted with this reply, and at once went off and consulted with his wife as to whether they could venture to substitute the second for the elder; and then her mother came and said to her, "That bad girl there won't obey her parents' commands; we wish, therefore, to put you in her place: will you consent to this arrangement?" The younger sister readily agreed, saying that had they told her to marry a beggar she would not have dared to refuse, and that she had not such a low opinion of Mr. Mao as all that. Her father and mother rejoiced exceedingly at receiving this reply; and dressing her up in her sister's clothes, put her in the bridal chair and sent her off. She proved an excellent wife, and lived in harmony with her husband; but she was troubled with a disease of the hair, which caused Mr. Mao some annoyance. Later on, she told him how she had changed places with her sister, and this made him think more highly of her than before. Soon after Mao took his bachelor's degree, and then set off to present himself as a candidate for the master's degree. On the way he passed by an inn, the landlord of which had dreamt the night before that a spirit appeared to him and said, "Tomorrow Mr. Mao, first on the list, will come. Some day he will extricate you from a difficulty." Accordingly the landlord got up early, and took especial note of all guests who came from the eastward, until at last Mao himself arrived. The landlord was very glad to see him, and provided him with the best of everything, refusing to take any payment for it all, but telling what he had dreamt the night before. Mao now began to give himself airs; and, reflecting that his wife's want of hair would make him look ridiculous, he determined that so soon as he attained to rank and power he would find another spouse. But alas! when the list of successful candidates was published, Mao's name was not among them; and he retraced his steps with a heavy heart, and by another road, so as to avoid meeting the innkeeper. Three years afterwards he went up again, and the landlord received him with precisely the same attentions as on the previous occasion; upon which Mao said to him, "Your former words did not come true; I am now ashamed to put you to so much trouble." "Ah," replied the landlord, "you meant to get rid of your wife, and the Ruler of the world below struck out your name.[237] My dream couldn't have been false." In great astonishment, Mao asked what he meant by these words; and then he learnt that after his departure the landlord had had a second dream informing him of the above facts. Mao was much alarmed at what he heard, and remained as motionless as a wooden image, until the landlord said to him, "You, Sir, as a scholar, should have more self-respect, and you will certainly take the highest place." By-and-by when the list came out, Mao was the first of all; and almost simultaneously his wife's hair began to grow quite thick, making her much better-looking than she had hitherto been.

Now her elder sister had married a rich young fellow of good family, who lived in the neighborhood, which made the young lady more contemptuous than ever; but he was so extravagant and so idle that their property was soon gone, and they were positively in want of food. Hearing, too, of Mr. Mao's success at the examination, she was overwhelmed with shame and vexation, and avoided even meeting her sister in the street. Just then her husband died and left her destitute; and about the same time Mao took his doctor's degree, which so aggravated her feelings that, in a passion, she became a nun. Subsequently, when Mao rose to be a high officer of state, she sent a novice to his *yamen* to try and get a subscription out of him for the temple; and Mao's wife, who gave several pieces of silk and other things, secretly inserted a sum of money among them. The novice, not knowing this, reported what she had received to the elder sister, who cried out in a passion, "I wanted money to buy food with; of what use are these things to me?" So she bade the novice take them back; and when Mao and his wife saw her return, they suspected what had happened, and opening the parcel found the money still there. They now understood why the presents had been refused; and taking the money, Mao said to the novice, "If one hundred ounces of silver is too much luck for your mistress to secure, of course she could never have secured a high official, such as I am now, for her

---

237 Here again we have the common Chinese belief that fate is fate only within certain limits, and is always liable to be altered at the will of heaven.

husband." He then took fifty ounces, and giving them to the novice, sent her away, adding, "Hand this to your mistress; I'm afraid more would be too much for her."[238] The novice returned and repeated all that had been said; and then the elder sister sighed to think what a failure her life had been, and how she had rejected the worthy to accept the worthless. After this, the innkeeper got into trouble about a case of murder, and was imprisoned; but Mao exerted his influence, and obtained the man's pardon.

47. Foreign[239] Priests

THE Buddhist priest, Ti Kong, relates that when he was at Qingzhou he saw two foreign priests of very extraordinary appearance. They wore rings in their ears, were dressed in yellow cloth, and had curly hair and beards. They said they had come from the countries of the west; and hearing that the Governor of the district was a devoted follower of Buddha, they went to visit him. The Governor sent a couple of servants to escort them to the monastery of the place, where the abbot, Lingpei, did not receive them very cordially; but the secular manager, seeing that they were not ordinary individuals, entertained them and kept them there for the night. Someone asked if there were many strange men in the west, and what magical arts were practiced by the Lohans;[240] whereupon one of them laughed, and putting forth his hand from his sleeve, showed a small pagoda, fully a foot in height, and beautifully carved, standing upon the palm. Now very high up in the wall there was a niche; and the priest threw the pagoda up to it, when lo! it stood there firm and straight. After a few moments the pagoda began to incline to one side, and a glory, as from a relic of some saint, was diffused throughout the room. The other priest then bared his arms and stretched out his left until it was five or six feet in length, at the same time shortening his right arm until it dwindled to nothing. He then stretched out the latter until it was as long as his left arm.

---

238 This is another curious phase of Chinese superstition, namely, that each individual is so constituted by nature as to be able to absorb only a given quantity of good fortune and no more, any superfluity of luck doing actual harm to the person on whom it falls.
239 The word here used is *fan*, generally translated "barbarian."
240 The disciples of Shakyamuni Buddha. Same as *Arkans*.

48. The Self-Punished Murderer

MR. LI was a *juren* of Yongnian.[241] On the 28th of the 9th moon of the 4th year of Kang Xi,[242] he killed his wife. The neighbors reported the murder to the officials, and the high authorities instructed the district magistrate to investigate the case. At this juncture Mr. Li was standing at the door of his residence; and snatching a butcher's knife from a stall hard by, he rushed into the Cheng-huang[243] temple, where, mounting the theatrical stage,[244] he threw himself on his knees, and spoke as follows: "The spirit here will punish me. I am not to be prosecuted by evil men who, from party motives, confuse right and wrong. The spirit moves me to cut off an ear." Thereupon he cut off his left ear and threw it down from the stage. He then said the spirit was going to fine him a hand for cheating people, out of their money; and he forthwith chopped off his left hand. Lastly, he cried out that he was to be punished severely for all his many crimes; and immediately cut his own throat. The Viceroy subsequently received the Imperial permission to deprive him of his rank[245] and bring him to trial; but he was then being punished by a higher power in the realms of darkness below. See the *Peking Gazette*.[246]

49. The Master Thief

BEFORE his rebellion,[247] Prince Wu frequently told his soldiers that if any one of them could catch a tiger unaided he would give him a handsome pension and the title of the Tiger Daunter. In his camp there was a man named Baozhu, as strong and agile as a monkey; and once when a new tower was being built, the wooden framework having only just been set up, Baozhu walked along the eaves, and finally got up on the very tip-top beam, where he ran backwards and forwards several times. He then jumped down, alighting safely on his feet.

---

241 In the province of zhili. "*Juren*" = second or master's degree.

242 In 1665, that is between fourteen and fifteen years previous to the completion of the *Liao Chat*.

243 See note 1 in tale number 1.

244 Religion and the drama work hand in hand in China.

245 Always the first step in the prosecution of a graduate. In this case, the accused was also an official.

246 Of what date, our author does not say, or it would be curious to try and hunt up the official record of this case as it appeared in the Government organ of the day. The unfortunate man was in all probability insane.

247 1675 CE. His full name was Wu Sangui.

Now Prince Wu had a favorite concubine, who was a skillful player on the guitar; and the nuts of the instrument she used were of warm jade,[248] so that when played upon there was a general feeling of warmth throughout the room. The young lady was extremely careful of this treasure, and never produced it for anyone to see unless on receipt of the Prince's written order. One night, in the middle of a banquet, a guest begged to be allowed to see this wonderful guitar; but the Prince, being in a lazy mood, said it should be exhibited to him on the following day. Baozhu, who was standing by, then observed that he could get it without troubling the Prince to write an order. Someone was therefore sent off beforehand to instruct all the officials to be on the watch, and then the Prince told Baozhu he might go; and after scaling numerous walls the latter found himself near the lady's room. Lamps were burning brightly within; the doors were bolted and barred, and it was impossible to effect an entrance. Under the verandah, however, was a cockatoo fast asleep on its perch; and Baozhu, first mewing several times like a cat, followed it up by imitating the voice of the bird, and cried out as though in distress, "The cat! the cat!" He then heard the concubine call to one of the slave girls, and bid her go rescue the cockatoo, which was being killed; and, hiding himself in a dark corner, he saw a girl come forth with a light in her hand. She had barely got outside the door when he rushed in, and there he saw the lady sitting with the guitar on a table before her. Seizing the instrument he turned and fled; upon which the concubine shrieked out "Thieves! thieves!" And the guard, seeing a man making off with the guitar, at once started in pursuit. Arrows fell around Baozhu like drops of rain, but he climbed up one of a number of huge ash trees growing there, and from its top leaped onto the top of the next, and so on, until he had reached the furthermost tree, when he jumped on to the roof of a house, and from that to another, more as if he were flying than anything else. In a few minutes he had disappeared, and before long presented himself suddenly at the banquet-table with the guitar in his hand, the entrance-gate having been securely barred all the time, and not a dog or a cock aroused.

---

248 Such is the literal translation of a term which I presume to be the name of some particular kind of jade, which is ordinarily distinguished from the imitation article by its comparative *coldness*.

50. A Flood

IN the twenty-first year of Kang Xi[249] there was a severe drought, not a
green blade appearing in the parched ground all through the spring and
well into the summer. On the 13th of the 6th moon a little rain fell, and
people began to plant their rice. On the 18th there was a heavy fall, and
beans were sown.

Now at a certain village there was an old man, who, noticing two
bullocks fighting on the hills, told the villagers that a great flood was at
hand, and forthwith removed with his family to another part of the country.
The villagers all laughed at him; but before very long rain began to fall
in torrents, lasting all through the night, until the water was several feet
deep, and carrying away the houses. Among the others was a man, who,
neglecting to save his two children, with his wife assisted his aged mother to
reach a place of safety, from which they looked down at their old home, now
only an expanse of water, without hope of ever seeing the children again.
When the flood had subsided, they went back, to find the whole place a
complete ruin; but in their own house they discovered the two boys playing
and laughing on the bed as if nothing had happened. Someone remarked
that this was a reward for the filial piety of the parents. It happened on the
20th of the 6th moon.[250]

51. Death by Laughing

A MR. SUN JINGXIA, a Director of Studies, told me that in his village there
was a certain man who had been killed by the rebels when they passed
through the place. The man's head was left hanging down on his chest;
and as soon as the rebels had gone, his servants secured the body and were
about to bury it. Hearing, however, a sound of breathing, they looked more
closely, and found that the windpipe was not wholly severed; and, setting
his head in its proper place, they carried him back home. In twenty-four

249 1682 CE; that is, three years after the date of our author's preface. See *Introduction*.
250 A curious note here follows in the original: "In 1696 a severe earthquake occurred at Pingyang,
and seven or eight out of every ten of the inhabitants were killed, the city and suburbs were utterly destroyed, only one house remaining uninjured—a house inhabited by a filial son. And thus, when in the
crash of a collapsing universe, filial piety is specially marked out for protection, who shall say that God
Almighty does not know black from white?"

hours he began to moan; and by dint of carefully feeding him with a spoon, within six months he had quite recovered.

Some ten years afterwards he was chatting with a few friends, when one of them made a joke which called forth loud applause from the others. Our hero, too, clapped his hands; but, as he was bending backwards and forwards with laughter, the seam on his neck split open, and down fell his head with a gush of blood. His friends now found that he was quite dead, and his father immediately commenced an action against the joker;[251] but a sum of money was subscribed by those present and given to the father, who buried his son and stopped further proceedings.

52. Playing at Hanging

A NUMBER of wild young fellows were one day out walking when they saw a young lady approach, riding on a pony.[252] One of them said to the others, "I'll back myself to make that girl laugh," and a supper was at once staked by both sides on the result. Our hero then ran out in front of the pony, and kept on shouting "I'm going to die! I'm going to die!" at the same time pulling out from over the top of a wall a stalk of millet, to which he attached his own waistband, and, tying the latter around his neck, made a pretence of hanging himself. The young lady did laugh as she passed by, to the great amusement of the assembled company; but as when she was already some distance off their friend did not move, the others laughed louder than ever. However, on going up to him they saw that his tongue protruded, and that his eyes were glazed; he was, in fact, quite dead. Was it not strange that a man should be able to hang himself on a millet stalk?[253] It is a good warning against practical joking.

---

251 The Chinese distinguish five degrees of homicide, of which accidental homicide is one (see *Penal Code*, Book VI.). Thus, if a gun goes off of itself in a man's hand and kills a bystander, the holder of the gun is guilty of homicide; but were the same gun lying on a table, it would be regarded as the will of Heaven. Similarly, a man is held responsible for any death caused by an animal belonging to him; though in such cases the affair can usually be hushed up by a money payment, no notice being taken of crimes in general unless at the instigation of a prosecutor, at whose will the case may be subsequently withdrawn. Where the circumstances are purely accidental, the law admits of a money compensation.
252 Women in China ride astride.
253 Which, although tolerably stout and strong, is hardly capable of sustaining a man's weight.

53. The Rat Wife

Xi SHAN was a native of Gaomi, and a trader by occupation. He used constantly to travel between Mengyin and Yishui (in Shandong). One day he was delayed on the road by rain, and when he arrived at his usual quarters it was already late in the night. He knocked at all the doors, but no one answered; and he was walking backwards and forwards in the piazza when suddenly a door flew open and an old man came out. He invited the traveler to enter, an invitation to which Xi Shan gladly responded; and, tying up his mule, he went in. The place was totally unfurnished; and the old man began by saying that it was only out of compassion that he had asked him in, as his house was not an inn. "There are only three or four of us," added he; "and my wife and daughter are fast asleep. We have some of yesterday's food, which I will get ready for you; you must not object to its being cold." He then went within, and shortly afterwards returned with a low couch, which he placed on the ground, begging his guest to be seated, at the same time hurrying back for a low table, and soon for a number of other things, until at last Xi Shan was quite uncomfortable, and entreated his host to rest himself awhile. By-and-by a young lady came out, bringing some wine; upon which the old man said, "Oh, our Aqian has got up." She was about sixteen or seventeen, a slender and pretty-looking girl; and as Xi Shan had an unmarried brother, he began to think directly that she would do for him. So he inquired of the old man his name and address, to which the latter replied that his name was Gu, and that his children had all died save this one daughter. "I didn't like to wake her just now, but I suppose my wife told her to get up." Xi Shan then asked the name of his son-in-law, and was informed that the young lady was not yet engaged—at which he was secretly very much pleased. A tray of food was now brought in, evidently the remains from the day before; and when he had finished eating, Xi Shan began respectfully to address the old man as follows: "I am only a poor wayfarer, but I shall never forget the kindness with which you have treated me. Let me presume upon it, and submit to your consideration a plan I have in my head. My younger brother, Sanlang, is seventeen years old. He is a student, and by no means unsteady or dull. May I hope that you will unite our families together, and not think it presumption on my part?" "I, too, am but a temporary sojourner," replied the old man, rejoicing; "and if you will only let me have a part of your house, I shall be very glad to come and live with you." Xi Shan consented to this, and got up and thanked him for the promise of his daughter; upon which the old man set to work to make him comfortable for the night, and then went away. At cock-crow he was outside, calling his guest to come and have a wash; and when Xi Shan had packed up ready to go, he offered to pay for his night's entertainment. This, however, the old man refused, saying, "I could hardly charge a stranger anything for a single meal; how much less could I take money from one who is to be a connection by marriage?" They then separated, and in about a month Xi Shan returned; but when he was a short distance from the village he met an old woman with a young lady, both dressed in deep mourning. As they approached he began to suspect it was Aqian; and the young lady, after turning around to look at him, pulled the old woman's sleeve, and whispered something in her ear, which Xi Shan himself did not hear. The old woman stopped immediately, and asked if she was addressing Mr. Xi; and when informed that she was, she said mournfully, "Alas! my husband has been killed by the falling of a wall. We are going to bury him today. There is no one at home; but please wait here, and we will be back by-and-by." They then disappeared among the trees; and, returning after a short absence, they walked along together in the dusk of the evening. The old woman complained bitterly of their lonely and helpless state, and Xi Shan himself was moved to compassion by the sight of her tears. She told him that the people of the neighborhood were a bad lot, and that if Aqian was to marry into his family, no time should be lost. Xi Shan said he was willing; and when they reached the house the old woman, after lighting the lamp and setting food before him, proceeded to speak as follows: "Knowing, Sir, that you would shortly arrive, we sold all our grain except about twenty piculs. We cannot take this with us so far; but a mile or so to the north of the village, at the first house you come to, there lives a man named Tan Erquan, who often buys grain from me. Don't think it too much trouble to oblige me by taking a sack with you on your mule and proceeding thither at once. Tell Mr. Tan that the old lady of the southern village has several piculs of grain which she wishes to sell in order to get money for a journey, and beg him to send some animals to carry it." The old woman then gave him a sack of grain; and Xi Shan, whipping up his mule, was soon at the place; and, knocking at the door, a great fat fellow came out, to whom he told his errand. Emptying the sack he had brought, he went back himself first; and before long a couple of men arrived leading five mules. The old woman took them into the granary, which was a cellar below ground, and Xi Shan, going down himself, held the measure and grasped the smoothing-bar, while the mother poured the grain into the measure and the daughter received it in the sack. In a little while the men had got a load, with which they went off, returning altogether four times before all the grain was exhausted. They then paid the old woman, who kept one man and two mules, and, packing up her things, set off towards the east. After traveling some seven miles day began to break; and by-and-by they reached a market-town, where the old woman hired animals and sent back Tan's servant. When they arrived at Xi Shan's home he related the whole story to his parents, who were very pleased at what had happened, and provided separate apartments for the old lady; and after choosing a lucky day, Aqian was married to Sanlang. The old woman prepared a handsome trousseau; and as for Aqian herself, she spoke but little, seldom losing her temper, and if anyone addressed her she would only reply with a smile. She employed all her time in spinning, and thus became a general favorite with all alike. "Tell your brother," said she to Sanlang, "that when he happens to pass our old residence he will do well not to make any mention of my mother and myself."

In three or four years' time the Xi family had made plenty of money, and Sanlang had taken his bachelor's degree, when one day Xi Shan happened to pass a night with the people who lived next door to the house where he had met Aqian. After telling them the story of his having had nowhere to sleep, and taking refuge with the old man and woman, his host said to him, "You must make a mistake, Sir; the house you allude to belongs to my uncle, but was abandoned three years ago in consequence of its being haunted. It has now been uninhabited for a long time. What old man and woman can have entertained you there?" Xi Shan was very much astonished at this, but did not put much faith in what he heard; meanwhile his host continued, "For ten years no one dared enter the house; however, one day the back wall fell down, and my uncle, going to look at it, found, half-buried underneath the ruins, a large rat, almost as big as a cat. It was still moving, and my uncle went off to call for assistance, but when he got back the rat had disappeared. Everyone suspected some supernatural agency to be at work, though on returning to the spot ten days afterwards nothing was to be either heard or seen; and about a year subsequently the place was inhabited once more." Xi Shan was more than ever amazed at what he now heard, and on reaching home told the family what had occurred; for he feared that his brother's wife was not a human being, and became rather anxious about him. Sanlang himself continued to be much attached to Aqian; but by-and-by the other members of the family let Aqian perceive that they had suspicions about her. So one night she complained to Sanlang, saying, "I have been a good wife to you for some years, but now I am no longer regarded as a human being. I pray you give me my divorce,[254] and seek for yourself some worthier mate." She then burst into a flood of tears; whereupon Sanlang said, "You should know my feelings by this time. Ever since you entered the house the family has prospered; and that prosperity is entirely due to you. Who can say it is not so?" "I know full well," replied Aqian, "what you feel; still there are the others, and I do not wish to share the fate of an autumn fan."[255] At length Sanlang succeeded in pacifying her; but Xi Shan could not dismiss the subject from his thoughts, and gave out that he was going to get a first-rate mouser, with a view to testing Aqian. She did not seem very frightened at this, though evidently ill at ease; and one night she told Sanlang that her mother was not very well, and that he needn't come to bid her good-night as usual. In the morning mother and daughter had disappeared; at which Sanlang was greatly alarmed, and sent out to look for them in every direction. No traces of the fugitives could be discovered, and Sanlang was overwhelmed with grief, unable either to eat or to sleep. His father and brother thought it was a lucky thing for him, and advised him to console himself with another wife. This, however, he refused to do; until, about a year afterwards, nothing more having been heard of Aqian, he could not resist their importunities any longer, and bought himself a concubine. But he never ceased to think of Aqian; and some years later, when the prosperity of the family was on the wane, they all began to regret her loss.

---

254 The Chinese acknowledge seven just causes for putting away a wife, (1) Bad behavior towards the husband's father and mother. (2) Adultery. (3) Jealousy. (4) Garrulity. (5) Theft. (6) Disease. (7) Barrenness. The right of divorce may not, however, be enforced if the husband's father and mother have died since the marriage, as thus it would be inferred that the wife had served them well up to the time of their death; or if the husband has recently risen to wealth and power (hence the saying, "The wife of my porridge days shall not go down from my hall"); or, thirdly, if the wife's parents and brothers are dead, and she has no home in which she can seek shelter.

255 This simile is taken from a song ascribed to Ban Jieyu, a favorite of the Emperor Cheng Di of the Han dynasty, written when her influence with the Son of Heaven began to wane. I venture to reproduce it here.

> "O fair white silk, fresh from the weaver's loom;
> Clear as the frost, bright as the winter's snow!
> See! friendship fashions out of thee a fan,
> Round as the round moon shines in heaven above
> At home, abroad, a close companion thou,
> Stirring at every move the grateful gale.
> And yet I fear, ah, me! that autumn chills,
> Cooling the dying Summer's torrid rage,
> Will see thee laid neglected on the shelf,
> All thought of bygone days, like them, bygone."

Now Sanlang had a step-brother, named Lan, who, when traveling to Jiaozhou on business, passed a night at the house of a relative named Lu. He noticed that during the night sounds of weeping and lamentation proceeded from their next-door neighbors, but he did not inquire the reason of it; however, on his way back he heard the same sounds, and then asked what was the cause of such demonstrations. Mr. Lu told him that a few years ago an old widow and her daughter had come there to live, and that the mother had died about a month previously, leaving her child quite alone in the world. Lan inquired what her name was, and Mr. Lu said it was Gu; "But," added he, "the door is closely barred, and as they never had any communication with the village, I know nothing of their antecedents." "It's my sister-in-law," cried Lan, in amazement, and at once proceeded to knock at the door of the house. Some one came to the front door, and said, in a voice that betokened recent weeping, "Who's there? There are no men in this house."[256] Lan looked through a crack, and saw that the young lady really was his sister-in-law; so he called out, "Sister, open the door. I am your step-brother Asui." Aqian immediately opened the door and asked him in, and recounted to him the whole story of her troubles. "Your husband," said Lan, "is always thinking of you. For a trifling difference you need hardly have run away so far from him." He then proposed to hire a vehicle and take her home; but Aqian replied, "I came hither with my mother to hide because I was not regarded as a human being, and should make myself ridiculous by now returning thus. If I am to go back, my elder brother Xi Shan must no longer live with us; otherwise, I will immediately poison myself." Lan then went home and told Sanlang, who set off and traveled all night until he reached the place where Aqian was. Husband and wife were overjoyed to meet again, and the following day Sanlang notified the landlord of the house where Aqian had been living. Now this landlord had long desired to secure Aqian as a concubine for himself; and, after making no claim for rent for several years, he began to hint as much to her mother. The old lady, however, refused flatly; but shortly afterwards she died, and then the landlord thought that he might be able to succeed. At this juncture Sanlang arrived, and the landlord sought to hamper him by putting in his claim for rent; and, as Sanlang was anything but well off at the moment, it really did annoy him very much. Aqian here came to the rescue, showing Sanlang a large quantity of grain she had in the house, and bidding him use it to settle accounts with the landlord. The latter declared he could not accept grain,

---

256 Signifying that it would be impossible for him to enter.

but must be paid in silver; whereupon Aqian sighed and said it was all her unfortunate self that had brought this upon them, at the same time telling Sanlang of the landlord's former proposition. Sanlang was very angry, and was about to take out a summons against him, when Mr. Lu interposed, and, by selling the grain in the neighborhood, managed to collect sufficient money to pay off the rent. Sanlang and his wife then returned home; and the former, having explained the circumstances to his parents, separated his household from that of his brother. Aqian now proceeded to build, with her own money, a granary, which was a matter of some-astonishment to the family, there not being a hundredweight of grain in the place. But in about a year the granary was full,[257] and before very long Sanlang was a rich man, Xi Shan remaining as poor as before. Accordingly, Aqian persuaded her husband's parents to come and live with them, and made frequent presents of money to the elder brother; so that her husband said, "Well, at any rate, you bear no malice." "Your brother's behavior," replied she, "was from his regard for you. Had it not been for him, you and I would never have met." After this there were no more supernatural manifestations.

54. The Man Who Was Thrown down a Well

MR. DAI, of An Qing, was a wild fellow when young. One day as he was returning home tipsy,[258] he met by the way a dead cousin of his named Ji; and having, in his drunken state, quite forgotten that his cousin was dead, he asked him where he was going. "I am already a disembodied spirit," replied Ji; "don't you remember?" Dai was a little disturbed at this; but, being under the influence of liquor, he was not frightened, and inquired of his cousin what he was doing in the realms below. "I am employed as scribe," said Ji, "in the court of the Great King." "Then you must know all about our happiness and misfortunes to come," cried Dai. "It is my

---

257 The result of Aqian's depredations as a rat.
258 I have already discussed the subject of drunkenness in China (*Chinese Sketches*, pp. 113, 114), and shall not return to it here, further than to quote a single sentence, to which I adhere as firmly now as when the book in question was published: "Who ever sees in China a tipsy man reeling about a crowded thoroughfare, or lying with his head in a ditch by the side of some country road?"

It is not, however, generally known that the Chinese, with their usual quaintness, distinguish between five kinds of drunkenness, different people being differently affected, according to the physical constitution of each. Wine may fly (1) to the heart, and produce maudlin emotions; or (2) to the liver, and incite to pugnacity; or (3) to the stomach, and cause drowsiness, accompanied by a flushing of the face; or (4) to the lungs, and induce hilarity; or (5) to the kidneys, and excite desire.

business," answered his cousin, "so of course I know. But I see such an enormous mass that, unless of special reference to myself or family, I take no notice of any of it. Three days ago, by the way, I saw your name in the register." Dai immediately asked what there was about himself, and his cousin replied, "I will not deceive you; your name was put down for a dark and dismal hell." Dai was dreadfully alarmed, and at the same time sobered, and entreated his cousin to assist him in some way. "You may try," said Ji, "what merit will do for you as a means of mitigating your punishment; but the register of your sins is as thick as my finger, and nothing short of the most deserving acts will be of any avail. What can a poor fellow like myself do for you? Were you to perform one good act every day, you would not complete the necessary total under a year and more, and it is now too late for that. But henceforth amend your ways, and there may still be a chance of escape for you." When Dai heard these words he prostrated himself on the ground, imploring his cousin to help him; but, on raising his head, Ji had disappeared; he therefore returned sorrowfully home, and set to work to cleanse his heart and order his behavior.

Now Dai's next-door neighbor had long suspected him of paying too much attention to his wife; and one day meeting Dai in the fields shortly after the events narrated above, he lured him into inspecting a dry well, and then pushed him down. The well was many feet deep, and the man felt certain that Dai was killed; however, in the middle of the night he came around, and sitting up at the bottom, he began to shout for assistance, but could not make any one hear him. On the following day, the neighbor, fearing that Dai might possibly have recovered consciousness, went to listen at the mouth of the well; and hearing him cry out for help, began to throw down a quantity of stones. Dai took refuge in a cave at the side, and did not dare utter another sound; but his enemy knew he was not dead, and forthwith filled the well almost up to the top with earth. In the cave it was as dark as pitch, exactly like the Infernal Regions; and not being able to get anything to eat or drink, Dai gave up all hopes of life. He crawled on his hands and knees further into the cave, but was prevented by water from going further than a few paces, and returned to take up his position at the old spot. At first he felt hungry; by-and-by, however, this sensation passed away; and then reflecting that there, at the bottom of a well, he could hardly perform any good action, he passed his time in calling loudly on the name of Buddha. Before long he saw a number of Will-o'-the-Wisps flitting over the water and illuminating the gloom of the cave; and immediately prayed to them, saying, "O Will-o'-the-Wisps, I have heard that ye are the shades of wronged and injured people. I have not long to live, and am without hope of escape; still I would gladly relieve the monotony of my situation by exchanging a few words with you." Thereupon, all the Wills came flitting across the water to him; and in each of them was a man of about half the ordinary size. Dai asked them whence they came; to which one of them replied, "This is an old coal-mine. The proprietor, in working the coal, disturbed the position of some graves;[259] and Mr. Longfei flooded the mine and drowned forty-three workmen. We are the shades of those men." He further said he did not know who Mr. Longfei was, except that he was secretary to the City God, and that in compassion for the misfortunes of the innocent workmen, he was in the habit of sending them a quantity of gruel every three or four days. "But the cold water," added he, "soaks into our bones, and there is but small chance of ever getting them removed. If, Sir, you someday return to the world above, I pray you fish up our decaying bones and bury them in some public burying-ground. You will thus earn for yourself boundless gratitude in the realms below." Dai promised that if he had the luck to escape he would do as they wished; "but how," cried he, "situated as I am, can I ever hope to look again upon the light of day?" He then began to teach the Wills to say their prayers, making for them beads[260] out of bits of mud, in order to keep record of the number of invocations uttered. He could not tell night from morning; he slept when he felt tired, and when he waked he sat up. Suddenly, he perceived in the distance the light of lamps, at which the shades all rejoiced, and said, "It is Mr. Longfei with our food." They then invited Dai to go with them; and when he said he couldn't because of the water, they bore him along over it so that he hardly seemed to walk. After twisting and turning about for nearly a quarter of a mile, he reached a place at which the Wills bade him walk by himself; and then he appeared to mount a flight of steps, at the top of which he found himself in an apartment lighted by a candle as thick around as one's arm. Not having seen the light of fire for some time, he was overjoyed and walked in; but observing an old man in a scholar's dress and cap seated in the post of honor, he stopped, not liking to advance further. But the old man had already caught sight of him, and asked him how he, a living man, had come there. Dai threw himself on the ground at his feet, and told him all; whereupon the old man cried out, "My great-grandson!" He then bade

---

259 A religious and social offence of the deepest dye, sure to entail punishment in the world to come, even if the perpetrator escapes detection in this life.
260 The Buddhist rosary consists of 108 beads, which number is the same as that of the compartments in the *Phrabat*, or sacred footprint of Buddha.

him get up; and offering him a seat, explained that his own name was Dai Qian, and that he was otherwise known as Longfei. He said, moreover, that in days gone by a worthless grandson of his named Tang had associated himself with a lot of scoundrels and sunk a well near his grave, disturbing the peace of his everlasting night; and that therefore he had flooded the place with salt water and drowned them. He then inquired as to the general condition of the family at that time.

Now Dai was a descendant of one of five brothers, from the eldest of whom Tang himself was also descended; and an influential man of the place had bribed Tang to open a mine[261] alongside the family grave. His brothers were afraid to interfere; and by-and-by the water rose and drowned all the workmen; whereupon actions for damages were commenced by the relatives of the deceased,[262] and Tang and his friend were reduced to poverty, and Tang's descendants to absolute destitution. Dai was a son of one of Tang's brothers, and having heard this story from his seniors, now repeated it to the old man. "How could they be otherwise than unfortunate," cried the latter, "with such an unfilial progenitor? But since you have come hither, you must on no account neglect your studies." The old man then provided him with food and wine, and spreading a volume of essays according to the old style before him, bade him study it most carefully. He also gave him themes for composition, and corrected his essays as if he had been his tutor. The candle remained always burning in the room, never needing to be snuffed and never decreasing. When he was tired he went to sleep, but he never knew day from night. The old man occasionally went out, leaving a boy to attend to his great-grandson's wants. It seemed that several years passed away thus, but Dai had no troubles of any kind to annoy him. He had no other book except the volume of essays, one hundred in all, which he read through more than four thousand times. One day the old man said to him, "Your term of expiation is nearly completed, and you will be able to return to the world above. My grave is near the coal-mine, and the grosser breeze plays upon my bones. Remember to remove them to the eastern plain."[263] Dai promised he would see to this; and then the old man summoned all the shades together and instructed them to escort Dai back

---

261 It here occurred to me that the word hitherto translated "well" should have been "shaft;" but the commentator refers expressly to the *Zuo Zhuan*, where the phrase for "a dry well," as first used, is so explained. We must accordingly fall back on the supposition that our author has committed a trifling slip.

262 See note 251 in tale number 51.

263 In order to profit by the vivifying influence of the east, the quarter associated with spring.

to the place where they had found him. The shades now bowed one after the other, and begged Dai to think of them as well, while Dai himself was quite at a loss to guess how he was going to get out.

Meanwhile, Dai's family had searched for him everywhere, and his mother had brought his case to the notice of the officials, thereby implicating a large number of persons, but without getting any trace of the missing man. Three or four years passed away, and there was a change of magistrate; in consequence of which the search was relaxed, and Dai's wife, not being happy where she was, married another husband. Just then an inhabitant of the place set about repairing the old well, and found Dai's body in the cave at the bottom. Touching it, he found it was not dead, and at once gave information to the family. Dai was promptly conveyed home, and within a day he could tell his own story.

Since he had been down the well, the neighbor who pushed him in had beaten his own wife to death; and his father-in-law having brought an action against him, he had been in confinement for more than a year while the case was being investigated.[264] When released he was a mere bag of bones;[265] and then hearing that Dai had come back to life, he was terribly alarmed and fled away. The family tried to persuade Dai to take proceedings against him, but this he would not do, alleging that what had befallen him was a proper punishment for his own bad behavior, and had nothing to do with the neighbor. Upon this, the said neighbor ventured to return; and when the water in the well had dried up, Dai hired men to go down and collect the bones, which he put in coffins and buried all together in one place. He next hunted up Mr. Longfei's name in the family tables of genealogy, and proceeded to sacrifice all kinds of nice things at his tomb. By-and-by the Literary Chancellor[266] heard this strange story, and was also very pleased with Dai's compositions; accordingly, Dai passed successfully through his examinations, and, having taken his master's degree, returned home and reburied Mr. Longfei on the eastern plain, repairing thither regularly every spring without fail.[267]

---

264 That is, as to whether or not there were extenuating circumstances, in which case no punishment would be inflicted.

265 Such is the invariable result of confinement in a Chinese prison, unless the prisoner has the wherewithal to purchase food.

266 The provincial examiner for the degree of bachelor.

267 To worship at his tomb.

55. The Virtuous Daughter-in-Law

DA CHENG was a Zhong Qing man. His father, who had gained the master's degree, died early; and his brother Er Cheng was a mere boy. He himself had married a wife from the Chen family, whose name was Shanhu; and this young lady had much to put up with from the violent and malicious disposition of her husband's mother.[268] However, she never complained; and every morning dressed herself up smart, and went in to pay her respects to the old lady. Once when Da Cheng was ill, his mother abused Shanhu for dressing so nicely; whereupon Shanhu went back and changed her clothes; but even then Mrs. An was not satisfied, and began to tear her own hair with rage. Da Cheng, who was a very filial son, at once gave his wife a beating, and this put an end to the scene. From that moment his mother hated her more than ever, and although she was everything that a daughter-in-law could be, would never exchange a word with her. Da Cheng then treated her in much the same way, that his mother might see he would have nothing to do with her; still the old lady wasn't pleased, and was always blaming Shanhu for every trifle that occurred. "A wife," cried Da Cheng, "is taken to wait upon her mother-in-law. This state of things hardly looks like the wife doing her duty." So he bade Shanhu begone,[269] and sent an old maid-servant to see her home: but when Shanhu got outside the village-gate, she burst into tears, and said, "How can a girl who has failed in her duties as a wife ever dare to look her parents in the face? I had better die." Thereupon she drew a pair of scissors and stabbed herself in the throat, covering herself immediately with blood. The servant prevented any further mischief, and supported her to the house of her husband's aunt, who was a widow living by herself, and who made Shanhu stay with her. The servant went back and told Da Cheng, and he bade her say nothing to any one, for fear his mother should hear of it. In a few days Shanhu's wound was healed, and Da Cheng went off to ask his aunt to send her away. His aunt invited him in, but he declined, demanding loudly that Shanhu should be turned out; and in a few moments Shanhu herself came forth, and inquired what she had done. Da Cheng said she had failed in her duty towards his mother; whereupon Shanhu hung her head and made no answer, while tears of blood[270] trickled from her eyes and stained her dress all over. Da Cheng was much touched

---

268 See note 215 in tale number 43.
269 See note 254 in tale number 53.
270 Such is the Chinese idiom for what we should call "bitter" tears. This phrase is constantly employed in the notices of the death of a parent sent around to friends and relatives.

by this spectacle, and went away without saying any more; but before long his mother heard all about it, and, hurrying off to the aunt's, began abusing her roundly. This the aunt would not stand, and said it was all the fault of her own bad temper, adding, "The girl has already left you, and do you still claim to decide with whom she is to live? Miss Chen is staying with me, not your daughter-in-law; so you had better mind your own business." This made Mrs. An furious; but she was at a loss for an answer, and, seeing that the aunt was firm, she went off home abashed and in tears.

Shanhu herself was very much upset, and determined to seek shelter elsewhere, finally taking up her abode with Mrs. An's elder sister, a lady of sixty odd years of age, whose son had died, leaving his wife and child to his mother's care. This Mrs. Yu was extremely fond of Shanhu; and when she heard the facts of the case, said it was all her sister's horrid disposition, and proposed to send Shanhu back. The latter, however, would not hear of this, and they continued to live together like mother and daughter; neither would Shanhu accept the invitation of her two brothers to return home and marry some one else, but remained there with Mrs. Yu, earning enough to live upon by spinning and such work.

Ever since Shanhu had been sent away, Da Cheng's mother had been endeavoring to get him another wife; but the fame of her temper had spread far and wide, and no one would entertain her proposals. In three or four years Er Cheng had grown up, and he had to be married first. His wife was a young lady named Zanggu, whose temper turned out to be something fearful, and far more ungovernable even than her mother-in-law's. When the latter only looked angry, Zanggu was already at the shrieking stage; and Er Cheng, being of a very meek disposition, dared not side with either. Thus it came about that Mrs. An began to be in mortal fear of Zanggu; and whenever her daughter-in-law was in a rage she would try and turn off her anger with a smile. She seemed never to be able to please Zanggu, who in her turn worked her mother-in-law like a slave, Da Cheng himself not venturing to interfere, but only assisting his mother in washing the dishes and sweeping the floor. Mother and son would often go to some secluded spot, and there in secret tell their griefs to one another; but before long Mrs. An was stretched upon a sick-bed with nobody to attend to her except Da Cheng. He watched her day and night without sleeping, until both eyes were red and inflamed; and then when he went to summon the younger son to take his place, Zanggu told him to leave the house. Da Cheng now went off to inform Mrs. Yu, hoping that she would come and assist; and he had hardly finished his tale of woe before Shanhu walked in. In great confusion at seeing her, he would have left immediately had not Shan held out her arms across the door; whereupon he bolted underneath them and escaped. He did not dare to tell his mother, and shortly afterwards Mrs. Yu arrived, to the great joy of Da Cheng's mother, who made her stay in the house. Every day something nice was sent for Mrs. Yu, and even when she told the servants that there was no occasion for it, she having all she wanted at her sister's, the things still came as usual. However, she kept none of them for herself, but gave what came to the invalid, who gradually began to improve. Mrs. Yu's grandson also used to come by his mother's orders, and inquire after the sick lady's health, besides bringing a packet of cakes and so on for her. "Ah, me!" cried Mrs. An, "what a good daughter-in-law you have got, to be sure. What have you done to her?" "What sort of a person was the one you sent away?" asked her sister in reply. "She wasn't as bad as someone I know of," said Mrs. An, "though not so good as yours." "When she was here you had but little to do," replied Mrs. Yu; "and when you were angry she took no notice of it. How was she not as good?" Mrs. An then burst into tears, and saying how sorry she was, asked if Shanhu had married again; to which Mrs. Yu replied that she did not know, but would make inquiries. In a few more days the patient was quite well, and Mrs. Yu proposed to return; her sister, however, begged her to stay, and declared she should die if she didn't. Mrs. Yu then advised that Er Cheng and his wife should live in a separate house, and Er Cheng spoke about it to his wife; but she would not agree, and abused both Da Cheng and Mrs. Yu alike. It ended by Da Cheng giving up a large share of the property, and ultimately Zanggu consented, and a deed of separation was drawn up. Mrs. Yu then went away, returning next day with a sedan-chair to carry her sister back; and no sooner had the latter put her foot inside Mrs. Yu's door, than she asked to see the daughter-in-law, whom she immediately began to praise very highly. "Ah," said Mrs. Yu, "she's a good girl, with her little faults like the rest of us; but even if your daughter-in-law were as good as mine, you would not be able to appreciate her." "Alas!" replied her sister, "I must have been as senseless as a statue not to have seen what she was." "I wonder what Shanhu, whom you turned out of doors, says of you?" rejoined Mrs. Yu "Why, swears at me, of course," answered Mrs. An. "If you examine yourself honestly and find nothing which should make people swear at you, is it at all likely you would be sworn at?" asked Mrs. Yu. "Well, all people are fallible," replied the other, "and as I know she is not perfect, I conclude she would naturally swear at me." "If a person has just cause for resentment, and yet does not indulge that resentment, it is obvious how he will repay kindness; or if any one has just cause for leaving another and yet does not do so, it is obvious how he will act under good treatment. Now, all the things that were sent when you were ill, and all the various little attentions, did not come from my daughter-in-law, but from yours." Mrs. An was amazed at hearing this, and asked for some explanation; whereupon Mrs. Yu continued, "Shanhu has been living here for a long time. Everything she sent to you was bought with money earned by her spinning, and that, too, continued late into the night." Mrs. An here burst into tears, and begged to be allowed to see Shanhu, who came in at Mrs. Yu's summons, and threw herself on the ground at her mother-in-law's feet. Mrs. An was much abashed, and beat her head with shame; but Mrs. Yu made it all up between them, and they became mother and daughter as at first. In about ten days they went home, and, as their property was not enough to support them, Da Cheng had to work with his pen while his wife did the same with her needle. Er Cheng was quite well off, but his brother would not apply to him, neither did he himself offer to help them. Zanggu, too, would have nothing to do with her sister-in-law, because she had been divorced; and Shanhu in her turn, knowing what Zanggu's temper was, made no great efforts to be friendly. So the two brothers lived apart;[271] and when Zanggu was in one of her outrageous moods, all the others would stop their ears, until at length there was only her husband and the servants upon whom to vent her spleen. One day a maid-servant of hers committed suicide, and the father of the girl brought an action against Zanggu for having caused her death. Er Cheng went off to the mandarin's to take her place as defendant, but only got a good beating for his pains, as the magistrate insisted that Zanggu herself should appear and answer to the charge, in spite of all her friends could do. The consequence was she had her fingers squeezed[272] until the flesh was entirely taken off; and the magistrate, being a grasping man, a very severe fine was inflicted as well. Er Cheng had now to mortgage his property before he could raise enough money to get Zanggu released; but before long the mortgagee threatened to foreclose, and he was obliged to enter into negotiations for the sale of it to an old gentleman of the village named

---

271 A disgraceful state of things, in the eyes of the Chinese. See the paraphrase of the *Sacred Edict*, Maxim I.

272 An illegal form of punishment, under the present dynasty, which authorizes only *bambooing* of two kinds, each of five degrees of severity; *banishment*, of three degrees of duration; *transportation* for life, of three degrees of distance; and *death*, of two kinds, namely, by strangulation and decapitation. That torture is occasionally resorted to by Chinese officials is an indisputable fact; that it is commonly employed by the whole body of mandarins could only be averred by those who have not had the opportunities or the desire to discover the actual truth.

Ren. Now Mr. Ren knowing that half the property had belonged to Da Cheng, said the deed of sale must be signed by the elder brother as well; however, when Da Cheng reached his house, the old man cried out, "I am Mr. An, M.A.; who is this Ren that he should buy my property?" Then, looking at Da Cheng, he added, "The filial piety of you and your wife has obtained for me in the realms below this interview;" upon which Da Cheng said, "O father, since you have this power, help my younger brother." "The unfilial son and the vixenish daughter-in-law," said the old man, "deserve no pity. Go home and quickly buy back our ancestral property." "We have barely enough to live upon," replied Da Cheng; "where, then, shall we find the necessary money?" "Beneath the crape myrtle-tree,"[273] answered his father, "you will find a store of silver, which you may take and use for this purpose." Da Cheng would have questioned him further, but the old gentleman said no more, recovering consciousness shortly afterwards[274] without knowing a word of what had happened. Da Cheng went back and told his brother, who did not altogether believe the story; Zanggu, however, hurried off with a number of men, and had soon dug a hole four or five feet deep, at the bottom of which they found a quantity of bricks and stones, but no gold. She then gave up the idea and returned home, Da Cheng having meanwhile warned his mother and wife not to go near the place while she was digging. When Zanggu left, Mrs. An went herself to have a look, and seeing only bricks and earth mingled together, she too, retraced her steps. Shanhu was the next to go, and she found the hole full of silver bullion; and then Da Cheng repaired to the spot and saw that there was no mistake about it. Not thinking it right to apply this heirloom to his own private use, he now summoned Er Cheng to share it; and having obtained twice as much as was necessary to redeem the estate, the brothers returned to their homes. Er Cheng and Zanggu opened their half together, when lo! the bag was full of tiles and rubbish. They at once suspected Da Cheng of deceiving them, and Er Cheng ran off to see how things were going at his brother's. He arrived just as Da Cheng was spreading the silver on the table, and with his mother and wife rejoicing over their acquisition; and when he had told them what had occurred, Da Cheng expressed much sympathy for him, and at once presented him with his own half of the treasure. Er Cheng was delighted, and paid off the mortgage on the land, feeling very grateful to his brother for such kindness. Zanggu, however, declared it was a proof

---

273 *Lagerstræmia indica*, L.
274 That is, old Mr. Ren's body had been possessed by the disembodied spirit of Da Cheng's father.

that Da Cheng had been cheating him; " for how otherwise," argued she, "can you understand a man sharing anything with another, and then resigning his own half?"

Er Cheng himself did not know what to think of it; but next day the mortgagee sent to say that the money paid in was all imitation silver, and that he was about to lay the case before the authorities. Husband and wife were greatly alarmed at this, and Zanggu exclaimed, "Well, I never thought your brother was as bad as this. He's simply trying to take your life." Er Cheng himself was in a terrible fright, and hurried off to the mortgagee to entreat for mercy; but as the latter was extremely angry and would hear of no compromise, Er Cheng was obliged to make over the property to him to dispose of himself. The money was then returned, and when he got home he found that two lumps had been cut through, showing merely an outside layer of silver, about as thick as an onion-leaf, covering nothing but copper within. Zanggu and Ercheng then agreed to keep the broken pieces themselves, but send the rest back to Da Cheng, with a message, saying that they were deeply indebted to him for all his kindness, and that they had ventured to retain two of the lumps of silver out of compliment to the giver; also that the property which remained to them was still equal to Da Cheng's, that they had no use for much land, and accordingly had abandoned it, and that Da Cheng could redeem it or not as he pleased. Da Cheng, who did not perceive the intention in all this, refused to accept the land; however, Ercheng entreated him to do so, and at last he consented. When he came to weigh the money, he found it was five ounces short, and therefore bade Shanhu pawn something from her jewel-box to make up the amount, with which he proceeded to pay off the mortgage. The mortgagee, suspecting it was the same money that had been offered him by Ercheng, cut the pieces in halves, and saw that it was all silver of the purest quality. Accordingly he accepted it in liquidation of his claim, and handed the mortgage back to Da Cheng. Meanwhile, Ercheng had been expecting some catastrophe; but when he found that the mortgaged land had been redeemed, he did not know what to make of it. Zanggu thought that at the time of the digging Da Cheng had concealed the genuine silver, and immediately rushed off to his house, and began to revile them all around. Da Cheng now understood why they had sent him back the money; and Shanhu laughed and said, "The property is safe; why, then, this anger?" Thereupon she made Da Cheng hand over the deeds to Zanggu. One night after this Ercheng's father appeared to him in a dream, and reproached him, saying, "Unfilial son, unfraternal brother, your hour is at hand. Wherefore usurp rights that do not belong to you?" In the morning Ercheng told Zanggu of his dream, and proposed to return the property to his brother; but she only laughed at him for a fool. Just then the eldest of his two sons, a boy of seven, died of small-pox, and this frightened Zanggu so that she agreed to restore the deeds. Da Cheng would not accept them; and now the second child, a boy of three, died also; whereupon Zanggu seized the deeds, and threw them into her brother-in-law's house. Spring was over, but the land was in a terribly neglected state; so Da Cheng set to work and put it in order again. From this moment Zanggu was a changed woman towards her mother and sister-in-law; and when, six months later, Mrs. An died, she was so grieved that she refused to take any nourishment. "Alas!" cried she, "that my mother-in-law has died thus early, and prevented me from waiting upon her. Heaven will not allow me to retrieve my past errors." Zanggu had thirteen children,[275] but as none of them lived, they were obliged to adopt one of Da Cheng's,[276] who, with his wife, lived to a good old age, and had three sons, two of whom took their doctor's degree. People said this was a reward for filial piety and brotherly love.

56. Dr. Zeng's Dream

THERE was a Fujian gentleman named Zeng, who had just taken his doctor's degree. One day he was out walking with several other recently elected doctors, when they heard that at a temple hard by there lived an astrologer, and accordingly the party proceeded thither to get their fortunes told. They went in and sat down, and the astrologer made some very complimentary remarks to Zeng, at which he fanned himself and smiled, saying, "Have I any chance of ever wearing the dragon robes and the jade girdle?"[277] The astrologer[278] immediately put on a serious face, and replied that he would be a Secretary of State during twenty years of national tranquility. Thereupon Zeng was much pleased, and began to give himself greater airs than ever. A slight rain coming on, they sought shelter in the priest's quarters, where they found an old Buddhist monk, with sunken eyes and a big nose, sitting

---

275 Five is considered a large number for an ordinary Chinese woman.
276 In order to leave someone behind to look after their graves and perform the duties or ancestral worship. No one can well refuse to give a son to be adopted by a childless brother.
277 That is, of rising to the highest offices of State.
278 The Chinese term used throughout is "star-man,"

upon a mat. He took no notice of the strangers, who, after having bowed to him, stretched themselves upon the couches to chat, not forgetting to congratulate Zeng upon the destiny which had been foretold him. Zeng, too, seemed to think the thing was a matter of certainty, and mentioned the names of several friends he intended to advance, amongst others the old family butler. Roars of laughter greeted this announcement, mingled with the patter-patter of the increasing rain outside. Zeng then curled himself up for a nap, when suddenly in walked two officials bearing a commission under the Great Seal appointing Zeng to the Grand Secretariat. As soon as Zeng understood their errand, he rushed off at once to pay his respects to the Emperor, who graciously detained him some time in conversation, and then issued instructions that the promotion and dismissal of all officers below the third grade[279] should be vested in Zeng alone. He was next presented with the dragon robes, the jade girdle, and a horse from the imperial stables, after which he performed the *ke-tou*[280] before His Majesty and took his leave. He then went home, but it was no longer the old home of his youth. Painted beams, carved pillars, and a general profusion of luxury and elegance, made him wonder where on earth he was; until, nervously stroking his beard, he ventured to call out in a low tone. Immediately the responses of numberless attendants echoed through the place like thunder. Presents of costly food were sent to him by all the grandees, and his gate was absolutely blocked up by the crowds of retainers who were constantly coming and going. When Privy Councillors came to see him, he would rush out in haste to receive them; when Under-Secretaries of State visited him, he made them a polite bow; but to all below these he would hardly, vouchsafe a word. The Governor of Shanxi sent him twelve singing-girls, two of whom, Nini and Fairy, he made his favorites. All day long he had nothing to do but find amusement as best he could, until he bethought himself that formerly a man named Wang had often assisted him with money. Thereupon he memorialized the Throne and obtained official employment for him. Then he recollected that there was another man to whom he owed a long-standing grudge. He at once caused this man, who was in the Government service, to be impeached and stripped of his rank and dignities. Thus he squared accounts with both. One day when out in his chair a drunken man bumped against one of his tablet-bearers.[281] Zeng had him seized and sent

---

279 Chinese official life is divided into nine grades.
280 Prostrating himself three times, and knocking his head on the ground thrice at each prostration.
281 The *retinue* of a high mandarin is composed as follows: First, gong-bearers, then banner-men, tablet-bearers (on which tablets are inscribed the titles of the official), a large red umbrella, mounted

in to the mayor's *yamen*, where he died under the bamboo. Owners of land adjoining his would make him a present of the richest portions, fearing the consequences if they did not do so; and thus he became very wealthy, almost on a par with the State itself. By-and-by, Nini and Fairy died, and Zeng was overwhelmed with grief. Suddenly he remembered that in former years he had seen a beautiful girl whom he wished to purchase as a concubine, but want of money had then prevented him from carrying out his intention. Now there was no longer that difficulty; and accordingly he sent off two trusty servants to get the girl by force. In a short time she arrived, when he found that she had grown more beautiful than ever; and so his cup of happiness was full. But years rolled on, and gradually his fellow-officials became estranged, Zeng taking no notice of their behavior, until at last one of them impeached him to the Throne in a long and bitter memorial. Happily, however, the Emperor still regarded him with favor, and for some time kept the memorial by him unanswered. Then followed a joint memorial from the whole of the Privy Council, including those who had once thronged his doors, and had falsely called him their dear father. The Imperial rescript to this document was "Banishment to Yunnan,"[282] his son, who was Governor of Pingyang being also implicated in his guilt. When Zeng heard the news, he was overcome with fear; but an armed guard was already at his gate, and the lictors were forcing their way into his innermost apartments. They tore off his robe and official hat, and bound him and his wife with cords. Then they collected together in the hall his gold, his silver, and bank-notes,[283] to the value of many hundred thousands of taels. His pearls, and jade, and precious stones filled many bushel baskets. His curtains, and screens, and beds, and other articles of furniture were brought out by thousands; while the swaddling-clothes of his infant boy and the shoes of his little girl were lying littered about the steps. It was a sad sight for Zeng; but a worse blow was that of his concubine carried off almost lifeless before his eyes, himself not daring to utter a word. Then all the apartments, store-rooms, and treasuries were sealed up; and, with a volley of curses, the

---

attendants, a box containing a change of clothes, bearers of regalia, a second gong, a small umbrella or sunshade, a large wooden fan, executioners, lictors from hell, who wear tall hats; a mace (called a "golden melon"), bamboos for "bambooing," incense-bearers, more attendants, and now the great man himself, followed by a body-guard of soldiers and a few personal attendants, amounting in all to nearly one hundred persons, many of whom are mere street-rowdies or beggars, hired at a trifling outlay when required to join what might otherwise be an imposing procession.

282 A land journey of about three months, ending in a region which the Chinese have always regarded as semi-barbarous.

283 From 1154 CE the use of paper money became quite common in China.

soldiers bade Zeng begone, and proceeded to leave the place, dragging him with them. The husband and wife prayed that they might be allowed some old cart, but this favor was denied them. After about ten *li*, Zeng's wife could barely walk, her feet being swollen and sore. Zeng helped her along as best he could, but another ten *li* reduced him to a state of abject fatigue. By-and-by they saw before them a great mountain, the summit of which was lost in the clouds; and, fearing they should be made to ascend it, Zeng and his wife stood still and began to weep: The lictors, however, clamored around them, and would permit of no rest. The sun was rapidly sinking, and there was no place at hand where they could obtain shelter for the night. So they continued on their weary way until about half-way up the hill, when his wife's strength was quite exhausted, and she sat down by the roadside. Zeng, too, halted to rest in spite of the soldiers and their abuse; but they had hardly stopped a moment before down came a band of robbers upon them, each with a sharp knife in his hand. The soldiers immediately took to their heels, and Zeng fell on his knees before the robbers, saying, "I am a poor criminal going into banishment, and have nothing to give you. I pray you spare my life." But the robbers sternly replied, "We are all the victims of your crimes, and now we want your wicked head." Then Zeng began to revile them, saying, "Dogs! though I am under sentence of banishment, I am still an officer of the State." But the robbers cursed him again, flourishing a sword over his neck, and the next thing he heard was the noise of his own head as it fell with a thud to the ground. At the same instant two devils stepped forward and seized him each by one hand, compelling him to go with them. After a little while they arrived at a great city where there was a hideously ugly king sitting upon a throne judging between good and evil. Zeng crawled before him on his hands and knees to receive sentence, and the king, after turning over a few pages of his register, thundered out, "The punishment of a traitor who has brought misfortune on his country: the cauldron of boiling oil!" To this ten thousand devils responded with a cry like a clap of thunder, and one huge monster led Zeng down alongside the cauldron, which was seven feet in height, and surrounded on all sides by blazing fuel, so that it was of a glowing red heat. Zeng shrieked for mercy, but it was all up with him, for the devil seized him by the hair and the small of his back and pitched him headlong in. Down he fell with a splash, and rose and sank with the bubbling of the oil, which ate through his flesh into his very vitals. He longed to die, but death would not come to him. After about half-an-hour's boiling, a devil took him out on a pitchfork and threw him down before the Infernal King, who again consulted his note-book, and said, "You relied on your position to treat others with contempt and injustice, for which you must suffer on the Sword-Hill." Again he was led away by devils to a large hill thickly studded with sharp swords, their points upwards like the shoots of bamboo, with here and there the remains of many miserable wretches who had suffered before him. Zeng again cried for mercy and crouched upon the ground; but a devil bored into him with a poisoned awl until he screamed with pain. He was then seized and flung up high into the air, falling down right on the sword-points, to his most frightful agony. This was repeated several times until he was almost hacked to pieces. He was then brought once more before the king, who asked what was the amount of his peculations while on earth. Immediately an accountant came forward with an abacus, and said that the whole sum was 3,210,000 taels, whereupon the king replied, "Let him drink that amount." Forthwith the devils piled up a great heap of gold and silver, and, when they had melted it in a huge crucible, began pouring it into Zeng's mouth. The pain was excruciating as the molten metal ran down his throat into his vitals; but since in life he had never been able to get enough of the dross, it was determined he should feel no lack of it then. He was half-a-day drinking it, and then the king ordered him away to be born again as a woman[284] in Ganzhou. A few steps brought them to a huge frame, where on an iron axle revolved a mighty wheel many hundred *yojanas*[285] in circumference, and shining with a brilliant light. The devils flogged Zeng on to the wheel, and he shut his eyes as he stepped up. Then whiz—and away he went, feet foremost, around with the wheel, until he felt himself tumble off and a cold thrill ran through him, when he opened his eyes and found he was changed into a girl. He saw his father and mother in rags and tatters, and in one corner a beggar's bowl and a staff,[286] and understood the calamity that had befallen him. Day after day he begged about the streets, and his inside rumbled for want of food; he had no clothes to his back. At fourteen years of age he was sold to a gentleman as concubine; and then, though food and clothes were not wanting, he had to put up with the scoldings and floggings of the wife, who one day burnt him with a hot iron.[287] Luckily the gentleman took a

284 This contingency is much dreaded by the Chinese.
285 A *yojana* has been variously estimated at from five to nine English miles.
286 The *patra* and *khakkharam* of the *bikshu* or Buddhist mendicant.
287 It is not considered quite correct to take a concubine unless the wife is childless, in which case it is held that the proposition to do so, and thus secure the much-desired posterity, should emanate from the wife herself. On page 41 of Vol. XIII. of this author, we read, "and if at thirty years of age you have no children, then sell your hair-pins and other ornaments, and buy a concubine for your husband. For the

fancy to him and treated him well, which kindness Zeng repaid by an irreproachable fidelity. It happened, however, that on one occasion when they were chatting together, burglars broke into the house and killed the gentleman, Zeng having escaped by hiding himself under the bed. Thereupon he was immediately charged by the wife with murder, and on being taken before the authorities was sentenced to die the "lingering death."[288] This sentence was at once carried out with tortures more horrible than any in all the Courts of Purgatory, in the middle of which Zeng heard one of his companions call out "Hello, there! you've got nightmare." Zeng got up and rubbed his eyes, and his friends said, "It's quite late in the day, and we're all very hungry." But the old priest smiled, and asked him if the prophecy as to his future rank was true or not. Zeng bowed and begged him to explain; whereupon the old priest said, "For those who cultivate virtue, a lily will grow up even in the fiery pit."[289] Zeng had gone thither full of pride and vain-glory; he went home an altered man. From that day he thought no more of becoming a Secretary of State, but retired into the hills, and I know not what became of him after that.

57. The Country of the Cannibals[290]

AT Jiaozhou[291] there lived a man named Xu, who gained his living by trading across the sea. On one occasion he was carried far out of his course by a violent tempest, and reached a country of high hills and dense jungle,[292] where, after making fast his boat and taking provisions with him, he landed, hoping to meet with some of the inhabitants. He then saw that the rocks were covered with large holes, like the cells of bees; and, hearing the sound

---

childless state is a hard one to bear;" or, as Victor Hugo puts it in his *Légende des Siècles*, there is nothing so sad as "la maison sans enfants."

288 This is the celebrated form of death, reserved for parricide and similar awful crimes, about which so much has been written. Strictly speaking, the malefactor should be literally chopped to pieces in order to prolong his agonies; but the sentence is now rarely, if ever, carried out in its extreme sense. A few gashes are made upon the wretched victim's body, and he is soon put out of his misery by decapitation.

289 Alluding to a well-known Buddhist miracle, in which a *bikshu* was to be thrown into a cauldron of boiling water in a fiery pit, when suddenly a lotus-flower came forth, the fire was extinguished, and the water became cold.

290 The Chinese term—here translated "cannibals"—is a meaningless imitation by two Chinese characters of the Sanscrit *yakcha*, or certain demons who feed upon human flesh.

291 Hué, the capital of Cochinchina.

292 The island of Hainan, inhabited as it was in earlier times by a race of savages, is the most likely source of the following marvelous adventures.

of voices from within, he stopped in front of one of them and peeped in. To his infinite horror he beheld two hideous beings, with thick rows of horrid fangs, and eyes that glared like lamps, engaged in tearing to pieces and devouring some raw deer's flesh; and, turning around, he would have fled instantly from the spot, had not the cannibals already espied him; and, leaving their food, they seized him and dragged him in. Thereupon ensued a chattering between them, resembling the noise of birds or beasts,[293] and they proceeded to pull off Xu's clothes as if about to eat him; but Xu, who was frightened almost to death, offered them the food he had in his wallet, which they ate up with great relish, and looked inside for more. Xu waved his hand to show it was all finished, and then they angrily seized him again; at which he cried out, "I have a saucepan in my boat, and can cook you some." The cannibals did not understand what he said; but, by dint of gesticulating freely, they at length seemed to have an idea of what he meant; and, having taken him down to the shore to fetch the saucepan, they returned with him to the cave, where he lighted a fire and cooked the remainder of the deer, with the flavor of which they appeared to be mightily pleased. At night they rolled a big stone to the mouth of the cave,[294] fearing lest he should try to escape; and Xu himself lay down at a distance from them in doubt as to whether his life would be spared. At daybreak the cannibals went out, leaving the entrance blocked, and by-and-by came back with a deer, which they gave to Xu to cook. Xu flayed the carcass, and from a remote corner of the cave took some water and prepared a large quantity, which was no sooner ready than several other cannibals arrived to join in the feast. When they had finished all there was, they made signs that Xu's saucepan was too small; and three or four days afterwards they brought him a large one, of the same shape as those in common use amongst men, subsequently furnishing him with constant supplies of wolf and deer,[295] of which they always invited him to partake. By degrees they began to treat him kindly, and not to shut him up when they went out; and Xu, too, gradually learnt to understand, and even to speak, a little of their language, which pleased them so much that they finally gave him a cannibal woman for his wife. Xu was horribly afraid of her; but, as she treated him with

---

293 To which sounds the languages of the West have been more than once likened by the Chinese. It is only fair, however, to the lettered classes to state that they have a similar contempt for their own local dialects; regarding *Mandarin,* or the Court dialect, as the only form of speech worthy to be employed by men.

294 The occasional analogies to the story of the Cyclops must be evident to all readers.

295 The animal here mentioned is the plain brown deer, or *Rusa Swinhoii,* of Formosa, in which island I should prefer to believe, but for the great distance from Hue, that the scenes here narrated took place.

great consideration, always reserving tidbits of food for him, they lived very happily together. One day all the cannibals got up early in the morning, and, having adorned themselves with strings of fine pearls, they went forth as if to meet some honored guest, giving orders to Xu to cook an extra quantity of meat that day. "It is the birthday of our King," said Xu's wife to him; and then, running out, she informed the other cannibals that her husband had no pearls. So each gave five from his own string, and Xu's wife added ten to these, making in all fifty, which she threaded on a hempen fiber and hung around his neck, each pearl being worth over a hundred ounces of silver. Then they went away, and as soon as Xu had finished his cooking his wife appeared and invited him to come and receive the King. So off they went to a huge cavern, covering about a mow[296] of ground, in which was a huge stone, smoothed away at the top like a table, with stone seats at the four sides. At the upper end was a dais, over which was spread a leopard's skin, the other seats having only deerskins; and within the cavern some twenty or thirty cannibals ranged themselves on the seats. After a short interval a great wind began to stir up the dust, and they all rushed out to a creature very much resembling themselves, which hurried into the cave, and, squatting down cross-legged, cocked its head and looked about like a cormorant. The other cannibals then filed in and took up their positions right and left of the dais, where they stood gazing up at the King with their arms folded before them in the form of a cross. The King counted them one by one, and asked if they were all present; and when they replied in the affirmative, he looked at Xu and inquired who he was. Thereupon Xu's wife stepped forward and said he was her husband, and the others all loudly extolled his skill in cookery, two of them running out and bringing back some cooked meat, which they set before the King. His Majesty swallowed it by handfuls, and found it so nice that he gave orders to be supplied regularly; and then, turning to Xu he asked him why his string of beads[297] was so short. "He has but recently arrived among us," replied the cannibals," and hasn't got a complete set; "upon which the King drew ten pearls from the string around his own neck and bestowed them upon Xu. Each was as big as the top of one's finger and as round as a bullet; and Xu's wife threaded them for him and hung them around his neck. Xu himself crossed his arms and thanked the King in the language of the country, after

---

296 About one-sixth of an acre. On old title-deeds of landed property in China may still be seen measurements calculated according to the amount of grain that could be sown thereon.

297 The king here uses the words "gu-tu-zi," which are probably intended by the author to be an imitation of a term in the savape tongue.

which His Majesty went off in a gust of wind as rapidly as a bird can fly, and the cannibals sat down and finished what was left of the banquet. Four years afterwards Xu's wife gave birth to a triplet of two boys and one girl, all of whom were ordinary human beings, and not at all like the mother; at which the other cannibals were delighted, and would often play with them and caress them.[298] Three years passed away, and the children could walk about, after which their father taught them to speak his own tongue; and in their early babblings their human origin was manifested. The boys, as mere children, could climb about on the mountains as easily as though walking upon a level road; and between them and their father there grew up a mutual feeling of attachment. One day the mother had gone out with the girl and one of the boys, and was absent for a long time. A strong north wind was blowing, and Xu, filled with thoughts of his old home, led his other son down with him to the beach, where lay the boat in which he had formerly reached this country. He then proposed to the boy that they should go away together; and, having explained to him that they could not inform his mother, father and son stepped on board, and after a voyage of only twenty-four hours, arrived safely at Jiaozhou. On reaching home Xu found that his wife had married again; so he sold two of his pearls for an enormous sum of money,[299] and set up a splendid establishment. His son was called Biao, and at fourteen or fifteen years of age the boy could lift a weight of three thousand catties[300] (4000 lb.). He was extremely fond of athletics of all kinds, and thus attracted the notice of the Commander-in-Chief, who gave him a commission as sub-lieutenant. Just at that time there happened to be some trouble on the frontier, and young Biao, having covered himself with glory, was made a colonel at the age of eighteen.

About that time another merchant was driven by stress of weather to the country of the cannibals, and had hardly stepped ashore before he observed a young man whom he knew at once to be of Chinese origin. The young man asked him whence he came, and finally took him into a cave hid away in a dark valley and concealed by the dense jungle. There he bade him remain, and in a little while he returned with some deer's flesh, which he gave the merchant to eat, saying at the same time that his own father was

---

298 Fondness for children is specially a trait of Chinese character; and a single baby would do far more to ensure the safety of a foreign traveler in China than all the usual paraphernalia of pocketpistols and revolvers.

299 Literally, "a million of taels."

300 Here again we have 100 *jun*, one *jun* being equal to about 40 *lb*. Chinese weights, measures, distances, numbers, etc., are often very loosely employed; and it is probable that not more than 100 *atties*, say 133 *lb.*, is here meant.

a Jiaozhou man. The merchant now knew that the young man was Xu's son, he himself being acquainted with Xu as a trader in the same line of business. "Why, he's an old friend of mine," cried the latter; "his other son is now a colonel." The young man did not know what was meant by a *colonel,* so the merchant told him it was the title of a Chinese mandarin. "And what is a *mandarin?*" asked the youth. "A mandarin," replied the merchant, "is one who goes out with a chair and horses; who at home sits upon a dais in the hall; whose summons is answered by a hundred voices; who is looked at only with sidelong eyes, and in whose presence all people stand aslant—this is to be a mandarin." The young man was deeply touched at this recital, and at length the merchant said to him, "Since your honored father is at Jiaozhou, why do you remain here?" "Indeed," replied the youth, "I have often indulged the same feeling; but my mother is not a Chinese woman, and, apart from the difference of her language and appearance, I fear that if the other cannibals found it out they would do us some mischief." He then took his leave, being in rather a disturbed state of mind, and bade the merchant wait until the wind should prove favorable,[301] when he promised to come and see him off, and charge him with a letter to his father and brother. Six months the merchant remained in that cave, occasionally taking a peep at the cannibals passing backwards and forwards, but not daring to leave his retreat. As soon as the monsoon set in the young man arrived and urged him to hurry away, begging him, also, not to forget the letter to his father. So the merchant sailed away and soon reached Jiaozhou, where he visited the colonel and told him the whole story. Biao was much affected, and wished to go in search of those members of the family; but his father feared the dangers he would encounter, and advised him not to think of such a thing. However, Biao was not to be deterred; and having imparted his scheme to the Commander-in-Chief, he took with him two soldiers and set off. Adverse winds prevailed at that time, and they beat about for half a moon, until they were out of sight of all land, could not see a foot before them, and had completely lost their reckoning. Just then a mighty sea arose and capsized their boat, tossing Biao into the water, where he floated about for some time at the will of the waves, until suddenly somebody dragged him out and carried him into a house. Then he saw that his rescuer was to all appearances a cannibal, and accordingly he addressed him in the language of the country, and told him whither he himself was bound. "It is my native place," replied the cannibal, in astonishment; "but

---

301 That is, until the change of the monsoon from S.W. to N.E.

you will excuse my saying that you are now 8000 *li* out of your course. This is the way to the country of the Poisonous Dragons, and not your route at all." He then went off to find a boat for Biao, and, himself swimming in the water behind, pushed it along like an arrow from a bow, so quickly that by the next day they had traversed the whole distance. On the shore Biao observed a young man walking up and down and evidently watching him; and, knowing that no human beings dwelt there, he guessed at once that he was his brother. Approaching more closely, he saw that he was right; and, seizing the young man's hand, he asked after his mother and sister. On hearing that they were well, he would have gone directly to see them; but the younger one begged him not to do so, and ran away himself to fetch them. Meanwhile, Biao turned to thank the cannibal who had brought him there, but he, too, had disappeared. In a few minutes his mother and sister arrived, and, on seeing Biao, they could not restrain their tears. Biao then laid his scheme before them, and when they said they feared people would ill-treat them, he replied, "In China I hold a high position, and people will not dare to show you disrespect." Thus they determined to go. The wind, however, was against them, and mother and son were at a loss what to do, when suddenly the sail bellied out towards the south, and a rustling sound was heard. "Heaven helps us, my mother!" cried Biao, full of joy; and, hurrying on board at once, in three days they had reached their destination. As they landed the people fled right and left in fear, Biao having divided his own clothes amongst the party; and when they arrived at the house, and his mother saw Xu, she began to rate him soundly for running away without her. Xu hastened to acknowledge his error, and then all the family and servants were introduced to her, each one being in mortal dread of such a singular personage. Biao now bade his mother learn to talk Chinese, and gave her any quantity of fine clothes and rich meats, to the infinite delight of the old lady. She and her daughter both dressed in man's clothes, and by the end of a few months were able to understand what was said to them. The brother, named Bao (Leopard), and the sister, Ye (Night), were both clever enough, and immensely strong into the bargain. Biao was ashamed that Bao could not read, and set to work to teach him; and the youngster was so quick that he learnt the Sacred Books[302] and histories by merely reading them once over. However, he would not enter upon a literary career, loving better to draw a strong bow or ride a spirited horse, and finally taking the highest military degree. He married the daughter of a

---

302 See note 204 in tale number 41.

post-captain; but his sister had some trouble in getting a husband, because of her being the child of a cannibal woman. At length a sergeant, named Yuan, who was under her brother's command, and had become a widower, consented to take her as his wife. She could draw a hundred-catty bow, and shoot birds at a hundred paces without ever missing. Whenever Yuan went on a campaign she went with him; and his subsequent rise to high rank was chiefly due to her. At thirty-four years of age Bao got a command; and in his great battles his mother, clad in armour and grasping a spear, would fight by his side, to the terror of all their adversaries; and when he himself received the dignity of an hereditary title, he memorialized the Throne to grant his mother the title of "lady."

58. Foot-Ball on Lake Dongting

WANG SHIXIU was a native of Luzhou, and such a lusty fellow that he could pick up a stone mortar.[303] Father and son were both good foot-ball players; but when the former was about forty years of age he was drowned while crossing the Money Pool.[304] Some eight or nine years later our hero happened to be on his way to Hunan; and anchoring in lake Dongting, watched the moon rising in the east and illuminating the water into a bright sheet of light. While he was thus engaged, lo! from out of the lake emerged five men, bringing with them a large mat, which they spread on the surface of the water so as to cover about six yards square. Wine and food were then arranged upon it, and Wang heard the sound of the dishes knocking together, but it was a dull, soft sound, not at all like that of ordinary crockery. Three of the men sat down on the mat and the other two waited upon them. One of the former was dressed in yellow, the other two in white, and each wore a black turban. Their demeanor as they sat there side by side was grave and dignified; in appearance they resembled three of the ancients, but by the fitful beams of the moon Wang was unable to see very clearly what they were like. The attendants wore black twill dresses, and one of them seemed to be a boy, while the other was many years older. Wang now heard the man in the yellow dress say, "This is truly a fine moonlit night for a drinking bout;" to which one of his companions replied, "It quite reminds

---

303 Used for pounding rice.
304 A fancy name for lake Dongting. See note 194 in tale number 38.

me of the night when Prince Guangli feasted at Pear-blossom Island."[305]
The three then pledged each other in bumping goblets, talking all the time
in such a low tone that Wang could not hear what they were saying. The
boatmen kept themselves concealed, crouching down at the bottom of the
boat; but Wang looked hard at the attendants, the elder of whom bore a
striking resemblance to his father, though he spoke in quite a different tone
of voice. When it was drawing towards midnight, one of them proposed a
game at ball; and in a moment the boy disappeared in the water, to return
immediately with a huge ball—quite an armful in fact—apparently full of
quicksilver, and lustrous within and without. All now rose up, and the man
in the yellow dress bade the old attendant join them in the game. The ball
was kicked up some ten or fifteen feet in the air, and was quite dazzling in
its brilliancy; but once, when it had gone up with a whish-h-h-h, it fell at
some distance off, right in the very middle of Wang's boat. The occasion
was irresistible, and Wang, exerting all his strength, kicked the ball with
all his might. It seemed unusually light and soft to the touch, and his foot
broke right through. Away went the ball to a good height, pouring forth a
stream of light like a rainbow from the hole Wang had made, and making
as it fell a curve like that of a comet rushing across the sky. Down it glided
into the water, where it fizzed a moment and then went out. "Ho, there!"
cried out the players in anger, "what living creature is that who dares thus
to interrupt our sport?" "Well kicked—indeed!" said the old man, "that's
a favorite drop-kick of my own." At this, one of the two in white clothes
began to abuse him, saying, "What! you old baggage, when we are all so
annoyed in this manner, are you to come forward and make a joke of it?
Go at once with the boy and bring back to us this practical joker, or your
own back will have a taste of the stick." Wang was of course unable to
flee; however, he was not a bit afraid, and grasping a sword stood there in
the middle of the boat. In a moment, the old man and boy arrived, also
armed, and then Wang knew that the former was really his father, and
called out to him at once, "Father, I am your son." The old man was greatly
alarmed, but father and son forgot their troubles in the joy of meeting once
again. Meanwhile, the boy went back, and Wang's father bade him hide, or
they would all be lost. The words were hardly out of his mouth when the
three men jumped on board the boat. Their faces were black as pitch, their
eyes as big as pomegranates, and they at once proceeded to seize the old
man. Wang struggled hard with them, and managing to get the boat free

---

305 The commentator declares himself unable to trace this allusion.

from her moorings, he seized his sword and cut off one of his adversaries' arms. The arm dropped down and the man in the yellow dress ran away; whereupon one of those in white rushed at Wang, who immediately cut off his head, and he fell into the water with a splash, at which the third disappeared. Wang and his father were now anxious to get away, when suddenly a great mouth arose from the lake, as big and as deep as a well, and against which they could hear the noise of the water when it struck. This mouth blew forth a violent gust, of wind, and in a moment the waves were mountains high and all the boats on the lake were tossing about. The boatmen were terrified, but Wang seized one of two huge stones there were on board for use as anchors,[306] about 130 lb. in weight, and threw it into the water, which immediately began to subside; and then he threw in the other one, upon which the wind dropped, and the lake became calm again. Wang thought his father was a disembodied spirit, but the old man said, "I never died. There were nineteen of us drowned in the river, all of whom were eaten by the fish-goblins except myself: I was saved because I could play foot-ball. Those you saw got into trouble with the Dragon King, and were sent here. They were all marine creatures, and the ball they were playing with was a fish-bladder." Father and son were overjoyed at meeting again, and at once proceeded on their way. In the morning they found in the boat a huge fin—the arm that Wang had cut off the night before.

59. The Thunder God

Yo YUNHAO and Xia Pingzi lived as boys in the same village, and when they grew up read with the same tutor, becoming the firmest of friends. Xia was a clever fellow, and had acquired some reputation even at the early age of ten. Yo was not a bit envious, but rather looked up to him, and Xia in return helped his friend very much with his studies, so that he, too, made considerable progress. This increased Xia's fame, though try as he would he could never succeed at the public examinations, and by-and-by he sickened and died. His family was so poor they could not find money for his burial, whereupon Yo came foward and paid all expenses, besides taking care of his widow and children.

---

306 These are bound in between several sharply pointed stakes, and serve their purpose very well in the inland waters of China.

Every peck or bushel he would share with them, the widow trusting entirely to his support; and thus he acquired a good name in the village, though not being a rich man himself he soon ran through all his own property. "Alas!" cried he, "where talents like Xia's failed, can I expect to succeed? Wealth and rank are matters of destiny, and my present career will only end by my dying like a dog in a ditch. I must try something else." So he gave up book-learning and went into trade, and in six months he had a trifle of money in hand.

One day when he was resting at an inn in Nanjing, he saw a great big fellow walk in and seat himself at no great distance in a very melancholy mood. Yo asked him if he was hungry, and on receiving no answer, pushed some food over towards him. The stranger immediately set to feeding himself by handfuls, and in no time the whole had disappeared. Yo ordered another supply, but that was quickly disposed of in like manner; and then he told the landlord to bring a shoulder of pork and a quantity of boiled dumplings. Thus, after eating enough for half a dozen, his appetite was appeased and he turned to thank his benefactor, saying, "For three years I haven't had such a meal." "And why should a fine fellow like you be in such a state of destitution?" inquired Yo; to which the other only replied, "The judgments of heaven may not be discussed." Being asked where he lived, the stranger replied, "On land I have no home, on the water no boat; at dawn in the village, at night in the city." Yo then prepared to depart; but his friend would not leave him, declaring that he was in imminent danger, and that he could not forget the late kindness Yo had shown him. So they went along together, and on the way Yo invited the other to eat with him; but this he refused, saying that he only took food occasionally. Yo marveled more than ever at this; and next day when they were on the river a great storm arose and capsized all their boats, Yo himself being thrown into the water with the others. Suddenly the gale abated and the stranger bore Yo on his back to another boat, plunging at once into the water and bringing back the lost vessel, upon which he placed Yo and bade him remain quietly there. He then returned once more, this time carrying in his arms a part of the cargo, which he replaced in the vessel, and so he went on until it was all restored. Yo thanked him, saying, "It was enough to save my life; but you have added to this the restoration of my goods." Nothing, in fact, had been lost, and now Yo began to regard the stranger as something more than human. The latter here wished to take his leave, but Yo pressed him so much to stay that at last he consented to remain. Then Yo remarked that after all he had lost a gold pin, and immediately the stranger plunged into the water again, rising at length to the surface with the missing article in his mouth, and presenting it to Yo with the remark that he was delighted to be able to fulfil his commands. The people on the river were all much astonished at what they saw; meanwhile Yo went home with his friend, and there they lived together, the big man only eating once in ten or twelve days, but then displaying an enormous appetite. One day he spoke of going away, to which Yo would by no means consent; and as it was just then about to rain and thunder, he asked him to tell him what the clouds were like, and what thunder was, also how he could get up to the sky and have a look, so as to set his mind at rest on the subject. "Would you like to have a ramble among the clouds?" asked the stranger, as Yo was lying down to take a nap; on awaking from which he felt himself spinning along through the air, and not at all as if he was lying on a bed. Opening his eyes he saw he was among the clouds, and around him was a fleecy atmosphere. Jumping up in great alarm, he felt giddy as if he had been at sea, and underneath his feet he found a soft, yielding substance unlike the earth. Above him were the stars, and this made him think he was dreaming; but looking up he saw that they were set in the sky like seeds in the cup of a lily, varying from the size of the biggest bowl to that of a small basin. On raising his hand he discovered that the large stars were all tightly fixed; but he managed to pick a small one, which he concealed in his sleeve; and then, parting the clouds beneath him, he looked through and saw the sea glittering like silver below. Large cities appeared no bigger than beans—just at this moment, however, he bethought himself that if his foot were to slip, what a tremendous fall he would have. He now beheld two dragons writhing their way along, and drawing a cart with a huge vat in it, each movement of their tails sounding like the crack of a bullock-driver's whip. The vat was full of water, and numbers of men were employed in ladling it out and sprinkling it on the clouds. These men were astonished at seeing Yo; however, a big fellow among them called out, "All right, he's my friend," and then they gave him a ladle to help them throw the water out. Now it happened to be a very dry season, and when Yo got hold of the ladle he took good care to throw the water so that it should all fall on and around his own home. The stranger then told him that he was an assistant to the God of Thunder,[307] and that he had just returned from a three years' punishment inflicted on him in consequence of some neglect of

---

307 This deity is believed to be constantly on the look-out for wicked people, aided by the Goddess of Lightning, who flashes a mirror on to whomsoever the God wishes to strike. "*The thief eats thunder-bolts,*" means that he will bring down vengeance from Heaven on himself. Tylor's *Primitive Culture*, Vol. I., p. 88.

his in the matter of rain. He added that they must now part and taking the long rope which had been used as reins for the cart, bade Yo grip it tightly, that he might be let down to earth. Yo was afraid of this, but on being told there was no danger he did so, and in a moment whish-h-h-h-h—away he went and found himself safe and sound on *terra firma*. He discovered that he had descended outside his native village, and then the rope was drawn up into the clouds and he saw it no more. The drought had been excessive; for three or four miles around very little rain had fallen, though in Yo's own village the water-courses were all full. On reaching home he took the star out of his sleeve, and put it on the table. It was dull-looking like an ordinary stone; but at night it became very brilliant and lighted up the whole house. This made him value it highly, and he stored it carefully away, bringing it out only when he had guests, to light them at their wine. It was always thus dazzling bright, until one evening when his wife was sitting with him doing her hair, the star began to diminish in brilliancy, and to flit about like a fire-fly. Mrs. Yo sat gaping with astonishment, when all of a sudden it flitted into her mouth and ran down her throat. She tried to cough it up, but couldn't, to the very great amazement of her husband. That night Yo dreamt that his old friend Xia appeared before him and said, "I am the Shaowei star. Your friendship is still cherished by me, and now you have brought me back from the sky. Truly our destinies are knitted together, and I will repay your kindness by becoming your son." Now Yo was thirty years of age, but without sons; however, after this dream his wife bore him a male child, and they called his name Star. He was extraordinarily clever, and at sixteen years of age took his master's degree.

60. The Gambler's Talisman

A TAOIST priest, called Han, lived at the Tianqi temple, in our district city. His knowledge of the black art was very extensive, and the neighbors all regarded him as an Immortal.[308] My late father was on intimate terms with him, and whenever he went into the city invariably paid him a visit. One day, on such an occasion, he was proceeding thither in company with my late uncle, when suddenly they met Han on the road. Handing them the key of the door, he begged them to go on and wait awhile for him, promising to

---

308 See note 13 in tale number 5.

be there shortly himself. Following out these instructions, they repaired to the temple, but on unlocking the door there was Han sitting inside—a feat which he subsequently performed several times.

Now a relative of mine, who was terribly given to gambling, also knew this priest, having been introduced to him by my father. And once this relative, meeting with a Buddhist priest from the Tianfo temple, addicted like himself to the vice of gambling, played with him until he had lost everything, even going so far as to pledge the whole of his property, which he lost in a single night. Happening to call in upon Han as he was going back, the latter noticed his exceedingly dejected appearance, and the rambling answers he gave, and asked him what was the matter. On hearing the story of his losses, Han only laughed, and said, "That's what always overtakes the gambler, sooner or later; if, however, you will break yourself of the habit, I will get your money back for you." "Ah," cried the other, "if I can only win back my money, you may break the dice with an iron pestle when you catch me gambling again." So Han gave him a talismanic formula, written out on a piece of paper, to put in his girdle, bidding him only win back what he had lost, and not attempt to get a fraction more. He also handed him 1000 *cash,* on condition that this sum should be repaid from his winnings, and off went my relative delighted. The Buddhist, however, turned up his nose at the small-ness of his means, and said it wasn't worth his while to stake so little; but at last he was persuaded into having one throw for the whole lot. They then began, the priest leading off with a fair throw, to which his opponent replied by a better; whereupon the priest doubled his stake, and my relative won again, going on and on until the latter's good luck had brought him back all that he had previously lost. He thought, however, that he couldn't do better than just win a few more strings of cash, and accordingly went on; but gradually his luck turned, and on looking into his girdle he found that the talisman was gone. In a great fright he jumped up, and went off with his winnings to the temple, where he reckoned up that after deducting Han's loan, and adding what he had lost towards the end, he had exactly the amount originally his. With shame in his face he turned to thank Han, mentioning at the same time the loss of the talisman; at which Han only laughed, and said, "That has got back before you. I told you not to be over-greedy, and as you didn't heed me, I took the talisman away."[309]

---

309 Gambling is the great Chinese vice, far exceeding in its ill effects all that opium has ever done to demoralize the country. Public gaming-houses are strictly forbidden by law, but their existence is winked at by a too venal executive. *Fandan* is the favorite game. It consists in staking on the remainder of an unknown number of cash, after the heap has been divided by four, namely, whether it will be three, two,

61. The Husband Punished

JING XING, of Wendeng, was a young fellow of some literary reputation, who lived next door to a Mr. Chen, their studios being separated only by a low wall. One evening Chen was crossing a piece of waste ground when he heard a young girl crying among some pine-trees hard by. He approached, and saw a girdle hanging from one of the branches, as if its owner was just on the point of hanging herself. Chen asked her what was the matter, and then she brushed away her tears, and said, "My mother has gone away and left me in charge of my brother-in-law; but he's a scamp, and won't continue to take care of me; and now there is nothing left for me but to die." Hereupon the girl began crying again, and Chen untied the girdle and bade her go and find herself a husband; to which she said there was very little chance of that; and then Chen offered to take her to his own home—an offer which she very gladly accepted. Soon after they arrived, his neighbor Jing thought he heard a noise, and jumped over the wall to have a peep, when lo and behold! at the door of Chen's house stood this young lady, who immediately ran away into the garden on seeing Jing. The two young men pursued her, but without success, and were obliged to return each to his own room, Jing being greatly astonished to find the same girl now standing at his door. On addressing the young lady, she told him that his neighbor's destiny was too poor a one for her,[310] and that she came from Shandong, and that her name was Qi Axia. She finally agreed to take up her residence with Jing; but after a few days, finding that a great number of his friends were constantly calling, she declared it was too noisy a place for her, and that she would only visit him in the evening. This she continued to do for a few days, telling him in reply to his inquiries that her home was not very far off. One evening, however, she remarked that their present *liaison* was not very creditable to either; that her father was a mandarin on the western frontier, and that she was about to set out with her mother to join him; begging him meanwhile to make a formal request for the celebration of their nuptials, in order to prevent them from being thus separated. She further said that they started in ten days or so, and then Jing began to reflect that if he married her she would have to take her place in the family, and that would make his first wife jealous; so he determined to get rid of the latter, and when she came in he began to abuse her right and left. His wife bore it as long as she

one or nothing; with other variations of a more complicated nature.
310 See note 238 in tale number 46.

could, but at length cried out it were better she should die; upon which Jing advised her not to bring trouble on them all like that, but to go back to her own home. He then drove her away, his wife asking all the time what she had done to be sent away like this after ten years of blameless life with him.[311] Jing, however, paid no heed to her entreaties, and when he had got rid of her he set to work at once to get the house whitewashed and made generally clean, himself being on the tip-toe of expectation for the arrival of Miss Axia. But he waited and waited, and no Axia came; she seemed gone like a stone dropped into the sea. Meanwhile emissaries came from his late wife's family begging him to take her back; and when he flatly refused, she married a gentleman of position named Xia, whose property adjoined Jing's, and who had long been at feud with him in consequence, as is usual in such cases. This made Jing furious, but he still hoped that Axia would come, and tried to console himself in this way. Yet more than a year passed away, and still no signs of her, until one day, at the festival of the Sea Spirits, he saw among the crowds of girls passing in and out one who very much resembled Axia. Jing moved towards her, following her as she threaded her way through the crowd as far as the temple gate, where he lost sight of her altogether, to his great mortification and regret. Another six months passed away, when one day he met a young lady dressed in red, accompanied by an old man-servant, and riding on a black mule. It was Axia. So he asked the old man the name of his young mistress, and learnt from him that she was the second wife of a gentleman named, Zheng, having been married to him about a fortnight previously. Jing now thought she could not be Axia, but just then the young lady, hearing them talking, turned her head, and Jing saw that he was right. And now, finding that she had actually married another man, he was overwhelmed with I rage, and cried out in a loud voice, "Axia! Axia! why did you break faith?" The servant here objected to his mistress being thus addressed by a stranger, and was squaring up to Jing, when Axia bade him desist; and, raising her veil, replied, "And you, faithless one, how do you dare meet my gaze?" "You are the faithless one," said Jing, "not I." "To be faithless to your wife is worse than being faithless to me," rejoined Axia; "if you behaved like that to her, how should I have been treated at your hands? Because of the fair fame of your ancestors, and the honors gained by them, I was willing to ally myself with you; but now that you have discarded your wife, your thread of official advancement has been cut short in the realms below, and Mr. Chen is to take the place that

---

311 See note 254 in tale number 53.

STRANGE TALES FROM A CHINESE STUDIO

should have been yours at the head of the examination list. As for myself, I am now part of the Zheng family; think no more of me." Jing hung his head and could make no reply; and Axia whipped up her mule and disappeared from his sight, leaving him to return home disconsolate. At the forthcoming examination, everything turned out as she had predicted; Mr. Chen was at the top of the list, and he himself was thrown out. It was clear that his luck was gone. At forty he had no wife, and was so poor that he was glad to pick up a meal where he could. One day he called on Mr. Zheng, who treated him well and kept him there for the night; and while there Zheng's second wife saw him, and asked her husband if his guest's name wasn't Jing. "It is," said he; "how could you guess that?" "Well," replied she, "before I married you, I took refuge in his house, and he was then very kind to me. Although he has now sunk low, yet his ancestors' influence on the family fortunes is not yet exhausted;[312] besides, he is an old acquaintance of yours, and you should try and do something for him." Zheng consented, and having first given him a new suit of clothes, kept him in the house several days. At night a slave-girl came to him with twenty ounces of silver for him, and Mrs. Zheng, who was outside the window, said, "This is a trifling return for your past kindness to me. Go and get yourself a good wife. The family luck is not yet exhausted, but will descend to your sons and grandchildren. Do not behave like this again, and so shorten your term of life." Jing thanked her and went home, using ten ounces of silver to procure a concubine from a neighboring family, who was very ugly and ill-tempered. However, she bore him a son, and he by-and-by graduated as doctor. Mr. Zheng became Vice-President of the Board of Civil Office,[313] and at his death Axia attended the funeral; but when they opened her chair on its return home, she was gone, and then people knew for the first time that she was not mortal flesh and blood! Alas! for the perversity of mankind, rejecting the old and craving for the new,[314] until at length the nest is overthrown and; the birds fly away. Thus does heaven punish such people.

---

312 The virtuous conduct of any individual will result not only in happiness and prosperity to himself, but a certain quantity of these will descend to his posterity, unless, as in the present case, there is one among them whose personal wickedness neutralizes any benefit that would otherwise accrue therefrom. Here we have an instance where the crimes of a descendant still left a balance of good fortune surviving from the accumulated virtue of generations.
313 One of the six departments of State administration.
314 This seems a curious charge to bring against a people who for a stolid and bigoted conservatism have rarely, if ever, been equalled. Mencius, however, uttered one golden sentence which might be brought to bear upon the occasionally foolish opposition of the Chinese to measures of proved advantage to the commonwealth. "Live," said the Sage, "in harmony with the age in which you are born."

62. The Marriage Lottery

A CERTAIN laborer, named Ma Tianrong, lost his wife when he was only about twenty years of age, and was too poor to take another. One day when out hoeing in the fields, he beheld a nice-looking young lady leave the path and come tripping across the furrows towards him. Her face was well painted,[315] and she had altogether such a refined look that Ma concluded she must have lost her way, and began to make some playful remarks in consequence. "You go along home," cried the young lady, "and I'll be with you by-and-by." Ma doubted this rather extraordinary promise, but she vowed and declared she would not break her word; and then Ma went off, telling her that his front door faced the north, etc. etc. At midnight the young lady arrived, and then Ma saw that her hands and face were covered with fine hair, which made him suspect at once she was a fox. She did not deny the accusation; and accordingly Ma said to her, "If you really are one of those wonderful creatures you will be able to get me anything I want; and I should be much obliged if you would begin by giving me some money to relieve my poverty." The young lady said she would; and next evening, when she came again, Ma asked her where the money was. "Dear me!" replied she, "I quite forgot it." When she was going away, Ma reminded her of what he wanted, but on the following evening she made precisely the same excuse, promising to bring it another day. A few nights afterwards Ma asked her once more for the money, and then she drew from her sleeve two pieces of silver, each weighing about five or six ounces. They were both of fine quality, with turned-up edges,[316] and Ma was very pleased and stored them away in a cupboard. Some months after this, he happened to require some money for use, and took out these pieces; but the person to whom he showed them said they were only pewter, and easily bit off a portion of one of them with his teeth. Ma was much alarmed, and put the pieces away directly; taking the opportunity when evening came of abusing the young lady roundly. "It's all your bad luck," retorted she; "real gold would be too much for your inferior destiny."[317] There was an end of that; but Ma went on to say, "I always heard that fox-girls were of surpassing beauty; how is it you are not?" "Oh," replied the young lady, "we always adapt ourselves to our company. Now you haven't the luck of an ounce of silver to call your

---

315 Only slave-girls and women of the poorer classes, and old women, omit this very important part of a Chinese lady's toilet.
316 Alluding probably to the shape of the "shoe" or ingot of silver.
317 See note 238 in tale number 46.

own; and what would you do, for instance, with a beautiful princess?[318] My beauty may not be good enough for the aristocracy; but among your big-footed, bent-backed rustics,[319] why, it may safely be called 'surpassing.'"

A few months passed away, and then one day the young lady came and gave Ma three ounces of silver, saying, "You have often asked me for money, but in consequence of your weak luck I have always refrained from giving you any. Now, however, your marriage is at hand, and I here give you the cost of a wife, which you may also regard as a parting gift from me." Ma replied that he wasn't engaged, to which the young lady answered that in a few days a go-between would visit him to arrange the affair. "And what will she be like?" asked Ma. "Why, as your aspirations are for 'surpassing' beauty," replied the young lady, "of course she will be possessed of surpassing beauty." "I hardly expect that," said Ma; "at any rate, three ounces of silver will not be enough to get a wife." "Marriages," explained the young lady, "are made in the moon;[320] mortals have nothing to do with them." "And why must you be going away like this?" inquired Ma. "Because," answered she, "for us to meet only by night is not the proper thing. I had better get you another wife and have done with you." Then when morning came, she departed, giving Ma a pinch of yellow powder, saying, "In case you are ill after we are separated, this will cure you." Next day, sure enough, a go-between did come, and Ma at once asked what the proposed bride was like; to which the former replied that she was very passable-looking. Four or five ounces of silver was fixed as the marriage present, Ma making no difficulty on that score, but declaring he must have a peep at the young lady.[321] The go-between said she was a respectable girl, and would never allow herself to be seen; however, it was arranged that they should go to the house together, and await a good opportunity. So off they went, Ma remaining outside while the go-between went in, returning in a little while to tell him it was all

---

318 Literally, "One who would make wild geese alight and fish dive down for shame;" or, as the next line from the same poem has it, "a beauty which would obscure the moon and put flowers to the blush."
319 Slave-girls do not have their feet compressed.
320 Wherein resides an old gentleman who ties together with a red cord the feet of those destined to become man and wife. From this bond there is no escape, no matter what distance may separate the affianced pair. The first go-between, Gu ci, was originally seen on ice, arranging matches with someone below:

> Marriage is not a trifling thing—
> The Book and the Vermilion String!
> On ice by moonlight may be seen
> The wedded couples' go-between.
> —*A Thousand Character Essays for Girls.*

Hence the common phrase "to do the ice (business)," *i.e.,* to arrange a marriage.
321 This proceeding is highly improper, but is winked at in a large majority of Chinese betrothals.

right. "A relative of mine lives in the same court, and just now I saw the young lady sitting in the hall. We have only got to pretend we are going to see my relative, and you will be able to get a glimpse of her." Ma consented, and they accordingly passed through the hall, where he saw the young lady sitting down with her head bent forward while some one was scratching her back. She seemed to be all that the go-between had said; but when they came to discuss the money, it appeared the young lady only wanted one or two ounces of silver, just to buy herself a few clothes, etc., which Ma thought was a very small amount, and gave the go-between a present for her trouble, which just finished up the three ounces his fox-friend had provided. An auspicious day was chosen, and the young lady came over to his house; when lo! she was humpbacked and pigeon-breasted, with a short neck like a tortoise, and regular beetle-crushers, full ten inches long. The meaning of his fox-friend's remarks then flashed upon him.

63. The Luocha Country and the Sea Market[322]

ONCE upon a time there was a young man, named Ma Zhun, who was also known as Longmei. He was the son of a trader, and a youth of surpassing beauty. His manners were courteous, and he loved nothing better than singing and playing. He used to associate with actors, and with an embroidered handkerchief around his head the effect was that of a beautiful woman. Hence he acquired the sobriquet of the Beauty. At fourteen years of age he graduated and began to make a name for himself; but his father, who was growing old and wished to retire from business, said to him, "My boy, book-learning will never fill your belly or put a coat on your back; you had much better stick to the old thing." Accordingly, Ma from that time occupied himself with scales and weights, with principal and interest, and such matters.

He made a voyage across the sea, and was carried away by a typhoon. After being tossed about for many days and nights he arrived at a country where the people were hideously ugly. When these people saw Ma they thought he was a devil, and all ran screeching away. Ma was somewhat alarmed at this, but finding that it was they who were frightened at him, he

---

322 The term "sea-market" is generally understood in the sense of *mirage,* or some similar phenomenon.

quickly turned their fear to his own advantage. If he came across people eating and drinking he would rush upon them, and when they fled away for fear, he would regale himself upon what they had left. By-and-by he went to a village among the hills, and there the people had at any rate some facial resemblance to ordinary men. But they were all in rags and tatters like beggars. So Ma sat down to rest under a tree, and the villagers, not daring to come near him, contented themselves with looking at him from a distance. They soon found, however, that he did not want to eat them, and by degrees approached a little closer to him. Ma, smiling, began to talk; and although their language was different, yet he was able to make himself tolerably intelligible, and told them whence he had come. The villagers were much pleased, and spread the news that the stranger was not a man-eater. Nevertheless, the very ugliest of all would only take a look and be off again; they would not come near him. Those who did go up to him were not very much unlike his own countrymen, the Chinese. They brought him plenty of food and wine. Ma asked them what they were afraid of. They replied, "We had heard from our forefathers that 26,000 *li* to the west there is a country called China. We had heard that the people of that land were the most extraordinary in appearance you can possibly imagine. Hitherto it has been hearsay; we can now believe it." He then asked them how it was they were so poor. They answered, "You see, in our country everything depends, not on literary talent, but on beauty. The most beautiful are made ministers of state; the next handsomest are made judges and magistrates; and the third class in looks are employed in the palace of the king. Thus these are enabled out of their pay to provide for their wives and families. But we, from our very birth, are regarded by our parents as inauspicious, and are left to perish, some of us being occasionally preserved by more humane parents to prevent the extinction of the family." Ma asked the name of their country, and they told him it was Luocha. Also that the capital city was some 30 *li* to the north. He begged them to take him there, and next day at cock-crow he started thitherwards in their company, arriving just about dawn. The walls of the city were made of black stone, as black as ink, and the city gate-houses were about 100 feet high. Red stones were used for tiles, and picking up a broken piece Ma found that it marked his fingernail like vermilion. They arrived just when the Court was rising, and saw all the equipages of the officials. The village people pointed out one who they said was Prime Minister. His ears drooped forward in flaps; he had three nostrils, and his eye-lashes were just like bamboo screens hanging in front of his eyes. Then several came out on horseback, and they said these were the privy councillors. So they went on, telling him the rank of all the ugly uncouth fellows he saw. The lower they got down in the official scale the less hideous the officials were. By-and-by Ma went back, the people in the streets marveling very much to see him, and tumbling helter-skelter one over another as if they had met a goblin. The villagers shouted out to reassure them, and then they stood at a distance to look at him. When he got back, there was not a man, woman, or child in the whole nation but knew that there was a strange man at the village; and the gentry and officials became very desirous of seeing him. However, if he went to any of their houses the porter always slammed the door in his face, and the master, mistress, and family, in general, would only peep at, and speak to him through the cracks. Not a single one dared receive him face to face; but, finally, the village people, at a loss what to do, bethought themselves of a man who had been sent by a former king on official business among strange nations. "He," said they, "having seen many kinds of men, will not be afraid of you." So they went to his house, where they were received in a very friendly way. He seemed to be about eighty or ninety years of age; his eyeballs protruded, and his beard curled up like a hedgehog. He said, "In my youth I was sent by the king among many nations, but I never went to China. I am now one hundred and twenty years of age, and that I should be permitted to see a native of your country is a fact which it will be my duty to report to the Throne. For ten years and more I have not been to Court, but have remained here in seclusion; yet I will now make an effort on your behalf." Then followed a banquet, and when the wine had already circulated pretty freely, some dozen singing girls came in and sang and danced before them. The girls all wore white embroidered turbans, and long scarlet robes which trailed on the ground. The words they uttered were unintelligible, and the tunes they played perfectly hideous. The host, however, seemed to enjoy it very much, and said to Ma, "Have you music in China?" He replied that they had, and the old man asked for a specimen. Ma hummed him a tune, beating time on the table, with which he was very much pleased, declaring that his guest had the voice of a phoenix and the notes of a dragon, such as he had never heard before. The next day he presented a memorial to the Throne, and the king at once commanded Ma to appear before him. Several of the ministers, however, represented that his appearance was so hideous it might frighten His Majesty, and the king accordingly desisted from his intention. The old man returned and told Ma, being quite upset about it. They remained together some time until they had drunk themselves tipsy. Then Ma, seizing a sword, began to pose for effect, smearing his face all over with coal-dust. He acted the part of Zhang Fei,[323] at which his host was so delighted that he begged him to appear before the Prime Minister in the character of Zhang Fei. Ma replied, "I don't mind a little amateur acting, but how can I play the hypocrite[324] for my own personal advantage?" On being pressed he consented, and the old man prepared a great feast, and asked some of the high officials to be present, telling Ma to paint himself as before. When the guests had arrived, Ma was brought out to see them; whereupon they all exclaimed, "Ai-yah! how is it he was so ugly before and is now so beautiful?" By-and-by, when they were all taking wine together, Ma began to sing them a most bewitching song, and they got so excited over it that next day they recommended him to the king. The king sent a special summons for him to appear, and asked him many questions about the government of China, to all of which Ma replied in detail, eliciting sighs of admiration from His Majesty. He was honored with a banquet in the royal guest-pavilion, and when the king had made himself tipsy he said to him, "I hear you are a very skillful musician. Will you be good enough to let me hear you?" Ma then got up and began to pose, singing a plaintive air like the girls with the turbans. The king was charmed, and at once made him a privy councillor, giving him a private banquet, and bestowing other marks of royal favor. As time went on his fellow officials found out the secret of his painted face,[325] and whenever he was among them they were always whispering together, besides which they avoided being near him as much as possible. Thus Ma was left to himself, and found his position anything but pleasant in consequence. So he memorialized the Throne, asking to be allowed to retire from office, but his request was refused. He then said his health was bad, and got three months' sick leave, during which he packed up his valuables and went back to the village. The villagers on his arrival went down on their knees to him, and he distributed gold and jewels amongst his old friends. They were all very glad to see him, and said, "Your kindness shall be repaid when we go to the sea-market; we will bring you some pearls and things." Ma asked them where that was. They said it was at the bottom of the sea, where the mermaids[326] kept their treasures, and that as many as twelve nations were accustomed to go thither to trade. Also that it was frequented by spirits, and that to get there it was necessary to

323 A famous General who played a leading part in the wars of the Three Kingdoms. See note 446 in tale number 93.
324 A hit at the hypocrisy of the age.
325 Showing that hypocrisy is bad policy in the long run.
326 The tears of Chinese mermaids are said to be pearls.

pass through red vapors and great waves. "Dear Sir," they said, "do not yourself risk this great danger, but let us take your money and purchase these rare pearls for you. The season is now at hand." Ma asked them how they knew this. They said, "Whenever we see red birds flying backwards and forwards over the sea, we know that within seven days the market will open." He asked when they were going to start, that he might accompany them; but they begged him not to think of doing so. He replied, "I am a sailor: how can I be afraid of wind and waves?" Very soon after this people came with merchandise to forward, and so Ma packed up and went on board the vessel that was going.

This vessel held some tens of people, was flat-bottomed, with a railing all around, and, rowed by ten men, it cut through the water like an arrow. After a voyage of three days they saw afar off faint outlines of towers and minarets, and crowds of trading vessels. They soon arrived at the city, the walls of which were made of bricks as long as a man's body, the tops of its buildings being lost in the Milky Way.[327] Having made fast their boat, they went in, and saw laid out in the market rare pearls and wondrous precious stones of dazzling beauty, such as are quite unknown amongst men. Then they saw a young man come forth riding upon a beautiful steed. The people of the market stood back to let him pass, saying he was the third son of the king; but when the prince saw Ma, he exclaimed, "This is no foreigner," and immediately an attendant drew near and asked his name and country. Ma made a bow, and standing at one side told his name and family. The prince smiled, and said, "For you to have honored our country thus is no small piece of good luck." He then gave him a horse and begged him to follow. They went out of the city gate and down to the sea-shore, whereupon their horses plunged into the water. Ma was terribly frightened and screamed out; but the sea opened dry before them and formed a wall of water on either side. In a little time they reached the king's palace, the beams of which were made of tortoise-shell and the tiles of fishes' scales. The four walls were of crystal, and dazzled the eye like mirrors. They got down off their horses and went in, and Ma was introduced to the king. The young prince said, "Sire, I have been to the market, and have got a gentleman from China." Whereupon Ma made obeisance before the king, who addressed him as follows: " Sir, from a talented scholar like yourself I venture to ask for a few stanzas upon our sea-market. Pray do not refuse." Ma thereupon made a ke-tou, and undertook the king's command. Using an

---

327 See note 103 in tale number 19.

ink-slab of crystal, a brush of dragon's beard, paper as white as snow, and ink scented like the larkspur,[328] Ma immediately threw off some thousand odd verses, which he laid at the feet of the king. When His Majesty saw them, he said, "Sir, your genius does honor to these marine nations of ours." Then, summoning the members of the royal family, the king gave a great feast in the Colored Cloud pavilion; and, when the wine had circulated freely, seizing a great goblet in his hand, the king rose and said before all the guests, "It is a thousand pities, Sir, that you are not married. What say you to entering the bonds of wedlock?" Ma rose blushing and stammered out his thanks; upon which the king, looking around, spoke a few words to the attendants, and in a few moments in came a bevy of Court ladies supporting the king's daughter, whose ornaments went tinkle, tinkle, as she walked along. Immediately the nuptial drums and trumpets began to sound forth, and bride and bridegroom worshipped Heaven and Earth together.[329] Stealing a glance, Ma saw that the princess was endowed with a fairy-like loveliness. When the ceremony was over she retired, and by-and-by the wine party broke up. Then came several beautifully dressed waiting-maids, who with painted candles escorted Ma within. The bridal couch was made of coral adorned with eight kinds of precious stones, and the curtains were thickly hung with pearls as big as acorns. Next day at dawn a crowd of young slave-girls trooped into the room to offer their services; whereupon Ma got up and went off to Court to pay his respects to the king. He was then duly received as royal son-in-law and made an officer of state. The fame of his poetical talents spread far and wide, and the kings of the various seas sent officers to congratulate him, vying with each other in their invitations to him. Ma dressed himself in gorgeous clothes, and went forth riding on a superb steed, with a mounted body-guard all splendidly armed. There were musicians on horseback and musicians in chariots, and in three days he had visited every one of the marine kingdoms, making his name known in all directions. In the palace there was a jade tree, about as big around as a man could clasp. Its roots were as clear as glass, and up the middle ran, as it were, a stick of pale yellow. The branches were the size of one's arm; the leaves like white jade, as thick as a copper cash. The foliage was dense, and beneath its shade the ladies of the palace were wont to sit

---

328 Good ink of the kind miscalled "Indian" is usually very highly scented; and from a habit the Chinese have of sucking their writing-brushes to a fine point, the phrase "to eat ink" has become a synonym of "to study."

329 This all-important point in a Chinese marriage ceremony is the equivalent of our own "signing in the vestry."

and sing. The flowers which covered the tree resembled grapes, and if a single petal fell to the earth it made a ringing sound. Taking one up, it would be found to be exactly like carved cornelian, very bright and pretty to look at. From time to time a wonderful bird came and sang there. Its feathers were of a golden hue, and its tail as long as its body. Its notes were like the tinkling of jade, very plaintive and touching to listen to. When Ma heard this bird sing, it called up in him recollections of his old home, and accordingly he said to the princess, "I have now been away from my own country for three years, separated from my father and mother. Thinking of them my tears flow and the perspiration runs down my back. Can you return with me?" His wife replied, "The way of immortals is not that of men. I am unable to do what you ask, but I cannot allow the feelings of husband and wife to break the tie of parent and child. Let us devise some plan." When Ma heard this he wept bitterly, and the princess sighed and said, "We cannot both stay or both go." The next day the king said to him, "I hear that you are pining after your old home. Will tomorrow suit you for taking leave?" Ma thanked the king for his great kindness, which he declared he could never forget, and promised to return very shortly. That evening the princess and Ma talked over their wine of their approaching separation. Ma said they would soon meet again; but his wife averred that their married life was at an end. Then he wept afresh, but the princess said, "Like a filial son you are going home to your parents. In the meetings and separations of this life, a hundred years seem but a single day; why, then, should we give way to tears like children? I will be true to you; do you be faithful to me; and then, though separated, we shall be united in spirit, a happy pair. Is it necessary to live side by side in order to grow old together? If you break our contract your next marriage will not be a propitious one; but if loneliness[330] overtakes you then choose a concubine. There is one point more of which I would speak, with reference to our married life. I am about to become a mother, and I pray you give me a name for your child." To this Ma replied, "If a girl I would have her called Longgong; if a boy, then name him Fuhai."[331] The princess asked for some token of remembrance, and Ma gave her a pair of jade lilies that he had got during his stay in the marine kingdom. She added, "On the 8th of the 4th moon, three years hence, when you once more steer your course for this country, I will give you up your child." She next packed a leather bag full of jewels and handed it to Ma, saying, "Take

---

330 Literally, "if you have no one to cook your food."
331 "Dragon Palace" "and "Happy Sea," respectively.

care of this; it will be a provision for many generations." When the day began to break a splendid farewell feast was given him by the king, and Ma bade them all adieu. The princess, in a car drawn by snow-white sheep, escorted him to the boundary of the marine kingdom, where he dismounted and stepped ashore. "Farewell!" cried the princess, as her returning car bore her rapidly away, and the sea, closing over her, snatched her from her husband's sight. Ma returned to his home across the ocean. Some had thought him long since dead and gone; all marveled at his story. Happily his father and mother were yet alive, though his former wife had married another man; and so he understood why the princess had pledged him to constancy, for she already knew that this had taken place. His father wished him to take another wife, but he would not. He only took a concubine. Then, after the three years had passed away, he started across the sea on his return journey, when lo! he beheld, riding on the wave-crests and splashing about the water in playing, two young children. On going near, one of them seized hold of him and sprang into his arms; upon which the elder cried until he, too, was taken up. They were a boy and girl, both very lovely, and wearing embroidered caps adorned with jade lilies. On the back of one of them was a worked case, in which Ma found the following letter:

"I presume my father and mother-in-law are well. Three years have passed away and destiny still keeps us apart. Across the great ocean, the letter-bird would find no path.[332] I have been with you in my dreams until I am quite worn out. Does the blue sky look down upon any grief like mine? Yet Changao[333] lives solitary in the moon, and Zhi Nü[334] laments that she cannot cross the Silver River. Who am I that I should expect happiness to be mine? Truly this thought turns my tears into joy. Two months after your departure I had twins, who can already prattle away in the language of childhood, at one moment snatching a date, at another a pear. Had they no mother they would still live. These I now send to you, with the jade lilies you gave me in their hats, in token of the sender. When you take them upon your knee, think that I am standing by your side. I know that you have kept your promise to me, and I am happy. I shall take no second husband, even unto death. All thoughts of dress and finery are gone from me; my looking-glass sees no new fashions; my face has long been unpowdered, my eyebrows

---

332 Alluding to an old legend of a letter conveyed by a bird.

333 See note 14 in tale number 5.

334 "The" Spinning Damsel," or name of a star in Lyra, connected with which there is a celebrated legend of its annual transit across the Milky Way.

unblacked. You are my Ulysses, I am your Penelope;[335] though not actually leading a married life, how can it be said that we are not husband and wife? Your father and mother will take their grandchildren upon their knees, though they have never set eyes upon the bride. Alas! there is something wrong in this. Next year your mother will enter upon the long night. I shall be there by the side of the grave, as is becoming in her daughter-in-law. From this time forth our daughter will be well; later on she will be able to grasp her mother's hand. Our boy, when he grows up, may possibly be able to come to and fro. Adieu, dear husband, adieu, though I am leaving much unsaid." Ma read the letter over and over again, his tears flowing all the time. His two children clung around his neck, and begged him to take them home. "Ah, my children," said he, "where is your home?" Then they all wept bitterly, and Ma, looking at the great ocean stretching away to meet the sky, lovely and pathless, embraced his children, and proceeded sorrowfully to return. Knowing, too, that his mother could not last long, he prepared everything necessary for the ceremony of interment, and planted a hundred young pine-trees at her grave.[336] The following year the old lady did die, and her coffin was borne to its last resting-place, when lo! there was the princess standing by the side of the grave. The lookers-on were much alarmed, but in a moment there was a flash of lightning followed by a clap of thunder and a squall of rain, and she was gone. It was then noticed that many of the young pine-trees which had died were one and all brought to life. Subsequently, Fuhai went in search of the mother for whom he pined so much, and after some days' absence returned. Longgong, being a girl, could not accompany him, but she mourned much in secret. One dark day her mother entered and bade her dry her eyes, saying, "My child, you must get married. Why these tears?" She then gave her a tree of coral eight feet in height, some Baroos camphor,[337] one hundred valuable pearls, and two boxes inlaid with gold and precious stones, as her dowry. Ma having found out she was there, rushed in, and, seizing her hand, began to weep for joy, when suddenly a violent peal of thunder rent the building and the princess had vanished.[338]

---

335 These are of course only the equivalents of the Chinese names in the text.

336 To keep off the much-dreaded wind, which disturbs the rest of the departed.

337 For which a very high price is obtained in China.

338 Episodes which appear in this story and in "The Princess of Lake Dongting" have been woven together to form the so-called Japanese "tale of Urashima, the fisher-lad who was beloved of the Sea King's daughter." See the *Fortnightly Review*, July 1906, p. 99, and Aston's *Japanese Literature*, p. 39.

64. The Fighting Cricket

DURING the reign of Xuande,[339] cricket fighting was very much in vogue at court, levies of crickets being exacted from the people as a tax. On one occasion the magistrate of Huayin, wishing to make friends with the Governor, presented him with a cricket which, on being set to fight, displayed very remarkable powers; so much so that the Governor commanded the magistrate to supply him regularly with these insects. The latter, in his turn, ordered the beadles of his district to provide him with crickets; and then it became a practice for people who had nothing else to do to catch and rear them for this purpose. Thus the price of crickets rose very high; and when the beadle's[340] runners came to exact even a single one, it was enough to ruin several families.

Now in the village of which we are speaking there lived a man named Cheng, a student who had often failed for his bachelor's degree; and, being a stupid sort of fellow, his name was sent in for the post of beadle. He did all he could to get out of it, but without success; and by the end of the year his small patrimony was gone. Just then came a call for crickets, and Cheng, not daring to make a like call upon his neighbors, was at his wits' end, and in his distress determined to commit suicide. "What's the use of that?" cried his wife. "You'd do better to go out and try to find some." So off went Cheng in the early morning, with a bamboo tube and a silk net, not returning until late at night; and he searched about in tumble-down walls, in bushes, under stones, and in holes, but without catching more than two or three, do what he would. Even those he did catch were weak creatures, and of no use at all, which made the magistrate fix a limit of time, the result of which was that in a few days Cheng got one hundred blows with the bamboo. This made him so sore that he was quite unable to go after the crickets any more, and, as he lay tossing and turning on the bed, he determined once again to put an end to his life.

---

339 Of the Ming dynasty; reigned 1426–1436 CE.

340 These beadles are chosen by the officials from among the respectable and substantial of the people to preside over a small area and be responsible for the general good behavior of its inhabitants. The post is one of honor and occasional emolument, since all petitions presented to the authorities, all mortgages, transfers of land, etc., should bear the beadle's seal or signature in evidence of their *bona-fide* character. On the other hand, the beadle is punished by fine, and sometimes bambooed, if robberies are too frequent within his jurisdiction, or if he fails to secure the person of any malefactor particularly wanted by his superior officers. And other causes may combine to make the post a dangerous one; but no one is allowed to refuse acceptance of it point-blank.

About that time a hump-backed fortune-teller of great skill arrived at the village, and Cheng's wife, putting together a trifle of money, went off to seek his assistance. The door was literally blocked up—fair young girls and white-headed dames crowding in from all quarters. A room was darkened, and a bamboo screen hung at the door, an altar being arranged outside at which the fortune-seekers burnt incense in a brazier, and prostrated themselves twice, while the soothsayer stood by the side, and, looking up into vacancy, prayed for a response. His lips opened and shut, but nobody heard what he said, all standing there in awe waiting for the answer. In a few moments a piece of paper was thrown from behind the screen, and the soothsayer said that the petitioner's desire would be accomplished in the way he wished. Cheng's wife now advanced, and, placing some money on the altar, burnt her incense and prostrated herself in a similar manner. In a few moments the screen began to move, and a piece of paper was thrown down, on which there were no words, but only a picture. In the middle was a building like a temple, and behind this a small hill, at the foot of which were a number of curious stones, with the long, spiky feelers of innumerable crickets appearing from behind. Hard by was a frog, which seemed to be engaged in putting itself into various kinds of poses. The good woman had no idea what it all meant; but she noticed the crickets, and accordingly went off home to tell her husband. "Ah," said he, "this is to show me where to hunt for crickets;" and, on looking closely at the picture, he saw that the building very much resembled a temple to the east of their village. So he forced himself to get up, and, leaning on a stick, went out to seek crickets behind the temple. Rounding an old grave, he came upon a place where stones were lying scattered about as in the picture, and then he set himself to watch attentively. He might as well have been looking for a needle or a grain of mustard-seed; and by degrees he became quite exhausted, without finding anything, when suddenly an old frog jumped out. Cheng was a little startled, but immediately pursued the frog, which retreated into the bushes. He then saw one of the insects he wanted sitting at the root of a bramble; but on making a grab at it, the cricket ran into a hole, from which he was unable to move it until he poured in some water, when out the little creature came. It was a magnificent specimen, strong and handsome, with a fine tail, green neck, and golden wings; and, putting it in his basket, he returned home in high glee to receive the congratulations of his family. He would not have taken anything for this cricket. He put it into a bowl, and fed it with white crab's flesh and with the yellow kernel of the sweet chestnut, tending it most lovingly, and waiting for the time when the magistrate should call upon him for a cricket.

Meanwhile, a son of Cheng's, aged nine, one day took the opportunity of his father being out to open the bowl. Instantaneously the cricket made a spring forward and was gone; and all efforts to catch it again were unavailing. At length the boy made a grab at it with his hand, but only succeeded in seizing one of its legs, which thereupon broke, and the little creature soon afterwards died. Cheng's wife turned deadly pale when her son, with tears in his eyes, told her what had happened. "Oh, you young rascal! won't you catch it when your father comes home," said she; at which the boy ran away, crying bitterly. Soon after Cheng arrived, and when he heard his wife's story he felt as if he had been turned to ice, and went in search of his son, who, however, was nowhere to be found, until at length they discovered his body lying at the bottom of a well. Their anger was thus turned to grief, and death seemed as though it would be a pleasant relief to them as they sat facing each other in silence in their thatched and smokeless[341] hut. At evening they prepared to bury the boy; but, on touching the body, lo! he was still breathing. Overjoyed, they placed him upon the bed, and towards the middle of the night he came around; but they found that his mind was weak, and he wanted to go to sleep. His father, however, caught sight of the empty bowl in which he had kept the cricket, and ceased to think any more about his son, never once closing his eyes all night; and as day gradually broke, there he lay stiff and stark, until suddenly he heard the chirping of a cricket outside the house door. Jumping up in a great hurry to see, there was his lost insect; but, on trying to catch it, away it hopped directly. At last he got it under his hand, though when he came to close his fingers on it, there was nothing in them. So he went on, chasing it up and down, until finally it hopped into a corner of the wall; and then, looking carefully about, he espied it once more, no longer the same in appearance, but small, and of a dark red color. Cheng stood looking at it, without trying to catch such a worthless specimen, when all of a sudden the little creature hopped into his sleeve; and, on examining it more nearly, he saw that it really was a handsome insect, with well-formed head and neck, and forthwith took it indoors. He was now anxious to try its prowess; and it so happened that a young fellow of the village, who had a fine cricket which used to win every bout it fought, and was so valuable to him that he wanted a high price for it, called on Cheng that very day. He laughed heartily at Cheng's champion, and, producing his own, placed it side by side, to the great disadvantage of the former. Cheng's countenance fell, and he no longer wished to back his

---

341   A favorite Chinese expression, signifying the absence of food.

cricket; however, the young fellow urged him, and he thought that there was no use in rearing a feeble insect, and that he had better sacrifice it for a laugh; so they put them together in a bowl. The little cricket lay quite still like a piece of wood, at which the young fellow roared again, and louder than ever when it did not move even though tickled with a pig's bristle. By dint of tickling it was roused at last, and then it fell upon its adversary with such fury, that in a moment the young fellow's cricket would have been killed outright had not its master interfered and stopped the fight. The little cricket then stood up and chirped to Cheng as a sign of victory; and Cheng, overjoyed, was just talking over the battle with the young fellow when a cock caught sight of the insect, and ran up to eat it. Cheng was in a great state of alarm; but the cock luckily missed its aim, and the cricket hopped away, its enemy pursuing at full speed. In another moment it would have been snapped up, when, lo! to his great astonishment, Cheng saw his cricket seated on the cock's head, holding firmly on to its comb. He then put it into a cage, and by-and-by sent it to the magistrate, who, seeing what a small one he had provided, was very angry indeed. Cheng told the story of the cock, which the magistrate refused to believe, and set it to fight with other crickets, all of which it vanquished without exception. He then tried it with a cock, and as all turned out as Cheng had said, he gave him a present, and sent the cricket in to the Governor. The Governor put it into a golden cage, and forwarded it to the palace, accompanied by some remarks on its performances; and when there, it was found that of all the splendid collection of His Imperial Majesty, not one was worthy to be placed alongside of this one. It would dance in time to music, and thus became a great favorite, the Emperor in return bestowing magnificent gifts of horses and silks upon the Governor. The Governor did not forget whence he had obtained the cricket, and the magistrate also well rewarded Cheng by excusing him from the duties of beadle, and by instructing the Literary Chancellor to pass him for the first degree. A few months afterwards Zheng's son recovered his intellect, and said that he had been a cricket, and had proved himself a very skillful fighter.[342] The Governor, too, rewarded Cheng handsomely, and in a few years he was a rich man, with flocks, and herds, and houses, and acres, quite one of the wealthiest of mankind.

---

342 That is to say, his spirit had entered, during his period of temporary insanity, into the cricket which had allowed itself to be caught by his father, and had animated it to fight with such extraordinary vigor in order to make good the loss occasioned by his carelessness in letting the other escape.

65. Taking Revenge

XIANG GAO, otherwise called Chudan, was a Taiyuan man, and deeply attached to his half-brother Sheng. Sheng himself was desperately enamoured of a young lady named Bosi,[343] who was also very fond of him: but the mother wanted too much money for her daughter. Now a rich young fellow named Zhuang thought he should like to get Bosi for himself, and proposed to buy her as a concubine. "No, no," said Bosi to her mother, "I prefer being Sheng's wife to becoming Zhuang's concubine." So her mother consented, and informed Sheng, who had only recently buried his first wife; at which he was delighted and made preparations to take her over to his own house. When Zhuang heard this he was infuriated against Sheng for thus depriving him of Bosi; and chancing to meet him out one day, set to and abused him roundly. Sheng answered him back, and then Zhuang ordered his attendants to fall upon Sheng and beat him well, which they did, leaving him lifeless on the ground. When Xiang heard what had taken place he ran out and found his brother lying dead upon the ground. Overcome with grief, he proceeded to the magistrate's, and accused Zhuang of murder; but the latter bribed so heavily that nothing came of the accusation. This worked Xiang to frenzy, and he determined to assassinate Zhuang on the high road; with which intent he daily concealed himself, with a sharp knife about him, among the bushes on the hillside, waiting for Zhuang to pass. By degrees, this plan of his became known far and wide, and accordingly Zhuang never went out except with a strong bodyguard, besides which he engaged at a high price the services of a very skillful archer, named Jiao Tong, so that Xiang had no means of carrying out his intention. However, he continued to lie in wait day after day, and on one occasion it began to rain heavily, and in a short time Xiang was wet through to the skin. Then the wind got up, and a hailstorm followed, and by-and-by Xiang was quite numbed with the cold. On the top of the hill there was a small temple wherein lived a Taoist priest, whom Xiang knew from the latter having occasionally, begged alms in the village, and to whom he had often given a meal. This priest, seeing how wet he was, gave him some other clothes, and told him to put them on; but no sooner had he done so than he crouched down like a dog, and found that he had been changed into a tiger, and that the priest had vanished. It

---

343   This is the term used by the Chinese for "Persia," often put by metonymy for things which come from that country, *sc.* "valuables." Thus, "to be poor in Persia" is to have but few jewels, gold and silver ornaments, and even clothes.

now occurred to him to seize this opportunity of revenging himself upon his enemy; and away he went to his old ambush, where lo and behold! he found his own body lying stiff and stark. Fearing lest it should become food for birds of prey, he guarded it carefully, until at length one day Zhuang passed by. Out rushed the tiger and sprang upon Chaung, biting his head off, and swallowing it upon the spot, at which Jiao Tong, the archer, turned around and shot the animal through the heart. Just at that moment Xiang awaked as though from a dream, but it was some time before he could crawl home, where he arrived to the great delight of his family, who didn't know what had become of him. Xiang said not a word, lying quietly on the bed until some of his people came in to congratulate him on the death of his great enemy Zhuang. Xiang then cried out, "I was that tiger," and proceeded to relate the whole story, which thus got about until it reached the ears of Zhuang's son, who immediately set to work to bring his father's murderer to justice. The magistrate, however, did not consider this wild story as sufficient evidence against him, and thereupon dismissed the case.

66. The Tipsy Turtle

At Lintiao there lived a Mr. Feng, whose other name the person who told me this story could not remember; he belonged to a good family, though now somewhat falling into decay. Now a certain man, who caught turtles, owed him some money which he could not pay, but. whenever he captured any turtles he used to send one to Mr. Feng. One day he took him an enormous creature, with a white spot on its forehead; but Feng was so struck with something in its appearance, that he let it go again. A little while afterwards he was returning home from his son-in-law's, and had reached the banks of the river,[344] when in the dusk of the evening he saw a drunken man come rolling along, attended by two or three servants. No sooner did he perceive Feng than he called out, "Who are you?" to which Feng replied that he was a traveler. "And haven't you got a name?" shouted out the drunken man in a rage, "that you must call yourself a traveler?" To

---

344 The name here used is the *Heng* or "ceaseless" river, which is applied by the Chinese to the Ganges. A certain number, extending to fifty-three places of figures, is called "Ganges sand," in allusion to a famous remark that "Buddha and the Bôdhisatras knew of the creation and destruction of every grain of dust in Jambudwipa (the universe); how much more the number of the sand-particles in the river Ganges?"

this Feng made no reply, but tried to pass by; whereupon he found himself seized by the sleeve, and unable to move. His adversary smelt horribly of wine, and at length Feng asked him, saying, "And pray who are you?" "Oh, I am the late magistrate at Nandu," answered he; "what do you want to know for?" "A nice disgrace to society you are, too," cried Feng; "however, I am glad to hear you are only *late* magistrate, for if you had been present magistrate there would be bad times in store for travelers." This made the drunken man furious, and he was proceeding to use violence, when Feng cried out, "My name is So-and-so, and I'm not the man to stand this sort of thing from anybody." No sooner had he uttered these words than the drunken man's rage was turned into joy, and, falling on his knees before Feng, he said, "My benefactor! pray excuse my rudeness." Then getting up, he told his servants to go on ahead and get something ready; Feng at first declining to go with him, but yielding on being pressed. Taking his hand, the drunken man led him along a short distance until they reached a village, where there was a very nice house and grounds, quite like the establishment of a person of position. As his friend was now getting sober, Feng inquired what might be his name. "Don't be frightened when I tell you," said the other; "I am the Eighth Prince of the Tiao river. I have just been out to take wine with a friend, and somehow I got tipsy; hence my bad behavior to you, which please forgive." Feng now knew that he was not of mortal flesh and blood; but, seeing how kindly he himself was treated, he was not a bit afraid. A banquet followed, with plenty of wine, of which the Eighth Prince drank so freely that Feng thought he would soon be worse than ever, and accordingly said he felt tipsy himself, and asked to be allowed to go to bed. "Never fear," answered the Prince, who perceived Feng's thoughts; "many drunkards will tell you that they cannot remember in the morning the extravagances of the previous night, but I tell you this is all nonsense, and that in nine cases out of ten those extravagances are committed wittingly and with malice prepense.[345] Now, though I am not the same order of being as yourself, I should never venture to behave badly in your good presence; so pray do not leave me thus." Feng then sat down again and said to the Prince, "Since you are aware of this, why not change your ways?" "Ah," replied the Prince, "when I was a magistrate I drank much more than I do now; but I got into disgrace with the Emperor and

---

345 Drunkenness is not recognised in China as an extenuating circumstance; neither, indeed, is insanity—a lunatic who takes another man's life being equally liable with ordinary persons to the forfeiture of his own.

was banished here, since which time, ten years and more, I have tried to reform. Now, however, I am drawing near the wood,[346] and being unable to move about much, the old vice has come upon me again; I have found it impossible to stop myself, but perhaps what you say may do me some good." While they were thus talking, the sound of a distant bell broke upon their ears; and the Prince, getting up and seizing Feng's hand, said, "We cannot remain together any longer; but I will give you something by which I may in part requite your kindness to me. It must not be kept for any great length of time; when you have attained your wishes, then I will receive it back again." Thereupon he spat out of his mouth a tiny man, no more than an inch high, and scratching Feng's arm with his nails until Feng felt as if the skin was gone, he quickly laid the little man upon the spot. When he let go, the latter had already sunk into the skin, and nothing was to be seen but a cicatrix well healed over. Feng now asked what it all meant, but the Prince only laughed, and said, "It's time for you to go," and forthwith escorted him to the door. The Prince here bade him adieu, and when he looked around, Prince, village, and house had all disappeared together, leaving behind a great turtle which waddled down into the water, and disappeared likewise. He could now easily account for the Prince's present to him; and from this moment his sight became intensely keen. He could see precious stones lying in the bowels of the earth, and was able to look down as far as Hell itself; besides which he suddenly found that he knew the names of many things of which he had never heard before. From below his own bedroom he dug up many hundred ounces of pure silver, upon which he lived very comfortably; and once when a house was for sale, he perceived that in it lay concealed a vast quantity of gold, so he immediately bought it, and so became immensely rich in all kinds of valuables. He secured a mirror, on the back of which was a phoenix, surrounded by water and clouds, and portraits of the celebrated wives of the Emperor Shun,[347] so beautifully executed that each hair of the head and eyebrows could easily be counted. If any woman's face came upon the mirror, there it remained indelibly fixed and not to be rubbed out; but if the same woman looked into the mirror again, dressed in a different dress, or if some other woman chanced to look in, then the former face would gradually fade away.

---

346 A favorite Chinese figure expressive of old age. It dates back to the celebrated commentary by Zuo-qiu Ming on Confucius' *Spring and Autumn* (see note 204 in tale number 41): "Xi is twenty-three and I am twenty-five; and marrying thus we shall approach the wood together;" the "wood" being, of course, that of the coffin.
347 See note 29 in tale number 8.

Now the third princess in Prince Su's family was very beautiful; and Feng, who had long heard of her fame, concealed himself on the Kongdong hill, when he knew the Princess was going there. He waited until she alighted from her chair, and then getting the mirror full upon her, he walked off home. Laying it on the table, he saw therein a lovely girl in the act of raising her handkerchief, and with a sweet smile playing over her face; her lips seemed about to move, and a twinkle was discernible in her eyes.[348] Delighted with this picture, he put the mirror very carefully away; but in about a year his wife had let the story leak out, and the Prince, hearing of it, threw Feng into prison, and took possession of the mirror. Feng was to be beheaded; however, he bribed one of the Prince's ladies to tell His Highness that if he would pardon him all the treasures of the earth might easily become his; whereas, on the other hand, his death could not possibly be of any advantage to the Prince. The Prince now thought of confiscating all his goods and banishing him; but the third princess observed, that as he had already seen her, were he to die ten times over it would not give her back her lost face, and that she had much better marry him. The Prince would not hear of this, whereupon his daughter shut herself up and refused all nourishment, at which the ladies of the palace were dreadfully alarmed, and reported it at once to the Prince. Feng was accordingly liberated, and was to informed of the determination of the Princess, which, however, he declined to fall in with, saying that he was not going thus to sacrifice the wife of his days of poverty,[349] and would rather die than carry out such an order. He added that if His Highness would consent, he would purchase his liberty at the price of everything he had. The Prince was exceedingly angry at this, and seized Feng again; and meanwhile one of the concubines got Feng's wife into the palace, intending to poison her. Feng's wife, however, brought her a beautiful present of a coral stand for a looking-glass, and was so agreeable in her conversation, that the concubine took a great fancy to her, and presented her to the Princess, who was equally pleased, and forthwith determined that they would both be Feng's wives.[350] When Feng heard of this plan, he said to his wife, "With a Prince's daughter there can be no distinctions of first and second wife;" but Mrs. Feng paid no heed to

---

348   . . . Move these eyes?
             . . . Here are severed lips.
                                        —*Merchant of Venice,* Act III., sc. 2.
349 See note 254 in tale number 53.
350 This method of arranging a matrimonial difficulty is a common one in Chinese fiction, but I should say quite unknown in real life.

him, and immediately sent off to the Prince such an enormous quantity of valuables that it took a thousand men to carry them, and the Prince himself had never before heard of such treasures in his life. Feng was now liberated once more, and solemnized his marriage with the Princess.

One night after this he dreamt that the Eighth Prince came to him and asked him to return his former present, saying that to keep it too long would be injurious to his chances of life. Feng asked him to take a drink, but the Eighth Prince said that he had forsworn wine, acting under Feng's advice, for three years. He then bit Feng's arm, and the latter waked up with the pain, to find that the cicatrix on his arm was no longer there.

67. The Magic Path

IN the province of Guangdong there lived a scholar named Guo, who was one evening on his way home from a friend's, when he lost his way among the hills. He got into a thick jungle, where, after about an hour's wandering, he suddenly heard the sound of laughing and talking on the top of the hill. Hurrying up in the direction of the sound, he beheld some ten or a dozen persons sitting on the ground engaged in drinking. No sooner had they caught sight of Guo than they all cried out, "Come along! just room for one more; you're in the nick of time." So Guo sat down with the company, most of whom, he noticed, belonged to the literati,[351] and began by asking them to direct him on his way home; but one of them cried out, "A nice sort of fellow you are, to be bothering about your way home, and paying no attention to the fine moon we have got tonight." The speaker then presented him with a goblet of wine of exquisite bouquet, which Guo drank off at a draught, and another gentleman filled up again for him at once. Now, Guo was pretty good in that line, and being very thirsty withal from his long walk, tossed off bumper after bumper, to the great delight of his hosts, who were unanimous in voting him a jolly good fellow. He was, moreover, full of fun, and could imitate exactly the note of any kind of bird; so all of a sudden

---

351 This term, while really including all literary men, of no matter what rank or standing, is more usually confined to that large section of unemployed scholarship made up of (1) those who are waiting to get started in an official career, (2) those who have taken one or more degrees and are preparing for the next, (3) those who have failed to distinguish themselves at the public examinations, and eke out a small patrimony by taking pupils, and (4) scholars of sufficiently high qualifications who have no taste for official life.

he began on the sly to twitter like a swallow, to the great astonishment of the others, who wondered how it was a swallow could be out so late. He then changed his note to that of a cuckoo, sitting there laughing and saying nothing, while his hosts were discussing the extraordinary sounds they had just heard. After a while he imitated a parrot, and cried, "Mr. Guo is very drunk: you'd better see him home;" and then the sounds ceased, beginning again by-and-by, when at last the others found out who it was, and all burst out laughing. They screwed up their mouths and tried to whistle like Guo, but none of them could do so; and soon one of them observed, "What a pity Madam Qing isn't with us: we must rendezvous here again at mid-autumn, and you, Mr. Guo, must be sure and come." Guo said he would, whereupon another of his hosts got up and remarked that, as he had given them such an amusing entertainment, they would try to show him a few acrobatic feats. They all arose, and one of them planting his feet firmly, a second jumped up on to his shoulders, a third on to the second's shoulders, and a fourth on to his, until it was too high for the rest to jump up, and accordingly they began to climb as though it had been a ladder. When they were all up, and the topmost head seemed to touch the clouds, the whole column bent gradually down until it lay along the ground transformed into a path. Guo remained for some time in a state of considerable alarm, and then, setting out along this path, ultimately reached his own home. Some days afterwards he revisited the spot, and saw the remains of a feast lying about on the ground, with dense bushes on all sides, but no sign of a path. At mid-autumn he thought of keeping his engagement; however, his friends persuaded him not to go.

68. The Faithless Widow[352]

MR. NIU was a Jiangxi man who traded in piece goods. He married a wife from the Zheng family, by whom he had two children, a boy and a girl. When thirty-three years of age he fell ill and died, his son Zhong being then

---

352 Unless under exceptional circumstances, it is not considered creditable in China for widows to marry again. It may here be mentioned that the honorary tablets conferred from time to time by His Imperial Majesty upon virtuous widows are only given to women who, widowed before the age of thirty, have remained in that state for a period of thirty years. The meaning of this is obvious; temptations are supposed to be fewer and less dangerous after thirty, which is the equivalent of forty with us; and it is wholly improbable that thirty years of virtuous life, at which period the widow would be at least fifty, would be followed by any act that might cast a stain upon the tablet thus bestowed.

only twelve and his little girl eight or nine. His wife did not remain faithful to his memory, but, selling off all the property, pocketed the proceeds and married another man, leaving her two children almost in a state of destitution with their aunt, Niu's sister-in-law, an old lady of sixty, who had lived with them previously, and had now nowhere to seek a shelter. A few years later this aunt died, and the family fortunes began to sink even lower than before; Zhong, however, was now grown up, and determined to carry on his father's trade, only he had no capital to start with. His sister marrying a rich trader named Mao, she begged her husband to lend Zhong ten ounces of silver, which he did, and Zhong immediately started for Nanjing. On the road he fell in with some bandits, who robbed him of all he had, and consequently he was unable to return; but one day when he was at a pawnshop he noticed that the master of the shop was wonderfully like his late father, and on going out and making inquiries he found that this pawnbroker bore precisely the same names. In great astonishment, he forthwith proceeded to frequent the place with no other object than to watch this man, who, on the other hand, took no notice of Zhong; and by the end of three days, having satisfied himself that he really saw his own father, and yet not daring to disclose his own identity, he made application through one of the assistants, on the score of being himself a Jiangzi man, to be employed in the shop. Accordingly, an indenture was drawn up; and when the master noticed Zhong's name and place of residence he started, and asked him whence he came. With tears in his eyes Zhong addressed him by his father's name, and then the pawnbroker became lost in a deep reverie, by-and-by asking Zhong how his mother was. Now Zhong did not like to allude to his father's death, and turned the question by saying, "My father went away on business six years ago, and never came back; my mother married again and left us, and had it not been for my aunt our corpses would long ago have been cast out in the kennel." Then the pawnbroker was much moved, and cried out, "I am your father!" seizing his son's hand and leading him within to see his step-mother. This lady was about twenty-two, and, having no children of her own, was delighted with Zhong, and prepared a banquet for him in the inner apartments. Mr. Niu himself was, however, somewhat melancholy, and wished to return to his old home; but his wife, fearing that there would be no one to manage the business, persuaded him to remain; so he taught his son the trade, and in three months was able to leave it all to him. He then prepared for his journey, whereupon Zhong informed his step-mother that his father was really dead, to which she replied in great consternation that she knew him only as a trader to the place, and that six years previously he had married her, which proved conclusively that he couldn't be dead. He then recounted the whole story, which was a perfect mystery to both of them; and twenty-four hours afterwards in walked his father, leading a woman whose hair was all dishevelled. Zhong looked at her, and saw that she was his own mother; and Niu took her by the ear and began to revile her, saying, "Why did you desert my children?" to which the wretched woman made no reply. He then bit her across the neck, at which she screamed to Zhong for assistance, and he, not being able to bear the sight, stepped in between them. His father was more than ever enraged at this, when, lo! Zhong's mother had disappeared. While they were still lost in astonishment at this strange scene, Mr. Niu's color changed; in another moment his empty clothes had dropped upon the ground, and he himself became a black vapor and also vanished from their sight. The stepmother and son were much overcome; they took Niu's clothes and buried them, and after that Zhong continued his father's business, and soon amassed great wealth. On returning to his native place he found that his mother had actually died on the very day of the above occurrence, and that his father had been seen by the whole family.

69. The Princess of Lake Dongting

CHEN BIJIAO was a Pekingese; and being a poor man he attached himself as secretary to the suite of a high military official named Jia. On one occasion, while anchored on lake Dongting, they saw a dolphin[353] floating on the surface of the water; and General Jia took his bow and shot at it, wounding the creature in the back. A fish was hanging on to its tail, and would not let go; so both were pulled out of the water together, and attached to the mast. There they lay gasping, the dolphin opening its mouth as if pleading for life, until at length young Chen begged the General to let them go again; and then he himself half-jokingly put a piece of plaster upon the dolphin's wound, and had the two thrown back into the water, where they were seen for some time afterwards diving and rising again to the surface. About a year afterwards, Chen was once more crossing lake Dongting on his way home,

353 Literally, a "pig old-woman dragon." Porpoise (Fr. Porc-poisson) suggests itself at once; but I think fresh-water dolphin is the best term, especially as lake Dongting is many hundred miles inland. The commentator explains it by to, which would be "alligator" or "cayman," and is of course out of the question.

when the boat was upset in a squall, and he himself only saved by clinging
to a bamboo crate, which finally, after floating about all night, caught in
the overhanging branch of a tree, and thus enabled him to scramble on
shore. By-and-by, another body floated in, and this turned out to be his
servant; but on dragging him out, he found life was already extinct. In
great distress, he sat himself down to rest, and saw beautiful green hills and
waving willows, but not a single human being of whom he could ask the
way. From early dawn until the morning was far advanced he remained in
that state; and then, thinking he saw his servant's body move, he stretched
out his hand to feel it, and before long the man threw up several quarts of
water and recovered consciousness. They now dried their clothes in the sun,
and by noon these were fit to put on; at which period the pangs of hunger
began to assail them, and accordingly they started over the hills in the hope
of coming upon some habitation of man. As they were walking along, an
arrow whizzed past, and the next moment two young ladies dashed by on
handsome palfreys. Each had a scarlet band around her head, with a bunch
of pheasant's feathers stuck in her hair, and wore a purple riding-jacket with
small sleeves, confined by a green embroidered girdle around the waist.
One of them carried a cross-bow for shooting bullets, and the other had on
her arm a dark-colored bow-and-arrow case. Reaching the brow of the hill,
Chen beheld a number of riders engaged in beating the surrounding cover,
all of whom were beautiful girls and dressed exactly alike. Afraid to advance
any further, he inquired of a youth who appeared to be in attendance, and
the latter told him that it was a hunting party from the palace; and then,
having supplied him with food from his wallet, he bade him retire quickly,
adding that if he fell in with them he would assuredly be put to death,
Thereupon Chen hurried away; and descending the hill, turned into a copse
where there was a building which he thought would in all probability be a
monastery. On getting nearer, he saw that the place was surrounded by a
wall, and between him and a half-open red door was a brook spanned by
a stone bridge leading up to it. Pulling back the door, he beheld within a
number of ornamental buildings circling in the air like so many clouds,
and for all the world resembling the Imperial pleasure-grounds; and
thinking it must be the park of some official personage, he walked quietly
in, enjoying the delicious fragrance of the flowers as he pushed aside the
thick vegetation which obstructed his way. After traversing a winding path
fenced in by balustrades, Chen reached a second enclosure, wherein were a
quantity of tall willow-trees which swept the red eaves of the buildings with
their branches. The note of some bird would set the petals of the flowers

fluttering in the air, and the least wind would bring the seed-vessels down from the elm-trees above; and the effect upon the eye and heart of the beholder was something quite unknown in the world of mortals. Passing through a small kiosk, Chen and his servant came upon a swing which seemed as though suspended from the clouds, while the ropes hung idly down in the utter stillness that prevailed.[354] Thinking by this that they were approaching the ladies' apartments,[355] Chen would have turned back, but at that moment he heard sounds of horses' feet at the door, and what seemed to be the laughter of a bevy of girls. So he and his servant hid themselves in a bush; and by-and-by, as the sounds came nearer, he heard one of the young ladies say, "We've had but poor sport today;" whereupon another cried out, "If the princess hadn't shot that wild goose, we should have taken all this trouble for nothing." Shortly after this, a number of girls dressed in red came in escorting a young lady, who went and sat down under the kiosk. She wore a hunting costume with tight[356] sleeves, and was about fourteen or fifteen years old. Her hair looked like a cloud of mist at the back of her head, and her waist seemed as though a breath of wind might snap it[357]—incomparable for beauty, even among the celebrities of old. Just then the attendants handed her some exquisitely fragrant tea, and stood glittering around her like a bank of beautiful embroidery. In a few moments the young lady arose and descended from the kiosk; at which one of her attendants cried out, "Is your Highness too fatigued by riding to take a turn in the swing?" The princess replied that she was not; and immediately some held her under the shoulders, while others seized her arms, and others, again, arranged her petticoats and supported her feet. Thus they helped her into the swing, she herself stretching out her shining arms, and putting her feet into a suitable pair of slippers;[358] and then—away she went, light as a flying-swallow, far up into the fleecy clouds. As soon as she had had enough, the attendants helped her out, and one of them exclaimed, "Truly,

---

354 Literally, in the utter absence of anybody.

355 In passing near to the women's quarters in a friend's house, it is etiquette to cough slightly, that inmates may be warned and withdraw from the doors or windows in time to escape observation. Over and over again at interviews with mandarins of all grades I have heard the rustling of the ladies' dresses from some coign of vantage, whence every movement of mine was being watched by an inquisitive crowd; and on one occasion I actually saw an eye peering through a small hole in the partition behind me.

356 Literally, "bald" —i.e., without the usual width and ornamentation of a Chinese lady's sleeve.

357 Small waists are much admired in China, but any such artificial aids as stays and tight lacing are quite unknown. A certain Prince Wei admitted none but the possessors of small waists into his harem; hence his establishment came to be called the *Palace of Small Waists*.

358 Probably of felt or some such material, to prevent the young lady from slipping as she stood, in this case, not sat, in the swing. Chinese girls swing either standing or sitting.

your Highness is a perfect angel!" At this the young lady laughed, and walked away, Chen gazing after her in a state of semi-consciousness, until, at length, the voices died away, and he and his servant crept forth. Walking up and down near the swing, he suddenly espied a red handkerchief near the paling, which he knew had been dropped by one of the young ladies; and, thrusting it joyfully into his sleeve, he walked up and entered the kiosk. There, upon a table, lay writing materials, and taking out the handkerchief he indited upon it the following lines:

What form divine was just now sporting nigh?—
'Twas she, I think, of "golden lily" fame;
Her charms the moon's fair denizens might shame,
Her fairy footsteps bear her to the sky.

Humming this stanza to himself, Chen walked along seeking for the path by which he had entered; but every door was securely barred, and he knew not what to do. So he went back to the kiosk, when suddenly one of the young ladies appeared, and asked him in astonishment what he did there. "I have lost my way," replied Chen; "I pray you lend me your assistance." "Do you happen to have found a red handkerchief?" said the girl. "I have, indeed," answered Chen, "but I fear I have made it somewhat dirty;" and, suiting the action to the word, he drew it forth, and handed it to her. "Wretched man!" cried the young lady, "you are undone. This is a handkerchief the Princess is constantly using, and you have gone and scribbled all over it; what will become of you now?" Chen was in a great fright, and begged the young lady to intercede for him; to which she replied, "It was bad enough that you should come here and spy about; however, being a scholar, and a man of refinement, I would have done my best for you; but after this, how am I to help you?" Off she then ran with the handkerchief, while Chen remained behind in an agony of suspense, and longing for the wings of a bird to bear him away from his fate. By-and-by the young lady returned and congratulated him, saying, "There is some hope for you. The Princess read your verses several times over, and was not at all angry. You will probably be released; but, meanwhile, wait here, and don't climb the trees, or try to get through the walls, or you may not escape after all." Evening was now drawing on, and Chen knew not, for certain, what was about to happen; at the same time he was very empty, and, what with hunger and anxiety, death would have been almost a happy release. Before long, the young lady returned with a lamp in her hand, and followed by a slave-girl bearing wine and food, which she forthwith presented to Chen. The latter asked if there was any news about himself; to which the young lady replied that she had just mentioned his case to the Princess, who, not knowing what to do with him at that hour of the night, had given orders that he should at once be provided with food, "which, at any rate," added she, "is not bad news." The whole night long Chen walked up and down, unable to take rest; and it was not until late in the morning that the young lady appeared with more food for him. Imploring her once more to intercede on his behalf, she told him that the Princess had not instructed them either to kill or to release him, and that it would not be fitting for such as herself to be bothering the Princess with suggestions. So there Chen still remained until another day had almost gone, hoping for the welcome moment; and then the young lady rushed hurriedly in, saying, "You are lost! Some one has told the Queen, and she, in a fit of anger, threw the handkerchief on the ground, and made use of very violent language. Oh dear! Oh dear! I'm sure something dreadful will happen." Chen threw himself on his knees, his face as pale as ashes, and begged to know what he should do; but at that moment sounds were heard outside, and the young lady waved her hand to him, and ran away. Immediately a crowd came pouring in through the door, with ropes ready to secure the object of their search; and among them was a slave-girl, who looked fixedly at our hero, and cried out, "Why, surely you are Mr. Chen, aren't you?" at the same time stopping the others from binding him until she should have reported to the Queen. In a few minutes she came back, and said the Queen requested him to walk in; and in he went, through a number of doors, trembling all the time with fear, until he reached a hall, the screen before which was ornamented with green jade and silver. A beautiful girl drew aside the bamboo curtain at the door, and announced, "Mr. Chen;" and he himself advanced, and fell down before a lady, who was sitting upon a dais at the other end, knocking his head upon the ground, and crying out, "Thy servant is from a far-off country; spare, oh! spare his life." "Sir!" replied the Queen, rising hastily from her seat, and extending a hand to Chen, "but for you, I should not be here today. Pray excuse the rudeness of my maids." Thereupon a splendid repast was served, and wine was poured out in chased goblets, to the no small astonishment of Chen, who could not understand why he was treated thus. "Your kindness," observed the Queen, "in restoring me to life, I am quite unable to repay; however, as you have made my daughter the subject of your verse, the match is clearly ordained by fate, and I shall send her along to be your handmaid." Chen hardly knew what to make of this extraordinary accomplishment of his wishes, but the marriage was solemnized there and then; bands of music struck up wedding-airs, beautiful mats were laid down for them to walk upon, and the whole place was brilliantly lighted with a profusion of colored lamps. Then Chen said to the Princess, "That a stray and unknown traveler like myself, guilty of spoiling your Highness's handkerchief, should have escaped the fate he deserved, was already more than could be expected; but now to receive you in marriage—this, indeed, far surpasses my wildest expectations." "My mother," replied the Princess, "is married to the King of this lake, and is herself a daughter of the River Prince. Last year, when on her way to visit her parents, she happened to cross the lake, and was wounded by an arrow; but you saved her life, and gave her plaster for the wound. Our family, therefore, is grateful to you, and can never forget your good act. And do not regard me as of another species than yourself; the Dragon King has bestowed upon me the elixir of immortality, and this I will gladly share with you." Then Chen knew that his wife was a spirit, and by-and-by he asked her how the slave-girl had recognized him; to which she replied, that the girl was the small fish which had been found hanging to the dolphin's tail. He then inquired why, as they didn't intend to kill him, he had been kept so long a prisoner. "I was charmed with your literary talent," answered the Princess, "but I did not venture to take the responsibility upon myself; and no one saw how I tossed and turned the livelong night." "Dear friend," said Chen; "but, come, tell me who was it that brought my food." "A trusty waiting-maid of mine," replied the Princess; "her name is Anian." Chen then asked how he could ever repay her, and the Princess told him there would be plenty of time to think of that; and when he inquired where the King, her father, was, she said he had gone off with the God of War to fight against Chiyou,[359] and had not returned. A few days passed, and Chen began to think his people at home would be anxious about him; so he sent off his servant with a letter to tell them he was safe and sound, at which they were all overjoyed, believing him to have been lost in the wreck of the boat, of which event news had already reached them. However, they were unable to send him any reply, and were considerably distressed as to how he would find his way home again. Six months afterwards Chen himself appeared, dressed in fine clothes, and riding on a splendid horse, with plenty of money,

---

359 A rebel chieftain of the legendary period of China's history, who took up arms against the Emperor Huang Di (2698–2598 BCE), but was subsequently defeated in what was perhaps the first decisive battle of the world.

and valuable jewels in his pocket—evidently a man of wealth. From that time forth he kept up a magnificent establishment; and in seven or eight years had become the father of five children. Every day he kept open house, and if any one asked him about his adventures, he would readily tell them without reservation. Now a friend of his, named Liang, whom he had known since they were boys together, and who, after holding an appointment for some years in Nanfu, was crossing lake Dongting, on his way home, suddenly beheld an ornamental barge, with carved woodwork and red windows, passing over the foamy waves to the sound of music and singing from within. Just then a beautiful young lady leant out of one of the windows, which she had pushed open, and by her side Liang saw a young man sitting, in a *négligé* attitude, while two nice-looking girls stood by and massaged[360] him. Liang, at first, thought it must be the party of some high official, and wondered at the scarcity of attendants;[361] but, on looking more closely at the young man, he saw it was no other than his old friend Chen. Thereupon he began almost involuntarily to shout out to him; and when Chen heard his own name, he stopped the rowers, and walked out towards the figurehead,[362] beckoning Liang to cross over into his boat, where the remains of their feast were quickly cleared away, and fresh supplies of wine, and tea, and all kinds of costly foods spread out by handsome slave-girls. "It's ten years since we met," said Liang, "and what a rich man you have become in the meantime." "Well," replied Chen, "do you think that so very extraordinary for a poor fellow like me?" Liang then asked him who was the lady with whom he was taking wine, and Chen said she was his wife, which very much astonished Liang, who farther inquired whither they were going. "Westwards," answered Chen, and prevented any further questions by giving a signal for the music, which effectually put a stop to all further conversation.[363] By-and-by, Liang found the wine getting into his head, and seized the opportunity to ask Chen to make him a present of one of his beautiful slave-girls. "You are drunk,[364] my friend," replied Chen; "however, I will give you the price of one as a pledge of our old friendship." And,

---

360 This favorite process consists in gently thumping the person operated upon all over the back with the soft part of the closed fists. Compare Lane, *Arabian Nights*, Vol. I., p. 551:—"She then pressed me to her bosom, and laid me on the bed, and continued gently kneading my limbs until slumber overcame me."

361 See note 281 in tale number 56. A considerable number of the attendants there mentioned would accompany any high official, some in the same, the rest in another barge.

362 Generally known as the "cut-wave God."

363 At all great banquets in China a theatrical troupe is engaged to perform while the dinner, which may last from four to six hours, drags its slow length along.

364 See note 258 in tale number 54.

turning to a servant, he bade him present Liang with a splendid pearl, saying, "Now you can buy a Green Pearl;[365] you see I am not stingy;" adding forthwith, "but I am pressed for time, and can stay no longer with my old friend." So he escorted Liang back to his boat, and, having let go the rope, proceeded on his way. Now, when Liang reached home, and called at Chen's house, whom should he see but Chen himself drinking with a party of friends! "Why, I saw you only yesterday," cried Liang, "upon the Dongting. How quickly you have got back!" Chen denied this, and then Liang repeated the whole story, at the conclusion of which Chen laughed, and said, "You must be mistaken. Do you imagine I can be in two places at once?" The company were all much astonished, and knew not what to make of it; and subsequently when Chen, who died at the age of eighty, was being carried to his grave, the bearers thought the coffin seemed remarkably light, and on opening it to see, found that the body had disappeared.[366]

70. The Princess Lily

At Jiaozhou there lived a man named Dou Xun, otherwise known as Xiaohui. One day he had just dropped off to sleep when he beheld a man in serge clothes standing by the bedside, and apparently anxious to communicate something to him. Dou inquired his errand; to which the man replied that he was the bearer of an invitation from his master. "And who is your master?" asked Dou. "Oh, he doesn't live far off," replied the other; so away they went together, and after some time came to a place where there were innumerable white houses rising one above the other, and shaded by dense groves of lemon-trees. They threaded their way past countless doors, not at all similar to those usually used, and saw a great many official-looking men and women passing and repassing, each of whom called out to the man in serge, "Has Mr. Dou come?" to which he always replied in the affirmative. Here a mandarin met them and escorted Dou into a palace, upon which the latter remarked, "This is really very kind of you; but I haven't the honor of knowing you, and I feel somewhat diffident about going in." "Our Prince," answered his guide, "has long heard of you as a man of good family and excellent principles, and is very anxious to make your acquaintance." "Who

365 The name of a celebrated beauty.
366 See note 338 in tale number 63.

is your Prince?" inquired Dou. "You'll see for yourself in a moment," said the other; and just then out came two girls with banners, and guided Dou through a great number of doors until they came to a throne, upon which sat the Prince. His Highness immediately descended to meet him, and made him take the seat of honor; after which ceremony exquisite viands of all kinds were spread out before them. Looking up, Dou noticed a scroll, on which was inscribed, *The Cassia Court*, and he was just beginning to feel puzzled as to what he should say next, when the Prince addressed him as follows: " The honor of having you for a neighbor is, as it were, a bond of affinity between us. Let us, then, give ourselves up to enjoyment, and put away suspicion and fear." Dou murmured his acquiescence; and when the wine had gone around several times there arose from a distance the sound of pipes and singing, unaccompanied, however, by the usual drum, and very much subdued in volume. Thereupon the Prince looked about him and cried out, "We are about to set a verse for any of you gentlemen to cap; here you are: *Genius seeks the Cassia Court*." While the courtiers were all engaged in thinking of some fit antithesis,[367] Dou added, *"Refinement loves the Lily flower*;" upon which the Prince exclaimed, "How strange! Lily is my daughter's name; and, after such a coincidence, she must come in for you to see her." In a few moments the tinkling of her ornaments and a delicious fragrance of musk announced the arrival of the Princess, who was between sixteen and seventeen, and endowed with surpassing beauty. The Prince bade her make an obeisance to Dou, at the same time introducing her as his daughter Lily; and as soon as the ceremony was over the young lady moved away. Dou remained in a state of stupefaction, and, when the Prince proposed that they should pledge each other in another bumper, paid not the slightest attention to what he said. Then the Prince, perceiving what had distracted his guest's attention, remarked that he was anxious to find a consort for his daughter, but that unfortunately there was the difficulty of *species,* and he didn't know what to do; but again Dou took no notice of what the Prince was saying, until at length one of the bystanders plucked his sleeve, and asked him if he hadn't seen that the Prince wished to drink with him, and had just been addressing some remarks to him. Thereupon Dou started, and, recovering himself at once, rose from the table and apologized to the Prince for his rudeness, declaring that he had taken so much wine he didn't know what he was doing. "Besides," said he, "your

---

367 In this favorite pastime of the literati in China the important point is that each word in the second line should be a due and proper antithesis of the word in the first line to which it corresponds.

Highness has doubtless business to transact; I will therefore take my leave."
"I am extremely pleased to have seen you," replied the Prince, "and only
regret that you are in such a hurry to be gone. However, I won't detain you
now; but, if you don't forget all about us, I shall be very glad to invite you
here again." He then gave orders that Dou should be escorted home; and on
the way one of the courtiers asked the latter why he had said nothing when
the Prince had spoken of a consort for his daughter, as his Highness had
evidently made the remark with an eye to securing Dou as his son-in-law.
The latter was now sorry that he had missed his opportunity; meanwhile
they reached his house, and he himself awoke. The sun had already set, and
there he sat in the gloom thinking of what had happened. In the evening
he put out his candle, hoping to continue his dream; but, alas! the thread
was broken, and all he could do was to pour forth his repentance in sighs.
One night he was sleeping at a friend's house, when suddenly an officer of
the Court walked in and summoned him to appear before the Prince; so
up he jumped, and hurried off at once to the palace, where he prostrated
himself before the throne. The Prince raised him and made him sit down,
saying that since they had last met he had become aware that Dou would be
willing to marry his daughter, and hoped that he might be allowed to offer
her as a handmaid. Dou rose and thanked the Prince, who thereupon gave
orders for a banquet to be prepared; and when they had finished their wine
it was announced that the Princess had completed her toilet. Immediately
a bevy of young ladies came in with the Princess in their midst, a red veil
covering her head, gliding with tiny footsteps as they led her up to be
introduced to Dou. When the ceremonies were concluded, Dou said to the
Princess, "In your presence, Madam, it would be easy to forget even death
itself; but, tell me, is not this all a dream?" "And how can it be a dream,"
asked the Princess, "when you and I are here together?"

Next morning Dou amused himself by helping the Princess to paint
her face,[368] and then with a girdle he began to measure the size of her
waist[369] and with his fingers the length of her feet. "Are you crazy?" cried
she, laughing; to which Dou replied, "I have been deceived so often by
dreams, that I am now making a careful record. If such it turns out to be,
I shall still have something as a souvenir of you." While they were thus
chatting a maid rushed into the room, shrieking out, "Alas! alas! a great
monster has got into the palace: the Prince has fled into a side chamber:

destruction is surely come upon us." Dou was in a great fright when he heard this, and rushed off to see the Prince, who grasped his hand and, with tears in his eyes, begged him not to desert them. "Our relationship," cried he, "was cemented when Heaven sent this calamity upon us; and now my kingdom will be overthrown. What shall I do?" Dou begged to know what was the matter; and then the Prince laid a despatch upon the table, telling Dou to open it and make himself acquainted with its contents. This despatch ran as follows: "The Grand Secretary of State, Black Wings, to His Royal Highness, announcing the arrival of an extraordinary monster, and advising the immediate removal of the Court in order to preserve the vitality of the empire. A report has just been received from the officer in charge of the Yellow Gate stating that, ever since the 6th of the 5th moon, a huge monster, 10,000 feet in length, has been lying coiled up outside the entrance to the palace, and that it has already devoured 13,800 and odd of your Highness's subjects, and is spreading desolation far and wide. On receipt of this information your servant proceeded to make a reconnaissance, and there beheld a venomous reptile with a head as big as a mountain and eyes like vast sheets of water. Every time it raised its head, whole buildings disappeared down its throat; and, on stretching itself out, walls and houses were alike laid in ruins. In all antiquity there is no record of such a scourge. The fate of our temples and ancestral halls is now a mere question of hours; we therefore pray your Royal Highness to depart at once with the Royal Family and seek somewhere else a happier abode."[370] When Dou had read this document his face turned ashy pale; and just then a messenger rushed in, shrieking out, "Here is the monster!" at which the whole Court burst into lamentations as if their last hour was at hand. The Prince was beside himself with fear; all he could do was to beg Dou to look to his own safety without regarding the wife through whom he was involved in their misfortunes. The Princess, however, who was standing by bitterly lamenting the fate that had fallen upon them, begged Dou not to desert her; and, after a moment's hesitation, he said he should be only too happy to place his own poor home at their immediate disposal if they would only deign to honor him. "How can we talk of *deigning*," cried the Princess, "at such a moment as this? I pray you take us there as quickly as possible." So Dou gave her his arm, and in no time they had arrived at Dou's house, which the Princess at once

---

370 The language in which this fanciful document is couched is precisely such as would be used by an officer of the Government in announcing some national calamity; hence the value of these tales—models as they are of the purest possible style.

pronounced to be a charming place of residence, and better even than their former kingdom. "But I must now ask you," said she to Dou, "to make some arrangement for my father and mother, that the old order of things may be continued here." Dou at first offered objections to this; whereupon the Princess said that a man who would not help another in his hour of need was not much of a man, and immediately went off into a fit of hysterics, from which Dou was trying his best to recall her, when all of a sudden he awoke and found that it was all a dream. However, he still heard a buzzing in his ears which he knew was not made by any human being, and, on looking carefully about, he discovered two or three bees which had settled on his pillow. He was very much astonished at this, and consulted with his friend, who was also greatly amazed at his strange story; and then the latter pointed out a number of other bees on various parts of his dress, none of which would go away even when brushed off. His friend now advised him to get a hive for them, which he did without delay; and immediately it was filled by a whole swarm of bees, which came flying from over the wall in great numbers. On tracing whence they had come, it was found that they belonged to an old gentleman who lived near, and who had kept bees for more than thirty years previously. Dou thereupon went and told him the story; and when the old gentleman examined his hive he found the bees all gone. On breaking it open he discovered a large snake inside of about ten feet in length, which he immediately killed, recognizing in it the "huge monster" of Dou's adventure. As for the bees, they remained with Dou, and increased in numbers every year.

71. The Donkey's Revenge

ZHONG QINGYU was a scholar of some reputation, who lived in Manchuria. When he went up for his master's degree, he heard that there was a Taoist priest at the capital who would tell people's fortunes, and was very anxious to see him; and at the conclusion of the second part of the examination,[371] he accidentally met him at Baotuquan.[372] The priest was over sixty years of age, and had the usual white beard flowing down over his breast. Around

---

371 The examination consists of three bouts of three days each, during which periods the candidates remain shut up in their examination cells day and night.
372 The name of a place.

him stood a perfect wall of people inquiring their future fortunes, and to each the old man made a brief reply: but when he saw Zhong among the crowd, he was overjoyed, and, seizing him by the hand, said, "Sir, your virtuous intentions command my esteem." He then led him up behind a screen, and asked if he did not wish to know what was to come; and when Zhong replied in the affirmative, the priest informed him that his prospects were bad. "You may succeed in passing this examination," continued he, "but on returning covered with honor to your home, I fear that your mother will be no longer there." Now Zhong was a very filial son; and as soon as he heard these words, his tears began to flow, and he declared that he would go back without competing any further. The priest observed that if he let this chance slip, he could never hope for success; to which Zhong replied that, on the other hand, if his mother were to die he could never hope to have her back again, and that even the rank of Viceroy would not repay him for her loss. "Well," said the priest, "you and I were connected in a former existence, and I must do my best to help you now." So he took out a pill which he gave to Zhong, and told him that if he sent it post-haste by someone to his mother, it would prolong her life for seven days, and thus he would be able to see her once again after the examination was over. Zhong took the pill, and went off in very low spirits; but he soon reflected that the span of human life is a matter of destiny, and that every day he could spend at home would be one more day devoted to the service of his mother. Accordingly, he got ready to start at once, and, hiring a donkey, actually set out on his way back. When he had gone about half-a-mile, the donkey turned around and ran home; and when he used his whip, the animal threw itself down on the ground. Zhong got into a great perspiration, and his servant recommended him to remain where he was; but this he would not hear of, and hired another donkey, which served him exactly the same trick as the other one. The sun was now sinking behind the hills, and his servant advised his master to stay and finish his examination while he himself went back home before him. Zhong had no alternative but to assent, and the next day he hurried through with his papers, starting immediately afterwards, and not stopping at all on the way either to eat or to sleep. All night long he went on, and arrived to find his mother in a very critical state; however, when he gave her the pill she so far recovered that he was able to go in and see her. Grasping his hand, she begged him not to weep, telling him that she had just dreamt she had been down to the Infernal Regions, where the King of Hell had informed her with a gracious smile that her record was fairly clean, and that in view of the filial piety of her son she was to have twelve years more of life. Zhong was rejoiced at this, and his mother was soon restored to her former health.

Before long the news arrived that Zhong had passed his examination; upon which he bade adieu to his mother, and went off to the capital, where he bribed the eunuchs of the palace to communicate with his friend the Taoist priest. The latter was very much pleased, and came out to see him, whereupon Zhong prostrated himself at his feet. "Ah," said the priest, "this success of yours, and the prolongation of your good mother's life, is all a reward for your virtuous conduct. What have I done in the matter?" Zhong was very much astonished that the priest should already know what had happened; however, he now inquired as to his own future. "You will never rise to high rank," replied the priest, "but you will attain the years of an octogenarian. In a former state of existence you and I were once traveling together, when you threw a stone at a dog, and accidentally killed a frog. Now that frog has reappeared in life as a donkey, and according to all principles of destiny you ought to suffer for what you did; but your filial piety has touched the Gods, a protecting star-influence has passed into your nativity sheet, and you will come to no harm. On the other hand, there is your wife; in her former state she was not as virtuous as she might have been, and her punishment in this life was to be widowed quite young; you, however, have secured the "prolongation of your own term of years, and therefore I fear that before long your wife will pay the penalty of death." Zhong was much grieved at hearing this; but after a while he asked the priest where his second wife to be was living. "At Zhongzhou," replied the latter; "she is now fourteen years old." The priest then bade him adieu, telling him that if any mischance should befall him he was to hurry off towards the south-east. About a year after this, Zhong's wife did die; and his mother then desiring him to go and visit his uncle, who was a magistrate in Jiangzi, on which journey he would have to pass through Zhongzhou, it seemed like a fulfilment of the old priest's prophecy. As he went along, he came to a village on the banks of a river, where a large crowd of people was gathered together around a theatrical performance which was going on there. Zhong would have passed quietly by, had not a stray donkey followed so close behind him that he turned around and hit it over the ears. This startled the donkey so much that it ran off full gallop, and knocked a rich gentleman's child, who was sitting with its nurse on the bank, right into the water, before any one of the servants could lend a hand to save it. Immediately there was a great outcry against Zhong, who gave his mule the rein and dashed away, mindful of the priest's warning, towards the south-east. After riding about seven miles, he reached a mountain village, where he saw an old man standing at the door of a house, and, jumping off his mule, made him a low bow. The old man asked him in, and inquired his name and whence he came; to which Zhong replied by telling him the whole adventure. "Never fear," said the old man; "you can stay here, while I send out to learn the position of affairs." By the evening his messenger had returned, and then they knew for the first time that the child belonged to a wealthy family. The old man looked grave and said, "Had it been anybody else's child, I might have helped you; as it is I can do nothing." Zhong was greatly alarmed at this; however, the old man told him to remain quietly there for the night, and see what turn matters might take. Zhong was overwhelmed with anxiety, and did not sleep a wink; and next morning he heard that the constables were after him, and that it was death to any one who should conceal him. The old man changed countenance at this, and went inside, leaving Zhong to his own reflections; but towards the middle of the night he came and knocked at Zhong's door, and, sitting down, began to ask how old his wife was. Zhong replied that he was a widower; at which the old man seemed rather pleased, and declared that in such case help would be forthcoming; "for," said he, "my sister's husband has taken the vows, and become a priest,[373] and my sister herself has died, leaving an orphan girl who has now no home; and if you would only marry her . . ." Zhong was delighted, more especially as this would be both the fulfilment of the Taoist priest's prophecy and a means of extricating himself from his present difficulty; at the same time, he declared he should be sorry to implicate his future father-in-law. "Never fear about that," replied the old man; "my sister's husband is pretty skillful in the black art. He has not mixed much with the world of late; but when you are married, you can discuss the matter with my niece." So Zhong married the young lady, who was sixteen years of age, and very beautiful; but whenever he looked at her he took occasion to sigh. At last she said, "I may be ugly; but you needn't be in such a hurry to let me know it;" whereupon Zhong begged her pardon, and said he felt himself only too lucky to have met with such a divine creature; adding that he sighed because he feared some misfortune was coming on them which

---

373 This interesting ceremony is performed by placing little conical pastilles on a certain number of spots, varying from three to twelve, on the candidate's head. These are then lighted add allowed to burn down into the flesh, while the surrounding parts are vigorously rubbed by attendant priests in order to lessen the pain. The whole thing lasts about twenty minutes, and is always performed on the eve of Shakyamuni Buddha's birthday. The above was well described by Mr. S. L. Baldwin in the *Foochow Herald*.

would separate them for ever. He then told her his story, and the young lady was very angry that she should have been drawn into such a difficulty without a word of warning. Zhong fell on his knees, and said he had already consulted with her uncle, who was unable himself to do anything, much as he wished it. He continued that he was aware of her power; and then, pointing out that his alliance was not altogether beneath her, made all kinds of promises if she would only help him out of this trouble. The young lady was no longer able to refuse, but informed him that to apply to her father would entail certain disagreeable consequences, as he had retired from the world, and did not any more recognize her as his daughter. That night they did not attempt to sleep, spending the interval in padding their knees with thick felt concealed beneath their clothes; and then they got into chairs and were carried off to the hills. After journeying some distance, they were compelled by the nature of the road to alight and walk; and it was only by a great effort that Zhong succeeded at last in getting his wife to the top. At the door of the temple they sat down to rest, the powder and paint on the young lady's face having all mixed with the perspiration trickling down; but when Zhong began to apologize for bringing her to this pass, she replied that it was a mere trifle compared with what was to come. By-and-by, they went inside; and threading their way to the wall behind, found the young lady's father sitting in contemplation,[374] his eyes closed, and a servant-boy standing by with a chowry.[375] Everything was beautifully clean and nice, but before the dais were sharp stones scattered about as thick as the stars in the sky. The young lady did not venture to select a favorable spot; she fell on her knees at once, and Zhong did likewise behind her. Then her father opened his eyes, shutting them again almost instantaneously; whereupon the young lady said, "For a long time I have not paid my respects to you. I am now married, and I have brought my husband to see you." A long time passed away, and then her father opened his eyes and said, "You're giving a great deal of trouble," immediately relapsing into silence again. There the husband and wife remained until the stones seemed to pierce into their very bones; but after a while the father cried out, "Have you brought the donkey?" His daughter replied that they had not; whereupon they were told to go and fetch it at once, which they did, not knowing what the meaning of this order was. After a few more days' kneeling, they suddenly heard that the murderer of the child had been caught and beheaded, and

---

374 There is a room in most Buddhist temples specially devoted to this purpose.
375 The Buddhist emblem of cleanliness; generally a yak's tail, and commonly used as a fly-brush.

were just congratulating each other on the success of their scheme, when a servant came in with a stick in his hand, the top of which had been chopped off. "This stick," said the servant, "died instead of you. Bury it reverently, that the wrong done to the tree may be somewhat atoned for."[376] Then Zhong saw that at the place where the top of the stick had been chopped off there were traces of blood; he therefore buried it with the usual ceremony, and immediately set off with his wife, and returned to his own home.

72. The Wolf Dream

MR. BAI was a native of Zhili, and his eldest son was called Jia. The latter had been some two years holding an appointment[377] as magistrate in the south; but because of the great distance between them, his family had heard nothing of him. One day a distant connection, named Ding, called at the house; and Mr. Bai, not having seen this gentleman for a long time, treated him with much cordiality. Now Ding was one of those persons who are occasionally employed by the Judge of the Infernal Regions to make arrests on earth;[378] and, as they were chatting together, Mr. Bai questioned him about the realms below. Ding told him all kinds of strange things, but Bai did not believe them, answering only by a smile. Some days afterwards, he had just lain down to sleep when Ding walked in and asked him to go for a stroll; so they went off together, and by-and-by reached the city. "There," said Ding, pointing to a door, "lives your nephew," alluding to a son of Mr. Bai's elder sister, who was a magistrate in Henan; and when Bai expressed his doubts as to the accuracy of this statement, Ding led him in, when, lo and behold! there was his nephew sitting in his court dressed in his official robes. Around him stood the guard, and it was impossible to get near him; but Ding remarked that his son's residence was not far off, and asked Bai if he would not like to see him too. The latter assenting, they walked along until they came to a large building, which Ding said was the place. However,

<hr/>

376 Tree-worship can hardly be said to exist in China at the present day; though at a comparatively recent epoch this phase of religious sentiment must have been widely spread. See *The Flower Nymphs* and *Mr. Willow.*
377 Literally, "had been allotted the post of Nanfu magistrate," such appointments being always determined by drawing lots.
378 Such is one common explanation of catalepsy (see note 5 in tale 1), it being further averred that the proper lictors of the Infernal Regions are unable to remain long in the *light* of the upper world.

there was a fierce wolf at the entrance,[379] and Mr. Bai was afraid to go in. Ding bade him enter, and accordingly they walked in, when they found that all the employes of the place, some of whom were standing about and others lying down to sleep, were all wolves. The central pathway was piled up with whitening bones, and Mr. Bai began to feel horribly alarmed; but Ding kept close to him all the time, and at length they got safely in. Bai's son, Jia, was just coming out; and when he saw his father accompanied by Ding, he was overjoyed, and, asking them to sit down, bade the attendants serve some refreshments. Thereupon a great big wolf brought in in his mouth the carcass of a dead man, and set it before them, at which Mr. Bai rose up in consternation, and asked his son what this meant. "It's only a little refreshment for you, father," replied Jia; but this did not calm Mr. Bai's agitation, who would have retired precipitately, had it not been for the crowd of wolves which barred the path. Just as he was at a loss what to do, there was a general stampede among the animals, which scurried away, some under the couches and some under the tables and chairs; and while he was wondering what the cause of this could be, in marched two knights in golden armor, who looked sternly at Jia, and, producing a black rope, proceeded to bind him hand and foot. Jia fell down before them, and was changed into a tiger with horrid fangs; and then one of the knights drew a glittering sword and would have cut off its head, had not the other cried out, "Not yet! not yet! that is for the fourth month next year. Let us now only take out its teeth." Immediately that knight produced a huge mallet, and, with a few blows, scattered the tiger's teeth all over the floor, the tiger roaring so loudly with pain as to shake the very hills, and frightening all the wits out of Mr. Bai—who woke up with a start. He found he had been dreaming, and at once set off to invite Ding to come and see him; but Ding sent back to say he must beg to be excused. Then Mr. Bai, pondering on what he had seen in his dream, despatched his second son with a letter to Jia, full of warnings and good advice; and lo! when his son arrived, he found that his elder brother had lost all his front teeth, these having been knocked out, as he averred, by a fall he had had from his horse when tipsy; and, on comparing dates, the day of that fall was found to coincide with the day of his father's dream. The younger brother was greatly amazed at this, and took out their father's letter, which he gave to Jia to read. The latter changed

---

379 Upon a wall at the entrance to every official residence is painted a huge fabulous animal, called *Greed*, in such a position that the resident mandarin must see it every time he goes out of his front gates. It is to warn him against greed and the crimes that are sure to flow from it.

color, but immediately asked his brother what there was to be astonished at in the coincidence of a dream. And just at that time he was busily engaged in bribing his superiors to put him first on the list for promotion, so that he soon forgot all about the circumstance; while the younger, observing what harpies Jia's subordinates were, taking presents from one man and using their influence for another, in one unbroken stream of corruption, sought out his elder brother, and, with tears in his eyes, implored him to put some check upon their rapacity. "My brother," replied Jia, "your life has been passed in an obscure village; you know nothing of our official routine. We are promoted or degraded at the will of our superiors, and not by the voice of the people. He, therefore, who gratifies his superiors is marked out for success;[380] whereas he who consults the wishes of the people is unable to gratify his superiors as well." Jia's brother saw that his advice was thrown away; he accordingly returned home and told his father all that had taken place. The old man was much affected, but there was nothing that he could do in the matter, so he devoted himself to assisting the poor, and such acts of charity, daily praying the Gods that the wicked son alone might suffer for his crimes, and not entail misery on his innocent wife and children. The next year it was reported that Jia had been recommended for a post in the Board of Civil Office,[381] and friends crowded the father's door, offering their congratulations upon the happy event. But the old man sighed and took to his bed, pretending he was too unwell to receive visitors. Before long another message came, informing them that Jia had fallen in with bandits while on his way home, and that he and all his retinue had been killed. Then his father arose and said, "Verily the Gods are good unto me, for they have visited his sins upon himself alone;" and he immediately proceeded to burn incense and return thanks. Some of his friends would have persuaded him that the report was probably untrue; but the old man had no doubts as to its correctness, and made haste to get ready his son's grave. But Jia was not yet dead. In the fatal fourth moon he had started on his journey and had fallen in with bandits, to whom he had offered all his money and valuables; upon which the latter cried out, "We have come to avenge the cruel wrongs of many hundreds of victims; do you imagine we want only *that*?" They then cut off his head, and the head of his wicked secretary, and the heads of several of his servants who had been foremost in carrying out his shameful orders, and were now accompanying him to the capital. They then divided

---

380 Such, indeed, is the case at the present day in China, and elsewhere.
381 See note 19 in tale number 7.

the booty between them, and made off with all speed. Jia's soul remained near his body for some time, until at length a high mandarin passing by asked who it was that was lying there dead. One of his servants replied that he had been a magistrate at such and such a place, and that his name was Bai. "What!" said the mandarin, "the son of old Mr. Bai? It is hard that his father should live to see such sorrow as this. Put his head on again."[382] Then a man stepped forward and placed Jia's head upon his shoulders again, when the mandarin interrupted him, saying, "A crooked-minded man should not have a straight body: put his head on sideways." By-and-by Jia's soul returned to its tenement; and when his wife and children arrived to take away the corpse, they found that he was still breathing. Carrying him home, they poured some nourishment down his throat, which he was able to swallow; but there he was at an out-of-the-way place, without the means of continuing his journey. It was some six months before his father heard the real state of the case, and then he sent off the second son to bring his brother home. Jia had indeed come to life again, but he was able to see down his own back, and was regarded ever afterwards more as a monstrosity than as a man. Subsequently the nephew, whom old Mr. Bai had seen sitting in state surrounded by officials, actually became an Imperial Censor, so that every detail of the dream was thus strangely realised.

73. The Unjust Sentence

MR. ZHU was a native of Yanggu, and, as a young man, was much given to playing tricks and talking in a loose kind of way. Having lost his wife, he went off to ask a certain old woman to arrange another match for him; and on the way he chanced to fall in with a neighbor's wife who took his fancy very much. So he said in joke to the old woman, "Get me that stylish-looking, handsome lady, and I shall be quite satisfied." "I'll see what I can do," replied the old woman, also joking, "if you will manage to kill her present husband;" upon which Zhu laughed and said he certainly would do so. Now about a month afterwards, the said husband, who had gone out to collect some money due to him, was actually killed in a lonely spot; and

---

382 The great sorrow of decapitation as opposed to strangulation is that the body will appear in the realms below without a head. The family of any condemned man who may have sufficient means always bribe the executioner to sew it on again.

the magistrate of the district immediately summoned the neighbors and beadle[383] and held the usual inquest, but was unable to find any clue to the murderer. However, the old-woman told the story of her conversation with Zhu, and suspicion at once fell upon him. The constables came and arrested him; but he stoutly denied the charge; and the magistrate now began to suspect the wife of the murdered man. Accordingly, she was severely beaten and tortured in several ways until her strength failed her, and she falsely acknowledged her guilt.[384] Zhu was then examined, and he said, "This delicate woman could not bear the agony of your tortures; what she has stated is untrue; and, even should her wrong escape the notice of the Gods, for her to die in this way with a stain upon her name is more than I can endure. I will tell the whole truth. I killed the husband that I might secure the wife: she knew nothing at all about it." And when the magistrate asked for some proof, Zhu said his bloody clothes would be evidence enough; but when they sent to search his house, no bloody clothes were forthcoming. He was then beaten until he fainted; yet when he came around he still stuck to what he had said. "It is my mother," cried he, "who will not sign the death-warrant of her son. Let me go myself and I will get the clothes." So he was escorted by a guard to his home, and there he explained to his mother that whether she gave up or withheld the clothes, it was all the same; that in either case he would have to die, and it was better to die early than late. Thereupon his mother wept bitterly, and going into the bedroom, brought out, after a short delay, the required clothes, which were taken at once to the magistrate's. There was now no doubt as to the truth of Zhu's story; and as

---

383 See note 340 in tale number 64.

384 Such has, doubtless, been the occasional result of torture in China; but the singular keenness of the mandarins, as a body, in recognizing the innocent and detecting the guilty—that is, when their own avaricious interests are not involved—makes this contingency so rare as to be almost unknown. A good instance came under my own notice at Swatow in 1876. For years a Chinese servant had been employed at the foreign Custom House to carry a certain sum of money every week to the bank, and at length his honesty was above suspicion. On the occasion to which I allude he had been sent as usual with the bag of dollars, but after a short absence he rushed back with a frightful gash on his right arm, evidently inflicted by a heavy chopper, and laying the bone bare. The money was gone. He said he had been invited into a tea-house by a couple of soldiers whom he could point out; that they had tried to wrest the bag from him, and that at length one of them seized a chopper and inflicted so severe a wound on his arm, that in his agony he dropped the money, and the soldiers made off with it. The latter were promptly arrested and confronted with their accuser; but, with almost indecent haste, the police magistrate dismissed the case against them, and declared that he believed the man had made away with the money and inflicted the wound on himself. And so it turned out to be, under overwhelming evidence. This servant of proved fidelity had given way to a rash hope of making a little money at the gaming-table; had hurried into one of these hells and lost everything in three stakes; had wounded himself on the right arm (he was a left-handed man), and had concocted the story of the soldiers, all within the space of about twenty-five minutes. When he saw that he was detected, he confessed everything, without having received a single blow of the bamboo; but up to the moment of his confession the foreign feeling against that police-magistrate was undeniably strong.

nothing occurred to change the magistrate's opinion, Zhu was thrown into prison to await the day for his execution. Meanwhile, as the magistrate was one day inspecting his jail, suddenly a man appeared in the hall, who glared at him fiercely and roared out, "Dull-headed fool! unfit to be the guardian of the people's interests!"—whereupon the crowd of servants standing around rushed forward to seize him, but with one sweep of his arms he laid them all flat on the ground. The magistrate was frightened out of his wits, and tried to escape, but the man cried out to him, "I am one of Guan Di's[385] lieutenants. If you move an inch you are lost." So the magistrate stood there, shaking from head to foot with fear, while his visitor continued, "The murderer is Gong Biao: Zhu had nothing to do with it." The lieutenant then fell down on the ground, and was to all appearance lifeless; however, after a while he recovered, his face having quite changed, and when they asked him his name, lo! it was Gong Biao. Under the application of the bamboo he confessed his guilt. Always an unprincipled man, he had heard that the murdered man was going out to collect money, and thinking he would be sure to bring it back with him, he had killed him, but had found nothing. Then when he learnt that Zhu acknowledged the crime as his own doing, he had rejoiced in secret at such a stroke of luck. How he had got into the magistrate's hall he was quite unable to say. The magistrate now called for some explanation of Zhu's bloody clothes, which Zhu himself was unable to give; but his mother, who was at once sent for, stated that she had cut her own arm to stain them, and when they examined her they found on her left arm the scar of a recent wound. The magistrate was lost in amazement at all this; unfortunately for him, the reversal of his sentence cost him his appointment, and he died in poverty, unable to find his way home. As for Zhu, the widow of the murdered man married him[386] in the following year, out of gratitude for his noble behavior.

---

385 See note 4 in tale number 1.
386 See note 352 in tale number 68. The circumstances which led to this marriage would certainly be considered "exceptional."

74. A Rip Van Winkle[387]

[THE story runs that a Mr. Jia, after obtaining, with the assistance of a mysterious friend, his master's degree, became alive to the vanity of mere earthly honors, and determined to devote himself to the practice of Taoism, in the hope of obtaining the elixir of immortality.[388]]

So early one morning Jia and his friend, whose name was Lang, stole away together, without letting Jia's family know anything about it; and by-and-by they found themselves among the hills, in a vast cave where there was another world and another sky. An old man was sitting there in great state, and Lang presented Jia to him as his future master. "Why have you come so soon?" asked the old man; to which Lang replied, "My friend's determination is firmly fixed: I pray you receive him amongst you." "Since you have come," said the old man, turning to Jia, "you must begin by putting away from you your earthly body." Jia murmured his assent, and was then escorted by Lang to a sleeping-chamber, where he was provided with food, after which Lang went away. The room was beautifully clean:[389] the doors had no panels and the windows no lattices; and all the furniture was one table and one couch. Jia took off his shoes and lay down, with the moon shining brightly into the room; and beginning soon to feel hungry, he tried one of the cakes on the table, which he found sweet and very satisfying. He thought Lang would be sure to come back, but there he remained hour after hour by himself, never hearing a sound. He noticed, however, that the room was fragrant with a delicious perfume; his viscera seemed to be removed from his body, by which his intellectual faculties were much increased; and every one of his veins and arteries could be easily counted. Then suddenly he heard a sound like that of a cat scratching itself; and, looking out of the window, he beheld a tiger sitting under the verandah. He was horribly frightened for the moment, but immediately recalling the admonition of the old man, he collected himself and sat quietly down again. The tiger seemed to know that there was a man inside, for it entered the room directly afterwards, and walking straight up to the couch sniffed at Jia's feet. Whereupon there was a noise outside, as if a fowl were having its legs tied, and the tiger ran away. Shortly afterwards a beautiful young girl came in, suffusing an exquisite fragrance around; and going up to the couch

---

387 This being a long and tedious story, I have given only such part of it as is remarkable for its similarity to Washington Irving's famous narrative.
388 See note 11 in tale number 4.
389 Borrowed from Buddhism.

where Jia was, she bent over him and whispered, "Here I am." Her breath was like the sweet odor of perfumes; but as Jia did not move, she whispered again, "Are you sleeping?" The voice sounded to Jia remarkably like that of his wife; however, he reflected that these were all probably nothing more than tests of his determination, so he closed his eyes firmly for a while. But by-and-by the young lady called him by his pet name, and then he opened his eyes wide to discover that she was no other than his own wife. On asking her how she had come there, she replied that Mr. Lang was afraid her husband would be lonely, and had sent an old woman to guide her to him. Just then they heard the old man outside in a towering rage, and Jia's wife, not knowing where to conceal herself, jumped over a low wall nearby and disappeared. In came the old man, and gave Lang a severe beating before Jia's face, bidding him at once to get rid of his visitor; so Lang led Jia away over the low wall, saying, "Because I entertained extravagant hopes of you, I made the mistake of too hastily introducing you; but now I see that your time has not yet come: hence this beating I have had. Good-bye: we shall meet again some day." He then showed Jia the way to his home, and waving his hand bade him farewell. Jia looked down—for he was in the moon— and beheld the old familiar village; and recollecting that his wife was not a good walker and would not have got very far, hurried on to overtake her. Before long he was at his own door, but he noticed that the place was all tumble-down and in ruins, and not as it was when he went away. As for the people he saw, old and young alike, he did not recognize one of them; and recollecting the story of how Liu and Yuan came back from heaven,[390] he was afraid to go in at the door. So he sat down and rested outside; and after a while an old man leaning on a staff came out, whereupon Jia asked him which was the house of Mr. Jia. "This is it," replied the old man;" you probably wish to hear the extraordinary story connected with the family? I know all about it. They say that Mr. Jia ran away just after he had taken his master's degree, when his son was only seven or eight years old; and that about seven years afterwards the child's mother went into a deep sleep from which she did not awake. As long as her son was alive he changed his mother's clothes for her according to the seasons, but when he died, her grandsons fell into poverty, and had nothing but an old shanty to put the sleeping lady into. Last month she awaked, having been asleep for over a

---

390 Alluding to a similar story, related in the *Record of the Immortals*, of how these two friends lost their way while gathering simples on the hills, and were met and entertained by two lovely young damsels for the space of half-a-year. When, however, they subsequently returned home, they found that ten generations had passed away.

hundred years. People from far and near have been coming in great numbers to hear the strange story; of late, however, there have been rather fewer." Jia was amazed when he heard all this, and, turning to the old man, said, "I am Jia Fengzhi." This astonished the old man very much, and off he went to make the announcement to Jia's family. The eldest grandson was dead; and the second, a man of about fifty, refused to believe that such a young-looking man was really his grandfather; but in a few moments out came Jia's wife, and she recognized her husband at once. They then fell upon each other's necks and mingled their tears together.

[After which the story is drawn out to a considerable length, but is quite devoid of interest.][391]

75. The Three States of Existence

A CERTAIN man of the province of Hunan could recall what had happened to him in three previous lives. In the first, he was a magistrate; and, on one occasion, when he had been nominated Assistant-Examiner, a candidate, named Xing, was unsuccessful. Xing went home dreadfully mortified, and soon after died; but his spirit appeared before the King of Purgatory, and read aloud the rejected essay, whereupon thousands of other shades, all of whom had suffered in a similar way, thronged around, and unanimously elected Xing as their chief. The Examiner was immediately summoned to take his trial, and when he arrived the King asked him, saying, "As you are appointed to examine the various essays, how is it that you throw out the able and admit the worthless?" "Sire," replied he, "the ultimate decision rests with the Grand Examiner; I only pass them on to him." The King then issued a warrant for the apprehension of the Grand Examiner, and as soon as he appeared, he was told what had just now been said against him; to which he answered, "I am only able to make a general estimate of the merits of the candidates. Valuable essays may be kept back from me by my

---

391 Besides the above, there is the story of a man named Wang, who, wandering one day in the mountains, came upon some old men playing a game of *weiqi*; and after watching them for some time, he found that the handle of an axe he had with him had mouldered away into dust. Seven generations of men had passed away in the interval. Also, a similar legend of a horseman, who, when riding over the hills, saw several old men playing a game with rushes, and tied his horse to a tree while he himself approached to observe them. A few minutes afterwards he turned to depart, but found only the skeleton of his horse and the rotten remnants of the saddle and bridle. He then sought his home, but that was gone too; and so he laid himself down upon the ground and died of a broken heart.

Associate-Examiners, in which case I am powerless."[392] But the King cried out, "It's all very well for you two thus to throw the blame on each other; you are both guilty, and both of you must be bambooed according to law." This sentence was about to be carried into effect, when Xing, who was not at all satisfied with its lack of severity, set up such a fearful screeching and howling, in which he was well supported by all the other hundreds and thousands of shades, that the King stopped short, and inquired what was the matter. Thereupon Xing informed His Majesty that the sentence was too light, and that the Examiners should both have their eyes gouged out, so as not to be able to read essays any more. The King would not consent to this, explaining to the noisy rabble that the Examiners did not purposely reject good essays, but only because they themselves were naturally wanting in capacity. The shades then begged that, at any rate, their hearts might be cut out, and to this the King was obliged to yield; so the Examiners were seized by the attendants, their garments stripped off, and their bodies ripped open with sharp knives. The blood poured out on the ground, and the victims screamed with pain; at which all the shades rejoiced exceedingly, and said, "Here we have been pent up, with no one to redress our wrongs; but now Mr. Xing has come, our injuries are washed away." They then dispersed with great noise and hubbub. As for our Associate-Examiner, after his heart had been cut out, he came to life again as the son of a poor man in Shaanxi; and when he was twenty years old he fell into the hands of the rebels, who were at that time giving great trouble to the country. By-and-by, a certain official was sent at the head of some soldiers to put down the insurrection, and he succeeded in capturing a large number of the rebels, among whom was our hero. The latter reflected that he himself was no rebel, and he was hoping that he would be able to obtain his release in consequence, when he noticed that the officer in charge was also a man of his own age, and, on looking more closely, he saw that it was his old enemy,

392 If there is one institution in the Chinese Empire which is jealously guarded and honestly administered, it is the great system of competitive examinations which has obtained in China now for many centuries. And yet frauds do take place, in spite of the exceptionally heavy penalties incurred upon detection. Friends are occasionally smuggled through by the aid of marked essays; and dishonest candidates avail themselves of "sleeve editions," as they are called, of the books in which they are to be examined. On the whole, the result is a successful one. As a rule, the best candidates pull through; while, in exceptional cases, unquestionably good men are rejected. Of the latter class, the author of this work is a most striking instance. Excelling in literary attainments of the highest order, he failed more than once to obtain his master's degree, and finally threw up in disgust. Thenceforward he became the enemy of the mandarinate; and how he has lashed the corruption of his age may be read in such stories as *The Wolf Dream*, and many others, while the policy that he himself would have adopted, had he been fortunate enough to succeed, must remain for ever a matter of doubt and speculation.

Xing. "Alas!" cried he, "such is destiny;" and so indeed it turned out, for all the other prisoners were forthwith released, and he alone was beheaded. Once more his spirit stood before the King of Purgatory, this time with an accusation against Xing. The King, however, would not summon Xing at once, but said he should be allowed to complete his term of official life on earth; and it was not until thirty years afterwards that Xing appeared to answer to the charge. Then, because he had made light of the lives of his people, he was condemned to be born again as a brute-beast; and our hero, too, inasmuch as he had been known to beat his father and mother, was sentenced to a similar fate. The latter, fearing the future vengeance of Xing, persuaded the King to give him the advantage of size; and, accordingly, orders were issued that he was to be born again as a big, and Xing as a little, dog. The big dog came to life in a shop in Shuntian Fu, and was one day lying down in the street, when a trader from the south arrived, bringing with him a little golden-haired dog, about the size of a wild cat, which, lo and behold! turned out to be Xing. The other, thinking Xing's size would render him an easy prey, seized him at once; but the little one caught him from underneath by the throat, and hung there firmly, like a bell. The big dog tried hard to shake him off, and the people of the shop did their best to separate them, but all was of no avail, and in a few moments both dogs were dead. Upon their spirits presenting themselves, as usual, before the King, each with its grievance against the other, the King cried out, "When will ye have done with your wrongs and your animosities? I will now settle the matter finally for you;" and immediately commanded that Xing should become the other's son-in-law in the next world. The latter was then born at Qing Yun, and when he was twenty-eight years of age took his master's degree. He had one daughter, a very pretty girl, whom many of his wealthy neighbors would have been glad to get for their sons; but he would not accept any of their offers. On one occasion he happened to pass through the prefectural city, just as the examination for bachelor's degree was over; and the candidate who had come out at the top of the list, though named Li, was no other than Mr. Xing. So he led this man away, and took him to an inn, where he treated him with the utmost cordiality, finally arranging that, as Mr. Li was still unmarried, he should marry his pretty daughter. Every one, of course, thought that this was done in admiration of Li's talents, ignorant that destiny had already decreed the union of the young couple. No sooner were they married than Li, proud of his own literary achievements, began to slight his father-in-law, and often passed many months without going near him; all of which the father-in-law bore very patiently, and when, at length,

Li had repeatedly failed to get on any farther in his career, he even went so far as to set to work, by all manner of means, to secure his success; after which they lived happily together as father and son.

76. In the Infernal Regions

XI FANGPING was a native of Dongan. His father's name was Xi Lian—a quick-tempered man, who had quarrelled with a neighbor named Yang. By-and-by Yang died; and some years afterwards, when Lian was on his death-bed, he cried out that Yang was bribing the devils in hell to torture him. His body then swelled up and turned red, and in a few moments he had breathed his last. His son wept bitterly and refused all food, saying, "Alas! My poor father is now being maltreated by cruel devils; I must go down and help to redress his wrongs." Thereupon he ceased speaking, and sat for a long time like one dazed, his soul having already quitted its tenement of clay. To himself he appeared to be outside the house, not knowing in what direction to go, so he inquired from one of the passers-by which was the way to the district city.[393] Before long he found himself there, and, directing his steps towards the prison, found his father lying outside[394] in a very shocking state. When the latter beheld his son, he burst into tears, and declared that the jailers had been bribed to beat him, which they did both day and night, until they had reduced him to his present sorry plight. Then Fangping turned around in a great rage, and began to curse the jailers. "Out upon you!" cried he; "if my father is guilty he should be punished according to law and not at the will of a set of scoundrels like you." Thereupon he hurried away, and prepared a petition, which he took with him to present at the morning session of the City God; but his enemy, Yang, had meanwhile set to work, and bribed so effectually, that the City God dismissed his petition for want of corroborative evidence.[395] Fangping was furious, but could do nothing; so he started at once for the prefectural city, where he managed to get his plaint received, though it was nearly a month before it

---

393 The Infernal Regions are supposed to be pretty much a counterpart of the world above, except in the matter of light.

394 The visitor to Canton cannot fail to observe batches of prisoners with chains on them sitting in the street outside the prisons, many of them engaged in plying their particular trades.

395 The judge in a Chinese court is necessarily very much dependent on his secretaries; and, except in special cases, he takes his cue almost entirely from them. They take theirs from whichever party to the case knows best how to "cross the palm."

came on for hearing, and then all he got was a reference back to the district city, where he was severely tortured, and escorted back to the door of his own home, for fear he should give further trouble. However, he did not go in, but stole away and proceeded to lay his complaint before one of the ten Judges of Purgatory; whereupon the two mandarins who had previously ill-used him, came forward and secretly offered him a thousand ounces of silver if he would withdraw the charge. This he positively refused to do; and some days subsequently the landlord of the inn, where he was staying, told him he had been a fool for his pains, and that he would now get neither money nor justice, the Judge himself having already been tampered with. Fangping thought this was mere gossip, and would not believe it; but, when his case was called, the Judge utterly refused to hear the charge, and ordered him twenty blows with the bamboo, which were administered in spite of all his protestations. He then cried out, "Ah! it's all because I have no money to give you;" which so incensed the Judge, that he told the lictors to throw Fangping on the fire-bed. This was a great iron couch, with a roaring fire underneath, which made it red-hot; and upon that the devils cast Fangping, having first stripped off his clothes, pressing him down on it, until the fire ate into his very bones, though in spite of that he could not die. After a while the devils said he had had enough, and made him get off the iron bed, and put his clothes on again. He was just able to walk, and when he went back into court, the Judge asked him if he wanted to make any further complaints. "Alas!" cried he, "my wrongs are still if unredressed, and I should only be lying were I to say I would complain no more." The Judge then inquired what he had to complain of; to which Fangping replied that it was of the injustice of his recent punishment. This enraged the Judge so much that he ordered his attendants to saw Fangping in two. He was then led away by devils, to a place where he was thrust in between a couple of wooden boards, the ground on all sides being wet and sticky with blood. Just at that moment he was summoned to return before the Judge, who asked him if he was still of the same mind; and, on his replying in the affirmative, he was taken back again, and bound between the two boards. The saw was then applied, and as it went through his brain he experienced the most cruel agonies, which, however, he managed to endure without uttering a cry. "He's a tough customer," said one of the devils, as the saw made its way gradually through his chest; to which the other replied, "Truly, this is filial piety; and, as the poor fellow has done nothing, let us turn the saw a little out of the direct line, so as to avoid injuring his heart." Fangping then felt the saw make a curve inside him, which caused him even more pain than before; and, in a few moments, he was cut through right down to the ground, and the two halves of his body fell apart, along with the boards to which they were tied, one on either side. The devils went back to report progress, and were then ordered to join Fangping together again, and bring him in. This they accordingly did—the cut all down Fangping's body hurting him dreadfully, and feeling as if it would re-open every minute. But, as Fangping was unable to walk, one of the devils took out a cord and tied it around his waist, as a reward, he said, for his filial piety. The pain immediately ceased, and Fangping appeared once more before the Judge, this time promising that he would make no more complaints. The Judge now gave orders that he should be sent up to earth, and the devils, escorting him out of the north gate of the city, showed him his way home, and went away. Fangping now saw that there was even less chance of securing justice in the Infernal Regions than upon the earth above; and, having no means of getting at the Great King to plead his case, he bethought himself of a certain upright and benevolent God, called Er Lang, who was a relative of the Great King's, and him he determined to seek. So he turned about and took his way southwards, but was immediately seized by some devils, sent out by the Judge to watch that he really went back to his home. These devils hurried him again into the Judge's presence, where he was received, contrary to his expectation, with great affability; the Judge himself praising his filial piety, but declaring that he need trouble no further in the matter, as his father had already been born again in a wealthy and illustrious family. "And upon you," added the Judge, "I now bestow a present of one thousand ounces of silver to take home with you, as well as the old age of a centenarian, with which I hope you will be satisfied." He then showed Fangping the stamped record of this, and sent him away in charge of the devils. The latter now began to abuse him for giving them so much trouble, but Fangping turned sharply upon them, and threatened to take them back before the Judge. They were then silent, and marched along for about half-a-day, until at length they reached a village, where the devils invited Fangping into a house, the door of which was standing half-open. Fangping was just going in, when suddenly the devils gave him a shove from behind, and   there he was, born again on earth as a little girl. For three days he pined and cried, without taking any food, and then he died. But his spirit did not forget Er Lang, and set out at once in search of that God. He had not gone far when he fell in with the retinue of some high personage, and one of the attendants seized him for getting in the way, and hurried him before his master. He was taken to a chariot, where he saw a handsome young man, sitting in great state; and thinking that now was his chance, he told the young man, who he imagined to be a high mandarin, all his sad story from beginning to end. His bonds were then loosed, and he went along with the young man until they reached a place where several officials came out to receive them; and to one of these he confided Fangping, who now learnt that the young man was no other than God himself, the officials being the nine princes of heaven and the one to whose care he was entrusted no other than Er Lang. This last was very tall, and had a long white beard, not at all like the popular representation of a God; and when the other princes had gone, he took Fangping into a court-room, where he saw his father and their old enemy, Yang, besides all the lictors and others who had been mixed up in the case. By-and-by, some criminals were brought in in cages, and these turned out to be the Judge, Prefect, and Magistrate. The trial was then commenced, the three wicked officers trembling and shaking in their shoes; and when he had heard the evidence, Er Lang proceeded to pass sentence upon the prisoners, each of whom he sentenced, after enlarging upon the enormity of their several crimes, to be roasted, boiled, and otherwise put to most excruciating tortures. As for Fangping, he accorded him three extra decades of life, as a reward for his filial piety, and a copy of the sentence was put in his pocket. Father and son journeyed along together, and at length reached their home; that is to say, Fangping was the first to recover consciousness, and then bade the servants open his father's coffin, which they immediately did, and the old man at once came back to fife. But when Fangping looked for his copy of the sentence, lo! it had disappeared. As for the Yang family, poverty soon overtook them, and all their lands passed into Fangping's hands; for as sure as any one else bought them, they became sterile forthwith, and would produce nothing; but Fangping and his father lived on happily, both reaching the age of ninety and odd years.[396]

77. A Singular Case of Ophthalmia

A MR. GU, of Jiangnan, was stopping in an inn at Jixia, when he was attacked by a very severe inflammation of the eyes. Day and night he lay on his bed groaning, no medicines being of any avail; and when he did get

---

396 The whole story is of course simply a satire upon the venality and injustice of the ruling classes in China.

a little better, his recovery was accompanied by a singular phenomenon. Every time he closed his eyes, he beheld in front of him a number of large buildings, with all their doors wide open, and people passing and repassing in the background, none of whom he recognized by sight. One day he had just sat down to have a good look, when, all of a sudden, he felt himself passing through the open doors. He went on through three court-yards without meeting anyone; but, on looking into some rooms on either side, he saw a great number of young girls sitting, lying, and kneeling about on a red carpet, which was spread on the ground. Just then a man came out from behind the building, and, seeing Gu, said to him, "Ah, the Prince said there was a stranger at the door; I suppose you are the person he meant." He then asked Gu to walk in, which the latter was at first unwilling to do; however, he yielded to the man's instances, and accompanied him in, asking whose palace it was. His guide told him it belonged to the son of the Ninth Prince, and that he had arrived at the nick of time, for a number of friends and relatives had chosen this very day to come and congratulate the young gentleman on his recent recovery from a severe illness. Meanwhile another person had come out to hurry them on, and they soon reached a spot where there was a pavilion facing the north, with an ornamental terrace and red balustrades, supported by nine pillars. Ascending the steps, they found the place full of visitors, and then espied a young man seated with his face to the north,[397] whom they at once knew to be the Prince's son, and thereupon they prostrated themselves before him, the whole company rising as they did so. The young Prince made Gu sit down to the east of him, and caused wine to be served; after which some singing-girls came in and performed the Huafengzhu.[398] They had got to about the third scene, when, all of a sudden, Gu heard the landlord of the inn and his servant shouting out to him that dinner was ready, and was dreadfully afraid that the young Prince, too, had heard. No one, however, seemed to have noticed anything, so Gu begged to be excused a moment, as he wished to change his clothes, and immediately ran out. He then looked up, and saw the sun low in the west, and his servant standing by his bedside, whereupon he knew that he had never left the inn. He was much chagrined at this, and wished to go back as fast as he could; he, therefore, dismissed his servant, and on shutting his eyes

---

397 In Book V. of Mencius' works we read that Shun, the perfect man, stood with his face to the south, while the Emperor Yao (see note 29 in tale number 8) and his nobles faced the north. This arrangement is said to have been adopted in deference to Shun's virtue; for in modern times the Emperor always sits facing the south.

398 Name of a celebrated play.

once more, he found everything just as he had left it, except that where, on the first occasion, he had observed the young girls, there were none now to be seen, but only some dishevelled humpbacked creatures, who cried out at him, and asked him what he meant by spying about there. Gu didn't dare reply, but hurried past them as quickly as he could, and on to the pavilion of the young Prince. There he found him still sitting, but with a black beard over a foot in length; and the Prince was anxious to know where he had been, saying that seven scenes of the play were already over. He then seized a big goblet of wine, and made Gu drink it as a penalty, by which time the play was finished, and the list was handed up for a further selection. The "Marriage of Peng Zu" was selected, and then the singing-girls began to hand around the wine in coconuts big enough to hold about five quarts, which Gu declined, on the ground that he was suffering from weak eyes, and was consequently afraid to drink too much. "If your eyes are bad," cried the young Prince, "the Court physician is at hand, and can attend to you." Thereupon, one of the guests sitting to the east came forward, and, opening Gu's eyes with his fingers, touched them with some white ointment, which he applied from the end of a jade pin. He then bade Gu close his eyes, and take a short nap; so the Prince had him conducted into a sleeping-room, where he found the bed so soft, and surrounded by such delicious perfume, that he soon fell into a deep slumber. By-and-by he was awaked by what appeared to be the clashing of cymbals, and fancied that the play was still going on; but on opening his eyes, he saw that it was only the inn-dog, which was licking an oilman's gong.[399] His ophthalmia, however, was quite cured; and when he shut his eyes again he could see nothing.

78. Zhou Kechang and His Ghost

AT Huaishang there lived a graduate named Zhou Tianyi, who, though fifty years of age, had but one son, called Kechang, whom he loved very dearly. This boy, when about thirteen or fourteen, was a handsome, well-favored fellow, strangely averse to study, and often playing truant from school, sometimes for the whole day, without any remonstrance on the part

---

399 These are about as big as a cheese-plate and attached to a short stick, from which hangs suspended a small button of metal in such a manner as to clash against the face of the gong at every turn of the band. The names and descriptions of various instruments employed by costermongers in China would fill a good-sized volume.

of his father. One day he went away and did not come back in the evening; neither, after a diligent search, could any traces of him be discovered. His father and mother were in despair, and hardly cared to live; but after a year and more had passed away, lo and behold! Kechang returned, saying that he had been beguiled away by a Taoist priest, who, however, had not done him any harm, and that he had seized a moment while the priest was absent to escape and find his way home again. His father was delighted, and asked him no more questions, but set to work to give him an education; and Kechang was so much cleverer and more intelligent than he had been before, that by the following year he had taken his bachelor's degree and made quite a name for himself. Immediately all the good families of the neighborhood wanted to secure him as a son-in-law. Among others proposed there was an extremely nice girl, the daughter of a gentleman named Zhao, who had taken his doctor's degree, and Kechang's father was very anxious that he should marry the young lady. The youth himself would not hear of it, but stuck to his books and took his master's degree, quite refusing to entertain any thought of marriage; and this so exasperated his mother that one day the good lady began to rate him soundly. Kechang got up in a great rage and cried out, "I have long been wanting to get away, and have only remained for your sakes. I shall now say farewell, and leave Miss Zhao for any one that likes to marry her." At this his mother tried to detain him, but in a moment he had fallen forwards on the ground, and there was nothing left of him but his hat and clothes. They were all dreadfully frightened, thinking that it must have been Kechang's ghost who had been with them, and gave themselves up to weeping and lamentation; however, the very next day Kechang arrived, accompanied by a retinue of horses and servants, his story being that he had formerly been kidnapped[400] and sold to a wealthy trader, who, being then childless, had adopted him, but who, when he subsequently had a son born to him by his own wife, sent Kechang back to his old home. And as soon as his father began to question him as to his studies, his utter dullness and want of knowledge soon made it clear that he was the real Kechang of old; but he was already known as a man who had got his master's degree (that is, the ghost of him had got it), so it was determined in the family to keep the whole affair secret. This Kechang was only too ready to espouse Miss Zhao; and before a year had passed over their heads his wife had presented the old people with the much-longed-for grandson.

---

400 See note 122 in tale number 23.

79. The Spirits of Lake Boyang

AN official, named Zhai, was appointed to a post at Raozhou, and on his way thither crossed the lake Boyang. Happening to visit the shrine of the local spirits, he noticed a carved image of the patriotic Ding Pulang,[401] and another of a namesake of his own, the latter occupying a very inferior position. "Come! come!" said Zhai, "my patron saint sha'n't be put in the background like that;" so he moved the image into a more honorable place, and then went back on board his boat again. Soon after, a great wind struck the vessel, and carried away the mast and sails; at which the sailors, in great alarm, set to work to howl and cry. However, in a few moments they saw a small skiff come cutting through the waves, and before long they were all safely on board. The man who rowed it was strangely like the image in the shrine, the position of which Zhai had changed; but they were hardly out of danger when the squall had passed over, and skiff and man had both vanished.

80. The Stream of Cash

A CERTAIN gentleman's servant was one day in his master's garden, when he beheld a stream of cash[402] flowing by, two or three feet in breadth and of about the same depth. He immediately seized two large handfuls, and then threw himself down on the top of the stream in order to try and secure the rest. However, when he got up he found that it had all flowed away from under him, none being left except what he had got in his two hands.

["Ah!" says the commentator, "money is properly a circulating medium, and is not intended for a man to lie upon and keep all to himself."][403]

---

401 A famous soldier, who distinguished himself at the battle of Boyang, 1363 CE. Even when his head had been taken off, he still grasped his sword and remained standing in an attitude of attack.
402 See note 7 in tale number 2.
403 The Chinese, fond as they are of introducing water, under the form of miniature lakes, into their gardens and pleasure-grounds, do not approve of a running stream near the dwelling-house. I myself knew a case of a man, provided with a pretty little house, rent-free, alongside of which ran a mountain rill, who left the place and paid for lodgings out of his own pocket rather than live so close to a stream which he averred *carried all his good luck away.* Yet this man was a fair scholar and a graduate to boot.

81. The Injustice of Heaven

MR. XU was a magistrate in Shandong. A certain upper chamber of his house was used as a store-room; but some creature managed so frequently to get in and make havoc among the stores, for which the servants were always being scolded, that at length some of the latter determined to keep watch. By-and-by they saw a huge spider as big as a peck measure, and hurried off to tell their master, who thought it so strange that he gave orders to the servants to feed the insect with cakes. It thus became very tame, and would always come forth when hungry, returning as soon as it had taken enough to eat.[404] Years passed away, and one day Mr. Xu was consulting his archives, when suddenly the spider appeared and ran under the table. Thinking it was hungry, he bade his servants give it a cake; but the next moment he noticed two snakes, of about the thickness of a chopstick, lying one on each side. The spider drew in its legs as if in mortal fear, and the snakes began to swell out until they were as big around as an egg; at which Mr. Xu was greatly alarmed, and would have hurried away, when crash! went a peal of thunder, killing every person in the house. Mr, Xu himself recovered consciousness after a little while, but only to see his wife and servants, seven persons in all, lying dead; and after a month's illness he, too, departed this life. Now Mr. Xu was an upright, honorable man, who really had the interests of the people at heart. A subscription was accordingly raised to pay his funeral expenses, and on the day of his burial the air was rent for miles around with cries of weeping and lamentation.

[Hereon the author makes the following remark: "That dragons play with pearls[405] I have always regarded as an old woman's tale. Is it possible, then, that the story is a fact? I have heard, too, that the thunder strikes only the guilty man; and, if so, how could a virtuous official be visited with this dire calamity?" Are not the inconsistencies of God Almighty many indeed?]

---

404 That Chinese man thinks his a hard lot who cannot "eat until he is full." It may be noticed here that the Chinese seem not so much to enjoy the process of eating, as the subsequent state of repletion. As a rule, they bolt their food, and get their enjoyment out of it afterwards.

405 The disc, spoken of as a pearl, which is often figured between two dragons, is really the symbol of thunder rolling.

82. The Sea-Serpent

A TRADER named Jia was voyaging on the south seas, when one night it suddenly became as light as day on board his ship. Jumping up to see what was the matter, he beheld a huge creature with its body half out of the water, towering up like a hill. Its eyes resembled two suns, and threw a light far and wide; and when the trader asked the boatmen what it was, there was not one who could say. They all crouched down and watched it; and by-and-by the monster gradually disappeared in the water again, leaving everything in darkness as before. And when they reached port, they found all the people talking about a strange phenomenon of a great light that had appeared in the night, the time of which coincided exactly with the strange scene they themselves had witnessed.[406]

83. The Magic Mirror[407]

". . . BUT if you would really like to have something that has belonged to me," said she, "you shall." Whereupon she took out a mirror and gave it to him, saying, "Whenever you want to see me, you must look for me in your books; otherwise I shall not be visible"—and in a moment she had vanished. Liu went home very melancholy at heart; but when he looked in the mirror, there was Fengxian, standing with her back to him, gazing, as it were, at someone who was going away, and about a hundred paces from her. He then bethought himself of her injunctions, and settled down to his studies, refusing to receive any visitors; and a few days subsequently, when he happened to look in the mirror, there was Fengxian, with her face turned towards him, and smiling in every feature. After this, he was always taking out the mirror to look at her; however, in about a month his good resolutions began to disappear, and he once more went out to enjoy himself and waste his time as before. When he returned home and looked in the mirror, Fengxian seemed to be crying bitterly; and the day after, when he looked at her again, she had her back turned towards him as on the day

---

406 The "sea-serpent" in this case was probably nothing more or less than some meteoric phenomenon.
407 The following is merely a single episode taken from a long and otherwise uninteresting story. Miss Fengxian was a fox; hence her power to bestow such a singular present as the mirror here described, the object of which was to incite her lover to success—the condition of their future union.

he received the mirror. He now knew that it was because he had neglected his studies, and forthwith set to work again with all diligence, until in a month's time she had turned around once again. Henceforward, whenever anything interrupted his progress, Fengxian's countenance became sad; but whenever he was getting on well, her sadness was changed to smiles. Night and morning Liu would look at the mirror, regarding it quite in the light of a revered preceptor; and in three years' time he took his degree in triumph. "Now," cried he, "I shall be able to look Fengxian in the face." And there, sure enough, she was, with her delicately-penciled arched eyebrows, and her teeth just showing between her lips, as happy-looking as she could be, when, all of a sudden, she seemed to speak, and Liu heard her say, "A pretty pair we make, I must allow"—and the next moment Fengxian stood by his side.

84. Courage Tested

MR. DONG was a Xuzhou man, very fond of playing broad-sword, and a light-hearted, devil-may-care fellow, who was often involving himself in trouble. One day he fell in with a traveler who was riding on a mule and going the same way as himself; whereupon they entered into conversation, and began to talk to each other about feats of strength and so on. The traveler said his name was Tong,[408] and that he belonged to Liaoyang; that he had been twenty years away from home, and had just returned from beyond the sea. "And I venture to say," cried Dong, "that in your wanderings on the Four Seas[409] you have seen a great many people; but have you seen any supernaturally clever ones?" Tong asked him to what he alluded; and then Dong explained what his own particular hobby was, adding how much he would like to learn from them any tricks in the art of broad-sword. "Supernaturals," replied the traveler, "are to be found everywhere. It needs but that a man should be a loyal subject and a filial son for him to know all that the super-naturals know." "Right you are,

---

408 Besides the all-important aspirate, this name is pronounced in a different *tone* from the first-mentioned "Dong;" and is, moreover, expressed in writing by a totally different character. To a Chinese ear, the two words are as unlikely to be confounded as Brown and Jones.

409 The Four Seas are supposed by the Chinese to bound the habitable portions of the earth, which, by the way, they further believe to be square. In the centre of all is China, extending far and wide in every direction—the eye of the universe, the Middle Kingdom. Away at a distance from her shores lie a number of small islands, wherein dwell such barbarous nations as the English, French, Dutch, etc.

indeed!" cried Dong, as he drew a short sword from his belt, and, tapping the blade with his fingers, began to accompany it with a song. He then cut down a tree that was by the wayside, to show Tong how sharp it was; at which Tong smoothed his beard and smiled, begging to be allowed to have a look at the weapon. Dong handed it to him, and, when he had turned it over two or three times, he said, "This is a very inferior piece of steel; now, though I know nothing about broad-sword myself, I have a weapon which is really of some use." He then drew from beneath his coat a sword, a foot or so in length, and with it he began to pare pieces off Dong's sword, which seemed as soft as a melon, and which he cut quite away like a horse's hoof. Dong was greatly astonished, and borrowed the other's sword to examine it, returning it after carefully wiping the blade. He then invited Tong to his house, and made him stay the night; and after begging him to explain the mystery of his sword, began to nurse his leg and sit listening respectfully without saying a word. It was already pretty late, when suddenly there was a sound of scuffling next door, where Dong's father lived; and, on putting his ear to the wall, he heard an angry voice saying, "Tell your son to come here at once, and then I will spare you." This was followed by other sounds of beating and a continued groaning, in a voice which Dong knew to be his father's. He therefore seized a spear, and was about to rush forth, but Tong held him back, saying, "You'll be killed for a certainty if you go. Let us think of some other plan." Dong asked what plan he could suggest; to which the other replied, "The robbers are killing your father: there is no help for you; but as you have no brothers, just go and tell your wife and children what your last wishes are, while I try and rouse the servants." Dong agreed to this, and ran in to tell his wife, who clung to him and implored him not to go, until at length all his courage had ebbed away, and he went upstairs with her to get his bow and arrows ready to resist the robbers' attack. At that juncture he heard the voice of his friend Tong, outside on the eaves of the house, saying, with a laugh, "All right; the robbers have gone;" but on lighting a candle, he could see nothing of him. He then stole out to the front door, where he met his father with a lantern in his hand, coming in from a party at a neighbor's house; and the whole court-yard was covered with the ashes of burnt grass, whereby he knew that Tong the traveler was himself a supernatural.[410]

---

410 The author adds a note to this story which might be summed up in our own—The [wo]man that deliberates is lost.

85. The Disembodied Friend

MR. CHEN, M.A., of Shuntian Fu, when a boy of sixteen, went to school at a Buddhist temple.[411] There were a great many scholars besides himself, and, among others, one named Chu, who said he came from Shandong. This Chu was a very hard-working fellow; he never seemed to be idle, and actually slept in the schoolroom, not going home at all. Chen became much attached to him, and one day asked him why he never went away. "Well, you see," replied Chu, "my people are very poor, and can hardly afford to pay for my schooling; but, by dint of working half the night, two of my days are equal to three of anybody else's." Thereupon Chen said he would bring his own bed to the school, and that they would sleep there together; to which Chu replied that the teaching they got wasn't worth much, and that they would do better by putting themselves under a certain old scholar named Lü. This they were easily able to do, as the arrangement at the temple was monthly, and at the end of each month anyone was free to go or to come. So off they went to this Mr. Lü, a man of considerable literary attainments, who had found himself in Shuntian Fu without a cash in his pocket, and was accordingly obliged to take pupils. He was delighted at getting two additions to his number; and Chu showing himself an apt scholar, the two soon became very great friends, sleeping in the same room and eating at the same table. At the end of the month Chu asked for leave of absence, and, to the astonishment of all, ten days elapsed without anything being heard of him. It then chanced that Chen went to the Tianning temple, and there he saw Chu under one of the verandahs, occupied in cutting wood for lucifer-matches.[412] The latter was much disconcerted by the arrival of Chen, who asked him why he had given up his studies; so the latter took him aside, and explained that he was so poor as to be obliged to work half a month to scrape together funds enough for his next month's schooling. "You come along back with me," cried Chen, on hearing this, "I will arrange for the payment," which Chu immediately consented to do on condition

---

411 Buddhist priests not unusually increase the revenue of their monastery by taking pupils; and it is only fair to them to add that the curriculum is strictly secular, the boys learning precisely what they would at an ordinary school and nothing else.

412 These consist simply of thin slips of wood dipped in brimstone, and resemble those used in England as late as the first quarter of the nineteenth century. They are said to have been invented by the people of Hangzhou, the capital of Zhejiang; but it is quite possible that the hint may have first reached China from the West. They were called *yin guang*, "bring light" (*lucifer*), *fa zhu*, "give forth illumination," and other names. Lucifer matches are now generally spoken of as *za lai huo*, "self-come fire," and are almost universally employed, except in remote parts where the flint and steel still hold sway.

that Chen would keep the whole thing a profound secret. Now Chen's father was a wealthy tradesman, and from his till Chen abstracted money wherewith to pay for Chu; and by-and-by, when his father found him out, he confessed why he had done so. Thereupon Chen's father called him a fool, and would not let him resume his studies; at which Chu was much hurt, and would have left the school too, but that old Mr. Lü discovered what had taken place, and gave him the money to return to Chen's father, keeping him still at the school, and treating him quite like his own son. So Chen studied no more, but whenever he met Chu he always asked him to join in some refreshment at a restaurant, Chu invariably refusing, but yielding at length to his entreaties, being himself loath to break off their old acquaintanceship.

Thus two years passed away, when Chen's father died, and Chen went back to his books under the guidance of old Mr. Lü, who was very glad to see such determination. Of course Chen was now far behind Chu; and in about six months Lü's son arrived, having begged his way in search of his father, so Mr. Lü gave up his school and returned home with a purse which his pupils had made up for him, Chu adding nothing thereto but his tears. At parting, Mr, Lü advised Chen to take Chu as his tutor, and this he did, establishing him comfortably in the house with him. The examination was very shortly to commence, and Chen felt convinced that he should not get through; but Chu said he thought he should be able to manage the matter for him. On the appointed day he introduced Chen to a gentleman who he said was a cousin of his, named Liu, and asked Chen to accompany this cousin, which Chen was just proceeding to do when Chu pulled him back from behind,[413] and he would have fallen down but that the cousin pulled him up again, and then, after having scrutinized his appearance, carried him off to his own house. There being no ladies there, Chen was put into the inner apartments; and a few days afterwards Liu said to him, "A great many people will be at the gardens today; let us go and amuse ourselves awhile, and afterwards I will send you home again." He then gave orders that a servant should proceed on ahead with tea and wine, and by-and-by they themselves went, and were soon in the thick of the fête. Crossing over a bridge, they saw beneath an old willow tree a little painted skiff, and were soon on board, engaged in freely passing around the wine. However, finding this a little dull, Liu bade his servant go and see if Miss Li, the famous singing-girl, was at home; and in a few minutes the servant returned bringing Miss Li with

413 The whole point of the story hinges on this.

him. Chen had met her before, and so they at once exchanged greeetings, while Liu begged her to be good enough to favor them with a song. Miss Li, who seemed laboring under a fit of melancholy, forthwith began a funeral dirge; at which Chen was not much pleased, and observed that such a theme was hardly suitable to the occasion. With a forced smile. Miss Li changed her key, and gave them a love-song; whereupon Chen seized her hand, and said, "There's that song of the Huansha river,[414] which you sang once before; I have read it over several times, but have quite forgotten the words." Then Miss Li began:

Eyes overflowing with tears, she sits gazing into her mirror;
Lifting the bamboo screen, one of her comrades approaches.
She bends her bead and seems intent on her bow-like slippers,
And forces her eyebrows to arch themselves into a smile.
With her scarlet sleeve she wipes the tears from her fragrant cheek,
In fear and trembling lest they should guess the thoughts that overwhelm her.

Chen repeated this over several times, until at length the skiff stopped, and they passed through a long verandah, where a great many verses had been inscribed on the walls,[415] to which Chen at once proceeded to add a stanza of his own. Evening was now coming on, and Liu remarked that the candidates would be just about leaving the examination-hall;[416] so he escorted him back to his own home, and there left him. The room was dark, and there was no one with him; but by-and-by the servants ushered in some one whom at first he took to be Chu. However, he soon saw that it was not Chu, and in another moment the stranger had fallen against him and knocked him down. "Master's fainted!" cried the servants, as they ran to pick him up; and then Chen discovered that the one who had fallen down was really no other than himself.[417] On getting up, he saw Chu standing by his side; and when they had sent away the servants the latter said, "Don't be alarmed: I am nothing more than a disembodied spirit. My time for reappearing on earth[418] is long overdue, but I could not forget your great

---

414 Beside which lived Xi Shi, the famous beauty of the fifth century after Christ.
415 The Chinese have precisely the same mania as our Browns, Joneses, and Robinsons, for scribbling and carving their names and compositions all over the available parts of any place of public resort. The literature of inn walls alone would fill many ponderous tomes.
416 The examination, which lasts nine days, has been going on all this time.
417 That is, his own body, into which Chu's spirit had temporarily passed, his own occupying, meanwhile, the body of his friend.
418 That is, for being born again, the sole hope and ambition of a disembodied shade.

kindness to me, and accordingly I have remained under this form in order to assist in the accomplishment of your wishes. The three bouts[419] are over, and your ambition will be gratified." Chen then inquired if Chu could assist him in like manner for his doctor's degree; to which the latter replied, "Alas! the luck descending to you from your ancestors is not equal to that.[420] They were a niggardly lot, and unfit for the posthumous honors you would thus confer on them." Chen next asked him whither he was going; and Chu replied that he hoped, through the agency of his cousin, who was a clerk in Purgatory, to be born again in old Mr. Lü's family. They then bade each other adieu; and, when morning came, Chen set off to call on Miss Li, the singing-girl; but on reaching her house he found that she had been dead some days.[421] He walked on to the gardens, and there he saw traces of verses that had been written on the walls, and evidently rubbed out, so as to be hardly decipherable. In a moment it flashed across him that the verses and their composers belonged to the other world. Towards evening Chu reappeared in high spirits, saying that he had succeeded in his design, and had come to wish Chen a long farewell. Holding out his open palms, he requested Chen to write the word *Chu* on each; and then, after refusing to take a parting cup, he went away, telling Chen that the examination-list would soon be out, and that they would meet again before long. Chen brushed away his tears and escorted him to the door, where a man, who had been waiting for him, laid his hand on Chu's head and pressed it downwards until Chu was perfectly flat. The man then put him in a sack and carried him off on his back. A few days afterwards the list came out, and, to his great joy, Chen found his name among the successful candidates; whereupon he immediately started off to visit his old tutor, Mr. Lü.[422] Now Mr. Lü's wife had had no children for ten years, being about fifty years of age, when suddenly she gave birth to a son, who was born with both fists doubled up so that no one could open them. On his arrival Chen begged to see the child, and declared that inside its hands would be found written the word Chu. Old Mr. Lü laughed at this; but no sooner had the child set eyes on Chen than both its fists opened spontaneously, and there was the word as Chen had said. The story was soon told, and Chen went home, after making a handsome present to the family; and later on, when Mr. Lü went up for his

---

419 See note 371 in tale number 71.
420 See note 312 in tale number 61.
421 His own spirit in Chu's body had met her in a disembodied state.
422 Such is the invariable custom. Large presents are usually made by those who can afford the outlay, and the tutor's name has ever afterwards an honorable place in the family records.

doctor's degree[423] and stayed at Chen's house, his son was thirteen years old, and had already matriculated as a candidate for literary honors.

86. The Cloth Merchant

A CERTAIN cloth merchant went to Qingzhou, where he happened to stroll into an old temple, all tumble-down and in ruins. He was lamenting over this sad state of things, when a priest who stood by observed that a devout believer like himself could hardly do better than put the place into repair, and thus obtain favor in the eyes of Buddha. This the merchant consented to do; whereupon the priest invited him to walk into the private quarters of the temple, and treated him with much courtesy; but he went on to propose that our friend the merchant should also undertake the general ornamentation of the place both inside and out.[424] The latter declared he could not afford the expense, and the priest began to get very angry, and urged him so strongly that at last the merchant, in terror, promised to give all the money he had. After this he was preparing to go away, but the priest detained him, saying, "You haven't given the money of your own free will, and consequently you'll be owing me a grudge: I can't do better than make an end of you at once." Thereupon he seized a knife, and refused to listen to all the cloth merchant's entreaties, until at length the latter asked to be allowed to hang himself, to which the priest consented; and, showing him into a dark room, told him to make haste about it.

At this juncture, a Tartar-General[425] happened to pass by the temple; and from a distance, through a breach in the old wall, he saw a damsel in

---

423 See note 241 in tale number 48.

424 The elaborate gilding and woodwork of an ordinary Chinese temple form a very serious item in the expense of restoration. Public subscriptions are usually the means employed for raising sufficient funds, the names of subscribers and amount given by each being published in some conspicuous position. Occasionally devout priests—black swans, indeed, in China—shut themselves up in boxes studded with nails, one of which they pull out every time a certain donation is given, and there they remain until every nail is withdrawn. But after all it is difficult to say whether they endure these trials so much for the faith's sake as for the funds from which they derive more of the luxuries of life, and the temporary notoriety gained by thus coming before the public. A Chinese proverb says, "The image-maker doesn't worship Buddha. He knows too much about it;" and the application of this saying may safely be extended to the majority of Buddhist priests in China.

425 This is the title generally applied to the Manchu commanders of Manchu garrisons, who are stationed at certain of the most important points of the Chinese Empire, and whose presence is intended as a check upon the action of the civil authorities.

a red dress pass into the priest's quarters. This roused his suspicions,[426] and dismounting from his horse, he entered the temple and searched high and low, but without discovering anything. The dark room above-mentioned was locked and double-barred, and the priest refused to open it, saying the place was haunted. The General in a rage burst open the door, and there beheld the cloth merchant hanging from a beam. He cut him down at once, and in a short time he was brought around and told the General the whole story. They then searched for the damsel, but she was nowhere to be found, having been nothing more than a divine manifestation. The General cut off the priest's head and restored the cloth merchant's property to him, after which the latter put the temple in thorough repair, and kept it well supplied with lights and incense ever afterwards.

Mr. Zhao, M.A., told me this story, with all its details.[427]

87. A Strange Companion

HAN GONGFU, of Yucheng, told me that he was one day traveling along a road with a man of his village, named Peng, when all of a sudden the latter disappeared, leaving his mule to jog along with an empty saddle. At the same moment, Mr. Han heard his voice calling for assistance, and apparently proceeding from inside one of the panniers strapped across the mule's back; and on looking closely, there indeed he was in one of the panniers, which, however, did not seem to be at all displaced by his weight. On trying to get him out the mouth of the pannier closed itself tightly; and it was only when he cut it open with a knife that he saw Peng curled up in it like a dog. He then helped him out, and asked him how he managed to get in; but this he was unable to say. It further appeared that his family was under fox influence, many strange things of this kind having happened before.

88. Spiritualistic Séances

IT is customary in Shandong, when any one is sick, for the womenfolk to engage an old sorceress or medium, who strums on a tambourine and

---

426 See note 17 in tale number 6.
427 The moral being, of course, that Buddha protects those who look after his interests on earth.

performs certain mysterious antics. This custom obtains even more in the capital, where young ladies of the best families frequently organize such *séances* among themselves. On a table in the hall they spread out a profusion of wine and meat, and burn huge candles which make the place as light as day. Then the sorceress, shortening her skirts, stands on one leg and performs the *shang-yang*,[428] while two of the others support her, one on each side. All this time she is chattering unintelligible sentences,[429] something between a song and a prayer, the words being confused but uttered in a sort of tune; while the hall resounds with the thunder of drums, enough to stun a person, with which her vaticinations are mixed up and lost. By-and-by her head begins to droop, and her eyes to look aslant; and but for her two supporters she would inevitably fall to the ground. Suddenly she stretches forth her neck and bounds several feet into the air, upon which the other women regard her in terror, saying, "The spirits have come to eat;" and immediately all the candles are blown out and everything is in total darkness. Thus they remain for about a quarter of an hour, afraid to speak a word, which in any case would not be heard through the din, until at length the sorceress calls out the personal name of the head of the family[430] and some others; whereupon they immediately relight the candles and hurry up to ask if the reply of the spirits is favorable or otherwise. They then see that every scrap of the food and every drop of the wine has disappeared. Meanwhile, they watch the old woman's expression, whereby they can tell if the spirits are well disposed; and each one asks her some question, to which she as promptly replies. Should there be any unbelievers among the party, the spirits are at once aware of their presence; and the old sorceress, pointing her finger at such a one, cries out, "Disrespectful mocker! where are your trousers?" upon which the mocker alluded to looks down, and lo! her trousers are gone—gone to the top of a tree in the court-yard, where they will subsequently be found.[431]

---

428 It is related in the *Family Sayings*, an apocryphal work which professes to give conversations of Confucius, that a number of one-legged birds having suddenly appeared in Qi, the Duke of Qi sent off to ask the Sage what was the meaning of this strange phenomenon. Confucius replied, "The bird is the *shang-yang*, and portends beneficial rain." And formerly the boys and girls in Shandong would hop about on one leg, crying, "The *shang-yang* has come;" after which rain would be sure to follow.

429 Speaking in the unknown tongue, like the Irvingites and others.

430 This is a clever hit. The "personal" name of a man may not be uttered except by the Emperor, his father or mother, grand-father, grandmother, etc. Thus, the mere use of the personal name of the head *of a family* proves conclusively that the spirit of some one of his ancestors must be present.

431 The above is a curious story to be found in a Chinese work over 200 years old; but no part of it more so than the forcible removal of some part of the clothing, which has been so prominent a feature in the *séances* of our own day. It may be added that in many a court-yard in Beijing will be found one or more trees, which cause the view from the city wall to be very pleasing to the eye.

Manchu women and girls, especially, are firm believers in spiritualism. On the slightest provocation they consult their medium, who comes into the room gorgeously dressed, and riding on an imitation horse or tiger.[432] In her hand she holds a long spear, with which she mounts the couch[433] and postures in an extraordinary manner, the animal she rides snorting or roaring fiercely all the time. Some call her Guan Di,[434] others Zhang Fei, and others, again, Zhou Gong, from her terribly martial aspect, which strikes fear into all beholders. And should any daring fellow try to peep in while the *séance* is going on, out of the window darts the spear, transfixes his hat, and draws it off his head into the room, while women and girls, young and old, hop around one after the other like geese, on one leg, without seeming to get the least fatigued.

89. The Mysterious Head

SEVERAL traders who were lodging at an inn in Beijing occupied a room which was divided from the adjoining apartment by a partition of boards from which a piece was missing, leaving an aperture about as big as a basin. Suddenly a girl's head appeared through the opening, with very pretty features and nicely dressed hair; and the next moment an arm, as white as polished jade. The traders were much alarmed, and, thinking it was the work of devils, tried to seize the head, which, however, was quickly drawn in again out of their reach. This happened a second time, and then, as they could see nobody belonging to the head, one of them took a knife in his hand and crept up against the partition underneath the hole. In a little while the head reappeared, when he made a chop at it and cut it off, the blood spurting out all over the floor and wall. The traders hurried off to tell the landlord, who immediately reported the matter to the authorities, taking the head with him, and the traders were forthwith arrested and examined; but the magistrate could make nothing of

---

432 The arrangement being that of the hobby-horse of bygone days.

433 The couches of the North of China are brick beds, heated by a stove underneath, and covered with a mat. Upon one of these is generally a dwarf table and a couple of pillows; and here it is that the Chinese man loves to recline, his wine-kettle, opium-pipe, or teapot within reach, and a friend at his side, with whom he may converse far into the night.

434 See note 4 in tale number 1. Zhang Fei was the bosom friend of the last, and was his associate-commander in the wars of the Three Kingdoms. Zhou Gong was a younger brother of the first Emperor of the Zhou dynasty, and a pattern of wisdom and virtue. He is said by the Chinese to have invented the compass; but the legend will not bear investigation.

the case, and, as no one appeared for the prosecution, the accused, after about six months' incarceration, were accordingly released, and orders were given for the girl's head to be buried.

90. The Spirit of the Hills

A MAN named Li, of Yidu, was once crossing the hills when he came upon a number of persons sitting on the ground engaged in drinking. As soon as they saw Li they begged him to join them, and vied with each other in filling his cup. Meanwhile, he looked about him and noticed that the various trays and dishes contained all kinds of costly food; the wine only seemed to him a little rough on the palate. In the middle of their fun up came a stranger with a face about three feet long and a very tall hat; whereupon the others were much alarmed, and cried out, "The hill spirit! the hill spirit!" running away in all directions as fast as they could go. Li hid himself in a hole in the ground; and when by-and-by he peeped out to see what had happened, the wine and food had disappeared, and there was nothing there but a few dirty potsherds and some pieces of broken tiles with newts and lizards crawling over them.[435]

91. Ingratitude Punished

KU DAYOU was a native of the Yang district, and managed to get a military appointment under the command of Zu Shushun.[436] The latter treated him most kindly, and finally sent him as Major-General of some troops by which he was then trying to establish the dynasty of the usurping Zhous. Ku soon perceived that the game was lost, and immediately turned his forces upon Zu Shushun, whom he succeeded in capturing, after Zu had been wounded in the hand, and whom he at once forwarded as a prisoner to headquarters. That night he dreamed that the Judge of Purgatory appeared to him, and, reproaching him with his base ingratitude, bade the devil-lictors seize him and scald his feet in a cauldron of boiling oil. Ku then woke up with a start,

---

435 Mr. Li had, doubtless, taken "a drop too much" before he started on his mountain walk.
436 Of whom I can learn nothing.

and found that his feet were very sore and painful; and in a short time they swelled up, and his toes dropped off. Fever set in, and in his agony he shrieked out, "Ungrateful wretch that I was indeed," and fell back and expired.

92. Smelling Essays[437]

NOW as they wandered about the temple they came upon an old blind priest sitting under the verandah, engaged in selling medicines and prescribing for patients. "Ah!" cried Song, "there is an extraordinary man who is well versed in the arts of composition;" and immediately he sent back to get the essay they had just been reading, in order to obtain the old priest's opinion as to its merits. At the same moment up came their friend from Yuhang, and all three went along together. Wang began by addressing him as "Professor;" whereupon the priest, who thought the stranger had come to consult him as a doctor, inquired what might be the disease from which he was suffering. Wang then explained what his mission was; upon which the priest smiled and said, "Who's been telling you this nonsense? How can a man with no eyes discuss with you the merits of your compositions?" Wang replied by asking him to let his ears do duty for his eyes; but the priest answered that he would hardly have patience to sit out Wang's three sections, amounting perhaps to some two thousand and more words. "However," added he, "if you like to burn it, I'll try what I can do with my nose." Wang complied, and burnt the first section there and then; and the old priest, snuffing up the smoke, declared that it wasn't such a bad effort, and finally gave it as his opinion that Wang would probably succeed at the examination. The young scholar from Yuhang didn't believe that the old priest could really tell anything by these means, and forthwith proceeded to burn an essay by one of the old masters; but the priest no sooner smelt the smoke than he cried out, "Beautiful indeed! beautiful indeed! I do enjoy this. The light of genius and truth is evident here." The Yuhang scholar was greatly astonished at this, and began to burn an essay of his own; whereupon the priest said, "I had had but a taste of that one; why change so soon to another?" "The first paragraph," replied the young man, "was by a friend; the rest is my own composition." No sooner had he uttered these words than the old priest

---

437 The following extract from a long and otherwise tedious story tells its own tale. Wang is the modest man, and the young man from Yuhang the braggart. Song is merely a friend of Wang's.

began to retch violently, and begged that he might have no more, as he was sure it would make him sick. The Yuhang scholar was much abashed at this, and went away; but in a few days the list came out, and his name was among the successful ones, while Wang's was not. He at once hurried off to tell the old priest, who, when he heard the news, sighed and said, "I may be blind with my eyes, but I am not so with my nose, which I fear is the case with the examiners. Besides," added he, "I was talking to you about composition: I said nothing about *destiny*."[438]

93. His Father's Ghost

A MAN named Tian Zicheng, of Jiangning, was crossing lake Dongting, when the boat was capsized, and he was drowned. His son, Liangsi, who, towards the close of the Ming dynasty, took the highest degree, was then a baby in arms; and his wife, hearing the bad news, swallowed poison forthwith,[439] and left the child to the care of his grandmother. When Liangsi grew up, he was appointed magistrate in Hubei, where he remained about a year. He was then transferred to Hunan, on military servce; but, on reaching lake Dongting, his feelings overpowered him, and he returned to plead inability as an excuse for not taking up his post. Accordingly, he was degraded to the rank of Assistant-Magistrate, which he at first declined, but was finally compelled to accept; and thenceforward gave himself up to roaming about on the lakes and streams of the surrounding country, without paying much attention to his official duties.

One night he had anchored his boat alongside the bank of a river, when suddenly the cadence of a sweetly-played flageolet broke upon his ear; so he strolled along by the light of the moon in the direction of the music, until, after a few minutes' walking, he reached a cottage standing by itself, with a few citron-trees around it, and brilliantly lighted inside. Approaching a window, he peeped in, and saw three persons sitting at a table, engaged in drinking. In the place of honor was a graduate of about thirty years of age; an old man played the host, and at the side sat a much younger man playing on the flageolet. When he had finished, the old man clapped his

---

438 This is one of our author's favorite shafts—a sneer at examiners in general, and those who rejected him in particular.
439 This would be regarded as a very meritorious act by the Chinese.

hands in admiration; but the graduate turned away with a sigh, as if he had not heard a note. "Come now, Mr. Lu," cried the old man, addressing the latter, "kindly favor us with one of your songs, which, I know, must be worth hearing." The graduate then began to sing as follows:

Over the river the wind blows cold on lonely me:
Each flow'ret trampled under foot, all verdure gone.
At home a thousand *li* away, I cannot be;
So towards the Bridge my spirit nightly wanders on.

The above was given in such melancholy tones that the old man smiled and said, "Mr. Lu, these must be experiences of your own," and, immediately filling a goblet, added, "I can do nothing like that; but if you will let me, I will give you a song to help us on with our wine." He then sang a verse from Li Taibo,[440] and put them all in a lively humor again; after which the young man said he would just go outside and see how high the moon was, which he did, and, observing Liangsi outside, clapped his hands, and cried out to his companions, "There is a man at the window, who has seen all we have been doing." He then led Liangsi in; whereupon the other two rose, and begged him to be seated, and to join them in their wine. The wine, however, was cold,[441] and he therefore declined; but the young man at once perceived his reason, and proceeded to warm some for him. Liangsi now ordered his servant to go and buy some more, but this his host would not permit him to do. They next inquired Liangsi's name, and whence he came, and then the old man said, "Why, then, you are the father and mother[442] of the district in which I live. My name is River: I am an old resident here. This young man is a Mr. Du, of Jiangzi; and this gentleman," added he, pointing to the graduate, "is Mr. Rushten,[443] a fellow-provincial of yours." Mr. Rushten looked at Liangsi in rather a contemptuous way, and without taking much notice of him; whereupon Liangsi asked him whereabouts he lived in Jiangning, observing that it was strange he himself should never have heard of such an accomplished gentleman. "Alas!" replied Rushten, "it is many a long day since I left my home, and I know nothing even of my

---

440 The Byron of China.

441 Chinese wine—or, more correctly, *spirits*—is always taken hot; hence the term wine-kettle, which frequently occurs in these pages.

442 The Magistrate; who is supposed to be towards the people what a father is to his children.

443 This singularly un-Chinese surname is employed to keep up a certain play upon words which exists in the original, and which is important to the *dénouement* of the story. "River" is the simple translation of a name actually in use.

own family. Alas, indeed!" These words were uttered in so mournful a tone of voice that the old man broke in with, "Come, come, now! talking like this, instead of drinking when we're all so jolly together; this will never do." He then drained a bumper himself, and said, "I propose a game of forfeits. We'll throw with three dice; and whoever throws so that the spots on one die[444] equal those on the other two shall give us a verse with a corresponding classical allusion in it." He then threw himself, and turned up an ace, a two, and a three; whereupon he sang the following lines:

> An ace and a deuce on one side, just equal a three on the other:
> For Fan a chicken was boiled, though three years had passed, by Zhang's
>   mother.[445]
> Thus friends love to meet!

Then the young musician threw, and turned up two twos and a four; whereupon he exclaimed, "Don't laugh at the feeble allusion of an unlearned fellow like me:

> Two deuces are equal to a four;
> Four men united their valor in the old city.[446]
> Thus brothers love to meet!"

Mr. Rushten followed with two aces and a two, and recited these lines:

> Two aces are equal to a two:
> Luxiang stretched out his two arms and embraced his father.[447]
> Thus father and son love to meet!

---

444 Chinese dice are the exact counterpart of our own, except that the ace and the four are colored red: the ace because the combination of black and white would be unlucky, and the four because this number once turned up in response to the call of an Emperor of the Tang dynasty, who particularly wanted a four to win him the *partie*. All letters, despatches, and such documents, have invariably something *red* about them, this being the lucky color, and to the Chinese emblematic of prosperity and joy.

445 Alluding to an ancient story of a promise by a Mr. Fan that he would be at his friend Zhang's house that day three years. When the time drew near, Zhang's mother ridiculed the notion of a man keeping a three years' appointment; but, acceding to her son's instances, she prepared a boiled chicken, which was barely ready when Fan arrived to eat of it.

446 Alluding to the celebrated oath of confederation sworn in the peach garden between Guan Yu, or Guan Di (see note 4 in tale number 1), Zhang Fei (see note 323 in tale number 63), Liu Bei, who subsequently proclaimed himself Emperor, 221 CE, and Zhuge Liang, his celebrated minister, to whose sage counsels most of the success of the undertaking was due.

447 Alluding to the story of a young man who went in search of his missing father.

Liang then threw, and turned up the same as Mr. Rushten; whereupon he said:

Two aces axe equal to a two:
Maorong regaled Linzong with two baskets.[448]
Thus host and guest love to meet!

When the *partie* was over Liangsi rose to go, but Mr. Rushten said, "Dear me! why are you in such a hurry; we haven't had a moment to speak of the old place. Please stay: I was just going to ask you a few questions." So Liangsi sat down again, and Mr. Rushten proceeded. "I had an old friend," said he, "who was drowned in lake Dongting. He bore the same name as yourself; was he a relative?" "He was my father," replied Liangsi; "how did you know him?" "We were friends as boys together; and when he was drowned, I recovered and buried his body by the river-side."[449] Liangsi here burst into tears, and thanked Mr. Rushten very warmly, begging him to point out his father's grave. "Come again tomorrow," said Mr. Rushten, "and I will show it to you. You could easily find it yourself. It is close by here, and has ten stalks of water-rush growing on it." Liangsi now took his leave, and went back to his boat, but he could not sleep for thinking of what Mr. Rushten had told him; and at length, without waiting for the dawn, he set out to look for the grave. To his great astonishment, the house where he had spent the previous evening had disappeared; but hunting about in the direction indicated by Mr. Rushten, he found a grave with ten water-rushes growing on it, precisely as Mr. Rushten had described. It then flashed across him that Mr. Rushten's name had a special meaning, and that he had been holding converse with none other than the disembodied spirit of his own father. And, on inquiring of the people of the place, he learnt that twenty years before, a benevolent old gentleman, named Gao, had been in the habit of collecting the bodies of persons found drowned, and burying them in that spot. Liang then opened the grave, and carried off his father's remains to his own home, where his grandmother, to whom he described Mr. Rushten's appearance, confirmed the suspicion he himself had formed. It also turned

---

448 Linzong saw his host kill a chicken which he thought was destined for himself. However, Maorong served up the dainty morsel to his mother, while he and his guest regaled themselves with two baskets of common vegetables. At this instance of filial piety, Linzong had the good sense to be charmed.
449 The Chinese recognize no act more worthy a virtuous man than that of burying stray bones, covering up exposed coffins, and so forth. By such means the favor of the Gods is most surely obtained, to say nothing of the golden opinions of the living.

out that the young musician was a cousin of his, who had been drowned when nineteen years of age; and then he recollected that the boy's father had subsequently gone to Jiangzi, and that his mother had died there, and had been buried at the Bamboo Bridge, to which Mr. Rushten had alluded in his song. But he did not know who the old man was.[450]

94. The Boat-Girl Bride

WANG GUIAN was a young man of good family. It happened once when he was traveling southwards, and had moored his boat to the bank, that he saw in another boat close by a young boat-girl embroidering shoes. He was much struck by her beauty, and continued gazing at her for some time, though she took not the slightest notice of him. By-and-by he began singing:

The Luoyang lady lives over the way:
[Fifteen years is her age I should say].[451]

to attract her attention, and then she seemed to perceive that he was addressing himself to her; but, after just raising her head and glancing at him, she resumed her embroidery as before. Wang then threw a piece of silver towards her, which fell on her skirt; however, she merely picked it up, and flung it onto the bank, as if she had not seen what it was, so Wang put it back in his pocket again. He followed up by throwing her a gold bracelet, to which she paid no attention whatever, never taking her eyes off her work. A few minutes after her father appeared, much to the dismay of Wang, who was afraid he would see the bracelet; but the young girl quietly placed her feet over it, and concealed it from his sight. The boatman let go the painter, and away they went down stream, leaving Wang sitting there, not knowing what to do next. And, having recently lost his wife, he regretted that he had not seized this opportunity to make another match; the more so, as when he came to ask the other boat-people of the place, no one knew anything about them. So Wang got into his own boat, and started off in pursuit; but evening came on, and, as he could see nothing of them, he was obliged to turn back

---

450 This is merely our author's way of putting the question of the old man's identity. He was the Spirit of the Waters—his name, it will be recollected, was River—just, in fact, as we say Old Father Thames.
451 From a poem by Wang Wei, a noted poet of the Tang dynasty; he lived 699–759 CE. The second line is not given in the text.

and proceed in the direction where business was taking him. When he had finished that, he returned, making inquiries all the way along, but without hearing anything about the object of his search. On arriving at home, he was unable either to eat or to sleep, so much did this affair occupy his mind; and about a year afterwards he went south again, bought a boat, and lived in it as his home, watching carefully every single vessel that passed either up or down, until at last there was hardly one he didn't know by sight. But all this time the boat he was looking for never reappeared.

Some six months passed away thus, and then, having exhausted all his funds, he was obliged to go home, where he remained in a state of general inaptitude for anything. One night he dreamed that he entered a village on the river-bank, and that, after passing several houses, he saw one with a door, towards the south, and a palisade of bamboos inside. Thinking it was a garden, he walked in, and beheld a beautiful magnolia, covered with blossoms, which reminded him of the line:

And Judas-tree in flower before the door.[452]

A few steps farther on was a neat bamboo hedge, on the other side of which, towards the north, he found a small house, with three columns, the door of which was locked; and another, towards the south, with its window shaded by the broad leaves of a plaintain-tree. The door was barred by a clothes-horse,[453] on which was hanging an embroidered petticoat; and, on seeing this, Wang stepped back, knowing that he had got to the ladies' quarters; but his presence had already been noticed inside, and, in another moment, out came his heroine of the boat. Overjoyed at seeing her, he was on the point of grasping her hand, when suddenly the girl's father arrived, and, in his consternation, Wang woke up, and found that it was all a dream.

---

452 From a poem by Pan Tangshen, which runs:

> Her rustic home stands by the Dongting lake.
> Ye who would there a pure libation pour,
> Look for mud walls, a roof of rushy make,
> And Judas-tree in flower before the door.

The Chinese believe that the Judas-tree will only bloom where fraternal love prevails.

453 I have already observed that men and women should not let their hands touch when passing things to each other (see note 200 in tale number 40); neither is it considered proper for persons of different sexes to hang their clothes on the same clothes-horse. (See note 700 in Appendix 1.)

With regard to shaking hands, I have omitted to mention how objectionable this custom is in the eyes of the Chinese, as in vogue among foreigners, without reference to sex. They believe that a bad man might easily secrete some noxious drug in the palm of his hand, and so convey it into the system of any woman, who would then be at his mercy.

Every incident of it, however, remained clear and distinct in his mind, and he took care to say nothing about it to anybody, for fear of destroying its reality.

Another year passed away, and he went again to Jinjiang, where lived an official, named Xu, who was an old friend of the family, and who invited Wang to come and take a cup of wine with him. On his way thither, Wang lost his way, but at length reached a village which seemed familiar to him, and which he soon found, by the door with the magnolia inside, to be identical in every particular with the village of his dream. He went in through the doorway, and there was everything as he had seen it in his dream, even to the boat-girl herself. She jumped up on his arrival, and, shutting the door in his face, asked what his business was there. Wang inquired if she had forgotten about the bracelet, and went on to tell her how long he had been searching for her, and how, at last, she had been revealed to him in a dream. The girl then begged to know his name and family; and when she heard who he was, she asked what a gentleman like himself could want with a poor boat-girl like her, as he must have a wife of his own. "But for you," replied Wang, "I should, indeed, have been married long ago." Upon which the girl told him if that was really the case, he had better apply to her parents, "although," added she, "they have already refused a great many offers for me. The bracelet you gave me is here, but my father and mother are just now away from home; they will be back shortly. You go away now and engage a match-maker, when I dare say it will be all right if the proper formalities are observed." Wang then retired, the girl calling after him to remember that her name was Meng Yun, and her father's Meng Jiangli. He proceeded at once on his way to Mr. Xu's, and after that sought out his intended father-in-law, telling him who he was, and offering him at the same time one hundred ounces of silver, as betrothal-money for his daughter. "She is already promised," replied the old man; upon which Wang declared he had been making careful inquiries, and had heard, on all sides, that the young lady was not engaged, winding up by begging to know what objection there was to his suit. "I have just promised her," answered her father, "and I cannot possibly break my word;" so Wang went away, deeply mortified, not knowing whether to believe it or not. That night he tossed about a good deal; and next morning, braving the ridicule with which he imagined his friend would view his wished-for alliance with a boat-girl, he went off to Mr. Xu, and told him all about it. "Why didn't you consult me before?" cried Mr. Xu; "her father is a connection of mine." Wang then went on to give fuller particulars, which his friend interrupted by saying, "Jiangli is indeed poor, but he has never been a boatman. Are you sure you are not making a mistake?" He then sent off his elder son to make inquiries; and to him the girl's father said, "Poor I am, but I don't *sell* my daughter.[454] Your friend imagined that I should be tempted by the sight of his money to forego the usual ceremonies, and so I won't have anything to do with him. But if your father desires this match, and, everything is in proper order, I will just go in and consult with my daughter, and see if she is willing." He then retired for a few minutes, and when he came back he raised his hands in congratulation, saying, "Everything is as you wish;" whereupon a day was fixed, and the young man went home to report to his father. Wang now sent off betrothal presents, with the usual formalities, and took up his abode with his friend, Mr. Xu, until the marriage was solemnized, three days after which he bade adieu to his father-in-law, and started on his way northwards. In the evening, as they were sitting on the boat together, Wang said to his wife, "When I first met you near this spot, I fancied you were not of the ordinary boating-class. Where were you then going?" "I was going to visit my uncle," she replied. "We are not a wealthy family, you know, but we don't want anything through an improper channel; and I couldn't help smiling at the great eyes you were making at me, all the time trying to tempt me with money. But when I heard you speak, I knew at once you were a man of refinement, though I guessed you were a bit of a rake; and so I hid your bracelet, and saved you from the wrath of my father." "And yet," replied Wang, "you have fallen into my snare after all;" adding, after a little pressure, "for I can't conceal from you much longer the fact that I have already a wife, belonging to a high official family." This she did not believe, until he began to affirm it seriously; and then she jumped up and ran out of the cabin. Wang followed at once, but, before he could reach her, she was already in the river; whereupon he shouted out to boats to come to their assistance, causing quite a commotion all around about; but nothing was to be seen in the river, save only the reflection of the stars shining brightly on the water. All night long Wang went sorrowfully up and down, and offered a high reward for the body, which, however, was not forthcoming. So he went home in despair, and then, fearing lest his father-in-law should come to visit his daughter, he started on a visit to a connection of his, who had an appointment in Henan. In the course of a year or two, when on his homeward journey, he chanced to be detained by bad weather at a roadside

---

454 Alluding to Wang's breach of etiquette in visiting the father himself, instead of sending a go-between, who would have offered the same sum in due form as the usual dowry or present to the bride's family.

inn of rather cleaner appearance than usual. Within he saw an old woman playing with a child, which, as soon as he entered, held out its arms to him to be taken. Wang took the child on his knee, and there it remained, refusing to go back to its nurse; and, when the rain had stopped, and Wang was getting ready to go, the child cried out, "Ba-ba gone!" The nurse told it to hold its tongue, and, at the same moment, out from behind the screen came Wang's long-lost wife. "You bad fellow," said she, "what am I to do with this?" pointing to the child; and then Wang knew that the boy was his own son. He was much affected, and swore by the sun[455] that the words he had uttered had been uttered in jest, and by-and-by his wife's anger was soothed. She then explained how she had been picked up by a passing boat, the occupant of which was the owner of the house they were in, a man of sixty years of age, who had no children of his own, and who kindly adopted her.[456] She also told him how she had had several offers of marriage, all of which she had refused, and how her child was born, and that she had called him Jisheng, and that he was then a year old. Wang now unpacked his baggage again, and went in to see the old gentleman and his wife, whom he treated as if they had actually been his wife's parents. A few days afterwards they set off together towards Wang's home, where they found his wife's real father awaiting them. He had been there more than two months, and had been considerably disconcerted by the mysterious remarks of Wang's servants; but the arrival of his daughter and her husband made things all smooth again, and when they-told him what had happened, he understood the demeanor of the servants which had seemed so strange to him at first.

---

455 Witnesses in a Chinese court of justice take no oath, in our sense of the term. Their written depositions, however, are always ended with the words "the above evidence is the truth!" In ordinary life people call heaven and earth to witness, or, as in this case, the sun; or they declare themselves willing to forfeit their lives; and so on, if their statements are not true. "Saucer-breaking" is one of those pleasant inductions from probably a single instance, which may have been the fancy of a moment; at any rate, it is quite unknown in China as a national custom. "Cock-killing" usually has reference to the ceremonies of initiation performed by the members of the numerous secret societies which exist over the length and breadth of the Empire, in spite of Government prohibitions, and the penalty of death incurred upon detection.

456 Adoption is common all over China, and is regulated by law. For instance, an adopted son excludes all the daughters of the family. A man is not allowed to marry a girl whom he has adopted until he shall have given her away to be adopted in a family of a *different surname from his own;* after which fictitious ceremony, his marriage with her becomes legal (see note 76 in tale number 15); for the child adopted takes the same surname as that of the family into which he is adopted, and is so far cut off from his own relations, that he would not venture even to put on mourning for his real parents without first obtaining the consent of those who had adopted him. A son or daughter may be sold, but an adopted child may not; neither may the adopted child be given away in adoption to any one else without the specific consent of his real parents. The general object in adopting children is to leave someone behind at death to look after the duties of ancestral worship. For this boys are preferred; but the *Fortunate Union* gives an instance in which these rites were very creditably performed by the heroine of the tale.

95. The Two Brides[457]

Now Jisheng, or Wang Sun, was one of the cleverest young fellows in the district; and his father and mother, who had foreseen his ability from the time when, as a baby in long clothes, he distinguished them from other people, loved him very dearly. He grew up into a handsome lad; at eight or nine he could compose elegantly, and by fourteen he had already entered his name as a candidate for the first degree, after which his marriage became a question for consideration. Now his father's younger sister, Erniang, had married a gentleman named Zheng Ziqiao, and they had a daughter called Guixiu, who was extremely pretty, and with whom Jisheng fell deeply in love, being soon unable either to eat or to sleep. His parents became extremely uneasy about him, and inquired what it was that ailed him; and when he told them, they at once sent off a match-maker to Mr. Zheng. The latter, however, was rather a stickler for the proprieties, and replied that the near relationship precluded him from accepting the offer.[458] Thereupon Jisheng became dangerously ill, and his mother, not knowing what to do, secretly tried to persuade Erniang to let her daughter come over to their house; but Mr. Zheng heard of it, and was so angry that Jisheng's father and mother gave up all hope of arranging the match.

At that time there was a gentleman named Zhang living near by, who had five daughters, all very pretty, but the youngest, called Wuke, was singularly beautiful, far surpassing her four sisters. She was not betrothed to any one, when one day, as she was on her way to worship at the family tombs, she chanced to see Jisheng, and at her return home spoke about him to her mother. Her mother guessed what her meaning was, and arranged with a match-maker, named Mrs. Yu, to call upon Jisheng's parents. This she did precisely at the time when Jisheng was so ill, and forthwith told his mother that her son's complaint was one she, Mrs. Yu, was quite competent to cure; going on to tell her about Miss Wuke and the proposed marriage, at which the good lady was delighted, and sent her in to talk about it to Jisheng herself. "Alas!" cried he, when he had heard Mrs. Yu's story, "you are bringing me the wrong medicine for my complaint." "All depends upon the efficacy of the medicine," replied Mrs. Yu; "if the medicine is good, it matters not what is the name of the doctor who administers the draught; while to set your heart on a particular person, and to lie there and die because that person doesn't come, is surely foolish in the extreme." "Ah," rejoined Jisheng, "there's no medicine under heaven that will do me any good." Mrs. Yu told him his experience was limited, and proceeded to expatiate by speaking and gesticulating on the beauty and liveliness of Wuke. But all Jisheng said was that she was not what he wanted, and, turning around his face to the wall, would listen to no more about her. So Mrs. Yu was obliged to go away, and Jisheng became worse and worse every day, until suddenly one of the maids came in and informed him that the young lady herself was at the door. Immediately he jumped up and ran out, and lo! there before him stood a beautiful girl, whom, however, he soon discovered not to be Guixiu. She wore a light yellow robe with a fine silk jacket and an embroidered petticoat, from beneath which her two little feet peeped out; and altogether she more resembled a fairy than anything else. Jisheng inquired her name; to which she replied that it was Wuke, adding that she couldn't understand his devoted attachment to Guixiu, as if there was nobody else in the world. Jisheng apologized, saying that he had never before seen any one so beautiful as Guixiu, but that he was now aware of his mistake. He then swore everlasting fidelity to her, and was just grasping her hand when he awoke and found his mother rubbing him. It was a dream, but so accurately defined in all its details that he began to think if Wuke was really such as he had seen her, there would be no further need to try for his impracticable cousin. So he communicated his dream to his mother; and she, only too delighted to notice this change of feeling, offered to go to Wuke's house herself; but Jisheng would not hear of this, and arranged with an old woman who knew the family to find some pretext for going there, and to report to him what Wuke was like. When she arrived Wuke was ill in bed, and lay with her head propped up by pillows, looking very pretty indeed. The old woman approached the couch and asked what was the matter; to which Wuke made no reply, her fingers fidgeting all the time with her waistband. "She's been behaving badly to her father and mother," cried the latter, who was in the room; "there's many a one has offered to marry her, but she says she'll have none but Jisheng: and then when I scold her a bit, she takes on and won't touch her food for days." "Madam," said the old woman, "if you could get that young man for your daughter they would make a truly pretty pair; and as for him, if he could only see Miss Wuke, I'm afraid it would be too much for him. What do you think of my going there and getting them to make proposals?" "No, thank you," replied Wuke; "I would rather not risk his refusal;" upon which the old woman declared she would succeed, and hurried off to tell Jisheng, who was delighted to find from her report that Wuke was exactly as he had seen her in his dream, though he didn't trust implicitly in all the old woman said. By-and-by, when he began to get a little better, he consulted with the old woman as to how he could see Wuke with his own eyes; and, after some little difficulty, it was arranged that Jisheng should hide himself in a room from which he would be able to see her as she crossed the yard supported by a maid, which she did every day at a certain hour. This Jisheng proceeded to do, and in a little while out she came, accompanied by the old woman as well, who instantly drew her attention either to the clouds or the trees, in order that she should walk more leisurely. Thus Jisheng had a good look at her, and saw that she was truly the young lady of his dream. He could hardly contain himself for joy; and when the old woman arrived and asked if she would do instead of Guixiu, he thanked her very warmly and returned to his own home. There he told his father and mother, who sent off a match-maker to arrange the preliminaries; but the latter came back and told them that Wuke was already betrothed. This was a terrible blow for Jisheng, who was soon as ill as ever, and offered no reply to his father and mother when they charged him with having made a mistake. For several months he ate nothing but a bowl of rice-gruel a day, and he became as emaciated as a fowl, when all of a sudden the old woman walked in and asked him what was the matter. "Foolish boy," said she, when he had told her all; "before you wouldn't have her, and do you imagine she is bound to have you now? But I'll see if I can help you; for were she the Emperor's own daughter, I should still find some way of getting her." Jisheng asked what he should do, and she then told him to send a servant with a letter next day to Wuke's house, to which his father at first objected for fear of another repulse; but the old woman assured him that Wuke's parents had since repented, besides which no written contract had as yet been made; "and you know the proverb," added she, "that those who are first at the fire will get their dinner first." So Jisheng's father agreed, and two servants were accordingly sent, their mission proving a complete success. Jisheng now rapidly recovered his health, and thought no more of Guixiu, who, when she heard of the intended match, became in her turn very seriously ill, to the great anger of her father, who said she might die for all he cared, but to the great sorrow of her mother, who was extremely fond of her daughter. The latter even went so far as to propose to Mr. Zheng that Guixiu should go as second wife, at which he was so enraged that he declared he would wash his hands of the girl altogether. The mother then found out when Jisheng's wedding was to take place; and, borrowing a chair and attendants from her brother under pretence of going to visit him, put Guixiu inside and sent her off to her uncle's house. As she arrived at the door, the servants spread a carpet for her to walk on, and the band struck up the wedding march. Jisheng went out to see what it was all about, and there met a young lady in a bridal veil, from whom he would have escaped had not her servants surrounded them, and, before he knew what he was doing, he was making her the usual salutation of a bridegroom. They then went in together, and, to his further astonishment, he found that the young lady was Guixiu; and, being now unable to go and meet Wuke, a message was sent to her father, telling him what had occurred. He, too, got into a great rage, and vowed he would break off the match; but Wuke herself said she would go all the same, her rival having only got the start of her in point of time. And go she did; and the two wives, instead of quarreling, as was expected, lived very happily together like sisters, and wore each other's clothes and shoes without distinction, Guixiu taking the place of an elder sister as being somewhat older than Wuke.[459] One day, after these events, Jisheng asked Wuke why she had refused his offer; to which she replied that it was merely to pay him out for having previously refused her father's proposal. "Before you had seen me, your head was full of Guixiu; but after you had seen me, your thoughts were somewhat divided; and I wanted to know how I compared with her, and whether you would fall ill on my account as you had on hers, that we mightn't quarrel about our looks." "It was a cruel revenge," said Jisheng; "but how should I ever have got a sight of you had it not been for the old woman?" "What had she to do with it?" replied Wuke; "I knew you were behind the door all the time. When I was ill I dreamt that I went to your house and saw you, but I looked upon it only as a dream until I heard that you had dreamt that I had actually been there, and then I knew that my spirit must have been with you." Jisheng now related to her the particulars of his vision, which coincided exactly with her own; and thus, strangely enough, had the matrimonial alliances of both father and son been brought about by dreams.

---

459 The *dénouement* of the *Yu Mao li,* a small novel which was translated into French by Rémusat, and again by Julien under the title of *Les Deux Cousines,* is effected by the hero of the tale marrying both the heroines.

96. A Supernatural Wife

A CERTAIN Mr. Zhao, of Changshan, lodged in a family of the name of Tai. He was very badly off, and, falling sick, was brought almost to death's door. One day they moved him into the verandah, that it might be cooler for him; and, when he awoke from a nap, lo! a beautiful girl was standing by his side. "I am come to be your wife," said the girl, in answer to his question as to who she was; to which he replied that a poor fellow like himself did not look for such luck as that; adding that, being then on his death-bed, he would not have much occasion for the services of a wife. The girl said she could cure him; but he told her he very much doubted that; "And even," continued he, "should you have any good prescription, I have not the means of getting it made up." "I don't want medicine to cure you with," rejoined the girl, proceeding at once to rub his back and sides with her hand, which seemed to him like a ball of fire. He soon began to feel much better, and asked the young lady what her name was, in order, as he said, that he might remember her in his prayers. "I am a spirit," replied she; "and you, when alive under the Han dynasty as Chu Suilang, were a benefactor of my family. Your kindness being engraven on my heart, I have at length succeeded in my search for you, and am able in some measure to requite you." Zhao was dreadfully ashamed of his poverty-stricken state, and afraid that his dirty room would spoil the young lady's dress; but she made him show her in, and accordingly he took her into his apartment, where there were neither chairs to sit upon, nor signs of anything to eat, saying, "You might, indeed, be able to put up with all this; but you see my larder is empty, and I have absolutely no means of supporting a wife." "Don't be alarmed about that," cried she; and in another moment he saw a couch covered with costly robes, the walls papered with a silver-flecked paper, and chairs and tables appear, the latter laden with all kinds of wine and exquisite viands. They then began to enjoy themselves, and lived together as husband and wife, many people coming to witness these strange things, and being all cordially received by the young lady, who in her turn always accompanied Mr. Zhao when he went out to dinner anywhere.[460] One day there was an unprincipled young graduate among the company, which she seemed immediately to become aware of; and, after calling him several bad names, she struck him on the

---

460 The sexes do not dine together. On the occasion of a dinner-party, private or official, the ladies give a separate entertainment to the wives of the various guests in the "inner" or women's apartments, as an adjunct to which a theatrical troupe is often engaged, precisely as in the case of the opposite sex. Singing-girls are, however, present at and share in the banquets of the *roués* of China.

side of the head, causing his head to fly out of the window while his body remained inside; and there he was, stuck fast, unable to move either way, until the others interceded for him and he was released. After some time visitors became too numerous, and if she refused to see them they turned their anger against her husband. At length, as they were sitting together drinking with some friends at the Duanyang festival,[461] a white rabbit ran in, whereupon the girl jumped up and said, "The doctor[462] has come for me;" then, turning to the rabbit, she added, "You go on: I'll follow you." So the rabbit went away, and then she ordered them to get a ladder and place it against a high tree in the back yard, the top of the ladder overtopping the tree. The young lady went up first and Zhao close behind her; after which she cabled out to anybody who wished to join them to make haste up. None ventured to do so with the exception of a serving-boy belonging to the house, who followed after Zhao; and thus they went up, up, up, up, until they disappeared in the clouds and were seen no more. However, when the bystanders came to look at the ladder, they found it was only an old door-frame with the panels knocked out; and when they went into Mr. Qiao's room, it was the same old, dirty, unfurnished room as before. So they determined to find out all about it from the serving-boy when he came back; but this he never did.

97. Bribery and Corruption

AT Baoding Fu there lived a young man, who having purchased the lowest[463] degree was about to proceed to Peking, in the hope of obtaining, by the aid of a little bribery, an appointment as District Magistrate. His boxes were already packed, when he was taken suddenly ill and was confined to his bed for more than a month. One day the servant entered and announced a visitor; whereupon our sick man jumped up and ran to the door as if there

---

461 This occurs on the 5th of the 5th moon, and is commonly known as the Dragon-Boat Festival, from a practice of racing on that day in long, narrow boats. It is said to have been instituted in memory of a patriotic statesman named Qu Yuan, who drowned himself (295 BCE) because his counsels were unheeded.

462 A hare or rabbit is believed to sit at the foot of the cassia-tree in the moon, pounding the drugs out of which is concocted the elixir of immortality. The first allusion to this occurs in the poems of Qu Yuan (see preceding note).

463 By which he would become eligible for Government employ. The sale of degrees has been extensively carried on under the present dynasty, as a means of replenishing an empty Treasury.

was nothing the matter with him. The visitor was elegantly dressed like a man of some position in society; and, after bowing thrice, he walked into the house, explaining that he was Gongsun Xia,[464] tutor to the Eleventh Prince, and that he had heard our Mr. So-and-so wished to arrange for the purchase of a magistracy. "If that is really so," added he, "would you not do better to buy a prefecture?" So-and-so thanked him warmly, but said his funds would not be sufficient; upon which Mr. Gongsun declared he should be delighted to assist him with half the purchase-money, which he could repay after taking up the post.[465] He went on to say that being on intimate terms with the various provincial Governors the thing could be easily managed for about five thousand taels; and also that at that very moment Zhending Fu being vacant, it would be as well to make an early effort to get the appointment. So-and-so pointed out that this place was in his native province;[466] but Gongsun only laughed at his objection, and reminded him that money[467] could obliterate all distinctions of that kind. This did not seem quite satisfactory; however, Gongsun told him not to be alarmed, as the post of which he was speaking was below in the infernal regions. "The fact is," said he, "that your term of life has expired, and that your name is already on the death list; by these means you will take your place in the world below as a man of official position. Farewell! In three days we shall meet again." He then went to the door and mounted his horse and rode away. So-and-so now opened his eyes and spoke a few parting words to his wife and children, bidding them take money from his strong room[468] and go buy large quantities of paper ingots,[469] which they immediately did, quite exhausting all the shops. This was piled in the court-yard with paper images of men, devils, horses, etc., and burning went on day and night until

---

464 Gongsun is an example of a Chinese double surname.
465 Such is the common system of repaying the loan, by means of which an indigent nominee is enabled to defray the expenses of his journey to the post to which he has been appointed, and other calls upon his purse. These loans are generally provided by some "western" merchant, which term is an ellipsis for a "Shanxi" banker, Shanxi being literally "west of the mountains." Some one accompanies the newly-made official to his post, and holds his commission in pawn until the amount is repaid; which settlement is easily effected by the issue of some well-understood proclamation, calling, for instance, upon the people to close all gambling-houses within a given period. Immediately the owners of these hells forward presents of money to the incoming official, the Shanxi banker gets his principal with interest, perhaps at the rate of 2 per cent *per month*, the gambling-houses carry on as usual, and everybody is perfectly satisfied.
466 Which fact would disqualify him from taking the post.
467 Literally, "square hole." A common name for the Chinese cash. See note 7 in tale number 2.
468 In the case of wealthy families these strong rooms often contain, in addition to bullion, jewels to a very great amount belonging to the ladies of the house; and, as a rule, the door may not be opened unless in the presence of a certain number of the male representatives of the house.
469 Pieces of silver and gold paper made up to represent the ordinary Chinese "shoes" of bullion (see note 101 in tale 18), and burnt for the use of the dead. Generally known to foreigners in China as "joss-paper."

the ashes formed quite a hill. In three days Gongsun returned, bringing with him the money; upon which So-and-so hurried off to the Board of Civil Office,[470] where he had an interview with the high officials, who, after asking his name, warned him to be a pure and upright officer, and then calling him up to the table handed him his letter of appointment. So-and-so bowed and took his leave; but recollecting at once that his purchased degree would not carry much weight with it in the eyes of his subordinates,[471] he sent off to buy elaborate chairs and a number of horses for his retinue, at the same time despatching several devil lictors to fetch his favorite wife in a beautifully adorned sedan-chair. All arrangements were just completed when some of the Zhending staff came to meet the new Prefect,[472] others awaiting him all along the line of road, about half a mile in length. He was immensely gratified at this reception, when all of a sudden the gongs before him ceased to sound, and the banners were lowered to the ground. He had hardly time to ask what was the matter before he saw those of his servants who were on horseback jump hastily to the ground and dwindle down to about a foot in height, while their horses shrank to the size of foxes or racoons. One of the attendants near his chariot cried out in alarm, "Here's Guan Di!"[473] and then he, too, jumped out in a fright, and saw in the distance Guan Di himself slowly approaching them, followed by four or five retainers on horseback. His great beard covered the lower half of his face, quite unlike ordinary mortals; his aspect was terrible to behold, and his eyes reached nearly to his ears. "Who is this?" roared he to his servants; and they immediately informed him that it was the new Prefect of Zhending. "What!" cried he; "a petty fellow like that to have a retinue like this?[474] Whereupon So-and-so's flesh began to creep with fear, and in a few moments he found that he too had shrunk to the size of a little boy of six or seven. Guan Di bade his attendants bring the new Prefect with them, and went into a building at the roadside, where he took up his seat facing the south[475] and calling for writing materials told So-and-so to write down his name and address. When this was handed to him he flew into a towering passion, and said, "The scribbly scrawl of a placeman, indeed![476]

---

470 See note 19 in tale 7. In this case the reference is to a similar Board in the Infernal Regions.

471 These would be sure to sneer at him behind his back.

472 A compliment usually paid to an incoming official.

473 See note 4 in tale number 1.

474 The retinue of a Mandarin should be in accordance with his rank. I have given elsewhere (see note 281 in tale number 56) what would be that of an official of the highest rank.

475 See note 397 in tale number 77.

476 Good writing holds a much higher place in the estimation of the Chinese than among Western

Can such a one be entrusted with the welfare of the people? Look me up the record of his good works." A man then advanced, and whispered something in a low tone; upon which Guan Di exclaimed in a loud voice, "The crime of the briber is comparatively trifling; the heavy guilt lies with those who sell official posts for money." So-and-so was now seized by angels in golden armor, and two of them tore off his cap and robes, and administered to him fifty blows with the bamboo, until hardly any flesh remained on his bones. He was then thrust outside the door, and lo! his carriages and horses had disappeared, and he himself was lying, unable to walk for pain, at no great distance from his own house. However, his body seemed as light as a leaf, and in a day and a night he managed to crawl home. When he arrived, he awoke as it were from a dream, and found himself groaning upon the bed; and to the inquiries of his family he only replied that he felt dreadfully sore. Now he really had been dead for seven days; and when he came around thus, he immediately asked for Alian, which was the name of his favorite wife. But the very day before, while chatting with the other members of the family, Alian had suddenly cried out that her husband was made Prefect of Zhending, and that his lictors had come to escort her thither. Accordingly she retired to dress herself in her best clothes, and, when ready to start, she fell back and expired. Hearing this sad story, So-and-so began to mourn and beat his breast, and he would not allow her to be buried at once, in the hope that she might yet come around; but this she never did. Meanwhile So-and-so got slowly better, and by the end of six months was able to walk again. He would often exclaim, "The ruin of my career and the punishment I received—all this I could have endured; but the loss of my dear Alian is more than I can bear."[477]

---

nations. The very nature of their characters raises calligraphy almost to the rank of an art.

477 The author here adds a somewhat similar case, which actually occurred in the reign of Kang Xi, of a Viceroy, who was modestly attended, falling in with the gorgeous retinue of a Magistrate, and being somewhat rudely treated by the servants of the latter. On arriving at his destination, the Viceroy sent for that Magistrate, and sternly bade him retire from office, remarking that no simple magistrate could afford to keep such a retinue of attendants unless by illegal exactions from the suffering people committed to his charge.

98. A Chinese Jonah

A MAN named Sun Bizhen was crossing the river[478] when a great thunder-squall broke upon the vessel and caused her to toss about fearfully, to the great terror of all the passengers. Just then, an angel in golden armor appeared standing upon the clouds above them, holding in his hand a scroll inscribed with certain characters, also written in gold, which the people on the vessel easily made out to be three in number, namely *Sun Bizhen*. So, turning at once to their fellow-traveler, they said to him, "You have evidently incurred the displeasure of Heaven; get into a boat by yourself, and do not involve us in your punishment." And without giving him time to reply whether he would do so or not, they hurried him over the side into a small boat and set him adrift; but when Sun Bizhen looked back, lo! the vessel itself had capsized.[479]

99. Zhang Buliang

A CERTAIN trader who was traveling in the province of Zhili, being overtaken by a storm of rain and hail, took shelter among some standing crops by the wayside. There he heard a voice from heaven, saying, "These are Zhang Buliang's fields; do not injure his crops." The trader began to wonder who this Zhang Buliang could be, and now, if he was *bu liang* (not virtuous), he came to be under divine protection; so when the storm was over and he had reached the neighboring village, he made inquiries on the subject, and told the people there what he had heard. The villagers then informed him that Zhang Buliang was a very wealthy farmer, who was accustomed every spring to make loans of grain to the poor of he district, and who was not too particular about getting back the exact amount he had lent—taking, in fact, whatever they brought him without discussion; hence the sobriquet of *bu liang*, "no measure" (*i.e.*, the man who doesn't measure the repayments of

---

478 The Yangtze: sometimes spoken of as the Long River.
479 The full point of this story can hardly be conveyed in translation. The man's surname was Sun, and his prænomen, Bizhen (which in Chinese *follows* the nomen), might be rendered "Must be saved." However, there is another word meaning "struck," precisely similar in sound and tone, though written differently, to the above *qin*; and, so far as the ear alone is concerned, our hero's name might have been either *Sun Must-be-saved* or *Sun Must-be-struck*. That the merchants mistook the character *Zhen*, "saved," for *zhen* "struck," is evident from the catastrophe which overtook their vessel, while Mr. Sun's little boat rode safely through the storm.

his loans).[480] After what, they all proceeded in a body to the fields, where it was discovered that vast damage had been done to the crops generally, with the exception of Zhang Buliang's, which had escaped uninjured.

100. The Dutch Carpet

FORMERLY, when the Red Heads[481] were permitted to trade with China, the officer in command of the coast defences would not allow them, on account of their great numbers, to come ashore. The Dutch begged very hard for the grant of a piece of land such as a carpet would cover; and the officer above-mentioned, thinking that this could not be very large, acceded to their request. A carpet was accordingly laid down, big enough for about two people to stand on; but by dint of stretching, it was soon enough for four or five; and so they went on, stretching and stretching, until at last it covered about an acre, and by-and-by, with the help of their knives, they had filched a piece of ground several miles in extent.[482]

101. Carrying a Corpse

A WOODSMAN who had been to market was returning home with his pole across his shoulder,[483] when suddenly he felt it become very heavy at the end behind him, and looking around he saw attached to it the headless trunk of a man. In great alarm, he got his pole quit of the burden and struck about him right and left, whereupon the body disappeared. He then hurried on to the next village, and when he arrived there in the dusk of the evening, he found several men holding lights to the ground as if looking for something.

---

480 Here again we have a play upon words similar to that in the last story.

481 We read in the *History of Amoy*: "In the year 1622 the red-haired barbarians seized the Pescadores and attacked Amoy." from the Pescadores they finally retired, on a promise that trade could be permitted, to Formosa, whence they were expelled by the famous Koxinga in 1662. "Red-haired barbarians," a term now commonly applied to all foreigners, was first used in the records the Ming dynasty to designate the Dutch.

482 Our author would here seem to have heard of the famous bull's hide which is mentioned in the first book of the *Æneid*. In any case, the substitution of "stretching" is no improvement on the celebrated device by which the bull's hide was made to enclose so large a space.

483 The common method of porterage in China is by a bamboo pole over the shoulder with well-balanced burdens hanging from each end. I have often seen children carried thus, sitting in wicket baskets; sometimes for long journeys.

On asking what was the matter, they told him that while sitting together a man's head had fallen from the sky into their midst; that they had noticed the hair and beard were all draggled, but in a moment the head had vanished. The woodsman then related what had happened to himself; and thus one whole man was accounted for, though no one could tell whence he came. Subsequently, another man was carrying a basket when some one saw a man's head in it, and called out to him; whereupon he dropped the basket in a fright, and the head rolled away and disappeared.

102. A Taoist Devotee

Ju Yaoru was a Qingzhou man, who, when his wife died, left his home and became a priest.[484] Some years afterwards he returned, dressed in the Taoist garb, and carrying his praying-mat[485] over his shoulder; and after staying one night he wanted to go away again. His friends, however, would not give him back his cassock and staff; so at length he pretended to take a stroll outside the village, and when there, his clothes and other belongings came flying out of the house after him, and he got safely away.

103. Justice for Rebels

During the reign of Shun Zhi,[486] of the people of Tengyi, seven in ten were opposed to the Manchu dynasty. The officials dared not touch them; and subsequently, when the country became more settled, the magistrates used to distinguish them from the others by always deciding any cases in their favor: for they feared lest these men should revert to their old opposition. And thus it came about that one litigant would begin by declaring himself to have been a "rebel," while his adversary would follow up by showing such statement to be false; so that before any case could be heard on its actual merits, it was necessary

---

484 It would be more usual to "renew the guitar string," as the Chinese idiom runs. In the paraphrase of the first maxim of the *Sacred Edict* we are told that "The closest of all ties is that of husband and wife; but suppose your wife dies, why, you can marry another. But if your brother were to die," etc. etc.

485 This, as well as the staff mentioned below, belongs to Buddhism. See note 11 in tale number 4.

486 The first Manchu ruler of the Empire of China. He came to the throne in 1644 CE.

to determine the status both of plaintiff and defendant, whereby infinite labor was entailed upon the Registrars.

Now it chanced that the yamen of one of the officials was haunted by a fox, and the official's daughter was bewitched by it. Her father, therefore, engaged the services of a magician, who succeeded in capturing the animal and putting it into a bottle; but just as he was going to commit it to the flames, the fox cried out from inside the bottle, "I'm a rebel!" at which the bystanders were unable to suppress their laughter.

104. Theft of the Peach

WHEN I was a little boy I went one day to the prefectural city.[487] It was the time of the Spring festival,[488] and the custom was that on the day before, all the merchants of the place should proceed with banners and drums to the judge's yamen: this was called "bringing in the Spring." I went with a friend to see the fun; the crowd was immense, and there sat the officials in crimson robes arranged right and left in the hall; but I was small and didn't know who they were, my attention being attracted chiefly by the hum of voices and the noise of the drums. In the middle of it all, a man leading a boy with his hair unplaited and hanging down his back, walked up to the dais. He carried a pole on his shoulder, and appeared to be saying something which I couldn't hear for the noise; I only saw the officials smile, and immediately afterwards an attendant came down, and in a loud voice ordered the man to give a performance. 'What shall it be?" asked the man in reply; whereupon, after some consultation between the officials on the dais, the attendant inquired what he could do best. The man said he could invert the order of nature; and then, after another pause, he was instructed to produce some peaches; to this he assented; and taking off his coat, laid it on his box, at the same time observing that they had set him a hard task, the winter frost not having broken up, and adding that he was afraid the gentlemen would be angry with him, etc., etc. His son here reminded him that he had agreed to the task and couldn't well get out of it; so, after fretting and grumbling awhile, he cried out, "I have it! with snow on the ground we shall never get

---

487 It is worth noting that the author professes actually to have witnessed the following extraordinary scene.
488 The vernal equinox, which would fall on or about the 20th of March.

peaches here; but I guess there are some up in heaven in the Royal Mother's garden,[489] and there we must try." How are we to get up, father?" asked the boy; whereupon the man said, "I have the means," and immediately proceeded to take from his box a cord some tens of feet in length. This he carefully arranged, and then threw one end of it high up into the air, where it remained as if caught by something. He now paid out the rope, which kept going up higher and higher until the end he had thrown up disappeared in the clouds and only a short piece was left in his hands. Calling his son, he then explained that he himself was too heavy, and, handing him the end of the rope, bade him go up at once. The boy, however, made some difficulty, objecting that the rope was too thin to bear his weight up to such a height, and that he would surely fall down and be killed; upon which his father said that his promise had been given and that repentance was now too late, adding that if the peaches were obtained they would surely be rewarded with a hundred ounces of silver, which should be set aside to get the boy a pretty wife. So his son seized the rope and swarmed up, like a spider running up a thread of its web; and in a few moments he was out of sight in the clouds. By-and-by down fell a peach as large as a basin, which the delighted father handed up to his patrons on the dais, who were some time coming to a conclusion whether it was real or imitation. But just then down came the rope with a run, and the affrighted father shrieked out, "Alas! alas! someone has cut the rope: what will my boy do now?" and in another minute down fell something else, which was found on examination to be his son's head. "Ah me!" said he, weeping bitterly and showing the head; "the gardener has caught him, and my boy is no more." After that, his arms, and legs, and body, all came down in like manner; and the father, gathering them up, put them in the box and said, "This was my only son, who accompanied me everywhere; and now what a cruel fate is his. I must away and bury him." He then approached the dais and said, "Your peach, gentlemen, was obtained at the cost of my boy's life; help me now to pay his funeral expenses, and I will be ever grateful to you." The officials, who had been watching the scene in horror and amazement, forthwith collected a good purse for him; and when he had received the money, he rapped on his box and said. " Pa-pa'rh! why don't you come out and thank the gentlemen?" Thereupon, there was a thump on the box from the inside, and up came the boy himself, who

---

489 A fabulous lady said to reside at the summit of the Kunlun mountain, where, on the border of the Gem Lake, grows the peach-tree of the Gods, the fruit of which confers immortality on him who eats it. For her identification with Juno, see *Adversaria Sinica*, No. 1, 1905.

jumped out and bowed to the assembled company. I have never forgotten this strange trick, which I subsequently heard could be done by the White Lily sect,[490] who probably got it from this source.[491]

105. Killing a Serpent

AT Guji island in the eastern sea, there were camellias of all colors which bloomed throughout the year. No one, however, lived there, and very few people ever visited the spot. One day, a young man of Dengzhou, named Zhang, who was fond of hunting and adventure, hearing of the beauties of the place, put together some wine and food, and rowed himself across in a small open boat. The flowers were just then even finer than usual, and their perfume was diffused for a mile or so around; while many of the trees he saw were several armfuls in circumference. So he roamed about and gave himself up to enjoyment of the scene; and by-and-by he opened a flask of wine, regretting very much that he had no companion to share it with him, when all of a sudden a most beautiful young girl, with extremely bright eyes, and dressed in red, stepped down from one of the camellias before him.[492] "Dear me!" said she, on seeing Mr. Zhang; "I expected to be alone here, and was not aware that the place was already occupied." Zhang, was somewhat alarmed by this apparition, and asked the young lady whence she came; to which she replied that her name was Jiaochang, and that she had accompanied thither a Mr. Hai, who had gone off for a stroll and had left her to await his return. Thereupon Zhang begged her to join him in a cup of wine, which she very willingly did, and they were just beginning to enjoy themselves when a sound of rushing wind was heard, and the trees

---

490 One of the most celebrated of the numerous secret societies of China, the origin of which dates back to about 1350 CE. Its members have always been credited with a knowledge of the black-art.
491 Of Chinese jugglers, Ibn Batuta writes as follows: "They produced a chain fifty cubits in length, and in my presence threw one end of it towards the sky, where it remained, as if fastened to something in the air. A dog was then brought forward, and, being placed at the lower end of the chain, immediately ran up, and reaching the other end immediately disappeared in the air. In the same manner a hog, a panther, a lion, and a tiger were alternately sent up the chain, and all equally disappeared at the upper end of it. At last they took down the chain, and put it into a bag, no one ever discerning in what way the different animals were made to vanish into the air in the mysterious manner above described. This, I may venture to affirm, was beyond measure strange and surprising."
    A propos of which passage, Mr. Maskelyne, the prince of all black-artists, ancient or modern, says: "These apparent effects were, doubtless, due to the aid of concave mirrors, the use of which was known to the ancients, especially in the East, but they could not have been produced in the open air."
492 See note 376 in tale number 71.

and plants bent beneath it. "Here's Mr. Hai!" cried the young lady; and jumping quickly up, disappeared in a moment. The horrified Zhang now beheld a huge serpent coming out of the bushes nearby, and immediately ran behind a large tree for shelter, hoping the reptile would not see him. But the serpent advanced and enveloped both Zhang and the tree in its great folds, binding Zhang's arms down to his sides so as to prevent him from moving them; and then raising its head, darted out its tongue and bit the poor man's nose, causing the blood to flow freely out. This blood it was quietly sucking up, when Zhang, who thought that his last hour had come, remembered that he had in his pocket some fox poison; and managing to insert a couple of fingers, he drew out the packet, broke the paper, and let the powder lie in the palm of his hand. He next leaned his hand over the serpent's coils in such a way that the blood from his nose dripped into his hand, and when it was nearly full the serpent actually did begin to drink it. And in a few moments the grip was relaxed; the serpent struck the ground heavily with its tail, and dashed away up against another tree, which was broken in half, and then stretched itself out and died. Zhang was a long time unable to rise, but at length he got up and carried the serpent off with him. He was very ill for more than a month afterwards, and even suspected the young lady of being a serpent, too, in disguise.

106. The Resuscitated Corpse

A CERTAIN old man lived at Caidian, in the Yangxin district. The village was some miles from the district city, and he and his son kept a roadside inn where travelers could pass the night. One day, as it was getting dusk, four strangers presented themselves and asked for a night's lodging; to which the landlord replied that every bed was already occupied. The four men declared it was impossible for them to go back, and urged him to take them in somehow; and at length the landlord said he could give them a place to sleep in if they were not too particular—which the strangers immediately assured him they were not. The fact was that the old man's daughter-in-law had just died, and that her body was lying in the women's quarters, waiting for the coffin, which his son had gone away to buy. So the landlord led them around thither, and walking in, placed a lamp on the table. At the further end of the room lay the corpse, decked out with paper robes, etc., in the usual way; and in the foremost section were sleeping couches for four people. The travelers were tired, and throwing themselves on the beds, were soon snoring loudly, with the exception of one of them, who was not quite off when suddenly he heard a creaking of the trestles on which the dead body was laid out, and opening his eyes, he saw by the light of the lamp in front of the corpse that the girl was raising the coverings from her and preparing to get down. In another moment she was on the floor and advancing towards the sleepers. Her face was of a light yellow hue, and she had a silk kerchief around her head; and when she reached the beds, she blew on the other three travelers, whereupon the fourth, in a great fright, stealthily drew up the bed-clothes over his face, and held his breath to listen. He heard her breathe on him as she had done on the others, and then heard her go back again and get under the paper robes, which rustled distinctly as she did so. He now put out his head to take a peep, and saw that she was lying down as before; whereupon, not daring to make any noise, he stretched forth his foot and kicked his companions, who, however, showed no signs of moving. He now determined to put on his clothes and make a bolt for it; but he had hardly begun to do so before he heard the creaking sound again, which sent him back under the bed-clothes as fast as he could go. Again the girl came to him, and, breathing several times on him, went away to lie down as before, as he could tell by the noise of the trestles. He then put his hand very gently out of bed, and, seizing his trousers, got quickly into them, jumped up with a bound, and rushed out of the place as fast as his legs would carry him. The corpse, too, jumped up; but by this time the traveler had already drawn the bolt, and was outside the door, running along and shrieking at the top of his voice, with the corpse following close behind. No one seemed to hear him, and he was afraid to knock at the door of the inn for fear they should not let him in in time; so he made for the highway to the city, and after awhile he saw a monastery by the roadside, and, hearing the "wooden fish,"[493] he ran up and thumped with all his might at the gate. The priest, however, did not know what to make of it, and would not open to him; and as the corpse was only a few yards off, he could do nothing but run behind a tree which stood close by, and there shelter himself, dodging to the right as the corpse dodged to the left, and so on. This infuriated the dead girl to madness; and at length, as tired and panting they stood watching each other on opposite

---

493 This instrument, used by Buddhist priests in the musical accompaniment to their liturgies, is said to be so called because a fish never closes its eyes, and is therefore a fit model of vigilance to him who would walk in the paths of holiness and virtue.

sides of the tree, the corpse made a rush forward with one arm on each side in the hope of thus grabbing its victim. The traveler, however, fell backwards and escaped, while the corpse remained rigidly embracing the tree. By-and-by the priest, who had been listening from the inside, hearing no sounds for some time, came out and found the traveler lying senseless on the ground; whereupon he had him carried into the monastery, and by morning they had got him around again. After giving him a little broth to drink, he related the whole story; and then in the early dawn they went out to examine the tree, to which they found the girl tightly fixed. The news being sent to the magistrate, that functionary attended at once in person,[494] and gave orders to remove the body; but this they were at first unable to do, the girl's fingers having penetrated into the bark so far that her nails were not to be seen. At length they got her away, and then a messenger was despatched to the inn, already in a state of great commotion over the three travelers, who had been found dead in their beds. The old man accordingly sent to fetch his daughter-in-law; and the surviving traveler petitioned the magistrate, saying, "Four of us left home, but only one will go back. Give me something that I may show to my fellow-townsmen." So the magistrate gave him a certificate and sent him home again.[495]

107. The Fisherman and His Friend

IN the northern parts of Zizhou there lived a man named Xu, a fisherman by trade. Every night when he went to fish, he would carry some wine with him, and drink and fish by turns, always taking care to pour out a libation on the ground, accompanied by the following invocation—"Drink too, ye drowned spirits of the river!" Such was his regular custom; and it was also noticeable that, even on occasions when the other fishermen caught nothing, he always got a full basket. One night, as he was sitting drinking by himself, a young man suddenly appeared and began walking up and down near him. Xu offered him a cup of wine, which was readily accepted, and they remained chatting together throughout the night, Xu meanwhile not catching a single fish. However, just as he was giving up all hope of doing

---

494 The duties of Coroner belong to the office of a District Magistrate in China.
495 Without such certificate he would be liable to be involved in trouble and annoyance at the will of any unfriendly neighbor.

anything, the young man rose and said he would go a little way down the stream and beat them up towards Xu, which he accordingly did, returning in a few minutes and warning him to be on the look-out. Xu now heard a noise like that of a shoal coming up the stream, and, casting his net, made a splendid haul—all that he caught being over a foot in length. Greatly delighted, he now prepared to go home, first offering his companion a share of the fish, which the latter declined, saying that he had often received kindnesses from Mr. Xu, and that he would be only too happy to help him regularly in the same manner if Mr. Xu would accept his assistance. The latter replied that he did not recollect ever meeting him before, and that he should be much obliged for any aid the young man might choose to afford him," regretting, at the same time, his inability to make him any adequate return. He then asked the young man his name and surname; and the young man said his surname was Wang, adding that Xu might address him when they met as Wang Liulang, he having no other name. Thereupon they parted, and the next day Xu sold his fish and bought some more wine, with which he repaired as usual to the river-bank. There he found his companion already awaiting him, and they spent the night together in precisely the same way as the preceding one, the young man beating up the fish for him as before. This went on for some months, until at length one evening the young man, with many expressions of his thanks and his regrets, told Xu that they were about to part for ever. Much alarmed by the melancholy tone in which his friend had communicated this news, Xu was on the point of asking for an explanation, when the young man stopped him, and himself proceeded as follows: "The friendship that has grown up between us is truly surprising, and, now that we shall meet no more, there is no harm in telling you the whole truth, I am a disembodied spirit—the soul of one who was drowned in this river when tipsy. I have been here many years, and your former success in fishing was due to the fact that I used secretly to beat up the fish towards you, in return for the libations you were accustomed to pour out. Tomorrow my time is up: my substitute will arrive, and I shall be born again in the world of mortals.[496] We have but this one evening left, and I therefore take advantage of it to express my feelings, to you." On hearing these words, Xu was at first very much alarmed; however, he had grown so accustomed to his friend's society, that his fears soon passed away; and, filling up a goblet, he said, with a sigh, "Liulang, old fellow, drink this up, and away with melancholy. It's hard to lose you; but I'm glad enough for

---

496 See note 234 in tale number 45.

your sake, and won't think of my own sorrow." He then inquired of Liulang who was to be his substitute; to which the latter replied, "Come to the river-bank tomorrow afternoon and you'll see a woman drowned: she is the one." Just then the village cocks began to crow, and, with tears in their eyes, the two friends bade each other farewell.

Next day Xu waited on the river-bank to see if anything would happen, and lo! a woman carrying a child in her arms came along. When close to the edge of the river, she stumbled and fell into the water, managing, however, to throw the child safely onto the bank, where it lay kicking and sprawling and crying at the top of its voice. The woman herself sank and rose several times, until at last she succeeded in clutching hold of the bank and pulled herself, dripping, out; and then, after resting awhile, she picked up the child and went on her way. All this time Xu had been in a great state of excitement, and was on the point of running to help the woman out of the water; but he remembered that she was to be the substitute of his friend, and accordingly restrained himself from doing so.[497] Then when he saw the woman get out by herself, he began to suspect that Liulang's words had not been fulfilled. That night he went to fish as usual, and before long the young man arrived and said, "We meet once again: there is no need now to speak of separation." Xu asked him how it was so; to which he replied, "The woman you saw had already taken my place, but I could not bear to hear the child cry, and I saw that my one life would be purchased at the expense of their two lives, wherefore I let her go, and now I cannot say when I shall have another chance.[498] The union of our destinies may not yet be worked out." "Alas!" sighed Xu, "this noble conduct of yours is enough to move God Almighty."

---

497 We have in this story the keynote to the notorious and much-to-be-deprecated dislike of the Chinese people to assist in saving the lives of drowning strangers. Some of our readers may, perhaps, not be aware that the Government of Hong-Kong has found it necessary to insert a clause on the junk-clearances issued in that colony, by which the junkmen are bound to assist to the utmost in saving life. The apparent apathy of the Chinese in this respect comes before us, however, in quite a different light when coupled with the superstition that disembodied spirits of persons who have met a violent death may return to the world of mortals if only fortunate enough to secure a substitute. For among the crowd of shades, anxious all to revisit their "sweet sons," may perchance be some dear relative or friend of the man who stands calmly by while another is drowning; and it may be that to assist the drowning stranger would be to take the longed-for chance away from one's own kith and kin. Therefore, the superstition-ridden Chinese person turns away, often perhaps, as in the story before us, with feelings of pity and remorse. And yet this belief has not prevented the establishment, especially on the river Yangtze, of institutions provided with lifeboats, for the express purpose of saving life in those dangerous waters; so true is it that when the Chinese people wish to move *en masse* in any given direction, the fragile barrier of superstition is trampled down and scattered to the winds.

498 As there are good and bad foxes, so may devils be beneficent or malicious according to circumstances; and Chinese apologists for the discourtesy of the term "foreign devils," as applied to Europeans and Americans alike, have gone so far as to declare that in this particular instance the allusion is to the more virtuous among the denizens of the Infernal Regions.

After this the two friends went on much as they had done before, until one day Liulang again said he had come to bid Xu farewell. Xu thought he had found another substitute, but Liulang told him that his former behavior had so pleased Almighty Heaven, that he had been appointed guardian angel of Wuzhen, in the Zhaoyuan district, and that on the following morning he would start for his new post. "And if you do not forget the days of our friendship," added he, "I pray you come and see me, in spite of the long journey." "Truly," replied Xu, "you well deserved to be made a God; but the paths of Gods and men lie in different directions, and even if the distance were nothing, how should I manage to meet you again?" "Don't be afraid on that score," said Liulang, "but come;" and then he went away, and Xu returned home. The latter immediately began to prepare for the journey, which caused his wife to laugh at him and say, "Supposing you do find such a place at the end of that long journey, you won't be able to hold a conversation with a clay image." Xu, however, paid no attention to her remarks, and traveled straight to Zhaoyuan, where he learned from the inhabitants that there really was a village called Wuzhen, whither he forthwith proceeded and took up his abode at an inn. He then inquired of the landlord where the village temple was; to which the latter replied by asking him somewhat hurriedly if he was speaking to Mr. Xu. Xu informed him that his name was Xu, asking in reply how he came to know it; whereupon the landlord further inquired if his native place was not Zizhou. Xu told him it was, and again asked him how he knew all this; to which the landlord made no answer, but rushed out of the room; and in a few moments the place was crowded with old and young, men, women, and children, all come to visit Xu. They then told him that a few nights before they had seen their guardian deity in a vision, and he had informed them that Mr. Xu would shortly arrive, and had bidden them to provide him with traveling expenses, etc. Xu was very much astonished at this, and went off at once to the shrine, where he invoked his friend as follows: "Ever since we parted I have had you daily and nightly in my thoughts; and now that I have fulfilled my promise of coming to see you, I have to thank you for the orders you have issued to the people of the place. As for me, I have nothing to offer you but a cup of wine, which I pray you accept as though we were drinking together on the river-bank." He then burnt a quantity of paper money,[499] when lo! a wind suddenly arose, which, after whirling around and around behind the

---

[499] See note 469 in tale number 97.

shrine, soon dropped, and all was still. That night Xu dreamed that his friend came to him, dressed in his official cap and robes, and very different in appearance from what he used to be, and thanked him, saying, "It is truly kind of you to visit me thus: I only regret that my position makes me unable to meet you face to face, and that though near we are still so far. The people here will give you a trifle, which pray accept for my sake; and when you go away, I will see you a short way on your journey." A few days afterwards Xu prepared to start, in spite of the numerous invitations to stay which poured in upon him from all sides; and then the inhabitants loaded him with presents of all kinds, and escorted him out of the village. There a whirlwind arose and accompanied him several miles, when he turned around and invoked his friend thus: "Liulang, take care of your valued person. Do not trouble yourself to come any farther.[500] Your noble heart will ensure happiness to this district, and there is no occasion for me to give a word of advice to my old friend." By-and-by the whirlwind ceased, and the villagers, who were much astonished, returned to their own homes. Xu, too, traveled homewards, and being now a man of some means, ceased to work any more as a fisherman. And whenever he met a Zhaoyuan man he would ask him about that guardian angel, being always informed in reply that he was a most beneficent God. Some say the place was Shikeng Zhuang, in Zhang Qin: I can't say which it was myself.

108. The Priest's Warning

A MAN named Zhang died suddenly, and was escorted at once by devil-lictors[501] into the presence of the King of Purgatory. His Majesty turned to Zhang's record of good and evil, and then, in great anger, told the lictors they had brought the wrong man, and bade them take him back again. As they left the judgment-hall, Zhang persuaded his escort to let him have a look at Purgatory; and, accordingly, the devils conducted him through the nine sections,[502] pointing out to him the Knife Hill,[503] the Sword Tree,

500 A phrase constantly repeated, in other terms, by a guest to a host who is politely escorting him to the door.
501 The spiritual lictors who are supposed to arrest the souls of dying persons are also believed to be armed with warrants signed and sealed in due form as in the world above.
502 Literally, the "nine dark places," which will remind readers of Dante of the nine "bolgie" of the *Inferno*.
503 This is a cliff over which sinners are hurled, to alight upon the upright points of knives below. The branches of the Sword Tree are sharp blades which cut and hack all who pass within reach.

and other objects of interest. By-and-by, they reached a place where there was a Buddhist priest, hanging suspended in the air head downwards, by a rope through a hole in his leg. He was shrieking with pain, and longing for death; and when Zhang approached, lo! he saw that it was his own brother. In great distress, he asked his guides the reason of this punishment; and they informed him that the priest was suffering thus for collecting subscriptions on behalf of his order, and then privately squandering the proceeds in gambling and debauchery.[504] "Nor," added they, "will he escape this torment unless he repents him of his misdeeds." When Zhang came around,[505] he thought his brother was already dead, and hurried off to the Xing-fu monastery, to which the latter belonged. As he went in at the door, he heard a loud shrieking; and, on proceeding to his brother's room, he found him laid up with a very bad abscess in his leg, the leg itself being tied up above him to the wall, this being, as his brother informed him, the only bearable position in which he could lie. Zhang now told him what he had seen in Purgatory, at which the priest was so terrified, that he at once gave up taking wine and meat,[506] and devoted himself entirely to religious exercises. In a fortnight he was well, and was known ever afterwards as a most exemplary priest.

109. Metempsychosis

Mr. Lin, who took his master's degree in the same year as the late Mr. Wen Bi,[507] could remember what had happened to him in his previous state of existence, and once told the whole story, as follows: I was originally of a good family, but, after leading a very dissolute life, I died at the age of sixty-two. On being conducted into the presence of the King of Purgatory, he received me civilly, bade me be seated, and offered me a cup of tea. I noticed, however, that the tea in His Majesty's cup was clear and limpid, while that in my own was muddy, like the lees of wine. It then flashed across me that this was the potion which was given to all disembodied spirits to render them oblivious of the past:[508] and, accordingly, when

504 Crimes by no means unknown to the clergy of China.
505 That is, when the lictors had returned his soul to its tenement.
506 See note 17 in tale number 6.
507 In 1621 CE.
508 According to the *Yu li chao* (see *Appendix,* 10th Court), this potion is administered by an old

the King was looking the other way, I seized the opportunity of pouring it under the table, pretending afterwards that I had drunk it all up. My record of good and evil was now presented for inspection, and when the King saw what it was, he flew into a great passion, and ordered the attendant devils to drag me away, and send me back to earth as a horse. I was immediately seized and bound, and the devils carried me off to a house, the door-sill of which was so high I could not step over it. While I was trying to do so, the devils behind lashed me with all their might, causing me such pain that I made a great spring, and—lo and behold! I was a horse in a stable. "The mare has got a nice colt," I then heard a man call out; but, although I was perfectly aware of all that was passing, I could say nothing myself. Hunger now came upon me, and I was glad to be suckled by the mare; and by the end of four or five years I had grown into a fine strong horse, dreadfully afraid of the whip, and running away at the very sight of it. When my master rode me, it was always with a saddle cloth, and at a leisurely pace, which was bearable enough; but when the servants mounted me barebacked, and dug their heels into me, the pain struck into my vitals; and at length I refused all food, and in three days I died. Reappearing before the King of Purgatory, His Majesty was enraged to find that I had thus tried to shirk working out my time; and, flaying me forthwith, condemned me to go back again as a dog. And when I did not move, the devils came behind me and lashed me until I ran away from them into the open country, where, thinking I had better die right off, I jumped over a cliff, and lay at the bottom unable to move. I then saw that I was among a litter of puppies, and that an old bitch was licking and suckling me by turns; whereby I knew that I was once more among mortals. In this hateful form I continued for some time, longing to kill myself, and yet fearing to incur the penalty of shirking. At length, I purposely bit my master in the leg, and tore him badly; whereupon he had me destroyed, and I was taken again into the presence of the King, who was so displeased with my vicious behavior that he condemned me to become a snake, and shut me up in a dark room, where I could see nothing. After a while I managed to climb up the wall, bore a hole in the roof, and escape; and immediately I found myself lying in the grass, a veritable snake. Then I registered a vow that I would harm no living

---

beldame, named Mother Meng, who sits upon the Terrace of Oblivion. "Whether they swallow much or little it matters not; but sometimes there are perverse devils who altogether refuse to drink. Then beneath their feet "Sharp blades start up, and a copper tube is forced down their throats, by which means they are compelled to swallow some."

thing, and I lived for some years, feeding upon berries and suchlike, ever remembering neither to take my own life, nor by injuring any one to incite them to take it, but longing all the while for the happy release, which did not come to me. One day, as I was sleeping in the grass, I heard the noise of a passing cart, and, on trying to get across the road out of its way, I was caught by the wheel, and cut in two. The King was astonished to see me back so soon, but I humbly told my story, and, in pity for the innocent creature that loses its life, he pardoned me, and permitted me to be born again at my appointed time as a human being.

Such was Mr. Lin's story. He could speak as soon as he came into the world; and could repeat anything he had once read. In the year 1621 he took his master's degree, and was never tired of telling people to put saddlecloths on their horses, and recollect that the pain of being gripped by the knees is even worse than the lash itself.

110. The Forty Strings of Cash

MR. JUSTICE WANG had a steward, who was possessed of considerable means. One night the latter dreamt that a man rushed in and said to him, "Today you must repay me those forty strings of cash." The steward asked who he was; to which the man made no answer, but hurried past him into the women's apartments. When the steward awoke, he found that his wife had been delivered of a son; and, knowing at once that retribution was at hand, he set aside forty strings of cash to be spent solely in food, clothes, medicines, and so on, for the baby. By the time the child was between three and four years old, the steward found that of the forty strings only about seven hundred cash remained; and when the wet-nurse, who happened to be standing by, brought the child and dandled it in her arms before him, he looked at it and said, "The forty strings are all but repaid; it is time you were off again." Thereupon the child changed color; its head fell back, and its eyes stared fixedly, and, when they tried to revive it, lo! respiration had already ceased. The father then took the balance of the forty strings, and with it defrayed the child's funeral expenses—truly a warning to people to be sure and pay their debts.

Formerly, an old childless man consulted a great many Buddhist priests on the subject. One of them said to him, "If you owe no one anything, and no one owes you anything, how can you expect to have children? A good son is the repayment of a former debt; a bad son is a dunning creditor, at whose birth there is no rejoicing, at whose death no lamentations."[509]

111. Saving Life

A CERTAIN gentleman of Shenyou, who had taken the highest degree, could remember himself in a previous state of existence. He said he had formerly been a scholar, and had died in middle life; and that when he appeared before the Judge of Purgatory, there stood the cauldrons, the boiling oil, and other apparatus of torture, exactly as we read about them on earth. In the eastern corner of the hall were a number of frames from which hung the skins of sheep, dogs, oxen, horses, etc.; and when anybody was condemned to reappear in life under any one of these forms, his skin was stripped off and a skin was taken from the proper frame and fixed on to his body. The gentleman of whom I am writing heard himself sentenced to become a sheep; and the attendant devils had already clothed him in a sheep's skin in the manner above described, when the clerk of the record informed the Judge that the criminal before him had once saved another man's life. The Judge consulted his books, and forthwith cried out, "I pardon him; for although his sins have been many, this one act has redeemed them all."[510] The devils then tried to take off the sheep's skin, but it was so tightly stuck on him that they couldn't move it. However, after great efforts, and causing the gentleman most excruciating agony, they managed to tear it off bit by bit, though not quite so cleanly as one might have wished. In fact, a piece as big as the palm of a man's hand was left near his shoulder; and when he was born again into the world, there was a great patch of hair on his back, which grew again as fast as it was cut off.

---

509 And such is actually the prevalent belief in China to this day.
510 Note 497 in tale number 107 should be read here. To save life is indeed the bounden duty of every good Buddhist, for which he will be proportionately rewarded in the world to come.

112. The Salt Smuggler

WANG SHI, of Gaowan, a petty salt huckster, was inordinately fond of gambling. One night he was arrested by two men, whom he took for lictors of the Salt Gabelle; and, flinging down what salt he had with him, he tried to make his escape.[511] He found, however, that his legs would not move with him, and he was forthwith seized and bound. "We are not sent by the Salt Commissioner," cried his captors, in reply to an entreaty to set him free; "we are the devil-constables of Purgatory." Wang was horribly frightened at this, and begged the devils to let him bid farewell to his wife and children; but this they refused to do, saying, "You aren't going to die; you are only wanted for a little job there is down below." Wang asked what the job was; to which the devils replied, "A new Judge has come into office, and, finding the river[512] and the eighteen hells choked up with the bodies of sinners, he has determined to employ three classes of mortals to clean them out. These are thieves, unlicensed founders,[513] and unlicensed dealers in salt, and, for the dirtiest work of all, he is going to take musicians."[514]

Wang accompanied the devils until at length they reached a city, where he was brought before the Judge, who was sitting in his Judgment-

---

511 Salt is a Government monopoly in China, and its sale is only permitted to licensed dealers. It is a contraband article of commerce, whether for import or export, to foreign nations trading with China. In an account of a journey from Swatow to Canton in March—April, 1877, I wrote: "*A propos* of salt, we came across a good-sized bunker of it when stowing away our things in the space below the deck. The boatmen could not resist the temptation of doing a little smuggling on the way up.... At a secluded point in a bamboo-shaded bend of the river, they ran the boat alongside the bank, and were instantly met by a number of suspicious-looking gentlemen with baskets, who soon relieved them of the smuggled salt and separated in different directions." Thus do the people of China seek to lighten the grievous pressure of this tax. A curious custom exists in Canton. Certain blind old men and women are allowed to hawk salt about the streets, and earn a scanty living from the profits they are able to make.
512 The Styx.
513 These words require some explanation. Ordinarily they would be taken in the sense of casting *cash* of a base description; but they might equally well signify the casting of iron articles of any kind, and thereby hang some curious details. Iron foundries in China may only be opened under license from the local officials, and the articles there made, consisting chiefly of cooking utensils, may only be sold within a given area, each district having its own particular foundries, from which alone the supplies of the neighborhood may be derived. Free trade in iron is much feared by the authorities, as thereby pirates and rebels would be enabled to supply themselves with arms. At the framing of the Treaty of Tianjin, with its accompanying tariff and rules, iron was not specified among other prohibited articles of commerce. Consequently, British merchants would appear to have a full right to purchase iron in the interior and convey it to any of the open ports under Transit-pass. But the Chinese officials steadily refuse to acknowledge, or permit the exercise of, this right, putting forward their own time-honored custom with regard to iron, and enumerating the disadvantages to China were such an innovation to be brought about.
514 The allusion is to women, of a not very respectable class.

hall. On turning up his record in the books, one of the devils explained that the prisoner had been arrested for unlicensed trading; whereupon the Judge became very angry, and said, "Those who drive an illicit trade in salt, not only defraud the State of its proper revenue, but also prey upon the livelihood of the people. Those, however, whom the greedy officials and corrupt traders of today denounce as unlicensed traders, are among the most virtuous of mankind—needy unfortunates who struggle to save a few cash in the purchase of their pint of salt.[515] Are they your unlicensed traders?" The Judge then bade the lictors buy four pecks of salt, and send it to Wang's house for him, together with that which had been found upon him; and, at the same time, he gave Wang an iron scourge, and told him to superintend the works at the river. So Wang followed the devils, and found the river swarming with people like ants in an anthill. The water was turbid and red, the stench from it being almost unbearable, while those who were employed in cleaning it out were working there naked. Sometimes they would sink down in the horrid mass of decaying bodies: sometimes they would get lazy, and then the iron scourge was applied to their backs. The assistant superintendents had small scented balls, which they held in their mouths. Wang himself approached the bank, and saw the licensed salt-merchant of Gaowan[516] in the midst of it all, and thrashed him well with his scourge, until he was afraid he would never come up again. This went on for three days and three nights, by which time half the workmen were dead, and the work completed; whereupon the same two devils escorted him home again, and then he woke up.

As a matter of fact, Wang had gone out to sell some salt, and had not come back. Next morning, when his wife opened the house door, she found two bags of salt in the court-yard; and, as her husband did not return, she sent off some people to search for him, and they discovered him lying senseless by the wayside. He was immediately conveyed home, where, after a little time, he recovered consciousness, and related what had taken place. Strange to say, the licensed salt-merchant had fallen down in a fit on the previous evening, and had only just recovered; and Wang, hearing that his body was covered with sores—the result of the beating with the iron scourge—went off to his house to see him; however, directly the wretched man set eyes on Wang, he hastily covered himself up with the bed-clothes,

---

515 No Chinese magistrate would pass sentence upon a man who stole food under stress of hunger, even if such a criminal were ever brought before him.
516 His own village.

forgetting that they were no longer at the infernal river. He did not recover from his injuries for a year, after which he retired from trade.[517]

113. Collecting Subscriptions

THE FROG-GOD frequently employs a magician to deliver its oracles to those who have faith. Should the magician declare that the God is pleased, happiness is sure to follow; but if he says the God is angry, women and children[518] sit sorrowfully about, and neglect even their meals. Such is the customary belief, and it is probably not altogether devoid of foundation.

There was a certain wealthy merchant, named Zhou, who was a very stingy man. Once, when some repairs were necessary to the temple of the God of War,[519] and rich and poor were subscribing as much as each could afford, he alone gave nothing.[520] By-and-by the works were stopped for want of funds, and the committee of management were at a loss what to do next. It happened that just then there was a festival in honor of the Frog-God, at which the magician suddenly cried out, "General Zhou[521] has given orders for a further subscription. Bring forth the books." The people all shouting assent to this, the magician went on to say, "Those who have already subscribed will not be compelled to do so again; those who have not subscribed must give according to their means." Thereupon various persons

---

517 The whole story is meant as a satire upon the iniquity of the Salt Gabelle.
518 The chief supporters of superstition in China.
519 See note 4 in tale number 1.
520 Such is one of the most common causes of hostile demonstration against Chinese Christians. The latter, acting under the orders of the missionaries, frequently refuse to subscribe to the various local celebrations and processions, the great annual festivities, and ceremonies of all kinds, on the grounds that these are idolatrous and forbidden by the Christian faith. Hence bad feeling, high words, blows, and sometimes bloodshed. I say "frequently," because many cases have come to light in which converts have quietly subscribed like other people rather than risk an *emeute*.

An amusing incident came under my own special notice not very long ago. A missionary appeared before me one day to complain that a certain convert of his had been posted in his own village, and cut off from his civic rights for two years, merely because he had agreed to let a room of his house to be used as a missionary *depot*. I took a copy of the placard which was handed to me in proof of this statement, and found it to run thus: "In consequence of — having entered into an agreement with a barbarian pastor, to lease to the said barbarian pastor a room in his house to be used as a missionary chapel, we, the elders of this village, do hereby debar — from the privilege of worshipping in our ancestral hall for the space of two years." It is needless, of course, to mention that Ancestral Worship is (or was) prohibited by all sects of missionaries in China alike; or that, when I pointed this out to the individual in question, who could not have understood the import of the Chinese placard, the charge was promptly withdrawn.

521 An historical character who was formerly among the ranks of the Yellow Turban rebels, but subsequently entered the service of Guan Yu (see note 4 in tale number 1), and was canonized by an Emperor of the last dynasty.

began to put down their names, and when this was finished, the magician examined the books. He then asked if Mr. Zhou was present; and the latter, who was skulking behind, in dread lest he should be detected by the God, had no alternative but to come to the front. "Put yourself down for one hundred taels," said the magician to him; and when Zhou hesitated, he cried out to him in anger, "You could give two hundred for your own bad purposes: how much more should you do so in a good cause?" alluding to a scandalous intrigue of Zhou's, the consequences of which he had averted by payment of the sum mentioned. This put our friend to the blush, and he was obliged to enter his name for one hundred taels, at which his wife was very angry, and said the magician was a rogue, and whenever he came to collect the money he was put off with some excuse.

Shortly afterwards, Zhou was one day going to sleep, when he heard a noise outside his house, like the blowing of an ox, and beheld a huge frog walking leisurely through the front door, which was just big enough to let it pass. Once inside, the creature laid itself down to sleep, with its head on the threshold, to the great horror of all the inmates; upon which Zhou observed that it had probably come to collect his subscription, and, burning some incense, he vowed that he would pay down thirty taels on the spot, and send the balance later on. The frog, however, did not move, so Zhou promised fifty, and then there was a slight decrease in the frog's size. Another twenty brought it down to the size of a peck measure; and when Zhou said the full amount should be paid on the spot, the frog became suddenly no larger than one's fist, and disappeared through a hole in the wall. Zhou immediately sent off fifty taels, at which all the other subscribers were much astonished, not knowing what had taken place. A few days afterwards the magician said Zhou still owed fifty taels, and that he had better send it in soon; so Zhou forwarded ten more, hoping now to have done with the matter. However, as he and his wife were one day sitting down to dinner, the frog reappeared, and, glaring with anger, took up a position on the bed, which creaked under it, as though unable to bear the weight. Putting its head on the pillow, the frog went off to sleep, its body gradually swelling up until it was as big as a buffalo, and nearly filled the room, causing Zhou to send off the balance of his subscription without a moment's delay. There was now no diminution in the size of the frog's body; and by-and-by crowds of small frogs came hopping in, boring through the walls, jumping on the bed, catching flies on the cooking-stove, and dying in the saucepans, until the place was quite unbearable. Three days passed thus, and then Zhou sought out the magician, and asked him what was to be done. The latter said he could manage it, and began by vowing on behalf of Zhou twenty more taels' subscription. At this the frog raised its head, and a further increase caused it to move one foot; and by the time a hundred taels was reached, the frog was walking out of the door. At the door, however, it stopped, and lay down once more, which the magician explained by saying, that immediate payment was required; so Zhou handed over the amount at once, and the frog, shrinking down to its usual size, mingled with its companions, and departed with them.

The repairs to the temple were accordingly completed, but for "lighting the eyes,"[522] and the attendant festivities, some further subscriptions were wanted. Suddenly, the magician, pointing at the managers, cried out, "There is money short; of fifteen men, two of you are defaulters." At this, all declared they had given what they could afford; but the magician went on to say, "It is not a question of what you can afford; you have misappropriated the funds[523] that should not have been touched, and misfortune would come upon you, but that, in return for your exertions, I shall endeavor to avert it from you. The magician himself is not without taint.[524] Let him set you a good example." Thereupon, the magician rushed into his house, and brought out all the money he had, saying, "I stole eight taels myself, which I will now refund." He then weighed what silver he had, and finding that it only amounted to a little over six taels, he made one of the bystanders take a note of the difference. Then the others came forward and paid up, each what he had misappropriated from the public fund. All this time the magician had been in a divine ecstasy, not knowing what he was saying; and when he came around, and was told what had happened, his shame knew no bounds, so he pawned some of his clothes, and paid in the balance of his

---

522 This curious ceremony is the final touch to a newly-built or newly-restored temple, and consists in giving expression to the eyes of the freshly-painted idols, which have been purposely left blank by the painter. Up to that time these blocks of clay or wood are not supposed to have been animated by the spiritual presence of the deity in question; but no sooner are the eyes lighted than the gratified God smiles down upon the handsome decorations thus provided by devout and trusting suppliants.

There is a cognate custom belonging to the ceremonies of ancestral worship, of great importance in the eyes of the Chinese. On a certain day after the death of a parent, the surviving head of the family proceeds with much solemnity to dab a spot of ink upon the memorial tablet of the deceased. This is believed to give to the departed spirit the power of remaining near to, and watching over the fortunes of, those left behind.

523 Such indeed is the fate of a percentage of all public subscriptions raised and handled by Chinese of no matter what class. An application was once made to me for a donation to a native foundling hospital at Swatow, on the ground that I was known as a "read (Chinese) book man," and that consequently other persons, both Chinese and foreigners, might be induced to follow my example. On my declining to subscribe, the manager of the concern informed me that if I would only put down my name for fifty dollars, say £10, no call should be made upon me for the money! What a blessing it is to live in Christian England, where peculation and corruption are unknown!

524 The reader must recollect that these are the words of the God, speaking from the magician's body.

own debt. As to the two defaulters who did not pay, one of them was ill for a month and more; while the other had a bad attack of boils.

114. Taoist Miracles

AT Jinan Fu there lived a certain priest: I cannot say whence he came, or what was his name. Winter and summer alike he wore but one unlined robe, and a yellow girdle about his waist, with neither shirt nor trousers. He combed his hair with a broken comb, holding the ends in his mouth, like the strings of a hat. By day he wandered about the market-place; at night he slept in the street, and to a distance of several feet around where he lay, the ice and snow would melt. When he first arrived at Jinan he used to perform miracles, and the people vied with each other in making him presents. One day a disreputable young fellow gave him a quantity of wine, and begged him in return to divulge the secret of his power; and when the priest refused, the young man watched him get into the river to bathe, and then ran off with his clothes. The priest called out to him to bring them back, promising that he would do as the young man required; but the latter, distrusting the priest's good faith, refused to do so; whereupon the priest's girdle was forthwith changed into a snake, several spans in circumference, which coiled itself around its new master's head, and glared and hissed terribly. The young man now fell on his knees, and humbly prayed the priest to save his life; at which the priest put his girdle on again, and a snake that had appeared to be his girdle, wriggled away and disappeared. The priest's fame was thus firmly established, and the gentry and officials of the place were constantly inviting him to join them in their festive parties. By-and-by the priest said he was going to invite his entertainers to a return feast;[525] and at the appointed time each one of them found on his table a formal invitation to a banquet at the Water Pavilion, but no one knew who had brought the letters. However, they all went, and were met at the door by the priest, in his usual garb; and when they got inside, the place was all desolate and bare, with no banquet ready. "I'm afraid I shall be obliged to ask you gentlemen to let me use your attendants," said the priest to his guests; "I am a poor man, and keep no servants myself." To this all readily

---

525 It is considered a serious breach of Chinese etiquette to accept invitations without returning the compliment at an early date.

consented; whereupon the priest drew a double door upon the wall, and rapped upon it with his knuckles. Somebody answered from within, and immediately the door was thrown open, and a splendid array of handsome chairs, and tables loaded with exquisite viands and costly wines, burst upon the gaze of the astonished guests. The priest bade the attendants receive all these things from the door, and bring them outside, cautioning them on no account to speak with the people inside; and thus a most luxurious entertainment was provided, to the great amazement of all present.

Now this Pavilion stood upon the bank of a small lake, and every year, at the proper season, it was literally covered with lilies; but, at the time of this feast, the weather was cold, and the surface of the lake was of a smoky green color. "It's a pity," said one of the guests, "that the lilies are not out"—a sentiment in which the others very cordially agreed, when suddenly a servant came running in to say that, at that moment, the lake was a perfect mass of lilies. Every one jumped up directly, and ran to look out of the window, and, lo! it was so; and in another minute the fragrant perfume of the flowers was borne towards them by the breeze. Hardly knowing what to make of this strange sight, they sent off some servants, in a boat, to gather a few of the lilies, but they soon returned empty-handed, saying, that the flowers seemed to shift their position as fast as they rowed towards them; at which the priest laughed, and said, "These are but the lilies of your imagination, and have no real existence." And later on, when the wine was finished, the flowers began to droop and fade; and by-and-by a breeze from the north carried off every sign of them, leaving the lake as it had been before.

A certain daotai[526] at Jinan, was much taken with this priest, and gave him rooms at his yamen. One day he had some friends to dinner, and set before them some very choice old wine that he had, and of which he only brought out a small quantity at a time, not wishing to get through it too rapidly. The guests, however, liked it so much that they asked for more; upon which the daotai said, "he was very sorry but it was all finished." The priest smiled at this, and said, "I can give the gentlemen some, if they will oblige me by accepting it;" and immediately inserted the wine-kettle[527] in his sleeve, bringing it out again directly, and pouring out for the guests. This wine tasted exactly like the choice wine they had just been drinking, and the

---

526 A high Chinese official, known to foreigners as Intendant of Circuit; the circuit being a circuit of Prefectures, over which he has full control, subject only to the approval of the highest provincial authorities. It is with this functionary that foreign Consols rank.
527 See note 441 in tale number 93.

priest gave them all as much of it as they wanted, which made the Daotai suspect that something was wrong; so, after the dinner, he went into his cellar to look at his own stock, when he found the jars closely tied down, with unbroken seals, but one and all empty. In a great rage, he caused the priest to be arrested for sorcery, and proceeded to have him bambooed; but no sooner had the bamboo touched the priest than the daotai himself felt a sting of pain, which increased at every blow; and, in a few moments, there was the priest writhing and shrieking under every cut,[528] while the Daotai was sitting in a pool of blood. Accordingly, the punishment was soon stopped, and the priest was commanded to leave Jinan, which he did, and I know not whither he went. He was subsequently seen at Nanjing, dressed precisely as of old; but on being spoken to, he only smiled and made no reply.

115. Arrival of Buddhist Priests

Two Buddhist priests having arrived from the West,[529] one went to the Wutai hill, while the other hung up his staff[530] at Taishan. Their clothes, complexions, language, and features were very different from those of our country. They further said they had crossed the Fiery Mountains, from the peaks of which smoke was always issuing as from the chimney of a furnace; that they could only travel after rain, and that excessive caution was necessary to avoid displacing any stone and thus giving a vent to the flames. They also stated that they had passed through the River of Sand, in the middle of which was a crystal hill with perpendicular sides and perfectly transparent; and that there was a defile just broad enough to admit a single cart, its entrance guarded by two dragons with crossed horns. Those who wished to pass prostrated themselves before these dragons, and on receiving permission to enter, the horns opened and let them through. The dragons were of a white color, and their scales and bristles seemed to be of crystal. Eighteen winters and summers these priests had been on the road; and of twelve who started from the West together, only two reached China.[531]

---

528 Of course only pretending to be hurt, the pain of the blows being transferred by his magical art to the back of the Daotai.

529 That is, missionaries from India.

530 See note 286 in tale number 56.

531 Much of the above recalls Fa Xian's narrative of his celebrated journey from China to India in the early years of the fifth century of our era, with which our author was evidently well acquainted. That courageous traveler complained that of those who had set out with him some had stopped on the way

These two said that in their country four of our mountains are held in great esteem, namely, Tai, Hua, Wutai, and Luojia. The people there also think that China[532] is paved with yellow gold, that Guanyin and Wenshu[533] are still alive, and that they have only come here to be sure of their Buddhahood and of immortal life. Hearing these words, it struck me that this was precisely what our own people say and think about the West; and that if travelers from each country could only meet half-way and tell each other the true state of affairs, there would be some hearty laughter on both sides, and a saving of much unnecessary trouble.

116. The Stolen Eyes

WHEN His Excellency Mr. Tang, of our village, was quite a child, a relative of his took him to a temple to see the usual theatrical performances.[534] He was a clever little fellow, afraid of nothing and nobody; and when he saw one of the clay images in the vestibule staring at him with its great glass[535] eyes, the temptation was irresistible; and, secretly gouging them out with his finger, he carried them off with him. When they reached home, his relative was taken suddenly ill, and remained for a long time speechless; at length, jumping up, he cried out several times in a voice of thunder, "Why did you gouge out my eyes?" His family did not know what to make of this, until little Tang told them what he had done; they then immediately began to pray to the possessed man, saying, "A mere child, unconscious of the wickedness of his act, took away in his fun thy sacred eyes. They shall be reverently replaced." Thereupon the voice exclaimed, "In that case, I shall go away;" and he had hardly spoken before Tang's relative fell flat upon the ground and lay there in a state of insensibility for some time. When he recovered, they asked him concerning what he had said; but he remembered nothing of it. The eyes were then forthwith restored to their original sockets.

---

and others had died, leaving him only his own shadow as a companion.

532 This may almost be said to have been the belief of the Arabs at the date of the composition of *The Arabian Nights*.

533 For Guanyin, see note 176 in tale number 33. Wenshu, or Manjusri, is the God of Wisdom, and is generally represented as riding on a lion, in attendance, together with Puxian, the God of Action, who rides an elephant, upon Shakyamuni Buddha.

534 See note 244 in tale number 48.

535 The term here used stands for a vitreous composition that has long been prepared by the Chinese.

117. The Invisible Priest

MR. HAN was a gentleman of good family, on very intimate terms with a skillful Taoist priest and magician named Dan, who, when sitting amongst other guests, would suddenly become invisible. Mr. Han was extremely anxious to learn this art, but Dan refused all his entreaties, "Not," as he said, "because I want to keep the secret for myself, but simply as a matter of principle. To teach the superior man[536] would be well enough; others, however, would avail themselves of such knowledge to plunder their neighbors. There is no fear that you would do this, though even you might be tempted in certain ways." Mr. Han, finding all his efforts unavailing, flew into a great passion, and secretly arranged with his servants that they should give the magician a sound beating; and, in order to prevent his escape through the power of making himself invisible, he had his threshing-floor[537] covered with a fine ash-dust, so that at any rate his footsteps would be seen and the servants could strike just above them.[538] He then inveigled Dan to the appointed spot, which he had no sooner reached than Han's servants began to belabor him on all sides with leathern thongs. Dan immediately became invisible, but his footprints were clearly seen as he moved about hither and thither to avoid the blows, and the servants went on striking above them until finally he succeeded in getting away. Mr. Han then went home, and subsequently Dan reappeared and told the servants that he could stay there no longer, adding that before he went he intended to give them all a feast in return for many things they had done for him. And diving into his sleeve he brought forth a quantity of delicious meats and wines, which he spread out upon the table, begging them to sit down and enjoy themselves. The servants did so, and one and all of them got drunk and insensible; upon which Dan picked each of them up and stowed them away in his sleeve. When Mr. Han heard of this, he begged Dan to perform some other trick; so Dan drew upon the wall a city, and knocking at the gate with his hand it was instantly thrown open. He then put inside it his wallet and clothes, and stepping through the gateway himself, waved his hand and bade Mr. Han farewell. The city gates were now closed, and Dan vanished from their sight. It was said that he appeared again in Qingzhou,

---

536 The perfect man, according to the Confucian standard.
537 A large, smooth area of concrete, to be seen outside all country houses of any size, and used for preparing the various kinds of grain.
538 Compare, "The not uncommon practice of strewing ashes to show the footprints of ghosts or demons takes for granted that they are substantial bodies."—Tylor's *Primitive Culture*, Vol. I., P. 455.

where he taught little boys to paint a circle on their hands, and, by dabbing this on to another person's face or clothes, to imprint the circle on the place thus struck without a trace of it being left behind upon the hand.

118. The Censor in Purgatory

JUST beyond Fengdu[539] there is a fathomless cave which is reputed to be the entrance to Purgatory. All the implements of torture employed therein are of human manufacture; old, worn-out shackles and fetters being occasionally found at the mouth of the cave, and as regularly replaced by new ones, which disappear the same night, and for which the magistrate of the district makes a formal charge[540] in his accounts.

Under the Ming dynasty, there was a certain Censor,[541] named Hua, whose duties brought him to this place; and hearing the story of the cave, he said he did not believe it, but would penetrate into it and see for himself. People tried to dissuade him from such an enterprise; however, he paid no heed to their remonstrances, and entered the cave with a lighted candle in his hand, followed by two attendants. They had proceeded about half a mile, when suddenly the candle was violently extinguished, and Mr. Hua saw before him a broad flight of steps leading up to the Ten Courts, or Judgment-halls, in each of which a judge was sitting with his robes and tablets all complete. On the eastern side there was one vacant place; and when the judges saw Mr. Hua, they hastened down the steps to meet him, and each one cried out, "So you have come at last, have you? I hope you have been quite well since last we met." Mr. Hua asked what the place was; to which they replied that it was the Court of Purgatory, and then Mr. Hua in a great fright was about to take his leave, when the judges stopped him, saying, "No, no. Sir! that is your seat there; how can you imagine you are to go back again?" Thereupon Mr. Hua was over-whelmed with fear, and

---

539 Fengdu is a district city in the province of Szechuen, and near it are said to be fire-wells, otherwise known as the entrance to Purgatory, the capital city of which is also called Fengdu.

540 To the Imperial Treasury. From what I know of the barefacedness of similar official impostures, I should say that this statement is quite within the bounds of truth. For instance, at Amoy 1 percent is collected by the local mandarins on all imports, ostensibly for the purpose of providing the Imperial table with a delicious kind of bird's nest said to be found in the neighborhood! Seven-tenths of the sum thus collected is pocketed by the various officials of the place, and with the remaining three-tenths a certain quantity of the ordinary article of commerce is imported from the Straits and forwarded to Beijing.

541 See note 165 in tale number 32.

begged and implored the judges to forgive him; but the latter declared they could not interfere with the decrees of fate, and taking down the register of Life and Death they showed him that it had been ordained that on such a day of such a month his living body would pass into the realms of darkness. When Mr. Hua read these words he shivered and shook as if iced water was being poured down his back, and thinking of his old mother and his young children, his tears began to flow. At that juncture an angel in golden armor appeared, holding in his hand a document written on yellow silk,[542] before which the judges all performed a respectful obeisance. They then unfolded and read the document, which was nothing more or less than a general pardon from the Almighty for the suffering sinners in Purgatory, by virtue of which Mr. Hua's fate would be set aside, and he would be enabled to return once more to the light of day. Thereupon the judges congratulated him upon his release, and started him on his way home; but he had not got more than a few steps of the way before he found himself plunged in total darkness. He was just beginning to despair, when forth from the gloom came a God with a red face and a long beard, rays of light shooting out from his body and illuminating the darkness around. Mr. Hua made up to him at once, and begged to know how he could get out of the cave; to which the God curtly replied, "Repeat the *sutras* of Buddha!" and vanished instantly from his sight. Now Mr. Hua had forgotten almost all the *sutras* he had ever known; however, he remembered a little of the diamond *sutra,* and, clasping his hands in an attitude of prayer, he began to repeat it aloud. No sooner had he done this than a faint streak of light glimmered through the darkness, and revealed to him the direction of the path; but the next moment he was at a loss how to go on, and the light forthwith disappeared. He then set himself to think hard what the next verse was, and as fast as he recollected and could go on repeating, so fast did the light reappear to guide him on his way, until at length he emerged once more from the mouth of the cave. As to the fate of the two servants who accompanied him it is needless to inquire.

---

542 An imperial mandate is always written on yellow silk, and the ceremony of opening and perusing it is accompanied by prostrations and other acts of reverential submission.

119. Mr. Willow and the Locusts

DURING the Ming dynasty a plague of locusts[543] visited Qingyan, and was advancing rapidly towards the I district, when the magistrate of that place, in great tribulation at the impending disaster, retired one day to sleep behind the screen in his office. There he dreamt that a young graduate, named Willow, wearing a tall hat and a green robe, and of very commanding stature, came to see him, and declared that he could tell the magistrate how to get rid of the locusts. "Tomorrow," said he, "on the south-west road, you will see a woman riding[544] on a large jennet: she is the Spirit of the Locusts; ask her, and she will help you." The magistrate thought this strange advice; however, he got everything ready, and waited, as he had been told, at the roadside. By-and-by, along came a woman with her hair tied up in a knot, and a serge cape over her shoulders, riding slowly northwards on an old mule; whereupon the magistrate burned some sticks of incense, and, seizing the mule's bridle, humbly presented a goblet of wine. The woman asked him what he wanted; to which he replied, "Lady, I implore you to save my small magistracy from the dreadful ravages of your locusts." "Oho!" said the woman, "that scoundrel, Willow, has been letting the cat out of the bag, has he? He shall suffer for it: I won't touch your crops." She then drank three cups of wine, and vanished out of sight. Subsequently, when the locusts did come, they flew high in the air, and did not settle on the crops; but they stripped the leaves off every willow-tree far and wide; and then the magistrate awoke to the fact that the graduate of his dream was the Spirit of the Willows. Some said that this happy result was owing to the magistrate's care for the welfare of his people.

120. Mr. Dong; or, Virtue Rewarded

AT Qingzhou there lived a Mr. Dong, President of one of the Six Boards, whose domestic regulations were so strict that the men and women servants were not allowed to speak to each other.[545] One day he caught

543 Innumerable pamphlets have been published in China on the best methods of getting rid of these destructive insects, but none to my knowledge contains much sound or practical advice.
544 See note 252 in tale 52. The mules of the North of China are marvels of beauty and strength; and the price of a fine animal often goes as high as £100.
545 See note 200 in tale number 40, and note 453 in tale number 94.

a slave-girl laughing and talking with one of his attendants, and gave them both a sound rating. That night he retired to sleep, accompanied by his *valet-de-chambre,* in his library, the door of which, as it was very hot weather, was left wide open. When the night was far advanced, the valet was awakened by a noise at his master's bed: and, opening his eyes, he saw, by the light of the moon, the attendant above mentioned pass out of the door with something in his hand. Recognizing the man as one of the family, he thought nothing of the occurrence, but turned around and went to sleep again. Soon after, however, he was again aroused by the noise of footsteps tramping heavily across the room, and, looking up, he beheld a huge being with a red face and a long beard, very like the God of War,[546] carrying a man's head. Horribly frightened, he crawled under the bed, and then he heard sounds above him as of clothes being shaken out, and as if someone was being massaged.[547] In a few moments, the boots tramped once more across the room and went away; and then he gradually put out his head, and, seeing the dawn beginning to peep through the window, he stretched out his hand to reach his clothes. These he found to be soaked through and through, and, on applying his hand to his nose, he smelt the smell of blood. He now called out loudly to his master, who jumped up at once; and, by the light of a candle, they saw that the bed-clothes and pillows were alike steeped in blood. Just then some constables knocked at the door, and when Mr. Dong went out to see who it was, the constables were all astonishment; "for," said they, "a few minutes ago a man rushed wildly up to our yamen, and said he had killed his master; and, as he himself was covered with blood, he was arrested, and turned out to be a servant of yours. He also declared that he had buried your head alongside the temple of the God of War; and when we went to look, there, indeed, was a freshly-dug hole, but the head was gone." Mr. Dong was amazed at all this story, and, on proceeding to the magistrate's yamen, he discovered that the man in charge was the attendant whom he had scolded the day before. Thereupon, the criminal was severely bambooed and released; and then Mr. Dong, who was unwilling to make an enemy of a man of this stamp, gave him the girl to wife. However, a few nights afterwards the people who lived next door to the newly-married couple heard a terrific crash in their house, and, rushing in to see what was the matter, found that husband and wife, and

---

546 See note 4 in tale number 1.
547 See note 360 in tale number 69.

the bedstead as well, had been cut clean in two as if by a sword. The ways of the God are many, indeed, but few more extraordinary than this.[548]

121. The Dead Priest

A CERTAIN Taoist priest, overtaken in his wanderings by the shades of evening, sought refuge in a small Buddhist monastery. The monk's apartment was, however, locked; so he threw his mat down in the vestibule of the shrine, and seated himself upon it. In the middle of the night, when all was still, he heard a sound of someone opening the door behind him; and looking around, he saw a Buddhist priest, covered with blood from head to foot, who did not seem to notice that anybody else was present. Accordingly, he himself pretended not to be aware of what was going on; and then he saw the other priest enter the shrine, mount the altar, and remain there some time, embracing Buddha's head and laughing by turns. When morning came, he found the monk's room still locked; and, suspecting something was wrong, he walked to a neighboring village, where he told the people what he had seen. Thereupon the villagers went back with him, and broke open the door, and there before them lay the priest weltering in his blood, having evidently been killed by robbers, who had stripped the place bare. Anxious now to find out what had made the disembodied spirit of the priest laugh in the way it had been seen to do, they proceeded to inspect the head of the Buddha on the altar; and, at the back of it, they noticed a small mark, scraping through which they discovered a sum of over thirty ounces of silver. This sum was forthwith used for defraying the funeral expenses of the murdered man.

122. The Flying Cow

A CERTAIN man, who had bought a fine cow, dreamt the same night that wings grew out of the animal's back, and that it had flown away. Regarding this as an omen of some pending misfortune, he led the cow off to market again, and sold it at a ruinous loss. Wrapping up in a cloth the silver he

---

548 It was the God of War who replaced Mr. Dong's head after it had actually been cut off and buried.

received, he slung it over his back, and was halfway home, when he saw a falcon eating part of a hare.[549] Approaching the bird, he found it was quite tame, and accordingly tied it by the leg to one of the corners of the cloth, in which his money was. The falcon fluttered about a good deal, trying to escape; and, by-and-by, the man's hold being for a moment relaxed, away went the bird, cloth, money, and all. "It was destiny," said the man every time he told the story; ignorant as he was, first, that no faith should be put in dreams;[550] and, secondly, that people shouldn't take things they see by the wayside.[551] Quadrupeds don't usually fly.

123. The "Mirror and Listen" Trick

AT Yidu there lived a family of the name of Zheng. The two sons were both distinguished scholars, but the elder was early known to fame, and, consequently, the favorite with his parents, who also extended their preference to his wife. The younger brother was a trifle wild, which displeased his father and mother very much, and made them regard his wife, too, with anything but a friendly eye. The latter reproached her husband for being the cause of this, and asked him why he, being a man like his brother, could not vindicate the slights that were put upon her. This piqued him; and, setting to work in good earnest, he soon gained a fair reputation, though still not equal to his brother's. That year the two went up for the highest degree; and, on New Year's Eve, the wife of the younger, very anxious for the success of her husband, secretly tried the "mirror and listen" trick.[552] She saw two men pushing each other in jest, and heard them say, "You go and get cool," which remark she was quite unable to interpret for good or for bad, so she thought no more about the matter. After the examination, the

---

549 See note 16 in tale number 6.
550 The highly educated Confucianist rises above the superstition that darkens the lives of his less fortunate fellow countrymen. Had such a dream as the above received an inauspicious interpretation at the hands of some local soothsayer the owner of the animal would in nine cases out of ten have taken an early opportunity of getting rid of it.
551 The Chinese love to refer to the "good old time" of their forefathers, when a man who dropped anything on the highway would have no cause to hurry back for fear of its being carried off by a stranger.
552 One method is to wrap an old mirror (formerly a polished metal disc) in a handkerchief, and then, no one being present, to bow seven times towards the Spirit of the Hearth: after which the first words heard spoken by any one will give a clue to the issue under investigation. Another method is to close the eyes and take seven paces, opening them at the seventh and getting some hint from the objects first seen in a mirror held in the hand, coupled with the words first spoken within the experimenter's hearing.

two brothers returned home; and one day, when the weather was extremely hot, and their two wives were hard at work in the cook-house, preparing food for their field-laborers, a messenger rode up in hot haste[553] to announce that the elder brother had passed. Thereupon his mother went into the cook-house, and, calling to her daughter-in-law, said, "Your husband has passed; *you go and get cool.*" Rage and grief now filled the breast of the second son's wife, who, with tears in her eyes, continued her task of cooking, when suddenly another messenger rushed in to say, that the second son had passed too. At this, his wife flung down her frying-pan, and cried out, "Now I'll *go and get cool*;" and as in the heat of her excitement she uttered these words, the recollection of her trial of the "mirror and listen" trick flashed upon her, and she knew that the words of that evening had been fulfilled.

124. The Cattle Plague

CHEN HUAFENG, of Mengshan, overpowered by the great heat, went and lay down under a tree, when suddenly up came a man with a thick comforter around his neck, who also sat down on a stone in the shade, and began fanning himself as hard as he could, the perspiration all the time running off him like a waterfall. Chen rose and said to him with a smile, "If, Sir, you were to remove that comforter, you would be cool enough without the help of a fan." "It would be easy enough," replied the stranger, "to take off my comforter; but the difficulty would be in getting it on again." He then went on to converse generally upon other matters, in a manner which betokened considerable refinement; and by-and-by he exclaimed, "What I should like now is just a draught of iced wine to cool the twelve joints of my oesophagus."[554] "Come along, then," cried Chen, "my house is close by, and I shall be happy to give you what you want." So off they went together; and Chen set before them some capital wine, which he produced from a cave, cold enough to numb their teeth. The stranger was delighted, and remained there drinking until late in-the evening, when, all at once, it began to rain.

---

553 In former days, these messengers of good tidings to candidates whose homes were in distant parts used to earn handsome sums if first to announce the news; but now the telegraph has taken their occupation from them.

554 Accurate anatomical descriptions must not be looked for in Chinese literature. "Man has three hundred and sixty-five bones, corresponding to the number of days it takes the heavens to revolve." From the *Xi yuan lu,* or *Instructions to Coroners,* Book I., ch. 12. See note 67 in tale number 14.

Chen lighted a lamp; and he and his guest, who now took off the comforter, sat talking together in *déshabillé*. Every now and again the former thought he saw a light coming from the back of the stranger's head; and when at length he had gone off into a tipsy sleep, Chen took the light to examine more closely. He found behind the ears a large cavity, partitioned by a number of membranes, and looking like a lattice, with a thin skin hanging down in front of each, the spaces being apparently empty. In great astonishment Chen took a hair-pin, and inserted it into one of these places, when pff! out flew something like a tiny cow, which broke through the window,[555] and was gone. This frightened Chen, and he determined to play no more tricks; just then, however, the stranger woke up. "Alas!" cried he, "you have been at my head, and have let out the Cattle Plague. What is to be done now?" Chen asked what he meant: upon which the stranger said, "There is no object in further concealment. I will tell you all. I am the Angel of Pestilence for the six kinds of domestic animals. That form which you have let out attacks oxen, and I fear that, for miles around, few will escape alive." Now Chen himself was a cattle-farmer, and when he heard this was dreadfully alarmed, and implored the stranger to tell him what to do. "What to do!" replied he; "why, I shall not escape punishment myself; how can I tell you what to do? However, you will find powdered *kucan*[556] an efficacious remedy—that is, if you don't keep it a secret for your private use."[557] The stranger then departed, first of all piling up a quantity of earth in a niche in the wall, a handful of which, he told Chen, given to each animal, might prove of some avail. Before long the plague did break out; and Chen, who was desirous of making a little money by it, told the remedy to no one, with the exception of his younger brother. The latter tried it on his own beasts with great success; while, on the other hand, those belonging to Chen himself died off, to the number of fifty head,[558] leaving him only four or five old cows, which showed every sign of soon sharing the same fate. In his distress, Chen suddenly bethought himself of the earth in the niche; and, as a last resource, gave some to the sick animals. By the next morning they were quite well, and then he knew that his secrecy about the remedy had caused it to have no effect. From that moment his stock went on increasing, and in a few years he had as many as ever.

---

555 See note 46 in tale number 10.
556 *Sophora flavescens*, Ait.
557 As the Chinese invariably do whenever they get hold of a useful prescription or remedy. Master workmen also invariably try to withhold something of their art from the apprentices they engage to teach.
558 The text has "of two hundred hoofs."

125. The Marriage of the Virgin Goddess

AT Guiji there is a shrine to the Plum Virgin, who was formerly a young lady named Ma, and lived at Dongwan. Her betrothed husband dying before the wedding, she swore she would never marry, and at thirty years of age she died. Her kinsfolk built a shrine to her memory, and gave her the title of the Plum Virgin. Some years afterwards, a Mr. Jin, on his way to the examination, happened to pass by the shrine; and entering in, he walked up and down thinking very much of the young lady in whose honor it had been erected. That night he dreamt that a servant came to summon him into the presence of the Goddess; and that, in obedience to her command, he went and found her waiting for him just outside the shrine. "I am deeply grateful to you, Sir," said the Goddess, on his approach, "for giving me so large a share of your thoughts; and I intend to repay you by becoming your humble handmaid." Mr. Jin bowed an assent; and then the Goddess escorted him back, saying, "When your place is ready, I will come and fetch you." On waking in the morning, Mr. Jin was not over-pleased with his dream; however, that very night every one of the villagers dreamt that the Goddess appeared and said she was going to marry Mr. Jin, bidding them at once prepare an image of him. This the village elders, out of respect for their Goddess, positively refused to do; until at length they all began to fall ill, and then they made a clay image of Mr. Jin and placed it on the left of the Goddess. Mr. Jin now told his wife that the Plum Virgin had come for him; and, putting on his official cap and robes, he straightway died. Thereupon his wife was very angry; and, going to the shrine, she first abused the Goddess, and then, getting on the altar, slapped her face well. The Goddess is now called Jin's virgin wife.

126. The Wine Insect

A MR. LIN of Changshan was extremely fat, and so fond of wine[559] that he would often finish a pitcher by himself. However, he owned about fifty acres of land, half of which was covered with millet, and being well off, he did not consider that his drinking would bring him into trouble. One day a foreign Buddhist priest saw him, and remarked that he appeared to be

---

559 The ordinary "wine" of China is a spirit distilled from rice. See note 441 in tale number 93.

suffering from some extraordinary complaint. Mr. Lin said nothing was the matter with him; whereupon the priest asked him if he often got drunk. Lin acknowledged that he did; and the priest told him that he was afflicted by the wine insect. "Dear me!" cried Lin, in great alarm, "do you think you could cure me?" The priest declared there would be no difficulty in doing so; but when Lin asked him what drugs he intended to use, the priest said he should not use any at all. He then made Lin lie down in the sun; and tying his hands and feet together, he placed a stoup of good wine about half a foot from his head. By-and-by, Lin felt a deadly thirst coming on; and the flavor of the wine passing through his nostrils seemed to set his vitals on fire. Just then he experienced a tickling sensation in his throat, and something ran out of his mouth and jumped into the wine. On being released from his bonds, he saw that it was an insect about three inches in length, which wriggled about in the wine like a tadpole, and had mouth and eyes all complete. Lin was overjoyed, and offered money to the priest, who refused to take it, saying, all he wanted was the insect, which he explained to Lin was the essence of wine, and which, on being stirred up in water, would turn it into wine. Lin tried this, and found it was so; and ever afterwards he detested the sight of wine. He subsequently became very thin, and so poor that he had hardly enough to eat and drink.

127. The Faithful Dog

A CERTAIN man of Lu'an, whose father had been cast into prison, and was brought almost to death's door,[560] scraped together one hundred ounces of silver, and set out for the city to try and arrange for his parent's release. Jumping on a mule, he saw that a black dog, belonging to the family, was following him. He tried in vain to make the dog remain at home; and when, after traveling for some miles, he got off his mule to rest awhile, he picked up a large stone and threw it at the dog, which then ran off. However, he was no sooner on the road again, than up came the dog, and tried to stop

---

560 In an entry on torture (see note 384 in tale number 73) which occurs in my *Glossary of Reference* I made the following statement: "The real tortures of a Chinese prison are the filthy dens in which the unfortunate victims are confined, the stench in which they have to draw breath, the fetters and manacles by which they are secured, the absolute insufficiency even of the disgusting rations doled out to them, and above all the mental agony which must ensue in a country with no *Habeas corpus* to protect the lives and fortunes of its citizens."

the mule by holding on to its tail. His master beat it off with the whip; whereupon the dog ran barking loudly in front of the mule, and seemed to be using every means in its power to cause his master to stop. The latter thought this a very inauspicious omen, and turning upon the animal in a rage, drove it away out of sight. He now went on to the city; but when, in the dusk of the evening, he arrived there, he found that about half his money was gone. In a terrible state of mind, he tossed about all night; then all of a sudden it flashed across him that the strange behavior of the dog might possibly have some meaning; so getting up very early, he left the city as soon as the gates were open,[561] and though, from the number of passers-by, he never expected to find his money again, he went on until he reached the spot where he had got off his mule the day before. There he saw his dog lying dead upon the ground, its hair having apparently been wetted through with perspiration;[562] and, lifting up the body by one of its ears, he found his lost silver. Full of gratitude he bought a coffin and buried the dead animal; and the people now call the place the Grave of the Faithful Dog.

128. An Earthquake

In 1668 there was a very severe earthquake.[563] I myself was staying at Jixia, and happened to be that night sitting over a kettle of wine with my cousin Li Du. All of a sudden we heard a noise like thunder, traveling from the south-east in a north-westerly direction. We were much astonished at this, and quite unable to account for the noise; in another moment the table began to rock, and the wine-cups were upset; the beams and supports of the house snapped here and there with a crash, and we looked at each other in fear and trembling. By-and-by we knew that it was an earthquake; and, rushing out, we saw houses and other buildings, as it were, fall down and get up again; and, amidst the sounds of crashing walls, we heard the shrieks of women and children, the whole mass being like a great seething cauldron. Men were giddy and could not stand, but rolled about on the ground; the river overflowed its banks; cocks crowed, and dogs barked from one end

---

561 For a small bribe, the soldiers at the gates of a Chinese city will usually pass people in and out by means of a ladder placed against the wall at some convenient spot.

562 I believe it is with us only a recently determined fact that dogs perspire through the skin.

563 The exact date is given—the 17th of the 6th moon, which would probably fall towards the end of June.

of the city to the other. In a little while the quaking began to subside; and then might be seen men and women running half naked about the streets, all anxious to tell their own experiences, and forgetting that they had on little or no clothing. I subsequently heard that a well was closed up and rendered useless by this earthquake; that a house was turned completely around, so as to face the opposite direction; that the Jixia hill was riven open, and that the waters of the I river flowed in and made a lake of an acre and more. Truly such an earthquake as this is of rare occurrence.

129. Making Animals

THE tricks for bewitching people are many. Sometimes drugs are put in their food, and when they eat they become dazed, and follow the person who has bewitched them. This is commonly called *daxuba*; in Jiangnan it is known as *chexu*. Little children are most frequently bewitched in this way. There is also what is called "making animals," which is better known on the south side of the River.[564]

One day a man arrived at an inn in Yangzhou, leading with him five donkeys. Tying them up near the stable, he told the landlord he would be back in a few minutes, and bade him give his donkeys no water. He had not been gone long before the donkeys, which were standing out in the glare of the sun, began to kick about, and make a noise; whereupon the landlord untied them, and was going to put them in the shade, when suddenly they espied water, and made a rush to get at it. So the landlord let them drink; and no sooner had the water touched their lips than they rolled on the ground, and changed into women. In great astonishment the landlord asked them whence they came; but their tongues were tied, and they could not answer, so he hid them in his private apartments, and at that moment their owner returned, bringing with him five sheep. The latter immediately asked the landlord where his donkeys were; to which the landlord replied by offering him some wine, saying, the donkeys would be brought to him directly. He then went out and gave the sheep some water, on drinking which they were all changed into boys. Accordingly, he communicated with the authorities, and the stranger was arrested and forthwith beheaded.

---

564 See note 478 in tale number 98

130. Cruelty Avenged

A CERTAIN magistrate caused a petty oil-vendor, who was brought before him for some trifling misdemeanor, and whose statements were very confused, to be bambooed to death. The former subsequently rose to high rank; and having amassed considerable wealth, set about building himself a fine house. On the day when the great beam was to be fixed in its place,[565] among the friends and relatives who arrived to offer their congratulations, he was horrified to see the oilman walk in. At the same instant one of the servants came rushing up to announce to him the birth of a son; whereupon, he mournfully remarked, "The house not yet finished, and its destroyer already here." The bystanders thought he was joking, for they had not seen what he had seen.[566] However, when that boy grew up, by his frivolity and extravagance he quite ruined his father. He was finally obliged himself to go into service; and spent all his earnings in oil, which he swallowed in large quantities.

131. The Weiqi Devil

A CERTAIN general, who had resigned his command, and had retired to his own home, was very fond of roaming about and amusing himself with wine and *weiqi*,[567] One day—it was the 9th of the 9th moon, when everybody goes up high[568]—as he was playing with some friends, a stranger walked up, and watched the game intently for some time without going away. He was a miserable-looking creature, with a very ragged coat, but nevertheless possessed of a refined and courteous air. The general begged him to be seated, an offer which he accepted, being all the time extremely

---

565 This corresponds to our ceremony of laying the foundation stone, except that one commemorates the beginning, the other the completion, of a new building.

566 That is, the disembodied spirit of the oilman.

567 A most abstruse and complicated game of skill, for which the Chinese claim an antiquity of four thousand years, and which I was the first to introduce to a European public through an article in the *Temple Bar Magazine* for January 1877. *A propos* of which, an accomplished American lady, Miss A. M. Fielde, of Swatow, wrote as follows: "The game seems to me the peer of chess... It is a game for the slow, persistent, astute, multitudinous Chinese; while chess, by the picturesque appearance of the board, the variety and prominent individuality of the men, and the erratic combination of the attack, is for the Anglo-Saxon."

568 On this day, annually dedicated to kite-flying, picnics, and good cheer, everybody tries to get up to as great an elevation as possible, in the hope, as some say, of thereby prolonging life. It was this day—4th October, 1878—which was fixed for the total extermination of foreigners in Foochow.

deferential in his manner. "I suppose you are pretty good at this," said the general, pointing to the board; "try a bout with one of my friends here." The stranger made a great many apologies in reply, but finally accepted, and played a game in which, apparently to his great disappointment, he was beaten. He played another with the same result; and now, refusing all offers of wine, he seemed to think of nothing but how to get someone to play with him. Thus he went on until the afternoon was well advanced; when suddenly, just as he was in the middle of a most exciting game, which depended on a single place, he rushed forward, and throwing himself at the feet of the general, loudly implored his protection. The general did not know what to make of this; however, he raised him up, and said, "It's only a game: why get so excited?" To this the stranger replied by begging the general not to let his gardener seize him; and when the general asked what gardener he meant, he said the man's name was Ma Cheng. Now this Ma Cheng was often employed as a lictor by the Ruler of Purgatory, and would sometimes remain away as much as ten days, serving the warrants of death; accordingly, the general sent off to inquire about him, and found that he had been in a trance for two days.[569] His master cried out that he had better not behave rudely to his guest, but at that very moment the stranger sank down to the ground, and was gone. The general was lost in astonishment; however, he now knew that the man was a disembodied spirit, and on the next day, when Ma Cheng came around, he asked him for full particulars. "The gentleman was a native of Huxiang," replied the gardener, "who was passionately addicted to *weiqi,* and had lost a great deal of money by it. His father, being much grieved at his behavior, confined him to the house; but he was always getting out, and indulging the fatal passion, and at last his father died of a broken heart. In consequence of this, the Ruler of Purgatory curtailed his term of life, and condemned him to become a hungry devil,[570] in which state he has already passed seven years. And now that the Phoenix Tower[571] is completed, an order has been issued for the literati to present themselves, and compose an inscription to be cut on stone, as a memorial thereof, by which means they would secure their own salvation as a reward. Many of the shades failing to arrive at the appointed time, God was very angry with the Ruler of Purgatory, and

---

569 See note 148 in tale number 26.

570 One of the *prêtas,* or the fourth of the six paths (*gati*) of existence; the other five being (1) angels, (2) men, (3) demons, (5) brute beasts, and (6) sinners in hell. The term is often used colloquially for a self-invited guest.

571 An imaginary building in the Infernal Regions.

the latter sent off me, and others who are employed in the same way, to hunt up the defaulters. But as you, Sir, bade me treat the gentleman with respect, I did not venture to bind him." The general inquired what had become of the stranger; to which the gardener replied, "He is now a mere menial in Purgatory, and can never be born again." "Alas!" cried his master, "thus it is that men are ruined by any inordinate passion." [572]

132. The Fortune-Hunter Punished

A CERTAIN man's uncle had no children and the nephew, with an eye to his uncle's property, volunteered to become his adopted son.[573] When the uncle died all the property passed accordingly to his nephew, who thereupon broke faith as to his part of the contract.[574] He did the same with another uncle, and thus united three properties in his own person, whereby he became the richest man of the neighborhood. Suddenly he fell ill, and seemed to go out of his mind; for he cried out, "So you wish to live in wealth, do you?" and immediately seizing a sharp knife, he began hacking away at his own body until he had strewed the floor with pieces of flesh. He then exclaimed, "You cut off other people's posterity and expect to have posterity yourself, do you?" and forthwith he ripped himself open and died. Shortly afterwards his son, too, died, and the property fell into the hands of strangers. Is not this a retribution to be dreaded?

133. Life Prolonged

A CERTAIN cloth merchant of Changqing was stopping at Taian, when he heard of a magician who was said to be very skilled in casting nativities. So he went off at once to consult him; but the magician would not undertake the task, saying, "Your destiny is bad: you had better hurry home." At this the merchant was dreadfully frightened, and, packing up his wares, set off

---

572 Mencius reckoned "to play *weiqi* for money" among the five unfilial acts.
573 See note 276 in tale number 55; and note 456 in tale number 94.
574 That is, in carrying out the obligations he had entered into, such as conducting the ceremonies of ancestral worship, repairing the family tombs, etc.

towards Changqing. On the way he fell in with a man in short clothes,[575] like a constable; and the two soon struck up a friendly intimacy, taking their meals together. By-and-by the merchant asked the stranger what his business was; and the latter told him he was going to Changqing to serve summonses, producing at the same time a document and showing it to the merchant, who, on looking closely, saw a list of names, at the head of which was his own. In great astonishment he inquired what he had done that he should be arrested thus; to which his companion replied, "I am not a living being: I am a lictor in the employ of the infernal authorities, and I presume your term of life has expired." The merchant burst into tears and implored the lictor to spare him, which the latter declared was impossible; "But," added he, "there are a great many names down, and it will take me some time to get through them: you go off home and settle up your affairs, and, as a slight return for your friendship, I'll call for you last." A few minutes afterwards they reached a stream where the bridge was in ruins, and people could only cross with great difficulty; at which the lictor remarked, "You are now on the road to death, and not a single cash can you carry away with you. Repair this bridge and benefit the public; and thus from a great outlay you may possibly yourself derive some small advantage." The merchant said he would do so; and when he got home, he bade his wife and children prepare for his coming dissolution, and at the same time set men to work and made the bridge sound and strong again. Some time elapsed, but no lictor arrived; and his suspicions began to be aroused, when one day the latter walked in and said, "I reported that affair of the bridge to the Municipal God,[576] who communicated it to the Ruler of Purgatory; and for that good act your span of life has been lengthened, and your name struck out of the list. I have now come to announce this to you." The merchant was profuse in his thanks; and the next time he went to Taian, he burnt a quantity of paper ingots,[577] and made offerings and libations to the lictor, out of gratitude for what he had done. Suddenly the lictor himself appeared and cried out, "Do you wish to ruin me? Happily my new master has only just taken up his post, and he has not noticed this, or where should I be?"[578]

---

575 The long flowing robe is a sign of respectability which all but the very poorest classes love to affect in public. At the port of Haiphong, *shoes* are the criterion of social standing; but, as a rule, the well-to-do native merchants prefer to go barefoot rather than give the authorities a chance of exacting heavier squeezes, on the strength of such a palpable acknowledgment of wealth.

576 See note 1 in tale number 1.

577 See note 283 in tale number 56; and note 469 in tale number 97.

578 The lictor had no right to divulge his errand when he first met the cloth merchant, or to remove the latter's name from the top to the bottom of the list.

The lictor then escorted the merchant some distance; and, at parting, bade him never return by that road, but, if he had any business at Taian, to go thither by a roundabout way.

134. The Clay Image

ON the river I there lived a man named Ma, who married a wife from the Wang family, with whom he was very happy in his domestic life. Ma, however, died young; and his wife's parents were unwilling that their daughter should remain a widow, but she resisted all their importunities, and declared firmly she would never marry again. "It is a noble resolve of yours, I allow," argued her mother; "but you are still a mere girl, and you have no children. Besides, I notice that people who start with such rigid determinations always end by doing something discreditable, and therefore you had better get married as soon as you can, which is no more than is done every day." The girl swore she would rather die than consent, and accordingly her mother had no alternative but to let her alone. She then ordered a clay image to be made, exactly resembling her late husband;[579] and whenever she took her own meals, she would set meat and wine before it, precisely as if her husband had been there. One night she was on the point of retiring to rest, when suddenly she saw the clay image stretch itself and step down from the table, increasing all the while in height, until it was as tall as a man, and neither more nor less than her own husband. In great alarm she called out to her mother, but the image stopped her, saying, "Don't do that! I am but showing my gratitude for your affectionate care of me, and it is chill and uncomfortable in the realms below. Such devotion as yours casts its light back on generations gone by; and now I, who was cut off in my prime because my father did evil, and was condemned to be without an heir, have been permitted, in consequence of your virtuous conduct, to visit you once again, that our ancestral line may yet remain unbroken."[580] Every morning at cock-crow her husband resumed his usual form and size as the clay image; and

---

579 The clay image makers of Tianjin are wonderfully clever in taking likenesses by these means. Some of the most skillful will even manipulate the clay behind their backs, and then, adding the proper colors, will succeed in producing an exceedingly good resemblance. They find, however, more difficulty with foreign faces, to which they are less accustomed in the trade.
580 See note 312 in tale number 61.

after a time he told her that their hour of separation had come, upon which husband and wife bade each other an eternal farewell. By-and-by the widow, to the great astonishment of her mother, bore a son, which caused no small amusement among the neighbors who heard the story; and, as the girl herself had no proof of what she stated to be the case, a certain beadle[581] of the place, who had an old grudge against her husband, went off and informed the magistrate of what had occurred. After some investigation, the magistrate exclaimed, "I have heard that the children of disembodied spirits have no shadow; and that those who have shadows are not genuine." Thereupon they took Ma's child into the sunshine, and lo! there was but a very faint shadow, like a thin vapor. The magistrate then drew blood from the child, and smeared it on the clay image; upon which the blood at once soaked in and left no stain. Another clay image being produced and the same experiment tried, the blood remained on the surface so that it could be wiped away.[582] The girl's story was thus acknowledged to be true; and when the child grew up, and in every feature was the counterpart of Ma, there was no longer any room for suspicion.

135. Dishonesty Punished

At Jiaozhou there lived a man named Liu Xiquan, who was steward to His Excellency Mr. Fa. When already over forty a son was born to him, whom he loved very dearly, and quite spoilt by always letting him have his own way. When the boy grew up he led a dissolute, extravagant life, and ran through all his father's property. By-and-by he fell sick, and then he declared that nothing would cure him but a slice off a fat old favorite mule they had; upon which his father had another and more worthless animal killed; but his son found out he was being tricked, and, after abusing his father soundly, his symptoms became more and more alarming. The mule was accordingly killed, and some of it was served up to the sick man; however, he only just tasted it and sent the rest away. From that time he got gradually worse and worse, and finally died, to the great grief of his father, who would gladly have died too. Three or four years afterwards, as some of the villagers

---

581 See note 340 in tale number 64.
582 Such is the officially authorized method of determining a doubtful relationship between a dead parent and a living child, substituting a bone for the clay image here mentioned.

were worshipping on Mount Dai, they saw a man riding on a mule, the very image of Mr. Liu's dead son; and, on approaching more closely, they saw that it was actually he.[583] Jumping from his mule,[584] he made them a salutation, and then they began to chat with him on various subjects, always carefully avoiding that one of his own death. They asked him what he was doing there; to which he replied that he was only roaming about, and inquired of them in his turn at what inn they were staying; "For," added he, "I have an engagement just now, but I will visit you tomorrow." So they told him the name of the inn, and took their leave, not expecting to see him again. However, the next day he came, and, tying his mule to a post outside, went in to see them. "Your father," observed one of the villagers, "is always thinking about you. Why do you not go and pay him a visit?" The young man asked to whom he was alluding; and, at the mention of his father's name, he changed color and said, "If he is anxious to see me, kindly tell him that on the 7th of the 4th moon I will await him here." He then went away, and the villagers returned and told Mr. Liu all that had taken place. At the appointed time the latter was very desirous of going to see his son; but his master dissuaded him, saying that he thought from what he knew of his son that the interview might possibly not turn out as he would desire; "Although," added he, "if you are bent upon going, I should be sorry to stand in your way. Let me, however, counsel you to conceal yourself in a cupboard, and thus, by observing what takes place, you will know better how to act, and avoid running into any danger." This he accordingly did, and, when his son came, Mr. Fa received him at the inn. "Where's Mr. Liu?" cried the son. "Oh, he hasn't come," replied Mr. Fa. "The old beast! What does he mean by that?" exclaimed his son; whereupon Mr. Fa asked him what *he* meant by cursing his own father. "My father!" shrieked the son; "why, he's nothing more to me than a former rascally partner in trade, who cheated me out of all my money, and for which I have since avenged myself on him.[585] What sort of a father is that, I should like to know?" He then went out of the door; and his father crept out of the cupboard from which, with the perspiration streaming down him and hardly daring to breathe, he had heard all that had passed, and sorrowfully wended his way home again.

---

583 "In various savage superstitions the minute resemblance of soul to body is forcibly stated."—*Myths and Myth-makers*, by John Fiske, p. 228.

584 An important point in Chinese etiquette. It is not considered polite for a person in a sitting position to address an equal who is standing.

585 By becoming his son and behaving badly to him. See note 509 in tale number 110, and the text to which it refers.

136. The Mad Priest

A CERTAIN mad priest, whose name I do not know, lived in a temple on the hills. He would sing and cry by turns, without any apparent reason; and once somebody saw him boiling a stone for his dinner. At the autumn festival of the 9th day of the 9th moon,[586] an official of the district went up in that direction for the usual picnic, taking with him his chair and his red umbrellas. After luncheon he was passing by the temple, and had hardly reached the door, when out rushed the priest, barefooted and ragged, and, himself opening a yellow umbrella, cried out as the attendants of a mandarin do when ordering the people to stand back. He then approached the official, and made as though he were jesting at him; at which the latter was extremely indignant, and bade his servants drive the priest away. The priest moved off with the servants after him, and in another moment had thrown down his yellow umbrella, which split into a number of pieces, each piece changing immediately into a falcon, and flying about in all directions. The umbrella handle became a huge serpent, with red scales and glaring eyes; and then the party would have turned and fled, but that one of them declared it was only an optical delusion, and that the creature couldn't do any hurt. The speaker accordingly seized a knife and rushed at the serpent, which forthwith opened its mouth and swallowed its assailant whole. In a terrible fright the servants crowded around their master and hurried him away, not stopping to draw breath until they were fully a mile off. By-and-by several of them stealthily returned to see what was going on; and, on entering, the temple, they found that both priest and serpent had disappeared. But from an old ash-tree hard by they heard a sound proceeding—a sound, as it were, of a donkey panting; and at first they were afraid to go near, though after a while they ventured to peep through a hole in the tree, which was an old hollow trunk; and there, jammed hard and fast with his head downwards, was the rash assailant of the serpent. It being quite impossible to drag him out, they began at once to cut the tree away; but by the time they had set him free he was already perfectly unconscious. However, he ultimately came around and was carried home; but from this day the priest was never seen again.[587]

---

586 See note 568 in tale number 131.
587 The story is intended as a satire on those puffed-up dignitaries who cannot even go to a picnic without all the retinue belonging to their particular rank. See note 281 in tale number 56.

137. Feasting the Ruler of Purgatory

AT Jinghai there lived a young man, named Shao, whose family was very poor. On the occasion of his mother completing her cycle,[588] he arranged a quantity of meat-offerings and wine on a table in the court-yard, and proceeded to invoke the Gods in the usual manner; but when he rose from his knees, lo and behold! all the meat and wine had disappeared. His mother thought this was a bad omen, and that she was not destined to enjoy a long life; however, she said nothing on the subject to her son, who was himself quite at a loss to account for what had happened. A short time afterwards the Literary Chancellor[589] arrived; and young Shao, scraping together what funds he could, went off to present himself as a candidate. On the road he met with a man who gave him such a cordial invitation to his house that he willingly accepted; and the stranger led him to a stately mansion, with towers and terraces rising one above the other as far as the eye could reach. In one of the apartments was a king, sitting upon a throne, who received Shao in a very friendly manner; and, after regaling him with an excellent banquet, said, "I have to thank you for the food and drink you gave my servants that day we passed your house." Shao was greatly astonished at this remark, when the King proceeded, "I am the Ruler of Purgatory. Don't you recollect sacrificing on your mother's birthday?" The King then bestowed on Shao a packet of silver, saying, "Pray accept this in return for your kindness." Shao thanked him and retired; and in another moment the palace and its occupants had one and all vanished from his sight, leaving him alone in the midst of some tall trees. On opening his packet he found it to contain five ounces of pure gold; and, after defraying the expenses of his examination, half was still left, which he carried home and gave to his mother.

138. The Picture Horse

A CERTAIN Mr. Cui, of Linqing, was too poor to keep his garden walls in repair, and used often to find a strange horse lying down on the grass inside. It was a black horse marked with white, and having a scrubby tail, which looked

---

588 See note 120 in tale number 23.
589 The examiner for the bachelor's, or lowest, degree.

as if the end had been burnt off;[590] and, though always driven away, would still return to the same spot. Now Mr. Cui had a friend, who was holding an appointment in Shanxi; and though he had frequently felt desirous of paying him a visit, he had no means of traveling so far. Accordingly, he one day caught the strange horse, and, putting a saddle on its back, rode away, telling his servants that if the owner of the horse should appear, he was to inform him where the animal was to be found. The horse started off at a very rapid pace, and, in a short time, they were thirty or forty miles from home; but at night it did not seem to care for its food, so the next day Mr. Cui, who thought perhaps illness might be the cause, held the horse in, and would not let it gallop so fast. However, the animal did not seem to approve of this, and kicked and foamed until at length Mr. Cui let it go at the same old pace; and by midday he had reached his destination. As he rode into the town, the people were astonished to hear of the marvelous journey just accomplished, and the Prince[591] sent to say he should like to buy the horse. Mr. Cui, fearing that the real owner might come forward, was compelled to refuse this offer; but when, after six months had elapsed, no inquiries had been made, he agreed to accept eight hundred ounces of silver, and handed over the horse to the Prince. He then bought himself a good mule, and returned home. Subsequently, the Prince had occasion to use the horse for some important business at Linqing; and when there it took the opportunity to run away. The officer in charge pursued it right up to the house of a Mr. Zeng, who lived next door to Mr. Cui, and saw it run in and disappear. Thereupon he called upon Mr. Zeng to restore it to him; and, on the latter declaring he had never even seen the animal, the officer walked into his private apartments, where he found, hanging on the wall, a picture of a horse, by Chen Ziang,[592] exactly like the one he was in search of, and with part of the tail burnt away by a joss-stick. It was now clear that the Prince's horse was a supernatural creature; but the officer, being afraid to go back without it, would have prosecuted Mr. Zeng, had not Cui, whose eight hundred ounces of silver had since increased to something like ten thousand, stepped in and paid back the original purchase-money. Mr. Zeng was exceedingly grateful to him for this act of kindness, ignorant, as he was, of the previous sale of the horse by Cui to the Prince.

---

590 The Chinese never cut the tails of their horses or mules.
591 One of the feudal Governors of bygone days.
592 656–698 CE. Better known as a poet.

139. The Butterfly's Revenge

MR. WANG, of Changshan, was in the habit, when a District Magistrate, of commuting the fines and penalties of the Penal Code, inflicted on the various prisoners, for a corresponding number of butterflies. These he would let go all at once in the court, rejoicing to see them fluttering hither and thither, like so many tinsel snippings borne about by the breeze; One night he dreamt that a young lady, dressed in gay-colored clothes, appeared to him and said, "Your cruel practice has brought many of my sisters to an untimely end, and now you shall pay the penalty of thus gratifying your tastes." The young lady then changed into a butterfly and flew away. Next day, the magistrate was sitting alone, over a cup of wine, when it was announced to him that the censor was at the door; and out he ran at once to receive His Excellency, with a white flower, that some of his women had put in his official hat, still sticking there. His Excellency was very angry at what he deemed a piece of disrespect to himself; and, after severely censuring Mr. Wang, turned around and went away. Thenceforward no more penalties were commuted for butterflies.

140. The Doctor

A CERTAIN poor man, named Zhang, who lived at I, fell in one day with a Taoist priest. The latter was highly skilled in the science of physiognomy;[593] and, after looking at Zhang's features, said to him, "You would make your fortune as a doctor." "Alas!" replied Zhang, "I can barely read and write; how then could I follow such a calling as that?" "And where, you simple fellow," asked the priest, "is the necessity for a doctor to be a scholar? You just try, that's all." Thereupon Zhang returned home; and, being very poor, he. simply collected a few of the commonest prescriptions, and set up a small stall with a handful of fishes' teeth and some dry honey-comb from a wasp's nest,[594] hoping thus to earn, by his tongue, enough to keep body and soul together, to which, however, no one paid any particular attention. Now it chanced that just then the Governor of Qingzhou was suffering from a bad cough, and had given orders to his subordinates to

---

593 Advertisements of these professors of physiognomy are to be seen in every Chinese city.
594 In order to make some show for the public eye.

send to him the most skillful doctors in their respective districts; and the magistrate of I, which was an out-of-the-way mountainous district, being unable to lay his hands on any one whom he could send in, gave orders to the beadle[595] to do the best he could under the circumstances. Accordingly, Zhang was nominated by the people, and the magistrate put his name down to go in to the Governor. When Zhang heard of his appointment, he happened to be suffering himself from a bad attack of bronchitis, which he was quite unable to cure, and he begged, therefore, to be excused; but the magistrate would not hear of this, and forwarded him at once in charge of some constables. While crossing the hills, he became very thirsty, and went into a village to ask for a drink of water; but water there was worth its weight in jade, and no one would give him any. By-and-by he saw an old woman washing a quantity of vegetables in a scanty supply of water, which was consequently, very thick and muddy; and, being unable to bear his thirst any longer, he obtained this and drank it up. Shortly afterwards he found that his cough was quite cured, and then it occurred to him that he had hit upon a capital remedy. When he reached the city, he learned that a great many doctors had already tried their hand upon the patient, but without success; so asking for a private room in which to prepare his medicines, he obtained from the town some bunches of bishop-wort, and proceeded to wash them as the old woman had done. He then took the dirty water, and gave a dose of it to the Governor, who was immediately and permanently relieved. The patient was overjoyed; and, besides making Zhang a handsome present, gave him a certificate written in golden characters, in consequence of which his fame spread far and wide;[596] and of the numerous cases he subsequently undertook, in not a single instance did he fail to effect a cure. One day, however, a patient came to him, complaining of a violent chill; and Zhang, who happened to be tipsy at the time, treated him by mistake for remittent fever. When he got sober, he became aware of what he had done; but he said nothing to anybody about it, and three days afterwards the same patient waited upon him with all kinds of presents to thank him for a rapid recovery. Such cases as this

---

595 See note 340 in tale number 64.

596 A doctor of any repute generally has large numbers of such certificates, generally engraved on wood, hanging before and about his front door. When I was stationed at Swatow, the Chinese writer at Her Majesty's Consulate presented one to Dr. E. J. Scott, the resident medical practitioner, who had cured him of opium-smoking. It bore two principal characters, "Miraculous Indeed!" accompanied by a few remarks, in a smaller-sized character, laudatory of Dr. Scott's professional skill. Banners, with graceful inscriptions written upon them, are frequently presented by Chinese passengers to the captains of coasting steamers who may have brought them safely through bad weather.

were by no means rare with him; and soon he got so rich that he would not attend when summoned to visit a sick person, unless the summons was accompanied by a heavy fee and a comfortable chair to ride in.[597]

141. Snow in Summer

ON the 6th day of the 7th moon[598] of the year *Dinghai* (1647) there was a heavy fall of snow at Soochow. The people were in a great state of consternation at this, and went off to the temple of the Great Prince[599] to pray. Then the spirit moved one of them to say, "You now address me as *Your Honor.* Make it *Your Excellency,* and, though I am but a lesser deity, it may be well worth your while to do so." Thereupon the people began to use the latter term, and the snow, stopped at once; from which I infer that flattery is just as pleasant to divine as to mortal ears.[600]

597 The story is intended as a satire upon Chinese doctors generally, whose ranks are recruited from the swarms of half-educated candidates who have been rejected at the great competitive examinations, medical diplomas being quite unknown in China. Doctors' fees are, by a pleasant fiction, called "horse-money;" and all prescriptions are made up by the local apothecary, never by the physician himself.
598 This would be exactly at the hottest season.
599 The *Jupiter Pluvius* of the neighborhood.
600 A sneer at the superstitious custom of praying for good or bad weather, which obtains in China from the Son of Heaven himself down to the lowest agriculturist whose interests are involved. Droughts, floods, famines, and pestilences are alike set down to the anger of Heaven, to be appeased only by prayer and repentance.

142. Planchette[601]

AT Changshan there lived a man, named Wang Ruiting, who understood the art of planchette. He called himself a disciple of Lü Dongbin,[602] and someone said he was probably that worthy's crane. At his *séances* the subjects were always literary—essays, poetry, and so on. The well-known scholar, Li Zhi, thought very highly of him, and availed himself of his aid on more than one occasion; so that by degrees the literati generally also patronized him. His responses to questions of doubt or difficulty were remarkable for their reasonableness; matters of mere good or bad fortune he did not care to enter into. In 1631, just after the examination at Jinan, a number of the candidates requested Mr. Wang to tell them how they would stand on the list; and after having examined their essays, he proceeded to pass his opinion on their merits.[603] Among the rest there happened to be one who was very intimate with another candidate, not present, whose name was Li Bian; and who, being an enthusiastic student and a deep thinker, was

---

601 Planchette was in full swing in China at the date of the composition of these stories, more than 200 years ago, and remains so at the present day. The character *ji*, used here and elsewhere for Planchette, is denned in the *Shuo Wen*, a Chinese dictionary, published 100 CE, "to inquire by divination on doubtful topics," no mention being made of the particular manner in which responses are obtained. For the purpose of writing from personal experience, I once attended a *séance* at a temple in Amoy, and witnessed the whole performance. After much delay, I was requested to write on a slip of paper "any question I might have to put to the God;" and, accordingly, I took a pencil and wrote down, "A humble suppliant ventures to inquire if he will win the Manila lottery." This question was then placed upon the altar, at the feet of the God; and shortly afterwards two respectable-looking Chinese men, not priests, approached a small table covered with sand, and each seized one arm of a forked piece of wood, at the fork of which was a stumpy end, at right angles to the plane of the arms. Immediately the attendants began burning quantities of joss-paper, while the two performers whirled the instrument around and around at a rapid rate, its vertical point being all the time pressed down upon the table of sand. All of a sudden the whirling movement stopped, and the point of the instrument rapidly traced a character in the sand, which was at once identified by several of the bystanders, and forthwith copied down by a clerk in attendance. The whirling movement was then continued until a similar pause was made and another character appeared; and so on, until I had four lines of correctly-rhymed Chinese verse, each line consisting of seven characters. The following is an almost word-for-word translation:

"The pulse of human nature throbs from England to Cathay,
And gambling mortals ever love to swell their gains by play;
For gold in this vile world of ours is everywhere a prize—
A thousand taels shall meet the prayer that on this altar lies."

As the question is not concealed from view, all that is necessary for such a hollow deception is a quick-witted versifier who can put together a poetical response *stans pede in uno*. But in such matters the unlettered masses of China are easily outwitted, and are a profitable source of income to the more astute of their fellow-countrymen.

602 A recluse who flourished in the eighth century of our era, and who, for his devotion to the Taoist religion, was subsequently canonized as one of the Eight Immortals. He is generally represented as riding on a crane.

603 That is, by means of the planchette-table.

confidently expected to appear among the successful few. Accordingly, the
friend submitted Mr. Li's essay for inspection; and in a few minutes two
characters appeared on the sand—namely, "Number one." After a short
interval this sentence followed: " The decision given just now had reference;
to Mr. Li's essay simply as an essay. Mr. Li's destiny is darkly obscured, and
he will suffer accordingly. It is strange, indeed, that a man's literary powers
and his destiny should thus be out of harmony.[604] Surely the Examiner will
judge of him by his essay; but stay: I will go and see how matters stand."
Another pause ensued, and then these words were written down: "I have
been over to the Examiner's yamen, and have found a pretty state of things
going on; instead of reading the candidates' papers himself, he has handed
them over to his clerks, some half-dozen illiterate fellows who purchased
their own degrees, and who, in their previous existence, had no status
whatever— 'hungry devils'[605] begging their bread in all directions; and who,
after eight hundred years passed in the murky gloom of the infernal regions,
have lost all discrimination, like men long buried in a cave and suddenly
transferred to the light of day. Among them may be one or two who have
risen above their former selves, but the odds are against an essay falling into
the hands of one of these." The young men then begged to know if there
was any method by which such an evil might be counteracted; to which
the planchette replied that there was, but, as it was universally understood,
there was no occasion for asking the question. Thereupon they went off and
told Mr. Li, who was so much distressed at the prediction that he submitted
his essay to His Excellency Sun Zimei, one of the finest scholars of the day.
This gentleman examined it, and was so pleased with its literary merit that
he told Li he was quite sure to pass, and the latter thought no more about
the planchette prophecy. However, when the list came out, there he was
down in the fourth class; and this so much disconcerted His Excellency
Mr. Sun, that he went carefully through the essay again for fear lest any
blemishes might have escaped his attention. Then he cried out, "Well, I
have always thought this Examiner to be a scholar; he can never have made
such a mistake as this; it must be the fault of some of his drunken assistants,
who don't know the mere rudiments of composition." This fulfilment of the
prophecy raised Mr. Wang very high in the estimation of the candidates,
who forthwith went and burned incense and invoked the spirit of the
planchette, which at once replied in the following terms: "Let not Mr. Li be

---

604 Our author was here evidently thinking of his own unlucky fate.
605 See note 570 in tale number 131.

disheartened by temporary failure. Let him rather strive to improve himself still further, and next year he may be among the first on the list." Li carried out these injunctions; and after a time the story reached the ears of the Examiner, who gratified Li by making a public acknowledgment that there had been some miscarriage of justice at the examination; and the following year he was passed high up on the list.[606]

143. Friendship with Foxes

A CERTAIN man had an enormous stack of straw, as big as a hill, in which his servants, taking what was daily required for use, had made quite a hole. In this hole a fox fixed his abode, and would often show himself to the master of the house under the form of an old man. One day the latter invited the master to walk into the cave, which he at first declined, but accepted on being pressed by the fox; and when he got inside, lo! he saw a long suite of handsome apartments. They then sat down, and exquisitely perfumed tea and wine were brought; but the place was so gloomy that there was no difference between night and day. By-and-by, the entertainment being over, the guest took his leave; and on looking back the beautiful rooms and their contents had all disappeared. The old man himself was in the habit of going away in the evening and returning with the first streaks of morning; and as no one was able to follow him, the master of the house asked him one day whither he went. To this he replied that a friend invited him to take wine; and then the master begged to be allowed to accompany him, a proposal to which the old man very reluctantly consented. However, he seized the master by the arm, and away they went as though riding on the wings of the wind; and, in about the time it takes to cook a pot of millet, they reached a city, and walked into a restaurant, where there were a number of people drinking together and making a great noise. The old man led his companion to a gallery above, from which they could look down on the feasters below; and he himself went down and brought away from the tables all kinds of nice food and wine, without appearing to be seen or noticed by any of the company. After awhile a man dressed in red garments came forward and laid upon the table some dishes of cumquats;[607] and the master at once

---

606 See note 392 in tale number 75.
607 Literally, "golden oranges." These are skillfully preserved by the Cantonese, and form a delicious

requested the old man to go down and get him some of these. "Ah," replied the latter, "that is an upright man: I cannot approach him." Thereupon the master said to himself, "By thus seeking the companionship of a fox, I then am deflected from the true course. Henceforth I, too, will be an upright man." No sooner had he formed this resolution, than he suddenly lost all control over his body, and fell from the gallery down among the revellers below. These gentlemen were much astonished by his unexpected descent; and he himself, looking up, saw there was no gallery to the house, but only a large beam upon which he had been sitting. He now detailed the whole of the circumstances, and those present made up a purse for him to pay his traveling expenses; for he was at Youtai—one thousand *li* from home.

144. The Great Rat

DURING the reign of the Emperor Wan Li,[608] the palace was troubled by the presence of a huge rat, quite as big as a cat, which ate up all the cats that were set to catch it. Just then it chanced that among the tribute offerings sent by some foreign State was a lion-cat, as white as snow. This cat was accordingly put into the room where the rat usually appeared; and, the door being closely shut, a secret watch was kept. By-and-by the rat came out of its hole and rushed at the cat, which turned and fled, finally jumping up on the table. The rat followed, upon which the cat jumped down; and thus they went on up and down for some time. Those who were watching said the cat was afraid and of no use; however, in a little while the rat began to jump less briskly, and soon after squatted down out of breath. Then the cat rushed at it, and, seizing the rat by the back of the neck, shook and shook while its victim squeaked and squeaked, until life was extinct. Thus they knew that the cat was not afraid, but merely waited for its adversary to be fatigued, fleeing when pursued and itself, pursuing the fleeing rat. Truly, many a bad swordsman may be compared with that rat!

---

sweetmeat for dessert.
608 1573–1620 CE, the epoch of the most celebrated "Blue China."

145. Wolves

I. A CERTAIN village butcher, who had bought some meat at market and was returning home in the evening, suddenly came across a wolf, which followed him closely, its mouth watering at the sight of what he was carrying. The butcher drew his knife and drove the animal off; and then reflecting that his meat was the attraction, he determined to hang it up in a tree and fetch it the next morning. This he accordingly did, and the wolf followed him no further; but when he went at daylight to recover his property, he saw something hanging up in the tree resembling a human corpse. It turned out to be the wolf, which, in its efforts to get at the meat, had been caught on the meat-hook like a fish; and as the skin of a wolf was just then worth ten ounces of silver, the butcher found himself possessed of quite a little capital. Here we have a laughable instance of the result of "climbing trees to catch fish."[609]

II. A butcher, while traveling aione at night, was sore pressed by a wolf, and took refuge in an old mat shed which had been put up for the watchman of the crops. There he lay, while the wolf sniffed at him from outside, and at length thrust in one of its paws from underneath. This the butcher seized hold of at once, and held it firmly, so that the wolf couldn't stir; and then, having no other weapon at hand, he took a small knife he had with him and slit the skin underneath the wolf's paw. He now proceeded to blow into it, as butchers blow into pork;[610] and after vigorously blowing for some time, he found that the wolf had ceased to struggle; upon which he went outside and saw the animal lying on the ground, swelled up to the size of a cow, and unable to bend its legs or close its open mouth. Thereupon he threw it across his shoulders and carried it off home. However, such a feat as this could only be accomplished by a butcher.

609 A satirical remark of Mencius (Book I.), used by the sage when combating the visionary projects of a monarch of antiquity.
610 This disgusting process is too frequently performed by native butchers at the present day, in order to give their meat a more tempting appearance. Water is also blown in through a tube, to make it heavier; and inexperienced housekeepers are often astonished to find how light ducks and geese become after being cooked, not knowing that the fraudulent poulterer had previously stuffed their throats as full as possible of sand.

146. A Singular Verdict

A SERVANT in the employ of a Mr. Sun was sleeping alone one night, when all of a sudden he was arrested and carried before the tribunal of the Ruler of Purgatory. "This is not the right man," cried His Majesty, and immediately sent him back. However, after this the servant was afraid to sleep on that bed again, and took up his quarters elsewhere. But another servant, named Guo An, seeing the vacant place, went and occupied it. A third servant, named Li Lu, who had an old standing grudge against the first, stole up to the bed that same night with a knife in his hand, and killed Guo An[611] in mistake for his enemy. Guo's father at once brought the case before the magistrate of the place, pleading that the murdered man was his only son on whom he depended for his living; and the magistrate decided that Guo was to take Li Lu in the place of his dead son, much to the discomfiture of the old man. Truly the descent of the first servant into Purgatory was not so marvelous as the magistrate's decision!

147. The Grateful Dog

A CERTAIN trader who had been doing business at Wuhu and was returning home with the large profits he had made, saw on the river-bank a butcher tying up a dog.[612] He bought the animal for much more than its value, and carried it along with him in his boat. Now the boatman had formerly been a bandit; and, tempted by his passenger's wealth, ran the boat among the rushes, and, drawing a knife, prepared to slay him. The trader begged the man to leave him a whole skin;[613] so the boatman wrapped him up in a carpet and threw him into the river. The dog, on seeing what was done, whined piteously, and, jumping into the river, seized the bundle with his teeth and did his best to keep the trader above water until at length a shallow spot was reached. The animal then succeeded by continuous barking in attracting the attention of some people on the bank, and they

---

611 This was the man whose destiny it was really to die just then, and appear before the Ruler of Purgatory.

612 The city of Canton boasts several "cat and dog" restaurants; but the consumption of this kind of food is much less universal than is generally supposed.

613 Not in our sense of the term. It was not death, but decapitation, or even mutilation, from which the trader begged to be spared. See note 382 in tale number 72.

hauled the bundle out of the river, and released the trader, who was still alive. The latter asked to be taken back to Wuhu, where he might look out for the robber boatman; but just as he was about to start, lo! the dog was missing. The trader was much distressed at this; and after spending some days at Wuhu without being able to find, among the forest of masts collected there, the particular boat he wanted, he was on the point of returning home with a friend, when suddenly the dog reappeared, and seemed by its barking to invite its master to follow in a certain direction. This the trader did, until at length the dog jumped on a boat and seized one of the boatmen by the leg. No beating could make the animal let go; and on looking closely at the man, the trader saw he was the identical boatman who had robbed and tried to murder him. He had changed his clothes and also his boat, so that at first he was not recognizable; he was now, however, arrested, and the whole of the money was found in his boat. To think that a dog could show gratitude like that! Truly there are not a few persons who would be put to shame by that faithful animal.[614]

148. The Great Test

BEFORE Mr. Yang Dahong[615] was known to fame, he had already acquired some reputation as a scholar in his own part of the country, and felt convinced himself that his was to be no mean destiny. When the list of successful candidates at the examination was brought to where he lived, he was in the middle of dinner, and rushed out with his mouth full to ask if his name was there or not; and on hearing that it was not, he experienced such a revulsion of feeling that what he then swallowed stuck fast like a lump in his chest and made him very ill. His friends tried to appease him by advising him to try at the further examination of the rejected, and when he argued that he had no money, they subscribed ten ounces of silver and started him on his way.

---

614 The Chinese dog is usually an ill-fed, barking cur, without one redeeming trait in its character. Valued as a guardian of house and property, this animal does not hold the same social position as wth us; its very name is a byword of reproach; and the people of Dongjing explain their filthy custom of blackening the teeth on the ground that a dog's teeth are white.
615 A celebrated scholar and statesman, who flourished towards the close of the Ming dynasty, and distinguished himself by his impeachment of the powerful eunuch, Wei Zhongxian—a dangerous step to take in those eunuch-ridden times.

That night he dreamt that a man appeared to him and said, "Ahead of you there is one who can cure your complaint: beseech him to aid you." The man then added:

A tune on the flute 'neath the riverside willow;
Oh, show no regret when 'tis cast to the billow!

Next day, Mr. Yang actually met a Taoist priest sitting beneath a willow tree; and, making him a bow, asked him to prescribe for his malady. "You have come to the wrong person," replied the priest, smiling; "I cannot cure diseases; but had you asked me for a tune on the flute, I could have possibly helped you." Then Mr. Yang knew that his dream was being fulfilled; and going down on his knees offered the priest all the money he had. The priest took it, but immediately threw it into the river, at which Mr. Yang, thinking how hardly he had come by his money, was moved to express his regret. "Aha!" cried the priest at this; "so you are not indifferent, eh? You'll find your money all safe on the bank." There indeed Mr. Yang found it, at which he was so much astonished that he addressed the priest as though he had been an angel. "I am no angel," said the priest, "but here comes one;" whereupon Mr. Yang looked behind him, and the priest seized the opportunity to give him a slap on the back, crying out at the same time, "You worldly-minded fellow!" This blow brought up the lump of food that had stuck in his chest, and he felt better at once; but when he looked around the priest had disappeared.[616]

149. The Alchemist[617]

AT Changan there lived a scholar named Jia Zilong, who one day noticed a very refined-looking stranger; and, on making inquiries about him, learnt that he was a Mr. Zhen who had taken lodgings hard by. Accordingly, next

---

616 Mr. Yang was a man of tried virtue, and had he been able to tolerate the loss of his money, the priest would have given him, not merely a cure for the bodily ailment under which he was suffering, but a knowledge of those means by which he might have obtained the salvation of his soul, and have enrolled himself among the ranks of the Taoist Immortals. "To those, however," remarks the author, "who lament that Mr. Yang was too worldly-minded to secure this great prize, I reply, 'Better one more good man on earth, than an extra angel in heaven.'"

617 Alchemy is first mentioned in Chinese history 133 BCE, and was widely cultivated in China during the Han dynasty by priests of the Taoist religion.

day Jia called and sent in his card, but did not see Zhen, who happened to be out at the time. The same thing occurred thrice, and at length Jia engaged someone to watch and let him know when Mr. Zhen was at home. However, even then the latter would not come forth to receive his guest, and Jia had to go in and rout him out. The two now entered into conversation, and soon became mutually charmed with each other; and by-and-by Jia sent off a servant to bring wine from a neighboring wineshop. Mr. Zhen proved himself a pleasant boon companion, and when the wine was nearly finished, he went to a box and took from it some wine-cups and a large and beautiful jade tankard, into the latter of which he poured a single cup of wine, and lo! it was filled to the brim. They then proceeded to help themselves from the tankard; but however much they took out, the contents never seemed to diminish. Jia was astonished at this, and begged Mr. Zhen to tell him how it was done. "Ah," replied Mr. Zhen, "I tried to avoid making your acquaintance solely because of your one bad quality— avarice. The art I practice is a secret known to the Immortals only: how can I divulge it to you?" "You do me wrong," rejoined Jia, "in thus attributing avarice to me. The avaricious, indeed, are always poor." Mr. Zhen laughed, and they separated for that day; but from that time they were constantly together, and all ceremony was laid aside between them. Whenever Jia wanted money, Mr. Zhen would bring out a black stone, and, muttering a charm, would rub it on a tile or a brick, which was forthwith changed into a lump of silver. This silver he would give to Jia, and it was always just as much as he actually required, neither more nor less; and if ever the latter asked for more, Mr. Zhen would rally him on the subject of avarice. Finally, Jia determined to try and get possession of this stone; and one day, when Mr. Zhen was sleeping off the fumes of a drinking-bout, he tried to extract it from his clothes. However, Zhen detected him at once, and declared that they could be friends no more, and next day he left the place altogether. About a year afterwards Jia was one day wandering by the river-bank, when he saw a handsome-looking stone, marvelously like that in the possession of Mr. Zhen; and he picked it up at once and carried it home with him. A few days passed away, and suddenly Mr. Zhen presented himself at Jia's house, and explained that the stone in question possessed the property of changing anything into gold, and had been bestowed upon him long before by a certain Taoist priest, whom he had followed as a disciple. "Alas!" added he, "I got tipsy and lost it; but divination told me where it was, and if you will now restore it to me, I shall take care to repay your kindness." "You have divined rightly," replied Jia; "the stone is with me; but recollect, if you please, that the indigent Guan Zhong[618] shared the wealth of his friend Bao Shu." At this hint Mr. Zhen said he would give Jia one hundred ounces of silver; to which the latter replied that one hundred ounces was a fair offer, but that he would far sooner have Mr. Zhen teach him the formula to utter when rubbing the stone on anything, so as just to try the thing once himself. Mr. Zhen was afraid to do this; whereupon Jia cried out, "You are an Immortal yourself; you must know well enough that I would never deceive a friend." So Mr. Zhen was prevailed upon to teach him the formula, and then Jia would have tried the art upon the immense stone washing-block[619] which was lying near at hand had not Mr. Zhen seized his arm and begged him not to do anything so outrageous. Jia then picked up half a brick and laid it on the washing-block, saying to Mr. Zhen, "This little piece is not too much, surely?" Accordingly, Mr. Zhen relaxed his hold and let Jia proceed; which he did by promptly ignoring the half brick and quickly rubbing the stone on the washing-block. Mr. Zhen turned pale when he saw him do this, and made a dash forward to get hold of the stone; but it was too late, the washing-block was already a solid mass of silver, and Jia quietly handed him back the stone. "Alas! alas!" cried Mr. Zhen in despair, "what is to be done now? For having thus irregularly conferred wealth upon a mortal,[620] Heaven will surely punish me. Oh, if you would save me, give away one hundred coffins[621] and one hundred suits of wadded clothes." "My friend," replied Jia, "my object in getting money was not to hoard it up like a miser." Mr. Zhen was delighted at this; and during the next three years Jia engaged in trade, taking care to be all the time fulfilling his promise to Mr. Zhen. At the expiration of that time Mr. Zhen himself reappeared, and, grasping Jia's hand, said to him, "Trustworthy and noble friend, when we last parted the Spirit of Happiness impeached me before God,[622] and my name was erased from the list of angels. But now that you have carried out my request, that sentence has accordingly been rescinded. Go on as you have begun, without ceasing." Jia asked Mr. Zhen what office he filled in heaven; to which the latter replied that he was only a fox, who,

---

619 These are used, together with a heavy wooden *bâton,* by the Chinese washerman, the effect being most disastrous to a European wardrobe.
620 For thus interfering with the appointments of Destiny.
621 To provide coffins for poor people has ever been regarded as an act of transcendent merit. The tornado at Canton in April 1878, in which several thousand lives were lost, afforded an admirable opportunity for the exercise of this form of charity—an opportunity which was very largely availed of by the benevolent.
622 For usurping its prerogative by allowing Jia to obtain unauthorized wealth.

by a sinless life, had finally attained to that clear perception of the Truth which leads to immortality. Wine was then brought, and the two friends enjoyed themselves together as of old; and even when Jia had passed the age of ninety years, that fox still used to visit him from time to time.

150. Raising the Dead

Mr. Tang Ping, who took the highest degree in the year 1661, was suffering from a protracted illness, when suddenly he felt, as it were, a warm glow rising from his extremities upwards. By the time it had reached his knees, his feet were perfectly numb and without sensation; and before long his knees and the lower part of his body were similarly affected. Gradually this glow worked its way up until it attacked the heart,[623] and then some painful moments ensued. Every single incident of Mr. Tang's life from his boyhood upwards, no matter how trivial, seemed to surge through his mind, borne along on the tide of his heart's blood. At the revival of any virtuous act of his, he experienced a delicious feeling of peace and calm; but when any wicked deed passed before his mind, a painful disturbance took place within him, like oil boiling and fretting in a cauldron. He was quite unable to describe the pangs he suffered; however, he mentioned that he could recollect having stolen, when only seven or eight years old, some young birds from their nest, and having killed them; and for this alone, he said, boiling blood rushed through his heart during the space of an ordinary meal-time. Then when all the acts of his life had passed one after another in panorama before him, the warm glow proceeded up his throat, and, entering the brain, issued out at the top of his head like smoke from a chimney. By-and-by Mr. Tang's soul escaped from his body by the same aperture, and wandered far away, forgetting all about the tenement it had left behind. Just at that moment a huge giant came along, and, seizing the soul, thrust it into his sleeve, where it remained cramped and confined, huddled up with a crowd of others, until existence was almost unbearable. Suddenly Mr. Dang reflected that Buddha alone could save him from this horrible state, and forthwith he began to call upon his holy name.[624] At the third or fourth invocation he fell out of the giant's sleeve, whereupon the latter picked him up and put him back; but

---

623 See note 64 in tale number 14.
624 See note 260 in tale number 54.

this happened several times, and at length the giant, wearied of picking him up, let him lie where he was. The soul lay there for some time, not knowing in which direction to proceed; however, it soon recollected that the land of Buddha was in the west, and westwards accordingly it began to shape its course. In a little while the soul came upon a Buddhist priest sitting by the roadside, and hastening forwards, respectfully inquired of him which was the right way. "The record of life and death for scholars," replied the priest, "is in the hands of Wenchang[625] and Confucius; any application must receive the consent of both." The priest then directed Mr. Tang on his way, and the latter journeyed along until he reached a Confucian temple, in which the Sage was sitting with his face to the south.[626] On hearing his business, Confucius referred him on to Wenchang; and, proceeding onwards in the direction indicated, Mr. Tang by-and-by arrived at what seemed to be the palace of a king, within which sat Wenchang precisely as we depict him on earth. "You are an upright man," replied the God, in reply to Mr. Tang's prayer, "and are certainly entitled to a longer span of life; but by this time your mortal body has become decomposed, and unless you can secure the assistance of Pusa,[627] I can give you no aid." So Mr. Tang set off once more, and hurried along until he came to a magnificent shrine standing in a thick grove of tall bamboos; and, entering in, he stood in the presence of the God, on whose head was the *ushnisha*[628] whose golden face was round like the full moon, and at whose side was a green willow-branch bending gracefully over the lip of a vase. Humbly Mr. Tang prostrated himself on the ground, and repeated what Wenchang had said to him; but Pusa seemed to think it would be impossible to grant his request, until one of the Lohans[629] who stood by cried out, "O God, Thou canst perform this miracle: take earth and make his flesh; take a sprig of willow and make his bones." Thereupon Pusa broke off a piece from the willow-branch in the vase beside him; and, pouring a little of the water upon the ground, he made clay, and, casting the whole over Mr. Tang's soul, bade an attendant lead the body back to the place where his coffin was. At that instant Mr. Tang's family heard a groan proceeding from within his coffin, and, on rushing to it and helping out the lately-deceased man, they found he had quite recovered. He had then been dead seven days.

---

625 The God of Literature.
626 See note 397 in tale number 77.
627 See note 150 in tale number 26.
628 A fleshy protuberance on the head, which is the distinguishing mark of a Buddha.
629 The eighteen personal disciples of Shâkyamuni Buddha. Sixteen of these are Hindoos, which number was subsequently increased by the addition of two Chinese Buddhists.

151. Fengshui[630]

AT Yizhou there lived a high official named Song, whose family were all ardent supporters of Fengshui; so much so, that even the women-folk read books[631] on the subject, and understood the principles of the science. When Mr. Song died, his two sons set up separate establishments,[632] and each invited to his own house geomancers from far and near, who had any reputation in their art, to select a spot for the dead man's grave. By degrees, they had collected together as many as a hundred apiece, and every day they would scour the country around, each at the head of his own particular regiment. After about a month of this work, both sides had fixed upon a suitable position for the grave; and the geomancers engaged by one brother, declared that if their spot was selected he would certainly some day be made a marquis, while the other brother was similarly informed, by his geomancers, that by adopting their choice, he would infallibly rise to the rank of Secretary of State. Thus, neither brother would give way to the other, but each set about making the grave in his own particular place— pitching marquees, and arranging banners, and making all necessary preparations for the funeral. Then when the coffin arrived at the point where roads branched off to the two graves, the two brothers, each leading on his own little army of geomancers, bore down upon it with a view to gaining possession of the corpse. From morn until dewy eve the battle raged; and as neither gained any advantage over the other, the mourners and friends, who had come to witness the ceremony of burial, stole away one by one; and the coolies, who were carrying the coffin, after changing the poles from one shoulder to another until they were quite worn out, put the body down by the roadside, and went off home. It then became necessary to make some protection for the coffin against the wind and rain; whereupon the elder brother immediately set about building a hut close by, in which he purposed leaving some of his attendants to keep guard; but he had no sooner begun

---

630 Literally, "wind and water," or that which cannot be seen and that which cannot be grasped. I have explained the term in my *Chinese Sketches*, p. 143, as "a system of geomancy, by the *science* of which it is possible to determine the desirability of sites—whether of tombs, houses, or cities, from the configuration of such natural objects as rivers, trees, and hills, and to foretell with certainty the fortunes of any family, community, or individual according to the spot selected; by the *art* of which it is in the power of the geomancer to counteract evil influences by good ones, to transform straight and noxious outlines into undulating and propitious curves, and rescue whole districts from the devastations of flood or pestilence."

631 As a rule, only the daughters of wealthy families receive any education to speak of.

632 A reprehensible proceeding in the eyes of all respectable Chinese, both from a moral and a practical point of view; "for when brothers fall out," says the proverb, "strangers get an advantage over them."

than the younger brother followed his example; and when the elder built a second and third, the younger also built a second and third; and as this went on for the space of three whole years, by the end of that time the place had become quite a little village. By-and-by, both brothers died, one directly after the other; and then their two wives determined to cast to the winds the decision of each party of geomancers. Accordingly, they went together to the two spots in question; and after inspecting them carefully, declared that neither was suitable. The next step was to jointly engage another set of geomancers, who submitted for their approval several different spots, and ten days had hardly passed away before the two women had agreed upon the position for their father-in-law's grave, which, as the wife of the younger brother prophesied, would surely give to the family a high military degree. So the body was buried, and within three years Mr. Song's eldest grandson, who had entered as a military cadet, actually took the corresponding degree to a literary master of arts.

["Fengshui," adds the author, "may or may not be based upon sound principles; at any rate, to indulge a morbid belief in it is utter folly; and thus to join issue and fight while a coffin is relegated to the roadside, is hardly in accordance with the doctrines of filial piety or fraternal love. Can people believe that mere position will improve the fortunes of their family? At any rate, that two women should have thus quietly settled the matter is certainly worthy of record."]

152. The Lingering Death

There was a man in our village who led an exceedingly disreputable life. One morning when he got up rather early, two men appeared, and led him away to the market-place, where he saw a butcher hanging up half a pig. As-they approached, the two men shoved him with all their might against the dead animal, and lo! his own flesh began to blend with the pork before him, while his conductors hurried off in an opposite direction. By-and-by the butcher wanted to sell a piece of his meat; and, seizing a knife, began to cut off the quantity required. At every touch of the blade our disreputable friend experienced a severe pang, which penetrated into his very marrow; and when, at length, an old man came and haggled over the weight given him, crying out for a little bit more fat, or an extra portion of lean,[633] then, as the butcher sliced away the pork ounce by ounce, the pain was unendurable in the extreme. By about nine o'clock the pork was all sold, and our hero went home, whereupon his family asked him what he meant by staying in bed so late.[634] He then narrated all that had taken place, and on making inquiries, they found that the pork-butcher had only just come home; besides which our friend was able to tell him every pound of meat he had sold, and every slice he had cut off. Fancy a man being put to the lingering death[635] like this before breakfast!

153. Dreaming Honors

WANG ZIAN was a Dongchang man, and a scholar of some repute, but unfortunate at the public examinations. On one occasion, after having been up for his master's degree, his anxiety was very great; and when the time for the publication of the list drew near, he drank himself gloriously tipsy, and went and lay down on the bed. In a few moments a man rushed in, and cried out, "Sir! you have passed!" whereupon Wang jumped up, and said, "Give him ten strings of cash."[636] Wang's wife, seeing he was drunk, and wishing to keep him quiet, replied, "You go on sleeping: I've given him the money." So Wang lay down again, but before long in came another man who informed Wang that his name was among the successful candidates for the highest degree. "Why, I haven't been up for it yet," said Wang; "how can I have passed?" "What! you don't mean to say you have forgotten the examination?" answered the man; and then Wang got up once more, and gave orders to present the informant with ten strings of cash. "All right," replied his wife; "you go on sleeping: I've given him the money." Another short interval, and in burst a third messenger to say that Wang had been elected a member of the National Academy, and that two official servants had come to escort him thither. Sure enough there were the two servants bowing at the bedside, and accordingly Wang directed that they should be served with wine and meat, which his wife,

---

633 Chinese tradesmen invariably begin by giving short weight in such transactions as these, partly in order to be in a position to gratify the customer by throwing in a trifle more and thus acquire a reputation for fair dealing.

634 It was only his soul that had left the house.

635 See note 288 in tale number 56.

636 See note 552 in tale number 123.

smiling at his drunken nonsense, declared had been already done. Wang now bethought him that he should go out and receive the congratulations of the neighbors, and roared out several times to his official servants; but without receiving any answer. "Go to sleep," said his wife, "and wait until I have fetched them;" and after a while the servants actually came in; whereupon Wang stamped and swore at them for being such idiots as to go away. "What! you wretched scoundrel," cried the servants, "are you cursing us in earnest, when we are only joking with you!" At this Wang's rage knew no bounds, and he set upon the men, and gave them a sound beating, knocking the hat of one off onto the ground. In the *mêlée,* he himself tumbled over, and his wife ran in to pick him up, saying, "Shame upon you, for getting so drunk as this!" "I was only punishing the servants as they deserved," replied Wang; "why do you call me drunk?" "Do you mean the old woman who cooks our rice and boils the water for your foot-bath," asked his wife, smiling, "that you talk of servants to wait upon your poverty-stricken carcass?" At this quip all the women burst out in a roar of laughter; and Wang, who was just beginning to get sober, woke up as if from a dream, and knew that there was no reality in all that had taken place. However, he recollected the spot where the servant's hat had fallen off, and on going thither to look for it, lo! he beheld a tiny official hat, no larger than a wine-cup, lying there behind the door. They were all much astonished, at this, and Wang himself cried out, "Formerly people were thus tricked by devils; and now foxes are playing the fool with me!"[637]

154. The She-Wolf and the Herd-Boys

Two herd-boys went up among the hills and found a wolf's lair with two little wolves in it. Seizing each of them one, they forthwith climbed two trees which stood there, at a distance of forty or fifty paces apart. Before long the old wolf came back, and, finding her cubs gone, was in a great state of distress. Just then, one of the herd-boys pinched his cub and made it squeak; whereupon the mother ran angrily towards the tree whence the sound proceeded, and tried to climb up it. At this juncture, the boy in the other tree pinched the other cub, and thereby diverted the wolf's attention

---

637 A common saying is, "Foxes in the north; devils in the south," as illustrative of the folk-lore of these two great divisions of China.

in that direction. But no sooner had she reached the foot of the second tree, than the boy who had first pinched his cub did so again, and away ran the old wolf back to the tree in which her other young one was. Thus they went on time after time, until the mother was dead tired, and lay down exhausted on the ground. Then, when after some time she showed no signs of moving, the herd-boys crept stealthily down, and found that the wolf was already stiff and cold. And truly, it is better to meet a blustering foe with his hand upon his sword-hilt, by retiring within doors, and leaving him to fret his violence away unopposed; for such is but the behavior of brute beasts, of which men thus take advantage.

155. Adulteration[638] Punished

AT Jinling there lived a seller of spirits, who was in the habit of adulterating his liquor with water and a certain drug, the effect of which was that even a few cups would make the strongest-headed man as drunk as a jelly-fish.[639] Thus his shop acquired a reputation for having a good article on sale, and by degrees he became a rich man. One morning, on getting up, he found a fox lying drunk alongside of the spirit vat; and tying its legs together, he was about to fetch a knife, when suddenly the fox waked up, and began pleading for its life, promising in return to do anything the spirit-merchant might require. The latter then released the animal, which instantly changed into the form of a human being. Now, at that very time, the wife of a neighbor was suffering under fox influence, and this recently-transformed animal confessed to the spirit-merchant that it was he who had been troubling her. Thereupon the spirit-merchant, who knew the lady in question to be a celebrated beauty, begged his fox friend to secretly introduce him to her. After raising some objections, the fox at length consented, and conducted the spirit-merchant to a cave, where he gave him a suit of serge clothes, which he said had belonged to his late brother, and in which he told him he could easily go. The merchant put them on, and returned home, when, to his great delight, he observed that no one could see him, but that if he changed

---

638 In no country in the world is adulteration more extensively practiced than in China, the only formal check upon it being a religious one—the dread of punishment in the world below.
639 The text has here a word (literally, "mud") explained to be the name of a boneless aquatic creature, which on being removed from the water lies motionless like a lump of mud. The common term for a jelly-fish is *shui mu*, "water-mother."

into his ordinary clothes everybody could see him as before. Accordingly he set off with the fox for his neighbor's house; and, when they arrived, the first thing they beheld was a charm on the wall, like a great wriggling dragon. At this the fox was greatly alarmed, and said, "That scoundrel of a priest! I can't go any farther." He then ran off home, leaving the spirit-merchant to proceed by himself. The latter walked quietly in, to find that the dragon on the wall was a real one, and preparing to fly at him, so he too turned, and ran away as fast as his legs could carry him. The fact was that the family had engaged a priest to drive away the fox influence; and he, not being able to go at the moment himself, gave them this charm to stick up on the wall. The following day the priest himself came, and, arranging an altar, proceeded to exorcise the fox. All the villagers crowded around to see, and among others was the spirit-merchant, who, in the middle of the ceremony, suddenly changed color, and hurried out of the front door, where he fell on the ground in the shape of a fox, having his clothes still hanging about his arms and legs. The bystanders would have killed him on the spot, but his wife begged them to spare him; and the priest let her take the fox home, where in a few days it died.

156. A Chinese Solomon

IN our district there lived two men, named Hu Cheng and Feng An, between whom there existed an old feud. The former, however, was the stronger of the two; and accordingly Feng disguised his feelings under a specious appearance of friendship, though Hu never placed much faith in his professions. One day they were drinking together, and being both of them rather the worse for liquor, they began to brag of the various exploits they had achieved. "What care I for poverty," cried Hu, "when I can lay a hundred ounces of silver on the table at a moment's notice?" Now Feng was well aware of the state of Hu's affairs, and did not hesitate to mock such pretensions, until Hu further informed him in perfect seriousness that the day before he had met a merchant traveling with a large sum of money and had tumbled him down a dry well by the wayside; in confirmation of which he produced several hundred ounces of silver, which really belonged to a brother-in-law on whose behalf he was managing some negotiations for the purchase of land. When they separated, Feng went off and gave information to the magistrate of the place, who summoned Hu to answer to the charge. Hu then told the actual facts of the case, and his brother-in-law and the owner of the land in question corroborated his statement. However, on examining the dry well by letting a man down with a rope around him, lo! there was a headless corpse lying at the bottom. Hu was horrified at this, and called Heaven to witness that he was innocent; whereupon the magistrate ordered him twenty or thirty blows on the mouth for lying in the presence of such irrefutable proof, and cast him into the condemned cell, where he lay loaded with chains. Orders were issued that the corpse was not to be removed, and a notification was made to the people, calling upon the relatives of the deceased to come forward and claim the body. Next day a woman appeared, and said the deceased was her husband; that his name was He, and that he was proceeding on business with a large sum of money about him when he was killed by Hu. The magistrate observed that possibly the body in the well might not be that of her husband, to which the woman replied that she felt sure it was; and accordingly the corpse was brought up and examined, when the woman's story was found to be correct. She herself did not go near the body, but stood at a little distance making the most doleful lamentations; until at length the magistrate said, "We have got the murderer, but the body is not complete; you go home and wait until the head has been discovered, when life shall be given for life." He then summoned Hu before him, and told him to produce the head by the next day under penalty of severe torture; but Hu only wandered about with the guard sent in charge of him, crying and lamenting his fate, but finding nothing. The instruments of torture were then produced, and preparations were made as if for torturing Hu; however, they were not applied,[640] and finally the magistrate sent him back to prison, saying, "I suppose that in your hurry you didn't notice where you dropped the head." The woman was then brought before him again; and on learning that her relatives consisted only of one uncle, the magistrate remarked, "A young woman like you, left alone in the world, will hardly be able to earn a livelihood. [Here she burst into tears and implored the magistrate's pity.] The punishment of the guilty man has been already decided upon, but until we get the head, the case cannot be closed. As soon as it is closed, the best thing you can do is to marry again. A young woman like yourself should not be in and out of a police court." The woman thanked the magistrate and retired; and the latter issued a notice to the people, calling upon them to make a search for the head. On the following day, a man named Wang, a fellow villager of

---

640 See note 384 in tale number 73.

the deceased, reported that he had found the missing head; and his report proving to be true, he was rewarded with 1,000 *cash*. The magistrate now summoned the woman's uncle above mentioned, and told him that the case was complete, but that as it involved such an important matter as the life of a human being, there would necessarily be some delay in closing it for good and all.[641] "Meanwhile," added the magistrate, "your niece is a young woman and has no children; persuade her to marry again and so keep herself out of these troubles, and never mind what people may say."[642] The uncle at first refused to do this; upon which the magistrate was obliged to threaten him, until he was ultimately forced to consent. At this, the woman appeared before the magistrate to thank him for what he had done; whereupon the latter gave out that any person who was willing to take the woman to wife was to present himself at his yamen. Immediately afterwards an application was made—by the very man who had found the head. The magistrate then sent for the woman and asked her if she could say who was the real murderer; to which she replied that Hu Cheng had done the deed. "No!" cried the magistrate; "it was not he. It was you and this man here. [Here both began loudly to protest their innocence.] I have long known this; but, fearing to leave the smallest loophole for escape, I have tarried thus long in elucidating the circumstances. How [to the woman], before the corpse was removed from the well, were you so certain that it was your husband's body? *Because you already knew he was dead.* And does a trader who has several hundred ounces of silver about him dress as shabbily as your husband was dressed? And you [to the man], how did you manage to find the head so readily? *Because you were in a hurry to marry the woman.*" The two culprits stood there as pale as death, unable to utter a word in their defence; and on the application of torture both confessed the crime. For this man, the woman's paramour, had killed her husband, curiously enough, about the time of Hu Cheng's braggart joke. He was accordingly released, but Feng suffered the penalty of a false accuser; he was severely bambooed, and banished for three years. The case was thus brought to a close without the wrongful punishment of a single person.

---

641   There is a widespread belief that human life in China is held at a cheap rate. This may be accounted for by the fact that death is the legal punishment for many crimes not considered capital in the West; and by the severe measures that are always taken in cases of rebellion, when the innocent and guilty are often indiscriminately massacred. In times of tranquillity, however, this is not the case; and the execution of a criminal is surrounded by a number of formalities which go far to prevent the shedding of innocent blood. The *Xi Yuan lu* (see note 67 in tale number 14) opens with the words, "There is nothing more important than human life."

642   See note 351 in tale number 67.

157. The Rukh

Two herons built their nest under one of the ornaments on the roof of a temple at Tianjin. The accumulated dust of years in the shrine below concealed a huge serpent, having the diameter of a washing-basin; and whenever the herons' young were ready to fly, the reptile proceeded to the nest and swallowed every one of them, to the great distress of the bereaved parents. This took place three years consecutively, and people thought the birds would build there no more. However, the following year they came again; and when the time was drawing nigh for their young ones to take wing, away they flew, and remained absent for nearly three days. On their return, they went straight to the nest, and began amidst much noisy chattering to feed their young ones as usual. Just then the serpent crawled up to reach his prey; and as he was nearing the nest the parent-birds flew out and screamed loudly in mid-air. Immediately, there was heard a mighty flapping of wings, and darkness came over the face of the earth, which the astonished spectators now perceived to be caused by a huge bird obscuring the light of the sun. Down it swooped with the speed of wind or falling rain, and, striking the serpent with its talons, tore its head off at a blow, bringing down at the same time several feet of the masonry of the temple. Then it flew away, the herons accompanying it as though escorting a guest. The nest too had come down, and of the two young birds one was killed by the fall; the other was taken by the priests and put in the bell tower, whither the old birds returned to feed it until thoroughly fledged, when it spread its wings and was gone.[643]

158. The Faithful Gander[644]

A SPORTSMAN of Tianjin, having snared a wild goose, was followed to his home by the gander, which flew around and around him in great distress, and only went away at nightfall. Next day, when the sportsman went out, there was the bird again; and at length it alighted quite close to his feet. He was on the point of seizing it when suddenly it stretched out its neck and

---

643 This story is inserted chiefly in illustration of the fact that all countries have a record of some enormous bird such as the *rukh* of *The Arabian Nights*.
644 See note 185 in tale number 35.

disgorged a piece of pure gold; whereupon, the sportsman, understanding what the bird meant, cried out, "I see! this is to ransom your mate, eh?" Accordingly, he at once released the goose, and the two birds flew away with many expressions of their mutual joy, leaving to the sportsman nearly three ounces of pure gold. Can, then, mere birds have such feelings as these? Of all sorrows there is no sorrow like separation from those we love; and it seems that the same holds good even of dumb animals.

159. The Elephants and the Lion

A HUNTSMAN of Guangxi, who was out on the hills with his bow and arrows, lay down to rest awhile, and unwittingly fell fast asleep. As he was slumbering, an elephant came up, and, coiling his trunk around the man, carried him off. The latter gave himself up for dead; but before long the elephant had deposited him at the foot of a tall tree, and had summoned up a whole herd of comrades, who crowded about the huntsman as though asking his assistance. The elephant who had brought him went and lay down under the tree, and first looked up into its branches and then looked down at the man, apparently requesting him to get up into the tree. So the latter jumped on the elephant's back and then clambered up to the topmost branch, not knowing what he was expected to do next. By-and-by a lion[645] arrived, and from among the frightened herd chose out a fat elephant, which he seemed as though about to devour. The others remained there trembling, not daring to run away, but looking wistfully up into the tree. Thereupon the huntsman drew an arrow from his quiver and shot the lion dead, at which all the elephants below made him a grateful obeisance. He then descended, when the elephant lay down again and invited him to mount by pulling at his clothes with its trunk. This he did, and was carried to a place where the animal scratched the ground with its foot, and revealed to him a vast number of old tusks. He jumped down and collected them in a bundle, after which the elephant conveyed him to a spot whence he easily found his way home.[646]

---

645 The term here used refers to a creature which partakes rather of the fabulous than of the real. The *Guang yun* says it is "a kind of lion;" but other authorities describe it as a horse. Its favorite food is tiger-flesh. Incense-burners are often made after the "lion" pattern and called by this name, the smoke of the incense issuing from the mouth of the animal, like our own gargoyles.

646 Compare the elephant story in the seventh voyage of Es-Sindibad of the Sea (Lane's *Arabian*

160 The Hidden Treasure

LI YUESHENG was a second son of a rich old man who used to bury his money, and who was known to his fellow-townsmen as "Old Crocks." One day the father fell sick, and summoned his sons to divide the property between them.[647] He gave four-fifths to the elder and only one-fifth to the younger, saying to the latter, "It is not that I love your brother more than I love you: I have other money stored away, and when you are alone I will hand that over to you." A few days afterwards the old man grew worse, and Yuesheng, afraid that his father might die at any moment, seized an opportunity of seeing him alone to ask about the money that he himself was to receive. "Ah," replied the dying man, "the sum of our joys and of our sorrows is determined by fate. You are now happy in the possession of a virtuous wife, and have no right to an increase of wealth." For, as a matter of fact, this second son was married to a lady from the Che family whose virtue equalled that of any of the heroines of history: hence his father's remark. Yuesheng, however, was not satisfied, and implored to be allowed to have the money; and at length the old man got angry and said, "You are only just turned twenty; you have known none of the trials of life, and were I to give a thousand ounces of gold, it would soon be all spent. Go! and, until you have drunk the cup of bitterness to its dregs, expect no money from me." Now Yuesheng was a filial son, and when his father spoke thus he did not venture to say any more, and hoped for his speedy recovery, that he might have a chance, of coaxing him to comply with his request. But the old man got worse and worse, and at length died; whereupon the elder brother took no trouble about the funeral ceremonies, leaving it all to the younger, who, being an open-handed fellow, made no difficulties about the expense. The latter was also fond of seeing a great deal of company at his house, and his wife often had to get three or four meals a day ready for guests; and, as her husband did very little towards looking after his affairs, and was further sponged upon by all the needy ones of the neighborhood, they were soon reduced to a state of poverty. The elder brother helped them to keep body and soul together, but he died shortly afterwards, and this resource was cut off from them. Then, by dint of borrowing in the spring and repaying in the

647 All sons, whether by wife or concubine, share equally, and in preference to daughters, even though there should be a written will in favor of the latter, the power of bequeathing by will, except as regards trifling matters of detail, being practically nonexistent.

autumn,[648] they still managed to exist, until at last it came to parting with their land, and they were left actually destitute. At that juncture their eldest son died, followed soon after by his mother; and Yuesheng was left almost by himself in the world. He now married the widow of a sheep-dealer, who had a little capital; and she was very strict with him, and wouldn't let him waste time and money with his friends. One night his father appeared to him and said, "My son, you have drained your cup of bitterness to the dregs. You shall now have the money. I will bring it to you." When Yuesheng woke up, he thought it was merely a poor man's dream; but the next day, while laying the foundations of a wall, he did come upon a quantity of gold. And then he knew what his father had meant by "when you are alone;" for of those about him at that time, more than half were gone.

161. The Boatmen of Laolong

WHEN His Excellency Zhu was Viceroy of Guangdong, there were constant complaints from the traders of mysterious disappearances; sometimes as many as three or four of them disappearing at once and never being seen or heard of again. At length the number of such cases, filed of course against some person or persons unknown, multiplied to such an extent that they were simply put on record, and but little notice was further taken of them by the local officials. Thus, when His Excellency entered upon his duties, he found more than a hundred plaints of the kind, besides innumerable cases in which the missing man's relatives lived at a distance and had not instituted proceedings. The mystery so preyed upon the new Viceroy's mind that he lost all appetite for food; and when, finally, all the inquiries he had set on foot resulted in no clue to an elucidation of these strange disappearances, then His Excellency proceeded to wash and purify himself, and, having notified the Municipal God,[649] he took to fasting and sleeping in his study alone. While he was in ecstasy, lo! an official entered, holding a tablet in his hand, and said that he had come from the Municipal temple with the following instructions to the Viceroy:

---

648 This has reference to the "seed-time and harvest."
649 See note 1 in tale number 1.

Snow on the whiskers descending:
Live clouds falling from heaven:
Wood in water buoyed up:
In the wall an opening effected.

The official then retired, and the Viceroy woke up; but it was only after a night of tossing and turning that he hit upon what seemed to him the solution of the enigma. "The first line," argued he, "must signify old [*lao* in Chinese]; the second refers to the *dragon*[650] [*long* in Chinese]; the third is clearly a *boat*; and the fourth a *door* [here taken in its secondary sense—*man*]" Now, to the east of the province, not far from the pass by which traders from the north connect their line of trade with the southern seas, there was actually a ferry known as the Old Dragon (Laolong); and thither the Viceroy immediately despatched a force to arrest those employed in carrying people backwards and forwards. More than fifty men were caught, and they all confessed at once without the application of torture. In fact, they were bandits under the guise of boatmen;[651] and after beguiling passengers on board, they would either drug them or burn stupefying incense until they were senseless, finally cutting them open and putting a large stone inside to make the body sink. Such was the horrible story, the discovery of which brought throngs to the Viceroy's door to serenade him in terms of gratitude and praise.[652]

162. The Pious Surgeon

A CERTAIN veterinary surgeon, named Hou, was carrying food to his field laborers, when suddenly a whirlwind arose in his path. Hou seized a spoon and poured out a libation of gruel, whereupon the wind immediately dropped. On another occasion, he was wandering about the municipal temple when he noticed an image of Liu Quan presenting the melon,[653] in

---

650 Clouds being naturally connected in every Chinese person's mind with these fabulous creatures, the origin of which has been traced by some to waterspouts. See note 405 in tale number 81.
651 "Boat-men" is the solution of the last two lines of the enigma.
652 The author actually supplies a list of the persons who signed a congratulatory petition to the Viceroy on the arrest and punishment of the criminals.
653 When the soul of the Emperor Tai Zong of the Tang dynasty was in the infernal regions, it promised to send Yenlo (the Chinese *Yama* or Pluto) a melon; and when His Majesty recovered from the trance into which he had been plunged, he gave orders that his promise was to be fulfilled. Just then a man, named Liu Quan, observed a priest with a hairpin belonging to his wife, and misconstruing the manner in which possession of it had been obtained, abused his wife so severely that she committed

whose eye was a great splotch of dirt. "Dear me, Sir Liu!" cried Hou, "who has been ill-using you like this?" He then scraped away the dirt with his finger-nail, and passed on. Some years afterwards, as he was lying down very ill, two lictors walked in and carried him off to a yamen, where they insisted on his bribing them heavily. Hou was at his wit's end what to do; but just at that moment a personage dressed in green robes came forth, who was greatly astonished at seeing him there, and asked what it all meant. Our hero at once explained; whereupon the man in green turned upon the lictors and abused them for not showing proper respect to Mr. Hou. Meanwhile a drum sounded like the roll of thunder, and the man in green told Hou that it was for the morning session, and that he would have to attend. Leading Hou within, he put him in his proper place, and, promising to inquire into the charge against him, went forward and whispered a few words to one of the clerks. "Oh," said the latter, advancing and making a bow to the veterinary surgeon, "yours is a trifling matter. We shall merely have to confront you with a horse, and then you can go home again." Shortly afterwards, Hou's case was called; upon which he went forward and knelt down, as did also a horse which was prosecuting him. The judge now informed Hou that he was accused by the horse of having caused its death by medicines, and asked him if he pleaded guilty or not guilty. "My lord," replied Hou, "the prosecutor was attacked by the cattle-plague, for which I treated him accordingly; and he actually recovered from the disease, though he died on the following day. Am I to be held responsible for that?" The horse now proceeded to tell his story; and after the usual cross-examination and cries for justice, the judge gave orders to look up the horse's term of life in the Book of Fate. Therein it appeared that the animal's destiny had doomed it to death on the very day on which it had died; whereupon the judge cried out, "Your term of years had already expired; why bring this false charge? Away with you!" and turning to Hou, the judge added, "You are a worthy man, and may be permitted to live." The lictors were accordingly instructed to escort him back, and with them went out both the clerk and the man in green clothes, who bade the lictors take every possible care of Hou by the way. "You gentlemen are very kind," said Hou, "but I haven't the honor of your acquaintance, and should be glad to know to whom I am so much indebted." "Three years ago," replied the man in green, "I was traveling in your neighborhood, and was suffering very much from

suicide. Liu Quan himself then determined to follow her example, and convey the melon to Yenlo; for which act he was subsequently deified. See the *Xi Yu qi*, Section XI.

thirst, which you relieved for me by a few spoonfuls of gruel. I have not forgotten that act." "And my name," observed the other, "is Liu Quan. You once took a splotch of dirt out of my eye that was troubling me very much. I am only sorry that the wine and food we have down here is unsuitable to offer you. Farewell." Hou now understood all that had happened, and went off home with the two lictors, where he would have regaled them with some refreshment, but they refused to take even a cup of tea. He then woke up and found that he had been dead for two days. From this time forth he led a more virtuous life than ever, always pouring out libations to Liu Quan at all the festivals of the year. Thus he reached the age of eighty, a hale and hearty man, still able to sit in the saddle; until one day he met Liu Quan riding on horseback, as if about to make a long journey. After a little friendly conversation, the latter said to him, "Your time is up, and the warrant for your arrest is already issued; but I have ordered the constables to delay awhile, and you can now spend three days in preparing for death, at the expiration of which I will come and fetch you. I have purchased a small appointment for you in the realms below,[654] by which you will be more comfortable." So Hou went home and told his wife and children; and after collecting his friends and relatives, and making all necessary preparations, on the evening of the fourth day he cried out, " Liu Quan has come!" and, getting into his coffin,[655] lay down and died.

163. Another Solomon

AT Taiyuan there lived a middle-aged woman with her widowed daughter-in-law. The former was on terms of too great intimacy with a notably bad character of the neighborhood; and the latter, who objected very strongly to this, did her best to keep the man from the house. The elder woman accordingly tried to send the other back to her family, but she would not go; and at length things came to such a pass that the mother-in-law actually went to the mandarin of the place and charged her daughter-in-law with the

---

654 As the Chinese believe that their disembodied spirits proceed to a world organized on much the same model as the one they know, so do they think that there will be social distinctions of rank and emolument proportioned to the merits of each.

655 A dying man is almost always moved into his coffin to die; and aged persons frequently take to sleeping regularly in the coffins provided against the inevitable hour by the pious thoughtfulness of a loving son. Even in middle life Chinese like to see their coffins ready for them, and store them sometimes on their own premises, sometimes in the outhouses of a neighboring temple.

offence she herself was committing. When the mandarin inquired the name of the man concerned, she said she had only seen him in the dark and didn't know who he was, referring him for information to the accused. The latter, on being summoned, gave the man's name, but retorted the charge on her mother-in-law; and when the man was confronted with them, he promptly declared both their stories to be false. The mandarin, however, said there was a *primâ facie* case against him, and ordered him to be severely beaten, whereupon he confessed that it was the daughter-in-law whom he went to visit. This the woman herself flatly denied, even under torture; and on being released, appealed to a higher court, with a very similar result. Thus the case dragged on, until a Mr. Sun, who was well known for his judicial acumen, was appointed district magistrate at that place. Calling the parties before him, he bade his lictors prepare stones and knives, at which they were much exercised in their minds, the severest tortures allowed by law being merely shackles and fetters.[656] However, everything was got ready, and the next day Mr. Sun proceeded with his investigation. After hearing all that each one of the three had to say, he delivered the following judgment: "The case is a simple one; for although I cannot say which of you two women is the guilty one, there is no doubt about the man, who has evidently been the means of bringing discredit on a virtuous family. Take those stones and knives there and put him to death. I will be responsible." Thereupon the two women began to stone the man, especially the younger one, who seized the biggest stones she could see and threw them at him with all the might of her pent-up anger; while the mother-in-law chose small stones and struck him on non-vital parts.[657] So with the knives: the daughter-in-law would have killed him at the first blow, had not the mandarin stopped her, and said, "Hold! I now know who is the guilty woman." The mother-in-law was then tortured until she confessed, and the case was thus terminated.

164. The Incorrupt Official

MR. WU, Sub-prefect of Jinan, was an upright man, and would have no share in the bribery and corruption which was extensively carried on, and

---

656 See note 384 in tale number 73.
657 The Chinese distinguish sixteen vital spots on the front of the body and six on the back, with thirty-six and twenty non-vital spots in similar positions, respectively. They allow, however, that a severe blow on a non-vital spot might cause death, and *vice versâ*.

at which the higher authorities connived, and in the proceeds of which they actually shared. The Prefect tried to bully him into adopting a similar plan, and went so far as to abuse him in violent language; upon which Mr. Wu fired up and exclaimed, "Though I am but a subordinate official, you should impeach me for anything you have against me in the regular way; you have not the right to abuse me thus. Die I may, but I will never consent to degrade my office and turn aside the course of justice for the sake of filthy lucre." At this outbreak the Prefect changed his tone, and tried to soothe him. . . . [How dare people accuse the age of being corrupt, when it is themselves who will not walk in the straight path.] One day after this a certain fox-medium[658] came to the Prefect's yamen just as a feast was in full swing, and was thus addressed by a guest: "You who pretend to know everything, say how many officials there are in this Prefecture" "*One*," replied the medium; at which the company laughed heartily, until the medium continued, "There are really seventy-two holders of office, but Mr. Sub-prefect Wu is the only one who can justly be called an official."

---

658 Certain classes of soothsayers are believed by the Chinese to be possessed by foxes, which animals have the power of looking into the future, etc., etc.

Appendix I

The *Yuli chao zhuan*

VISITORS to Chinese temples of the Taoist persuasion usually make at once for what is popularly known amongst foreigners as the "Chamber of Horrors." These belong specially to Taoism, or the ethics of Right in the abstract, as opposed to abstract Wrong, and are not found in temples consecrated to the religion of Buddha. Modern Taoism, however, once a purely metaphysical system, is now so leavened with the superstitions of Buddhism, and has borrowed so much material from its younger rival, that an ordinary observer can hardly tell one from the other, and generally regards them as to all intents and purposes the same. These rightly-named Chambers of Horrors—for Madame Tussaud has nothing more ghastly to show in the whole of her wonderful collection—represent the Ten Courts of Purgatory, through some or all of which erring souls must pass before they are suffered to be born again into the world under another form, or transferred to the eternal bliss reserved for the righteous alone. As a description of these Ten Courts may not be uninteresting to some of my readers, and as the subject has a direct bearing upon many of the stories in the previous collection, I hereto append my translation of a well-known Taoist work[659] which is circulated gratuitously all over the Chinese Empire by people who are anxious to lay up a store of good works against the day of reckoning to come. Those who are acquainted with Dante's *Divine Comedy* will recollect that the poet's idea of a Christian Purgatory was a series of nine lessening circles arranged one above the other, so as to form a cone. The Taoist believes that his Purgatory consists of Ten Courts of Justice situated in different positions at the bottom of a great ocean which lies down in the depths of the earth. These are subdivided into special wards, different forms of torture being inflicted in each. A perusal of this work will show what punishments the wicked Chinese person has to expect in the unseen world, and by what means he may hope to obtain a partial or complete remission of his sins.

---

659 The *Yuli chao zhuan*, or *Divine Panorama*.

STRANGE TALES FROM A CHINESE STUDIO

The Divine Panorama, published by the Mercy of Yu Di[660] *that Men and Woman may repent them of their faults and make Atonement for their Crimes.*

On the birthday of the Saviour Pusa,[661] as the spirits of Purgatory were thronging around to offer their congratulations, the ruler of the Infernal Regions spake as follows: "My wish is to release all souls, and every moon as this day comes around I would wholly or partially remit the punishment of erring shades, and give them life once more in one of the Six Paths.[662] But alas! the wicked are many and the virtuous few. Nevertheless, the punishments in the dark region are too severe, and require some modification. Any wicked soul that repents and induces one or two others to do likewise shall be allowed to set this off against the punishments which should be inflicted." The Judges of the Ten Courts of Purgatory then agreed that all who led virtuous lives from their youth upwards shall be escorted at their death to the land of the Immortals; that all whose balance of good and evil is exact shall escape the bitterness of the Three States,[663] and be born again among men; that those who have repaid their debts of gratitude and friendship, and fulfilled their destiny, yet have a balance of evil against them, shall pass through the various Courts of Purgatory and then be born again amongst men, rich, poor, old, young, diseased or crippled, to be put a second time upon trial. Then, if they behave well they may enter into some happy state; but if badly, they will be dragged by horrid devils through all the Courts, suffering bitterly as they go, and will again be born, to endure in life the uttermost of poverty and wretchedness, in death the everlasting tortures of hell. Those who are disloyal, unfilial, who commit suicide, take life, or disbelieve the doctrine of Cause and Effect,[664] saying to themselves that when a man dies there is an end of him, that when he has lost his skin[665] he has already suffered the worst that can befall him, that living men can be tortured, but no one ever saw a man's ghost in the pillory, that after death all is unknown, etc., etc.—truly these men do not know that the body alone perishes but the soul lives for ever and ever; and that whatsoever evil they do in this life, the same will be done unto them in the life to come. All who commit such crimes are handed over to the everlasting tortures

---

660 The Divine Ruler, immediately below God Himself.
661 See note 150 in tale number 26.
662 See Author's Own Record (in the Introduction), note 53.
663 The three worst of the Six Paths.
664 That the state of one life is the result of behavior in a previous existence.
665 *Lit*—the skin purse (of his bones).

of hell; for alas! in spite of the teachings of the Three Systems[666] some will persist in regarding these warnings as vain and empty talk. Lightly they speak of Divine mercy, and knowingly commit many crimes, not more than one in a hundred ever coming to repentance. Therefore the punishments of Purgatory were strictly carried out and the tortures dreadfully severe. But now it has been mercifully ordained that any man or woman, young, old, weak or strong, who may have sinned in any way, shall be permitted to obtain remission of the same by keeping his or her thoughts constantly fixed on Pusa and on the birthdays of the Judges of the Ten Courts, by fasting and prayer, and by vows never to sin again. Or for every good work done in life they shall be allowed to escape one ward in the Courts below. From this rule to be excepted disloyal ministers, unfilial sons, suicides, those who plot in secret against good people, those who are struck by lightning (*lit.* thunder), those who perish by flood or fire, by wild animals or poisonous reptiles[667]—these to pass through all the Courts and be punished according to their deserts. All other sinners to be allowed to claim their good works as a set-off against evil, thus partly escaping the agonies of hell and receiving some reward for their virtuous deeds.

This account of man's wickedness on the earth and the punishments in store for him was written in language intelligible to every man and woman, and was submitted for the approval of Pusa, the intention being to wait the return[668] of some virtuous soul among the sons of men, and by these means publish it all over the earth. When Pusa saw what had been done, he said it was good; and on the 3rd of the 8th moon proceeded with the ten Judges of Purgatory to lay this book before God.[669]

Then God said, "Good indeed! Good indeed! Henceforth let all spirits take note of any mortal who vows to lead a virtuous life and, repenting, promises to sin no more. Two punishments shall be remitted him. And if, in addition to this, he succeeds in doing five virtuous acts, then he shall escape all punishment and be born again in some happy state—if a woman she shall be born as a man. But more than five virtuous acts shall enable such a soul to obtain the salvation of others, and redeem wife and family from the tortures of hell. Let these regulations be published in the *Divine Panorama*

---

666 Buddhism, Taoism, and Confucianism.
667 Violent deaths are regarded with horror by the Chinese. They hold that a truly virtuous man always dies either of illness or old age.
668 Good people go to Purgatory in the flesh, and are at once passed up to Heaven without suffering any torture, or are sent back to earth again.
669 The Supreme Ruler.

and circulated on earth by the spirits of the City Guardians.[670] In fear and trembling obey this decree and carry it reverently into effect."

The First Court

HIS Infernal Majesty Qin Guang is specially in charge of the register of life and death both for old and young, and presides at the judgment-seat in the lower regions. His court is situated in the great Ocean, away beyond the Wujiao rock,[671] far to the west near the murky road which leads to the Yellow Springs.[672] Every man and woman dying in old age whose fate it is to be born again into the world, if their tale of good and evil works is equally balanced, are sent to the First Court, and thence transferred back to Life, male becoming female, female male, rich poor, and poor rich, according to their several deserts. But those whose good deeds are outnumbered by their bad are sent to a terrace on the right of the Court, called the Terrace of the Mirror of Sin, ten feet[673] in height. The mirror is about fifty feet" in circumference and hangs towards the east. Above are seven characters written horizontally: "Sin Mirror Terrace upon no good men." There the wicked souls are able to see the naughtiness of their own hearts while they were among the living, and the danger of death and hell. Then do they realise the proverb:

Ten thousand taels of yellow gold cannot be brought away:
But every crime will tell its tale upon the judgment day.

When the souls have been to the Terrace and seen their wickednesses, they are forwarded into the Second Court, where they are tortured and dismissed to the proper hell.

Should there be anyone enjoying life without reflecting that Heaven and Earth produce mortals, that father and mother bring the child to maturity—truly no easy matter; and, ignoring the four obligations,[674] before receiving the summons, lightly sever the thread of their own existence by cutting their throats, hanging, poisoning, or drowning themselves—then such suicides,

---

670 See note 1 in tale number 1.
671 Supposed to be the gate of the Infernal Regions.
672 Hades
673 Literally ten armfuls."
674 To Heaven, Earth, sovereign, and relatives.

if the deed was not done out of loyalty, filial piety, chastity, or friendship, for which they would go to Heaven, but in a trivial burst of rage, or fearing the consequences of a crime which would not amount to death, or in the hope of falsely injuring a fellow-creature—then such suicides, when the last breath has left their bodies, shall be escorted to this Court by the Spirits of the Threshold and of the Hearth. They shall be placed in the Hunger and Thirst Section, and every day from seven until eleven o'clock they will resume their mortal coil, and suffer again the pain and bitterness of death. After seventy days, or one or two years, as the case may be, they will be conducted back to the scene of their suicide, but will not be permitted to taste the funeral meats, or avail themselves of the usual offerings to the dead. Bitterly will they repent, unable as they will be to render themselves visible and frighten people,[675] vainly striving to procure a substitute.[676] For when the substitute shall have been harmlessly entrapped, the Spirits of the Threshold and Hearth will reconduct the erring soul back to this Court, whence it will be sent on to the Second Court, where its balance of good and evil will be struck, and dreadful tortures applied, being finally passed on through the Various Courts to the utter misery of hell. Should anyone have such intention of suicide and thus threaten a fellow creature, even though he does not commit the act but continues to live not without virtue, yet shall it not be permitted in any way to remit his punishment. Any soul which after suicide shall not remain invisible, but shall frighten people to death, will be seized by black-faced, long-tusked devils and tortured in the various hells, to be finally thrust into the great Gehenna, forever to remain hung up in chains, and not permitted to be born again.

Every Buddhist or Taoist priest who receives money for prayers and liturgies, but skips over words and misses out sentences, on arriving at this, the First Court, will be sent to the section for the completion of Prayer, and there in a small dark room he shall pick out such passages as he has omitted, and make good the deficiency as best he can, by the uncertain light of an infinitesimal wick burning in a gallon of oil. Even good and virtuous priests must also repair any omissions they may have (accidentally) made, and so must every man or woman who in private devotion may have omitted or wrongly repeated any part of the sacred writings from over-earnestness, their attention not being properly fixed on the actual words they repeat.

675 Held to be a great relief to the spirits of the dead.
676 It Is commonly believed that if the spirit of a murdered man can secure the violent death of some other person he returns to earth again as if nothing had happened, the spirit of his victim passing into the world below and suffering all the misery of a disembodied soul In his stead. See note 234 in tale number 45.

The same applies to female priests. A dispensation from Buddha to remit such punishment is put in force on the first day of each month when the names are entered in the register of the virtuous.

O ye dwellers upon earth, on the 1st day of the 2nd moon, fasting turn to the north and make oath to abstain from evil and fix your thoughts on good, that ye may escape hell! The precepts of Buddha are circulated over the whole world to warn mankind to believe and repent, that when the last hour comes their spirits may be escorted by dark-robed boys to realms of bliss and happiness in the west.

The Second Court

HIS Infernal Majesty Chu Jiang reigns at the bottom of the great Ocean. Away to the south, below the Wujiao rocks, he has a vast hell, many leagues in extent, and subdivided into sixteen wards, as follows:

In the first, nothing but black clouds and constant sand-storms. In the second, mud and filth. In the third, *chevaux de frise.* In the fourth, gnawing hunger. In the fifth, burning thirst. In the sixth, blood and pus. In the seventh, the shades are plunged into a brazen cauldron (of boiling water). In the eighth, the same punishment is repeated many times. In the ninth, they are put into iron clothes. In the tenth, they are stretched on a rack to regulation length. In the eleventh, they are pecked by fowls. In the twelfth, they have only rivers of lime to drink. In the thirteenth they are hacked to pieces. In the fourteenth, the leaves of the trees are as sharp as sword-points. In the fifteenth they are pursued by foxes and wolves. In the sixteenth, all is ice and snow.

Those who lead astray young boys and girls, and then escape punishment by cutting off their hair and entering the priesthood;[677] those who filch letters, pictures, books, etc., entrusted to their care, and then pretend to have lost them; those who injure a fellow-creature's ear, eye, hand, foot, fingers, or toes; those who practice as doctors without any knowledge of

---

677 A very common trick in China. The drunken bully Lu Da in the celebrated novel *Shuihu zhuan* saved himself by these means, and I have heard that the Mandarin who in the war of 1843 spent a large sum in constructing a paddle-wheel steamer to be worked by men, hoping thereby to match the wheel-ships of the Outer Barbarians, is now expiating his failure at a monastery in Fujian. *A propos* of which, it may not be generally known at this moment (1880) there are small paddle-wheel boats for Chinese passengers, plying up and down the Canton River, the wheels of which are turned by gangs of coolies, who perform a movement precisely similar to that required on the treadmill.

the medical art; those who will not ransom grown-up slave-girls;[678] those who, contracting marriage for the sake of gain, falsely state their ages; or those who in cases of betrothal, before actual marriage, find out that one of the contracting parties is a bad character, and yet do not come forward to say so, but inflict an irreparable wrong on the innocent one; such offenders, when their quota of crime has been cast up, their youth or age and the consequences of their acts taken into consideration, will be seized by horrid red-faced devils and thrust into the great Hell, and thence dispatched to the particular ward in which they are to be tormented. When their time of suffering there has expired, they will be moved into the Third Court, there to be tortured and passed on to Gehenna.

O ye men and women of the world, take this book and warn all sinners, or copy it out and circulate it for general information! If you see people sick and ill, give medicine to heal them. If you see people poor and hungry, feed them. If you see people in difficulties, give money to save them. Repent your past errors, and you will be allowed to cancel that evil by future good, so that when the hour arrives you will pass at once into the Tenth Court, and thence return again to existence on earth.

Let such as love all creatures endowed with life, and do not recklessly cut and slay, but teach their children not to harm small animals and insects—let these, on the 1st of the 3rd moon, register an oath not to take life, but to aid in preserving it. Thus they will avoid passing through Purgatory, and will also enter at once the Tenth Hall, to be born again in some happy state.

The Third Court

His Infernal Majesty Song Di reigns at the bottom of the great Ocean, away to the south-east, below the Wujiao rock, in the Gehenna of Black Ropes. This Hall is many leagues wide, and is subdivided into sixteen wards, as follows:

In the first everything is Salt; above, below, and all around, the eye rests upon Salt alone. The shades feed upon it, and suffer horrid torments in consequence. When the fit has passed away they return to it once again, and suffer agonies more unutterable than before. In the second, the erring shades are bound with cords and carry heavily-weighted *cangues*. In the third, they are perpetually pierced through the ribs. In the fourth, their

---

678 In order that their marriage destiny may not be interfered with. It is considered disgraceful not to accept the ransom of a slave girl of fifteen or sixteen years of age. See note 153 in tale number 26.

faces are scraped with iron and copper knives. In the fifth, their fat is scraped away from their bodies. In the sixth, their hearts and livers are squeezed with pincers. In the seventh, their eyes are gouged. In the eighth, they are flayed. In the ninth, their feet are cut off. In the tenth, their finger-nails and toe-nails are pulled out. In the eleventh, their blood is sucked. In the twelfth, they are hung up head downwards. In the thirteenth, their shoulder-bones are split. In the fourteenth, they are tormented by insects and reptiles. In the fifteenth, they are beaten on the thighs. In the sixteenth, their hearts are scratched.

Those who enjoy the light of day without reflecting on the Imperial bounty;[679] officers of State who revel in large emoluments without reciprocating their sovereign's goodness; private individuals who do not repay the debt of water and earth;[680] wives and concubines who slight their marital lords; those who fail in their duties as acting sons,[681] or such as reap what advantages there are and then go off to their own homes; slaves who disregard their masters; official underlings who are ungrateful to their superiors; working partners who behave badly to the moneyed partner; culprits who escape from prison or abscond from their place of banishment; those who break their bail and get others into trouble; and those infatuated ones who have long omitted to pray and repent—all these, even though they have a set-off of good deeds, must pass through the misery of every ward. Those who interfere with another man's *fengshui*; those who obstruct funeral obsequies or the completion of graves; those who in digging come on a coffin and do not immediately cover it up, but injure the bones; those who steal or avoid paying up their quota of grain;[682] those who lose all record of the site of their family burying-place; those who incite others to commit crimes; those who promote litigation; those who write anonymous placards; those who repudiate a betrothal; those who forge deeds and other documents; those who receive payment of a debt without signing a receipt or giving up the IOU; those who counterfeit signatures and seals; those who alter bills; those who injure posterity in any way—all these, and similar offenders, shall be punished according to the gravity of each offence. Devils

---

679 The soil of China belongs, every inch of it, to the Emperor. Consequently, the people owe him a debt of gratitude for permitting them to live upon it.
680 Do their duty as men and women.
681 A Chinese man may have three kinds of fathers: (1) his real father, (1) an adopted father, such as an uncle without children to whom he has been given as heir, and (3) the man his widowed mother may marry. The first two are to all intents and purposes equal; the third is entitled only to one year's mourning instead of the usual three.
682 As taxes.

with big knives will seize the erring ones and thrust them into the great Gehenna; besides which they shall expiate their sins in the proper number of wards, and shall then be forwarded to the Fourth Court, where they shall be tortured and dismissed to the general Gehenna.

O ye sons of men, on the 8th day of the 2nd moon, register an oath that ye will do no evil. Thus you may escape the bitterness of these hells.

The Fourth Court

THE Lord of the Five Senses reigns at the bottom of the great Ocean, away to the east below the Wujiao rock. His Court is many leagues wide, and is subdivided into sixteen wards, as follows: In the first, the wicked shades are hung up and water is continually poured over them. In the second, they are made to kneel on chains and pieces of split bamboo. In the third, their hands are scalded with boiling water. In the fourth, their hands swell and stream with perspiration. In the fifth, their muscles are cut and their bones pulled out. In the sixth their shoulders are pricked with a trident and the skin rubbed with a hard brush. In the seventh, holes are bored into their flesh. In the eighth, they are made to sit on spikes. In the ninth, they wear iron clothes. In the tenth they are placed under heavy pieces of wood, stone, earth, or tiles. In the eleventh, their eyes are put out. In the twelfth, their mouths are choked with dust. In the thirteenth, they are perpetually dosed with nasty medicines. In the fourteenth, it is so slippery, they are always falling down. In the fifteenth, their mouths are painfully pricked. In the sixteenth, their bodies are buried under broken stones, etc., the head alone being left out.

Those who cheat the customs and evade taxes; those who repudiate their rent, use weighted scales, sell sham medicines, water their rice,[683] utter base coin, get deeply in debt, sell doctored[684] silks and satins, scrape[685] or add size to linen cloth; those who do not make way for the cripples, old and young; those who encroach upon petty trade rights[686] of old or young; those who

---

683 Visitors to Beijing may often see the Junkmen at Tongzhou pouring water by the bucketful onto newly arrived cargoes of Imperial rice in order to make up the right weight and conceal the amount they have filched on the way.

684 That is, with a false gloss on them.

685 In order to raise the nap and give an appearance of strength and goodness.

686 Costermongers and others acquire certain rights to doorsteps or snug corners in Chinese cities which are not usually infringed by competitors in the same line of business. Chair-coolies, carrying-coolies, ferrymen, etc., also claim whole districts as their particular field of operations, and are very

delay in delivering letters entrusted to them; steal bricks from walls as they pass by, or oil and candles from lamps;[687] poor people who do not behave properly and rich people who are not compassionate to the poor; those who promise a loan and go back on their word; those who see people suffering from illness yet cannot bring themselves to part with certain useful drugs they may have in their possession; those who know good prescriptions but keep them secret; those who throw vessels which have contained medicine or broken cups and bottles into the street; those who allow their mules and ponies to be a nuisance to other people; those who destroy their neighbor's crops or his walls and fences; those who try to bewitch their enemies,[688] and those who try to frighten people in any way—all these shall be punished according to the gravity of their offences, and shall be thrust by the devils into the great Gehenna until their time arrives for passing into the Fifth Court.

O ye children of this world, if on the 18th day of the 2nd moon you register an oath to sin no more, then you may escape the various wards of this Hall; and if to this book you add examples of rewards and punishments following upon virtues and crimes, and hand them down to posterity for the good of the human race, so that all who read may repent them of their wickedness—then they will be without sin, and you not without merit!

The Fifth Court

HIS Infernal Majesty Yan Luo[689] said, "Our proper place is in the First Court; but, pitying those who die by foul means, and should be sent back to earth to have their wrongs redressed, we have moved our judgment-seat to the great hell at the bottom of the Ocean, away to the north-east below the Wujiao rock, and have subdivided this hell into sixteen wards for the torment of souls. All those shades who come before us have already suffered long tortures in the previous four Courts, whence, if they are

---

jealous of any interference. I know of a case in which the right of "scavengering" a town had been in the same family for generations, and no one dreamt of trying to take it out of their hands.

687 Chiefly alluding to small temples where some pious spirit may have lighted a lamp or candle to the glory of his favorite Pusa.

688 This is done either by makng a figure of the person to be injured and burning it in a slow fire, like the old practice of the wax figure in English history; or by obtaining his nativity characters, writing them out on a piece of paper and burning them in a candle, muttering all the time whatsoever mischief it is hoped will befall him.

689 Popularly known as the Chinese Pluto. The Indian *Yama*.

hardened sinners, they are passed on after seven days to this Court, where, if again found to be utterly hardened, corruption will overtake them by the fifth or seventh day. All shades cry out either that they have left some vow unfulfilled, or that they wish to build a temple or a bridge, make a road, clean out a river or well, publish some book teaching people to be virtuous, that they have not released their due number of lives, that they have filial duties or funeral obsequies to perform, some act of kindness to repay, etc., etc. For these reasons they pray to be allowed to return once more to the light of day, and are always ready to make oath that henceforth they will lead most exemplary lives. We, hearing this, reply—In days gone by ye openly worked evil, but now that your boat has reached the midstream, ye bethink yourselves of caulking the leak. For although Pusa in his great mercy decreed that there should be a modification of torture, and that good works might be set off against evil, the same being submitted to God and ratified by Divine Decree, to be further published in the realms below and in the Infernal City—yet we Judges of the Ten Courts have not yet received one single virtuous man amongst us, who, coming in the flesh, might carry this *Divine Panorama* back with him to the light of day. Truly those who suffer in hell and on earth cannot complain, and virtuous men are rare! But now ye have come to my Court, having beheld your own wickedness in the mirror of sin. No more—bull-headed, horse-faced devils, away with them to the Terrace[690] that they may once more gaze upon their lost homes!" This Terrace is curved in front like a bow; it looks east, west, and south. It is eighty-one *li* from one extreme to the other. The back part is like the string of the bow; it is enclosed by a wall of sharp swords. It is 490 feet high; its sides are knife-blades; and the whole is in sixty-three stories. No good shade comes to this Terrace; neither do those whose balance of good and evil is exact. Wicked souls alone behold their homes close by and can see and hear what is going on. They hear old and young talking together; they see their last wishes disregarded and their instructions disobeyed. Everything seems to have undergone a change. The property they scraped together with so much trouble is dissipated and gone. The husband thinks of taking another wife; the widow meditates second nuptials.[691] Strangers are in possession of the old estate; there is nothing to divide amongst the children. Debts long since paid are brought again for settlement, and the survivors are called upon to acknowledge

---

690 The celebrated "See-one's-home Terrace."
691 Regarded by the Chinese with intense disgust.

claims upon the departed. Debts owed are lost for want of evidence, with endless recriminations, abuse, and general confusion, all of which falls upon the three families[692] of the deceased. They in their anger speak ill of him that is gone. He sees his children become corrupt, and his friends fall away. Some, perhaps, for the sake of bygone times, may stroke the coffin and let fall a tear, departing quickly with a cold smile. Worse than that, the wife sees her husband tortured in the yamen; the husband sees his wife victim to some horrible disease, lands gone, houses destroyed by flood or fire, and everything in an unutterable confusion—the reward of former sins.[693] All souls, after the misery of the Terrace, will be thrust into the great Gehenna, and, when the amount of wickedness of each has been ascertained, they will be passed through the sixteen wards for the punishment of evil hearts. In the Gehenna they will be buried under wooden pillars, bound with copper snakes, crushed by iron dogs tied tightly hand and foot, be ripped open and have their hearts torn out, minced up and given to snakes, their entrails being thrown to dogs. Then, when their time is up, the pain will cease and their bodies become whole once more, preparatory to being passed through the sixteen wards.

In the first are non-worshippers and sceptics. In the second, those who have destroyed or hurt living creatures. In the third, those who do not fulfill their vows. In the fourth, believers in false doctrines, magicians, and sorcerers. In the fifth, those who tyrannize over the weak but cringe to the strong; also those who openly wish for another's death. In the sixth, those who try to put their misfortunes on to other people's shoulders. In the seventh, those who lead immoral lives. In the eighth, those who injure others to benefit themselves. In the ninth, those who are parsimonious and will not help people in trouble. In the tenth, those who steal and involve the innocent. In the eleventh, those who forget kindness or seek revenge. In the twelfth, those who by pernicious drugs stir up others to quarrel, keeping themselves out of harm's way. In the thirteenth, those who deceive or spread false reports. In the fourteenth, those who love brawling and implicate others. In the fifteenth, those who envy the virtuous and wise. In the sixteenth, those who are lost in vice, evil speakers, slanderers, and such.

---

692 Father's, mother's, and wife's families.
693 I know of few more pathetic passages throughout all the exquisite imagery of the "Divine Comedy" than this in which the guilty soul is supposed to look back to the home he has but lately left and gaze in bitter anguish on his desolate hearth and broken household gods. For once the gross tortures of Chinese Purgatory give place to as refined and as dreadful a punishment as human ingenuity could well devise.

All who disbelieve the doctrine of Cause and Effect, who obstruct good works, make a pretence of piety, talk of other people's sins, burn or injure religious books, omit to fast when praying for the sick, interfere with the adoration of Buddha, slander the priesthood, or, if scholars, abstain from instructing women and children; those who dig up graves and obliterate all traces thereof, set light to woods and forests, allow their servants to be careless in handling fire and thus endanger their neighbors' property; those who wantonly discharge arrows and bolts, who try their strength against the sick or weak, throw potsherds over a wall, poison fish, let off guns, catch birds either with net, sticky pole,[694] or trap; those who throw down salt to kill plants, who do not bury dead cats and venomous snakes deep in the ground, who dig out corpses, who break the soil or alter their walls and stoves at wrong seasons,[695] who encroach on the public road or take possession of other people's land, who fill up wells and drains etc., etc.—all these, when they return from the Terrace, shall first be tortured in the great Gehenna, and then such as are to have their hearts minced shall be passed into the sixteen wards, thence to be sent on to the Sixth Court for the punishment of other crimes. Those who in life have not been guilty of the above sins, or, having sinned, did on the 8th day of the 1st moon, fasting, register a vow to sin no more, shall not only escape the punishments of this Court, but shall also gain some further remission of torture in the Sixth Court. Those, however, who are guilty of taking life, of gross immorality, of stealing and implicating the innocent, of ingratitude and revenge, of infatuated vice which no warnings can turn from its course—these shall not escape one jot of their punishments.

The Sixth Court

THIS Court is situated at the bottom of the great Ocean, due north of the Wujiao rock. It is a vast, noisy Gehenna, many leagues in extent, and around it are sixteen wards.

In the first, the souls are made to kneel for long periods on iron shot. In the second, they are placed up to their necks in filth. In the third, they are pounded until the blood runs out. In the fourth their mouths are opened

---

694 A long pole tipped with a kind of birdlime is cautiously inserted between the branches of a tree and then suddenly dabbed on to some unsuspecting sparrow.
695 If this is done in winter or spring the Spirits of the Hearth and Threshold are liable to catch cold.

with iron pincers and filled full of needles. In the fifth, they are bitten by rats. In the sixth, they are enclosed in a net of thorns and nipped by locusts. In the seventh, they are crushed to a jelly. In the eighth, their skin is lacerated and they are beaten on the raw. In the ninth, their mouths are filled with fire. In the tenth, they are licked by flames. In the eleventh, they are subjected to noisome smells. In the twelfth, they are butted by oxen and trampled on by horses. In the thirteenth, their hearts are scratched. In the fourteenth, their heads are rubbed until their skulls come off. In the fifteenth; they are chopped in two at the waist. In the sixteenth, their skin is taken off and rolled up into spills.

Those discontented ones who rail against Heaven and revile Earth, who are always finding fault either with the wind, thunder, heat, cold, fine weather or rain; those who let their tears fall towards the north,[696] who steal the gold from the inside[697] or scrape the gilding from the outside of images; those who take holy names in vain, who show no respect for written paper, who throw down dirt and rubbish near pagodas or temples, who use dirty cookhouses and stoves for preparing the sacrificial meats, who do not abstain from eating beef and dog flesh;[698] those who have in their possession blasphemous or obscene books and do not destroy them, who obliterate or tear books which teach man to be good, who carve on common articles of household use the symbol of the origin of all things,[699] the Sun and Moon and Seven Stars, the Royal Mother and the God of Longevity on the same article,[700] or representations of any of the Immortals; those who embroider the Svastika[701] on fancy work, or mark characters on silk, satin, or cloth, on banners, beds, chairs, tables, or any kind of utensil; those who secretly wear clothes adorned with the dragon and the phœnix[702] only to be trampled under foot, who buy up grain and hold until the price is exorbitantly high—all these shall be thrust into the great and noisy Gehenna, there to be examined as to their misdeeds and passed accordingly into one of the sixteen wards, whence, at the expiration of their time, they will be sent for further questioning on to the Seventh Court.

---

696 I presume because God sits with his face to the south.
697 Pious and wealthy people often give orders for an image of a certain Pusa to be made with an ounce or so of gold inside.
698 Primarily, because no living thing should be killed for food. The ox and the dog are specified because of their kindly services to man in tilling the earth and guarding his home.
699 The symbol of the Yin and the Yang.
700 One being male and the other female. This calls to mind the extreme modesty of a celebrated French lady, who would not put books by male and female authors on the same shelf.
701 The symbol on Buddha's heart; more commonly known to the Western world as Thor's Hammer.
702 Emblems of Imperial dignity.

All dwellers upon earth who on the 8th day of the 3rd moon, fasting, register a vow from that date to sin no more, and, on the 14th and 15th of the 5th moon, the 3rd of the 8th moon, and the 10th of the 10th moon, to practice abstinence, vowing, moreover, to exert themselves to convert others—these shall escape the bitterness of all the above-mentioned wards.

The Seventh Court

His Infernal Majesty Tai Shan reigns at the bottom of the great Ocean, away to the north-west, below the Wujiao rock. His is a vast, noisy Court, measuring many leagues in circumference and subdivided into sixteen wards, as follows:

In the first, the wicked, souls are made to swallow their own blood. In the second, their legs are pierced and thrust into a fiery pit. In the third, their chests are cut open. In the fourth, their hair is torn out with iron combs. In the fifth, they are gnawed by dogs. In the sixth, great stones are placed on their heads. In the seventh, their skulls are pierced. In the eighth, they wear fiery clothes. In the ninth, their skin is torn and pulled by pigs. In the tenth, they are pecked by huge birds. In the eleventh, they are hung up and beaten on the feet. In the twelfth, their tongues are pulled out and their jaws bored. In the thirteenth, they are disembowelled. In the fourteenth, they are trampled on by mules and bitten by badgers. In the fifteenth, their fingers are ironed with hot irons. In the sixteenth, they are boiled in oil.

All mortals who practice eating red lead[703] and certain other nauseous articles,[704] who spend more than they should upon wine, who kidnap human beings for sale, who steal clothes and ornaments from coffins, who break up dead men's bones for medicine, who separate people from their relatives, who sell the girl brought up in the house to be their son's wife, who allow their wives[705] to drown female children, who stifle their illegitimate offspring, who unite to cheat another in gambling, who act as tutors without being properly strict, and thus wrong their pupils, who beat and injure their slaves without estimating the punishment by the fault, who regard districts entrusted to their charge in the light of so much spoil, who disobey their elders, who talk at random and go back on their word,

---

703 Supposed to confer immortality.
704 Unfit for translation.
705 This is ingeniously expressed, as if *mothers* were the prime movers in such unnatural acts.

who stir up others to quarrel and fight—all these shall, upon verification of their sins, be taken from the great Gehenna and passed through the proper wards, to be forwarded when their time has expired to the Eighth Court, again to be tortured according to their deserts. All things may not be used as drugs. It is bad enough to slay birds, beasts, reptiles, and fishes, in order to prepare medicine for the sick; but to use red lead and many of the filthy messes in vogue is beyond all bounds of decency, and those who foul their mouths with these nasty mixtures, no matter how virtuous they may otherwise be, will not only derive no benefit from saying their prayers, but will be punished for so doing without mercy.

Ye who hear these words, make haste to repent! From today forbear to take life, buy many birds and animals in order to set them free,[706] and every morning when you wash your teeth mutter a prayer to Buddha. Thus, when your last hour comes, a good angel will stand by your side and purify you of your former sins.

Some steal the bones of people who have been burnt to death or the bodies of illegitimate children, for the purpose of compounding medicines; others steal skulls and bones (from graves) with the same object. Worst of all are those who carry off bones by the basketful, using the hard ones for making various articles and grinding down the soft ones for the manufacture of pottery.[707] These, no matter what may have been their good works on earth, will not obtain thereby any remission of punishment; but when they are brought down below, the Ruler of the Infernal Regions will first pass them from the great Gehenna into the proper wards, and will send instructions to the Tenth Court that when they are born again on earth it shall be either without ears, or eyes, hand, foot, mouth, lips, or nose, or maimed in some way or other. Yet such as have thus sinned may still avoid this punishment, if only they are willing to pray and repent, vowing never to sin again. Or if they buy coffins for the poor and persuade others to do likewise, by these means giving a decent burial to many corpses—then, when the death-summons comes, the Spirits of the Home and Hearth will make a black mark upon the warrant, and punishment will be remitted.

Sometimes, when there is a famine, people have nothing to eat and die of hunger, and wicked men, almost before the breath is out of their bodies, cut them up and sell their flesh to others for food—a horrid crime indeed.

---

706 On fête days at temples it is not uncommon to see cages full of birds hawked about among the holiday-makers, that those who feel twinges of conscience may purchase a sparrow or two and relieve themselves from anxiety by the simple means of setting them at liberty.

707 Bones are used in glazing porcelain, to give a higher finish.

Those who are guilty of such practices will, on arrival in the lower regions, be tortured in the various Courts for the space of forty-nine[708] days, and then the judge of the Tenth Court will be instructed to notify the judge of the First Court to put them down in his register for a new birth—if among men, as hungry, famished outcasts, and if among animals as loathing the food that falls to their lot, and by-and-by perishing of hunger. Such is their reward. Besides the above, those who have eaten what is unfit for food and willingly continue to do so, will be punished either among men or animals according to their deserts. Their throats will swell, and though devoured by hunger they will be unable to swallow, and thus die. Those who do not err a second time may be forgiven as they deserve; but those who in times of distress subscribe money for the sufferers, prepare gruel, give away rice to the needy, or distribute ginger tea[709] and soup in the open street, and thus sustain life a little longer and do real good to their fellow creatures—all these shall not only obtain remission of their sins, but carry on a balance of good to their account which shall ensure them a happy old age in the life to come.[710]

Of the above three clauses, two were proposed by the officials attached to this Seventh Court, the third by the Chief Justice of the great Gehenna, and the whole submitted together for the approval of God, the following Rescript being obtained: "Let it be as proposed; let the three clauses be copied into the *Divine Panorama,* and let the officials concerned be promoted or rewarded. Also, in case of crimes other than those already provided for, let such be punished according to the statutes of the Rulers of the Four Continents on earth, and let any evasion of punishment and implication of innocent people be at once reported by the proper officials for our consideration. This from the Throne! Obey!"

O ye sons and daughters of men, if on the 27th of the 3rd moon, fasting and turned towards the north, ye register a vow to pray and repent, and to publish the whole of the *Divine Panorama* for the enlightenment of mankind, then ye may escape the bitterness of this Seventh Court.

---

708 The seven periods of seven days each which occur immediately after a death and at which the departed shade is appeased with food and offerings of various kinds.
709 To warm them.
710 When they are born again on earth.

The Eighth Court

His Infernal Majesty Du Shi reigns at the bottom of the great Ocean, due east below the Wujiao rock, in a vast noisy Court many leagues in extent, subdivided into sixteen wards as follows:

In the first, the wicked souls are rolled down mountains in carts. In the second, they are shut up in huge saucepans. In the third, they are minced. In the fourth, their noses, eyes, mouths, etc., are stopped up. In the fifth, their uvulas are cut off. In the sixth they are exposed to all kinds of filth. In the seventh, their extremities are cut off. In the eighth, their viscera[711] are fried. In the ninth; their marrow is cauterised. In the tenth, their bowels are scratched. In the eleventh, they are inwardly burned with fire. In the twelfth, they are disembowelled. In the thirteenth, their chests are torn open. In the fourteenth, their skulls are split and their teeth dragged out. In the fifteenth, they are hacked and gashed. In the sixteenth, they are pricked with steel prongs.

Those who are unfilial, who do not nourish their relatives while alive or bury them when dead, who subject their parents to fright, sorrow, or anxiety—if they do not quickly repent them of their former sins, the Spirit of the Hearth will report their misdoings and gradually deprive them of what prosperity they may be enjoying. Those who indulge in magic and sorcery will, after death, when they have been tortured in the other Courts, be brought here to this Court, and dragged backwards by bull-headed, horse-faced devils to be thrust into the great Gehenna. Then when they have been tortured in the various wards they will be passed on to the Tenth Court, whence at the expiration of a *kalpa*[712] they will be sent back to earth with changed heads and faces forever to find their place amongst the brute creation. But those who believe in the *Divine Panorama,* and on the 1st of the 4th moon make a vow of repentance, repeating the same every night and morning to the Spirit of the Hearth, shall, by virtue of one of three characters, *obedient, acquiescent,* or *repentant,* to be traced on their foreheads at death by the Spirit of the Hearth, escape half the punishments from the First to the Seventh Court, inclusive, and escape this Eighth Court altogether, being passed on to the Ninth Court, where cases of arson and poisoning are investigated, and finally born again from the Tenth Court among mankind as before.

---

711 Heart, lungs, spleen, liver, and kidneys.
712 Many millions of years.

To this God added, "Whosoever may circulate the *Divine Panorama* for the information of the world at large shall escape all punishment from the First to the Eighth Court, inclusive. Passing through the Ninth and Tenth Courts, they shall be born again amongst men in some happy state."

The Ninth Court

HIS Infernal Majesty Ping Teng reigns at the bottom of the great Ocean, away to the south-west, below the Wujiao rock. His is the vast, circular hell of Abi, many leagues in breadth, jealously enclosed by an iron net, and subdivided into sixteen wards, as follows:

In the first, the wicked souls have their bones beaten and their bodies scorched. In the second, their muscles are drawn out and their bones rapped. In the third, ducks eat their heart and liver. In the fourth, dogs eat their intestines and lungs. In the fifth, they are splashed with hot oil. In the sixth, their heads are crushed in a frame, and their tongues and teeth are drawn out. In the seventh, their brains are taken out and their skulls filled with hedgehogs. In the eighth, their heads are steamed and their brains scraped. In the ninth, they are dragged about by sheep until they drop to pieces. In the tenth, they are squeezed in a wooden press and pricked on the head. In the eleventh, their hearts are ground in a mill. In the twelfth, boiling water drips on to their bodies. In the thirteenth, they are stung by wasps. In the fourteenth, they are tortured by ants and maggots; they are then stewed, and finally wrung out (like clothes). In the fifteenth, they are stung by scorpions. In the sixteenth, they are tortured by venomous snakes, crimson and scarlet.

All who on earth have committed one of the ten great crimes, and have deserved either the lingering death, decapitation, strangulation, or other punishment, shall, after passing through the tortures of the previous Courts, be brought to this Court, together with those guilty of arson, of making *gu* poison,[713] bad books, stupefying drugs, and many other disgraceful acts. Then, if it be found that, hearkening to the words of the *Divine Panorama,* they subsequently destroyed the blocks of these books,

---

713 The following recipe for this deadly poison is given in the well-known Chinese work *Instructions to Coroners*: "Take a quantity of insects of all kinds and throw them into a vessel of any kind; cover them up, and let a year pass away before you look at them again. The insects will have killed and eaten each other, until there is only one survivor, and this one is *Gu*."

burnt their prescriptions, and ceased practising the magical art, they shall escape the punishments of this Court and be passed on to the Tenth Court, thence to be born again amongst the sons of men. But if, having heard the warnings of the *Divine Panorama,* they still continue to sin, from the Second to the Eighth Court their tortures shall be increased. They shall be bound on to a hollow copper pillar, clasping it around with their hands and feet. Then the pillar shall be filled with fierce fire, so as to burn into their heart and liver; and afterwards their feet shall be plunged into the great Gehenna of Abi, knives shall be thrust into their lungs, they shall bite their own hearts, and gradually sink to the uttermost depths of hell, there to endure excruciating torments until the victims of their wickedness have either recovered the property out of which they were cheated, or the life that was taken away from them, and until every trace of book, prescription, picture, etc., formerly used by these wicked souls has disappeared from the face of the earth. Then, and only then, may they pass into the Tenth Court to be born again in one of the Six States of existence.

O ye who have committed such crimes as these, on the 8th of the 4th moon, or the 1st or 15th (of any moon), fasting swear that you will buy up all bad books and magical pamphlets and utterly destroy them with fire; or that you will circulate copies of the *Divine Panorama* to be a warning to others! Then, when your last moment is at hand, the Spirit of the Hearth will write on your forehead the two words *He obeyed,* and from the Second up to the Ninth Court your good deeds will be rewarded by a diminution of such punishments as you have incurred. People in the higher ranks of life who secure incendiaries or murderers, who destroy the blocks of bad books, or publish notices warning others, and offer rewards for the production of such books, will be rewarded by the success of their sons and grandsons at the public examinations. Poor people who, by a great effort, manage to have the *Divine Panorama* circulated for the benefit of mankind, will be forwarded at once to the Tenth Court, and thence be born again in some happy state on earth.

The Tenth Court

His Infernal Majesty Zhuan Lun[714] reigns in the Dark Land, due east, away below the Wujiao rock, just opposite the Wuzhuo of this world. There he has six bridges, of gold, silver, jade, stone, wood, and planks, over which all souls must pass: He examines the shades that are sent from the other courts, and, according to their deserts, sends them back to earth as men, women, old, young, high, low, rich, or poor, forwarding monthly a list of their names to the judge of the First Court for transmission to Fengdu.[715]

The regulations provide that all beasts, birds, fishes, and insects, whether biped, quadruped, or otherwise, shall after death become *jian*,[716] to be born again for long and short lives alternately. But such as may possibly have taken life, and such as must necessarily have taken life, will pass through a revolution of the Wheel, and then, when their sins have been examined, they will be sent up on earth to receive the proper retribution. At the end of every year a report will be forwarded to Fengdu.

Those scholars who study the Book of Changes, or priests who chant their liturgies, cannot be tortured in the Ten Courts for the sins they have committed. When they come to this Court their names and features are taken down in a book kept for the purpose, and they are forwarded to Mother Meng, who drives them on to the Terrace of Oblivion and doses them with the draught of forgetfulness. Then they are born again in the world for a day, a week, or it may be a year, when they die once more; and now, having forgotten the holy words of the Three Religions,[717] they are carried off by devils to the various Courts, and are properly punished for their former crimes.

All souls whose balance of good and evil is exact, whose period of punishment is completed, or whose crimes are many and good deeds few, as soon as their future state has been decided—man, woman, beautiful, ugly, comfort, toil, wealth, or poverty, as the case may be—must pass through the Terrace of Oblivion.

Amongst those shades, on their way to be born again in the world of human beings, there are often to be found women who cry out that they have some old and bitter wrong to avenge,[718] and that rather than be

---

714 He who "turns the wheel;" a *chakravartti raja.*
715 The capital city of the Infernal Regions.
716 The ghosts of dead people are believed to be liable to death. The ghost of a ghost is called *jian.*
717 Confucianism, Buddhism, and Taoism.
718 Women are considered in China to be far more revengeful than men. *Cf.* "Sweet is revenge, espe-

born again amongst men they would prefer to enter the ranks of hungry devils.[719] On examining them more closely it generally comes out that they are the virtuous victims of some wicked student, who may perhaps have an eye to their money, and accordingly dresses himself out to entrap them, or promises marriage when sometimes he has a wife already, or offers to take care of an aged mother or a late husband's children. Thus the foolish women are beguiled, and put their property in the wicked man's hands. By-and-by he turns around upon and reviles them, and, losing face in the eyes of their relatives and friends, with no one to redress their wrong, they are driven to commit suicide. Then, hearing[720] that their seducer is likely to succeed at the examination, they beg and implore to be allowed to go back and compass his death. Now, although what they urge is true enough, yet that man's destiny may not be worked out, or the transmitted effects of his ancestors' virtue may not have passed away;[721] therefore, as a compromise, these injured shades are allowed to send a spirit to the Examination Hall to hinder and confuse him in the preparation of his paper, or to change the names on the published list of successful candidates; and finally, when his hour arrives, to proceed with the spirit who carries the death-summons, seize him, and bring him to the First Court for judgment.

Ye who on the 17th of the 4th moon swear to carry out the precepts of the *Divine Panorama,* and frequently make these words the subject of your conversation, may in the life to come be born again amongst men and escape official punishments, fire, flood, and all accidents to the body.

The place where the Wheel of Fate goes around is many leagues in extent, enclosed on all sides by an iron palisade. Within are eighty-one subdivisions, each of which has its proper officers and magisterial appointments. Beyond the palisade there is a labyrinth of 108,000 paths leading by direct and circuitous routes back to earth. Inside it is as dark as pitch, and through it pass the spirits of priest and layman alike. But to one who looks from the outside everything is seen as clear as crystal, and the attendants who guard the place all have the faces and features they had at their birth. These attendants are chosen from virtuous people who in life were noted for filial piety, friendship, or respect for life, and are sent here to look after the working of the Wheel and such duties. If for a space of five years they make

---

cially to women."
719 See Author's Own Record (in the Introduction), note 53.
720 While in Purgatory.
721 It was mentioned above that the rewards for virtue would be continued to a man's sons and grand-sons.

no mistakes they are promoted to a higher office; but if found to be lazy or careless they are reported to the Throne for punishment.

Those who in life have been unfilial or have destroyed much life, when they have been tortured in the various Courts are brought here and beaten to death with peach twigs. They then become *jian,* and with changed heads and altered faces are turned out into the labyrinth to proceed by the path which ends in the brute creation.

Birds, beasts, fishes, and insects may after many myriads of *kalpas* again resume their original shapes; and if there are any that during three existences do not destroy life, they may be born amongst human beings as a reward, a record being made and their names forwarded to the First Court for approval. But all shades of men and women must proceed to the Terrace of Oblivion.

Mother Meng was born in the Earlier Han Dynasty. In her childhood she studied books of the Confucian school; when she grew up she chanted the liturgies of Buddha. Of the past and the future she had no care, but occupied herself in exhorting mankind to desist from taking life and become vegetarians. At eighty-one years of age her hair was white and her complexion like a child's. She lived and died a virgin, calling herself simply Meng; but men called her Mother Meng. She retired to the hills and lived as a *religieuse* until the Later Han. Then because certain evil-doers, relying on their knowledge of the past, used to beguile women by pretending to have been their husbands in a former life, God commissioned Mother Meng to build the Terrace of Oblivion, and appointed her as guardian, with devils to wait upon her and execute her commands. It was arranged that all shades who had been sentenced in the Ten Courts to return in various conditions to earth, should first be dosed by her with a decoction of herbs, sweet, bitter, acrid, sour, or salt. Thus they forget everything that has previously happened to them, and carry away with them to earth some slight weaknesses, such as the mouth watering at the thought (of something nice), laughter inducing perspiration, fear inducing tears, anger inducing sobs, or spitting from nervousness. Good spirits who go back into the world will have their senses of sight, hearing, smell, and taste very much increased in power, and their physical strength, and constitution generally will be much bettered. But evil spirits will experience the exact contrary of this, as a reward for previous sins and as a warning to others to pray and repent.

The Terrace is situated in front of the Ten Courts, outside the six bridges. It is square, measuring ten (Chinese) feet every way, and surrounded by 108 small rooms. To the east there is a raised path, one foot four inches in breadth, and in the rooms above-mentioned are prepared cups of forgetfulness ready for the arrival of the shades. Whether they swallow much or little it matters not; but sometimes there are perverse devils who altogether refuse to drink. Then beneath their feet sharp blades start up, and a copper tube is forced down their throats, by which means they are compelled to swallow some. When they have drunk, they are raised by the attendants and escorted back by the same path. They are next pushed onto the Bitter Bamboo floating bridge, with torrents of rushing red water on either side. Half-way across they perceive written in large characters on a red cliff on the opposite side the following lines:

> To be a man is easy, but to act up to one's responsibilities as such is hard.
> Yet to be a man once again is perhaps harder still.
> For those who would be born again in some happy state there is no great difficulty;
> It is only necessary to keep mouth and heart in harmony.

When the shades have read these words they try to jump on shore, but are beaten back into the water by two huge devils. One has on a black official hat and embroidered clothes; in his hand he holds a paper pencil, and over his shoulder he carries a sharp sword. Instruments of torture hang at his waist, fiercely he glares out of his large round eyes and laughs a horrid laugh. His name is *Short Life*. The other has a dirty face smeared with blood; he has on a white coat, an abacus in his hand and a rice sack over his shoulder. Around his neck hangs a string of paper money; his brow contracts hideously, and he utters long sighs. His name is *They have their reward,* and his duty is to push the shades into the red water. The wicked and foolish rejoice at the prospect of being born once more as human beings; but the better shades weep and mourn that in life they did not lay up a store of virtuous acts, and thus pass away from the state of mortals for ever.[722] Yet they all rush on to birth like an infatuated or drunken crowd; and again, in their early childhood, hanker after the forbidden flavors.[723] Then, regardless of consequences, they begin to destroy life, and thus forfeit all claims to the mercy and compassion of God. They take no thought as to the end that must overtake them; and finally, they bring themselves once more to the same horrid plight.

---

722 That is, go to heaven.
723 Of meat, wine, etc.

Appendix III

Cultural Notes

Ancestral Worship

"THE rudimentary form of all religion is the propitiation of dead ancestors, who are supposed to be still existing, and to be capable of working good or evil to their descendants."—SPENCER'S ESSAYS. Vol. iii., p. 102—*The Origin of Animal Worship.*

Bilocation

"As a general rule, people are apt to consider it impossible for a man to be in two places at once, and indeed a saying to that effect has become a popular proverb. But the rule is so far from being universally accepted, that the word 'bilocation' has been invented to express the miraculous faculty possessed by certain saints of the Roman Church, of being in two places at once; like St. Alfonso di Liguori, who had the useful power of preaching his sermon in church, while he was confessing penitents at home."—TYLOR'S *Primitive Culture.* Vol. i., p. 447.

Burial Rites

"HENCE the various burial rites—the placing of weapons and valuables along with the body, the daily bringing of food to it, etc. I hope hereafter to show that with such knowledge of facts as he has, this interpretation is the most reasonable the savage can arrive at."—SPENCER'S ESSAYS. Vol. iii., p. 104.—*The Origin of Animal Worship.*

Dreams

"THE distinction so easily made by us between our life in dreams and our real life is one which the savage recognizes in but a vague way; and he cannot express even that distinction which he perceives. When he awakes, and to those who have seen him lying quietly asleep, describes where he has been, and what he has done, his rude language fails to state the difference between seeing and dreaming that he saw, doing and dreaming that he did. From this inadequacy of his language it not only results that he cannot truly represent this difference to others, but also that he cannot truly represent it to himself."—SPENCER'S ESSAYS. Vol. iii., pp. 103, 104.

Shade or Shadow

"THE ghost or phantasm seen by the dreamer or the visionary is an unsubstantial form, like a shadow, and thus the familiar term of the *shade* comes in to express the soul. Thus the Tasmanian word for the shadow is also that for the spirit; the Algonquin Indians describe a man's soul as *otahchuk,* 'his shadow;' the Quiché language uses *natub* for 'shadow, soul;' the Arawac *ueja* means 'shadow, soul, image;' the Abipones made the one word *loákal* serve for 'shadow, soul, echo, image.'"—TYLOR'S *Primitive Culture.* Vol. i., p. 430.

Shadow

"THUS the dead in Purgatory knew that Dante was alive when they saw that, unlike theirs, his figure cast a shadow on the ground." —TYLOR'S *Primitive Culture.* Vol. i., p. 431.

The Soul

"THE savage, conceiving a corpse to be deserted by the active personality who dwelt in it, conceives this active personality to be still existing, and his feelings and ideas concerning it form the basis of his superstitions."—SPENCER'S ESSAYS. Vol. iii., p. 103.—*The Origin of Animal Worship.*

Transmigration

"Whether the Buddhists receive the full Hindu doctrine of the migration of the individual soul from birth to birth, or whether they refine away into metaphysical subtleties the notion of continued personality, they do consistently and systematically hold that a man's life in former existences is the cause of his now being what he is, while at this moment he is accumulating merit or demerit whose result will determine his fate in future lives."—Tylor's *Primitive Culture*. Vol. ii., p. 12.

"Memory, it is true, fails generally to recall these past births, but memory, as we know, stops short of the beginning even of this present life."—Tylor's *Primitive Culture*. Vol. ii., p. 12.

"As for believers, savage or civilised, in the great doctrine of metempsychosis, these not only consider that an animal may have a soul, but that this soul may have inhabited a human being, and thus the creature may be in fact their own ancestor or once familiar friend."—Tylor's *Primitive Culture*. Vol. i., p. 469.

Tree-Souls

"Orthodox Buddhism decided against the tree-souls, and consequently against the scruple to harm them, declaring trees to have no mind nor sentient principle, though admitting that certain dewas or spirits do reside in the body of trees, and speak from within them."—Tylor's *Primitive Culture*.—Vol. i., p. 475.

Appendix III

Herbert Allen Giles
(December 18, 1845–February 13,1935)

WHEN Herbert Giles translated his *Strange Tales from a Chinese Studio* he was in Shantou, China, stationed with Her Britannic Majesty's Consular Service. Although Giles is often described as a "diplomat," this word hardly describes the hands-on involvement he had with local Chinese life and governance. The Consular Service had been newly established in China after the Opium Wars, its officers seizing the affairs of the decaying coastal cities. They mediated in all matters: whether of taxation and transport, of protection of trade, or of legal cases and local politics.[724]

Giles arrived in China for his employment in the Consular Service in February 1867, leaving behind a childhood marked by his father's bitter—and impoverishing—controversies with the Anglican Church. At twenty-one Giles turned his back on college-studies, took the Consular exam, and set out for China. In Beijing he satisfied the requisite one-year of intensive language study and was then appointed as lowly "Student Interpreter." In his quarter-century of mixed success in the Service, he served as Interpreter, Assistant Consul, and eventually Consul, at a series of Treaty Ports and cities "opened" to foreign control: Shanghai, Tianjin, Ningbo, Hankou, Shantou and Danshui.

Giles began his long career in the field of sinology as a frustrated student with a mission to improve the world of language study. He began by correcting existing dictionaries and primers; and ended up writing more practical primers and aids. His furious improvements, for example, of Sir Thomas Wade's romanization system led to the Wade-Giles system; his innovations produced a romanized version of Chinese that is still, to some extent, in use today. He became perforce an autodidact: in China he read widely—with the help of tutors—in Chinese literature. His self-determined training and later his scholarship were surprisingly liberal, however. He did not limit himself to the literati orthodoxies of classical training, but took rather a broader view of culture. Giles had an ear, not only for language,

---

724 D. C. M. Platt, "The Role of the British Consular Service in Overseas Trade, 1825–1914," *The Economic History Review*, New Series, Vol. 15, No. 3 (1963), p 496.

but for the larger linguistic culture of China. He studied, and ultimately translated works of "light literature" as he called them, reading—well ahead of his time—the long and difficult novels of early vernacular fiction, as well as drama and, of course, classical fiction of the strange. Thus his discovery of Pu Songling, a work that was much loved, but was not formally recognized as suitable for genteel studies. He succeeded at reportage as well. While in China he published *Chinese Sketches* a study of Chinese city-life. He was like Pu Songling, catholic in his view.

After a total of twenty-six years in China and eleven books, Giles returned to Great Britain in 1893, to Aberdeen Scotland. In 1897 he became Professor of Chinese at Cambridge University—still with no specialized, institutional training or formal degrees—where he remained for thirty-five years. Giles produced over time, not only translations of literature, but also his valuable *Chinese Biographical Dictionary* and his *Chinese English Dictionary*, as well as volumes of intelligent, plainly told narratives on Chinese History, Chinese Religion, Chinese Art and contemporaneous Chinese society.

If he was independent in his taste, he was, like many Victorians, a contentious advocate. This was an era of "zealous pugnaciousness,"[725] when scholarship was marked by vitriol. His diary is filled with the gleeful depiction of scholarly disputes. Often he "took up the cudgels"[726][727] against one translator or another. His critical comments were famously caustic: "The work... seemed to me to be a tissue of inaccuracies, relieved chiefly by serious mistakes." And for those of us who assumed the Wade-Giles system reflected a cooperative effort: "I further seized the opportunity of a slap at Sir T. Wade for his egregious mistranslations of a Chinese proverb..."[728]

Indeed, truculent agnosticism marked his work; he tells us proudly that in "1909 I was elected to an Honorary Member of the (society of) Heretics."[729] Combativeness affected his later life, however. When his son, Lancelot, wrote letters home from China describing the violence of the anti-foreign riots of the North, his father, "would hear no wrong" about the China that he recalled. His son "began to find that his letters were being returned to him embellished with savage critical comments

---

725 Norman J. Girardot, The Victorian Translation of China: James Legge's Oriental Pilgrimage. Berkeley, CA: University of California Press, 2002, p. 107.
726 Charles Aylmer, "The Memoirs of H. A. Giles," East Asian History, 13/14 (June/December 1997), p. 34.
727 Ibid. p. 34.
728 Ibid. p. 18.
729 Ibid. p. 27.

by his father."[730] His second son, Lionel—who became the prolific and brilliant translator of the Chinese classics—was the only child to remain on speaking terms with him.

Of Giles' more than one hundred publications: translations, grammars and dictionaries, histories, pamphlets, journal pieces and essays, he seems to have had a special fondness for his *Strange Tales from a Chinese Studio*. His own memoirs—so animated by disdain—ended on an elegiac note, with a quotation from Pu Songling: "The interest in China... will no doubt quicken some day in the future: but I, who would have loved above all things to witness its growth and expansion, shall by that time be a dweller with Pu Songling "down in that bosky grove, wrapped in that impenetrable gloom."[731]

730 Lancelot Giles, The Siege of the Peking Legations, a Diary, edited, with an Introduction, "Chinese Anti-Foreignism and the Boxer Rebellion," by L. R. Marchant. Nedlands, Western Australia: University of Western Australia Press, 1970, p. xxiv.
731 Aylmer, p. 86.

Appendix IV

Suggested Readings

Selections from *Liaozhai zhiyi* and Other Anthologies

Bauer, Wolfgang and Herbert Franke, *The Golden Casket, Chinese Novellas of Two Millennia* (tr. Christopher Levenson). Baltimore, MD: Penguin Books Inc.,1967.

Feng Menglong, *Stories from a Ming Collection: The Art of the Chinese Storyteller* (tr. Cyril Birch). New York: Grove Press, 1958.

Karl S. Kao, ed. *Classical Chinese Tales of the Supernatural and the Fantastic: Selections from the Third to the Tenth Century*. Bloomington: Indiana University Press, 1985.

Li Yu, *Silent Operas* (tr. Patrick Hanan). Honk Kong: Renditions Paperback, 1990.

Pu Songling, *Chroniques de l'étrange* (tr. André Lévy). Paris: Editions Philippe Picquier, 2005.

Pu Songling, *Strange Tales from a Chinese Studio* (tr. John Minford). London: Penguin, 2006.

Pu Songling, *Strange Tales from Make-do Studio* (tr. Denis C. & Victor H. Mair). Beijing: Foreign Languages Press, 1989.

Pu Songling. *Strange Tales of Liaozhai* (tr. Lu Yunzhong, Chen Tifang, Yang Liyi and Yang Zhihong). Hong Kong: Commercial Press. 1982.

Criticism

Barr, Allan, "The Textual Transmission of *Liaozhai zhiyi*," HJAS vol 44, No. 2 (Dec., 1 984).

------------ "Disarming Intruders: Alien Women in *Liaozhai zhiyi*," *HJAS*, 49.2 (Dec. 1989): 501–517.

Chang Chun-shu and Chang Hsueh-lun, *Redefining History: Ghosts, Spirits, and Human Society in P'u Sung-ling's World, 1640–1715*. Ann Arbor, MI: University of Michigan Press, 1998.

Hunington, Rania, *Alien Kind: Foxes and Late Imperial Chinese Narrative*. Cambridge, MA: The Harvard University Asian Center, 2003.

Li Wai-yee, *Enchantment and Disenchantment: Love and Illusion in Chinese Literature*. Princeton: Princeton University Press, 1993

Luo Hui, "The Ghost of *Liaozhai*: Pu Songling's Ghostlore and its History of Reception," Ph D thesis, University of Toronto, 2009.

Minford, John and Tong Man, "Whose Strange Stories? P'u Sung-ling (1640–1715), Herbert Giles (1845-1935) and the *Liao-chai chih-I*," *East Asian History* 17/18(1999).

Prusek, Jaroslav, "P'u Sung-ling and His Work." *Chinese History and Literature: Collection of Studies*. Dordrecht: Reidel, 1970, pp. 109–38.

Zeitlin, Judith T., *Historian of the Strange: Pu Songling and the Chinese Classical Tale*. Stanford: Stanford University Press, 1983.

Background: History, Religion and Mythology

Cass, Victoria, *Dangerous Women, Warriors, Grannies and Geishas of the Ming*. Lanham, Maryland: Rowman and Littlefield, 1999.

----------------- *In the Realm of the Gods, Lands, Myths and Legends of China*. San Francisco: Long River Press, 2007.

Mann, Susan, *Precious Records: Women in China's Long Eighteenth Century*. Stanford: Stanford University Press, 1997.

De Groot, J.J.M., *The Religious System of China*, 6 volumes. Leiden, 1892–1910.

Robinet, Isabelle, *Taoism: Growth of a Religion* (tr. Phyllis Brooks). Stanford, CA: Stanford University Press, 1997.

Robinson, Richard H. and Willard L. Johnson, *The Buddhist religion, A Historical Introduction*. Belmont, California: Wadsworth, 1982.

Rowe, William T., *China's Last Empire: the Great Qing*. Cambridge, Mass.: Belknap Press of Harvard University Press, 2009.

Schafer, Edward, *The Divine Woman, Dragon Ladies and Rain Maidens in Tang Literature*. Berkeley, Los Angeles: University of California, Press, 1973.

Schipper, Kristofer, *The Taoist Body* (tr. Karen Duval). Berkeley & Los Angeles: University of California Press, 1993.

Spence, Jonathan D., *The Death of Woman Wang*. New York: Viking, 1978.

Strassberg, Richard, *A Chinese Bestiary, Strange Creatures from the Guideways through Mountains and Seas*. Berkeley & Los Angeles: University of California Press, 2002.

Watt, James C. Y., "The Literati Environment," and Chu-Tsing Li, "The Literati Life," in Chu-Tsing Li, James C. Y. Watt, eds., *The Chinese Scholar's Studio, Artistic Life in the Late Ming Period*. New York: Thames and Hudson, 1987.